Dragon's Rook

The Lost Sword, Book 1

KEANAN BRAND

Penwor†hy
Press

www.penworthypress.com

revised September 2015

DEDICATED

To My Family

Our story deserves its own novel.

Contents

I

The Heir of Uartha

He squats in the dust beside a dead man and draws designs in the dirt, letters someone taught him in a gentle voice and a patient manner. He does not know what words the letters form, but singsongs their sounds in a monotonous drone. It soothes him. He almost forgets the dead man.

His quill is a dagger as long as his leg. The hilt grows warm. He drops it and stands. Dark trees line the road. They do not frighten him but whisper, D'urnythn. We have been waiting.

D'urnythn. *He looks down at the letters drawn in the dirt. Which ones spell the mysterious word? As he studies, he tosses blue sparks back and forth between his hands.*

Vibrations rumble along the road and through his feet. He closes his fists and looks up.

Dust floating behind their heavy wooden wheels, farm wagons approach. A man leaps from the first cart. He kneels beside the body and waves away flies. Then his gaze fastens on the dagger.

"Donnegan?" someone calls, and other farmers leave their wagons.

Alarmed, the boy grabs the dagger and shouts in a language he does not understand. Puzzlement on their faces, the men back away.

"Come, lad," says Donnegan. "We mean no harm. Put away the blade and tell us your name."

Name? The dagger wavers.

"Was this man your father?"

The boy shakes his head.

"How came you here? Did you see what happened?"

Words balk, refusing to push past his teeth.

1

Donnegan turns his head to speak over his shoulder. "Search the clothing. Bury the body."

Voices rumble: "I say we take both to Shea. The body and the boy."

"What if Baron Markha comes lookin' for 'im?"

"Not dressed like anyone from this province."

"Not Skardian."

"Dissonay? One of the Ethem?"

"Ain't no Ethem anymore."

"Wealthy, by the look of 'im."

Donnegan pushes the corpse's shoulder, rolling it on to its side. "Wounds on his back, one in his chest. Brigands."

Then he stands, and the other farmers bring spades from their carts and walk to a stand of trees on a hillock near the road. Working in silence, some dig a grave while others wrap the corpse in empty grain sacks. They lower the body into the hole and stand a few moments with bowed heads. Then they fill the grave with earth, and each man places a large stone over the fresh mound.

Shouldering their spades, the farmers return to the carts, nodding as they pass the boy.

Donnegan kneels once more. "A fine blade. May I?"

The boy's grip tightens, but then he offers the dagger, blade down. On the hilt glows blue chasing set with a letter, one the boy had drawn in the dirt.

Donnegan gasps. Lifts a stunned gaze. Swallows. "You are a Kel."

The boy frowns, not understanding.

Careful not to touch the chasing, Donnegan grabs the blade near the guard, cuts a strip from the hem of his belted tunic, and wraps the dagger's hilt in the cloth.

"Ho, Donnegan!" calls a gruff voice. "Stop tinkering and move out!"

He tucks the dagger under the bench in the first wagon, lifts the boy to the plank seat, then climbs up beside him, and grabs the reins. The oxen strain forward, the wagon lurches, and the boy grips the front edge of the bench to hold himself steady. The road bends and the trees lean close.

"I am not a farmer but a blacksmith," says Donnegan, "and you are not just any boy. A king was killed because of what you are."

He lowers his voice. "Whatever your name before, now you are

Kieran, for you have seen darkness and you seem a brave lad. When my wife and daughters ask who you are, we will tell them you are an orphan and my new apprentice."

Reins in one hand, he reaches over and plucks at the shoulder of the dirty blue tunic with colorful stitching around the hem and sleeves. "Do you wear an undertunic? No one will believe our story if you walk around in this."

The boy unbuckles his belt then pulls the silk over his head and tosses it into the wagon bed.

Donnegan narrows his eyes at the white linen shirt—"Still too fine, but better"—and the boy picks up his belt. As he tugs the ends together, he slides off the bench but catches himself on one foot, his other heel kicking the dagger.

In a voice lower still, and with words sharp as blades, Donnegan warns, "Never show that dagger to anyone. Not if you want to live. Understand?"

The boy nods. He hoists himself back onto the seat and finishes buckling the belt.

"Never. Swear on it."

He places a closed fist over his heart.

Donnegan nods, but the grim light in his eyes does not dim. "Now, we practice your story."

This time, speech is smooth as trout gliding through water. "My name is Kieran, an orphan and your new apprentice."

Donnegan laughs. "And with a fine, strong voice." He grows solemn again. "Keen wits and a good arm will take you far. Learn a trade and do it well, and you will live."

And so he does.

1 ~ CAPTAIN

The chains of a many-headed flail wrapped the longsword in iron tentacles and wrenched the two-fisted hilt from Gaerbith's grasp.

"Bark, dog!" The Skardian laughed, shaking chains dripping with the blood of other men. "I do not fear your curséd magic!"

Gaerbith drew a flat knife from the sheath tied just behind his neck, ducked beneath the Skardian's arm, and thrust the knife into the man's armpit, twisting the flail from his hand even as the blade drove deep. With a grunt, the Skardian slumped to his knees.

Gaerbith pulled the knife free. "This dog bites."

The Skardian swayed as if undecided about dying, then tumbled forward and lay still.

With a flick of Gaerbith's wrist, the knife hurtled through the air and sank into another Skardian's thigh. The man's leg buckled but he remained upright, fumbling at the haft, his sword tipping downward.

Gaerbith freed his own sword from the tangled flail, took two long strides forward and swung the flail. The chains caught a third opponent around the ribs in a bloody embrace, and the spikes bit into the mail and leather armor. The man gave a strangled gasp then fell.

The second man had pulled the knife from his leg, but blood gushed and he collapsed, his face pale. He was not long for this world. With shaking hands, he lifted his sword in surrender.

Gaerbith nodded and stepped back. Some might call him unwise for not disarming an enemy, even a dying one, but there was a certain honor due.

He whirled and met yet another opponent who, upon crossing swords with him, grew as white of face as a snow-mantled mountain. Snatching aside his blade, the man turned and ran.

Gaerbith was an island of life in a sea of corpses. Battle raged beyond him, Dissonay against Skardian, but none stood forth to challenge him.

He picked up his knife and wiped it clean against his thigh before tucking the blade into his belt. The sun lowered. The armies were thin and ragged in their formations. No new strategies had been employed other than meeting the enemy blade-to-blade on the field. Such warfare could not long be sustained.

The men of the Fourth Lachmil fought well and soon stood as he did, exhausted, unopposed. Skardian troops had not yet withdrawn from the field, but had contracted to the northern end of the vale, far from the Fourth and nearer their own lines. In such fashion they had been pushed back until Disson's army had moved beyond the Territories and stood well within Skarda's borders. Disson wanted to go home and be left alone—but not until Skarda ceased aggression and swore to leave the Territories free. In the beginning, most of the Fourth had been Territory men, but as war lengthened and losses increased, the *lachmil* had gained a greater mix of origins, good men all. Gaerbith lifted his sword to signal them, and turned toward the Dissonay lines.

Between the Fourth and the straggling remnants of battle, a pale youth quailed before a Young Wolf, one of the elite Skardian guards. The boy's blade was broken. The Wolf swatted him aside with the back of a gauntleted hand, knocking him to the ground. Then the Wolf lifted his sword arm, preparing to strike.

Gaerbith ran at the Young Wolf, and as he ran, he drew back the longsword over his left shoulder and swung it down, catching the man below the ribs. Propelled by momentum, by the force of the swing and the weight of the sword—and by something other—the blade broke the links of mail, sliced through the leather jerkin underneath, scraped across bone, and tore free just above the right hip, slinging a crimson arc. Divided at the waist, the Wolf toppled in two.

Gaerbith yanked the blood-spattered Dissonay youth to his feet and pulled him close, nose to nose, and glared into his fear-widened eyes. "Leave this field!"

"Captain—"

A short spear whistled past their heads.

"Go!" He released him with a shove.

The youth stumbled backward a few steps then hesitated.

Gaerbith pointed his sword at him.

The boy turned and ran toward Dissonay lines.

"Captain!" someone shouted.

Even as Gaerbith turned, pain seared his sword arm from shoulder to fingertips. He tossed the hilt into his other hand, but new pain cut into his back, slicing along his hip and down the side of his right leg. He staggered as he turned. A traditional Skardian sword, thin-bladed and wicked sharp, wavered before his eyes.

"You are the captain with the magic?"

Point digging the earth, only Gaerbith's longsword kept him upright. "Not. Magic."

He grit his teeth against the pain, and blinked at the blurred shadow of his enemy. Another Young Wolf. This one smiled.

"Only mortal after all." The Wolf drew back his sword.

His body jerked. Eyes widened in surprise then in realization. The bit of an axe, its edge appearing to be a seam in his surcoat, traced a line down his chest. Frothy lung blood bubbled from his mouth. The Wolf fell to his knees.

Clad in a stained and slashed surcoat bearing the green Oak of Disson, an enormous man with shaggy hair loomed behind the Skardian. Pulling the axe free, he kicked the dying man aside.

"Up with ye now, captain." His voice sounded distant.

Gaerbith squinted. "Turi?"

The big man tossed him over his shoulder, where Gaerbith flopped as loose as an old shirt, breath rushing out in a sharp gust. In the same hand as his axe, Turi carried Gaerbith's sword, and his heels left deep gouges as he strode over broken bodies and trampled earth.

On the battlefield—a broad, shallow vale in the northern shadow of the Highlands—men still cleared away the dead or bore the wounded to the healing tents. Cayn the Keeper stood outside such a tent, his clasped hands covered by the generous sleeves of his pale grey robe, and watched Lord Boorn approach.

The nobleman bowed. "Greetings, Elder."

Cayn inclined his head.

Boorn straightened, his silver hair gilded by late sunlight. Servants, bland-faced and rigid, arrayed behind him like the train of a long cloak. "I had not yet caught sight of camp when a messenger brought word of Captain Gaerbith's fate."

And how quick you are to test the truth of it. Cayn offered the fragment of a smile. "He yet lives—"

Lord Boorn's mouth opened then closed.

"—but every life's passing must be marked, and the pyres are burning," Cayn continued smoothly. "Perhaps your messenger mistook the captain for someone else?"

Boorn bowed slightly. "Captain Gaerbith is beloved of the king. All but a son. Should he die, there will be great mourning in Disson."

He extended his arm, ushering the Keeper away from the healing tent. Cayn's jaw tightened. This talking around a matter annoyed him. Boorn's real question had not yet been asked. Cayn would not spare him the asking.

"I cannot build higher walls around my vineyards," Boorn said after several steps in silence. "It is vital this war end soon."

"It is vital this war end well." Cayn reined in his pace so that he not out-stride the nobleman. "The Territories must remain free, else—"

"Come, come, Elder! This is a spat between brothers!"

"Kin by marriage. The only blood between them is the blood they shed on that field."

Boorn clasped has hands behind his back. "You are the master healer of the Dissonay army. You wield great power. Did you command other Keepers join their virtue to yours, you could end this war. Yet you do nothing."

"You would have us seek power too great for the frail arms of Men. I answer to the Voice, and to the king."

Boorn persisted. "What marks Captain Gaerbith in the king's eyes? Or in yours? He is nothing but a shepherd from the Hills, yet the men swear he wields magic. Even our enemies regard him."

Aye. Cayn looked to the distant line of Skardian tents. On the battlefield they did not know whether to fear Gaerbith or fight him.

When the captain first came to Disson, he knew nothing of war or weaponry. He spoke in an accent different from others in the Territories, and the king's guards did not understand the travel-stained stranger who beat his staff against the gate and brashly demanded to see Damanthus face to face. A shepherd confront a king? Yet Gaerbith brought the first warning: farmers and herdsmen had barely held back the advance troops Skarda sent to lay claim to the Thynathel Hills.

Hunters, herders, and vinedressers fought from thickets and from behind outcroppings. They knew the terrain, and harried the soldiers, picking them off as if harvesting fruit, and only occasionally engaging in true battle. Yet, though strong of heart and limb, the men of the Hills were poorly-armed and would soon be overrun.

As soon as he heard Gaerbith's message, King Damanthus sent arms and men. While they pushed the Skardians out of the Hills, he prepared his armies for war.

Curious. Boorn's vast vineyards had not been harmed in the first attack by the enemy, nor his men-at-arms sent to battle. Rather, they guarded his estate. His quest for position was rivaled only by his desire for self-preservation.

Had Gaerbith gone to him for aid but been turned away? Were that so, the shepherd would have had no other recourse than the king himself.

What if Gaerbith had not made the long journey? What if he had been injured, slain, indolent, afraid?

Cayn pushed speculation aside.

He continued between two rows of deer-hide tents before which men gathered in small groups, weary after battle.

Boorn lowered his voice to a grumble. "Wine from my vineyards may grace the king's table, but my sons are not invited to join the king's guard."

Cayn halted to face the nobleman. "You ask why your wealth attains little next to Gaerbith's poverty."

"Yes, Elder, tell me." The corners of Boorn's mouth tightened. "Tell me what my sons must do to gain favor with Damanthus."

"Where are your sons?"

"In the vineyards, making wine for the king's table."

"Perhaps they should be here, defending those vineyards."

"Not every man can go to war. Some must stay, make provision for the armies and for the families left behind."

"True," said Cayn, "but the Territories belong to no king. Damanthus need not defend them. After all, Morfran is not attacking him, but his neighbors. Nor has Damanthus demanded tribute of the Territories in exchange for his armies. Yet men and provisions arrive from the Calhoun Forest, from the Thynathel Hills and the Western Wood."

Two healers' apprentices passed, exchanging nods with the Keeper, and approached a fire where another apprentice burned old bandages and garments, anything that might bring disease.

"This is not the time for fear, Lord Boorn. Other men, poorer men, brave the journey. They combat ill weather, brigands, the Nar'ath—and they do it again and again, bringing necessary things to soldiers fighting to protect those very men, their families, and their land.

"Your sons desire the king's favor? Let them prove their worth."

Turi shook his head to fling water from his eyes. He grabbed a tattered piece of rough towel, rubbed it over his hair, face, and neck, then scrubbed dirt and dried blood from his arms and hands. With an almost-clean corner, he daubed a cut on his cheek.

Provender wagons arrived, glittering with bits of polished metal, sharp stones, knife-edged shells from the far western sea, all dangling from the cart railings or strung like barbed wreaths over the covered beds. On either side of each wagon rode archers on swift horses. They were guards against Nar'ath, great black birds that attacked with random, brutal malice.

As the caravan slowed to a stop in the center of the camp, soldiers hastened to unload barrels, sacks, and crates. Captains oversaw the dividing. Turi considered claiming his share, but he ate well enough: deer, fish, and whatever herbs, nuts, and berries he found in the wood near the Highlands. He even had a small clay jar filled with honey richer than the thin-tasting stuff brought in casks from Disson.

Carrying a yoke of buckets—one filled with water, the other with cellar vegetables, well past ripe though not yet rotten—a youth hurried past.

Palm flat against the boy's chest, Turi stopped him. "Owen."

Owen looked away.

"Step on the battlefield again, I will not save ye as the captain did." Turi released him. "Go. Take the haunch of venison hanging by my tent. The men are hungry."

The boy struggled to unhook the meat. He dropped it across the bucket with the vegetables and carried it to the main fire in the Fourth Lachmil's camp. The men sitting around the fire moved away, re-gathering into smaller groups. None spoke to Owen, or even looked at the boy.

The hem of a robe murmured through the grass. A Keeper approached. The pale-clad elder's only signs of great age were the clusters of lines at the corners of his eyes and the timelessness in his gaze. "He is young."

"His desire to be a warrior nigh killed the captain. The men will not forget."

"And you?"

Turi did not reply.

Owen sliced turnips into a pot. The boy's shoulders hunched, his head bent over his task.

"He knows his wrong," said Cayn, "That knowledge and his shame are greater punishment than shunning. Even now, if he could, Captain Gaerbith would sit by the fire, eat the soup, and speak to the lad of home."

Turi tossed aside the wadded towel. "How fares the captain?"

"He dreams old things."

Did not every soldier dream of life before the war? "But will he live?"

"I will send word when he wakes." Then Cayn turned his sharp gaze toward Turi. "On the morrow, beware the vineyard. From twisted grapes come twisted men."

The Keeper departed, robe whispering as he walked.

Turi frowned. Did Cayn speak of drunkenness? Poison? Keepers all sounded alike, uttering comprehensible words but incomprehensible matters. Captain Gaerbith understood them, but he was as odd as they.

On the far side of the battlefield, campfires flickered in the twilight. Beyond them, dark smoke marked the funeral pyres. In that, at least, Skarda and Disson were akin, sending souls at sundown when the path to the Otherland lay clear.

There was another place for the fallen, for the murdered and the war dead. They were said to cry in eternal grief and bitterness, trapped on the Highlands, separated from kindred until a blue sun rose in the west. Their howls were nothing more than wind through stones, but even Turi would go no closer to the Highlands than the wood. After all, what defense was a sword against a spirit?

He tilted back his head and looked up at the ribboned sky. *Omwen'din?*

A sudden breeze set banners waving, snapping the green Oak of Disson in a brisk salute.

When will those distant fires be the fires of home?

The breeze died. The first stars of evening winked in the sky.

"Tell me, Turi, how fares Captain Gaerbith?"

The fire's upward light created shadows that cut deep into the old man's face. King Damanthus winced, leaning on a wooden camp table that wobbled beneath the pressure. A wide bandage thickened his torso, and another wrapped his throat.

Turi stepped inside the tent, letting the flap drop closed behind him. "Be at peace, m'lord. The Otherland beckons, yet he lives."

Damanthus sighed. "If I had a thousand men like him, even then would Skarda defeat us. They are too strong, we are too few." He pressed his fist down on a sheaf of dispatches. "The Keepers assure me Omwen'din does not will our destruction, yet why is He silent before Skarda's dark arts?"

"M'lord, 'tis the Skardians say Gaerbith is magic."

The king snorted in derisive laughter then winced again, pressing his forearm against his middle. "Blood and bone!"

Turi helped him to the cot and settled him against a pile of cushions bearing the mark of the Keepers: a white bloom broidered by a thin outline of vibrant blue. "Should ye be about, my lord? Where is yer servant?"

"I am Damanthus of Disson, my mother is long dead, and I do not take orders from a mountain."

Smiling, Turi sat back on his haunches and looked up into the king's lined face. "Forgive me, my lord, I forgot my place."

Damanthus shot him a sour look. "Nor do I suffer liars."

Sweat glistened on his brow. His long grey hair, a few thin locks of it braided, hung in damp twists.

"Have ye eaten, m'lord?"

"Not hungry." The king closed his eyes. After a moment, he murmured, "I will drink a little water."

A jug of fresh water stood beside a cup made of silver-trimmed horn. Turi filled the cup then helped Damanthus sit upright, and held the vessel to the king's lips. The older man swallowed then coughed.

"Truly, m'lord, where is your servant?"

"Walking the camp." The king lay back once more, his voice thready for want of breath. "If the men see him about, they will think I do not need him. If I do not need him, my wounds must not be grave. If my wounds are not grave, then all is well."

Placing the cup on the tray, Turi said nothing.

Damanthus opened his eyes and smiled wryly. "I know what you are thinking."

"My lord?"

"You are thinking, 'He does not suffer lies. He encourages them.'"

Turi squatted beside the fire and pushed a half-burned brand back into the flames. "I was thinking of what the Young Wolf said."

"What? Oh. Magic." The king made a rude gesture. "Superstition."

Turi studied the glowing coals among the ashes. "Nothing touched the captain. Nothing grave. Until that fool Owen took up a sword. The boy should be home in the Hills, tending sheep. Not out on a field of battle, doing his clumsy worst to get the captain killed."

With the toe of his boot, Damanthus shoved Turi's shoulder. "Be at peace. Young fool Owen will grow wise with years. He is an impatient lad guided by a steady hand. My word as a father, he will be as good a man and as good a warrior as any I know."

"As ye say, m'lord."

The king's laughter descended into a cough. "Be gone, mountain. I have maps to study and dispatches to write. Tell one of the guards to send for my messengers."

As Turi pushed aside the tent flap, Damanthus added, "Fret not, Turi. Your captain is not visited by the dark arts. He is not magic but something more, and will reveal it soon enough."

Neither reassured nor comprehending, Turi bowed and ducked out of the tent. He dispatched a guard to find the messengers then searched the camp until he found the king's servant, Thael, playing at bones with a group of brown-clad soldiers from western Disson.

"Thael."

The young man put up a finger to signal *a moment* then scooped up a trio of knucklebones and rattled them in his fist.

Turi yanked Thael up by his tunic.

"What—!" Thael's legs flailed, seeking the ground. "My money!"

Setting the man on his feet, Turi plucked the fat purse from Thael's belt and poured half the coins back into the circle drawn in the dirt. Thael squawked in protest, but Turi pried the playing knuckles from the servant's fist and tossed them among the coins. All three bones landed alike.

Thael groaned. "A crown! You lost me a crown!"

12

The other men laughed, hooting jibes, grabbing up the money, huddling over the circle once more.

"I demand to know—"

"Then ye shall be disappointed." Turi dragged Thael through the camp.

"I warn you, the king will not be pleased if I come to harm!"

Turi spun about. "Did ye possess more wit and less greed, ye would have stayed with the king."

Thael's eyes widened. "Is he well?"

"If ye be not in his tent by the time I pass by, ye will not live to say a last prayer."

Turi released Thael, and the servant hastened away without a backward glance.

The Fourth Lachmil had pitched the southernmost camp of the Dissonay, and set a watch in the small, dense wood. The northern wall of the Highlands rose sheer behind the trees and wore a misty crown silvered by the moon's rising glow. Ever since the fighting had advanced deep in to Skarda, the Fourth had kept this ghostly post.

Eating or quietly speaking, men lingered around fires and tended their armor or weapons, or fashioned whatever necessary things could not be bought from the provender wagons. Exhausted but his mind too lively to let him sleep, Turi stood in the shadows.

Owen sat beyond the fires. Beside him rose a jumbled pile of weapons and armor scavenged by the men after the battle. He sorted usable items in one pile, repairable in another, and what needed to be melted down and reforged in yet another pile. As if feeling the weight of Turi's gaze, Owen looked up.

"Turi!" called an archer named Fremmen. "What happens on the morrow?"

Both armies had withdrawn from the field, but they did not retreat. Losses were heavy on both sides, and if the wind switched 'round, the thick smell of the funeral pyres would reach even the Fourth's camp.

Turi stepped forward into the light, and kept his words pitched low lest there be more than his own men standing watch in the wood. "Lord Padraig arrives soon with reinforcements. Even if they train for war as they march, they will be raw, untested. The Fourth, the First, and the Seventh are the most experienced *lachmil*. Damanthus may hold one of these in reserve to harbor the new troops."

Fremmen grimaced in annoyance. Other men did likewise, and some protested in rumbling murmurs.

"How long before Captain Gaerbith returns?" asked a grizzled warrior named Warrten.

The men quieted, their hands still, their eyes alert. From the shadows, Owen's face was a pallid gleam.

Turi took a deep breath. There was no softening the truth. "Captain Gaerbith might never leave the healing tent. If he lives, he may not walk nor swing a sword. Pray Omwen'din he does both, and soon."

No one looked at Owen directly, though some turned their heads a little as if pulled by their thoughts.

After a short silence, Warrten stood, stretching his arms out from his sides, shoulder-high and palms up. Setting aside tools, bowls, and weapons, the rest of the men joined him, and recited *Uûrun Trancta*, the warrior's prayer.

Omwen'din, hear my cry
and give me strength like the oak.
Make my back strong for the burden,
my arms mighty for the sword,
my legs swift in the chase,
and my will resolute in the tumult.

May I die a soldier,
blade in hand, honor in heart, pure in purpose.
When my shield is shattered
and the last blow falls,
may I look upon Your face
and be at peace.

The words swelled until the reverent *may I look upon Your face* fell to the longing of *be at peace.*

Turi forced down the emotion fisted in his throat. What would happen if Morfran succeeded in gaining the Territories? That question kept these men fighting. Peace and home was their greatest wish. They would have neither if Skarda took Disson.

As the men banked fires, changed watch, and prepared for sleep, Turi dug in his satchel for his food bowl then crossed the camp. Owen still crouched beside the mounded metal refuse. He started to stand, but Turi put a hand on his shoulder.

"Come dawn, take a bow and bring back more meat. Then finish this." Turi gestured at the pile.

The cauldron still hung over a low-burning fire. He filled his bowl and returned to his tent.

Gaerbith dreamed. Armies clad in ancient armor gathered near a tangle of massive trees. In the distance, tribes crossed forested hills, bearing bows and clubs and axes. The scene became a rout, one army chasing another to a river fouled black with blood. Blue light flared then faded. The vision changed. Again he saw the tangled wood. A man, old and bent, stood in the branches of a tree, his tattered robes hanging from his limbs in ragged ribbons. The old man spoke, but the words were snatched away, stolen by the wind.

A sword flashed. A child died. A warrior stood alone in the ruins of tumbled stone. He turned, despair in his eyes. Blood dripped from his sword, streaked his arms, matted his hair. "Uártha's heir, make haste. Haste, ere the Dark Voice find the heir of Kel."

Pale smoke shrouded the man.

"Wait!" Gaerbith reached out a hand, but his fingers passed through air, and smoke swirled around them, parting in pallid wisps.

The warrior was gone.

A quavering voice crooned in an ancient tongue, and gentle hands washed Gaerbith's limbs. Light flickered beyond his eyelids, but he could not open them to see if it was merely a Keeper's candle or the torch to light his funeral pyre.

Something brushed his face and touched his hair. Then a broad cloth wrapped his chest. So. He would not be burned on the battlefield. He would be swaddled in herbs and taken home to be buried in the Thynathel Hills.

I am coming, Father. Look for me.

2 ~ Dragon

Icy moonlight speared a hole in the dome of the cavern. A chained Dragon crouched. Golden scales gleamed. Green eyes glared. Wings scraped the walls, sending down rock in sharp cascades.

Torches were brought. A wheeled cage rumbled into the space just between the Dragon's forelegs, and held a man so beaten his features were masked by blood. A second cage was placed beside the first, its prisoner unmarked. The Dragon's head turned downward, and black-robed men hastened away from the cavern's mouth. Nostrils spouting steam, the creature sniffed each cage. The prisoners gagged on the foul air.

"Who are these men?" murmured a hooded observer clad in a black robe far finer than that of his companion, one of the Hôk Nar. Both men held damp scented cloths across their mouths and noses.

"The first is a Kel, my lord, and the other a commoner caught burning wood."

The Dragon hesitated a moment then—in one smooth, decisive motion—arched its neck and shot forth a concentrated stream of fire, consuming the first cage, leaving nothing but molten puddles on the stone floor.

The second prisoner cowered and cried out, but his cage was untouched.

A sense of supreme power pounded like blood through the observer. "It knows its prey every time?"

"Yes, my lord. Every time."

"How did Heolstor contrive to capture a full-grown Gremian?"

"Praise Nar Cahm, who renders the impossible possible."

"Praise *me*," the observer's voice grew chill, "for believing impossible was but a myth. I am the one who put forth the plan and refused to fail. I. Morfran, King of Skarda."

The Hôk Nar bowed. "Yes, my lord."

Morfran held up a thin scrap of gold, translucent, strong, and strangely warm. "Bind me to this Dragon."

"But, my lord, Heolstor has not found the binding ceremony in any of the scrolls. The Nar'ath report the Keepers walk in open sight, but the Elders among them have fallen away from scholarship and are now only healers. If we knew where to find the Great Archive—"

"The Great Archive does not exist."

"Your pardon, my lord"—the superior tone of the Hôk Nar's voice robbed his words of respect, and he swept the hood from his head —"but if that is so, what then do the Keepers keep?"

"Secrets."

Stirred by the Dragon's wings and its massive tail, ash floated in the air. The black robes of the two men turned grey, and the king's eyes stung.

"The Keepers know where hides the Kel-child. Once I am bound to this Dragon, the secrets of the Elders will be revealed, the sword will be found, and the Kel-child will be mine."

The Dragon turned its head and caught the king in the glow of one green eye, narrowed as if in thought. Transfixed, Morfran stared up at the gold-flecked iris. There he saw deepest knowledge, and hatred so ancient it could not be measured by so short a span as centuries.

It was for that knowledge the Gremian had been captured, and for that simmering desire for vengeance. Most other imprisoned Dragons were hatchlings—useful to Morfran's purpose only if he contrived to live a few hundred years past his appointed life—but now, *now*, he witnessed the fruition of dreams.

"It cannot be done, my lord," said the Hôk Nar, as if reading Morfran's mind. "None has survived the binding."

The king returned the scale to a small drawstring bag hanging from his belt. Then, smiling, he drew his sword from the folds of his robe. The Black Hood stuttered an apology, but Morfran gathered all the force of a man strengthened by years of battle and struck the head from Brother Terren's shoulders.

A Skardian sword might seem too thin and light for such a task, but it made a fine headsman's tool. He wiped the blade clean on the hem of Terren's robe before the Black Hood's body disintegrated into ashes and blew away.

Sheathing his sword, Morfran chuckled. What need had he for magic? He held the key to the Dragon's mind.

Yet, staring once more at the glittering, glassy scale, he felt the press of history, of the promises made, of his own ambitions. He had been reduced to a slave the moment he became king and took the Dragon Crown of Skarda. Yet here he held freedom. Here he held power. Here he held all the knowledge of the world.

He lifted the scale and looked into the Dragon's great eye. "Give me what I want, and I shall set you free."

The Dragon looked down on him in silence.

3 ~ CHALLENGE

In the darkness beyond the campfires, Morfran alit from the back of a Nar'ath and strode toward his tent, the golden Dragon scale clutched in his fist. Uncurling his fingers, he thrust the scale at the bearded ancient who greeted him.

"The creature mocked me. It looked on me and revealed nothing."

"Come inside, my lord," uttered the grey-clad counselor in a rasping whisper as he held aside the tent flap, "and we shall speak of the matter less widely."

Morfran ducked into the tent and gestured curtly at his manservant, Imre, who rushed to remove the king's cloak and unbuckle his sword. Then Morfran whirled on Heolstor. "Why did it not work?"

"We have not yet found a binding ritual in any of our texts. Perhaps in the Great Archive—"

"Speak to me no more of myths." Morfran's hand sliced the air between them, cutting off the counselor's request, one the old man had made countless times. Did it exist, the Archive was hidden well and guarded by Keepers. A battle conducted by magic and powers beyond his ken did not appeal to Morfran. Give him a good sword, and he would solve the matter himself. "Tell me, how do your Black Hoods keep a Dragon imprisoned by no more than a single chain and this bit of nothing?"

Heolstor looked at the thin disc in the king's palm. "The Gremians are warriors, strongest of the Dragon-kin. The one in the cave is a chieftain. He scarce fought when I plucked this scale from the floor of his lair and ordered him to yield his will to me. He *let* us capture him. And yet—" The counselor stretched forth a skeletal hand and touched the scale, his long nails clicking against the glittering surface. "And yet, he revealed no knowledge. He came quietly, but he did not open his mind to us or impart any power."

Withdrawing his hand, Heolstor wrapped it around his carven staff and moved toward the fire.

"So much for your great arts." Tossing the scale onto a table, Morfran dropped into a chair, and Imre put a goblet of wine into his hand. Morfran drained the cup and held it out for more. "The most devoted servant of Nar Cahm claims to read the thoughts of Men, yet he cannot plumb the depths of a brute beast."

Heolstor's thick grey brows drew together. "And yet I felt the essence of Brother Terren depart this world the moment his head left his body."

Morfran opened his mouth to reply, but loud voices lifted outside the tent. Leaving the goblet in Imre's hand, he stood and strode to the opening, and shoved aside the flap. His guards, their pikes crossed, stood before a group of barons whose anger was writ plain across their scowling faces.

Morfran stepped from the tent. "What matter is this?"

A portly baron stood forth. "My lord, Disson's armies are but half our number, we have superior warriors, and the Nar'Ath spy for us. Yet the Young Wolves lost five this day—all taken by the captain from the Thynathel Hills. The men are saying he is possessed of a magic greater even than Nar Cahm's. He must be stopped before his name drains courage from Skarda."

"Baron Hargow"—Morfran shouldered aside his guards—"if you persist in mongering fear, I will order the Hôk Nar to impose on your armies the same loyalty my own warriors endure when they first join my ranks."

Hargow put up a hand and backed away a step or two. "My lord, I assure you, such measures are not necessary. Yet can nothing be done to stop this captain?"

"We could stop the entire Dissonay army if your archers would ascend the Highlands and attack from the stone crown." Morfran glanced back at Heolstor, who stood behind the guards. "But even the dreaded Hôk Nar dare not scale those heights, and the Nar'ath do not fly too near."

Wine cup in hand, Imre stood beside Heolstor. Morfran beckoned him near.

Another noble, Baron Chennam in a striped surcoat, came forward and inclined his head in a brief bow. "My lord king, your son is the greatest warrior in Skarda. None stand before his blade. Mayhap he can seek out this man in battle and—"

"And do what?" A tall, slender young man with long golden hair emerged from the shadows. Dark half-moons beneath his eyes spoke his weariness, but his back was straight and his jaw firm.

Pride rose in Morfran whenever he looked upon his son, heir to the throne of Skarda and a colder warrior even than himself. He clapped Arien on the shoulder and offered him the goblet Imre carried. "We need to kill a Dissonay dog."

Arien's mouth pulled up at one corner. "Are they not all dogs?"

His companions—a cousin, Ûtgar, and two Young Wolves, Rhôn and Gurn—laughed at the old jest, their eyes bright with strong spirits.

Arien drank deep from his goblet then wiped his mouth with the back of his hand. "You will pardon me, Baron Hargow, but the fifth Wolf was slain by an axe, not a sword. Before he died, he might very well have killed the man you fear."

"Fear?" Hargow sputtered. "I do not—"

"He lives." Heolstor's harsh whisper was so jagged it hurt Morfran's throat. "The Nar'ath saw him being carried to a healing tent. He has not left it."

Arien raised the cup in mocking salute. "May he rise from his bed, the sooner to meet my blade."

"And Lord Padraig of Disson?" inquired Baron Chennam in a hesitant tone. "He alone has felled more of our men than that captain from the Hills."

Mouth a rigid line, Arien's face took on an expression Morfran knew well and relished, for it was a look of determination, an answer to a challenge. "Him I shall kill before this war is over."

"Indeed," agreed Morfran. "We cannot leave Disson a champion."

"To that end, my lord," Heolstor said, "I have a plan."

Gaerbith opened his eyes. A dark expanse arched above him, and somewhere near the head of his cot, beyond sight, a soft light wavered, perhaps a candle burning low in a stand.

As his eyes grew accustomed to the darkness, he saw a faint glow on the other side of the expanse. Dawn approached. He had not traveled to the Otherland.

Gritting his teeth, he turned onto his left side. The effort took more strength than he had. He leaned his weight on his elbow and forearm, sweating, cursing under his breath.

An urgent voice murmured, *Uártha's heir, make haste. Haste!*

He pushed aside the blanket and struggled into an almost upright position, left leg over the edge of the cot. He sucked in his breath as sundered muscles pulled and burned beneath their bandages. He was clad in a loose white garment with long sleeves. Where were his clothes? His sword? His knives?

Grasping the candle stand, Gaerbith pulled himself to his feet. Heat burst against his back and wicked down his leg. A torn sound, agonized and angry, ripped from his throat.

"Captain!" A Keeper rushed toward him. "What are you doing?"

"Sword—"

"You are bleeding again. Captain, you must lie down."

"Haste." Gaerbith fell to his knees. "Haste." His sight wavered. Candle flames blurred into long whips of light.

"He burns with fever." Cayn's familiar face appeared over the other Keeper's shoulder.

"It is the dream again," someone said, and Gaerbith felt himself lifted to the cot.

A damp cloth touched his brow, and another draped his throat. The shock of cold roused him to clarity. He grabbed Cayn's sleeve. "Elder, there is no time. I must find the Kel-child."

The Keeper bent toward him and waved a vial of bittersweet herbs before his face. "First, captain, you must mend. What use will you be if you rend these sinews past healing?"

"The warrior summoned me. He called me Uártha's heir."

Cayn's eyes twitched, as if brows and pupils drew tight for a worried instant, then his gaze cleared once more. "Nothing odd in that. You are heir to everything she taught you before she died."

"Not what he meant." Gaerbith's fist loosened. "Not what he meant."

The deer drank from a wee brook.

Owen crouched in a thicket.

The doe looked up, her ears flicking, water dripping from her lower jaw. Her large brown eyes seemed to stare straight at him.

He hesitated.

She bent her head once more to the water.

His arrow shot true, striking just behind her shoulder and piercing her chest. Her neck arched downward. Graceful legs collapsed.

He did not rise, but remained hidden. Countless animals had fed his family, clothed them, provided tools. Never had he thought overmuch on the necessity, nor on the ease with which he hunted. This day, though, guilt plucked at his sleeve and crouched beside him in the thicket.

But the guilt was not so much for the doe as for the captain. Staying here mended nothing.

Owen rose, slung the bow on his back, and descended the slope to where the doe lay. The arrow had broken when she fell. He pulled the shaft free then scooped water from the brook to cleanse it and the arrowhead. After putting the pieces in his quiver, he drew a knife from his belt and placed a hand on the doe's neck. She was still warm, her hide soft.

Returning the knife to its sheath, Owen removed his bow and quiver, propping them against a tree. He hefted the deer onto his back so that the forelegs hung over his left shoulder and the hind legs over his right. Then, after grabbing the bow and the quiver, he wrapped his hands around the doe's legs and pushed himself to his feet. The weight pressed them deep into the damp earth of the brookside, and the small slope seemed to grow steeper with every step he took.

Morning had come, and sun brightened the wood, rose light warming the cool green until it became a rich mantle.

On the edge of the wood, just beyond the camp, Owen hung the carcass by the hind legs and rough-dressed it. The blood he captured in a pot, and some of the organs he placed in a small cauldron so they might be boiled and chopped for stews. Unusable parts he burned lest they draw flies or animals to the camp.

Leaving the deer to drain completely of blood, he cleaned his hands with cool ashes, set a cauldron over the main fire in camp, then set to work sorting the weapons and armor from yesterday's battle.

Aside from a few guards, and archers making arrows, the entire Dissonay encampment was quiet. The army was gone to hurl themselves at the enemy once more—except for the troops Damanthus kept hidden lest the Skardians tried to attack them from behind.

Dissonay rarely wore helms, but everything salvageable was gleaned from the field. Owen stacked helms in the re-forging pile, along with shattered swords and other broken weapons. Mail birnies and hauberks with broken links made an almost cheery jingle as he dropped them in a shapeless heap. Three of his elder brothers had not been wrapped for burial, but carried home in rended mail shirts, and his father Forba had refused to clean the bodies or remove the garments of war.

"Bury them as they died," Father had said, "and let Omwen'din give them robes fitting of heroes."

The third brother had been brought home by the fourth, and that was when Owen had decided he, too, would go to war.

Fool. He slammed down a buckler.

It slewed the pile askew. Something glinted deep in the unsorted pile. Shoving aside a pair of greaves, a tooled vambrace, and a shield, he reached down and drew out a fancywork hilt. A stub of jagged blade remained near the guard. His arm still felt the shuddering blow that paralyzed him with fear when the Wolf broke that blade.

His memory filled with his first dazzled sight of the sword. Sleek and deadly, it had glittered against the sumptuous cloth lining the carven maple box in the back of a peddler's cart. The guard was a voluptuous curve. Wire-of-gold twined the hilt. No matter that the gem in the pommel was mere colored glass—it was a beautiful sword, and not too costly for a shepherd's son.

"So conceited a blade cannot be sound," his father warned, counting out coins in exchange for a new axe head.

The peddler shrugged one shoulder and said nothing.

A slight frown drawing his brows together, Owen's brother shook his head, and that silent no was like a hand on Owen's shoulder, drawing him away from the cart. He took a step or two backward.

Then his sight snagged on the hilt jutting up from the scabbard strapped to his brother's back. Named Bítan, the ancestral sword had been given to the eldest son of the eldest son for seven generations, and on its blade was graven a warning in an ancient tongue: *I will taste the flesh of my enemies and drink their blood.* So it had done during the war, and so it had served the first three sons. Now it had come to the eldest son yet living.

Why must a younger son be cast aside simply because he had not the fortune to be born first?

If Owen would not be given favor, perhaps he could earn it. What better way to prove mettle—and love for his brother—than to take up a sword and join him in the fight? Besides, Bítan was unadorned, a mere tool, and the sword in the cart was a magnificent weapon.

Owen poured his coin into the peddler's palm, and counted himself fortunate to own such a handsome blade. But now? Now it seemed tawdry, a cheap woman in a broidered gown.

He cursed himself; he cursed the sword; he cursed his ignorant arrogance; and as he cursed, he wiped the hilt clean, digging filth from the crevices with his thumbnail and polishing surfaces with a soft cloth. Using a rasp, he dulled the broken blade until it was no longer an edge, merely an uneven lump. Then he set out for the main camp.

He remembered the day he left the Hills: his father's farewell hand on his shoulder, the weight of the pack on his back, his brother's long strides consuming the road—a seasoned soldier reluctantly leading a foolish youth toward battle. Yesterday proved it. Though man-grown, Owen had been frightened, powerless, still a boy.

The Keeper outside the door of the healing tent stepped aside and drew back the flap so Owen might enter. Cots marched in tidy rows. The wounded or ill lay clad in pale tunics. Fragrance tickled his nose, and he saw bundles of herbs hanging in iron bowls suspended above scattered candelabra. Though the light was muted, the tent was not dark. He walked slowly past the cots, looking at each man's face but not finding the captain.

The day Owen bought the sword, he declared he wanted to join the Fourth. Gaerbith had looked at him, somber and sharp.

"You may serve," the captain said at last, "but you will put away that pretty sword. Pray Omwen'din we never need send boys or old men to face the enemy. You come with me, you care for the camp. Nothing more."

Owen had brought the sword anyway, hiding it among the tent poles. Would that he had cut off his arm instead.

Near the back of the healing tent, separated from the others by a thin curtain spanning the foot of his cot, lay Captain Gaerbith. Bandages thickened his body and bound his sword arm to his side; his free hand rested on his chest.

Owen wanted to say something, but excuse and apology seemed

too close kin. He wrapped the captain's lax fingers around the gaudy hilt and set it on Gaerbith's chest.

The captain's head moved on the pillow, and he muttered something in a tongue Owen could not understand. He should have paid heed when Mother tried teaching the old language to her squirming, inattentive children.

Voices stilled, and even moans ceased. The tent filled with sudden silence. Candle stands wobbled and the earth trembled as if shaken by the march of many feet. There were no clashing swords or sounding horns, yet men propped themselves up on elbows, their faces alert. Some of the wounded grabbed weapons from beneath their cots and struggled to their feet.

Owen ran to the tent door.

Clouds splayed grey hands over the sun, chilling the air, bringing the damp bite of winter to a spring morning. The rains had not yet come. When they did, armies would be mired in mud.

Disson stood ready, most of its *lachmil* arrayed in open sight on the field. The ranks were already sparse, but a few *lachmil* had hidden before dawn in flanking formation behind rising ground.

Yet the enemy, superior in number, did not attack nor did its armies stand forth from their camps. Nar'ath did not sweep down from the sky. Scores of the winged spies had been killed by Dissonay bowmen throughout the war, until Mad Morfran no longer used them in battle.

A lone horseman rode onto field, his sword held above his head—hilt in one hand, flat of the blade in the other—then threw the sword down, burying its point in the ground.

He waited.

Damanthus, pale and silent, sat his warhorse by will alone. He gestured to Turi, a flick of the fingers commanding him go. Turi tapped his heels against his mount's flanks, and rode forward. Wary of treachery, he stopped four horse-lengths from the Skardian and waited for the man to speak. A long silence passed as each warrior examined the other.

Then, in a quick smooth movement, the Skardian tossed a small leather tube.

It fell into Turi's palm with a crisp slap, and he wrapped his fingers around it.

With a curt nod, the Skardian pulled his sword free of the earth, sheathed it then turned his horse, kicking it into a run toward his camp.

Turi rode back to Dissonay lines at a leisurely walk, waiting the whole while for an arrow to put an end to his insolence, but he would not let his enemies think he valued any message from their hands.

He held out the dispatch case, but the king shook his head.

"Read it to me." Damanthus gripped the reins with white-knuckled strength.

"My lord, I cannot read Skardian."

"Thael—" The king clamped his lips shut and swayed in the saddle.

The manservant ran forward and, standing beside the king's stirrup, took the case and drew out a scroll of pliable calf-skin. He scanned the message silently then translated aloud in Dissonay: "'Morfran of Skarda sends greeting to Damanthus of Disson, and proposes an end to this conflict. Let us send forth champions, one from Skarda, one from Disson. Let them meet on the field of battle with what weapons they choose. Let the victor's king be ruler of the Territories. Let the defeated be mourned with all honors and rites. I, Morfran of Skarda, do set my seal and swear upon it.'"

Damanthus bowed his head and sighed. "Send word throughout the ranks. Tell them to return to their tents but remain ready. To the troops in hiding, send no message. They will see us leave the field, and will know we do not fight."

Thael bowed then hastened to his task. Captains and lords ordered their *lachmil* to turn ranks and return to camp. The Fourth remained, waiting their signal from Turi.

"Do I even answer this lie?" Damanthus curled his lip. "Morfran will send his son, Lord Arien, the most storied warrior in Skarda. Whom shall I send?" He looked across the vale. "Whom shall I decree worthy of death?"

"I will go, my lord," said Turi. "My axe is more than a match for any scrawny Skardian sword."

The king shook his head. "I need you with the Fourth."

"Send me, Father." A man who might have been Damanthus in younger days rode from the ranks and reined his horse beside the king.

"Padraig! You are come!"

"But with fewer reinforcements than we need." Padraig gestured; behind the gathered army stood a weary-looking mass of men in the varied garments of farmers, hunters, miners, craftsmen. "I turned some away. If I brought all, there would be none to tend the land or protect the families."

"The sea folk do not join us?"

Padraig shook his head.

"The mountain folk?"

"Only three clans."

Damanthus slumped a little to the side.

"Send me, Father."

"You are my son! My son! You will not—" Damanthus bent over his horse's neck, coughing.

Arm around the king's shoulders, Padraig looked over his father's head and said to Turi, "Summon a Keeper to tend him. Call the captains to my tent. Bring Gaerbith."

"He, too, is sore wounded, my lord."

Grim-faced, Padraig gazed across the battlefield.

Struggling to sit upright, Damanthus wheezed, "You shall not fall into Morfran's trap, Padraig. Nor you, Turi. I forbid you answer the challenge."

Neither man replied, but turned their horses and escorted the king to the Keepers.

4 ~ WAITING

Gaerbith knew he had dreamed again, but all he could recall was the voice of Uártha, long dead. She had spoken words over him as she lay dying, stricken by Heolstor, servant of Nar Cahm.

Nar Cahm, who spread confusion and fear and madness, so that all who followed that fell voice believed lies were truth and truth was the enemy.

Gaerbith opened his eyes. The sun was high, its light overspreading the far side of the tent. Had he forgotten truth in pursuit of folly? Did he remain here when he should be seeking the Kel-child?

No. He was protecting his homeland. This is where he belonged.

Then why did the warrior appear to him in dreams and bid him to the search?

He could not stay here, in this tent, in this cot, in this soft clean garb. Gaerbith lifted his free hand to cast aside the blanket, felt the metal he clasped, and recognized the colored glass in the pommel of the broken sword. He stared at it, watching light refract through the facets and cast rainbows in the air. How frail it seemed, this stub of sword—more gilt than guard—and how very useless.

Is that how Owen felt? Useless?

There came a time when every youth took a single step forward, from child to man, and any wise kin—or captain—would let the lad's foot fall on the path of his own choosing, for good or ill.

Pray Omwen'din it was for good.

Gaerbith dropped the hilt onto the cot then struggled to stand, canting his body and rolling out of the cot until his left foot could support his weight. Using the candle stand as a walking staff, he blew out the candle's flame, lifted the stand just enough to turn himself around, and surveyed the space beyond his curtained alcove. There was a clear aisle to the door, and the Keepers seemed occupied.

He lurched and scooted toward the door, the grass dampening the thud of the four-legged candle stand. Other men lay and watched him, some with puzzled frowns, some with conspiratorial smiles. He nodded as he inched past, sweat streaming down his face.

A shadow crossed his path.

"Good day, captain." Amusement touched the corners of Cayn's mouth.

Gaerbith did not stop. He shuffled onward with a sketchy bow and a breathless "Elder."

"Indeed, I am." Cayn walked beside him. "You know better than any healer how to care for those wounds?"

Gaerbith reached out to the tent flap, but Cayn pushed it aside and secured it open by tying it back against the side of the tent. Gaerbith tottered outside, squinting, then bid one of the guards exchange his spear for the candle stand—which the man did with a surprised chuckle.

Gaerbith pressed on, delighting in sunshine and movement, though he trembled in exhaustion and his wounds pained him.

"Where are you going, captain?"

"Fourth."

"Forth?" Cayn chuckled at his own joke, and Gaerbith smiled. "The Fourth is preparing to move camp after dark." A short silence, then, "The other captains are gathered in Lord Padraig's tent."

Gaerbith altered his course, and the Keeper followed, neither helping nor admonishing, but taking slow steps beside him. Before they reached the tent, however, Cayn put a hand on his shoulder, and Gaerbith halted—not because the Keeper demanded it, he told himself, but because he needed to catch his breath. No point in appearing at council gasping for air.

"Few know the truth," said Cayn. "If the enemy discovers who you are—"

"I did not choose to be Uártha's heir."

"Every man decides his destiny, even he who refuses to choose."

Gaerbith did not answer.

"You walk now only because Uártha imparted to you some of her strength before she died. You are a soldier, but you will never find rest from the dreams until you answer the summoning and become yourself a Keeper."

"Can I not do the Voice's bidding without swearing to it?" Bitterness bit Gaerbith's tongue. "Was not Uártha slain because of her oath?"

"She was slain because she shielded you, and because she held a secret. That secret is now yours, be you Keeper or no, but it will only be unlocked once you take the vow."

Gaerbith looked at him for a long silence then continued toward Lord Padraig's tent, alone.

"Aye," he told the startled guards, "your sight is true."

"Captain," said one with a nod after a slight pause. "The spear—"

Gaerbith handed it to him and entered the council.

Turi saw him first, then Lord Padraig. The other captains and lords turned more slowly, disbelief on every face.

"Welcome, captain." Padraig gestured to a stool near his chair.

"If it please you, my lord"—Gaerbith inclined his head—"I will stand."

Turi rose to stand beside him.

Face flushed, perhaps from the heat inside the tent, perhaps from anger, Lord Boorn stared at Gaerbith. "How is it you are here?"

"I walked."

Chuckles rumbled, and Captain Yerrin said, "At last! A man who speaks to the point!"

Lord Padraig leaned a forearm on the collapsible wooden table. "We were discussing a challenge issued by Morfran of Skarda." He read the message aloud then tossed it atop a stack of maps and dispatches. "What say you, captain? Do we answer?"

Every man looked to Gaerbith.

"Mad Morfran is much influenced by Heolstor of the Hôk Nar, who rarely speaks the truth, my lord, and even what little he utters is surely by accident."

Padraig smiled somberly. "Then you say we set a plan of battle rather than send one warrior?"

"That message is from a desperate king who has no more men to throw into battle." Gaerbith shuffled forward a few steps. "Our archers have felled most of his Nar'ath, and few of his spies have returned to his camp. Even his Brethren of the Black Hood are hindered in their magic."

Captain Yerrin added, "I say we attack—in full force—and finish this."

"And lose more men?" Lord Boorn stood. "We have precious few. Before any great endeavor, one must consider if it is worth the risk."

Lord Ában spoke from across the tent. "Wise words for any venture, but what lies behind them? True, we must consider the cost, but is that rigid accounting for the kingdom's sake or for your own purse?"

Boorn folded his arms. "If my purse is thin, I cannot serve the king."

"Gaerbith here is a shepherd and by no means a wealthy man. Does he serve the king no less than I, who have wealth enough to thatch every roof and repair every wall in my village?"

"Foolish generosity becomes foolish poverty."

"Indeed." Lord Ában nodded. "There is a time to open the hand, and a time to close the fist. Not every man who desires aid requires it. Many a man would be content to let others work while he lies at ease."

Boorn snorted. "Do continue, my lord. We are eager to hear more of your boasting disguised as wisdom."

Padraig drummed his fingers on the table. "The question of risk or retreat is mine to answer—or my father's, should he wake." He looked from one lord to the other. "Every action is peril, for consequence attends it. If we meet the enemy, we die. If we retreat, we concede the field. Either way, the dead will have died in vain."

"Even if we retreat, we die," said Captain Yerrin. "Skarda will gain courage and pursue us to the Territories."

Another captain added, "They have been holding back the Nar'ath. But if Skarda discards all caution in one last battle, they may send the Nar'ath at our archers again and overwhelm them." He hesitated. "We are short of arrows."

No one spoke. In the silence, men made the sign of Omwen'din, touching the joint of right thumb to chin, mouth, and brow. Each great black bird could lift an armed man wearing armor and tear him apart.

Gaerbith asked Padraig, "Where is Damanthus?"

"In the Keepers' care."

"It is grave?"

"He bleeds inside." Padraig rubbed his eyes with thumb and forefinger. "Does Omwen'din call him to the Otherland, I will be king by morning."

"Then we can give no answer, my lord, for you are the best warrior among us"—the captains nodded in murmured agreement—"and if you should fall, who will lead us?"

Rumors that Lord Padraig had best look to his inheritance were untrue. Gaerbith wanted no place in ruling Disson, nor did he go seeking approval. He wanted only to live in peace, his remaining kindred unmolested and well for the rest of their days, without a king to tax or oppress them. Yet he loved Damanthus as one of close blood, and Padraig as a brother.

"Send another, my lord, to face Lord Arien." Lord Boorn sank to his seat but leaned toward Padraig, his face and voice persuading, one hand outflung, open then fisted in emphasis. "There are great warriors in our ranks." He looked to Gaerbith. "Any captain but one is more than able to face Morfran's son."

"What if the challenger is Morfran himself?" Captain Yerrin also leaned forward. "Some say he is protected by the very breath of Nar Cahm, who suffers no hurt to befall him." Yerrin spat into the fire. "I stand with Gaerbith. This is a trap. Our best answer is silence."

Boorn raised his voice in protest, Yerrin replied, and then the others joined the argument.

"This is how it has been, captain," Turi said to Gaerbith through the din. "We are stirred to strife. Ye missed the argument over the way the new troops are dispersed."

Swaying, Gaerbith caught himself by grasping Turi's shoulder. "How fares the Fourth?"

"Only ten men wounded past fighting. And yerself."

"The other *lachmil*?"

"The Twelfth only has thirty men."

"Blood and bone."

"Aye."

The tent wavered and light swirled, turning the gesturing men to blurs of moving color.

Lord Padraig's palm slapped bare wood, and the table shuddered. Startled, the captains and nobles grew quiet. In the sudden silence, the king's son glared from beneath lowered brows, and it seemed a young Damanthus glowered upon the gathering. "Go. I shall make my decision before dawn tomorrow."

The men stood to leave. Padraig thrust a forefinger at Lord Boorn. "You. Return to the Thynathel Hills. Tonight."

Boorn bowed stiffly. "My lord."

As he departed, such hatred burned in the nobleman's eyes as they met Gaerbith's that the captain felt the scald of it on his skin, as if he passed through flame.

Only Gaerbith and Turi remained with Lord Padraig, who leaned forward, elbows on table, forehead resting against clasped hands. He sat so still he seemed not even to breathe.

Turi jerked his chin toward the door. Gaerbith nodded, and they started to leave the tent.

"My father once said you trained with a powerful teacher." Padraig lowered his hands and looked up. "One who stood face to face with the enemy and did him much harm."

Gaerbith hesitated. "Aye, my lord."

"Your teacher—she was a Keeper?"

Gaerbith inclined his head.

"Is it possible, then, that you might heal my father?"

"Uártha was a scholar, my lord. She taught me words, not remedies. I am not a Keeper, nor have I the skill—"

"But if you took the oath!" Padraig leapt to his feet, face intense, then almost at the same instant waved a hand. "No. No. That I cannot ask. Centuries of life shortened only on the edge of a blade? No. Nor would my father ask it of you." A wry smile. "If he roused from his bed because you took the oath and cured him, he would find some other way to die."

"He is obstinant."

"Obstinant." He passed a hand down his red beard braided here and there with bits of graven stone. "That is too small a word."

He fixed Gaerbith and Turi with a somber stare. "Should my father die, and should I fall"—he touched a scroll sealed in green wax—"the army is yours to lead until my brothers are of age. The choosing of my sisters' husbands is yours, as well." He added, "Captain Yerrin has caught Astara's eye."

Gaerbith bowed his head in consent as Turi replied for them both: "We will do yer will, my lord."

Padraig's shoulders eased. "I will give this to Thael's keeping. He bears the only other key to this box"—he placed the scroll inside a small carven chest—"and we will speak of it no more."

The atmosphere inside Lord Padraig's tent was thick with the odor of battle and sweat, leather and metal. Cayn tied the flap open to admit only slightly fresher air.

Padraig sat at the campaign table and stared at the tent wall. Cayn waited.

"Can it be done?"

"You know your father's words."

Padraig nodded. "This will not break his command—he never mentioned Gaerbith—but it will certainly strain his will."

"He who takes the Keeper's oath without first hearing the Voice's call forfeits his life. Gaerbith has been called, but he refuses. Keepers share their strength with one another, but we do not know what will happen if we give that strength to a mortal."

With both hands, Padraig pushed back his red hair and tied it with a leather string. Then he stood and leaned forward, palms pressed against the table top. "He rose from his death bed and walked in his own strength to this very tent." Padraig looked at Cayn. "He can absorb your power."

"For how long? And at what cost?"

Padraig's desperation was troubling yet understandable. The king lay dying while a man who should be dead walked the camp. What military leader would not want to make use of such a weapon?

"Would you risk your own brothers to an untried measure?" Cayn asked. "Would you go yourself?"

Padraig looked away.

Morfran paced his tent. He had issued challenge to Damanthus, that stone-headed brother of his faithless wife, but had received no reply.

No matter. Morfran would be the victor. That was the plan. Heolstor had vowed it could not fail.

Yet, away from the old counselor's raspy voice and slippery reasoning, Morfran doubted. Had he not cause? Heolstor had promised to bind Morfran to the creature, but the Dragon yielded neither will nor knowledge.

Morfran halted before a small square table covered by a rough cloth. It held the crown of Skarda: in the shape of a Dragon, its arching neck rising at the front, and its outspread wings forming the sides. The tail wrapped the back of the crown and met the left wing, completing the circle. Rubies glittered in the eyes, but he had read in the archives that all golden Dragons—the Gremian kindred—had green eyes.

When he had first worn the crown, the gold was as red as the rubies, covered with the blood of Vegeir, whose head parted company with his body. Morfran had taken the crown from the dead king's brow and placed it on his own, then knelt before Heolstor for Nar Cahm's black blessing.

Heolstor's thirst for power was greater than his own. He had determined many times to cast out the Master of the Black Hoods, yet the old man remained.

There was a dark magic at work—

"My lord." Imre, his servant, ducked into the tent and brought a tray bearing a steaming bowl of stew, a small loaf of bread, and a wizened apple that had likely spent a long winter in a barrel.

Morfran put back the crown. Imre set the tray on another table, but Morfran strapped on a sword, pulled on supple leathern gloves, and tucked a coiled whip into his belt.

"Come, Imre. I am going to the hold."

After a startled pause, Imre gathered his quills and ink pots, and several parchments scraped free of old dispatches, and packed them in his messenger pouch. He wrote a fair hand and had a way with details. When Morfran read of his own deeds, recorded in books kept locked in a private chamber in the Keep, he marveled at vivid descriptions so sharp and filled with sensation that they seemed more real than his own memories.

A pity Imre spoke more poorly than he wrote.

Located in the midst of the camp, its walls constructed of tall poles sharpened to wicked points, the hold was a roofless structure in which prisoners were tied to posts and, whenever Morfran felt restless, tortured. This day, only one man was staked in the center of the enclosure, his body sagging in his bonds. His leg had been crudely set between two crooked sticks bound in place by dirty rags. He was not Dissonay but one of Morfran's own soldiers, caught stealing a horse so he could flee back to his village.

He should never have remembered he had a home other than the Skardian army. Save the Young Wolves or those who joined the barons' troops of their own will, all men in the king's service were conscripted, their memories swept clean, replaced by loyalty to Morfran and devotion to Nar Cahm.

And yet the magic of the Hôk Nar had availed nothing. This man's mind was his own, and would not be turned again.

Uncoiling the whip, Morfran studied him: filthy, his scarlet surcoat a ragged mess, rivulets of dried blood trailing from his ears, crusting his beard. The Brethren had been fervent in their task.

"I will not bow." The man raised his head—slowly, slowly—and glared defiantly at the king. "I am not a beast but a man, and I will not bow."

"Then I will make those you love bow, and those you call friend bow, and all who live in your village bow." Morfran let the whip sway back and forth. "What say you to that?"

Silence.

Morfran flicked the whip. The tip of it licked a red line across the prisoner's face; the man scarce moved.

Morfran felt the bite of anger, but he pushed it aside. He would extinguish that fire of rebellion in the prisoner's eyes.

"Imre, bid the guard bring coals—thriving coals—and step sharp!"

Once the pot of coals had been brought, Morfran plunged the tip of his sword into their glowing heart then touched the flat of the red-hot blade to the prisoner's ear. His reward was a scream so pure it chilled his skin.

He smiled. Heating the blade anew, he watched the man writhe, teeth bared, face contorted, skin seared like cooked meat.

"Now"—Morfran branded the side of the prisoner's neck, and shuddered with gratitude at the shrill agony of a fresh scream—"we will talk of many things." He let the tip of the sword hover near the man's right eye. "Tell me, where is this village? The one you stole a horse to find? In which province does it lie?"

Nostrils flaring, the man took quick breaths. The muscles in his neck and jaw were tight, vessels and sinews standing sharp beneath his skin. Before Morfran could turn aside, the prisoner spat. Mucous fouled the king's beard.

Morfran slapped him with the back of a gloved hand, slamming the man's head against the wooden post.

"Imre." Morfran's voice shook with wrath, and that increased his anger. "I require a flat club, a cauldron of hot water, and pincers. Bid the guards build a fire here, in the pit."

The unconscious prisoner's head had fallen forward so that his chin rested on his chest.

"We will be some time."

Though of the original men half the count remained, the Fourth had lost twice its number since the beginning of the war.

Only a few of the dead had been carried home. The rest were burned in pits or on pyres that left great charred circles in the earth as the Dissonay pushed deeper into Skarda, away from the scarred timber of the Calhoun, where Mad Morfran had first tried to defeat Damanthus. Morfran had set fire to the forest, then—on the other side of the flames, standing in his stirrups with his fist in the air—shouted a mockery of the Dissonay death blessing: "Nar Cahm, I give to you these mongrel dogs! Diseased, dishonored dead!"

In perfect Dissonay, it was, so they all might hear and understand.

And the Dissonay roared, swords held high, "Omwen'din, we give to Thee the honored dead!"

Then, with pots and cauldrons and cups, they cast water on the flames, dug trenches with their swords, felled trees, scooped dirt with their hands, and killed the fire. By then, however, two whole days had passed, and the enemy had retreated far into the Lowlands.

Not retreated, perhaps, but sped well on its way lest the grasslands, too, catch fire and chase the army across the Plains.

Turi smiled in somber humor. Skarda should have looked over its shoulder—should have turned sooner upon the weary, smoke-blackened Dissonay—if it meant to win the war.

Too late, the magicians of Nar Cahm sent their birds to spy out the smoldering ruins and report on the number of dead. The archers of Disson brought down many a Nar'ath that day. The warriors, thinking to feast, found the birds' flesh inedible and rank, and subsisted on what few berries and nuts they could scavenge. Deer and other animals had fled the fire.

So time has flown, and we be only this deep into the enemy's kingdom. Too far from home, and too long away.

Gaerbith stumbled. Turi thrust out his arm, and Gaerbith's chest caught up against it. The captain retrieved his breath after a moment, his face paler than when he first entered Lord Padraig's tent for the council.

"What happened yesterday? Why did we withdraw from the field, and why did not Skarda pursue?"

"Ye said it yerself, captain. Skarda's losses are as great as our own. " Angry, though he could not have told why, Turi added with a mutter, "Or perhaps yer magic saved us."

Ice-blue eyes studied him.

Turi looked aside. He was a tall man, taller than the captain, and larger than most men in the Dissonay army. He knew he intimidated. It was no wonder young Owen seemed to shrink into himself yesternight. Yet the captain, wounded, weak, and a head shorter, had the strength in one long look to make him feel like a petulant youth picking a fight.

When Lord Padraig chose Turi to serve in the Fourth Lachmil, Gaerbith himself had trained him in swordcraft. Turi preferred the axe. He carried one on his back, next to his longsword.

In the great fire, the Second lost its captain. King Damanthus appointed Padraig to the post and elevated Gaerbith to captain the Fourth. Gaerbith continued to train Turi,.and put him in command of the newer soldiers. They were of an age, he and the captain, and of similar humor. Had they been men of the same village, they might have been lifelong friends.

A cartwright by trade, Turi had been the first in his village to join the men marching from Disson through the Territories. He had more cause than mere loyalty to a king and countrymen. Walking through a meadow one day, his wife and eldest son, a lad of eight, were slain by two Nar'ath. Turi came upon the birds as they feasted on the flesh. The first he killed with a well-thrown stone through the eye; the second he tore asunder with his hands.

Then, collapsing in the bloody grass, he wept.

The birds were burned by the villagers, who also gathered what remained of Turi's wife and son and buried them. The next day, Turi sold or burned all his possessions, placed his daughter and infant son in the care of his sister in a nearby village, and walked to where the army camped.

He wished he were only a cartwright again who knew nothing of war, who closed his shop at sunset every day and entered a well-kept cottage, made welcome by his children and his wife, but there was no mending the past. He would not cease until vengeance had been wrought on those who commanded the Nar'ath.

With formidable reach and strength in battle, he was a warrior unafraid. Yet even he was uneasy enough to make the sign of Omwen'din when the wind howled down from the Highlands. Perhaps the revelation that Gaerbith was somehow touched by the power of the Keepers should not have roused such apprehension in him, or such anger. Yet it did.

He forced himself to meet the captain's steady gaze.

"You doubt me, Turi?" The question was quiet. "I will not fight beside a man I cannot trust."

Stung, he spoke what he did not intend. "Not trust me? Yer one of them!"

"If I were, it would only make me a better soldier."

Turi snorted.

"Keepers are called to service by Omwen'din, and He it is gives them long life and strength. Likewise, far sight and great knowledge are His. I would not turn away such gifts."

"And yet ye do not take the oath."

Gaerbith limped onward, a misshapen creature, thick bandages enlarging his entire right side as if he were a being made of two different men. "I am as mortal as you. This strength that lets me live when I should have died? Merely the residue of one Keeper's ebbing life."

Turi hesitated. Then, taking a single stride, he caught up with him. "Why are they all healers?"

"Keepers are farmers, craftsmen, merchants. They appear as any other men or women."

"But why are they called Keepers? What do they keep?"

"Ancient knowledge. Books, craft, music, medicine, husbandry. They teach Men, but they also guard truth and history in the Great Archive. Other than the Voice Himself, they are the greatest enemies of Nar Cahm."

The healing tent loomed near. Gaerbith's breath came in gasps. His leg was red with blood.

"Rest, captain. Obey the Keepers. Yer not the only soldier defending the Territories."

"You think I seek glory on the field?" He seemed too weary to be angry. "I lost brothers there, and friends. What do I tell the families of the fallen? How do I write them letters that the village priest or the magistrate must read to them? My book of names grows heavy, and my store of words grows light."

"I do not doubt ye, Gaerbith. I have counted ye friend since Lord Padraig was our captain, but—"

Silence grew deep between them, a wide river without a bridge.

Gaerbith gripped one of the ropes securing the healing tent to its stakes. "Padraig did not learn of it from me. I did not think it worth the telling."

"A Keeper's heir? Not worth the telling?"

"The men might see only an unknowable power and think it magic. They might refuse my lead, and no longer count me one of them."

Turi crossed his arms. "They know something already. They know. It is in yer dreams. Ye speak in riddles and in other tongues. Ye speak of a place of stone. A place ye expect to die."

"Even Keepers die."

"Aye. On the edge of a blade."

"We are warriors, and this is war."

"And there"—Turi jerked his chin toward the Highlands—"is stone."

5 ~ HIGHLANDS

The sheer scarp of rock rose high above the small woodland at its base. The top of the cliff was marked by a crown of standing stones, some leaning against one another, some toppled. Twisted trees clung to the wind-scoured heights, and water trickled down in small cascades over the ribbed rock, feeding brooks and pools in the wood. When Gaerbith looked on the Highlands, he felt only welcome, never the fear that drove other men to kiss their thumbs and mutter prayers when the night wind howled like murdered souls.

His weary sight blurred at the edges, slurring sunlight into bright smears. He blinked the world into clarity once more, gave Turi a few instructions for the Fourth, then turned toward the healing tent.

"The wanderer returns"—Cayn stepped forward, accompanied by two other healers—"but not to rest. We go where few journey but the dead."

His companions laid Gaerbith's arms across their shoulders, holding him upright.

"We will return your captain," the Keeper said to Turi, "but whether alive or dead is his choice and the will of Omwen'din."

The healers led him away from the tent. He stumbled along, questions crowding his thoughts, but they required too much effort to speak.

His senses grew hazy until the only thing he knew for certain was the pain piercing his leg and back with each slogging step. Yet the healers pressed forward, beyond the camp, across the open space then into the wood, through undergrowth that slapped at his legs and tangled his steps. The healers came upon a narrow footpath, and the struggle was not so great here.

"Here we must leave you." Cayn's voice behind seemed far away, as if speaking across a vast distance. "The rest of the journey you must take alone."

The healers released him and stepped back. He almost fell, but tottered forward a few steps and caught himself.

"We will wait until you return."

He looked back. Cayn and the others were vague shapes obscured by a white curtain of mist-like brilliance. Their pale robes melded with it, as if made of light, and their stillness assured him they would remain.

Gaerbith trudged onward.

Uártha walked beside him, speaking words in a tongue he had not heard since boyhood. *Enë iri ark.* She reached toward him, her eyes sad. *Enë nythn tae dyn clahdá, o enë rhoclárho pyrvínë.*

It was something she told him often in his childhood, always in ancient Kelden rather than common Dissonay: *Your anger break. Your peace it will steal, and your soul poison.*

He wanted to tell her there was no need for such warning. He had not been squabbling with his brothers but fighting the army of a greedy king mad to possess what was not his. Surely such anger was necessary?

The path broke free of the trees and cut through rock—rising, rising—then it disappeared, overtaken by thick moss carpeting the earth around and amid a ring of standing stones.

From the stones themselves stepped figures as grey and fluid as the rain.

The spirit of Rabb, his eldest brother, caught him as he fell, and laid him on the spongy ground. Kneeling, the shade took his chin in a cold hand and looked into his eyes. *Gaerbith, my brother. Listen well.*

He stood looking down at himself: pale, tattered, bloody. He felt no pain, but agony showed on his face. How sunken were his eyes, how hollow his cheeks. His yellow hair straggled across the ground, long, braided here and there as was the custom of Lord Padraig and others among the Dissonay.

Though his body lay on its back, he saw what lay hidden. He saw the groove across his shoulder and deep behind his chest, saw the long cut down his back, hip and thigh. Bone glistened white beneath sundered muscles.

Was he dead?

This was not how he envisioned the Otherland. He looked around, but the dead were gone. He stood alone in the ring of stones.

WHAT DESIRE YOU MOST, GAERBITH THA FORBA?

Whirling, he saw only mist and a soft light. Whoever spoke knew Kelden—an ancient tongue spoken by only a few—for "tha" meant "son", and Gaerbith had not heard that name since leaving his father's house.

"Omwen'din?"

OMWEN'DIN. MYMNA TOR. THE VOICE. ALL THOSE NAMES AND MORE.

Gaerbith dropped to one knee, but he did not feel the press of mossy ground or even his own weight. When he bowed his head, he saw the rusty green of the moss shimmering through the translucence of his thigh.

WHAT DO YOU DESIRE?

Words shot like arrows from a taut bow. "I want to be free of my inheritance. I do not wish to be a Keeper. Let me walk beside my brother. Let us go home and live peaceful and free. Let me embrace my sisters and clasp my father's hand. Let me bow at the graves of my brothers. Let me hang my sword above the door and take down the shepherd's crook. Let me live."

WHAT GOOD IS LIFE TO A MAN WOUND TIGHT IN HIS GRAVE CLOTHES?

"You stole my mother's life!" Gaerbith rose shouting, his fist punching the air. "If I die, if Owen dies, you leave my father without sons! You let a madman threaten our freedom and our peace! Why stand aside and let all that is beautiful die?"

BEAUTY IS OF MY OWN MAKING. I WILL NOT SEE IT DESTROYED ENTIRE OR FOREVER.

"And yet You will see it destroyed for a time? What is the good in that?"

Anger bleeding from him, Gaerbith sank to sit on a fallen monolith, sudden exhaustion taking his ghostly limbs. "What is the good in that?"

Wind mourned among the stones. Almost he heard the voices of the dead.

Omwen'din held His peace.

Gaerbith looked over at his prone body. How oft of late had he been trying to do everything alone? He had not asked for help of his men in sending tokens, letters, or possessions back to the families of the fallen men; the drivers of the provender wagons were always willing to deliver messages. Nor had he let the men see him mourn. He led them into battle, but he fought alone. He had grown proud in his skills, in being nigh untouchable.

Untouchable no longer.

There he lay, a crippled warrior of no use to anyone if he did not heed the healers and let his body mend. Not even the Keepers had skill to knit together one who would not submit to what must be done.

Submission implied weakness. He was a warrior. How could he stand back and let anyone else—even the almighty Voice—accomplish a task that was his alone?

Gaerbith looked up and saw the past: a grey-hooded figure clutching a pale carven staff, and a tall woman with long golden hair and clad in blue the color of a clear summer sky. The supreme servant of Nar Cahm the Dark Voice challenging Uártha, Keeper, servant of Omwen'din.

"Tell me where it lies," the grey-clad man orders in a jagged whisper, "and the boy will live."

Uártha says nothing at first. At her feet lies a boy of thirteen summers, bleeding. He looks up at her, refusing to let her see how much he hurts.

"I will not bargain with Nar Cahm or his hireling." Uártha holds a book in her hand. It is a rare thing, for it is bound and not a scroll. "I will not render to my enemies my greatest treasure."

The boy thinks she means the book, or the secret demanded by the servant of Nar Cahm. Then she looks down at him, and in her eyes is such a light he lifts a hand to ward against the brilliance.

"Ta na—ta cahm ni æa—claehdas frilë dur lel medë."

No one—no enemy or friend—takes him from my hand.

She thrusts the book toward Nar Cahm's servant, and unseen power bursts from it, silent shocks that shudder the air and thunder in the boy's ears.

Lifted from his feet, the grey man flies backward and falls, but he leaps up like a cat, twirling the long staff and directing it toward Uártha. Smoke—pure darkness—shoots from it and wraps her throat.

She shrugs, and the black rope uncoils.

She holds the open book in both hands, offering it toward the sky. Light blazes from its pages, and golden words cut the air, myriad daggers flying at the grey man.

He cowers on one knee, the staff raised above his head, his shoulders hunched. Not all the words are held at bay. Some slip past his shield and leave trails of dark blood along his pale arms and hands. One dagger slashes the fabric of his hooded robe, and even darker blood spills from his side. He cries out and does not rise.

Uártha helps the boy to his feet. Looking over her shoulder at the grey man, "Ta na," she says, cold warning in her voice. No one.

She touches the boy's shoulder, and he follows her from the stony heights of the mount on the Isle of Morga and down to the edge of the Dävra Sea. Uártha steps into a boat, and the boy takes an oar.

Cawing shrill and harsh, one of the Nar'ath flies from the depths of the forest. The boy whirls, oar raised. The boat rocks as he strikes at the giant bird. It reels but returns, flying lower, its claws gleaming.

Uártha utters a word. The crow flaps and struggles but is held midair, caught like a fish in an invisible net.

From the shadows lurches the grey man, blood oozing from his side. He thrusts out a hand, and the Nar'ath breaks free, diving once more.

Uártha steps from the boat and stands in the water. The blue of her garments joins the sea until she seems made of water and light.

Again the boy strikes at the bird, but not before it rakes his chest and shoulder with its claws, toppling him into the shallows. Salt stings his wounds. He can scarce breathe. Somehow he stands again, flinging wet hair from his eyes and lifting the oar.

"What we fight is not that creature," Uártha says. "Remember, Gaerbith. What we fight is not blood and bone."

But when the Nar'ath swoops again, the golden words fly from her book and slay it, follow as it tumbles to the sandy shore, and there cut it to bits.

The grey man staggers. Planting the butt of the staff in the sand, he lifts both his arms and summons a billowing cloud of darkness. It rolls from his sleeves, his hem, his hood, surrounding him, swallowing him.

Light embraces Uártha, and she stretches out her arms to the boy, bidding him enter that protection.

Dropping the oar into the boat, he splashes toward her, water and sand sucking at his legs and feet.

A bolt of black power shoots from the dark cloud. He cannot move—

She sweeps in front of him, her arms still outstretched, her body jolting with the impact of the bolt. Light stretches and twists, absorbing the shock.

Smoke sucks backward until it disappears, revealing once more the grey man.

Uártha crumples into the lapping sea.

The man pulls the staff from the sand.

"Mymna Tor take you!" the boy shouts, tears streaming down his face. He grabs up the book bobbing in the water and shoves it toward the enemy.

Nothing happens.

Laughing, wheezing, the grey man limps away.

A hand clamps the boy's ankle. Dropping the book into the boat, he kneels, and lifts Uártha's head from the water. Long hair floats around her in gilded waves.

She places a trembling hand on his head and utters a blessing that is not a blessing: "What strength is mine, I give to thee—"

"No!" Gaerbith leapt up and, with a sharp chop of his hand, waved away the memory. "No!"

He stood amid the stones, challenging the Voice. "Who am I that she would save me rather than kill him? Who am I that she would die in my place? Who am I—"

HER SON.

He dropped to his knees. Wind wept through the stones and swirled around him in mournful embrace. He bent forward, pounded a fist against his chest, but refused to weep.

IN YOU DWELLS UÁRTHA'S SECRET, BESTOWED BY HER AND HELD UNTIL THE KEL-CHILD IS READY.

Why keep it from him, like child's treasure kept on a high shelf? Why only reveal it if he took the Keeper's oath? What purpose did that serve?

THE TASK IS YOURS, FOR YOU ARE NOT EASILY SWAYED. YOU WILL SEE A MATTER ACCOMPLISHED.

The wind strengthened, whistling then crying, pushing through his ghostly form and sweeping away tears. He clamped down the anger and rose to his feet. "The warrior pursues me in dreams, telling me to make haste, and yet You say the secret must be revealed when the true king is ready." Knowing it was hubris, he shouted, "Why not tell the Kel-child Yourself?"

Silence.

"Why this roundabout and backward—"

WILL YOU HEED ME, GAERBITH? WILL YOU TRUST YOUR FUTURE TO ME?

"I cannot."

The wind ceased as suddenly as a door slams, shutting out the noise and the tumult.

GO. BE A SHEPHERD IN YOUR FATHER'S FIELDS. GROW WEALTHY, MARRY, RAISE CHILDREN FEARLESS AND STRONG. SERVE PADRAIG AS CAPTAIN. TRAIN OTHER WARRIORS. HEAP HONOR ON YOUR HEAD. BE A SCRIBE IN A VILLAGE. TEACH ITS CHILDREN TO READ AND WRITE. BE REVERED AS A SAGE. BE ANYTHING YOU DESIRE.

"I need not become a Keeper? You are setting me free?"

YOU HAVE ALWAYS BEEN FREE. MEN ARE NOT PUSHED AROUND THE EARTH AS IF THEY ARE THE PLAYING PIECES ON A *JHYLA* BOARD. EACH MAN MUST CHOOSE FOR HIMSELF.

"What choice is this?" He flung his arms wide and lifted his gaze to the sky. "You offer freedom in one hand and servitude in the other!"

FREEDOM AND SERVITUDE RESIDE IN THE SAME HAND.

The Voice quieted, as if speaking while walking away.

THEIR COMRADES, THEIR KINDRED, THEMSELVES, A KING NOT THEIR OWN—ALL MEN SERVE SOMEONE.

A breath of wind ruffled the grass.

A BIRD FLIES, NOT ONLY BECAUSE IT SPREADS ITS WINGS, BUT BECAUSE IT RELEASES THE BRANCH.

Gaerbith walked over and looked down at himself.

He wanted to live. He wanted to see an end to this war.

But the Keeper's oath? What kind of Keeper would he be? Uártha had died before teaching him all she knew, and he had forgotten much of what he had learned. He was not wise or mannered or skilled in anything beyond sheep-herding and warfare. He spoke three languages, but many men knew how to get along in tongues not their own.

"I will not take the oath"—Gaerbith drew a deep breath, as if plunging into cold water—"but in all other ways, I will serve You, Omwen'din."

HALF-HEART IS NO HEART AT ALL.

Gaerbith lowered to one knee, and bowed his head. "It is because I cannot offer whole heart that I ask Your patience, Omwen'din, and Your guidance until the day I give all."

Like the pause after a great sigh, silence filled the circle of stones.

I HAVE NEVER CEASED TO SPEAK, YET THERE ARE FEW WHO HEAR. OF THOSE WHO HEAR, EVEN FEWER KNOW MY VOICE. THEREFORE I SEND YOU AS MY EMISSARY, TO SPEAK MY WORDS AS WITNESS.

RISE, GAERBITH THA FORBA.

Light filled the body lying on the moss. Bandages loosened and fell away. Sinews tightened, muscles drew together, flesh pulled closed. Scars, pale and ridged, formed over the hurts.

The tension around his mouth eased, and his face warmed with a healthy flush. His eyes closed, and his head turned to the side.

He was at peace.

The dead returned, whispering just beyond his ken, lifting him to his feet. Their cool touch wakened him completely, and when he took a step, they moved back, watching.

He walked around the ring of stones. His shoulder was stiff, and his leg was like new leather not yet loosened with wear and weather. Pain fled, yet an ache lived deep in his wounds. Why had the Voice not taken that, too?

He lived. Complaint was ingratitude.

His brothers came from the ranks of the dead. His mother, too. They walked with him to the edge of the Highlands, where Cayn and the healers waited and the stone path descended to the wood far below.

Gaerbith took the cool hand of each of his clear-eyed brothers—Rabb, Cuin, Ard—and they nodded their farewells. Uártha took him by the shoulders and kissed his brow then stepped back to join her other sons.

He missed them. He loved them. But saying so seemed— "Mymna Tor keep you."

Ard and Cuin smiled. Rabb nodded.

Then all turned west, and as they walked over the rim of the

Highlands they rose, the ground beneath their feet unseen. Brothers draped arms around each other's shoulders or linked arms with their mother. Behind the family trailed the Fourth's fallen, nodding to Gaerbith as they passed.

Why had they not yet traveled the sunset path? Why had they stayed until this day?

The last man paused, and he smiled. "Thank you, captain. Our service is done." He gripped Gaerbith's shoulder. "You will do well."

Then he, too, stepped into nothing and out of sight.

On the wind whispered the barest murmur. *Ta na.*

6 ~ RUINS

Ro'Ar approached the ring of massive trees, the sun behind him, its lowering rays gilding the leaves. The tall grasses of the Plains bowed, bent by the evening breeze.

A faint shadow in the grass marked the line of the Old Road, and Ro'Ar turned his mount to meet it, the horse descending a small slope before entering the deep cut of the roadbed. Grass grew here, too, in clumps or in narrow lines between ruts, but there were signs of regular travel that kept the road from succumbing completely to the Plains. Hoofprints and footprints over-marked the tracks of wagon wheels, and there was animal sign, too, most of it a skitter of paw prints crossing the road, or droppings in the grass along the edges.

The road broadened as it neared the trees, and the horse quickened its pace. Ro'Ar patted its neck and smiled a little. Rest waited them, and home.

The land rose toward the first ring of trees, whose ancient girths were so broad that their base formed a wall. The road ended in a tangle of roots, each root as thick as a man's torso. Yet, at Ro'Ar's word, branches loosened and roots unwound, and—with a cracking groan, as if in protest—two giant trunks drew apart to reveal the rest of the way. It passed through all three rings of Guardians, trees that had lived since the earliest days of the House of Kel and now protected the Ruins, the broken remains of Havyn duru Asryn, the House of the Sky.

The shadowed path led up the rise, and in the distance burbled a merry spring flowing over stones in the courtyard and down into a quiet stream that he would soon cross. He had been here almost every night in dreams. How long since he had walked this wood? His time was measured *before the reign of Adwr* and *after the fall of Adwr,* and all the days and years since seemed only passages that he paced, awaiting the Day. Here, though, his sojourn seemed short, and his hope renewed.

The horse, Brythn, splashed through the clear stream and surged up the opposite bank. Ro'Ar's heart leapt to see the crumbled white walls surrounding the Ruins, the tower rising above all. Brythn crossed a wooden bridge, its timbers still sound, and entered the courtyard through an arch once guarded by heavy gates, the only remainder of which were twisted hinges crusted with rust. The spring, protected by a low wall, bubbled from the earth and down through a small arched opening in the stones.

Opposite the spring, on the left side of the entrance, the Broken Flame lay covered in moss and dirt. Fashioned from grey-veined white stone quarried in the Craydaeg Mountains, the Flame had been a gift from the ancestors of the Krûdhírri, the Hidden Ones, a tribal folk. The fall of the House of Kel and the ensuing wars had driven them into the deep fastness of the mountains. The only way to reach them was through Brona's Veil. Never having traveled the Craydaegs nor seen any maps of the region, Ro'Ar did not know what that veil might be: a tumble of stone or a field of snow? The clouds ringing the mountain peaks?

Perhaps it was best the Krûdhírri no longer walked among other Men. They did not see their gift lay broken among the Ruins.

Ro'Ar dismounted, and a man in plain garments came forward and led Brythn to the stables.

A tall white figure emerged from the shadowed door of the tower and stepped out on to the broad expanse of the portico, then descended the wide, shallow stairs leading down to the yard.

"Wyn!" Ro'Ar strode forward, arms outstretched.

The man in white embraced him with a chuckle and a few hearty claps on the back.

Wyn had been a Keeper as many centuries as Ro'Ar, both of them drawn to the Ruins by the Voice. Their faces scarce showed the years. Ro'Ar still looked and felt an able warrior. Wyn's white hair and beard made him appear a venerable mortal elder, but he had been already old when he uttered the Keeper's oath.

"Come." Wyn turned to walk up the steps. "The others are waiting."

Blown by the wind, leaves and twigs piled in corners or crunched beneath Ro'Ar's boots as he followed Wyn into the tower. Their footsteps echoed in the cavernous hall, its shadows relieved by the soft evening light from windows set high in the walls.

At the head of the room and surmounting a set of three circular steps—one set upon another to form a dais—stood a white marble chair. A great crack from head to foot had riven the throne so that each side tilted away from the other. Dirt and leaves collected in the opening. Birds or mice had constructed a nest.

In the wall behind the chair, and high above it, thin panes of colored glass and clear formed a round window depicting the seal of the House of Kel: a blue sword crossed by a white bloom of dragon's bane.

On either side of the hall marched rows of simple columns, and from the passages behind each colonnade appeared men and women dressed in pale garments of every color. Ro'Ar still wore his travel clothes—dusty, stained, infused with the odor of sweat and horse—yet his fellow Keepers greeted him with embraces and smiles, drawing him from the great hall to a room lit with candles and a healthy fire on the hearth. A table was set with platters of food and jugs of wine, water, and milk. Dried herbs smoldered in wee clay pots to sweeten the air.

The others chose their seats, laughing softly, speaking in low pleasant voices. Everything the Keepers did had a quietness about it. Standing vigil in the Highlands, Ro'Ar did not often gather with them, but now he let the comfort of their presence enfold him, content to stand aside and watch them as a father might his children.

The first Keeper, he was in a sense their father. It was too great an honor. They prized his words, sang songs he wrote, played instruments he made, yet his secret was an invisible wall, closing him away from all but the Voice. If the other Keepers knew why he was first called to take the oath, they would turn away in shame at his foolhardy arrogance.

They were, after all, still subject to the pangs of Men. Though Keepers were set apart, they hungered, thirsted, dreamed, loved. Hated. Their oath of service conveyed long life and far sight, but it did not make them untouchable. Yet, taken unworthily, the oath could kill.

There were days Ro'Ar longed for an end.

Brin, the man who had stabled Brythn, entered the room and

nodded at Ro'ar, then handed him the saddlebags and found a seat at the table. The Keepers spoke to one another but none ate, for they would not partake until Ro'Ar took his proper place.

The bags draped across his shoulder, he walked the length of the table, bringing forth gifts—a wooden flute for Brin and a reed whistle for Eldwar; a fan of feathers for Lyra; ribbons of dyed, plaited Plains grass for Hetta, at whose touch his fingertips tingled—and by the time he reached his chair, the bags were empty. He stood looking along the table, smiling to see the pleasure on the faces of his friends.

Two new Keepers brought a pitcher of water, a basin, and a towel. "Welcome, First Keeper."

He set down the saddlebags, washed his hands and face, and handed back the grubby towel. "Thank you."

The new Keepers backed away and bowed their heads.

"Ro'Ar?" Hetta, with apple-red cheeks and gentle brown eyes, seemed no older than eighteen but was in truth approaching two hundred.

At her question, all eyes turned toward him. Gifts were placed beside empty plates.

Ro'Ar stood and held out his hands, palms up. "The grace of Mymna Tor, and blessings on thy way."

"And grace to thee," said the Keepers in one voice.

Wyn sat on Ro'Ar's right. As food was passed around the table, he leaned over and murmured, "Any news of Uártha's heir?"

Ro'Ar heaped potatoes, stewed meat, and fried carrots onto his plate. "He fights in Disson's army. And he lives."

He gave a brief account of the war as seen from the Highlands, facts and stark numbers only. Soon everyone was exchanging news from the various provinces. A Keeper from the East assured everyone the Kel-child had not been found by King Morfran's spies.

"Sibyl sends word the heir of Kel is safe and well," reported a huntress named Madda. "He is restless, though, and she fears he will set forth too soon." Madda drained her cup of wine.

"Does he know his true name?" Emara the healer, sweet-voiced and wide-eyed, tucked a strand of hair behind her ear. "Is it not time?"

Eldwar set his knife across his plate. "I hear he is still a blacksmith."

Broad-shouldered Brin leaned forward to look down the table and said in a rough voice, "A fine craft! No better skill the Kel-child needs for beating down the enemy!"

Eldwar inclined his head. "I meant no dishonor, Brin, but that it may not be wise to keep the truth secret any longer."

Ro'Ar listened to the debates in silence, weariness overtaking him until he stared at his plate, his mind elsewhere.

The first time he sat at this table, he was a young soldier in the king's guard. Thoughts drifted into memories, the voices of the Keepers became the voices of his comrades in arms, and the debate over the Kel-child's name and Uártha's heir slurred into the sounds of laughter, the clinks of ale mugs, and the shuffle of boots across the stone floor. The fragrance of herbs was overcome by the strong smell of men fresh from the training ground, their tunics dark with sweat, their hair dripping and their faces damp. There were boasts and jests and salutes with ale, and there was young Ro'Ar in the corner, watching it all.

He jolted awake. He lay on a soft bed in a dark room, and a blanket covered him. Someone had removed his boots. From elsewhere in the room came the gentle breathing of souls asleep. Ro'Ar lay looking up into the darkness.

How long, Mymna Tor, before my task is done? How long before I live again?

Havyn duru Asryn had been built on rising ground, overlooking the Plains. With the fall of the House of Kel, however, and the passing of centuries, the tower became overshadowed by the three rings of Guardians, and any chance passerby would never know an ancient fortress stood crumbling behind those old trees. Ro'Ar walked among them, his way lit only by whatever starglow traversed the overhanging boughs. His feet needed no guidance to tread the paths etched into the earth by generations of Kels and the guards who once paced their watch among the trees.

Somewhere in the oaks and lindens, the pines and elms, the fir, spruce, and apples that had sprung up together in a strange mix, there dwelt an ageless wisdom whose name Ro'Ar did not know but whose voice he heard in memory and in dreams. Centuries past, if King Adwr had heeded that voice, the House of Kel might yet be strong and the sword of Kel might not be lost.

Not lost. Hidden.

"Grandfather," he called, "what do you see?"

The branches rustled overhead as if in laughter. "I see a familiar face, and shoulders weary with their burden." There was a pause and the sense of deep study. "Welcome home, Ro'Ar. You have been too long away."

Ro'Ar smiled. "You sound like Wyn."

"Good." Grandfather chuckled. "The lad is learning at last."

"Lad?" Ro'Ar looked up at the pale blade of light hovering in the notch of an elm. "Wyn was a lifetime older than I before we became Keepers."

"Ah, but I was a lifetime older than he when I came to Adwr's court. Age is nothing if a man does not use his years wisely."

There was a tang of regret in the words.

Ro'Ar had spent his years as a soldier then a scholar, and now he was a watcher. To what purpose? "A thousand years and more, Grandfather. Why?"

The presence did not answer the question. Instead, he asked his own: "How many Kels remain in Skarda?"

"I do not know." Ro'Ar leaned his shoulder against a tree and plucked the odd bits of leaves and twigs from a branch he had found at his feet. "Disson has become a haven, and lands to the east and south have received them well."

The light in the elm took shape until it became a robed figure seated on a bough. "Have you considered what might happen if the Kel-child dies before he finds the sword? Is there another who will rise in his place?"

"There can be no other!" Ro'Ar straightened and stared up at the figure. "Who will restore the House of Kel if all we thought true becomes false? There can be no other."

"Ah, but why?"

"Because—" Ro'Ar fumbled for words as a man might try to gather leaves scattered by a sudden wind. "Because truth is constant. The Voice speaks only truth. The Kel-child is the closest heir of Kel High King, and he bears the gift. He is the one the Voice said will rise up and restore the House."

"Aye, truth remains constant, but what we believe is true may change. Or, perhaps, how we perceive truth. A blind man cannot see the sun, therefore he declares the sun does not exist. Does he cease, then, to feel its warmth upon his face?"

It was a question to ask a lazy-minded young scholar. Ro'Ar was being led somewhere. "No, Grandfather. Neither the blind man's words nor his disbelief would make the sun cease to exist."

"So"—the figure shifted, casting its light upon Ro'Ar as if leaning closer—"if truth remains true, and the Voice speaks only truth, what does that mean for a Keeper who wanders the wood and thinks he serves no purpose?"

"But I cannot discern a purpose, Grandfather!" The words exploded from a bleak ball of anger in his chest. "Others look on me as their leader, but I am the cause—"

He could not speak the reality and release it to the wind.

"You are the blind man, Ro'Ar. A linden tree becomes a log becomes a brand in the fire becomes a pile of ash. Always, it is linden. You were once a boy. Now you are a man. One day, you will be only a soul. Always, you are Ro'Ar."

Grandfather's voice gentled. "Were it not for you, there would be no Great Archive, nor would the sword of Kel be protected all these long years. You serve so great a purpose, Ro'Ar, it cannot be measured in mere words."

Leaning on the branch in his hand as on a staff, Ro'Ar bowed slightly. "In my weariness, I did not think to lift my head and see beyond my feet. Forgive me."

Grandfather's warm light touched on Ro'Ar's shoulder. "For centuries, these trees have embraced me as I wait the Day as a young man waits his sweetheart—eagerly, impatiently, straining his eyes to see her blue dress coming down the road."

Ro'Ar closed his eyes as the warmth blessed his brow.

"Just as the maiden may wear the brown dress and not the blue, so the Day may not appear as we expect, but it *will* come. We must not turn away, lest it pass us by."

Light glowed beyond Ro'Ar's eyelids, and fingers of heat trailed across his face.

"Sleep, Ro'Ar. Be at peace."

The captured light of morning slanted across the chamber. Ro'Ar tucked his hands behind his head and looked up at the ceiling, at the graceful meeting of arches and columns. He was in no hurry to rise.

None of the other beds were occupied, but distant voices echoed in vast stone chambers or murmured along pillared halls. He could almost imagine this was the soldiers' barracks, long before it had crumbled into dust, and that those voices belonged to other men of the king's guard or were the everyday conversations of servants going about their tasks. Almost this could be any day in the High King's household, before the death of Adwr and the fall of the House of Kel.

Almost.

Ro'Ar lowered one of his arms and let it rest across his chest. When would he no longer mourn for what could not be undone? Would there come a day when all he could see was the future?

His thoughts turned to Hetta, with her sweet face and pleasing plumpness. Other Keepers married after taking the oath, though some came to the enclave already wed. Wyn or even Grandfather could perform the rite—

But he was ahead of himself. He had neither wooed nor won her. What had he to offer a cheerful soul as she? Yet what a comfort it would be to be joined by such a companion while on his travels or while standing watch in the Highlands.

What had he to offer her but solitude and harsh living? The Voice had called her to the Ruins, and here she stayed, restoring and tending the gardens, preparing medicines, making all manner of garments, keeping linens clean and in readiness for weary wandering Keepers. She had a comfortable life, surrounded by Brin the blacksmith and his wife, and there was Emara the healer, and other Keepers who came and went. Hetta would be mad to leave such a life.

Swinging his legs over the side of the bed, he sat on the edge a few moments before rising to wash in the wooden tub filled with lukewarm water, sheltered by a woven screen of slender limbs. Fresh garments—a long shirt of soft blue, and loose trews of deeper hue—had been laid out on a chair, and these he donned along with a soft pair of deerskin shoes. His boots he stood on the floor at the foot of his bed, and the travel-stained garments he folded and placed underneath, next to his saddlebags and sword.

On his way to the kitchen, he passed the great hall. The sleeping chamber was on the east, filled with the direct light of morning, but the colored window over the riven throne faced north, and soft light cast a glow over all.

A voluminous apron covering her from neck to ankles, her hair gathered in a loose knot at the nape of her neck and covered by a kerchief, Hetta wielded a twig broom and swept up the detritus that had blown in from the woodland. Motes of dust swirled around her, gilding the air.

Firm, crisp steps entered through the open wooden doors.

Ro'Ar moved behind a column.

Draken the hunter approached. Hetta straightened and smiled, running the back of her wrist across her brow as she watched him draw near.

Jealousy licked through Ro'Ar. He tried quenching it with reason, but his teeth still bit together when Draken greeted her with a kiss on the brow. She did not draw back from his hands on her shoulders.

Ro'Ar forced himself to turn away. Appetite lost, he crossed the kitchen, stalked through the garden door, strode past the stables to the armorer's shop, and asked to be given a task, preferably something difficult and mindless. Brin protested, but one look at Ro'Ar's face silenced him, and he set the First Keeper to work cleaning old armor found in a store room.

So Ro'Ar polished rusted birnies and hauberks in barrels of sand. Long he labored, but could not push from his mind the way Hetta smiled at Draken.

Past midday, he paused to rest on one of the barrels in deep shade beneath a wide oak.

PEACE, RO'AR.

He fell to one knee. Placing a palm over his thudding heart, he bowed his head. "Mymna Tor."

PREPARE TO LEAVE ON A JOURNEY A SEVEN-NIGHT HENCE, NORTH TO THE CRAYDAEG MOUNTAINS. CHOOSE THREE TO JOIN YOU: A HEALER, A WARRIOR, AND A HUNTER. IN THE KELCEY FOREST, NEAR THE FOOTHILLS, YOU WILL BE MET BY ONE WHOM I WILL SEND.

"How will I know him?"

HE WILL BE LAME IN ONE LEG, AND SCARRED PAST MORTAL HEALING. TO HIM YOU WILL GIVE THE ROBES OF A KEEPER. WITH HIM WILL BE AN EXILE. BRING HER TO THE RUINS.

"Is she, too, a Keeper?"

SHE IS THE OIL IN THE FIRE.

Then the Voice withdrew—PEACE, RO'AR, AND SWIFT THE JOURNEY

—and he was alone beneath the sheltering tree.

From his stool set before a tall desk, Wyn rose, clasped his hands behind his back, and looked out a nearby window. Afternoon light shone full on his face, turning his hair and beard so dazzling white that Hetta blinked.

"He came neither to breakfast nor dinner, he worked at the smithy, now he locks himself away in the observatory." She ran the back of her wrist across her forehead, and felt what was surely a muddy mix of dust and sweat. "He has spoken to no one but Brin. And after last night, falling asleep at supper, him being so tired and all—"

What was there to say that Wyn did not already know?

The old Keeper turned from the window.

Hetta set some books upright on their shelf and used the corner of her apron to dust their spines. Blinking, she wiped an invisible spot from a shiny silver candlestick. Blast all this dust! Dry weather always made her eyes sting.

"I see." Wyn's voice sounded especially gruff, but when Hetta looked at him, she thought a smile fled his lips. His brows lowered and he frowned, nodding. "I see."

He reached into a shallow drawer meant to hold quills, and removed a large key. "Prepare his favorite supper. I shall see that he is there."

Though the Ruins were just that—ruins—the central structure of Havyn duru Asryn remained sound. Council chambers and grand galleries, bright sitting rooms and comfortable bedchambers, were now pantries, storerooms, a kitchen, even an apothecary. Only two rooms were for sleeping, not just for one or two occupants but for dozens. The outer chambers existed only in remnants, open to the sky.

Above the great hall, where the riven throne waited the restoration of the House of Kel, a small observatory had somehow survived the destruction of war and time. It had been built on the roof for Meresh, a king of Skarda when the land was still called Kell, so he could study stars and whatever bodies dwelt above the earth.

As Wyn mounted the steps leading up what was now the outside of the keep, he saw the glint of the scope's long barrel, turned northward toward mountains rather than sky. A few steps more, and into sight came the roof of a little house made of glass, the upper panels propped open to catch the breezes. Even on cool days, the observatory was warm. Inside sat Ro'Ar, polishing the scope's eyepiece with a cloth. Spread about him on low tables were sheaves of paper, a pot of ink, a few quills, and a lute that looked as battered and travel-stained as he had been yesternight. His mouth moved, and one knee bounced a rhythm as he worked. He paused, wrote something on one of the pages, tapped a finger on the table, wrote a little more, then returned to polishing the eyepiece.

Wyn smiled. Ascending the last few steps, he crossed the roof of the keep and tapped on the glass nearest Ro'Ar.

Startled, Ro'Ar looked up with a frown.

Wyn dangled a key at him as if to say, *I will come in anyway, so you may as well open the door.*

He set aside the cloth and the eyepiece, and flipped the latch.

Wyn ducked inside. "Composing?"

Ro'Ar nodded.

Wyn sat on the short stool, leaving Ro'Ar to stand in what room remained. Every space was well used: beneath the tables lining the walls were shelves filled with scrolls, charts, and sundry supplies and instruments, the useful as well as the musical.

"A bit like being in the Highlands, isn't it?" Wyn looked around. "A view of trees and sky. And, with that"—he gestured at the scope —"distances farther even than our Keepers' sight."

Again, Ro'Ar nodded. A snatch of melody hummed in his thoughts, and he bent to scribble it on the page. "What are you not saying, Wyn?"

"You missed two meals you are too thin to miss, and now you are hiding." The old man's voice was flat, but Ro'Ar heard its edge. "And you know very well the scope needs no more polishing. Hetta cleaned it as soon as we knew you were coming."

Tossing down the quill, Ro'Ar crossed his arms and stared at the westward arc of the Guardians glowing gold in the setting sun. "How long has Draken been here?"

"Just arrived today. More hunters are coming soon, and healers from the south and west. Except Sibyl."

Sibyl spoke with the Voice more often than most, and was a faithful Keeper. She had been set a task that tethered her to a particular village. Her comings and goings worried him not.

"How often does he visit the Ruins?"

"Draken? No more than two or three times this year."

"How long since I was here last?"

"Two years. Not since the summoning when Heolstor of the Black Hoods sent his Nar'ath against us."

Two years? Indeed, time had fled.

Looking down at the scrawled musical notations, at the uneven lines and the oft-corrected rhymes, Ro'Ar asked as casually as he could muster, "Why must he journey here so often? Does the Voice summon him?"

"You know how it is, being sent on solitary tasks. Any chance for company is embraced."

Wyn rose and moved toward the door.

Ro'Ar straightened, and opened his mouth to speak.

Glancing at the scope, Wyn said, "Hetta makes the polish herself. Ask her how at supper. We are having meat pies, I think."

The crusts were buttery and crisp, the fillings oozed succulent juices, and Ro'Ar ate two pies, scarce looking up from his plate.

Upon entering the room, he had noticed Hetta wore braided in her hair the ribbons of plaited grass he had dyed and woven while in the Highlands. Their hues warmed her face and seemed to him more vibrant than jewels. She did not look at him—though, until blessing was spoken and the food served, he could not stop looking at her.

Then she lifted her gaze and he looked down. He had been looking down ever since.

Even as a youth, he courted with little aptitude. When not training at sword or standing guard, he read books or played music, yet for all his skill with words sung or written, speech fit his tongue like an ill-made garment. Asking a maiden to stand up with him for a dance was akin to running in shoes that kept falling off his feet.

Yet there had been young women intrigued by his station as one of the king's guards. Their boldness often eliminated his need to talk, for they carried on quite well by themselves. Hetta, though— She frightened away even stumbling speech, and he found himself conversing only in nods, smiles, or gestures with those who sat nearest him at supper.

"Excellent!" Wyn declared, a little too loudly, raising his empty plate, and other Keepers praised Hetta's cooking.

Setting aside his napkin and taking a deep breath, Ro'Ar stood.

Quieting, the others looked toward him.

"The healers with the Dissonay army shall remain at their posts. Our scribes are here"—he bowed his head at the gathered scholars, who returned the courtesy—"but most of our ranks have yet to arrive. Our tradesmen, artisans, craftsmen, hunters, and husbandmen will arrive as they are able, and when all are come, the purpose of this High Summoning will be revealed.

"Until then, the Voice has set me a task—to journey northward and meet two whom He will send. I must choose as my companions a healer, a hunter, and a warrior."

Almost before Ro'Ar finished speaking, Craddoch, a dark-skinned, curly-haired warrior from the Mynoth Mountains in the south, rose to his feet. "If it please you, Eldest, I will journey with you."

Ro'Ar inclined his head. "I welcome your company, Craddoch." He smiled.

Draken stood next, but Madda was just as quick. They spoke over one another: "I will go!" "Take me, Eldest!"

Madda frowned at Draken, whose own brow creased as he looked at her.

"I need but one hunter." Ro'Ar kept his words quiet. "You may decide between you before sunset tomorrow."

Draken bowed his head—"Of course, Eldest"—and resumed his seat.

After a small hesitation, Madda also agreed and sank down again beside Wyn, though her mouth was rigid and her eyes determined.

Silence lengthened, and the Keepers looked at one another, but no healers rose to join the company. They were not required to do so, nor would anyone look on them ill for choosing not to go. Each man or woman must do only as he or she willed. The Voice never forced a soul into service. Yet Ro'Ar grew tense, wondering how soon other healers might arrive from the provinces, and if any of them would be ready in time for yet another long journey.

Hetta rose slowly from her chair and smoothed her crisp apron. Her gaze did not quite meet his.

"I may be a Keeper of the Ruins, but I also trained as a healer, and I make many of Emara's medicines to take to those few villages still living on the Plains." Taking a breath, lifting her chin, she seemed to gather her courage. "I have scarce left Havyn duru Asryn since I swore the oath." Her brown eyes almost pleaded. "If the Voice wills it, I would join the Eldest on his journey."

From the corner of his eye, Ro'Ar saw a smile pull at Wyn's mouth.

"Then you are most welcome, Hetta." Ro'Ar surprised himself: his voice was calm and his hands steady. "We leave a seven-night hence."

"I will be ready."

Someone called for music, and tables were cleared and pushed aside, chairs were set upon them, and the room filled with dancing, laughter, and song. With a flute of carved bone, Ro'Ar played fluid melodies that wove together like wind in the grass.

Hetta clapped her hands or swayed with the music, or danced with whoever asked. Once, eyes sparkling, she threw back her head and laughed. Ro'Ar closed his eyes and played to that image.

The sun had been low when the Keepers sat down to supper. Now its light seemed to blaze beyond his eyelids, and he saw the vale where Disson battled Skarda; watched the vision of Hetta's face fade until the brightness of her eyes became the glitter of swords meeting in relentless dispute. Flames rose. Smoke filled the vale.

As soon as another song began—a spritely air carried by lute, pipe, and tabor—Ro'Ar ceased playing. He rose and took the flute up to the observatory, and there he scarce heard the merriment below as he recorded all he saw in his mind, his quill scratching across parchment as fast as he could form visions into words.

All the days since he left the Highlands were revealed, and he wrote them in the scroll. He heard the screams from the Hold; heard Damanthus order his son not to answer Skarda's challenge; saw two great warriors fall.

Then, as urgency died and his pen slowed, Ro'Ar saw the face of Uártha's heir.

Stars threaded the cloak of night, and she needed no candle to light her way up the steps and across the stone roof.

A stub of candle still flickered inside the observatory, but Ro'Ar slept, head cradled on his arms, his upper torso resting on the small table, obscuring part of a long, outspread scroll.

Hetta pinched the flame and set aside the candle lest he knock it over in his sleep, capped the inkwell and removed the quill from his ink-stained fingers, and set the flute and the battered lute on a shelf, along with a sheaf of parchments covered in musical notation. Using one arm to gently push his chest up from the table, she lifted his head and arms just enough to pull the scroll from beneath him and push her folded shawl into place as a pillow. She had brought a blanket; this she draped across his shoulders, smoothing away the folds, letting her hands linger just a moment on the breadth of his back.

Despite her curiosity to read what had drawn him from the dance, she rolled the scroll into a neat cylinder and set it beside him. She would rather he spoke to her about it himself than read words he did not intend her to see.

Hetta closed the observatory door behind her and descended the steps.

7 ~ FATHERS AND SONS

The sons of provincial barons and wealthy merchants, Young Wolves did not mingle with common soldiers, but pitched their scarlet tents nearest the king, whose broad square tent marked the very center of the camp. They were only a ceremonial guard. The men who stood around the king's tent had been turned, their memories wiped clean by the Brethren, but the Young Wolves retained their identities. Yet the only true loyalty they held was to themselves.

They might defend the pack from outsiders, but within the troop they fought for supremacy: for Morfran's esteem, for Arien's friendship, for Yanámari's favor. If those prizes were out of reach, they might gain renown in battle, proving their value by killing more dogs—more Dissonay—than their comrades.

The Young Wolves fallen in yesterday's battle had all pursued the captain who hailed from the Thynathel Hills. Only that captain. Now his body lay in a healing tent, theirs in the flames.

Arien drained his cup, then shook his head at the servant waiting to refill it. The heat of the pyre was almost too searing to endure, yet still he stood at its foot, watching black surcoats curl back from the flames, gilt embroidery melting. On the other side of the pyre stood a hooded figure in a black robe. From its belt hung a drawstring bag. The fine powder inside it, poured on the ground in a precise circle, had ignited the instant the Black Hood spoke a word, guttural and low. Then the Young Wolves had lifted their cups, shouted a salute, and drunk down the wine in a single gulp. Such was the Wolves' funeral rite.

Gurn told a jest; the others laughed. Ûtgar clapped him on the back and called for more wine.

"Why are we here?" Like Arien, Gurn's cousin Rhôn did not join the raucous mourning. He tipped back his head as sparks and ash flew skyward.

"Why were we born," Arien asked, "or why are we at war?"

"Both, I suppose."

"The first I cannot answer. As for the second, my father's mad greed."

"Skarda has traded with the Territories for centuries. Why must Morfran possess them now?"

"It is not about the land, or the forests, or the vineyards. He hates."

"Hates whom?"

Arien remained silent.

"You are not like him." Lifting his wooden mug, Rhôn gestured toward the other Wolves. "You are not like them. Why are you here?"

"I was made for war."

Rhôn drank deep. "Kill him and take the crown. You would be a far better king."

Charred wood crumbled, and two bodies shifted on the pyre then dropped toward the middle of the fire. On the other side of the flames, the Black Hood lifted his head. Though no face or even eyes could be seen in the depths of the cowl, Arien felt the weight of the stare.

Turning from the fire, Arien waved his cup at a servant, who brought a jug of wine and filled the mug. "Morfran sacrifices to Nar Cahm, who will see no hurt befall him."

Rhôn chuckled. "So. You have at least thought of it."

Mindful of the watching Hood, Arien turned the discussion. "My sister Yanámari comes of age soon, and must choose a husband. If she marries Padraig of Disson, we might have peace. What think you?"

Rhôn did not answer at once. Arien cursed inwardly. His question had been thoughtless and cruel. Rhôn had loved Yanámari since he first came to the king's household as a youth.

"I think Ûtgar will be the likeliest choice," Rhôn said at last, looking toward the shadows beyond the pyre.

Arien cleared his throat in loud disgust.

"He is the son of your father's cousin. Now that his father, Baron Markha, is dead, Ûtgar is closest kin."

"Yanámari is too strong of will, and Ûtgar is too prone to power. I do not see her letting him be king."

Brows lifting, Rhôn stared at him. "You do not think to live long enough to wear the crown?"

"I am not graced with the protection that my father enjoys. Beside, if I, being skilled only in war and not in courtesies, might be a better king than he"—Arien walked toward his tent, keeping his voice low —"how much better might Yanámari? She could be the wisest ruler Skarda has seen in many an age."

Laughing, they passed Heolstor and Morfran with tipsy bows and over-careful greetings, then—once the king and his counselor were out of sight—returned to steady walks and circumspect speech. His father might be nigh unkillable, but Arien would be cursed before he gave the man more respect than he was due.

"Father?"

Damanthus opened his eyes. "Padraig."

The king's son sat on a low stool beside his father's cot and bent forward, placing his hand over the king's fist pressed against fresh bandages staining again with blood and the corrupt discharge of a fevered wound. The hurt was past even a Keeper's skills to cure.

With a small bow, Cayn withdrew to stand beside the table piled with clean bandages, pouches of herbs, and small pots of ointment. He packed them away in his healer box while Thael, the king's servant, disposed of soiled bandages and fouled water.

"The Woodsman's horn calls me to the Otherland." Damanthus spoke in a wheezing whisper. "Do not weep, my son. It is a call I long to answer."

"I would be your general, Father, not your heir. Not yet." Padraig bowed his head. "Stay, Father. Disson has need of you."

"Nay, my son. Disson has need of you."

Damanthus turned his head on the pillow and looked toward Cayn.

Blinking once or twice—even Keepers were allowed their grief—Cayn unlocked a square wooden box and lifted from it the plain gold circlet that was the crown of Disson. "My lord Padraig, kneel and receive your place among the kings of the House of Rhobarrd."

Thael hastened to place a cushion on the ground beside the cot. Padraig drew his sword and, holding it across his palms, knelt one knee on the cushion, tears unheeded on his face.

Cayn held the crown above Padraig's head. "Omwen'din, Thy

blessings be on one who offers his sword to Thy service, his ear to Thy wisdom, and his soul to Thy care."

Placing the tip of the sword to the ground, Padraig took the hilt in both hands and bowed until his forehead rested on his thumbs covering the pommel.

Damanthus lifted his right hand and placed it on Padraig's head in blessing. "My son, peace in the deepest corners of your being. Such peace cannot be destroyed—not by war or troubles or the workings of other men. May truth be your constant companion and wisdom your faithful guide. Be no man's slave but every man's servant, and the crown shall rest light upon your brow." The long speech left him gasping. His hand trembled. "Be of clear purpose and strong action, then you need never remind any man you are king. With your kindred be kind. With your enemies be just. Let not wroth rule your hand, nor confuse petty temper with rightful anger. One wounds, the other sets right." His hand slipped to Padraig's shoulder, and breath whistled harsh through his throat. "Serve Omwen'din, for even a king must remember there is a power beyond him."

Padraig lifted his head. "I hear the admonition of my king, and vow to fulfill all his commands."

Thael brought a longsword and laid it flat along the king's body. Damanthus clutched the hilt to his chest. "Take the sword Rhobarrd, and in the taking seal your vow."

An exchange was made—Padraig's blade for the heirloom of his house, an ancient sword with little decoration. He kissed the pommel. Then—back straight, eyes forward—he returned to the same posture with which he began the ceremony, holding a blade across his palms in offering.

Cayn lowered the simple crown, and it fit Padraig's brow as if fashioned just for him. In a voice thick with emotion, the Keeper spoke the final words of the rite: "Arise, Padraig Damanthusson, king of Disson."

As Padraig rose, he sheathed Rhobarrd in the scabbard on his back.

Thael wrote an account of the brief ceremony. Damanthus was too weak to hold his hand steady, so Cayn helped him press his signet in the green wax, and the parchment was sealed.

Damanthus closed his eyes. Uncurling slowly, as if reluctant to loose its grip on life, his hand slid away from the hilt.

Quiet, unhurried, Keepers prepared the body of Damanthus for its journey home to Sonndin, to be laid with the bones of his forefathers in the walls surrounding the oaken throne.

In Dissonay lore, though the souls of the ancient ones dwelt in the Otherland, their wisdom whispered to any king who spoke true the vows when receiving the crown. And, if he inherited a sword one of them had wielded, the blade remembered, and imparted those memories to its new master. Rhobarrd was such a sword. Named for the first king of Kellish blood to sit on the throne of Disson, it was a renowned sign of kingship.

Padraig wrapped the hilt in old cloth—he was not ready to announce his father's death—then Cayn handed him a key. He locked the crown in the box, and stood staring down at the oak tree graven on the lid. Limbs reaching wide, roots spreading broad and deep, it was his father: tenacious defender, generous guardian, resolute foe.

"I am a sapling in his shade."

Cayn spoke after a short silence. "How will you answer Morfran's challenge?"

"How would you?"

"I am not king."

Padraig studied the Elder's calm face. Were all Keepers devoid of deep feeling, or so unhelpful in their speech?

"If you see matters beyond the ken of mortals, why can you not see a way to win this war?" Padraig slapped the table, and the Keepers who cared for his father's corpse looked up from their silent task. "And if you do see a way, why will you not tell me what it is?"

"Keepers are still but Men. We see what Omwen'din chooses to reveal. The rest we trust to Him."

Turning from that gaze, Padraig watched the Keepers wrap the body in layers of white cloths and herbs. "Is Omwen'din against us?"

Cayn took the coronation parchment from Thael, who was passing by, and looked down at the scroll wrapped in green oilcloth and tied with a leather string. "This account of your crowning will go in to the box. In that same box with the crown is kept Mahyla, the Sea Stone, a symbol of great wisdom. But even greater than the Sea Stone is Omwen'din, who speaks wisdom to those willing to listen."

He held out the scroll. "My first act of service to Padraig

Damanthusson is this. The wee *lynneth* birds have a way of playing weak or wounded in order to lure predators away from nests or vulnerable flocks. Then, once predators are in pursuit, other *lynneth* swoop from hiding and overcome the hunters.

"It works very well with Men, too."

Hours before dawn, the entire Dissonay army moved, no torches lit, no words spoken louder than a breath. Warhorses wore cloths tied around their hooves, and soft muzzles over their mouths and noses. Tents were struck and supply wagons packed, men working together in a succession of lines, passing items from one person to another so that movement was minimal, reducing the chances of tripping, knocking into one another, dropping something.

Owen led the captain's mount—a wily old creature named Kraekor —away from the other wounded horses kept apart until their hurts healed. Most warhorses that suffered injury also lost their masters at the same time. When Gaerbith had dismounted to lift a comrade onto Kraekor's back, Young Wolves ran at him in a rushing attack. The horse rose on his hind legs and knocked the Skardians to the ground, killing at least one of them with a blow to the head. He held them off until the captain and the wounded man ran behind a line bristling with swords in the hands of the Fourth.

Kraekor had suffered injuries that, come to think on it, resembled Gaerbith's: a deep wound to the shoulder and back, a long cut to the leg. Owen walked slowly, letting the warhorse limp beside him in silence, no muzzle needed.

At the healing tents, apprentices rolled back supple walls and removed poles, and Keepers placed the ill and wounded on carts or sledges. On another wain draped with a large cloth, once the standard above the king's tent, lay the body of Damanthus.

Owen rubbed the back of his hand across his mouth. No time to mourn. Perhaps when war was over, when Skarda was vanquished—

A tap on the shoulder. He looked up into a shadowed face.

The man jerked his head: *Follow me.*

Then he turned. A strange shape hung from a strap on the man's shoulder. Only Warrten carried a mace fashioned as a many-blossomed flower. It was shielded in a thick leathern pouch. The petals and leaves were like razors, and a careless man might find himself short a finger or two.

Past the camp, past the last line of wagons, into the wood at the base of the Highlands—and still neither Owen nor Warrten spoke. Kraekor's movements were clumsy, but the old horse kept pace. Water murmured nearby.

From the Highlands came low, piteous moaning. It chilled Owen's skin. Kraekor tossed his head and balked. Warrten, however, did not stop.

"Come, lad," Owen whispered, coaxing the trembling horse forward, and forcing his own feet to keep walking. "For the captain."

By the time they reached the *lachmil* hidden behind the horn of the Highlands, the air smelt of rain and Owen felt as if he hadn't slept in a month.

Captain Gaerbith had not been among the wounded back in the camp, nor was he among the men of the Fourth now gathered on the western side of the Highlands. Neither Warrten nor Turi would reveal where he was, and the other men still maintained their aloof silence with Owen.

He fed Kraekor and smeared fresh salve on the wounds then searched for a place to sleep. But, just as he found a hollow in the ground between two rocks and settled in, half-propped against one of the stones, Turi stood over him and held out a sack of provisions.

"Can ye find yer way back?"

With a sinking sensation in his chest, Owen nodded.

"Be swift and silent. Keep a sharp eye. Report anything odd to Lord Padraig."

Owen took the sack and forced himself to his feet.

"Might need yer bow."

Morning dawned cold and clouds veiled the sun. In the north, dark shrouds draped the Thynathel Hills, and the Grimë Mountains disappeared in the grey rain. A chill wind blew, billowing the tents, snapping the banners.

Behind the camp, Arien dueled an invisible foe, and Morfran watched with pride the fluid line of arm and sword, the dance of block and strike and whirl away, the agility of lithe youth suckled on battle's bloody milk. A worthy heir to the Dragon Crown, greater even than his father.

Beyond Arien, Young Wolves broke their fast while lounging on the ground beneath a wide canopy, as if in their provincial gardens rather than a battle camp. One Wolf laughed, gesturing with his goblet. Ûtgar had golden hair like Arien's, a common trait among the men of Morfran's family.

Family was growing thin. Morfran's cousin and Ûtgar's father, Baron Markha, was dead. Sometime in the autumn, was it? A servant girl had killed him with a pair of sewing shears.

There was something special about her, something the baron had been holding over the king. It mattered little now, the baron's scheme to put Ûtgar on the throne. Besides, Morfran's spies would find the girl. They were relentless.

"No shield, my son?" Morfran stepped from behind the line of provender wagons. "No helm? Even the least among the Dissonay can reach inside your defense with his longsword."

Arien sheathed his sword. Damp twists of bright yellow hair hung past his shoulders, and his sun-browned face dripped sweat.

"Why such exertions?" asked Morfran. "You will be victorious, no matter whom Damanthus sends."

"What is it? Scold or praise?"

Morfran spread his arms, inviting embrace. "I am a father."

Arien did not move. "The man in the Hold."

"Dead."

"He told you nothing."

"Not a word."

"Your Dragon army."

"Still too young and unruly."

"Our kinsmen."

Morfran dropped his arms to his sides. "The Nar'ath report Padraig has returned, yet Damanthus sends no reply. My hidden troops were forced to swing wide to flank Disson's lines." He studied his son's impassive face. "You challenge me as king to king."

After a short, heavy silence, Arien replied, almost as if speaking to himself, "Fighting the Dissonay is like fighting a stone wall. We beat against it, and beat against it, and beat against it, and we break chips and shards of it, but we do not defeat it. Why, then, do we remain?"

Anger burned in Morfran's veins. "I will not be doubted! Not by my own blood! Not by the son of a faithless mother!"

The insult did not stab deep enough to rouse answering anger in

Arien. His expression never altered. "What happens to the throne if I fall? Will you name Yanámari queen?"

"Yanámari!" Morfran turned his back to Arien. "Yanámari!"

Fair-skinned and raven-haired, with large eyes the color of twilight, she was the image of Una, Morfran's erstwhile queen who had sought other arms than his. He could see no trace of himself in Yanámari's features. While there was such doubt, he would not overthrow tradition and give the rule of Skarda to a woman who might be the daughter of a common man.

"She is strong," said Arien, "and keen-witted. Without a tutor, she teaches herself. She can even read Dissonay, though she does not speak it well. She can wield a sword. She is decisive." He almost smiled. "The barons will not easily sway her to their causes. If you wish me to stand as Skarda's champion, give your word my sister will wear the crown."

Drawing his sword, Morfran wheeled to meet Arien's blade, drawn the instant the king's hand twitched.

Morfran attacked with swift, brutal force. Arien blocked and countered.

"Want to kill me as you did the prisoner in the Hold?" He slid his sword under Morfran's and tapped the king's side before leaping back to safer distance.

Morfran rushed. Laughing, Arien stepped aside. Unable to stop in time, Morfran ran past—and received a swat across his back from the flat of Arien's blade.

"Nar Cahm's protection has made you reckless, Father."

Shamed before the watching Wolves, Morfran would not let it happen twice. Wheeling, he pressed his attack until Arien was backed against one of the wagons, and still the impudent boy laughed.

"I would rather name Ûtgar an heir—No! I would kill you—before letting that strumpet sit on the throne of Skarda."

Arien pushed against their locked swords, and Morfran tottered backward a few stuttering steps.

"Give Lord Arien what he wants." As grey as the northern sky, Heolstor leaned on his staff as if too frail to stand without it. "There is nothing to fear. Give your word, my lord. There will be no need to honor it. All signs assure us victory."

Hatred flickered in Arien's eyes—purple like Yanámari's. Like Una's. They were directed toward Heolstor.

The boy was right to distrust the old man. Heolstor was concerned only for Heolstor, and any form of *we* was merely the collection of other voices that might live in his head. Morfran himself harbored a few.

Stepping backward, Morfran sheathed his sword. "Yanámari shall wear the Dragon Crown."

After a short silence, Arien slammed his sword into its scabbard and stalked toward the tents.

Near midday, a misty rain falling, two emissaries met on the battlefield. The Dissonay messenger tossed something to the Skardian then both men returned to their own lines.

From a notch in a tall tree, Owen watched the exchange. The Dissonay lines were only two long rows, one behind the other, staggered so that—from the front—they appeared to be the full army. Empty tents remained, and a few fires burned, the smoke hovering rather than rising in the burdened air. In healers' robes or in common garb, Keepers walked here and there, giving the appearance of life to the abandoned camp.

Nar'ath wheeled overhead. Owen hoped they might wander within range of his bow, but they did not approach any nearer than the middle of the vale. Perhaps they saw the waiting archers among the Dissonay, and feared to tempt them.

A tall, broad-shouldered man with fiery hair rode onto the battlefield. From the Skardian camp came a slender, golden-haired warrior who cast aside his helm as he approached his challenger. It was an honor, letting his enemy see his face, a sign of respect between equals. More than equals in rank or skill, however, they were also close blood—cousins who had, in all the war, never crossed swords, seeing one another only at a distance on the battlefield. So said men telling tales around campfires at night. The two lords faced one another now to draw blood, not to acknowledge it.

They dismounted in the center of the vale, in the sight of armies standing in rigid silence. Padraig and Arien raised their swords. From this distance and through the leaden air, Owen could scarce hear the clang of metal on metal, for the sound came long after each blow was struck. Neither man gave ground nor faltered, nor did either appear wounded. Long the challenge waged, and Owen grew cramped and cold in his perch.

Tremors shook the tree. Shouts cut the air. Owen looked westward.

North of the camp, men battled. Some wore the scarlet, yellow, or black that marked most provincial Skardian men-at-arms, and some wore blue. With the Skardians came Hôk Nar—the Black Hoods—and with them came Nar'ath. Shrieking, the great black ravens swooped down on roaring troops clad in the bright earth-green of Disson, men rising as if from the ground, coming out of hiding at last.

Bark tearing his hands, limbs tugging his clothes and snatching at his bow, he scrambled down the tree.

Skardians ran down a rise behind the camp and set tents ablaze. Yet, at the edge of the battlefield, the two thin lines of Dissonay warriors did not move from their place. Instead, Keepers surrounded the Skardian raiders and set upon them with longswords.

One foot on a branch stub and the other dangling in the air, Owen clung to the tree and watched in amazement. He had never thought of Keepers as anything more than quiet healers, almost priests. Their skill with longswords was beautiful to behold.

A few Keepers did not engage the attackers. Rather, they walked through the camp as if strolling in a garden, their steps measured, their postures calm. Quietude walked in their wake. Past the easternmost tents they stopped, bowed their heads, lifted their arms out from their sides until their hands were level with their shoulders, and turned palms upward as if to catch the favor of Omwen'din.

Owen scrambled the rest of the way down the tree and ran, sliding and stumbling through wet grass and mud. Whoever stood as King Padraig's second in command must be told about the attack, yet when Owen reached the army and approached the man who stood in front of it—in the very center—he found not the king's second but the king himself.

"My lord!" Owen almost fell backward, he stopped so quickly.

Damp red hair clinging to his brow, beard curling in the rain, Padraig scarce glanced at him. "Do you disobey your captain yet again, young Owen?"

"Nay, my lord. I bring news—"

"We are under attack." The king's gaze fixed on the two men still fighting in the vale. "I trust our troops are doing well?"

"Aye, though there are Nar'ath and Black Hoods among the

Skardians."

"The Keepers will hold back the darkness."

His voice bold, his face calm, Padraig seemed so confident that Owen, too, quieted. The chaos in the camp had been foreseen by the king—and, perhaps, invited. Then who had ridden Padraig's warhorse onto the battlefield to answer Mad Morfran's challenge?

There was something about how the Dissonay champion stood, how he wielded the longsword, something about the longsword itself.

Gaerbith?

No. No, the captain scarce survived the last battle. He had not the strength even to stand.

As if the question had been asked aloud, Padraig replied, "A bit of dye. A few stones woven into his beard."

"Impossible! His wounds!"

"Aye, his wounds are grave, but just as yon Keepers push back the magic of the Hôk Nar, there is more at work than you or I can see." The king did not explain further, but turned his head and looked across the vale once more.

Rain poured. Thunder growled. Owen folded his arms across his chest to harbor what little warmth he could.

The champions battled on, mud splashing until their legs and surcoats were heavy and brown, their hair swinging in long wet ropes as they whirled and dodged and struck. Here, the sound of their swords was clear, each ringing blow like a bell.

If Gaerbith should slip on the mud or the slick grass—

Padraig reached back and pulled his sword from its scabbard. A sodden cloth wrapped the hilt.

From behind came shouts and shrill caws, louder as the Skardians pushed deeper into the camp. Padraig nodded to the men on his left and right, and murmurs rippled down the lines. Swords were loosed and arrows nocked.

"Go back to your watch," the king told Owen. "If Gaerbith falls, leave your father at least one son to bear his name."

8 ~ Arien

Gaerbith saw it all with Keeper's sight.

Time stretched. Action slowed. Every blow he blocked or struck vibrated along his arms and through his body, quaking the mud, shuddering the ground. He anticipated—though he knew not how—every move Lord Arien made, from the swing of his blade to the flicker of his expression.

Sword on sword cracked the air, yet Gaerbith heard the whisper of raindrops sliding on grass stems. Borne on the wings of the storm, the cool green scent of spring blew down from the distant, snow-mantled mountains. The tang of lightning and metal bit his tongue.

Sodden hair obscured his sight. Red tinted the water streaming into his eyes. The dye in his hair would soon be gone.

Rain hindered his opponent, as well, and whips of wet hair clung to Arien's face. The men stepped back from one another and stood catching their breath, swords ready. Arien nodded. Gaerbith shrugged one shoulder. While they waited, the rain eased then ceased.

Arien attacked, but his mightiest efforts could not gain advantage. Another warrior seemed to command Gaerbith's arms and legs, giving him force and agility he did not possess on his own.

Three Keepers—Cayn among them—had surrendered a portion of their grace. A mighty gift, it was not imparted lightly. Though their oaths assured them a well of strength, Gaerbith was still only a mortal, and Men who had not taken the oath were subject to death if they sought the power of a Keeper apart from the sacrifice of a Keeper. He did not know how long he could fight before he reached the limits of this temporary strength.

He brought the tip of his longsword up beneath his opponent's arm, a move he used often in battle.

Arien's eyes widened. He whirled away, knocking aside Gaerbith's blade then turning again and stepping forward, inside Gaerbith's reach. It was a neat gamble. It assumed Gaerbith could not bring the longsword to bear before the smaller Skardian blade thrust home.

Gaerbith caught Arien's sword on his vambrace, deflecting the edge. The tip caught his sleeve but no more. Slanting the longsword between himself and the Skardian, he brought it up at an angle, catching Arien across the chest. It was not a perfect move nor should it have cut as deeply as it did, being at an awkward bent and without the full force of Gaerbith's strength.

Apology sprang before he could stop it. "I did not mean—"

Arien stared, swaying, blood pouring down his body. "Not—Padraig."

The beat of advancing armies pounded like thunder in Gaerbith's ears. The roars of men were an angry wind; the glint of steel and the flash of arrows, lightning in a storm.

Tendons tensing in his neck, Arien lifted his sword. "You—killed—me." He sounded surprised. The most celebrated warrior in Skarda had vanquished all who stood against him—until this moment. The fear in his eyes was like that of young Owen clutching a broken sword, terror stark on his face.

Swatting Arien's weapon aside, Gaerbith stepped inside the reach of the blade, pulled off his glove and tucked it into his belt, then pressed his palm to the wound.

Armies clashed, but silence enfolded him. Power had surged through Gaerbith's being with Uártha's blessing long ago, and it had done so this day with the gift of the three Keepers. Now a searing essence flared deep in his chest, flowed down his arm and out his hand, heating the air.

Blood still stained Arien's rent surcoat, the mail was still sundered, yet he no longer paled nor did he stagger, but stood straight. He looked on Gaerbith in wonder. "Who are you?"

"A shepherd."

"You are the one Heolstor fears. The captain with the magic."

Gaerbith sighed. "Not magi—"

Arien jerked. The sword dropped from his slack hand, and he fell forward, his chin catching on Gaerbith's shoulder as if he embraced a friend. An arrow pierced his back. It bore the scarlet fletching of Mad Morfran's archers.

Gaerbith's mind fogged with curses, questions, inarticulate grief.

Sound assaulted him: anguished cries, ringing swords, pounding hooves. The Wolves were on horseback, slashing with their elegant sharp swords. No Dissonay stood before them.

Gaerbith cast a hasty look 'round for King Padraig's horse, but perhaps the warhorse had returned to its master during the challenge. Lord Arien's horse remained, heedless of battle, and approached his fallen master with an enquiring nicker. Gaerbith lifted Arien to lie across the horse's back, and returned the Skardian's sword to its sheath. The arrow he did not remove.

He slapped the horse on its flanks, sending it back through the battle, then he stepped into the fight. Men fell before his blade, but his movements, once fluid and precise, became sluggish and awkward. He stumbled. He had given away the virtue of the Keepers in vain.

Forked lightning licked the earth. Thunder roared, so close and loud Gaerbith's chest hurt. Rain pinged against helms and shields— and then the skies let loose.

King Padraig plunged into a knot of Skardian foot soldiers, breaking their shields, knocking men to the ground.

With a bludgeoning blow, Gaerbith felled an opponent by force rather than skill. The effort of lifting a sword made his arms tremble. He pushed toward Padraig. Wind-driven rain stung his eyes.

The battle had pushed closer to the Dissonay camp. Fires died, their flames drowned by the storm. Among the spoiled tents, skirmishers still fought and Nar'ath swooped down to feed on the fallen.

Gritting his teeth, forcing his body to obey, Gaerbith limped onward. He struck at enemy soldiers, every blow a towering effort.

Something bumped his shoulder, and warm breath chuffed against his neck. He turned.

Lord Arien's horse.

9 ~ AFTER THE BATTLE

Slung on Owen's back by a length of sodden rope, a Skardian sword hung beside his bow and quiver. He'd taken the sword from the dead hand of the soldier who killed Cayn Elder.

Rain eased to a fine mist, and a faint sunset glimmered beyond the grey clouds.

Long past hunger, his head foggy and his arms heavy, Owen helped clear away the carnage. The fallen formed row upon lengthy row, Skardian and Dissonay mingling in the same muddy graves. The Keepers who survived began the burial rites, sending forth the dead to the Otherland, though how the souls of so many warriors could find their way in such weak light, Owen did not know.

He stopped to rest, tip of his wooden shovel planted in the churned earth, and blinked away sweat stinging his eyes.

A ghost limped from the dripping twilight. Yellow hair hung in damp twists, and the white and green surcoat glowed pallid in the shadows. The hilt of a longsword jutted over his shoulder.

Forgetting exhaustion, forgetting Gaerbith's command to always address him as captain, Owen ran and embraced him, laughing, weeping, calling him brother.

Ro'Ar wiped the nib of the quill clean, then set the pen across the inkwell and stared at the fresh-written parchment before him. A tidy, neatly-lettered record of destruction, madness, death.

Morfran of Skarda wanted more land. Well, that and revenge on his faithless wife. No one knew if she had truly been unfaithful, but the king banished her when he began to doubt the queen's daughter was also his. Royal kinsmen and the people of Disson were not to blame, but they were hers and must pay the price. Such was the logic of mortals.

The Skardian king's jealousy and greed were likely goaded by another thing he could not control. In the Dissonay kings still flowed a trace of Kellish blood. One of them—Padraig, perhaps—might find Azrin, the sword of Kel, and declare himself ruler of Skarda.

Unlikely. There was a closer heir to the throne. A true heir. Direct in the line of Kel.

As soon as Morfran took the Dragon Crown and became king of Skarda, he had hunted and killed Kels. It mattered not which branch of Kel's descendents, or how far removed from the direct line, anyone who might lay claim as the true ruler of Skarda was slain. Even now, spies lurked in diverse guises, and folk were killed on mere suspicion.

In truth, Kels had lived so long in fear, so far removed from their history, they posed no real threat.

Yet a threat did exist.

The true heir of Kel lived in Markha Province, hidden in plain sight in a small village on the Romney Road. The Kel-child did not know who he was, but he knew he was something more.

Before he could take his rightful place, the lost sword must call to him and tell its hiding place. Or perhaps it was other other way 'round: the heir must call out the sword.

There was another man who could find Azrin. He was not a Kel. He was not a Keeper. He was the heir of Uártha. Inside his mind hid the—

"Ro'Ar?"

Startled, he jerked his hand, almost marring the perfection of the words he had just written. Hetta stood in the observatory doorway, a covered tray in her hands, the shawl over her head and shoulders darkened by damp. Only a light, steady rain fell on the Ruins, but Ro'Ar's visions had shown the storm in the battle vale.

Standing, he beckoned her to enter the cramped room. The smell of warm food woke his hunger, but he set the tray aside and offered Hetta the stool.

She shook her head and gestured toward the scroll. "I will not keep you—"

"Please."

A puzzled look in her brown eyes, she sat. When she removed the shawl, candlelight caught the red and gold in her brown hair.

The cloudy day had been cool, but now Ro'Ar felt a trickle of sweat crawl down his back. He leaned a hip against one of the tables and crossed his arms, looking down at the floor. "We leave in six days."

"Emara has been helping me fill a healer's box with what medicines might be hardest to find or prepare on our journey."

"A healer's box?" He smiled, still not meeting her gaze. "An honor."

Hetta's gentle voice quickened. "She made it for me many weeks ago, but was waiting the anniversary of my oath-day."

He rubbed the toe of one shoe against the stone floor. "Do you regret your decision?"

"No." It was immediate and firm. Then, less decided, "Do you not wish me to go?"

"It will be a long and difficult journey. No shelter. No comforts. No Guardians to keep you safe."

"There will be you. And Craddoch."

She did not mention Draken. Again, Ro'Ar smiled.

"And Madda or Draken," she added.

He straightened and turned, looking out at the darkening twilight, at the drops tracing curving trails down the overspreading panes of glass.

"Damanthus of Disson is dead. Lord Arien of Skarda is slain. Morfran has fled the field. Uártha's heir has been to the Highlands, but what happened there, I cannot see."

"Morfran has fled?" Her reflection smiled, and her garments rustled as she rose from the stool. "Then war is over!"

"It is only interrupted."

She had been staring at his back; now her gaze dropped.

He turned, and handed her the folded blanket and the shawl he had slept on, her fragrance still clinging to it. "Some other plan is being worked, darker and more serpentine than I can tell." He drew a deep breath then released it. "There are other healers—"

She smoothed the blanket then stared up at him with a determined look until he glanced away. Then she left the observatory without bidding him goodnight.

His cloak covering the scarlet tunic he wore as Morfran's servant, Imre stood aft and watched the wake as the oarsmen pulled the ship against the current, up the River Sonndin toward the Dävra Sea and thence to the River Thrayne. The battle vale was hidden by distance, by mist and darkness and the deceptive rises and hollows that marked the Lowland plains.

A few men—the king and Imre among them—had flown to the waiting ships on the backs of Nar'ath. Imre disliked the creatures, but he was grateful for a few days shorter journey and a dry bed tonight. The rest of the army camped in the mud.

King Morfran sheltered in a small tent on deck. With him were a handful of nobles and Heolstor, planning their newest strategy. No doubt this retreat was nothing more than a ploy to regain strength of arms and men. If it was a full retreat, however, and the king returned to Elycia, there was a certain handmaid Imre longed to see. How long since he had bidden Elta farewell?

One of the Hôk Nar Brethren glided sure-footedly past as if the deck did not tilt beneath his feet.

The Black Hoods were only rumored to read one's thoughts, but Imre took no chances, pushing Elta from his mind and staring at the river. Torches lit reflected fires in the water, but in his mind he saw a man slumped against a post and bloody, his arms chained above his head, his head fallen forward until chin rested on chest. The soldier who had attempted to escape the king's army and go home.

Beaten, burned, broken, silenced.

A wise man would take warning.

Mayhap I am not wise.

Anger flared in Imre, only to be squelched as soon as he caught sight again of the Black Hood's robe swaying with the tilt of the ship. Surely—surely—there would come a day when Skardians lived free. But with such evil abroad as the Hôk Nar and men like King Morfran, and with such silent and cowardly opposition as his own, Imre doubted that day would come soon.

"You there!" A short sailor beckoned him. "The king calls."

Imre pushed away from the rail and obeyed.

Captain Gaerbith's limp seemed no more than an annoyance in his stride as he entered Padraig's tent. Looking at him, one might never know he had almost set foot on the path to the Otherland.

"Wounded, my lord?"

Padraig cradled his injured forearm. "Have you magic to spare?"

"None, my lord." Gaerbith smiled a little. He looked too weary to do more. "And all the Keeper's virtue I gave away." The smile fled. "Wasted."

He squatted beside the small fire in the center of the tent and, using one of his famed throwing knives, hooked the blade into the handle of a metal cup and lifted it out of the flames. Then he passed the cup beneath his nose, nodded, and poured the contents into a bowl on a low table in front of Padraig.

"So many Keepers were killed"—Padraig winced as he shifted on the folding stool—"we must heal ourselves."

Gaerbith spread the steaming poultice on the raw wound. Padraig sucked in his breath and gripped his forearm, but strength could not strangle pain.

First creating a thick pad to cover the stinky goo, Gaerbith then wrapped a clean bandage around Padraig's arm and knotted the ends. Then he lifted the cup and gestured with it. "The arrow was tipped in poison, else you would not be using this foul stuff. How long?"

"Near the end. Just before Morfran blew his horn." Blast, but the remedy set a fire in the wound.

"It is unwise to wait so long." Gaerbith touched the back of his hand to Padraig's brow then the side of his neck. "No fever."

"Yet."

"Blurred sight?"

Padraig nodded.

"The cramping will come just before the fever. If you drink what is left"—Gaerbith swished the contents of the cup, and the vile fumes stung Padraig's nostrils—"you might prevent all ill effects but a strong headache. Which is, unfortunately, a result of the cure."

Padraig stared at him. "You took the oath."

Gaerbith shook his head. Reaching into a healer's box open on the table, he found a pot of clover honey and dropped a dollop into the concoction. "Drink."

Bracing himself, Padraig studied the greenish froth floating on the liquid's surface like scum on stagnant water, then swallowed the medicine in one gulp. With a grimace and a shudder and a raw cough, he set the cup on the table. "I cannot say it compares well with the wine from your Hills, but it has a certain—essence."

The captain handed him a waterskin, and Padraig rinsed the foul taste from his mouth. "Why must what is good for the body not also be pleasant to the tongue?"

"When you return to Disson, drink mint tea. Good for the digestion, good for the soul." Gaerbith closed the healer's box, and rested his hand on the unadorned lid. "No healer leaves his box open and untended."

Padraig pulled a chain from beneath his tunic. A silver key dangled from the chain. Cayn had left it with him before the battle. Perhaps he knew. "A good archer, Owen is. He killed the man who killed Cayn."

Gaerbith sat back on his haunches, his eyes bleak. After a silent moment he took the cup and looked into the fire as if he sought answers among the flames, his hands scrubbing the metal clean with ashes.

He rinsed the cup, set it on the table, then dusted his hands and stood. "Where is Thael, my lord, and the other servants?"

Padraig's eyelids drooped. Gaerbith's voice seemed distant and faint. What had he asked?

"Morfran retreated." Padraig's tongue was thick and uncooperative. "Left Arien. Why would a king—even one so mad as my uncle—leave his son's body? Retreat is no excuse. There is a certain honor due."

He was weary past reckoning. His father was dead. All but a handful of Keepers were dead. If his clumsy attempt at preparing a remedy did not work, he too would soon be dead. Questions were pointless. He persisted. "Arien. Shot by his father's own archers. Not an accident of war."

His head fell forward.

"My lord?"

Stop shaking me. Stop shouting.

"Padraig!"

A rough-skinned hand touched his brow and tipped back his head.

He still had to tell Gaerbith—what?

"Captain Gaerbith." The voice of Thael, his father's servant. "I have brought a healer's apprentice. They have been so busy—"

"Too busy to come to Padraig? He is your king!"

Gaerbith's harsh voice jarred Padraig, forcing open his eyes, and he caught the captain's arm. "The Fourth fought well, brother. Tell them their king is pleased."

"Shall I stay, my lord?"

Padraig shook his head. "You look like a ghost. Pray do not frighten your men. Disson still needs them."

With a faint smile more grave than amused, Gaerbith bowed and departed.

Owen fell into step beside him without a word. Something had changed in the boy.

Something had changed in himself. Something had loosened and unwound, like a banner unfurled: wherever he went depended on the wind, yet he was anchored still, kept by an unseen hand from blowing away in the storm.

Was it the residue of Omwen'din? Traces of Keepers' virtue?

Ask Cayn—

Cayn was dead.

Jaw clenched, Gaerbith looked around at the scattered lachmil, their fires few and small, the men around them hunched, wounded, silent. Did the Skardian army return, Disson could not give a defense.

If the Skardians—the common folk, not just the nobles—rose up and refused Morfran's mad rule, would anything change? Would the brother kingdoms still rage? If so, how long before the free Territories fell?

The Thynathel Hills with their abundant vineyards and flocks of fine-wooled sheep would be taken first, being closest to Morfran's fortified cities and without the rugged defense of stony heights or thick forests; only open rolling slopes and inviting valleys of rich farmland, and the thinnest ranks of border guards. Would his father, his sisters and their husbands and children, be willing to leave the green Hills and return to the long-ago haven in the wastes of the Grimë Mountains?

If the time came, would he remember the way?

"Owen."

The boy kept walking.

Gaerbith put a hand on Owen's shoulder. The muscles bunched, repelling his touch.

The boy halted, his face turned toward the darkness. Beyond him, Captain Yerrin crouched beside a fire, his head bound by what might have been the remnants of a tunic. He looked up, nodded at Gaerbith then cast a puzzled glance at Owen. Gaerbith raised a hand in greeting and walked onward. Owen stirred then followed, no longer beside but slightly behind.

Gaerbith walked a tenuous path. As reticent as he could be, his brother could match him for silence.

Owen had seen Cayn die.

"The death of a Keeper is— When Uártha died—"

When she placed her hand on his head and blessed him, power had thundered through him like rivers over-rushing their banks, sweeping everything before them. His senses sharpened. His mind saw memories not his. The light surrounding his mother had not faded but grew until the air gleamed silver, and her body rose, limp as a child's in the arms of her father. Then she disappeared, fading into whiteness. He had been left, alone, kneeling in the water beside an empty boat.

"If you wish to tell what you saw, Owen, I will listen."

Owen walked, and did not speak.

Turi stared at the silent figure standing on the cusp of darkness.

Streaked with blood and earth, the man's surcoat gaped at the chest. A slash cut the green Oak of Disson broidered there, as if someone had tried to hew him down. His hair was indeterminate color, being yellow but with streaks of red, and his beard was a similar tangle of hues. Ice-blue eyes looked out of a face at once familiar and strange.

Other men turned. Had they been speaking or laughing, their silence might have been taken for astonishment. Their shoulders sagged, their movements slow, their faces etched by weariness. Most of them wore bloodied rags wrapped around their wounds.

Turi rose from his place by the fire. "Captain."

Men struggled to stand, but Captain Gaerbith stepped forward into the meager light.

The Fourth had been hidden so they might come back around the Highlands with the intent of catching the enemy unaware. Instead, the enemy had caught them, and the Fourth had lost so many men that to call the end of the battle a victory was a vile jest. The pristine little wood with its brooks and small bits of beauty was now a ruin, the streams muddy and fouled with blood. The hillocks around its edges were new graves.

Yet here stood the captain as if he had never taken near-mortal wounds only two days past. Where had he been during the worst of the fighting? Not with the ill or wounded in the carts driven far from battle. Not with his own men.

Turi took the captain's right forearm in greeting, but anger tightened his grasp. Gaerbith said nothing at the fierce grip on his arm nor did anger flare in his gaze. Rather, there was understanding. Then, with a clap on Turi's shoulder, he limped toward the one fire the men had been able to light, and accepted a bowl of soup from Fremmen.

"Captain."

Gaerbith turned to meet Turi's stare.

The men looked first at the captain then at his second then back again. The captain lifted the bowl by its rim and drank down the soup. Handing the bowl to Fremmen, he wiped his mouth with the back of his hand.

Turi hitched his belt, adjusted the baldric, crossed his arms. "Ye did not fight with us."

He waited.

Gaerbith studied him with that same odd look, as if Turi could say whatever he liked but the captain already understood.

"He did not fight with the Fourth"—young Owen strode from the darkness to stand beside the captain—"because he fought in King Padraig's stead."

"I fight my own battles, Owen," murmured the captain.

The lad stepped backward, bowing his head a little though not bending his spine. Pride stiffened him like a frozen shirt.

Turi spat. "King's favor means more than comrades' blood?"

Gaerbith's eyes were steady. "Skardians fell before my blade this day. If I slew them while leading the Fourth or while standing for the king on the battlefield, they fell. I am confident my second in command led my men to do what must be done."

Turi could almost hear the question left unspoken: *Did he?*

Shamed now—not because he had failed, but because he had doubted his captain—he lifted his chin and set his jaw.

The captain looked around at the watching soldiers. "Whom have we lost?"

Warrten held out a piece of rough cloth on which he had written names with charcoal. "Over half, captain. Padraig sent reinforcements, but we lost many."

Taking the cloth, Gaerbith stared down at it, his thumb rubbing the edge. "Has the death blessing been said?"

"Aye, captain. We only now returned to camp."

"Wounded?"

"Nigh all of us. We bound our own wounds."

"Missing?"

"If they are not here, captain, they are dead."

A horse limped into view, the rope that had tied him to a tree frayed on one end and trailing beside him. He tossed his head and nickered.

"Kraekor!" Gaerbith threw his arms around the horse's neck. Kraekor, his chin resting on the man's shoulder, snuffled the captain's hair and cheek. The captain ran his hand lightly along the horse's shoulder, not touching the still-healing wound. "We are a matched pair, eh, old friend?"

It was a common thing for a soldier and his warhorse to have a kinship beyond that of master and beast. In battle they must act as one being, as if Omwen'din had put a little bit of one's mind into the other's, enabling them to think alike. So it was with the captain and Kraekor.

The old horse had missed his master indeed if he had chewed through his lead. The frayed rope could not have tasted nearly as sweet as the apples he was forever seeking—and Kraekor was renowned for his fine tastes. He had once disdained a rosy but common Calhoun Forest apple from Turi's own hand, only to follow a soldier from the Western Wood who happened to be munching on a golden autumn apple from the Thynathel Hills. Kraekor had nosed the man's arm and butted his shoulder until he turned and offered the rest of the apple to the old rogue.

"Our enemy is fled," said Gaerbith, "but I doubt it is a true retreat."

"Captain," Fremmen said, "we had hoped to go home."

Turi looked down at the trampled ground. Home. Where was that?

If he returned to Disson, would his children know him? His daughter might, but to his son he would be a stranger. Did they call his sister mother? Her husband father?

"Would that we were going home." The captain's voice was heavy with things he did not say. "Meantime, I will stand with the first watch."

Turi said, "I stand second watch."

So it went, men calling out their watch, and then the first being taken while the rest of the men wrapped themselves in still-damp blankets, leaned against trees, and tried to sleep standing.

After stringing his bow, Owen climbed a tree.

Turi watched him, seeing in the youth a change similar to Gaerbith's. Not the result of battle—that affected everyone—but a shaping, as if unseen hands had reached out to form the clay but molded the soul.

Settling his mind on matters he better understood, Turi unfurled his old stained blanket, draped it over his shoulders and, finding a stone near a tree, sat on the rock and propped his back against the trunk, and prayed he did not waken with more aches than he already owned.

Face hollowed by weariness, Fremmen handed Gaerbith a bundle wrapped in the remnants of an old blanket.

Gaerbith unwrapped the books: his journal listing the names of the fallen, and an older book, its leather and pages water-stained. He opened the journal, riffling the pages. He chose a clean page, and placed there the piece of cloth covered with the newest names, then closed the journal and slid the other book from beneath it. This he did not open, but laid his palm flat against the cover.

"I was a cooper. I taught my sons. I was good. Strong barrels. Water-tight buckets. Even made a few shields." Fremmen let out a long sigh. "Now my sons are dead, and war is all I know."

"You will be a cooper again." Gaerbith wrapped the blanket scrap over the books, and tucked the bundle under his arm. "The dead know we have not forgotten."

The fire was banked and the first watch hidden, so still and quiet Owen could not discern men from shadows.

Sitting in a sturdy notch of a tree, with a third branch against which he could recline, he rolled a ball of wax between his fingers until it was soft, then he rubbed it along the length of the bowstring, feeling for thin places, lumps, any weakness or oddity that would prevent his arrows from shooting true. The string thrummed at his touch. Still taut, still good.

Only three or four hours remained until sunrise. Resting the bow across his legs, Owen leaned back and closed his eyes. He did not fear he would miss an enemy creeping on the camp. He may not make a warrior, but he was a hunter. He would hear.

10 ~ THE MESSAGE

Brittle edges rained brown flecks on the table. The scroll was held open by smooth stones anchoring each corner of the delicate material. Neither parchment nor vellum nor any kind of animal skin, it was fibrous, made of plants. The faded script was Old Kelden, not the tongue spoken among the Keepers but its ancestor, a language birthed from the coming together of clans under the rule of Kel High King.

Doth na arka tahn
dyn urk fril rívae
enkára mahyla sthyn
Doth thén fril théně ta
Toth elae fril llúmë ta
E totha théneth lae llúm
o griára duru sthyn

Twice a broken sword
shall cripple he who comes
seeking inheritance lost
Twice dead he dies not
Thrice born he lives not
In third death is life
and finding of the lost

In the dawn light peeking through the library window, Ro'Ar stared at the words. Cripple and break were related in Old Keldon, and were sometimes interchanged. Was the man lame? Was his mind be broken?

Captain Gaerbith, heir of Uártha, had been nigh crippled, but by a whole blade. The broken sword had been his brother's, not an enemy's. Yet there were no strictures in the ancient text, no detailing of how the weapon might be applied. And it was because the youth's sword had been broken that the captain sprang to his aid and received grievous wounds. The words implied treachery, as if swords—inanimate, unaware objects—could seek out a particular man to do him harm.

And what was this matter of "twice dead, thrice born"?

Ro'Ar closed his eyes and tilted his head back against the stone of the casement. Was "the lost" the heir of Kel? The sword Azrin? The restoration of the people to freedom and prosperity?

In customary vagary of thought, Ro'Ar's mind leapt to other ideas —to Dragons exiled and heirs hidden, to swords concealed and Kels slain—and in the wandering he saw a band of men standing at the foothills of the Craydaeg Mountains and looking upward. Somewhere in those mountains lurked treachery, yet the men did not hesitate but pressed onward, advancing to their doom.

In truth, they were not there yet. They still lingered near the battlefield.

Ro'Ar opened his eyes and looked once more at the scroll.

A quiet cough startled him.

"Your pardon, First Keeper," said Madda the huntress, standing beside Draken in the doorway. "We cannot come to agreement on which of us shall accompany you on the journey."

Despite her quiet words, determination gleamed in her eyes, and from the thrust of Draken's chin, he would not yield.

One might think that Keepers, as skilled and wise and old as most of them were, would not be subject to the ill humors of Men. Ro'Ar knew better than anyone that service to the Voice did not free one from folly.

Stifling a sigh, he put away the scroll and prepared for the storm.

Gripping the silver cord that acted as a rein on the great raven, Imre squinted against the wind tugging at his cloak. Far below and distant glinted wavering pinpricks of light, the scattered small campfires of the Dissonay. His current state—cold, tired, afraid—could have been worse. He could have been forced to sleep in the mud. As it was, he had been allowed a few hours of rest aboard ship before being sent with a message to Damanthus, king of Disson.

Why Morfran should send *him*, though, Imre did not know. There were couriers and spies still stationed at outposts. A leather cylinder could have been strapped to the leg of a Nar'ath trained to fly between two specific points, and thus a courier could have received the orders and taken the message to the Dissonay. And thus Imre, the royal manservant, would not be forced to struggle against his fear of the great black birds.

But he had been summoned, and there was no denying King Morfran, even by a servant of long standing.

A stranger had knelt before the king. The man spoke garbled Skardian with a strong Dissonay accent. Morfran, leaning forward with an intent gaze, hushed the man almost as soon as Imre lifted the tent flap to enter, but Imre had already deciphered something about a captain and grapes, and a phrase that might describe either bargain or revenge.

Morfran spared Imre half a glance, ordering him to write a letter. Then, once the king had signed and folded the parchment and sealed it with his ring, he placed it inside a messenger pouch. "Deliver this to Damanthus. Return before sunset with a reply from that king of dogs." He handed the bag to Imre. "Sunset."

It was spoken in the same flat voice and sharp look with which Morfran had ordered the archer to shoot Lord Arien.

The stinging wind pricked Imre's eyes. He looked over his shoulder. Beyond the far Craydaeg Mountains and the Kelcey Forest, dawn cut the eastern horizon, a knife-edge of light slashing the darkness. He turned the Nar'ath south, hoping to reach the wood near the Highlands before the bird was seen by a vigilant archer. Imre could not signal from this height that he was merely a messenger, but if he could land some distance outside the camp and dismount, perhaps the barbarians would let him live.

The fires were closer now. Mounds, long and wide, filled the vale. Men still moved among them, burying the last of the dead. A man gestured skyward with his spade, and his fellows looked up. One of them ran toward a waiting horse and leapt astride. Another man grabbed up a bow.

Swallowing hard, tightening his grip on the silver cord, Imre urged the Nar'ath to go higher—

Something shot from deep in the wood. The bird wheeled then dove. The arrow missed. As if taunting the unseen archer, the bird shrieked, plunging toward the trees.

Imre closed his eyes. Who would take the news of his demise to sweet Elta?

The Nar'ath jerked. Another shrill cry.

Imre's stomach seemed to claw its way up his throat as he clung to the tumbling bird. Wind screamed in his ears.

Something hit him with the crushing force of a falling wall, and sensation ceased.

"Gaerbith? Captain?"

He blinked and groaned. He had just closed his eyes. Surely it was firelight he saw, and not the sun.

Turi leaned over him, for an instant blocking the light. "Come see what young Owen caught."

Pushing himself up from the hollow where he rested and sheathing his sword, Gaerbith shook tangled hair back from his face and wished for a basin of cold water to pour over his head and shock his senses to clarity. Instead, he drank the mug of ale Turi thrust into his hand.

In the center of the camp stood Owen. At his feet knelt a blindfolded and beardless youth, hands bound behind his back. Blood poured from a wound on his head.

"Says he is an emissary of King Morfran. He brings this." Owen tossed a messenger pouch.

Gaerbith caught it in his free hand, then passed the pouch to Turi. Inside was a sealed parchment, folded not rolled, and the red wax bore the imprint of a Dragon.

Crouching before the prisoner, Gaerbith examined the wound. The youth flinched, his breath coming in thready gasps, either from fear or pain, or both. He leaned to one side, likely favoring a broken rib.

"We are short of healers." Gaerbith dredged up his best Skardian, not spoken in many a day. "Deliver your message to the king, then we find you aid. Can you walk?"

The prisoner nodded.

Gaerbith helped him stand. Owen grasped the prisoner's elbow to lead him away.

"Wait." Gaerbith held out the mug.

Owen frowned.

"It may help calm him."

Owen held it to the youth's lips. "Drink!"

Ale stained the corners of the prisoner's mouth and dripped from his chin. When the boy coughed, Owen withdrew the mug and handed it to Gaerbith who passed it to Turi—"Break camp and meet at the king's standard"—in exchange for the messenger pouch and an old rucksack.

"Come along, you." Owen jerked the prisoner's arm. The youth clamped his teeth over a short cry of pain, and lurched beside him.

No older than Owen, the boy wore a torn scarlet tunic broidered with the Dragon of the House of Morfran, and his hands were soft, the fingers stained with ink. A servant or a scribe, and a royal one. Why send him and not a seasoned messenger?

"Peace, Owen, walk easy. He is not a soldier, nor has he done us harm."

"He is Skardian, and he rode a Nar'ath. The bird is dead. I would have killed the Skardian, too, but for Turi."

Gaerbith met his brother's hard gaze and shook his head, but Owen thrust out his chin, yanking the prisoner over the uneven ground.

"Halt."

The command brought Owen up short, his stance rigid, eyes defiant.

"Remove the blindfold."

After a tense silence, Owen snatched the cloth from the prisoner's eyes then let him go with a shove. Gaerbith grabbed the boy just in time to keep him upright.

"Report to Turi. Now."

With a hot glare, Owen stalked away, muttering an oath.

Omwen'din, give me wisdom. To the watching prisoner, Gaerbith said, "It is yet some distance. There, to the green pennant."

The boy nodded, freckles dark against his pallor. "I see it."

"We shall walk slow, then, and you will tell me of your home."

"My home is wherever my lord commands. I am Imre, servant to Morfran of Skarda. I stand in the king's chamber and beside his throne. I record what he wishes in the archives. I scribe his letters and taste his wine. I care for his garments and tend his armor. I do whatever he bids.

"I was born in Cäldon, but was taken very young to Elycia, there to serve in the king's household. Unlike many other servants or the king's own soldiers, my mind is still my own."

From the corner of his eye, Gaerbith considered him. Intelligent but too open, especially for one who served a notorious cunning master. "You reveal so much on such slight command that one might think you are hiding something greater."

"I have nothing to conceal, my lord. It is all in the letter."

"I am captain, Imre, not lord. And I do not believe you."

The sun warmed the chill morning just enough to keep his breath from misting in the air. Lachmil were breaking camp, packing what little remained of their possessions. Few fires burned. There was scant wood dry enough to kindle and nothing to cook. Disson was an army of skeletons and ghosts.

"Are you going to kill me, my lor—captain?"

"If you are, as you claim, merely a messenger, why do you ask?"

"The Dissonay are barbarians. They eat the flesh of their enemies, and drink their blood."

Hiding sudden dark humor behind a grim glare, Gaerbith drew his sword. It came free with a sliding twist, scraping along the edges of the scabbard's deep open V that allowed the longsword to be unsheathed with ease. With a squawk of fear, Imre tottered sideways, his feet sliding in mud not yet dried from yesterday's storm.

"This"—Gaerbith looked up the entire length of the sword's shuddering blade—"is Bítan." He sliced it downward, the flat of it stopping a hand's breadth from the boy's face. "See the ancient words graven there? 'I will taste the flesh of my enemies and drink their blood.' And it has. Indeed, it has." He studied the wide-eyed youth. "Blood keeps the metal supple, and many an hour has passed since Bítan last tasted Skardian."

Hiding a smile, he sheathed the sword and walked onward. A moment later, he heard Imre shuffling to follow him.

"So, you do not mean to kill me."

"Not without cause."

"There is a captain with magic to rival Heolstor's. Are you—"

"Owen slew your Nar'ath. You have no way back to your king but your own two feet. If our king chooses, you will be a prisoner."

Imre's words trembled a little. "If I cannot complete this task, I would rather you slew me before Heolstor sends his magic."

Gaerbith felt anew the stinging rip of Nar'ath claws tearing his chest, saw again his mother's book of golden words and the dark blood streaming down an arm paler than bleached bone. How old was that old man? What poison had he whispered in the ears of Skardian kings, century after century?

If Gaerbith took the oath of a Keeper, he would have what he lacked as a boy—the power to exact vengeance. Would hatred for Heolstor push him past fear of the oath?

Heolstor had slain Keepers beyond number. Repeating mere words could not defeat such an ancient and dominant foe.

"Will you, captain?"

"What?" Yanked from his thoughts, Gaerbith spoke sharp, hard.

"Kill me."

"No promises, young Imre."

Captains and nobles were already gathered before Padraig's tent. When they saw Gaerbith and the prisoner, their weary faces grew alert. Drooped postures straightened. Hands gripped on hilts.

Captain Yerrin, still wearing a bloody rag around his head, jerked his chin at Imre. "I heard the rumors among the men that a Nar'ath had been killed."

"His." Gaerbith hooked a thumb in Imre's direction. "He brings a message for the king. Is there a healer about?"

Yerrin ducked into the king's tent and returned with a Keeper whose pale robe was spattered with blood and smeared with grime. The healer went straight to Imre and examined the head wound then pressed his thumbs lightly against ribs. Imre sucked in his breath and winced.

"Has the king woken?" asked Gaerbith quietly.

The Keeper's eyes were grave. "He is gripped with fever. Someone tended his poisoned wound, however, and that may save his life."

Gaerbith patted Imre's shoulder. "Is there medicine for this one?"

The Keeper untied Imre's hands and led him away. Standing outside the king's tent, Thael watched them go then he approached Gaerbith.

"Captain." The servant bobbed his head in an almost-bow. He held out a small key.

Seeing it, Gaerbith grew still. It was the key to the casket where the scroll was kept—the scroll giving him and Turi authority over all the lachmil and making them governors of the kingdom of Disson. He did not want that key.

Thael continued to offer it, a curious look on his thin face.

"Bring the box. I will open it here, before witnesses."

Turi arrived, nodding to Gaerbith and greeting the others. Beyond him, soldiers gathered, keeping a distance between themselves and the men near the king's tent. They were waiting orders. Gaerbith's throat tightened How few they were, how gaunt and weary.

Thael returned with the casket, and held it while Gaerbith unlocked and lifted the lid. Inside were stacked several scrolls, each with a notation on the edge near the seal. He chose the first: *Gaerbith, Captain of the Fourth Lachmil, to be read by him in the presence of the captains.*

Breaking the wax with a clean snap, he unfurled the thin parchment and, without first reading it to himself, read aloud.

Should death take me, I, Padraig Damanthusson, king of Disson, do entrust the armies of Disson and the guardianship of the House of Rhobarrd to Gaerbith son of Forba, to Turi of the Calhoun Forest, and to Yerrin of Sonndin, until my brother Daman Damanthusson gains the twentieth anniversary of his birth.

The seal of the House of Rhobarrd shall wait the day the king takes it up again. Nobles and captains of Disson, do not supplant the guardians until the trust is fulfilled. A copy of this trust has been delivered to the House of Rhobarrd in Sonndin, and another to the scribes of the archive, that there may be no argument.

So declared on this day, One hundred fifteenth day of the year, Second day of the reign of Padraig Damanthusson, king of Disson.

The king's bold signature was followed by a round medallion of green wax in which was pressed the image of the Oak.

Gaerbith passed the parchment to Captain Párhetton on his left, who glanced at the seal then passed it on around the circle. Men read in silence.

"Captain Gaerbith," sneered a familiar voice. "You are looking well. Your magic stands you in good stead."

Lord Boorn stood just beyond the gathering. Captain Yerrin

cursed. Someone else muttered something obscene.

"I was summoned to return." Lord Boorn waved a folded piece of parchment. "It seems King Damanthus has countered Lord Padraig's order, and has asked—most graciously—if I would return. He has a matter of great importance he wishes me to undertake."

"But," Yerrin began, "Damanthus is d—"

"Departed." Gaerbith trod lightly on the toe of Yerrin's boot, and Lord Symon quickly furled the scroll and slipped it up his ample sleeve. "Gone to Sonndin with the wounded."

"If the king is gone, why is not Padraig standing here with you? Is he wounded as well?"

Boorn started toward the tent, but Gaerbith held up another scroll from the box. "The king left this for you, Lord Boorn."

The writing near the seal did indeed say *Boorn, a lord of Disson and the king's winemaker, to be read by him in the presence of the lords and captains of Disson.* Which king, however, there was no name written.

Warning whispered in Gaerbith's mind, and seemed to have traveled among the gathered men, for none of them revealed to Boorn that Damanthus was dead.

Boorn snatched the scroll from Gaerbith's grasp and started to break the seal, but Lord Áben, a slight man with grey streaks near his temples and a humorous quirk to his mouth, leaned forward. "May we delay your matter a little, Lord Boorn, until we have heard what King Morfran has written?"

There was no way Boorn could disagree and do so with any grace.

His eyes narrowed. "Morfran has sent a message? Does he ask for treaty?"

Lord Áben inclined his head. "We shall know in a moment."

Gaerbith opened the Skardian messenger's pouch, withdrew the letter sealed in scarlet wax, and offered it to Áben. "If you please, my lord."

Áben cleared his throat. "My Skardian is none too easy." He broke the red wax seal, opened the folded page, and in halting phrases read aloud:

To Damanthus, king of Disson, born brother of Una, queen of Skarda, and sworn brother of Morfran, king of Skarda, greeting.

The letter that followed was so astonishing that even Lord Boorn was struck dumb—until the arguing began.

Two Nar'ath appeared near midday, one of them bearing a rider. Archers nocked arrows but did not loose them, and men drew swords, watching as the rider in a hooded black robe simply waited instead of dismounting. Around the neck of each bird was looped a silver cord.

Imre was released, his injuries neatly bound, the strap of the messenger pouch slung over his shoulder. He hobbled out to meet the Black Hood but could not mount. Gaerbith sent two men: one to lift Imre, the other to stand with weapon ready.

Though restive, the Nar'ath did not attack. Once Imre was settled, the silver cord wrapped about his hand for grip, the great black birds rose, their wings conjuring a wind that whipped the hair and beards of men standing at a distance. With Imre went a scroll—signed by Padraig's hand, but bearing the name of Damanthus.

Gaerbith assembled his *lachmil*. The sick, wounded, or unwilling, he sent with the caravans returning west. To those who remained, he revealed the king's plan: escort an emissary to Elycia, capital city of Skarda, there to treat with King Morfran for peace between the two kingdoms.

"I have little liking for Lord Boorn," said Turi, "and even less now that he bears a new title. High Lord, the king's own emissary. A little man puffed with his own greatness."

"Aye!"

"Why him?"

"Are ye sure Padraig was in his right mind?"

Gaerbith raised his hands to quiet the protests. "We do not go for High Lord Boorn, but for our families, for our people and our land. Say nothing about the death of Damanthus. Refer to our king as Lord Padraig, and speak as if Damanthus were merely wounded and will recover soon."

Someone laughed. "So, you do not trust Boorn either, eh, captain?"

"Only as far as my sword will reach."

Amid more raucous speculation about the worthiness of the new emissary, "Why do we go to Mad Morfran's house, captain?" asked Trag, one of the new warriors, with a belligerent tilt of his jaw. "Why not bid him crawl to ours?"

"Aye," said Fremmen, crossing his arms upon his chest and planting his feet wide. "My bow is strong, and my arrows fleet. Let me slay *Bachaná* and be done with this." He spat *Bachaná*, the old word for *butcher*, as if it left a foul taste in his mouth.

Their grand words spilled from frustration and anger, not from any real power, for neither weapon nor warrior were threat to Mad Morfran. Arrows glanced off his helm, swords slid harmlessly across mail, lances pierced only air. The king of Skarda fought inside an invisible shield said to have been fashioned from the breath of Nar Cahm, darkness himself.

Gaerbith looked into the faces of his men as they gathered beside the burial mounds. They knew something was amiss, for treaty was always conducted on the ground between two armies, not in the home of either.

"We go to treat for peace, but we go also for a purpose I cannot yet see. Padraig has a plan, but he did not reveal the end, neither in written words nor spoken. We are asked to do this task without knowing why. We are hunters. Trappers. He could tell nothing more before the fever took him again. Our prey is for us to discover."

"I know my prey." Warrten slapped the handle of his wicked mace. "A quick tap with this wizarding rod, and the Butcher is beef."

Turi hefted his axe handle in one huge hand and tapped the flat of the head in the other large palm. Men chuckled and jests flew like arrows, describing Morfran and Skarda in increasingly gruesome and ribald terms, until Gaerbith had to raise his voice to be heard.

"Your families wait your return," he said, "and your comrades prepare to journey home. This is a difficult thing I ask. I do not plead your loyalty or trust. I leave you to choose."

Their ready humor fell silent. Men turned away their faces from him, shifted stances, examined well-kept weapons. In their hearts, they wanted to go home. Most were men of the Territories, and therefore without a king. They fought by choice. The journey to Elycia would be dangerous, and the risk too high to demand their compliance. Yet, if an end of war could be achieved—

"Captain?"

"Owen?" Anger tugged at Gaerbith's brows. "I sent you with the others. Why are you yet here?"

"I am going to Elycia with you."

"I sent you with the others so that you may return to the Thynathel

Hills and home."

"Aye, captain, and I choose to go with you."

Owen's words were flames kindling latent coals. If a youth who was not yet a warrior had the courage to go, how could the others remain?

With audacious laughter and bold words, every able-bodied man agreed to the journey.

In the dining hall of Havyn duru Asryn, the gathered Keepers marked a solemn ceremony. With but one date painted, and one picture—that of a Keeper wielding a sword, a healer's box at his feet—to represent all who fell in the Lowland vale between the River Sonndin and the Highlands, each fallen healer's name was inscribed on the wall, one by one, a thin brush dipped in the pot, used, and then passed to the next Keeper who stepped forward to write the next name.

When all were written, Ro'Ar lifted his arms out from his sides, palms upward, and bowed his head. The other Keepers did the same.

"Omwen'din, we give to Thee the honored dead. May their feet find a sure path, and their souls find peace."

And the Keepers responded, "It is so."

Then, after all the gathered Keepers took candles from the stands, Ro'Ar led them down echoing colonnades to the Great Hall. Mounting the three steps of the round dais, he stood before the broken throne. When he spoke, the vast space expanded his voice.

"The time for departure draws near. Ere we go, we pray for wisdom, for strength to stand when our hearts despair, for skill and patience to do what must be done."

Kneeling on one knee, hands clasped on the other, each person sank into an attitude of silent prayer. In their pale garments and with candles set on the floor before them, the Keepers formed circles of light like ripples in water. Ro'Ar stood a moment looking at them, wondering how many would remain when he returned, and how many would be remembered by pictures on a wall.

II

BLACKSMITH, LAUNDRESS,
HEALER, PRIEST

Risá El ethem, Mymna Tor
Risá duru Nar Cahm enkára lenë llumim
Risá nen, o pyrvië grimladh

Save Your people, Mighty Lord
Save from the Dark Enemy seeking our lives
Save us, and vanquish evil

> *ancient prayer sung by the remnant of the House of Kel*
> *as they flee hunters, from the fall of Adwr to this day*

11 ~ BLACKSMITH

Under the sign of the Blue Oak, wood painted bright but cracked with age, the inn door stood wide to admit the mild night air and release the pipe smoke clouding the great room. Dice players gambled with polished river stones. The first man whose pile of pebbles disappeared bought his fellows a round of ale. Master Clem the innkeeper traded jests with a merchant, and a scarlet-clad stranger ate alone.

Kieran Smith hooked a foot around a thick-legged stool and sat at an empty table.

A serving lass brought him a cup of ale and lingered, a saucy glimmer in her eyes. "Will you dance this year at the Faere, Master Smith?" Sally possessed a winsome smile, and when she leaned forward, her low bodice brushed his cheek.

Heat crept up his neck. "I am not, ah, much of a dancer."

Sally chuckled, and swayed across the room.

"Studying?" A ruddy-cheeked young man with merry blue eyes and curly blond hair sat on the bench opposite Kieran. A knowing smile lit his sun-browned face.

"I am free to look, Harry. You, however, had best keep your eyes on Jenny—"

"—or the Highlands for me." Harry crossed his eyes and made a face, drawing a finger across his throat.

"Aye, my friend, and I shall hie you there myself."

"No need." Harry placed his hands over his heart, affecting a lovelorn expression. "Jenny is the love of my life. But she is not the only woman walking the earth, and that you know right well." He signaled for ale. "Never was a more somber lad than Kieran Smith. You laugh too rare, my friend. Get you a wife."

Sally brought Harry's drink, setting it on the table with another flirtatious glance at Kieran. He flushed again.

Harry laughed. "You cannot run from it, lad. They will make you a husband, whether you will or no." Harry quaffed his ale and ran the back of his hand across his mouth. "I am a married man now. The wisdom of the ages is mine."

Kieran chuckled. "And what, pray tell, is this wisdom?

"Woman will have what she will have, and there is naught man may do about it."

"Jenny's strong mind is no secret, but I thought you a man well able to stand his ground."

"I have no weapons against tears or ill-cooked meat or-or withheld affections. There's no fighting such things."

"And you wish them on me? And to think I called you friend."

Harry slapped the table. "You made a jest, my friend. Well done!"

Kieran kicked the bench, knocking Harry to the floor.

Grinning, the farmer picked himself up, righted the bench, sat, and leaned across the table like a gossip. "Back to husbands and wives. What of Kathleen?"

"John Oakley."

Harry frowned. "But there is an understanding—"

Kieran pressed a fist to his forehead. He could work all day in a hot smithy, yet mere conversation drummed a pounding fist on his skull.

"Old Donnegan cared not which of his daughters you took to wife, but now there is only Kathleen." Harry's mouth tipped up. "Get over it, lad. I was just too handsome for Jenny to resist."

Yet he did not wake Kieran's humor, and the men drank in silence.

Standing, Harry laid a coin on the table and clapped Kieran on the back. "Come see my orchard soon. The blue apples are improving."

He left, and the corpulent innkeeper approached. Kieran ordered bread and a bowl of stew. "Unless," he added in a murmur, "you have any poached venison?"

"All our meat is roasted." A twinkle danced in Master Clem's eyes. "We serve nothing poached, not even eggs." He lowered his voice. "But we are not wasteful. Why turn away whatever wanders into bowshot?"

Chuckling, Master Clem set off for the kitchen, passing the stranger's table without a glance.

Leaning back, Kieran crossed his arms over his chest and listened to other customers grumble over the war between Skarda and Disson, grouse about the latest tax, and confirm rumors of another conscription patrol sighted on the Romney Road.

Farmer Connor, drinking more than customary, dared speak against the baron. He stood swaying, and raised his tankard. "We are but seed for the baron's crops, grist for his mills. He steals our goods, conscripts our sons, and handles our women. I say we leave our fields and turn our plows on him!"

"Beware, friend," one of his fellows warned in a low voice. "Denouncing the baron is denouncing the king."

"Spies," added another.

Someone grunted. "A baron with spies."

"The king has spies."

"Aye, and he thinks Kels still haunt the kingdom."

A sleepy, ale-slurred voice asked, "What're Kels?"

"Dangerous men! Dangerous men," declared drunken Farmer Connor, "but only in our mad king's mind. And the king is the baron's cousin. Madmen all. Anyone seen the baron making his circuit 'round the province? Must have gathered his courage and gone to war."

Silence circled the room like a noose.

Looking anywhere but at each other, the other customers busied themselves with their dinners. The farmer plopped onto his bench and stared into his ale.

Someone at last braved the silence. Conversation turned to less troublesome topics—crops and livestock, and the hubbub of the coming Faere. Gossip circulated concerning a foul wind stirred by an invisible creature distressing the hamlets somewhere east of Shea. The monster stole cattle or burned cottages, although no folk had been killed. Some had seen a light burning deep inside Dragon's Rook. Lurid details were added as successive listeners recalled something they had heard from a friend's brother's son-in-law, or some other such eyewitness.

The scarlet-clad stranger rose and came to stand before Kieran.

"Good even." He placed a closed fist over his heart then lowered his hand and opened it, the greeting of a Southman. The blacksmith studied the outstretched palm. It bore no calluses or scars—as soft as a noblewoman's. "I am Teag," said the stranger. "A minstrel."

Kieran neither answered nor extended his own hand in greeting.

Teag's mouth tightened, but he maintained a smile and sat on the opposite bench just as Sally arrived with the food.

While the minstrel ordered a tankard and offered florid flattery to Sally, Kieran studied the man's clothes: a short tunic, scarlet hose, feathered cap, yellow undershirt. He could not be from a sensible farming village like Shea, where the men dressed in sturdy breeches tied from ankle to knee with leather laces and wore thick-soled leather shoes, and wore knee-length tunics called blouses, belted at the waist. The women, too, clad themselves in simple clothes, kirtles and aprons with little adornment, more practical than pretty. Where in the kingdom did men dress in such a festival fashion as this Teag?

"Do we hear a song?" Kieran tore the loaf of bread in half, dipping part of it in the stew. "Or a bright tune?"

"My lute was rendered in payment for a debt." Teag's thin face took on a look of faint regret. "Perchance I shall acquire a new one at the Faere."

Kieran continued eating.

The silence grew long. Teag shifted on the bench.

"People expect music with their songs. A minstrel merely plays, they say, but a skald tells a tale." Teag seemed a man eager to cover skittishness with conversation. "Do you know of the lands to the west where our countrymen now fight the Dissonay dogs?"

"A bit."

Let the man reveal his purpose. Kieran would eat.

The minstrel leaned forward. "The Plains are uninhabited but by animals that burrow beneath the earth. Many generations past, the Plains existed only in the south and were smaller. Then trees were cut for war machines, and the land cleared for fields. Clans fought for slaves and land, and the grasslands were alive with people.

"With the coming of peace and Kel Dragonslayer, change was wrought. Dragons disappeared, the earth grew fertile once more, and Men turned from war to husbandry." Teag tipped his head to one side and gestured at nothing in particular. "Such a golden age could not last, could it? Havyn duru Asryn. The House of the Sky. You may know it as the Ruins of Kel, the rubble that was the seat of High Kings for a thousand years—"

Sally brought a tankard. Teag winked at her over the rim, but she turned a stiff shoulder.

He drank deeply, wiped his upper lip then set down the tankard, resting his arms atop the table once more. Despite his relaxed posture, there was a watchfulness about him. Teag waited for something. Or someone.

A young woman, her russet braids pinned up like a crown, crossed from the kitchen to ascend the stairs, bearing a basket filled with herbs and flowers tied in bundles to be hung over the beds and sweeten the air. No doubt the rooms would soon need more than a few flowers to freshen them after a sennight of carousing Faere-goers.

Teag's face took on the look of a ferret, lean and tense. Picking up his tankard, he held it poised for drinking, his gaze fixed on the girl. It was a casual trick, hiding his face while giving him cover to watch the stairs until Maggie's bare feet disappeared from sight at the landing. A moment later, he glanced at Kieran and shrugged with a smile, as if embarrassed to be caught staring. "You know her?"

"Not a talkative lass." Kieran drank from his tankard. "Any man challenged by her silence will soon regret waking her wit."

Teag's brows rose. "You do not like her."

"Her words are green berries. Apt to give a man indigestion."

"Comely wench."

Kieran shrugged.

"What is her name?"

Kieran spun the tankard back and forth between his palms.

"Has she always been here? In the village?"

"Long enough."

"Pleasant to look at, eh?"

Kieran stood. "A wise man will keep free of her."

Teag leaned back. "You do not dislike her. Not at all."

Kieran paid Master Clem then strode outside. He walked upriver until only fields bounded the water. The Renfrew curved east then. Were this cloudless day instead of starry evening, he might see Dragon's Rook in the distance.

It was said the mountain birthed the Renfrew, one of two rivers in Skarda that flowed north. The other was the River Kel, streaming from the fabled Stone of Oswyn to join the Renfrew in the Lowlands, there merging with the River Thrayne to empty into the Dävra Sea.

Kieran longed to see what lay beyond the Kelcey Forest. He had heard tales of the Plains to the west, of the Craydaeg Mountains to the north. Beyond the Plains lay another forest, darker than the Kelcey, guarded by the Black River and the haunted Highlands. The stories fed the restlessness in Kieran's soul. Sometimes the fire built, demanding he close the smithy and walk until the fury died. Whither he went depended on the whimsy of his feet. This night, he sought the openness of the fields and the gentle Renfrew River.

He pulled off his boots, waded into the chill shallows at the edge of the river, and searched for silvery fish flickering like stars in the cold rippling depths that tugged at his knees and overturned the smooth, shifting pebbles beneath his feet. Fish slipped through his hands, swished around his ankles, nibbled at his toes.

A blue glow pulsed in the water.

Kieran looked around. Perhaps the strange light was a reflection of flame behind a veil—but no torch or lantern was nearer than the distant village, and none cast a blue light.

His hands tingled in the cold water. He warmed them by rubbing them against one another, but the strange sensation grew stronger.

The blue light swelled.

Kieran's heart thudded. He knew this light.

It waned a little, drawing into itself, revealing three rough lumps among the smoother river stones. He plunged his hand into the water and brought up the stones in one fist. They warmed in his palm like birds settling into a nest.

They were ore, dull rock veined with ribbons almost the sheen of forged steel. Once smelted, the deep blue metal might be desirable as a large brooch for a nobleman's cloak, or a bracelet for a fine lady's white arm. A clever smith might make his fortune on one beautiful but useless trinket.

Something rustled in the fallow field nearby—perhaps only a rabbit or a field mouse. The grain stalks did not stand high enough to hide a man unless he crouched low to the ground.

Kieran closed his fist around the stones then dropped them into his scrip, drawing the string tight to conceal the glow. He splashed out of the riverside weeds, climbed the embankment, tugged on socks and boots, then strode toward the village. Around the bend and nearing the kirk, he glanced backward.

Nothing that should not be there.

Yet there was a waiting among the trees across the river, and an awareness in the shadows. Whatever it was, the presence did not want him.

Not yet.

Home was a small room behind the forge. Old Donnegan had been neither stonemason nor carpenter. This was borne out by the smithy's squat shape, resembling a crouching ogre in the darkness. There was no uglier building in the entire village.

Unlocking the door to his room, Kieran nudged it open with his foot. The shuttered window over his cot let in a miserly glow through the slats, but he needed no light to find his way.

He sat on the bed and removed his shoes, then pulled off his belt with the scrip and tossed it onto the lone chair. A basin of clean water waited, but he did not have the energy to rise again and wash. His body slumped, his mind clamored. Lying on the too-narrow, too-short cot, he raised one arm over his head and rested the other on his chest.

His eyes would not close.

Rolling to his side, he reached under the bed and drew out a dagger. The metal warmed in his hand, and the chasing on the hilt glowed dull in the thin moonlight.

The weapon had been tucked into the leg of his breeches the day Donnegan brought him to work in the smithy, and for all the years since, Kieran had hidden the dagger from the rest of the smith's family. What they did not know could not be tortured from them.

A gust of wind slammed into the shutters, pulling the latch free, slapping them back against the wall with a sharp crack. He leapt to the window.

Treetops bent under a violent wind. A foul stench filled his nostrils. The river mists parted. The stars remained brilliant, yet sky seemed to ripple around them like water around stones.

The dagger flared. Fingers of blue light groped from the mouth of his scrip.

The wind whipped 'round—a living thing—clapping the shutters closed then open again.

Kieran closed his hand over the dagger's hilt, and the light turned his skin a translucent blue.

The wind turned once more, and the odor dissipated as quickly as it came, sucked along in the wake of an invisible storm.

Out in the street, someone swore, and a woman uttered an urgent prayer for protection from Nardha's fell schemes. Other voices joined in wonder and fear.

The trees swayed gently for a time then stilled. The mists swirled back together as if they had never been sundered. The dagger grew dull again. Light from the stones withdrew into the scrip.

All was as it should be.

Had he not heard cursing and praying, Kieran might have pushed the storm aside as a waking dream, just another vision among many since he was a child. He might almost believe the rumors about Dragon-folk.

He was tired. His head ached. Pulling in the shutters, he latched them, and slept with the dagger under his pillow.

12 ~ The Healer's Apprentice

Maggie Finney knelt beside the Renfrew River and gathered the succulent greens growing in the moist earth of the riverbank. Proper healers kept good habits, but Maggie had overslept. The hour was late, encroaching on one of Mother Crumb's strictest lessons: Aside from elfwort, which must be gathered at night, never harvest leaves but in early morning before sun dries the dew and makes them bitter.

A blue light pulsed in the shallows, sparkling in shadows where the sun did not penetrate.

She slipped her left hand into the river until the chill water rose to her elbow. The blue light expanded. The water grew warm. Her fingers closed around a small, heavy sphere. It thrummed against her skin, as warm and steady as a heartbeat, and she stood, holding the stone up to the sun, water dripping from her hand and streaming down her arm.

A fish jumped, its scales a flashing rainbow, and returned to the river with a delicate splash. A woman laughed.

Maggie dropped the stone into her apron pocket.

On the opposite shore, raven-haired Kathleen Donnegan walked with John Oakley. The young farmer gazed as if at a marvel, and Kathleen smiled up at him with a saucy pair of dimples.

Poor Johnny.

Maggie brushed dirt from her knees and hung the basket of dock leaves in the crook of her arm.

A breeze caught Kathleen's hair, and she swept the long black strands away from her face. As she did, she turned, and her gaze snagged on Maggie's twisted right hand.

The ill-knit bones ached under the pressure of Kathleen's disdain. Maggie stood rigid. She had been in Shea only a few months, and folk looked at her sideways. Were she merely an outsider, their suspicion would fade with time and her continued quiet industry. She bore a twisted hand, though, and that proclaimed her a witch. No amount of medicine or hard work would change their minds.

This mind—Kathleen's—opened a little. Behind bold eyes swirled myriad thoughts, none of them settled. Kathleen knew her own beauty, knew its power, but was afraid it might not be enough. She liked John, but he was not the one she wanted. As for Maggie's hand, Kathleen feared it as a mark of Nardha, and she hated it for the attention it took away from her. The attention of—

A wise healer does not delve into minds without welcome.

Chastened by Mother Crumb's warning, Maggie shuttered her gift.

Another toss of glossy hair, another laugh at John's words, and Kathleen pulled the young farmer toward the road leading into Shea.

Maggie kneaded the claw-like fingers, trying to push the pain from swollen joints, willing knotty bones to grow slender and straight. The only way to fix them was to break them again and reset the bones, but her knees weakened at the memory of the flat of an iron axe-head whistling down, crushing her hand against a chopping block.

She turned from the river and followed a faint path, one of many secret ways deep in the forest.

Rimmed by tall ferns, a willow tree stood in a dusty beam of light. Maggie passed through its vines and the supple limbs parted, a green curtain opening to reveal a cottage beyond. The cottage door stood open, releasing the gentle converse of two familiar voices. Father Donovan, the traveling priest, spoke in a lilting cadence edged with humor, even while delivering somber homilies in the kirk. Mother Crumb's matter-of-fact tones were spiced with irony and mellowed by mirth. The voices embraced Maggie, welcoming her. This was her home now.

She stood and listened, imagining the two old friends. Father Donovan would be poking through the piles of powders and dried petals, his curiosity never satisfied and his experiments rarely successful. That little thump might be Mother Crumb placing a mug of steaming elderberry tea on the table, and the soft scrape would be the small pot of honey scooting along the oak surface. The priest always sweetened his tea.

"—but it might rouse the king's attention," Mother Crumb was saying. "He still searches for Kels. What bloodlust would send him forth if he heard a Kellish prayer?"

"His rage would be opportunity. When he comes forth from his mountain hold, we will meet him with grand rebellion!" Father Donovan spoke treason with a humorous tilt, and only partly in jest.

A chair gritted along the stone floor as if the healer had pulled it away from the table in order to sit. "A score of years in Mymna Tor's service, and you cannot forget the sword. You are no longer a bandit, Donovan."

They fell silent, drinking their tea in that certain companionship that comes only after many years, requiring neither words nor perfection of one another, simply content to be. Maggie envied them.

She also envied their faith. Her own prayers were mere mouth offerings, dry husks of empty devotion. She doubted the Voice's existence yet had a rare gift, allowing her to mend body and soul, and Mother Crumb said that was proof enough.

Upon first meeting Father Donovan, Maggie had stared. A scar ran from the priest's hairline to jaw, cutting across his right eye and clipping the corner of his mouth, a pale slash in his sun-browned face. Yet, when his thoughts passed over it, she sensed only gratitude, a sublime thankfulness for life. He knew himself and was at peace.

Few mortals know themselves. Few examine their own souls—yet another of Mother Crumb's precepts. A healer with the gift helped folk see clearly and without force. Every mortal must discover certain truths for himself.

Did healers themselves ever fail to see?

Maggie stepped toward the cottage door, but the priest's questions stayed her feet: "How fares young Kieran Smith? Come to a decision yet about Kathleen Donnegan?"

"All he thinks and feels is bound inside him. A tight ball of yarn. He keeps his secrets, but he cannot unravel them." Mother Crumb sighed. "I vowed not to tell the truth before its time, but it troubles me to see him restless, torn between duty and dreams." Then, after a heavy silence, "Would that I could consult the Keepers."

"Are there none nearby?"

"The Voice has called them to the Summoning."

A shiver slithered up Maggie's spine.

"In the villages near Dragon's Rook," the priest said,"the people tell of a strange light glowing inside the mountain, of foul winds at night. Some suffer scorched fields and missing livestock. Something dark is moving abroad. I feel it in me very bones."

Mother Crumb drew a deep breath and expelled it slowly.

Maggie entered the cottage and set the basket of leaves on the table. She nodded at the priest. "Good day, Father Donovan."

"Aye, 'tis." He smiled.

To Mother Crumb she said, "Carts arrived just after dawn. Folk are already gathering for the Faere. I will take the linens to Mistress Clem, and be back in time to help you in the garden."

Mother Crumb gestured to a deep basket piled with fresh folded bed sheets beside the door. "Careful. With all those folk, it is certain there will be soldiers sent to find you."

"I have ways."

"No doubt you do, but Mistress Clem will have another basket or two of soiled linens for you to wash. Best ask her to send Sally to help you carry the load. And"—Mother Crumb pressed some coins into her hand—"ask Kieran Smith if he has repaired my cooking pot."

Maggie dropped the coins into her apron pocket where they clinked against the strange blue stone, then she bent to grasp the woven handles of the basket. As she straightened, pain shot through her fingers. She gasped, almost dropping the clean linens onto the dirt floor.

Father Donovan grabbed the basket and set it on the table. He lifted her crippled hand. "The old complaint?"

She winced even at that gentle touch.

"There be no shame in admitting pain. Cannot abide anyone touching this hand, can thee, even when it does not hurt? Well, then. I shall take this hand until thee think no more about it."

From an applewood casket, a healer's box, Mother Crumb took a strong-smelling ointment of licorice and black mustard, rubbed it into the hand and worked away the pain.

"What a healer I will make, so in need of healing myself," said Maggie.

Mother Crumb gave quiet reply: "Who better to heal than one who has known pain?"

Bitterness twisted its knife in Maggie's throat. "Who will seek the help of a witch?"

Thryffin halted his barrow and bent to pick up sticks near a thicket. He had brought an axe to chop fallen logs, too, gathering hardwood useful for the charcoal pit. It was a rare day when Master Smith could not simply fill the leather belly of the bellows with air and bring coals to life.

The bellows was large, used by pushing down the top to meet the bottom, thus expelling the air. Its top handle was too high for Thryffin's reach, but he leapt up each day, vowing that when he could wrap his fingers around it while standing with both feet on the floor he would no longer be a lad but a man.

One day, he would be a proper bellows-tender and learn to fashion iron. One day, he would be as Master Smith and have the admiration of young women in the village. One day, he would be strong and tall and broad-shouldered, the envy of all the boys who mocked him now. One day, he would be rich and have the respect of men.

One day.

Master Smith had given him two pennies this morning. Thryffin had used one for breakfast at the Blue Oak, tied the other into the hem of his tunic for later, sharpened the axe, laid it in the barrow, then trundled the barrow across the mill bridge and along the Romney Road that led north out of Shea. The forest undergrowth was not so thick along the road, and he could scavenge for wood with ease. Already, the barrow groaned with its load.

He bent to pick up another stick.

Scarlet flickered through the trees, stopping beside the thicket.

He remained in a crouch, still clutching the stick on the ground.

The scarlet was a tunic hanging from the slender shoulders of a man in a feathered cap. He looked north, his features sharp. He tapped a scroll against his thigh, and strode back and forth behind the thicket.

Thryffin slowed his breathing, kept his muscles as still as the dead wood lying around him.

Billowing dust and the crisp sound of hooves on hard-packed earth signaled a rider. The man in scarlet strode from the trees as a young messenger reined the horse to a halt. The man tossed the scroll The courier caught it then slid it into a round leather case slung across his back like a quiver of arrows. "Nelek arrives tonight."

The man in scarlet nodded once. "Any word on the rumors?"

"A female escaped. It is she in the Rook."

The man cursed.

"Her mate is still in Elycia."

"They captured her younglings, too, I suppose?"

The rider nodded.

"Fools!" The man in scarlet clenched his fist. "They wake the beast, and the people pay for it." His voice quieted. "Best go before we are seen. Tell Nelek I have found the Kel-child. He is here."

Turning his mount, the rider kicked the horse's flanks and returned the way he came.

The man in scarlet watched for a moment before darting across the road and slipping into the trees.

Thryffin waited until the last bit of red disappeared. Then, tossing his armload of wood into the barrow, he hastened to the village.

Impossible.

Kieran had melted down the blue stones, and now stood poised to skim the slag—impurities rising to the top of molten ore—but there was none. The bluish soup in the crucible changed to a midnight hue. It should have glowed red or orange, some shade indicating the heat applied to it. Instead, it deepened almost to black. Altogether, the liquid in the crucible appeared enough for a sturdy knife, a set of hinges, or perhaps a fine door latch.

A small collection of molds littered a dusty upper shelf high on the wall above the workbench. Before heating the ore, Kieran had chosen a mold, cleaned and tempered it, then buried it in a box of sand and earth, covering all but the mouth of the spout. Now, with a steady hand, he poured the molten ore down the spout.

The shimmering liquid adhered to itself, pulling every last drop of itself behind it, leaving no residue in the crucible.

"Master Smith?" inquired a crisp female voice.

Startled, he whirled, the bellows sighing as he knocked the handle. His elbow hit a pair of tongs hanging on a post, jostling them from their nail. They landed squarely on his foot. Cursing, he bent to pick them up but struck his forehead on the anvil. He blinked, groaned, straightened. A row of horseshoes hanging from a beam whacked the back of his skull. Cursing again, he clapped a hand to his head. Spots danced before his eyes in a dizzying rainbow of sparks.

A firm hand grasped his arm, guiding him to a stool just inside the door. He blinked against the slanting rays of morning sun, then surrendered and closed his eyes. Liquid warmth trickled down his face. Blood?

Something plunged into the bucket of water beside the anvil then a wet cloth draped over his forehead.

"Thank you," he said.

Fingers light as butterfly steps probed the back of his head. He sucked in his breath, inhaling the mingled scents of flowers, the tang of herbs, the clean essence of soap. Only one woman walked in that diverse fragrance. His ears and neck grew hot.

The cloth was removed. Squinting, he fixed his limited vision on the sun-gilded face above him. *Blast.*

Maggie Finney's brows rose, and her mouth quirked into a brief smile. "Your sight is intact. You have a bruise"—she pressed the damp cloth to the skin just above his left brow—"and a gash."

Lightning shot up his arm when she took his hand, lifting it to place it over the cloth. She stepped back, her face rosy beneath the tan. Too late he remembered that, even as a novice healer, Maggie had likely read every nuance of his thoughts.

Embarrassment sharpened his words. "What do you want, Maggie Finney? I've nothing for you to wash."

She wrinkled her nose, a glint of sly amusement in her forest-green eyes. "Something needs washing."

He glared, head aching, but she was nowise daunted. Rather, her smile deepened. "I came for Mother Crumb's kettle."

"Ah, not quite ready."

"Father Donovan has returned for the Faere. He and Mother Crumb will soon be concocting all sorts of interesting brews, like as not." She chuckled. "They are like children making mud pies. The special ingredients are a secret all their own."

Maggie removed her white apron and bent to dampen it in the bucket. He felt drunk, sight fuzzy, head pounding. His mouth was dry. He couldn't swallow. She straightened, and lightly patted the moist fabric over his face and neck. Again he drew a deep breath, but not because of his wounds.

"Your pain speaks well of your work." She smiled. "Confront it with something as strong as your head, it defends itself well."

"I must diminish the quality against future clumsiness."

She laid a hand on his brow, pushed back his hair, looked into his eyes. "Lie down while I fetch Mother Crumb."

"I am not a child."

"A ninny, perhaps"—her mouth grew firm, ruining the gentle curve of the lips—"but not a child. If you will not lie down, then at least remain seated here until we return." She soaked the apron again and draped it around his neck. "Keep it pressed to the cut."

Maggie lifted the shawl from her shoulders and covered her pinned-up braids, obscuring her face, then picked up a basket of linens, propping it on her hip. In spite of the encumbrance, her steps were sure, her back straight, as if the crown of Skarda rested atop her russet head. What was a blacksmith to royalty?

Especially a great oaf of a blacksmith who cannot even turn around in his own smithy without damaging himself? You made a fine sight, lad. A fine sight. She will be laughing for days about how she but spoke your name and turned you into a fool.

He leaned against the wall, bumping the knot forming at the back of his head. Grumbling a curse, he hunched forward again, resting his elbows on his knees.

Did it truly matter how he appeared to Maggie Finney? After all, what would he want with a woman who could read his mind? He was not one to lie or hold secrets—one or two secrets, perhaps—but why give up his freedom to think about whatever he wished?

Ah, but the truth, lad, is that she is in your thoughts too much already.

A shadow passed over him. He lifted his head with effort. A tall, slender woman stood outside the smithy, the sun burnishing her black hair.

"Kathleen."

"A brawl at the Blue Oak?"

"The anvil."

Kathleen glanced down the street in the direction of Maggie's departure, then turned back to him with a too-bright smile. She held a covered basket smelling of warm bread. "Breakfast. For John Oakley."

"Wish John good day for me."

Kathleen lifted her chin. "How many days since you looked in on Jenny or saw Harry's orchard? Longer still since you walked with me." Her blue eyes narrowed. "Do you break your promise to Father?"

This one thing the old blacksmith had asked on his deathbed: that Kieran marry one of Donnegan's daughters and raise up sons to carry on the family trade. Kieran cared for Jenny and Kathleen as his sisters, nothing more. He could not lie, but he could not leave the dying man without hope, so he did not reply.

Jenny had not waited for him to choose. She wed Harry, and Kieran had stood in her father's stead last spring, placing the coin in the groom's hand as a sign that Jenny was now in Harry's care and he must set her needs above his own. Harry was young, but he had done well. No doubt John Oakley would do as well for Kathleen.

The elder of the two Donnegan sisters, she was the village beauty. Many a young man in Shea had wooed her, captured by her changeful eyes or silky black hair. Quick to laugh, she was just as quick to round on a man, lashing him with sharp words. All guile and no grace.

He gestured to the basket of bread. "John will welcome such an offering more if it is still warm."

Kathleen stepped back, expression rigid. She opened her mouth to say more but turned and walked away—and then, as if unable to resist knowing whether or not Kieran watched her, she looked over her shoulder. He lifted a corner of the damp apron, waving it like a kerchief and smiling. Raising her chin, she faced forward just in time to avoid an oxcart lumbering down the middle of the street.

Kieran leaned forward, propped his elbows on his knees, and stared down at the dusty stone floor, seeing instead a pair of smiling green eyes.

Thryffin ran, the barrow's wooden wheel bounding over bumps, shaking the load of sticks. The axe shifted with each turn.

He thought he heard voices somewhere off to his right, maybe the push of bodies through the undergrowth, but it might only have been his imagination and the scuffle and thud of the barrow's contents.

In sight of the mill bridge, he felt the wheel strike something large. The barrow stopped but he did not, catching his middle on the edge and flipping over the mounded wood to land on his backside in the middle of the road.

For an instant, he felt no pain, only the shock of being unable to move or breathe.

The hardpacked earth of the Romney Road vibrated with hoofbeats he could not yet hear. Or perhaps they were the footsteps of an approaching band of king's men. Breath sobbing, backside bruised and aching, Thryffin scrambled to his feet, righted the barrow, and limped toward Shea.

"You are in more pain than you admit."

Seated in a chair, eyes closed, Kieran made no reply. Argument required effort. Let Maggie read his thoughts.

Mother Crumb unlocked her medicine casket with a crisp click. She emptied the box, setting bottles and bags of herbs on the smithy worktable with soft thumps. Then came the solid clunk of mortar and pestle, the dry rustle of leaves and roots. The old healer was seldom in a hurry. She was never taken by surprise. All things seemed to happen at her own pace.

The quick, restive movements belonged to Maggie. Even her stride was expeditious. The sooner one task was accomplished, the sooner she could begin another. Caring for Kieran's injury was simply one of those tasks.

Mother Crumb gave her a quiet correction. "Careful, child. Any more, and he will sleep for a sennight."

So, Maggie Finney, do you wear a lofty look now?

Mother Crumb chuckled. "Say something, Kieran?"

He shook his head.

"I thought not."

He opened his eyes. The two women had turned his room into an apothecary, setting a kettle over the fire and dropping in handfuls of chopped root or pinches of powder. An aromatic mist filled the air.

Maggie had borrowed one of his threadbare tunics from a nail on the wall and tied the arms around her waist. Her dampened apron was still draped around Kieran's neck.

Mother Crumb applied balm to the gash on his forehead and spooned foul elixir down his throat. Then she applied a broad leaf to his brow and bound a wide bandage around his head to hold the poultice in place.

Maggie frowned a little as she poured and measured. A flush crept up her cheeks. Perhaps the heat of the day or the fire rosied her face. He liked that face, dusky-skinned and set with clear green eyes. Wisps of russet hair fell from her pinned-up braids, curling at her temples and at the nape of her neck.

With a sound half between a laugh and a harrumph, Mother

Crumb shook her head. She handed him another cup of elixir. "Drink this."

Grimacing, he obeyed.

Maggie scooped or poured medicines into bowls while the healer instructed Kieran on when to drink this or apply that. Then, while Maggie cleaned, Mother Crumb placed stoppered bottles and leather pouches inside the applewood casket, replaced the mortar and pestle, then locked the box with a silver key kept on a chain around her neck. She tucked the box under her arm—"Lock up the forge and get you to bed"—and moved toward the open door.

A small shadow fell across the opening. Thryffin's thin face, dirt-smeared and wide-eyed, peered into the room. His gaze landed on Maggie, and he hesitated then took a tentative step, staring past her to Kieran. "Are you ill?"

"A bump on the head, nothing more."

Thryffin shot an uncertain glance at Maggie. She reached out to lay her good hand on Thryffin's shoulder, but he jerked away before she could touch him. She covered the crippled hand with the whole, and stood as rigid as stone.

Mother Crumb washed the cuts on the boy's face and arms, and *tsk-tsked* the large bruise on his back. She spread ointment over it, spoke a few low sharp phrases Kieran could not hear, then signaled Maggie, and the women left.

Thryffin watched them depart, an unreadable expression on his narrow face.

"What is it, Thryff? Did the bullies have at you again?"

The boy gripped the edge of the table.

"Out with it, Thryff."

"There is a spy in Shea."

"A spy? He the one gave you those bruises?"

"He never saw me. I was gathering wood. There was a rider, too, and the spy passed him a message. He said a name. Nelek."

Kieran cudgeled his thoughts. "You know this Nelek?"

"No. The spy said, 'He is here.' They are looking for someone." Thryffin leaned forward, his knuckles white. "Who could they want? It is not yet time for spring taxes. Surely no one in Shea has broken the baron's law?"

"Laws are only for peaceable men." Kieran's tongue slurred the words.

"Are you not afraid, Master Smith?"

Aye.

Kieran bought from Baron Markha only a small amount of the hardwood necessary to make charcoal for his forge. The rest he purchased at a much cheaper price from a skilled tree poacher—one of the baron's own foresters and a friend of Jack the ironmonger. Perhaps the forester had been caught in the act of cutting or hauling trees, and now a spy had been sent to find the man's conspirator.

Best not frighten the boy. "Likely the spy seeks someone who has come for the Faere. What is his appearance?"

"Not very big, shorter than you, with a..." Thryffin's voice bent, distorting his words. They faded into a distant mumble, then snapped back to clarity again."...doesn't sound like a villager." The boy looked down. "What if he is one of the baron's men, and takes someone else away this time? Farmer Harry's wife, Jenny? Or Kathleen? Or—or someone?"

Kieran rose, swayed, caught himself by gripping the table. "Lock the smithy. Do not go back to the mill. Sleep here tonight, Thryff. Just in case."

He stumbled across the room and dropped onto his cot. The herbs dulling his pain tricked his senses. Fire danced higher and higher on the clay-plastered walls. The sinuous play of shadow and light became the waving grasses of the Plains then lightning over the mountains. Trees swayed, limbs reaching to clutch him in tangled arms, whispering, *Welcome, D'urnythn.*

13 ~ At River's Edge

He woke in darkness. The air was chill and smelled of dew. Dawn was near. He swung his legs over the side of the cot, rubbed his face with both hands, and sat a moment before rising. Pain returned, harsh around the gash on his forehead.

He shuffled out to the well in the village square and drew a bucket of water. A few scattered cottages had candles in the windows to dispel the greyness before dawn.

Maggie Finney crossed the bridge. He knew her by the basket propped on her hip and by her purposeful stride. There was little feminine about her walk, yet her dress swayed with each step. It was not the simple kirtle that village women wore. Rather, Maggie's had a high collar wrapping her throat, wide sleeves ending at her elbows, and a shape that curved in at the waist and fell in grey folds over the hips like a fluid bell.

As if his watchfulness were a sound, she turned toward him. Breath abandoned him. A long look, suspended like a bird gliding above the trees—then Maggie bent her head and turned away. Passing the mill, she walked downriver and out of sight.

Tall grasses and reeds damp with dew brushed against her, chilling her bare feet and legs as she trod the narrow path along the riverbank. The cool of morning scrubbed sleep from her eyes.

Maggie set the laden basket on her favorite little shingle, a sandy shelf perfect for kneeling beside the water. She kept a bucket and a washtub tipped on its side under the sheltering overhang of a weather-rounded boulder. Pulling out the tub, she knocked loose any insects that tried to shelter there, then dumped the soiled linens into it and used the bucket to fill it with water.

She and Mother Crumb had attended a difficult birth yesternight in an outlying hamlet. As was the old healer's custom, she had brought fresh linens as a gift to replace those bloodied in the birthing. Maggie soaked the soiled sheets in the tub. Even the strongest soap was not always successful in whitening bloodstained cloth, and not even Mother Crumb's friendship could calm every fear. The mother had seemed comforted by the old woman's quiet presence, but the anxious father barred the cottage door against Maggie.

She built a fire to boil water, then stood outside the open window and watched the healer's sure hands, heard her calming words to the agonized young mother. Maggie passed fresh buckets of water across the window sill, and carried away the pans of bloody toweling. In a clean tub of just-warm water, she washed the newborn babe. A boy. The child had tried to suckle her crooked fingers.

Maggie passed the wrapped infant to the healer, who nestled him in the crook of his mother's arm. Then the old woman pulled off her apron, handed it and the bundled sheets and mother's soiled garments to Maggie, and went out to speak to the father.

I am well, Maggie had told herself as she washed the instruments and basins in boiling water, then bundled the soiled sheets and towels. *I helped the hands that ushered that child into the world.*

Yet, as she followed Mother Crumb home, each woman's back bent under its burden, she glanced back at the cottage and caught a glimpse of the young husband watching them from the open door. He made the sign of the Shepherd, warding off the evil of the witch with the crippled hand.

Only two hours past, it had been, yet were it a lifetime, she would still feel the sting.

Pulling a bar of soap and a small knife from her apron pocket, Maggie knelt, shaving slivers of soap into the tub. When the top of the water was afloat with creamy yellow curls, she pulled the linens up and down, agitating water and soap into a pale froth.

The sun rose, its rays coloring the clear depths of the Renfrew with bright threads of light, stringing together the stones on the riverbed like beads on a giant's necklace.

The strange stone in her apron pocket grew warm, and she drew it forth. Its blue glow pulsed in her hand.

A warning stilled her. Something probed her senses—tentative, as one gropes in the dark. It settled on her twisted fingers gripping the stone. Incoherent questions clamored in her mind. She dropped the stone into her pocket again and turned, searching the forest behind her, seeing nothing.

The gift did not come. In time, she would learn to call on it at will as she would any tool—like a hammer, like the knife in her hand—and she needed but to pick it up to use it.

The pressure of the questions withdrew. Likely a curious child, hiding to spy on the witch.

Maggie relaxed, but only a little, and returned to her washing.

Free of the mold, the blue cuff lay on the workbench beside a set of engraving tools. Wide and smooth, a broad bead rimming top and bottom, the bracelet resembled those the Northmen wore on their upper arms, but smaller, more fitted to a woman than to a man.

It glowed through the window as Kieran sharpened a kitchen knife outside at the grindstone. He was grateful Thryffin had been required by Miller George to help grind the last of the stored winter grain, else the boy would pester him to explain that inexplicable light.

The bracelet drew him like an alluring voice, and Kieran gave in at last. He slid the repaired kitchen knife into its sheath, wiped his hands clean of the grinding dust, then picked up the bracelet, turning it, examining its plain face, wondering what images to grave there. If he followed the Voice—the mighty being Mother Crumb called Mymna Tor, and Father Donovan named Creator—he might shun this thing as magic, and therefore evil.

Yet if there was evil, was there not also good? Magic and mundane? Right and wrong? Nature and that which transcended nature? How could a man always know one from the other?

Deep in the metal, a glow limned a faint tracery of twining leaves and flowers. He knew that design. He had never seen it before, but he knew it. Kieran's pulse beat in his temples. His fingertips tingled.

He took up the graving chisel.

He set down the tool.

Picked it up.

Laid it down.

His stomach complained its hunger. The mundane overcame the magical, and he shoved the bracelet into the scrip on his belt. The morning was not so spent that Mistress Clem would refuse him the remnants of breakfast.

"Ho, the smithy!"

Pulled by a team of ponies, a sturdy wagon piled with iron rods and bars lurched to a halt in the smithy yard.

Kieran despised giving coin to Baron Markha, yet he had no means of smelting large amounts of iron for himself nor the wherewithal to mine the ore. However, Jack the ironmonger was not above a bit of poaching. He mined and smelted ore for the baron and a few other men of rank, but he kept a little aside for his friends. They tended to pay better, and at once.

Jack was a short stout man with thick shoulders and a neck like a tree stump. He greeted Kieran with a nod, Kieran dropped a few coins into his palm, and the two men hauled rods from the cart and piled them in the shed against the smithy, laboring in silence until the cart stood half empty. The rest of the iron was destined for another village.

Kieran wiped the back of his hand across his brow, and nodded toward the inn across from the smithy. "A tankard, Jack?"

The ironmonger grinned. "Aye." He grasped the bridles of the two ponies still hitched to the wagon. "They will not be unhappy for a drink either, I wager."

"Take them to the stableyard, then, and I will order a meal for us."

"You will not be telling me twice, Master Smith."

That was the extent of Jack's loquacity. Once presented with a tankard of ale, a loaf of bread, and a plate of stew, he spoke no more. When he finished eating, Jack tossed back the last of his ale, dropped a coin on the table to pay his part, and stood.

"Midsummer," he said with a nod and departed.

Kieran lingered over his tankard perhaps a quarter hour then paid his reckoning, standing aside as a clutch of young men pushed their noisy way into the inn, laughing, calling for food and drink, one of them planting a smacking kiss on Sally's cheek.

Kieran stepped into the street. In the square stood a half-finished platform for the dancing during the Faere, and carts and caravans filled the open space between it and the village well. Music and juggling and the building of bright booths transformed the high street into a festival of noise.

Perhaps the river might settle his thoughts, ease the throbbing in his skull. He walked west this time, opposite the direction that led him to the blue stones.

Maggie Finney knelt beside the river, on a gentle slope of sandy earth sheltered by a moss-covered rock. Water washed over the ridges of her gnarled fingers. Some rumors said she was a changeling of the forest folk and the hand was a tree root, proof of imperfect transformation. Others said it was Nardha's black blessing. None dared treat her ill. Who knew but that she had some dark power to harm them?

He could scarce begin a conversation with such a question.

"There is always the weather, or the Faere, or the war." She spoke without turning around. Pulling the linen from the water, she rubbed it with soap. "Well, Kieran Smith, and what brings you to the river?"

"The smithy is too confining, and my head is not quite ready for the heat."

Maggie pushed the cloth underwater again. "And you are confused. You question something."

"Aye, and you are never confused. You have the gift."

She twisted the sheet, wringing water from it. "I am still learning."

He wondered at the dark shadows under her eyes.

"A birthing," she replied, again as if he asked the question aloud.

He could stand there, awkwardness gripping him like a callow lad of thirteen, or he could behave as if conversing with a russet-haired witch were an everyday thing.

He sat in the sand beside her, stretching out his legs, leaning back against the rock. "I am accustomed to Mother Crumb reading my thoughts. She has done so since I was a child. Until you came, I never encountered another who used such magic."

"There is none less magical than Maggie Finney."

The bracelet grew warm against his hip, reminding him of things he did not understand. "You arrived in Shea in a howling snowstorm, and survived such cold as we have not endured for many a year. Surely you must have a *little* magic?"

She stood and snapped the linen. It unfurled, broad and sinuous as a war banner. "The only magic is woven by Mother Crumb, and even it is common sense." She looked down at him with a sting in her gaze. "Are you magic?"

"I am a blacksmith. That is all."

"Nay, Master Smith. Not all."

"You see more? My future, perhaps?"

"We none of us know the future. Anyone who claims he does is lying." She spread the sheet on a low-growing bush to dry. "Healers do not practice magic. They are too wise to think they can harness the supernatural."

Then, when he said nothing, she added, "You are great deal more civil now than yesterday."

"A man cannot be held to account when his head is spinning."

Smiling, she knelt to wash another length of linen.

Neither spoke for a time, and the river's music filled the quiet. Kieran leaned his head back against a soft patch of dry moss on the rock, and watched Maggie.

"What does it say to you?" she asked.

He raised his brows in question.

"The river. What does it say?"

"We are old friends, the Renfrew and I. If I am sad, it cries. If I am happy, it laughs. At this moment, it is content."

She looked to the opposite bank. Trees grew thick to the water's edge. "When first I crossed the river, it was frozen, but water ran sluggish beneath the ice. Snow blinded me. My shoes were rags. I thought I would die. A voice compelled me onward. I heard it in the river."

She had blown into the village on a January wind. What secrets did she keep?

"If you befriend me, you may regret it."

He reached into the soapy water and gently lifted her crippled hand. Her breath drew in, and her eyes widened. With his other hand, he covered hers. "Can anything be done?"

After a moment of rigid stillness, she pulled away from him and bent to her work again. "Good day, Master Smith."

Kathleen shrank back into the trees as Kieran turned from the river, his long strides consuming the distance to the village, his mouth set, a determined look she knew well from childhood.

After the smith passed, a stranger slipped from behind a large old elm, cast a glance at Maggie, then followed Kieran toward the village. Passing a clump of wildflowers, the stranger snapped off a blossom and let the stem dangle from his fingers.

Kathleen smoothed her hair, straightened her kirtle, and stepped from her hiding place.

The man halted as if jerked up by a rope. "G-Good day." He removed his cap.

Ah, this appeared good sport. Handsome, albeit a bit thin, well-dressed, with a ready smile and the proper admiration in his eyes.

"Good day." Her gaze traveled his person. "Are you come for the Faere?"

He bowed with a flourish. "A minstrel. Teag, at your service." He straightened, replacing his cap at a jaunty angle. "And you, sprite—have you a name?"

"Kathleen."

"Kathleen." He said it like a prayer. "Are you as innocent and charming as your name?"

"Does it matter?"

"Such beauty declares a nature to match." He offered his arm, and she slipped a slender hand through the crook of his elbow.

"A flower for a lucky maiden?" She plucked it from his fingers and stuck it in her hair with a laugh. "You shall just have to pick her another. Better still, forget her altogether and sing me a song."

"Sweet maid, anything you wish."

14 ~ Advice

Rumors traveled with the caravans coming to Shea. Stories hummed in the air like dread bees gathering poisonous honey. A fearsome beast had been sighted in the sky, its body so great it shadowed the sun, and spewed fire as it flew. Kieran heard the tale many times through the afternoon, and the details changed with the telling. Customers recounted it while he shod their horses or welded their broken knives. Two men even came to blows over the matter.

"Y'sayin' me boy is a liar? If he says he saw one o' the Dragon-folk, he saw one o' the Dragon-folk!"

"If he saw a Dragon, his head is full o' mush, or his da is as daft as he!"

The men shoved and punched, rolling in the dirt, shouting inarticulate epithets impeded by bites to fingers or fists to jaws.

Kieran set aside tongs and hammer. Grabbing their shirts, he pulled the men apart. They staggered, gasping and bloody, propped up by Kieran's fists clenched against their chests. Both men shot him resentful looks as if they cursed his interference.

"Now, lads," he said in a calm voice, "I have very likely botched a shoe because of you. Take your disagreement elsewhere. Go to the river. Come back after a good soaking. The horse will be ready when you return."

Kieran released them. One man shrugged, the other tilted his head, popping the bones in his neck, and both departed in the direction of the river. After a few moments, they reached out to clap one another's shoulder, raising clouds of dust from torn, dirty tunics. Smiling, Kieran shook his head.

Beyond the square, Kathleen leaned on the arm of a stranger. Both were laughing. Another victim. Poor fellow.

The man wore scarlet and a feather-cocked cap.

Teag the minstrel. Thryffin's spy?

The pair entered a fortune-teller's cart in the encampment at the edge of the village.

Moments later, Kieran mounted the steps and shoved aside the stained purple curtain. His body filled the opening, shutting out the light. Kathleen turned, startled. Teag rose from a stool, his hand covering the hilt of the short sword at his belt, his movement making the candles gutter. Eyes half-closed, the seer—a young man—remained impassive. His hands hovered over garish painted cards spread across a small round table draped in threadbare black velvet.

Kathleen's brows drew together. "What do you want, Kieran?"

"Come with me."

"I am busy."

"I am not asking."

She stood, running her hands over her waist and hips as if to smooth her kirtle but Kieran knew her ways.

Teag stepped forward, pulling his sword partly out of the scabbard.

"Put it away," said Kieran. "This is a family matter."

He took Kathleen by the arm, descended the steps, and walked several paces from the cart before letting her go and turning to face her. She stood with arms folded, face harsh with anger.

"What are you doing?" Kieran kept his voice low. "How do you know that man?"

"What is that to you?"

He waited for a better answer.

She tilted her head. "He is handsome. He amuses me."

"He is a spy. Whether he serves the king or the baron, it matters not. He is dangerous."

"A minstrel?" Kathleen laughed. "What harm is there in that?" Hands on her hips, she lifted one shoulder in a provocative shrug that tugged the fabric of her kirtle just so. It was dyed to match her eyes. "But if his attention means that I now have yours, then I shall gladly leave him to the care of some other willing maid."

"You already have John Oakley. Let this man be."

"You are neither father nor brother to me. Nor husband."

"I am still the head of the Donnegan family," but even as he said it, Kieran knew the argument was lost.

So did Kathleen. A triumphant smile curved her lips.

She returned to the fortune-teller's cart.

Kieran stalked through the village, the long leather smock flapping around his knees.

Did Kathleen not mind her ways, she might suffer her mother's fate. They were of similar beauty, tall and dark. Mistress Donnegan had lived modestly, laughing and working alongside her husband, but Kathleen lived with her arms flung open, embracing and encouraging the notice of men. No matter the repeated warnings, no matter the number of women taken by the baron, she refused to alter her ways.

There was John Oakley, too, a love-blind innocent.

Kieran's temper cooled as he walked. He turned toward the kirk. A white banner floated from the roof. Father Donovan had returned.

Except for the mill, the kirk was the northernmost building in Shea. A stone wall surrounded the chapel and grounds. On the side closest to the river was a wooden wicket strengthened by young tree limbs woven around the slats and appearing like one side of a basket. Kieran unlatched the little gate then closed it behind him.

Sibley, Father Donovan's grey donkey, grazed on the tall grass near the wall. One ear drooped like a perpetual wink, the result of a tangle with a wild dog some time in the donkey's youth. Kieran rubbed Sibley's blaze and murmured a welcome.

Father Donovan wore a simple brown robe belted at the waist with a length of rope and surmounted by a cowl that could be raised to cover his head. With his compact build and scarred face, he seemed a man at odds with his habit, looking more soldier than priest.

He was on his knees among the overgrown flowers, tearing up weeds and tossing them into a pile on the path. He muttered something that might have been a curse. It could just as well have been an angry prayer. The priest looked up with a frown as Kieran approached, then smiled and rose, brushing dirt from square-fingered hands. "Ah, Kieran lad! How fare thee?"

"I am well. You are in good health?"

"Aye, aye. Kathleen?"

"John Oakley could tell you more, Father."

The priest gestured toward a stone bench. They sat in silence. Kieran leaned forward, resting elbows on knees covered by the stained and burned leather smock.

"Excellent man, John Oakley," said Father Donovan at last. "Hardworking. Keeps a fine farm."

Kieran nodded.

The priest waited.

"Sometimes I am so bound to Shea that I will never leave the village." Kieran pulled a long blade of grass, and twirled it between his thumb and forefinger. "Then there are times I shake myself awake and realize I have walked a dozen furlongs along the Romney Road."

"Running from Kathleen? Or from what happened to her mother, Mistress Donnegan?"

Kieran drew in a long breath then let it out. He stared at the ground between his feet. A ladybug waddled on a leaf.

"Anger and hatred be twin hounds baying at thy heels. They will never harm the baron." Father Donovan put a hand on Kieran's shoulder. "Only the man they hunt."

Kieran shrugged off the priest's hand, rose, and stalked back and forth on the flagstone path. "Did Baron Markha have ought to do with Maggie Finney's twisted hand?"

"She will not speak of it. 'Twas more than accident."

"It is a cruel thing to cripple a woman, to cast her outside society and steal her means of earning bread."

"Thee cannot add Maggie's troubles to thy list of hates."

"Why not?" Kieran's fists opened and closed.

Father Donovan stood. "Walk with me."

In the orchard lay brown desiccated remains of last year's windfalls, whatever the birds did not claim.

"Thee be acquainted with life and death, with the turning of seasons, the ending of one thing so another may begin." Father Donovan spread his arms and looked around at the limbs in need of pruning. "Were I not a traveling priest, I would dig and tear and cut to restore these grounds to health and beauty. I would kill something to let another live."

Kieran's neck and jaw tensed. He remembered Mistress Donnegan's body thrown against the smithy door, her bruised face pale with death, and the anguish in Donnegan's eyes as he sat in the dirt and cradled his beloved in the grey dawn. "Are you saying all the baron's thieving of people, all the king's murder for pleasure, is *just*?"

"D'not be daft, lad!" The priest swung around, his brow creased. "Want to leave the village? Then end something. Want a new life? Kill the old."

His expression relaxed into patience, master addressing pupil. "A young man without a wife, in a village with young women needing husbands. Smithing comes easy to thy hands. When Old Donnegan took thee in, the villagers extended to thee their regard for him. Never had to earn anyone's respect. Perhaps it is time to leave Shea."

"Who would take my place at the smithy?"

The silvery eyes smiled. "Let Mymna Tor worry about that."

Kieran ducked into the smithy, closed the door, hung his smock on its nail, banked the remaining coals, then leaned back against the worktable, arms folded.

He had a forge and a room. A living. A place of his own. Something to rely on. He was a freeman, unbound by debt or land belonging to Baron Markha. He could leave the village, the province, even the kingdom, if he so wished. What did he want? To see the rest of the kingdom? Find adventure?

A wise man would stay. He would not throw away friends or kindred—even kindred by adoption—nor would he risk not having a home when he returned.

What would become of Thryffin? His father had abandoned the boy because he could no longer face living out the days set before him. In exchange for occasional work, Miller George let the lad sleep among the grain sacks, but he seemed in no hurry to train him in his trade. Thryffin wanted to learn smithing. He believed whatever Kieran said, imitated his walk, his gestures, his ways of speaking. How could Thryffin be left behind simply to fulfill a selfish wish?

Maybe Father Donovan could take Thryffin to the abbey. Full of curious questions, the boy would drive the poor brothers mad with his thirst to know everything. Yet where better for an eager mind to be but among scholars?

Kieran knew how to read and write—Father Donovan had taught him—but there was very little to read in Shea, other than occasional notices posted by the baron's men or the traveling magistrates. Monasteries had libraries. Perhaps Thryffin could spend part of the year learning from the scholars, and part of the year learning a trade. Then, when he was older, he could decide what he wanted to do with his life. An enviable choice.

Kieran pulled the blue bracelet from his scrip and rolled it back and forth along his fingertips. It glowed a little.

This bracelet had something to do with the dagger hidden under his bed, but what? Other than the blue metal, how were they akin?

He worked until sundown then went to the inn for supper.

Teag bore no great admiration for Captain Nelek, a short fellow whose arrogance far outstripped his stature. He was an ambitious man, however, and that Teag well understood.

Outside the village, near an abandoned woodcutter's cottage on the fringe of the forest, a sentry blocked his path.

Teag said, "To the coming age."

The silent guard stepped aside and let him pass. Two more soldiers stood guard at the door. They moved to allow Teag entrance to the leaning cottage, part of its thatched roof open to the night sky, the air dank and smelling of old things.

Someone had lit a small fire in the crumbling fireplace. Nelek stood before it, flames echoing the scarlet of his tunic. "So, he is here." His nostrils flared and his chest expanded with a deep breath. "And the girl?"

"She is here, too."

"Well, then, we will take them—"

"There will be no killing. Yet. The king has need of him."

"Morfran's prisoners never live long. Nor do mine."

Few men were as cheerfully cold-blooded as Captain Nelek. Baron Markha took what he wanted by whatever means he chose, King Morfran heard voices commanding absurdities, but Nelek enjoyed killing like other men thirsted for cold ale on a hot day.

"Morfran requires a smith capable of forging a replica of Azrin," said Teag. "All other captive smiths have died trying."

Nelek smiled. "Poor souls."

He appeared nowise grieved by their demise. If death came not by his own hand, he gladly stood by to watch the slaughter. The loss of excellent craftsmen seemed little consequence to his sport.

"The problem lies in finding enough etherium for a sword, and in convincing the smith to perform the king's will."

Nelek scoffed. "A commoner does not argue with the king."

"If you kill this commoner, the king will decorate the walls of Elycia with your bones."

Nelek paced the dirt floor. "What does Morfran intend?"

"To prove himself a true descendent of Kel, of course."

"And how will he do that with a false sword?"

"None living know the fashion of the first Azrin. It matters not how this one is forged, so long as it is etherium."

The captain halted, anger flickering in his eyes. "Morfran is not a Kel. No matter what he does to conjure up a sword to convince the people, he can never wield it."

"Neither can you."

Nelek's mouth tightened. "There are ways."

"None that will not leave you mad or dead."

"There are ways," he growled. "Yon blacksmith, the only man in the kingdom able to touch etherium and live—"

"I have not the truth of that yet—"

"—will simply give up his right to the throne and make a sword that proves a usurper is the rightful ruler?"

"The smith is a large man, slow in his manner of speech, and likely slow of foot and mind, as well." Teag recalled Kieran filling the doorway of the fortuneteller's caravan, blocking the light. "I doubt he has ever fought, even for a friendly wager. A mannerly mountain."

Nelek swatted at cobwebs. "Do not mistake long-suffering for slow wit. The dangerous thing about such a man is his ability to wait."

Homeless, a large spider scurried away from the torn wall of webs.

"He lulls you into thinking you can do anything to him, that he will never retaliate."

The spider crawled across the toe of his boot and down to the floor again.

"No one bears a grudge like a quiet man."

With a sickening crunch, the spider died beneath Nelek's heel.

The guards at the open door bent over, covering their mouths, shoulders heaving. Someone retched. Strong wind shuddered the old cottage, and a malodorous fog entered the room. Nelek and Teag whipped their cloaks over the lower portions of their faces.

"What is that?" demanded Nelek as soon as the strange stench passed. "Worse than a slaughter yard!"

Teag coughed, certain his face was the same unpleasant white-green as the captain's. "Dragon."

"Dragon? Dragon!" Nelek laughed, then wiped the corners of his eyes with a gloved knuckle. "I did not think you a simpleton."

"This from a man who cannot even read the old scrolls."

"I am not lost in a world of words and nonsense."

"Whether you choose to believe or not, captain, Dragons are not dead. Had you read the courier dispatches these past three months, you might have known the news from Heolstor's own pen."

"The old vulture. How is it he still lives?"

"We cannot rely only on this night's strange wind," said Teag. "We must know the proper history of the blacksmith."

"We know enough. We know a few old farmers recall finding a boy playing beside a dead man a score of years past. We know the boy wielded an unusual weapon. We know the dead man wore clothes unseen in this province. We know the boy spoke in a language no one had ever heard."

"What we do not know, captain, is whether or not Kieran Smith is that boy." Teag leaned forward with the force of his argument. "The people have forgotten how he came to be among them. Kieran Smith bears the authority of an eldest son. None question his right."

Then Teag ran a hand over his face and took a step back. "If the dagger in the boy's hand was as fantastical as those old farmers described, why did none of them take it from him? He could scarce have resisted."

Nelek pushed the toe of his boot against the spider's squashed remains. "The honesty of men like them informs the dishonesty of men like us."

Teag could not disagree.

Kieran Smith would not willingly give up his right and make the sword. However, if he succumbed to illusions of royalty or power—

"He has sisters and a few friends."

"Kith and kin." The captain tapped his chin with one gauntled fingertip. "A man will do almost anything to preserve the lives of those he loves. Even give his own."

Nelek strode to the door then looked back. "Three days."

"And the girl?"

"No need to alert the village of our presence. If this smith is a Kel, we take him and the girl at the same time."

"And if not?"

"Kill him."

In his cell behind the chancel of the kirk, Father Donovan lay on his bed in a pool of moon-glow, unable to sleep. The soothing song of the river usually lulled him, but now it only roused him to fretting wakefulness.

He prayed, but years of discipline were for naught. His mind wandered down paths not of his choosing. Awash in blood, the past rose up, a gory brigand. His fist clenched as if around a sword, his muscles sore and aching as though battle weary. He fought memories.

The foul storm blew its stench through the cell, and he knew fear as he had never known it, immediate and beyond his control. It signaled what was to come, prophecies written in ink centuries old on parchments crumbling to dust.

Sleep enfolded him at last, but the dream returned. It unfurled before his mind like a living banner, like a tale he had heard many times, always expecting the end to be different. It was always the same.

He jolted awake, hands trembling, breath ragged. "Mymna Tor, forgive me."

He drank from the tumbler of water at his bedside. Then, kneeling on the cold stone floor, he prayed.

15 ~ SECRETS

Maggie arrived at the smithy in early morning, her expression stiff. Without a word, Kieran handed her the repaired kettle for Mother Crumb. He wanted to speak, wanted her to say something sharp, something Maggie-ish, but she was as silent as he.

She held out a few copper coins.

Shaking his head, he turned from her and busied his hands by hanging tools and shifting projects on the workbench. He listened for her departure, yet her shadow remained in the doorway.

Then came the bright sounds of coins falling on the anvil and the swish of her kirtle as she left.

He plied the bellows with far more force than necessary, raising a cloud of ashes as he sought to rekindle the fire.

The coals were dead.

He reduced the pile of old ashes by a pailful, and stacked fresh charcoal and kindling on the hearth. Then Kieran lit a small pile of tinder with a flint and watched the tiny curl of smoke spiral upward, his thoughts a turmoil of spies and bracelets and mysterious storms—and offended laundresses.

Teag watched from the orchard as Kathleen Donnegan bid farewell to John Oakley. She brushed her lips across the young farmer's sunburned cheek and let her hand linger on his sinewy arm. Then, fingertips trailing along his skin, she moved slowly away, smiling over her shoulder. He stared at the door long after she entered her cottage.

Teag frowned. She would never fasten her affections on a man like himself. He appeared a stripling beside the broad-shouldered farmer. No matter. Teag had a quick wit and a ready poem. Charm was his game. He played it well.

He waited until Oakley was well away before approaching the cottage. Chickens scattered, squawking, as he trod across the corn scattered on the packed earth of the yard. Laundered garments flapped in a gust of wind that tugged the cord stretching from cottage to tree.

He reached out to knock, but the door opened and Kathleen stood in the doorway, smiling. Another woman appeared, suspicion in her face as she looked at him over Kathleen's shoulder. Teag recognized her as Jenny, the pragmatic and strong-minded younger sister wed to Harry, a promising young farmer.

Teag doffed his cap and bowed. "Good day to you both."

Jenny stared at him; Kathleen smiled.

"May I have a word with you?" he asked.

"And what word would that be?" Kathleen's voice sent small shudders through him. "Will you sing it to me?"

He pretended to clear his throat, holding a gloved fist to his mouth, trying to remember why he came.

"Who is this man?" Jenny's eyes narrowed. "And what does he want with you? Is he the one Kieran warned against?"

Kathleen's smile thinned. "All is well, Jenny. He is but a minstrel come for the Faere."

Putting on his blandest demeanor, Teag placed his cap over his heart in what he hoped was the very essence of sincerity. "Being new-come to this part of the province and finding it exceeding lovely, I would see more." He gestured at the fields surrounding the cottage. "Among the finest crops I ever beheld."

Jenny snorted. "And the poorest liar I ever heard. Crops not even knee-high, nor will they be for many days. You have a pretty tongue, stranger, but my sister has a sharp mind. I trust she will cut to the truth." Jenny stepped back into the cottage and closed the door, leaving him alone with Kathleen.

If one could be alone in the presence of so many chickens.

"Since you were such an agreeable companion yesterday," he began, the pitch of his voice changing with mortifying rapidity. He cleared his throat in earnest. "You were such an agreeable companion yesterday, I wondered if you might be my guide and pass the time until the Faere."

She leaned against the door, laughter dancing in her eyes.

He spread his hands. "Well?"

"Well what, Master Teag? I have not heard the question."

He bowed. "Will you act as my guide?"

"Gladly." She stepped into the yard. Black hair caught fire, turning red in the sunlight. "What would you see first? The river? The forest? My brother-in-law's orchard?"

"I heard tell of a healer with an unusual garden."

"Good minstrel, I warn you, she is a witch."

"I have never seen a witch. Haggish, is she?"

Kathleen's blue-grey eyes resembled granite. "Not her apprentice. You have seen Maggie Finney. The trollop with the twisted hand? Thinks herself better than the rest of us. No one crosses her, or speaks ill of her in Mother Crumb's hearing. They are afraid of Maggie. And she ignores them. Like some condescending queen of the damned."

Well, now, here is poison. He put on another smile and offered his arm. "Shall we venture forth?"

"If you are a brave man, go alone." Kathleen turned back to the cottage. "Beware your thoughts. The healer knows them all."

Kieran entered the Blue Oak for a midday tankard and found the inn alive with newcomers. Sally and Mistress Clem, both rosy-cheeked, hair straggling about their faces, strove to serve customers through the din of converse, the air grey with pipe smoke. He found a place to stand at the high counter where Master Clem dispensed ale and wine.

The innkeeper tossed the smith a harried smile. Kieran stepped behind the counter, and the two men worked side by side, sliding mugs, cups, and tankards down the bar, and handing out plates from the kitchen. The cook called out that the mutton was gone, then the stew, and finally all the bread and chicken. By then, however, customers pushed away from tables, settling back to enjoy their pipes.

Wiping his sleeve across his forehead, Kieran leaned against a cask, regretting his rumbling stomach. A bit of bread and cheese remained in his meager larder. "I'll be off, then."

"Nay!" Master Clem ran his palms over his apron. "We always save a bit for ourselves." He patted his round stomach, chuckling. "And today you do not pay. Come to the kitchen."

Sally slumped at the worktable, resting her chin in her hands. Mistress Clem eyed the piled wooden bowls and horn cups, shaking her head and speaking with the cook, a village woman so thin she appeared comical beside the two corpulent innkeepers.

A customer called for another round of ale. Sally grimaced, pushing herself to her feet. "Best be handsome."

Lacking a clean vessel, Kieran used his knife to spear a chunk of meat from the spit in the fireplace and a slab of bread from the cutting board. Thanking Master Clem, he went out the back door of the kitchen and sat on a sturdy wooden bench. The inn's stables bordered a livestock pen and the chicken coop. The wind being westerly, the barnyard smell did not steal his appetite, though he doubted much could interfere with it now.

Finished eating, Kieran wiped the knife clean on his breeches and stood to sheath it. The bracelet fell from the open mouth of his scrip and wobbled along the dirt. He bent to take it up again. A shadow moved across the ground, a feathery shape bobbing at its head. A red boot clamped the bracelet to earth.

Kieran grew still. The wound over his eye ached.

"Good day, Master Smith."

Kieran straightened.

Teag reached down then snatched back his hand. Kieran bent once more to retrieve the broad circlet, but Teag grabbed his wrist.

"Did you trade for it with a merchant?" The man's hungry gaze was that of a hawk on a hunt. "I have never seen its like. Surely you did not craft it yourself?"

Kieran twisted his arm, and Teag's fingers slipped his wrist like loose ribbons. Picking up the bracelet, Kieran dropped it into his scrip and pulled the laces tight. He turned his back on the pinch-faced minstrel and strode to the village square.

People and animals milled in the wide space, raising dust, filling the air with strong odors of sweat and dung. A small shape darted along the edge of his vision and ran in stooped fashion toward the smithy. Kieran rounded the building and met Thryffin at the door to the room behind the forge. Straw stuck up from the boy's hair and through holes in his clothing.

Kieran pushed open the door. "Well, lad, why the skulking?"

"The man in the stableyard"—Thryffin followed him inside—"he is the spy!"

"I thought as much."

"I followed him."

Kieran frowned.

"Did I do wrong, Master Smith?"

"It is a dangerous thing, spying on a spy."

"He crossed the bridge twice. I saw him from the mill when I helped Mistress George sew new grain sacks. The spy went up the Romney Road a bit again. He even visited Kathleen."

"At Harry's farm?"

Thryffin nodded. "What does he want?"

No use waking the lad's fears. Kieran's own were enough. "Maybe a fugitive from Cameron, or a poacher. Perhaps a conscript who has decided the king's army is not for him."

"What does he want with you?"

"If he crossed the bridge, did he go to Mother Crumb?"

Thryffin shrugged. "He does not look ill."

"Mayhap she cured him."

"The spy has been asking about you. I told him nothing."

"You are a true friend, Thryff."

A startled smile warmed the boy's face.

"You should not come to the smithy again."

"But—!"

"Only until the spy leaves Shea. Give him no cause to suspect you."

Confusion shadowed Thryffin's eyes. "What do you mean?"

"Do you remember the stories of what happened before you were born? Of when King Morfran and his men rode through the province?"

The boy nodded. "Aye, they killed folk for sport."

"And information."

"About what?"

"About people who do not exist. People who died centuries ago."

"Why would the king kill for that?"

"He is mad."

"Will he do it again?"

"Aye."

"Does he think you are one of the people who do not exist?"

"How could I be?" Kieran plucked straw from the boy's hair. "I am a blacksmith." He stepped to the door. "Take to the woods behind the shop, then circle 'round to the mill."

Thryffin hunched his shoulders as if hiding. "He will not see me."

"Good lad." Kieran hesitated. "Do not come tomorrow. Do not

speak to me at the Faere. If he asks, give him no reply. "

The boy gave a single nod and slipped out the door. Kieran stood staring at its aged and knotted wood. What danger lurked at the edges of Shea's hard-won prosperity and uneasy peace? What part did he—Kieran Smith—play in the danger?

He removed the dagger from hiding and cradled it in his open palms, willing himself to remember.

To him, life began when he was found by the farmers and brought to Shea. How had this dagger, likely the treasured possession of a wealthy man, come to him? Why had the farmers or Donnegan not taken it from him, a child far too small to defend himself?

A glow emanated from the chasing that twined the haft, shining through the skin of his hand as if he were a bodiless shade. Echoing the hot gleam of the weapon, the bracelet thrummed against his hip. He pulled it from the scrip and laid it on the table, setting the dagger beside it. Blue incandescence filled the room.

Teag knows what it is.

He must. His bit of mummery in the stable yard was stiff and contrived. He had not touched the bracelet.

He is afraid of it. Why?

There was one person who would know.

On the ancient stone steps stood an over-dressed fellow Father Donovan had seen lurking about the village. The man seemed too watchful to be a mere Faere-goer.

He removed his feathered cap. "Good day, Father."

"Aye, 'tis. Would thee be needing prayer? A bit of counsel?"

"Answers."

Father Donovan stepped aside, pulling wide the door.

The kirk's simple lines bespoke it as a remnant of the Keldon Age. The windows, tall and squared at either end, marched down the sides of the nave like lean soldiers guarding the simple benches. There were no doors but the one opening on the priest's small cell behind the altar. Chaste wood formed the low altar but, on the side away from the benches, a poem had been carved in crude Kellish runes. Father Donovan could see it when he stood to address the villagers, and he often wondered if it had been the desperate prayer of Kels taking refuge in the tiny chapel centuries ago.

Beyond the altar hung the many-hued tapestry of a shepherd and flock. Aye, it was threadbare in patches, and the edges had been fraying long before Father Donovan traveled his first circuit through Shea, but it was a majestic piece that any nobleman would covet. How it remained here, out of Baron Markha's clutches, he did not know.

The stranger's narrow handsome face seemed an axe blade, cunning and sharp. He turned around in the aisle between the two rows of rough-hewn benches worn smooth by generations, his gaze flicking back and forth as if he sought a secret hiding place.

"Tell me, Father," he said, a smile on his lips but not in his eyes. "Your face catches at my memory. Were you ever confessor to Baron Markha?"

"I bring comfort to the common people."

"You dislike the nobility?"

"All men be within Mymna Tor's scope. Whom do thee seek?"

"An enemy of the king."

"Have the Dissonay marched so deep past Skardian ranks?"

"Not all his foes are Dissonay. Some are his own subjects."

"This be a peaceable village in a loyal province."

"In words, perhaps. Deeds speak other allegiances."

"Make thy speech plain."

"What do you know of the blacksmith?"

"Old Donnegan?"

"You know right well of whom I speak. Kieran Smith."

Father Donovan folded his hands and did not reply.

Stepping back, the stranger half-turned, presenting his profile.

Aye, he does have a familiar look.

"You, Father, seem impatient I leave."

"I must prepare for tonight."

"Indeed." The man faced the cleric again. "Did you perform the naming rite for Kieran Smith when he was new-born? Does he bear any marks? Do you know his parents?"

The priest weighed knowledge with truth. "They were long dead ere I came to Shea."

"You did not perform the naming rite. What of any marks?"

"I rescued him from the river when he was but a lad learning to swim. There are none."

"I am Teag, emissary of His Majesty King Morfran, empowered to take any who threaten the throne." Teag studied him. "Are you

Morfran's loyal subject?"

Hidden within the long sleeves of his coarse brown habit, the priest's hands gripped one another. "I keep laws and render taxes."

"Those are mere facts, Father. What is the truth? Your brown robe will not save you. Measure well your words."

The priest's fingers itched for a sword.

"Tell me, Father, what you know of Maggie Finney."

"Thee have yet to say why Kieran Smith threatens the throne."

"He lives. And your life hangs by your tongue. What do you know of Maggie Finney?"

Staring into those hard eyes, Father Donovan prayed for wisdom. "A priest of the Order of the Holy Shepherd, I am bound by oaths to tell the truth, to guide the people, and to protect them from wolves."

"So you do hold an allegiance higher than the king."

"Aye, and Him thee cannot threaten."

The spy's nostrils flared. "The foul wind yesternight. You know whence it came. Once the smith leaves Shea, the threat will be gone as well. What matters most, Father? One man? Or an entire province?"

Teag stalked back through the nave and out the door, sunlight brightening his tunic to the hue of fresh blood.

A pair of grey-bodied birds with blue wings wheeled and above the weeping willow tree, and a wheelbarrow trundled before Mother Crumb as she rounded the cottage, her apron dirt-streaked, her straw hat askew. She smiled up at Kieran—"What brings you, lad?"—as she pushed the barrow through the garden.

"Possible magic."

She left the barrow beside an elevated herb bed, brushed her hands together, and pulled off her hat. Inside the cottage, she hung the hat and apron on pegs beside the door, slipped her feet from the wooden clogs and into soft slippers. Hers was one of the rare cottages boasting a stone floor. Most were of earth, tamped down to the consistency of rock.

An age-blackened oak table ruled the room. A bent-willow rocking chair sat near the hearth. Bundles of dried herbs and flowers hung from the rafters. Phials and jars lined shelves on the walls. Antler hooks held a collection of shiny steel knives. Two pairs of clogs, dirt still clinging to their soles, flanked the doorway. Woolen shawls hung from pegs, awaiting winter. A hoe leaned against the wall. Peace was almost a living presence.

The healer's time-worn hands cleared the table of jars and pouches. Kieran took the medicine box and put it atop the applewood cabinet for her.

Mother Crumb gestured for him to bend down, and she examined his head. "You will have a scar, but it will not be your first. Are you hungry? Thirsty?"

"Thirsty. Has someone been here? A stranger?"

"A man did come." Mother Crumb pushed a mug of tea toward him. Kieran drew a chair forward and sat at the table. "He lurked in the forest and watched me go about the garden. He is anxious but uncertain. There is a task he must do, and he has little time."

"Did he wear a feather-cocked hat and scarlet?"

"He did." She sipped her tea. "Tell me of this magic."

Kieran laid his hands on the table, wondering what to tell first.

Mother Crumb reached across the table and grasped his hands in her own. "These are capable hands. Good hands." She traced an old scar slashing across one callused palm. "You were no more than twelve when you saved Jenny's life." She curled his fingers over the scar, closing them into a fist. "You could have lost the hand."

"I could not cut wood for weeks." He chuckled. "Poor Donnegan. Jenny was afraid of the axe, I was wounded, and Kathleen would not be persuaded to roughen her skin."

"But these hands crafted something special." Mother Crumb released him and leaned back in her chair. "Tell me."

He examined his fingernails, blackened and chipped by his work. "I found three small lumps of strange ore in the river."

Pulling the bracelet from his scrip, he placed it between them on the table. Light ignited in the healer's eyes. She reached out then pulled back her hand.

"What is it?" Kieran asked. "The man you saw in the forest—Teag —he seemed afraid of this, too. As if it somehow lives."

"Indeed, it does. He saw it. Did he touch it?"

"He did the same as you."

"Etherium answers certain people, just as you and I answer one another. It makes itself known only to those who may master it, and it glows only in their presence or at their touch. Otherwise, it appears as grey and lifeless as any other stone." She clutched her tea mug. "You have found the source of the sword of Kel."

The dagger, tucked into his belt, grew hot.

He knew the legend of Kel. Every child in Shea knew it. They heard the tale from their elders, and even the most skeptical of the villagers had uttered—at one time or another—a wish for the return of the golden age of the Kels.

His fingertips tingled.

"Has that happened before?" she asked in an odd voice. "The strange sensation in your hands?"

He nodded.

"*Ru Karrohm*. It made you an excellent smith, but remained quiet until wakened by the etherium."

"What is it? Magic?"

"A form of *ru Bená*, the gift. Keepers have it, or descendents of artisans who lived in the Keldon Age. Or Kels themselves."

"What does this mean?"

"That is a wide tale. You heard the legend of Kel since you were a boy, but you do not know all. Few people do. The Keepers know. It is a tale written long ago. I will tell you what I may. The rest shall keep."

In the darkness of the Prymmiddion Age, when clan fought clan and chaos ruled, Dragons broke their bond with Men.

Attor Dragonking, a vile creature, worst of his brethren, plagued the people for generations but did not utterly consume them. Toward Dar Gûm Ethem, the People of the Golden Land, he showed special malice, poisoning fields with his fumes, stealing livestock to feed his young, and feasting upon the children of Men.

The Ethem crafted weapons to kill Attor and his kin-Dragons, but nothing prevailed against the steely scales.

Yet hope remained.

A youth named Kel stood at Council to vow vengeance for his parents burned to death in their field. He would enter the great wyrm's lair and steal a scale from the Dragonking. Thus would he have power over Attor, and be able to bend the creature to his will, preserve his people, and learn the ancient knowledge locked inside the Dragon's mind.

The chieftains feared Kel's success. They might have a new enemy in the guise of this young sprig if he rid them of Attor—for, by controlling the Dragon, he would control them, as well. They sought to deflect his purpose, even restrain him, but he slipped their bonds and set forth.

The Dragon flew far and fast, striking at flatlands and clearings then retreating to the mountains. Kel journeyed long to find Attor's den. He entered the dark eastern forest and followed the Renfrew River south until Dragon-stench led him to where Attor dwelt in a vast cavern.

Kel searched for a way to climb the mountain. Dragons are keen of smell, however, and Attor knew the youth lurked at the bottom of the stony height. The beast flew from his lair, and thus began a great race. Attor pursued him through the forest to the Plains. Then Kel turned back and ran into the river to dampen the wyrm's fire. There Kel saw a blue sun glowing in the river. He grabbed it up, and escaped to a small cave we now call Dragon's Rook.

Attor clawed at the mountainside, shot fire into the opening, thrust his talons into the cave's mouth. Kel struck him with the blue ore. Attor's talon broke and lay glittering on the cavern floor. Screaming in agony, the Dragon flew away.

The great broken talon he tied to his pack then climbed down the mountain and searched the river for the curious blue metal he called etherium for its otherworldly light. He gathered more than he could carry. Fashioning a sledge, he piled it with etherium, and traveled until he found a village where he begged the use of a forge.

He was a farmer, not a smith, yet his hands were guided by skills not his own. He crafted a beautiful longsword. A simple weapon, unadorned, flexible, and strong. Perfectly balanced. The sword glowed blue whenever he drew near. Villagers called it magic. Kel called it Azrin.

He returned to the mountain to face the Dragon.

Kel no longer wanted power over the Dragon. He could not leave the people in the shadow of evil, no matter how much knowledge might be gained. Were Attor Dragonking slain, other Dragons might cease their marauding ways.

The sword's light was a beacon, taunting Attor, yet he did not come forth until sunset, awaiting the darkness when Dragons may become invisible at will.

Kel knew the beast's smell, an odor of death and brimstone, but he did not know if the beast lay in wait for him, or if Attor's stealth *was such that he made no sound as he hunted. If Attor flew, his invisible form would shroud the stars and his wings would stir the air. Kel only knew Attor was aground.*

The youth stood in the center of the Renfrew and waited. The moon rose. On the eastern bank of the river, darker than the trees, appeared the liquid outline of the Dragon

Attor's foul breath washed over Kel. A ball of flame shot forth. Kel raised the sword, and fire slanted off the flat of the blade, setting the trees ablaze. In the firelight, the Dragon shed his invisibility.

Flames burned before and behind Kel, turning the river into a dazzling ribbon of gilt and scarlet. Standing firm in the center of the river, deflecting what fire he could, he waited for a moment he was not certain would come.

Attor reared up, opening his mouth to send another stream of fire, and Kel threw the sword. It lodged deep in the Dragon's mouth. Beams shot forth. Attor roared, tossed his head, clawed his throat. Light grew until Kel turned his head to shield his eyes. Rays lanced the sky, seen for such great distance that stories are still told of them in the Craydaeg Mountains and the Calhoun Forest.

The Dragon burst into a golden blaze. His scales rained into the river, sizzling as they fell. The sword remained suspended, a needle threading the air, until the last piece of Attor disappeared. Then, as if guided by an unseen hand, the sword slipped into Kel's grasp.

He returned to his people and presented the broken talon to his chieftain, who knelt at Kel's feet and swore to serve the Dragonslayer.

Clans of Ethem gathered from mountain, forest, and plain to see the Dragon's claw, and the chieftains counseled together for many days, debating the wisdom of setting Kel Dragonslayer as ruler over all the tribes. Kel protested, for he knew nothing of leading clans or armies, but the beautiful blue sword drew the chieftains. In its presence, they forgot what grudges they held, and looked on one another as brothers. The golden talon was mounted in the tent where the chieftains met, and none among them challenged the man who had slain the Dragonking.

They reached accord, and journeyed to the Stone of Oswyn to crown Kel High King. As the circle of gold was placed on his brow, a spring bubbled from beneath the stone, becoming a brook, then a stream, then a river. Growing wide, it flowed north and became the

River Kel.

The High King returned to his village, wed a farmer's daughter, and established his rule.

Great good came of the House of Kel. His descendents built the fortress of Havyn duru Asryn, the House of the Sky, and reigned for a thousand years, fostering artisans, scholars, craftsmen, and ideas. New farming practices rose, and the people flourished.

Afraid of Azrin, the Slayer's sword, Attor's kin-dragons left the Ethem unmolested and faded into memory. The Plains people, content and prosperous, forgot why Kel's sword was forged or how peace came to their land.

Adwr, the last Kellish king and guided by a mysterious counselor named Heolstor, heeded not the justice and mercy of his ancestors. Generosity died in his grasp. Proud Adwr no longer aided the people but oppressed them. He promised high wage to any who would become his soldiers, and increased tax on all who would not. Clan chieftains held power under previous kings, but Adwr claimed all power as his own.

One day, an ancient scribe entered the court and prophesied Dragons would have their vengeance on Men, but not before the white throne lay broken in the House of Kel. Adwr scoffed and ordered the old man tossed outside the gates.

To prove his contempt for the prophecy, the king brought forth Azrin with his own hand, for none but a true descendent of Kel could touch forged etherium and live. Adwr mounted the sword on the wall above his throne, but the blade would not glow blue as it had in the presence of other Kellish kings.

Within a fortnight, war burst upon the land, led by a conspiracy of chieftains. They drew out the king's army and pushed between Adwr and the three rings of trees that guarded the fortress.

Adwr fled, falling on the banks of the Black River, so named for the quantities of dark blood fouling its waters.

On the day the Kels fled was Adwr's family slain, and Azrin stolen from the dead king's hand. Even now, a thousand years later, the one proof of true sovereignty remains lost.

And in the east, a fire burns in Dragon's Rook.

Her gaze pinioned him. "You, Kieran Smith, are a Kel."

"I am an orphan. No one."

"What has that to do with anything?"

"All the Kels are dead."

"Except the ones King Morfran still hunts."

"But I am a blacksmith."

"Aye. A Kellish blacksmith."

The bracelet pulsed on the table, and the dagger threatened to burn its way through his tunic. Uttering an oath, he stood, flinging the dagger to the floor. It skittered across the stone hearth, its point catching on a chair leg.

The healer stared at the weapon. "The decoration is etherium."

"I am not a Kel."

"None but a Kel may touch etherium and live. Even simply being near it has driven some men mad. You are quite sane."

He thought of Thryffin and all the other children who played near the river. "What if someone picks up a stone in innocence?"

"Etherium in its rough state will not only look ordinary but behave ordinary. Not until it is forged is it deadly."

Mother Crumb rose from the table and lifted the cheesecloth covering the mouth of a jar on the windowsill. The pungent scent of elfwort wafted across the room. "A bit of infused honey. Almost ready. Farmer William's children have summer colds." She replaced the cloth.

"Now, about *ru Karrohm*. Not all Kels have it, just as all healers do not have *ru Bená*. We are chosen, you and I." She gestured at the dagger. "So, my fine young fellow, all your arguments are vain."

He reached down and felt the hilt. It was cool. She handed him a length of ragged cloth. He wrapped it around the dagger then tied it to his leg, just below the knee, and slid the bracelet back in to his scrip.

The healer stooped to stir a pot over the small fire. She straightened, rubbing her lower back with both hands. Kieran had never thought of her as truly old, but Mother Crumb's lined face looked weary, its creases deep.

"Few Kels escaped their attackers," she said. "They fled across the Plains, some into the Kelcey Forest and others into the Calhoun. Generations later, few traditions survive. The mark remains. Kels brand the royal crest between their shoulder blades, where the neck meets the back, so they might know one another."

"I bear no brand."

"The spy saw you touch etherium and live. You need no brand."

She sat once more at the table. "King Morfran has been searching for survivors ever since he took the throne. Even the most indirect descendent of Kel High King is a threat to him."

Taking his hand in hers, she turned it over and traced the scar across his palm with her thumb. Power jolted along his arm.

"Mad Morfran's hunters have done their job well, but you, Kieran Smith, can overcome him."

She released his hand, and he held it to his chest. The residual tremble of lightning shuddered down his spine. Who—what—was she?

The healer leaned forward, her eyes taking on a fierce light. "Did you feel the wind stir yesternight, and smell the fetid air? Did the stars dance behind a veil of water?"

Chills raced along his skin. "The Dragon."

"Aye, the Dragon. Find Azrin, the lost sword of Kel. Only an etherium blade will slay the Dragon. It is already marauding in the east, and will soon bring destruction here. If I recall the prophecy aright, it is Attor's kin-dragon, and thus the foretold one who will seek vengeance on the House of Kel. The kin-dragon will not cease hunting until the true heir is dead. Save the people, and prove irrefutably your lineage."

The cottage seemed close, hot. Kieran ducked out the doorway and stood with his face turned to the sky, eyes closed, measuring his breaths with deep draughts of cool air.

The healer's soft footfalls sounded behind him, and she touched the middle of his back as Mistress Donnegan had done when he was a child. Quiet reassurance.

"Where do I look?" he asked after a time. "If the sword has been lost for generations, how shall I find it? And how does one kill a Dragon?"

"Listen to the Voice. He will guide you."

"I cannot believe. I try, but I have no faith."

"He will give it to you."

"If I succeed in finding Azrin, what then?"

The old woman donned her floppy straw hat again, and pulled on her dirt-stained gloves. "The people wait the return of the House of Kel, but they have lost hope. The sword will be their banner. They will follow the man who wields it against Mad Morfran and all his host."

Once more, the bracelet warmed and the dagger heated.

"The real question," Mother Crumb continued as she walked away, "is whether or not you are willing to lead a collection of farmers, herders, tradesmen, and petty merchants against so fierce a king as Mad Morfran?"

Kieran followed her. Fear and anticipation tumbled in his belly like stones in a stream. "What would we do for weapons? And what of the barons with their own armies? The wealthy merchants with their mercenaries? Might they want favor with the king and turn their guards against an army of commoners? Rebels would be defeated before they ever went to war!"

The healer attacked weeds with a hoe, slicing between rows of just-greening strawberry plants with precision born of long skill.

"Where do I begin?" he asked, holding his arms out from his sides as if measuring the vastness of the task.

Leaning on the hoe, she looked up at him. "The people have long needed a leader. They talk about how someone should do something, yet few have risked a whit to see justice done. Would you let the unknown stand in your way? Fear will bind you with a thousand ropes. It will sap your life like a river of leeches. It will steal your soul like a dream-thief. Fear will leave you an old man, sitting and wondering what might have been."

Impatience crackled through him. Thin, bright flames sparked among his fingertips and sizzled in the air. A fly bumbled into the web of blue light and fell to the ground, a tiny black crisp.

Chuckling, Mother Crumb returned to her gardening.

III

THE LADY OF SKARDA

She wipes bloody hands on the hem of his white tunic. A black flood spills down his side, soaking the threadbare blanket. She yanks the sewing shears from his chest, polishes them clean on his sleeve, and tucks them into her belt.

Her belongings are few: a journal, a quill and inkwell, one change of clothing, a sewing kit, a shawl, a patched pair of shoes. She gathers all into a length of sturdy cloth and knots it.

She opens the garret door and steps out to the narrow landing. The household sleeps, quiet and dark. She keeps to the wall, her bare feet skimming the stairs with the sureness of long familiarity. In the great hall, the stone floor is cool and smooth.

Baron Markha's massive chair looms like a bear in the hall's shadowed depths. His dogs loll at his feet there during the day but guard his chamber tonight. A cold humor draws up the corners of her mouth. The beasts guard an empty bed. He had tried to invade hers. His final mistake. The women of Markha Province are safe.

At the main entry, she places her bundle on the floor with the same careful steadiness with which she once cut cloth. Again, she listens. No guards. No dogs. The only sound is her breathing.

She slides the lock bar from its iron cradle and tugs the door. It groans, swinging wide to admit a pale luminescence. Beyond the harvested fields, the forest waits.

Inhaling the brisk autumn air and thankful for her woolen shawl, she steps into the courtyard and closes the door.

16 ~ The Letter

Ashen-peaked Mount Cathál resisted the sun's embrace. Clouds shadowed its head and spiraled down into green-cloaked ravines. Just above the tree line, where great boulders thrust out of the snow, a waterfall rushed down in a crashing sheet to join the River Thrayne far below, hidden but not unheard. Yanámari leaned her head against the stone casement of her chamber window, and watched rainbows leap like gleaming trout in the misty spray of the waterfall. Brona's Veil.

In legend, Brona demeaned the love of an honest commoner and encouraged the suit of a highborn rogue. "I will have fire and splendor," she said. "I cannot be a merchant's wife."

One day, a wise-woman from the deep reaches of the Craydaeg Mountains cursed Brona: she would never wear bride clothes but in death.

Brona pleaded for mercy, and it was granted. She would die full of years at the end of a well-lived life if after twelve moons she could but answer one question: above all else, what matters most?

Each storyteller had his own ending. One said love, another said honor, yet another said wisdom. Hope? Strength? Friendship? Humility? Faith? Noble things all, but which had she chosen? Did she complete her journey? Marry? Live the promised long life? One thing was certain: she ventured beyond the bounds of Elycia's high stone walls and traversed the realm.

Such daring drew Yanámari. She had never been outside the city, nor was she ever likely to leave it. Even when she wed, she would not travel to her husband's ancestral home. No, her father would insist he, too, stay in Elycia. She would exchange one gaoler for another.

She felt least fettered when gazing at the rushing freedom of

Brona's Veil. Elder servants said it was best appreciated from the highest tower in Elycia, but the King's Keep was locked to all but her father and his counselor.

Why the King's Keep was abandoned, she did not know. The most fortified part of the city, its upper levels once served as the royal residence, and its lower reaches comprised the dungeon. After the sudden death of her mother when Yanámari was still an infant, the dungeon had been cleared and the convicts sent to fill the king's army. One prisoner remained in the Keep, but not in the cells. In the uppermost chamber, a face sometimes appeared at the window, and a hand at the bars. Conjecture ran through the city, but the king kept his own counsel.

The present royal dwelling was fashioned from an ample tower in an impregnable portion of the city wall, carved from the mountain itself. The tower had served as the dwelling of the Hôk Nar, the Brethren of the Black Hood. That was before Heolstor had purged the ranks of his minions and moved the new recruits to the caves below the city. Most traces of torture and the dark arts were removed. Yanámari remembered no other home.

Her chamber overlooked a grey cliff rising from the river gorge. She stood often on the window ledge. There was no rail to prevent falling, but she feared no height. The ledge was broad and deep, and she sometimes sat and dangled her feet over the edge. Many a shoe had been lost to the river.

Someday she would follow them.

The heavy door of the chamber scraped open. Yanámari looked over her shoulder.

"My lady." A diminutive handmaiden, Elta, offered a leather cylinder. "A letter from Lord Arien."

Yanámari stepped down from the window and met her in the middle of the chamber. "Who brought the letter?"

"Not the Brethren, my lady."

Yanámari raised her brows. Elta blushed.

"He arrived on the back of a Nar'ath, straight from the battlefield." The maid's voice softened to almost a whisper. "He looked injured or ill, my lady. He did not even alight, but tossed messages for you and the steward, and flew away."

Yanámari also lowered her voice, though—unlike elsewhere in the tower—there were no secret rooms or passages leading from her chamber, and therefore little chance unwanted listeners might overhear. "Imre?"

Elta nodded.

Odd. Why send as messenger so valuable a servant?

Elta slid the cap off the end of the cylinder and tipped the tube. A scroll and a long, cloth-wrapped bundle dropped into her hand. She handed the letter to Yanámari. The black wax seal bore the impression of a wolf's head. Yanámari broke the seal and held the letter to the light. The writing was tidy, the letters thin and upright.

To Yanámari, beloved sister.

Your betrothal day fast approaches. Choose well, and please our father the king, thereby pleasing me. Dear sister, be guided by me in this. Were you not always governed by my advice?

Elta covered her mouth, her eyes laughing, and Yanámari smiled. She was apt to disagree—loudly—but she trusted him.

Arien's writing was overdone, much grander than he spoke. Pretty phrases hid pointed meaning. Brother and sister had learned in childhood to disguise their speech and thoughts lest Heolstor know all. It was the price they paid for keeping their own minds, for not having their memories stripped bare by the Brethren.

As for our friend, the little mouse who yet keeps company with my few possessions is well, bright-eyed, and resourceful. He looks on war and anguish, on the deeds of evil men, and still he cleans his whiskers and washes his paws, and finds enough scraps on which to live. Perhaps we should heed the mouse, and find what peace we may for as long as it remains.

"Imre," breathed Elta.

"You sigh like a heroine in a skald's tale."

"As would you, my lady, if you knew his kisses."

"If I did, we might be tearing out one another's hair rather than sharing a letter."

Elta smiled. "Read on, my lady."

The mighty guided by a mouse. Well you may laugh at such a jest, but he is wise. We bear burdens unknown to other creatures.

Remember you once complained women were not allowed to be warriors? In youthful pride, I declared only men may fight or rule, for women have not the strength for it, nor the wit. Then you demonstrated which end of the sword did the most damage to an arrogant backside.

Did Father allow me to return home as oft as he, I would test your swordsmanship, dear sister, and hear once more your sensible counsel.

Despite the war, the king came to Elycia often, arriving on the back of a Nar'ath and disappearing into the mountain. He rarely spoke to Yanámari. When he did, it was to express displeasure over her appearance or her lack of countenance, or to press for her choice of husband.

During such visits, he smelled of sulfur and smoke, and sometimes arrived at table with soot streaks on his face and hands, or with ashes in his hair. Rumor among the servants said a mighty beast lived within the caves, and the Black Hoods fed it the flesh of Elycians accused of crimes against the king.

Likely the beast was simply one of the great fires used to burn the city's waste—but why would the king, so fond of war, leave the battle only to spend hours among the dung heaps?

It was not for nothing Morfran was considered mad.

Yanámari continued reading.

Meantime, wear this knife in your sleeve.

She looked up with a puzzled frown, and Elta unrolled the length of cloth, revealing a thin-bladed knife in a tooled sheath.

Never reveal you can fight until you must fight.

Then the writing changed. It became untidy, scrawled, as if written in haste.

Dawn is near. Soon I face Disson's champion to decide an end to this war.

If you are reading this, Mári, I am dead. Do not grieve. I pray I died well.

Leave Elycia. Find a way. Fear nothing but enslavement. Forgive me, sister, I rather you die than continue his prisoner.
I entrust this letter to the mouse.

Yanámari stared at the blurring words. The letter fell from her slack grasp and landed on the stone floor, the edges of the scroll curling closed.

17 ~ JOURNEY

Gaerbith hunched, pulling his cloak tight about him. He could not stop shivering, nor could he sleep. Disson was a land of gentler hills than these rugged giants called the Craydaeg Mountains. His men were hardy but not mountain folk. None were prepared for bitter winds, thin air that left them gasping and tired, or the treacherous road winding up along cliffs and often scarce wide enough for a man, let alone a horse. If not for ropes and quick action, one man and two pack animals would have been lost to the plunging chasm roaring with the waters of the River Thrayne.

If Gaerbith failed, the journey back down the mountains would be one of flight before the swords of Skarda. Even the renowned Fourth Lachmil would not survive a fighting retreat.

He climbed to stand on the barren height above the camp. His cloak swirled and danced, now tugging away from his body, now binding his legs. Clinging to niches in the rocks, scrub trees bent or twisted with every new whim of the wind. Their tough dry wood made hot, long-burning fires, if the flames could be sheltered from the mountain's shrieking breath. Only four fires still survived this night, and men huddled so close, so tightly shoulder-to-shoulder, that they propped up one another in sleep. In front of a deep cleft wide enough for three horses to stand abreast, the packs had been piled to help shield the animals, who cropped what little grass grew among the stones, or ate the more tender tops of scrub trees.

High Lord Boorn sat with his back to a boulder, his body swallowed in a thick, fur-lined cloak boasting an extra cape across the shoulders and a hood drawn low to cover the face. The men had accorded him a place near the fire, but he drew himself apart. Perhaps he knew their distrust, or perhaps he refused to sully himself by sitting with common folk.

Boorn had attained the rank of lord as a reward for his service to the king's table, but it was rumored his marriage into a wealthy vintner clan sped his rise. Damanthus had not been a king who could be bought, but perhaps long friendship with the clan had guided him in naming Boorn among the lords. Whatever the reason, Boorn felt his rank keenly, and seemed bent on everyone knowing it.

Gaerbith could recall nothing—no careless words, no discourteous acts—that might explain Boorn's hatred of him or his brothers. Other nobles came to the battles to provide troops; Boorn arrived in splendor with wine and servants. He braved the Nar'ath and brigands on the road just to hover behind the army and insinuate himself into battlefield councils. But why? High Lord Boorn did nothing without an eye for gain.

Perhaps this moment, this task, was his reward. He acted in the king's stead as emissary.

A heady thing, power.

Gaerbith turned his back to the wind and looked southward, toward the Plains and the Kelcey Forest. The moon was hidden for another seven-night at least, but no clouds obscured the stars, and he saw a great distance from this height. Still, a ridge of mountain stood in his way, and he could only imagine what lay beyond, down where land was gentle and forested and growing warm with spring.

But he was here, wondering if he might be more than a little mad. The fate of a kingdom rested on his decisions, on what he said and did. The weight of it pressed like a millstone, grinding his thoughts.

When King Padraig roused from his fever to dictate letters to Boorn and Morfran, it had not been Thael, the royal manservant, who wrote them, but the Keeper who tended the king's wounds. There were things written that Thael was not supposed to know. Yet the servant held the only other key to the casket containing Padraig's correspondence. Was there something other than letters in that box?

"You guard Disson best by accompanying Boorn to the treaty council," Padraig had commanded Gaerbith and Turi. "He and Morfran must believe I am well and my father lives. The Territories remain free only as long as a king of the House of Rhobarrd sits on the throne." A tremor took him, and only the Keeper's arm held him upright. "Become hunters. Stalk your prey by walking beside him. It is the last thing he will expect."

"My lord, what is our goal in Elycia?" Gaerbith asked. "Alliance, or the death of Morfran?"

The question went unanswered. Soaked with sweat, Padraig bent forward, convulsed.

"Bring more water!" the Keeper snapped. "And find me a healer's apprentice."

Gaerbith offered his own waterskin then sent men to find more. Turi grabbed the first apprentice he saw. When the Fourth Lachmil left the battlefield, High Lord Boorn in their midst, buckets and waterskins were still being brought to the tent.

That was ten days past.

"Omwen'din, guide us," Gaerbith prayed through lips stiff with cold. "May we do what must be done, and not falter in the doing."

He returned to camp. Little fires still burned, and the lack of wind made the space among the rocks seem almost warm. He slept.

"Get up, you!" High Lord Boorn kicked his fallen horse. The beast lifted its head, but did not rise.

Boorn drew back his boot to kick again, but Gaerbith thrust a foot in his way. "A little rest, then he must be led. The way is too steep for him to carry a rider."

His own horse, Kraekor, rested his unlovely head on Gaerbith's shoulder, ears pricked forward as if comprehending this exchange.

Boorn swung 'round and kicked a small stone, sailing into across the road and into the chasm.

Kneeling, Gaerbith stroked the fallen horse's neck. Kraekor nickered softly, touching the horse's nose with his own. The animal's breathing eased.

Here the road was broad again, and more level than the distance they had just climbed from last night's camp. The Fourth had traveled afoot the entire distance from the Lowlands to the Craydaeg Mountains. Only High Lord Boorn rode, but his mount, like the other animals, was not accustomed to the heights or the sharp air. It was a marvel the horse had endured this long.

"*Nyth, drengná. Lyrë gol.*" Rest, brave one. Breathe deep.

The horse obeyed, exhaling a gust rather than a wheeze.

"Where are the lookouts?" Boorn demanded. "What if Morfran's men are waiting in the rocks to kill us with arrows? Or the Nar'ath are released?"

"What good would that do him, my lord?" Gaerbith strove to keep his voice steady, free of anger. "Morfran wants something of us, and he will not obtain it if we are dead."

"Always an answer," Boorn sneered.

Gearbith leaned forward to address the horse once more. The beast's ears twitched. "*Magh. Lae bryn.*" Stand. Be strong.

Rich brown coat layered with dust and flecked with sweat, the horse gathered his legs beneath him and heaved himself upright, trembling. A small cheer went up from the men, and someone tossed a withered carrot that missed its mark, landing in the dirt. The horse lipped it up from the ground, crunching the thick barrel of the carrot.

"Trag, lead him. Owen, find something to rub him down."

Boorn snatched the bridle from Gaerbith's hand, yanking the animal's head down and to the side. "I am the king's emissary! I do not answer to a mere captain, nothing more than a common sheepherder and of questionable blood. Was not your father the defiler of another man's wife?"

Gaerbith's hand clenched, and his fingers itched for the hilt of his longsword. *Enë iri ark*, whispered Uártha's remembered voice.

"High Lord Boorn, you are the king's emissary, but we are the king's men. If you would see your task accomplished, we must do ours. With what dignity will you enter the gates of Elycia if your mount dies on the road?"

Boorn opened his mouth, but Gaerbith shook his head. "Nay, my lord, Kraekor will not suffer you to ride him."

Face ruddied by wind and sun and the dark flush of anger, Boorn glared at Gaerbith. Then he released the bridle. "Arrogant puppy, to think I would sit astride your ugly beast."

He stomped up the incline, his boots crunching over the stony ground, wind catching his cloak.

Kraekor bumped his nose against Gaerbith's arm, and received an absent-minded scratch on the forelock. Owen found a rag and wiped down the lord's winded horse. Men adjusted packs on their laden animals, and others took advantage of the break in the journey to tear their ration of tough bread into chewable chunks or to drink cold water from a snowmelt streaming down a nearby boulder.

Turi pushed away from the rock on which he leaned, and stood on the other side of Kraekor, speaking quietly over the warhorse's back. "No fresh sign, captain. No wagon ruts, no dung nor footprints. The

Skardians did not pass this way."

Squinting against bright sun on unbroken snow, Gaerbith looked to the far side of the chasm, his left hand kneading the top of his right shoulder, rubbing away the deep ache. "Nor could they journey up the River Thrayne. The water is too surly, and bounded by rugged cliffs. Armies and merchant caravans need to move with ease and safety. There must be another pass that leads to the city."

"Should we turn back? Try to find it?"

Gaerbith glanced toward High Lord Boorn, who had ceased stamping and stood in an attitude of impatience, arms crossed. "I have no kindness for Boorn, but our task is greater than my dislike. He is anxious to reach Elycia, and we are already halfway up the mountain."

"Padraig said we would walk beside our enemy," said Turi. "Maybe he meant Morfran's tricks, or maybe one of our own is a traitor. Y'know as well as I, captain, how Lord Boorn thinks he is ill-used."

After a short silence, Gaerbith nodded. "Say nothing."

Lifting a hand, he signaled the men, and the Fourth continued their slow way up the southern rim of the River Thrayne.

18 ~ SHOES

Freedom—what little she enjoyed in her father's absence—was at an end. Scarlet banners flew on the city walls, and a narrow line of them snaked up the mountain.

In the waxing morning light, Yanámari pinned up her gleaming black plaits then Elta helped her don a blood-red gown, tugging the skirt so that the folds fell and the fabric clung in the proper places.

As dressed as a boar served at banquet. Yanámari kicked at the tongue of the gold-broidered girdle resting on the swell of her hips. *All I am missing is an apple in my teeth.*

"Elta, remain here, lest your joy on seeing Imre give you away."

"But my lady—"

Yanámari strode toward the door. Then, recalling her training under the guidance of a skittish noblewoman held captive until Yanámari had learned proper ways, she shortened her steps. A lady must not appear coarse. The king might not pay her much heed, but he was quick to see any flaws.

"I will find a way for you and Imre to meet in secret."

"Perhaps I may watch from Lord Arien's window?"

Yanámari looked over her shoulder.

"The shutter will scarce move, my lady."

Uneasy, Yanámari nodded once and departed.

In the great hall, she met the steward, Gwar, a tall man with greying hair and an agitated manner. She calmed his flustered exclamations—"But the king is early, my lady! The meat has only now been put on the spit, and the wine not yet brought from the cellar!"—and reminded him the day was scarce begun. The king would not sit down to banquet the instant he rode through the gates. Best tell the servants to look sharp to their duties, and send someone to lay precious wood on the raised hearth in the center of the hall. With a relieved expression, Gwar hastened to do her bidding.

He scurried down the dim corridor toward the kitchens. Some folk lived in constant uncertainty, afraid to displease. She might look on them in derision, if not for her own lack of courage.

Leaving the tower, Yanámari walked the city wall then descended steep steps and passed through a small garden. It grew in clay pots and or in raised beds lined by stones, filled with soil dug from Mount Cathál and worked fine by Yanámari's own hands. Aside from rare window boxes on hovels, the garden and the sward surrounding it were the only green in the city.

In the stableyard bordering the Court of Soldiers, she waited, chin raised, shoulders back. As soon as the column approached down a narrow street, she forced a stiff smile to her lips.

How cold and callus she must be to smile at all—somewhere in that procession was the body of her brother—but no letter had arrived from the king. Did Morfran think to humble her? To shock her to tears by revealing in front of his men the news of Arien's death?

She smiled. Pain amused the king. She would not oblige.

Three wolves, tall and grey, trotted beside the king's black warhorse, their keeper following close behind. The king seemed to love nothing more than those wolves. Love them so much that he did not permit them near the battlefield but kept them in the city. They stayed near him now as he dismounted.

Yanámari's hands closed into fists hidden in the folds of her gown.

As a child, she had found the hidden door at the rear of her father's chamber. The king had fallen asleep in his chair, an overturned goblet and a broken wine jug on the floor beside him. The wolves surged up from their place near his feet and lunged at her. She stumbled backward into the secret passage, kicking the door closed just before the first wolf could leap through. Its body thudded against the wall. Claws scratched the stones. She ran to her chamber and barred the door, afraid even to let servants enter.

Now Yanámari looked for her brother's horse—for any horse bearing a body across its saddle. There was none.

Maintaining a respectful distance between the king and his wolves, men and animals filled the stableyard, but the only lifeless things were bedrolls and packs.

Back toward the gate, the sky blackened with Nar'ath as the Brethren of the Black Hood returned. The great birds wheeled above the city then dove into the chasm of the River Thrayne. They and their masters dwelt in a cavern in the cliff's face. If there were dead to be ritually burned, the Hôk Nar would have entered the city and prepared the bodies.

For one hope-filled instant, Arien still lived.

Then King Morfran, pulling off his leather gauntlets and tucking them into his belt, looked toward her. He did not speak, but seemed to take her measure, studying her face.

She lowered her head in a brief bow. "Welcome home, my lord."

He said nothing.

"Where is Lord Arien? Do his men arrive soon?"

"He is dead."

Unbidden, one fist pressed against her chest, pushed back the grief. *No. I will not weep.*

The sharp, rhythmic echo of hoofbeats announced the returning Young Wolves.

"Bid them welcome. Among them you choose a husband. I will not have you look forlorn. No soldier wants to be greeted by a hagged face, nor by an insincere smile. Never give your husband reason to think your heart is anywhere but with him. No tears. Smile. Your traitorous brother deserves no pity."

He motioned the keeper of the wolves to come forward. A massive man with three heavy chains across his shoulders uttered a sharp command, and the wolves sat on their haunches as he attached the chains to their thick spiked collars. He led them toward the city side of the tower where a small door, heavily guarded, gave entrance to the lower reaches.

Yanámari gulped thready breaths of air. Traitor? Arien?

A slight young man bowed stiffly and with little grace. "My lady."

"Imre."

He straightened, wincing. Fading bruises marked his face. "I mourn with you, my la—"

"What cause have I to mourn?"

Imre's brows drew together, a question in his eyes.

"Go," she murmured. "Attend the king."

After another pain-stiff bow, he hastened to carry Morfran's pack.

When the king at last quitted the stableyard for the tower, Yanámari followed him as far as the great hall, and there he bade her return to her chamber until he required her presence.

Then Morfran turned, looked at her from hem to hair, and grunted a sound almost akin to approval. "When the Dissonay arrive, wear the white gown."

"Yes, my lord."

He smiled, and Yanámari shivered.

"Yes," he said in a musing voice. "Yes. Arien was right."

But about what Arien had been right, he did not say.

Yanámari forced herself to climb the stairs, floor after floor. Her legs shook and her throat constricted. Thoughts were numb and body cold, as if she lingered too long in the snow. When she reached her chamber, she stood outside the door and stared at it, at the ancient writing graven on it in letters like those on the city gates.

Then she pushed open the heavy door and shut it behind her, shoving home the bolt. Stepping out of her soft shoes, she walked across the cold stones, mounted the short steps to the center window, and stood in the opening, shoving wide the shutters with such force that she leaned out, the wind catching her hair and tugging her gown.

Today she would follow the lost shoes.

Water dripped from the melting layer of thick ice covering the hole in the cavern's dome. The ice was clear, admitting a cold light at odds with the heat filling the vast space. Into the cavern was led a line of prisoners linked by chains hand and foot, captured from a band of travelers on their way to one of the many spring Faeres.

Dragon stench compounded with lingering ash and smoke, making the air nigh unbreathable. Morfran covered his nose and mouth with a damp, herb-scented cloth, and watched from his accustomed place, a scooped-out space high on the wall, reached by steps carved into the stone and half-hidden by a thin curtain of rock shielding it as a hand shields a face.

Behind the prisoners, Black Hoods pulled down the necks of tunics or pushed aside hair, searching for the mark of the House of Kel. The captives were then unlocked and separated into two large cages rolled into place before the Dragon.

Pulsing fire glowed between gleaming teeth. Large eyes were lidded green slits glinting like new moons. The creature saw the busyness—and scorned it.

This beast was a ruler. Morfran's fist tightened around the golden scale. Surely the Gremian Kindred want their revenge on the House of Kel. *Why will he not join me in search of Kel's heir?*

A greater question remained. Why did Heolstor's dark magic not prevail against the Dragon's will, forcing it to submit, to be so bound to Morfran that king and king, Man and Dragon, shared the same mind?

Other caverns held other Dragons. Stolen from their nests by the Hôk Nar, the hatchlings grew quickly. Their scales remained pliable, easily pierced or cut, but only until the legs began to grow, and the wings. Then the stinging fangs no longer emitted venom, but closed and grew long and sharp, and fire spat from the younglings' jaws in unpredictable bursts. As with the children of Men on the brink of manhood, their moods became capricious and their control feeble.

In two or three months, their musculature expanded and their bodies lengthened, tails became distinct, and ridges of upright scales formed along their spines. By six months, their skin was impenetrable, the scales harder than iron. No blade could harm them, nor mar their glittering beauty.

Fed human flesh since their capture, the younglings grew to distinguish province from province, clan from clan. They learned—by smell and taste, and perhaps by sight—the difference between a common Skardian and anyone in whose veins flowed the merest hint of Kellish blood.

Like the king's soldiers whose minds had been cleared of memory until they knew nothing but service to Morfran, the Dragons forgot they ever had mothers, and the only fathers they knew wore dark robes and were of a race unlike themselves.

When old enough to shed scales, each youngling underwent rituals to bind it to one of the Brethren, to reveal one mind to the other, but the links never lasted longer than a few moments. Though instructed in war and hunger, in hatred and revenge, the young did not possess the knowledge—the vast, deep wells of power and history—hidden inside the massive chieftain of the Gremian Kindred, whose years were calculated in centuries, and whose strength was beyond measure.

Yet the Dragon had allowed himself to be captured, to be brought here and imprisoned by a single chain in a cavern high in the Craydaeg Mountains. That thought alone shivered Morfran's spine and weakened his joints, for it meant the Dragon and not Morfran held the advantage.

To what end?

Before entering the cavern, the prisoners had been given strong drink mixed with herbs. Now, as the potion ceased to calm them, they clung to one another, weeping, crying out, some clutching the bars of the cages and staring in terror. Yet the Dragon did not move, wings folded to his sides, tail coiled around his feet, eyes almost closed.

"Observe, my lord." Heolstor appeared at Morfran's side, his rasping whisper loud in the hiding place. "He waits. He toys with the prisoners."

"He defies me." Morfran ground his teeth.

"A cage filled with Kels, my lord, and he refuses to consume them? He wants to torture them first."

"The Kel he seeks is not among them."

"Perhaps. But he has killed every Kel we set before him."

"Why then, Longbeard, do you not set before him his enemy? Is the long arm of your magic shortened? You serve the great Nar Cahm, the master of darkness. Why can you not see in the dark and find the heir of Kel?"

"The House of Kel serves Mymna Tor, my lord, who will not suffer the loss without a fight."

"Man is but a plaything for the gods."

Heolstor spread his hands in a gesture of unknowing.

That and the Dragon's mockery angered Morfran. Coupled with the humiliating defeat at the hands of the Dissonay, it pushed him almost past rational thought.

No. Not defeat.

The appearance of defeat.

He would never concede that those Dissonay dogs were superior to his Young Wolves, or even to his common soldiers. No. He was Morfran. He did not suffer defeat. Did not the enemy even now walk open-eyed into his trap?

I am a spider, alert and motionless. I spread before my enemies a banquet where they shall sit and I shall feed.

"My lady?"

Something heavy pounded against the chamber door, and Elta's calls sounded faint on the far side of the thick oak.

"My lady! Please! Open the door!"

Yanámari pulled pins from her plaits, letting them drop behind her to the stone floor with a light, almost musical, sound. Then, when the last of the bone and silver pins had fallen, she drew a plait over her shoulder and unraveled the glossy black skeins, her fingers slipping through the rippling hair like fish through water.

"Please, please, my lady! Open the door!"

Arien once told her Mother's hair had been long and black. Morfran—before his madness became acute—would brush its soft waves and whisper and laugh with Mother. After Yanámari's birth, however, affection ceased and madness grew. And Mother died.

Pulling the other plait forward, Yanámari worked languidly, the loosened hair brushing her knees. She laughed mirthlessly. Clad in red and with hair like night, she was her father's seal, the colors of his kingdom.

Wind grabbed her hair, tossing it across her face.

Is that what she would see at the end? Only darkness?

A sharp crack split the air, and the door crashed open.

She turned, detached but curious.

Face streaked with tears, Elta rushed forward, her blue kirtle rumpled.

In the doorway swayed a Young Wolf, Rhôn, a length of hewn log in his gauntleted hands. He cast the wood aside and walked slowly toward Yanámari. "My lady." He sounded short of breath. "Forgive me, but your handmaid thought you ill."

Odd that he should worry so. She was only going for a walk to find her lost shoes.

"I have something to tell you, my lady." Rhôn spoke each word clear and unhurried. "It is about your brother, Lord Arien."

She smiled. "You have seen him? He is here?"

Elta clamped a hand over her mouth, and sank to the rug near the bed.

A strange tremor took Rhôn's voice. "Come away from the window, my lady, and I will tell you of him."

Yanámari considered. She looked over her shoulder at the waterfall, at the dark roaring chasm and the wild peaks glimpsed between the wind-whipped ribbons of her hair. So desolate. So cold. Walking there would be no different from walking the corridors of the tower.

But her brother was here—

Hands gripped her waist. Before she could brace herself against the casement, she was lifted from the window and carried to the bed.

"No. No!" She reached for the window. Elta closed and latched the shutters, casting out the light.

Rhôn took Yanámari's face in his hands, looking into her eyes. "Peace, my lady. Peace."

"Arien?"

He took a cloth from Elta and touched it to Yanámari's brow. She closed her eyes. When had summer come? Her face felt hot, and her body ached as with fever.

"What happened?" he murmured, and Elta replied, "I do not know. She went down to greet the king, and I waited elsewhere. When I returned, well, you know the rest."

The rest? Had something else befallen while she watched Brona's Veil? Something else as terrible as—

"Rhôn, do you know?" Yanámari opened her eyes. "Arien is dead."

He nodded. When he spoke, his voice was gruff and his eyes glistened. "Yes, my lady, I know."

"My brother is dead, Rhôn." Rolling to her side, she drew her knees toward her chest and stared at a sliver of light slicing beneath a shutter. "Elta, my brother is dead."

19 ~ Reflection

Too distant to kill even with a well-sped arrow, Nar'ath glided and wheeled over the road ahead of the Fourth. Westering sun blazed against the slopes of the Craydaegs, and the road wound back and forth across the face of the mountain, so steep now that the men and animals kept moving lest they not begin again.

Gaerbith's lungs burned and legs trembled. Steps became shuffles, breaths were gasps, and every sinew rebelled. His recent wounds, though closed by the Voice, burned like coals banked beneath his skin. His right leg trembled. Keeping his gaze on the next step, he thrust all other thought from his mind.

Just when the effort of pushing himself upward seemed impossible, level ground stumbled him. His knees crashed, his hands too late to break his fall. He tried to crawl, but his strength was as water, and he fell forward, heedless of sharp stones.

Kraekor moved him. Taking Gaerbith's tunic and baldric between his teeth, the old warhorse dragged the man toward the center of the flat, broad space curving into the mountainside. With his nose, Kraekor turned his master over so that Gaerbith lay, arms outflung, looking at the sky.

Men collapsed around him. Gaerbith had not the strength to sit up or even speak. Shredded clouds flamed in the setting sun before he finally sat upright and looked around. Horses stood with bent heads and sweat-streaked sides, their packs gone or severely lightened. Men sat or lay, and some walked about slowly like decrepit elders, trying to keep their legs limber after so long a strain.

Did we—" Gaerbith's voice was a whispered croak. He pushed himself upright and drank a little from a skin. The cool water was like honey to his ravaged throat. "Did we lose anyone?"

They looked around at one another, silent questions asked and answered in glances, shrugs, expressions, nods.

Turi said, "We are all here. Even the horses."

Unlooked-for good news. Leaning most of his weight on his left leg, Gaerbith stood and surveyed their resting place. The road entered it on the north, for the sun was lowering to his left, and the western curve was bounded by upright stones, untooled but resembling posts, like a giant's fence. The southern curve cut deep into the mountain and was overhung by a shelf of rock, forming a shallow cave large enough to shelter them all.

The eastern edge was also protected, but there were crude steps carved into the mountainside leading up from the landing—the expanse seemed very much like the turning in a stair—and guarded on both sides by high walls of rock. The steps had likely been fashioned with pack animals in mind, for the rise was shallow but the run deep, and horses could climb them far more easily than the steep ascent that led to the landing.

"Captain."

He turned. Owen and Trag carried coiled ropes draped over their shoulders and chests like baldrics.

"We ask to scout ahead while the others rest." Owen's expression was guarded. "If there is another portion of road like that"—he gestured back the direction the Fourth had just arrived—"we can prepare for it."

Gaerbith wanted to ask if they were rested, if they had food enough and water, if they had regained their strength for the task, but he did not. He merely studied them for a moment then nodded. "You will have little light, and we have no wood."

Owen's shoulders eased, and Trag said, "If we find any scrub, we will make a torch, and bring some back for a fire."

They climbed the steps then disappeared around a turn.

Fremmen grunted. "Youth."

Turi clapped him on the back, and the older man stuttered forward with the force of the blow. Laughter echoed from stone to stone, and Gaerbith remembered why he would rather command the Fourth than any other *lachmil* in Disson or the Territories.

Beneath the stone shelf, High Lord Boorn pushed his prone body into a sitting position and wrapped his fur-lined cloak around his shoulders. The day's journey had been hard on everyone, but more so on the nobleman unaccustomed to any great exertion other than riding a horse or walking his vineyards.

Gaerbith squatted beside him and held out a waterskin. "Drink, my lord. We will prepare what supper we may, and rest the night here. There will be no fire, but we can tie the horses at the cave's mouth, and so keep out some of the wind."

"I have my own waterskin." Boorn lifted his head, his face pale with exhaustion. "And my own food. Your task, captain, as you so clearly pointed out this morning, is to take me to Elycia. That is all. You need not play nursemaid."

Gaerbith stood, hanging the strap of the waterskin around his neck and across his shoulder so that the skin rested between his right elbow and his side. "I know not what enmity lies between us, my lord, but I cannot make amends for a wrong I do not recall."

Boorn turned his face toward the cave's shadows. "Amends, captain, are already being made."

Gaerbith left him and went to stand between two of the tall stones. He looked into the glare of the setting sun, and felt a measure of peace. His home was there, and all he loved: his father, his sisters and their families, the graves of his brothers. The rolling green of the Thynathel Hills and the quiet majesty of the Western Wood.

But his home—his true home—lay in the reaches of the Grimë Mountains, between the Thynathel Hills and the Great North Sea, in caverns and tunnels in which grew whole forests, both leafy and fruit-bearing, and swards of green grass as thick as any in a rich man's garden. Berries, flowers, and vines throve there, as well as all manner of animals and birds. Sun and rain nurtured all things, the roofs of the caves being pierced here and there, admitting the sky.

To Gaerbith, his true life was those days before the thieves came. He had lived as free and content as any child who knows no hardships in life nor comprehends the evils his father keeps at bay. Even now, after long years spent in the open as a shepherd and as a soldier, he still dreamt of the caves. Timelessness resided under the gnarled trees. From fruit that grew nowhere else in the world, flavors unknown burst on the tongue like celebrations. Neither winter's cold nor summer's heat fell too harshly there. Who would wish to quit this life when there was such a place to be found in the realms of Men?

But bandits found the caves, and the family was forced elsewhere.

The other children and Father had liked the caves well enough, but they loved the Thynathel Hills more.

Only Mother—Uártha—had stood with him when he closed his eyes and communed with the Voice, wishing for those early days and demanding a reason why they had to end. Come to think on it, those conversations were not unlike the confrontation in the Highlands, Gaerbith shouting, the Voice replying in quiet patience. However, He had never spoken to him as to a child, but called Gaerbith to a hard task. Take the oath, find the Kel-child.

Was the child hidden in Elycia?

Nay, child no longer.

Gaerbith closed his eyes, the last rays of sun warm on his face. Arms outstretched, hands braced against the standing stones on either side of him, he listened for the Voice. What he heard was not words but a deep quiet. He breathed it in, felt it pool in his belly and seep into his bones.

Kraekor nudged his shoulder. Opening his eyes, Gaerbith chuckled, scratching Kraekor between the eyes. "Old rogue. Come begging apples? I have none." He glanced to the far side of the river chasm. Only bleak, rugged mountains. "We shall have to be patient, my friend, and savor our memories."

Behind him, men talked and laughed as they had in the earliest days of the war, after the great fire when Disson chased Skarda and thought the war would be won in a seven-night. Tomorrow they ventured into the very lair of Mad Morfran, but there was ease in their voices and freedom in their laughter. They jested, spoke of their families and villages, traded jibes. He looked over his shoulder. Even the new men had fallen into the habits of seasoned warriors. Before eating, they tended their horses. Before sleeping, they mended garments or bridles, sharpened weapons, repaired boots. There were no complaints about hardship or lack.

Catching Gaerbith's eye, Turi thrust his chin toward the gathering, and Gaerbith nodded.

Aye. The Fourth.

Warrten approached and stood with him in the gathering shadows, arms folded, one shoulder leaning against a standing stone. Hair and beard grizzled, his years of war stretching back before Gaerbith was born, Warrten nevertheless seemed ageless. He might almost have been Turi's father or close kin, for the two men stood alike, feet planted wide and arms crossed, and they both spoke little except when thoughts pressed themselves into words. His silent presence was welcome.

The dying sun smeared crimson on the horizon, a thin swath nearly obliterated by night.

When Gaerbith finally spoke, he did not look at the older man, but kept his gaze on the fading light. "You were once a captain. Would you have led your men on such a journey as this?"

"I was young and foolish," said Warrten. "In my thirst for glory, I thought to win the battle with only a handful of men. We fell into an ambush. I alone survived.

"Our skirmish alerted the other *lachmil*, who rose to arms and defeated the surrounding enemy. I and my lost men were counted heroes, but I knew the truth. I returned to my village, married, raised crops and children. To this day, I do not know whether to curse my pride or praise it."

He paused and Gaerbith thought him finished, but Warrten shifted his feet, settled back against the stone, and continued. "Wealth or rank do not make men good or wise, but they do make men cautious, for wealth and rank must be protected. Though Padraig named two young commoners as guardians of Disson, the nobles are content to let the king's will stand. They do not contend for the honor of guardianship because they are relieved they need not risk their own lives to do what must be done.

"They know the guardians are honorable men and keep good counsel. The favor of two wise kings—though one be dead and the other still young—can only reassure that Disson and the Territories will not be presented to Skarda as careless gifts. Like all of us, the nobles and captains are weary. Their hope fades, and they do not trust any sign of friendship from Skarda. But they do trust the captain of the Fourth."

Gaerbith looked toward the darkness and blinked against the sudden sting in his eyes.

Warrten gripped his shoulder then returned to the cave.

New steps crunched beside Gaerbith. Turi's massive form stood against a frosty expanse of stars. His gruff voice rumbled. "Trag and Owen are back. They wanted to report, but I bid them rest."

He seemed hesitant, as if he had more to say but was unsure how to say it. Gaerbith waited.

"Young Owen. Until this morning, when Boorn mistreated that

horse, ye spoke not a word to him since the Lowlands."

Young Owen indeed. Too young.

Gaerbith crossed his arms. "What drives a lad not quite sixteen to leave a good life and a sure inheritance to follow four brothers all doomed to die?"

"Not all."

"Not yet."

"Let the lad go."

"Trag is the only one who speaks to him with any friendship. The rest of you ignore him."

"Aye, we do. Owen disobeyed orders and nigh cost our captain's life." Turi rubbed a knuckle across his chin. "But blood is blood."

In trying to show his brother no favor, Gaerbith showed him no friendship, either. The men treated him as any other soldier who had lost their trust, but shunning was a hard thing to accept, and Owen had shown courage coming with them to Elycia. Yet that, too, cost their trust, for it was but another instance of disrespect toward their captain—who should not have brooked the boy's disobedience.

"He should not be here. I should not have allowed it."

"If he were in the Hills, he would be nigh a man. In the Lowlands, he saw war and wielded a sword. He is already a man."

"Owen is the son of our father's old age. How will Forba look on me if I do not bring Owen home?"

"Ye think Forba will grieve yer death any less?"

Gaerbith stood long in the cold dark, cloak wrapped tight around him, and pondered the knowledge given him in dreams. He would die in a place of stone. If in the Craydaeg Mountains or in the walls of Elycia, what did it matter? And what of his other task—finding the heir of Kel?

Thoughts spiraled down their old paths. Why must he be the one in whom a secret dwelt? Why must it remain hidden unless he took the oath of a Keeper? Curse and vexation! He had not asked for this. He had not asked for any of it.

Deep ache roused in his shoulder, and as he rubbed away the pain, he remembered the Voice and the faces of the dead in the mists of the Highlands.

And he knew he would not turn back.

20 ~ RESOLVE

Yanámari walked around the table piled with gifts from the families of the Young Wolves. Firelight warmed cold silver and pale bone brooches, set fire to jewels, caressed vibrant fabrics.

Elta dozed in a chair near the fire, a blanket drawn up to her chin. She had snatched a few moments with Imre—who helped deliver these fine, unwanted offerings—and clicked her tongue at his bruises and broken ribs. He shrugged, but let her slather his wounds with herbs and fragrant salves.

This had been done under the watch of Rhôn and his cousin Gurn, who established themselves outside the chamber door, should Yanámari again try to harm herself. None said a word about her grief.

She trailed her fingers along a bolt of green wool, soft as down. These gifts were meant to capture her favor. Only Rhôn had refrained. He was Arien's closest friend, and she would choose him if he but showed the slightest sign of anything more than brotherly kindness. He had seen her weakness, pulled her from the brink of death, and in all things been correct and thoughtful, but he bestowed no presents nor made speeches, his expression closed and his manner formal. He was a soldier doing his duty.

It was less shaming than if he showed pity.

Gurn, however, was effusive and bold, kissing her hand, giving not one gift but three, and declaring himself superior among the Wolves, then laughing at his own boast and treating it as jest. A pair of hideous silver horse-head candlesticks surmounted another of his gifts—a silver casket—in the center of the table. She tossed a length of purple linen over them then turned toward the fire.

"My lady?" Elta stretched and sat upright, the blanket falling to her lap. "Shall I fetch anything? Food or drink?"

Yanámari shook her head.

Once she regained her right thinking, she had drunk one of Elta's concoctions and slept for hours. Then, wakened and made presentable, she received the Young Wolves and their offerings, but did not go to the great hall. A message was sent to the king, praying he excuse her. A message was returned, saying he expected her at table on the morrow.

The hour was late, perhaps after midnight, but her feet were restless and her thoughts vagabond. Lines from Arien's last letter repeated in her mind: *Mári, I am dead. Do not grieve. I pray I died well. Leave Elycia. Find a way.*

How dare he tell her not to grieve!

She unclenched her fists. How could she leave? The Nar'ath and the Hôk Nar saw everything. Common folk caught trying to leave the city were tortured before they were killed. She could not go to her little garden or wander the tower without being watched—unless she used the hidden passages, but none led outside the tower. There was no escape.

"Come, my lady, you must rest. The Dissonay—"

"—arrive on the morrow. Yes, I will rest."

Abandoning the fireside, she paced the darkness, the hem of her fur-lined robe whispering along the stones. No one would see her ever again as she had been when Rhôn took her from the window ledge. She would be as cold as Arien when he chose, as rigid and inscrutable.

If she could hide nowhere else, she would hide inside herself.

21 ~ THE MAD KING

Imre tried to ignore the pain from pummeled ribs as he heaved a hauberk up to hang from the shoulders of a dummy formed in the size and general shape of the king. The chain-mail unrolled until the tunic hem stopped just short of the block of wood anchoring the armor stand. He buckled the leather straps that closed the back of the hauberk, then settled a helm on the wooden sphere attached to the dummy's shoulders by a thick dowel. The swordbelt he draped over the bed's headboard, and propped up the scabbard against the bedpost. Thus was the king's armor kept at hand, and the sword within easy reach during the night.

Near the fire, Morfran brooded, a jug of wine on the table at his left elbow, an empty cup dangling from his right hand. His wolves lay at his feet like loyal dogs.

The king had been thwarted again by the Dragon. Imre knew it the moment Morfran returned from the caverns, slamming his sword, scabbard and all, to the floor and casting a disk into the flames. The Dragon scale did not burn but rolled out onto the hearth, bringing ashes and coals with it. Morfran stomped it, cursed it, hacked at it with his sword, but the scale appeared as burnished and perfect as ever. Large as the palm of a man's hand, the disk was translucent, glittering, and somehow always warm, even if it had lain untouched for hours in the chill of the king's chamber.

Curiosity was one of Imre's failings.

He went about his duties as quietly as possible then stood in the shadows until called upon. Sometimes Morfran stared at nothing for hours while Imre stood attendance, his feet, back and legs aching. Even now, his eyes burned and his shoulders tensed. In the morning, he would waken to stiff joints and aching muscles, his movements those of an old man instead of a youth.

Elta had a way with ointments and cures. She had a way with him, too. Tomorrow, when she went with Lady Yanámari to tend the herb garden, he might escape his duties long enough to visit the grotto and let his wounds be treated. And steal a kiss.

The king shifted in his chair. Perhaps Morfran roused from his dark mood to call for a pair of jesters and another flagon of wine, or to summon a pair of his mind-turned soldiers to fight to the death and leave the stones slick with blood.

Imre had been in Morfran's service since childhood. He remembered little of life in Cäldon before the king's men gathered folk to serve in Elycia. He had been fortunate, chosen to learn the duties of a royal manservant. He had food enough, and fine clothes, a warm place to sleep when winter howled through the Craydaeg Mountains, and the deference of other servants. There were worse fates.

But the madness and the deaths—

Morfran stood, placing his cup on the small table. The wolves stirred, their ears alert, their eyes watching. "Stay, lads." They lowered their chins to their forepaws. "Come, Imre. Bring your scribing tools."

Imre obeyed, but his hands were clumsy as he gathered ink, quills, and parchments into his goatskin bag, donned a knee-length woolen cloak lined in fleece, and tugged warm supple gloves over fingers grown colder than they should be. He followed the king, who had buckled on his sword belt and gathered a few other items of his own into a pouch with a long strap and red-brown stains that were neither soil nor sweat.

Down the stairs, down, down, past the corridors where the barons slept, past the great hall and the kitchens, past the storerooms, through a great locked door opened by a heavy key kept on the king's belt, through the silent dungeon empty of prisoners, and down a long dank tunnel lit only by occasional torches, a steady progress into the heart of the mountain.

No guards were posted to prevent servants or anyone else, either lost or curious, who might wander these dark ways. There was no need. Imre could enter because he walked with Morfran, the protected of Nar Cahm. Only the king or the Hôk Nar could open the doors. To all others they were unseen—and, were they not, they would still be impassable. Heolstor had marked the doors with his staff. Anyone entering without the company of the Brethren would be stricken, burned by unseen fire, and reduced to ash.

The tunnel ended in a hub of tunnels, a vast echoing cavern from which other passages led, the black legs of a hollow spider. Morfran's stride lengthened as he led the way across the cavern, and there was laughter in his quickened breath. Who would die tonight?

The tunnel smelled so foul that Imre's stomach revolted. He stopped, leaning his forehead against damp stone to cool his face.

"Weakness, Imre. Weakness."

The king disdained weakness almost as much as he hated disloyalty, yet would not continue toward the Dragon without a scribe to record his cleverness.

Imre pushed away from the wall. *One day, he will turn his amusement on me, and another will write the bloody tale.*

The tunnel forked, and Morfran chose the branch that took a sharp turn upward. It soon became stairs. When the smoke thickened, no longer the result of noxious torches, a Black Hood stepped from one of the hollowed-out rooms that were part of each tunnel. He offered damp rags soaked in an infusion of herbs. Imre tied the cloth behind his head, masking his nose and mouth, but it was only slight help against the fumes.

The stairs seemed endless, but the rigor and the darkness helped Imre sweep his mind, clearing away, bit by bit, everything that made him Imre. If his mind were to survive what was to come, it must not know itself at the end, after the last screams died and the king's restlessness slept. It must not remember the night's evil when Imre next stood in the clear light of morning. It must not betray the vile deeds his eyes had seen.

Lest he turn from himself and seek solace in madness.

The stair twisted yet again. On the left, a box big enough for three or four people to stand inside was secured to the wall by a rope wound around a double-headed hook. Once the rope was freed, the box swung away from the wall and could be lowered to stair level. Imre held open the narrow door—it reached no higher than his waist —and steadied the box for the king before stepping inside and latching the door. He grasped the pulley rope, and the box lifted into a lightless shaft above the tunnel.

The box rose in absolute darkness, the rope creaking a little, in need of oiling. Imre continued his cleansing, scrubbing away Elta's features, her voice, her touch. Then he worked backward, through his duties as a manservant, through the years spent in battle camps in the Lowlands then the Calhoun Forest, back to the day he was taken captive as a boy, and then—the very last vestige of himself—the removal of his name.

Fatherless and unknown, the scribe grabbed the double-headed hook and secured the rope to it. His master disembarked before the scribe could hold the door for him. By the time the Brethren had brought a table and a chair and set a candle before him, by the time parchments and quills were arrayed on the table before a great golden Dragon with mocking green eyes, the scribe was attuned to every detail, every breath and word and gesture of his master.

He began to write.

Two cages remained, full of captives undevoured. Morfran studied them, his hands behind his back, ignoring the Dragon.

Some prisoners lay as if asleep. Perhaps they were. Perhaps they had succumbed to the smoke and even now stumbled toward the Otherland, not able to see the path, for the sun had long set and the way was dark. Other prisoners sat in attitudes of defeat, heads hanging, shoulders slumped. Three still stood, clinging to the bars.

Morfran raised a hand, and one of the Hôk Nar glided from the shadows.

"Unlock the Kels."

"Yes, my lord."

The cage door opened, but the prisoners only stared up at him. Hope was long fled, taking with it any thought of escape.

Morfran grabbed the nearest captive, a woman. She whimpered, and the small sound annoyed him. Turning her so that her back was to the Dragon, he yanked her hair to the side and pulled down the neck of her kirtle, revealing the brand of the House of Kel.

"You see this, Dragon? You see this? It is the mark of your enemies. And yet you refuse to consume this woman. Are you frightened? Weak? How else could the chieftain of the Gremian Kindred be captured and led here, held thrall by a single iron chain?"

A snort of sulfurous smoke, yet the eyes did not widen nor the head lift. The chieftain derided Morfran's insults.

"Well, then, Dragonking. See now my malice toward those who would pretend to the throne of Skarda."

Taking a dagger from his belt, Morfran drew a neat square around the brand on the base of the Kellish woman's neck. Her whimpering grew louder, but his tight clamp around her torso, binding her arms to her sides, kept her in place. Thin red lines welled beneath the dagger's point.

"I will add your mark to the others already adorning my wall," he murmured against her thick hair, "and treasure the memory of this moment every time I look on it."

The tip of the dagger retraced each line, cutting deeper, spilling crimson across her white neck, along her white shoulders, down her white back. She writhed in his grip, and he smiled.

"You will tell me everything you know about the heir of Kel. If you speak the truth, your death will be quick and painless. If you lie, you will live as long as I choose, but you will pray for the edge of my blade as a thirsty man prays for water."

Weeping, she gasped, "Please, please, my lord! I know nothing!"

Trailing the bloody dagger lightly along her cheek, he shook his head and said gently, "That truly is a lovely brand. A work of craftsmanship. One wonders why you Kels persist in making yourselves such easy prey. One would think you would realize—"

"Please, my lord!"

"—that bearing such a mark, always the same place, always the same sign, would be foolish when your people are being hunted."

She babbled broken phrases, but he paid no heed. Could they not look on one another and see the bloodline? Could they not almost *smell* their ancestry?

Yet, holding the woman and studying the other wide-eyed Kellish captives, he conceded that centuries had corrupted their blood, for there was little similarity in their features.

But wait. Look there. That man in the corner—the shape of his eyes is akin to the youth's standing by the bars. And the white-faced woman rocking the infant has thick hair the same color and texture as does this woman I hold. Yes. One Kel should know another, regardless of this pretentious mark on their backs.

He ripped the patch of skin from her neck—she screamed then fainted—and a waiting Brother caught the scrap in a pan of saltwater brought from the Dävra Sea for this purpose. Morfran let go, and the woman slithered to the floor.

The prisoners cried out, some calling curses upon his head, others wailing, thinking the woman already dead. He turned from them and looked up at the Dragon.

"There are other Dragons here. Younglings. Surely some are your own offspring, so large and hearty are they, and stubborn. They will welcome a feast. But you? You shall starve until you open your mind to me and find for me the heir of Kel."

The green eyes glittered and the great head lowered, the nostrils blowing a hot foul wind that pushed Morfran backward a few steps. A growl rumbled deep inside that massive chest, and shook the floor.

Morfran smiled. "Brethren, wake the woman. Bring the prisoners." He cleaned the blade on the hem of her kirtle then sheathed the dagger. "Come, Imre."

When Imre did not stir, the king kicked the table, rousing him.

The younglings were kept in a warren of small caves, and each cave was secured by doors of iron plates welded to the bars of old cages. Small openings in the doors allowed the younglings to look out into a common area linking the caves, as a courtyard links a group of buildings. Spurts of flame and smoke pushed through the openings, and the eager sounds of hungry Dragons echoed through the common.

One by one, prisoners were questioned and tortured, and the frenzy grew among the Dragon young. Screams whetted their appetites, and the smell of blood crazed their minds. When all the Kellish brands were floating in the basin of seawater, and all the Kels lay broken and too wounded to flee, the Brethren opened the cave doors.

From his place just inside a tunnel, Morfran laughed to see the younglings spew their fire on one another, tear each other's wings with razor-like talons, crush the Kels with one stamp of their clawed feet. Their dispute sent stones raining, and he covered his head with his arms. Fire belched from the mountain, and the glow of it blazed against the far side of the River Thrayne, as if the broad fields of snow had been set alight.

Beside him, face impassive, motions unhurried and steady, Imre wrote.

The Dragon young quieted, circling, snatching at Kellish flesh, growling low in their throats, eating while keeping watch on one another.

Into the slow-gathering calm roared a sudden thunder, deep inside the mountain.

Morfran turned toward the sound, raised his fist, and shouted, "I will rule you yet! I! Morfran of Skarda! I shall be the Dragonking, and you, o great one, shall be my slave!"

He laughed as the patches of skin were skimmed from the basin and dropped into his bag, adding to its stains. He laughed as Imre packed away the scribing. He laughed through the tunnels and across the central cavern and down the echoing paths of the dungeon. He laughed as he staggered like a drunken man through the storerooms and past the kitchens. Only when he fumbled for a sturdy shoulder to lean on did he realize Imre's expression was still blank, his manner still unnaturally calm.

"Imre lad"—Morfran draped one arm across the servant's shoulders and slapped him in the chest with the palm of the other hand—"You need wine. I need wine. The wolves need wine. We all need wine. Except for the chieftain. But he will bow. Never doubt that. His children are my slaves. And the skins! I wonder how many Kellish brands it takes to make a cloak?"

In his chamber, he dropped his sword and the bag, stumbled toward the tall curtained bed, scrambled up the steps, and flopped across the soft expanse. The wolves moved to lie on the floor beside him.

He slept without dreams and woke refreshed, though he could not understand why he was fully clothed or why his hands and garments were stained with blood. When he asked Imre, the boy replied in vague phrases.

There were shadows under Imre's eyes. Morfran admonished him to get more rest, and not stay up reading scrolls or copying texts. Then the king tore a leg from the small roast fowl on his tray, gulped a cup of iced wine, and told Imre to take a message to Lady Yanámari, reminding her to wear the white gown tonight, the one with the black Dragon on the sleeve.

A fine day this would be. A very fine day.

191

22 ~ ELYCIA

Gaerbith woke to a sense of something out of place. It was not yet dawn. The horses stood tied at the cave's mouth, the men slept, but something was not right.

He shifted his body enough that he could look behind him. At the rear of the cave, a light glowed just enough to reveal High Lord Boorn's face. He gazed into his hands from whence the light came, his expression almost triumphant.

The earth trembled. Horses neighed, tossed their heads, pulled against their ropes. Boorn looked up. The light disappeared.

Thunder growled through the mountain. In the river chasm, light flamed, illuminating the distant cliffs.

"The ground shakes!"

"Look! The standing stones are moving!"

"Bring the horses inside!"

Across the chasm, boulders bounded down the mountainside, and a field of loose stones slipped and tumbled in its wake. Dirt rained from the cave roof, silting through unseen cracks and gritting Gaerbith's eyes.

"What kind of war machine makes fire?"

"Not a machine—a monster!"

"The magic of the Hôk Nar."

Watching the majestic storm, men stood at the cave's mouth, heedless of the danger, until the cracked earth yielded no more fire and the thunder faded to a rumbling echo. The standing stones wavered but did not fall.

In the silence, some men wandered back to their places and settled down to sleep. Others wanted to inspect the damage, but Gaerbith ordered them remain. The sun at least two hours from rising, there was no point in exploring until they had light.

No sooner he spoke than the thunder returned, and fire belched from high in the east, smoke billowing like wind-driven clouds, wreathing the peaks. An odor drifted down—the smell of decay and filth and brimstone. Then, as before, the world fell silent, and the only fire kindled was that of the cold stars, their pale flames glittering in a lucid sky of deepest blue.

Gaerbith lay back and stared up into the arching expanse, but not long. Neither earthquake nor fire nor the threat of the road being blocked by a rockslide could keep his eyes from closing or his thoughts from sinking into dreams. He saw again the blood-streaked warrior, heard again the plea to find the heir of Kel, but his bones were too soft and his sinews too rigid, and he could not summon any urgency great enough to move his body from its chosen place.

When he woke again, the sun was high. He was not alone in sleeping late. A few men rose soon after he did, but most remained curled or sprawled on the cave floor, their usual acute senses dulled by prolonged weariness.

Young Trag was one of the early risers. He greeted Gaerbith with a nod then tended High Lord Boorn's horse, feeding it a bit of grain from the bags, letting Owen make the report on the scouting yesternight.

Gaerbith listened in silence as his brother described in straightforward tones the stair and the wide sloping curve of the road as it neared the city, whose distant walls could be seen after perhaps an hour's journey. The Fourth could be in Elycia by sunset.

As he pondered the piled stones at his feet, Gaerbith became aware that Owen had asked a question. He looked up.

"Will you show me how to fight?"

"Axe, knife, mace, or sword?"

"Sword. Father taught us all the knife."

"Aye. Sword it is."

Gaerbith drew Bítan, and Owen struggled to untie the single-edged Skardian sword that hung down his back.

Turi made a short, sharp motion, and those men who were awake leapt to help clear rubble from the open space. They pushed it with their feet, piled it with their hands, and some even sacrificed the edges of their swords to scrape the ground clean.

"Set aside your bow and quiver," Gaerbith instructed, "and take my sword for yours."

"But—"

"Take it."

Frowning in concentration, Owen lifted Bítan until its blade rose at a dangerous angle toward his shoulder and neck.

"Turn it. Yes, like that. Plant your feet. Extend the blade. Straight out, shoulder high. Both hands. Excellent. Now one hand."

Bítan tipped toward the ground.

"Your sword must be as supple as your own hands, your own skin. Would you let your fingers trail in the dirt while you shot your bow? Lift the sword. One hand."

The cords of his neck standing stark and rigid, Owen obeyed.

"Now the other hand. Good. Good. Straight out to the left. Now the right. Know its length. Feel the wind's breath along its edges. Hear the blade hum? It speaks. It knows what it can do. All that remains is for you to learn what you can do."

The Skardian blade felt like a twig in Gaerbith's hand, light as a child's toy, and for a moment he felt lost without the solid, familiar weight of the longsword. "Attack."

Owen stared at him.

"Attack!"

The boy started forward at a staggering run, and Gaerbith stepped left—Owen's right—and tapped his brother's sword arm with the flat of the Skardian blade. "Never expect your opponent to stand still and wait for you. Try again."

Owen's eyes sparked, and Gaerbith smiled. Let anger overcome uncertainty, and something might actually be accomplished.

Two passes later, their blades rang together, the sound sharp and clean. Gaerbith laughed aloud, Owen snarled, and the lesson truly began.

Gaerbith slipped and danced the lighter blade under and inside the reach of the longsword, but there were a few times when the sheer weight and length of Bítan almost gave Owen victory. Sweat stood out on the boy's brow and soaked his tunic. His movements were slow and awkward, but as the drill continued, he gained a measure of grace.

"Hold." Gaerbith stepped back, lifting the tip of his sword skyward and catching the blade in a loose grasp. "The day grows old, and I am hungry."

Owen's arms trembled, and he had stumbled on that last attack, but Gaerbith would not shame him by acknowledging it. They exchanged weapons again, and Gaerbith clapped him on the shoulder. When Owen joined Trag by the horses, Warrten nodded at him. The boy ducked his head.

High Lord Boorn led his horse toward the stair. "Finished playing, captain?"

Gaerbith tore off a piece of dried meat with his teeth and chewed the tough mouthful without haste. He washed it down with a swallow of musty water from the skin then nodded.

Kraekor followed him without having to be called or led. The emissary let Gaerbith and the warhorse pass, and the Fourth fell in behind. The climb was a stroll compared to the scrabbling ascent of yesterday, and Gaerbith relished the stretch and bunch of muscles being put to their normal use. Perhaps an hour into the climb, he realized he breathed easier, as if the mountain no longer withheld its precious store of air. When the Fourth passed through a thin layer of fog—a ring of clouds, in truth—he paused to look back and down, amazed at the clarity of light and the blue-hazed distances visible from the height.

He could nigh forget he walked into a trap.

The sun had begun its western descent by the time the stair ended and the road broadened. Gaerbith saw no other road leading onto it. If there was a safer pass through the Craydaegs, it did not enter here.

Though the way was still bounded by granite cliffs on one side and a sheer drop on the other, the angle was not steep, seeming more a wide path up a gentle rise rather than the last distance to a mountain city. Like old scars long-healed but still marring the skin, ancient chisel marks gleamed pale on the cliffs where workmen had peeled away slabs of rock to broaden the road. The slabs had been used to build Elycia.

The Fourth rounded a turn. The road straightened, and before them stood the grey gates. Corpses rotted in iron cages hung from gibbets on either side of the road. Crows plucked at the carrion, or flew away with hanks of flesh draped from their beaks.

Turi muttered, "An omen."

"We will not be fodder for crows."

Turi's expression twitched.

"Smile, my friend," Gaerbith murmured as High Lord Boorn

halted nearby. "We know our enemy. He does not know us."

"Small comfort," but the bear-like man attempted a smile that might have given nightmares to small children.

"I will ride into the city," High Lord Boorn announced, looking up at the city gates. "You, too, captain. And all men with fit horses."

By *fit*, Boorn did not mean horses in good health but ones with good height and pleasing appearance. Only two or three answered to that description. The rest were sturdy work animals.

Gaerbith examined Kraekor's wounds. They had healed nicely, though the hide was still bald around them. He slathered fresh salve on the tender new skin and placed a folded blanket across the horse's back. The saddle had been left with the men who returned home, for Kraekor had been unable to wear it when the journey began, and there was no reason to burden another horse with the weight of an extra saddle. The blanket served very well.

From his pack Gaerbith took a bundle of sticks, evenly shaped and sanded smooth. Fitting nub end to bored end and twisting, he fashioned a staff, and on it he tied the Dissonay standard: green broidered on white, the Oak of Disson, its limbs widespread, its trunk broad. In ancient time, the oak was revered as the dwelling place of Turwen, god of the forest, but the old gods had died, replaced by one almighty being—Omwen'din, the Voice, maker of the oak, who freely offered wisdom to Men.

"Captain."

Looking up, Gaerbith met the emissary's cool gaze.

The man had brushed his fur cloak, and restored order to his garments. "If you are ready, captain."

Gaerbith gave Kraekor a pat on the chest; the horse knelt, Gaerbith sat astride, and Kraekor rose with easy grace despite his burden.

High Lord Boorn harrumphed, kicked his mount's flanks, and led the remaining distance to Elycia.

The Fourth strode forward with knocked arrows or drawn swords, watchful eyes scanning the cliffs, but there was no ambush, no Nar'ath, only the cawing crows with their feast.

Sculpted of granite hewn from the surrounding mountains, the closed gates presented the carved image of a black Dragon, wings outspread, stone fire spewing from open jaws. Kellish letters arched over the whole.

Yevahn Nar Sal
Yevahn Drekáthim
Yevahn Ven Ethem
Yevahn Tahrn Asryn

Gaerbith caught himself after the first three words: *Rise, Dark Voice*—not a prayer he would willingly pray.

Watchers on the walls shouted to one another and the gates opened, the great hinges and pins moving as easily as water slipping over stones, laying bare the city. The Dissonay entered. Strangely silent common folk gathered in a spacious square surrounded by massive stone buildings. Lord Boorn halted. Gaerbith looked around.

A disturbance arose in a narrow street, pushing people against the walls and scattering the crowd in the square. Clad in scarlet tunics, Young Wolves arrived. At their head rode a dark-bearded man in a similar surcoat, a gold Dragon blazoned across the chest: Morfran, king of Skarda. A madman with sword and dagger, the king's mastery seemed only to grow in battle's heat, and no man could stand against him. For his violent gift, the Dissonay called him *Bachaná*, the Butcher.

Gaerbith had never crossed swords with him. What kind of warrior was he? What quirks and tricks did he employ in combat? Every man had a weakness. It was just a matter of finding the breach, however small, for even the sharpened end of a quill pen could kill if rightly applied.

A tall man, the king sat his horse as a tower dominates a town, his steed one or two hands higher than the largest horse among those of his guards. Halting, he uttered a sharp command. Three wolves, tongues lolling, trotted from the ranks of the king's men. Their hides glittered as if each hair were tipped in metal. On large paws fitted with gleaming claws, they paced back and forth, in and out, tracing a menacing pattern between the king and High Lord Boorn.

Tossing its head, the emissary's mount backed away.

Kraekor shifted his hooves but otherwise stood still. A shiver twitched under his skin. The old roan had been through many a battle and faced foes fierce as any wolf. He would be alert but unafraid.

Gaerbith lowered the Dissonay standard in an ancient sign of truce, showing that the blunted tip of the staff was not a spear.

The king nudged his horse forward, parting the wolves, and

clasped Boorn's forearm, greeting him in Skardian. "Welcome. I trust your journey was well-sped."

"Peace is an eager guide." Boorn's Skardian was crude but serviceable.

They smiled, but not in amusement. This was a subtle dance between words and meaning.

Boorn continued, "How fortunate if our meeting be not vain."

"Indeed." Morfran turned to one of his men. "Prepare quarters for these men with all haste."

The Young Wolf nodded crisply and clattered away to do the king's bidding.

The hospitality was all show. With Nar'ath watching the road, Morfran had known precisely when the Dissonay would arrive, and had already set aside a place where they could be easily watched. Indeed, they likely seemed easy prey—outnumbered, almost all on foot, weary, hungry, needing drink—but, from the wary way the Skardians stared at them, the pureblood Young Wolves feared the bite of mongrel dogs.

Gaerbith chuckled.

"You are amused?" A Wolf's eyes narrowed. "Tell me your name that I may spit when I hear it."

"Gaerbith tha Forba, captain of the Fourth Lachmil. Your name I need not know. I would only forget it."

All heads turned toward him, gazes fixed in keen awareness.

The other man opened his mouth, but Morfran said, "Peace, Gurn. You will have time enough for sport when you meet in the Court of Soldiers. There will be no blood shed this night."

With a glare that promised he would not forget the insult, Gurn made way for the king and the emissary. He let Gaerbith pass but turned his mount too quickly, ramming Kraekor's shoulder. The warhorse's hooves scrabbled on the slick stones paving the square, and he fought for footing. Gaerbith spoke soothing words and patted Kraekor's neck. Gurn sneered as he returned to the ranks of the Young Wolves.

Beyond them, ranged against the city wall, stood a line of narrow wagons piled with goods. A merchant caravan. Surely it did not use the old pass. There must be another path. Gaerbith would speak to the head merchant and learn how the carts traversed the mountains.

King Morfran led High Lord Boorn through a street so narrow

their boots almost touched the walls on either side. People scurried out of the way, squeezing into available doorways as Morfran passed, his wolves as escort. Behind them were the Fourth, and further behind them the Young Wolves. The only sound was the solid beat of hooves echoing between the high walls of the narrow streets. Colorless gloom lay over the city. Late afternoon sunlight struck the upper reaches of the walls, leaving the streets in shadow. The one bright thing was the Dissonay standard, yet even its green branches hung slack in the breezeless streets.

The strange quake yesternight had left detritus in the city, broken stones of varied hue and grain, the broken edges of dressed stones paler than their weathered, discolored faces. Some were piled, some swept against the buildings, perhaps in hasty effort to clear the streets.

Other than the damaged stones, everything was square, orderly. Drains marked the streets at intervals, and the usual foul waste odors did not exist. When streets turned, they did so at clean angles. There was nothing that invited one to wander the city or linger in company of friends. There were few signs over doors—Gaerbith saw two alehouses, a bootmaker's shop, and the crossed chisel and mallet indicating a stonemason—and there seemed to be fewer people than there were houses, which themselves had the same haunted look as their dwellers, blank-eyed and pale. Why did the people not leave this place and seek the softer, warmer Lowlands?

Houses rose skyward, hovel stacked on hovel. He could not imagine living penned like an animal in a cramped cage. No space, little color, stark mountains hoarding the city in a chill embrace—it was no strange thing that the people were silent and hunched. He might have thought the folk were mind-turned but for the fear lurking in their eyes.

Uártha's words from long ago: *Where fear has taken hold, there is no need for magic. Men will bind themselves, and have no need of gaolers.*

Somewhere in the mountain, thunder rolled.

"They come, my lady!"

Yanámari looked up from the text she studied. She sat near the fire, a sheaf of pages stacked into two piles—read and unread—on a wide table that also held a candlestick, an inkwell, and a cup of wine. "The Dissonay?"

"Oh, yes, them, of course. But I meant the merchants!" Elta grabbed her mistress's hand and knelt beside her chair. "Now I can tell you my plan."

"You are a lively mystery, Elta," but Yanámari waited, smiling.

"I have discovered a use for that ugly brace of horse-head candlesticks."

"I noticed they went missing this morning. Thank you."

"We will ride out of the city on the backs of those horses."

Near the base of the royal tower, and separated from it by a vast complex of stables, lay the Court of the Soldiers, comprised of low stone longhouses arranged around small courtyards. In the center of each courtyard bubbled a fountain.

Nickering, Kraekor tugged the reins, and Gaerbith's parched throat ached for a taste of fresh water.

The barracks were austere, with a few small windows high in the walls and only one door on the end of each longhouse, yet the short passages between the courtyards were broad enough for two or three horsemen to ride abreast.

To the right, a great tower built into the city wall pushed up to a dizzying height, and on the far side of the stables was a similar tower, though it appeared to stand free, unattached to anything around it. What need there was for such massive keeps, or the archers and spearmen on the walls? Did not the mountains stand guard, and the elements? Elycia had been fashioned from living stone. It would not fall to the brave remnants of a ragged Dissonay *lachmil.*

Gaerbith drew a deep breath. He looked up into the wide sky alight with sunset and felt tension uncoil in his chest, as if a rope loosened and unwound. Come what may—

Their escort stopped beside barracks where the door stood open. A fountain chuckled, however, and the Dissonay surrounded it, lifting dripping handfuls of icy water to thirsty mouths.

"Nay, captain," said Morfran as Gaerbith started to dismount. "You accompany High Lord Boorn."

Someone laughed, and Morfran continued, his voice almost pleasant. "Your men will be quite safe here, captain, among the barons' men. My foot soldiers are lodged nearest the stables, and the Young Wolves, of course, do not mix with common soldiers, so there will be little need for concern."

As if such long-standing enemies as Skardian soldiers and Dissonay warriors would remain neatly in their little boxes like obedient children sent to their beds.

Turning to follow the king and the emissary from the courtyard, Gaerbith cast a quick warning glance to Turi, who lifted his chin in acknowledgment.

Aye, captain, said that slight gesture. *We will look behind us and remember we are the hunted.*

23 ~ ALLIANCE

Nothing adorned the white gown but a black Dragon broidered on one wide sleeve. Yanámari turned, holding up her hair so Elta could tug the gown closed and secure the strings in a sturdy tie at the nape of her neck. Brushed to a high sheen, Yanámari's hair was unbound, its thick waves warming her back and shoulders. The gown was light, meant for summer's heat and not the lingering chill of mountain spring, but she was not allowed the warmth of a shawl lest it obscure the mark of the House of Morfran.

Elta uncoiled a black and silver girdle. The belt was heavy, made of leather and metal, ungainly, meant for nothing more than drawing attention to Yanámari's shape. The king had sent it, however, so it must be worn. It circled Yanámari's hips, Elta buckled it closed, and the tongue of the girdle fell to the hem of the gown, swaying with every step.

Yanámari kicked at it and muttered an oath.

Then she shook back her left sleeve and buckled the slim straps of a slender sheath to the inside of her arm. With the fluid fabric covering her hand to the base of the thumb, the knife's silver haft was concealed, its shape nigh invisible beneath the loose sleeve.

Elta handed her a thumb-sized scrap of cloth on which a single word was written: *Now*. The message was for Imre.

Having paid the lead merchant to hide them among the carts when the caravan left the city, Elta would wait in the shadows near the gates. Imre and Yanámari would meet her there and exchange fine clothes for common.

As Yanámari tucked the cloth into the sheath, she hoped there would be opportunity at banquet to slip the message to Imre, and wished again that the secret passages led outside the tower. "Have you ever wondered why we never encounter anyone else in the passageways?"

Elta slid her arms into the holes of a sleeveless overdress a shade or two lighter in color than her kirtle, and short enough to let the other garment's hem show beneath it in a wide band of dark blue. "No, my lady."

Yanámari turned to look at the fire. "Arien"—she could almost say his name without her throat clenching off the syllables—"Arien once said he doubted anyone else knew about them."

"Not even Heolstor?" Elta's pleasant round face seemed scooped and hollowed by the shadows as she turned from the firelight. "After all, the Brethren used to live here."

"Have you the candles?"

Elta patted the side of her skirt, where a hidden pocket was sewn in her blue kirtle. "And more here." She lifted a woven basket piled with laundry. It hid changes of clothes, food tied in a bundle, and coins from selling the candlesticks.

A prayer leapt into Yanámari's mouth, but who would hear? She could not ask help of Nar Cahm, and did any good deity exist? So she swallowed the words, smiled thanks at her maid, and led the way down to the great hall.

The basket at their feet, she and Elta stood in the shadows outside the hall, and watched others enter.

With a few youthful exceptions, the Dissonay were tall men, broad at the shoulder. They arrived at banquet in simple garb, their leather armor and mail covered by stained and patched white tunics that had seen much service and were blazoned with the green Oak of Disson. Thick-soled leather boots covered their feet, and baldrics crossed their chests, securing scabbards on their backs. Wild-haired and bearded, the Dissonay walked with bold strides. At the fore strode a grey-haired man of distinguished mien, accompanied by a stern-faced man with a neat beard and a slight halt to one leg.

"Their names?" Yanámari whispered.

"The old one is High Lord Boorn, the king of Disson's emissary," Elta replied. "The young one is a captain and Lord Boorn's guard, and the soldiers say he is magic, but the servants did not know his name."

They were followed by the Young Wolves, who arrived in long

black surcoats blazoned with a gold wolf's head. They wore ceremonial swords, the blades of which could still kill if need be, and their feet were shod in supple leather rather than the metal-heeled boots worn in battle. In their wake came a clutch of servants, among them Imre carrying a jug of wine marked with the king's seal and meant only for the king's goblet.

In the shadows, unseen by Imre, Elta touched her soft brown hair and tugged at the strained bodice of her plain blue gown. Yanámari pressed her lips shut to keep from smiling. Elta caught her glance, frowned, then blushed.

Three Black Hoods passed on their way to banquet.

Yanámari clasped Elta's hand then let it go. Farewell—for the moment. The maid picked up the basket then disappeared into the darkness.

Yanámari shivered. Could she do this? Would her courage fail?

A soft footfall. The murmur of cloth on stone.

She turned.

A Black Hood stood just inside a circle of torchlight, one shoulder and the side of his cowl illuminated, the rest darkness.

Again a prayer for help without anywhere to direct it. Yanámari let the words plead for her in silence.

She drew a deep breath, stepped from the shadows and into the corridor, and met Gwar the steward at the door of the great hall. He nodded to the musicians, thudded a thick oaken staff on the stone floor, and called out, "Yanámari, Lady of Skarda!"

Beside him, a servant struck a bell hung from a frame as tall as he. The Young Wolves formed two facing ranks on either side of the doorway and stood shoulder to shoulder as she entered. Mouth stiff, she smiled, nodding to one or another of the young men along the living corridor. She tried not to see how they looked not toward her face but to where the heavy girdle accented her movements, circling her hips, swaying between her knees as she walked to the high table.

Rhôn bowed his head as she passed. "My lady."

"Thank you," she murmured.

If she chose him—

On the dais sat the stern-faced man. The enemy.

He met her gaze, and his eyes narrowed a little. The heat of shame crept along her skin. Did he see her humiliation beneath the rigid smile?

Her chin raised a fraction, and humor roused in his ice-colored eyes. She almost smiled in return.

Yanámari mounted the steps to her place. Seated beside her father, she was unable to see the man. Relief mingled with disappointment.

Fire-haired Rhôn Bergsson and dark Gurn Grumësson raised their goblets to her and drank, Gurn staring at her over the rim of his cup. She smiled and lifted her goblet but drank to neither one, pretending to be distracted by the servants bringing trays of dried fruit, roast fowl, and fresh-baked bread. She ate little. Hands trembling slightly, she touched the corners of her mouth with a napkin after almost every bite and sipped at her wine, making the appearance of a hearty appetite.

As another course was served, the Dissonay emissary and the captain were introduced, and Skardian nobles and provincial barons came forward, bowing to King Morfran as their names were announced by the steward, then returning to their tables.

Ûtgar, son of Baron Markha, the king's cousin, was rarely parted from his comrades-in-arms yet his place at the table sat empty. With Arien dead, he was a close contender for the throne of Skarda. Unless he, too, had been killed in battle.

Yanámari cut her meat into small bites, working up her courage. "Father, where is my cousin?"

"We parted ways in the Lowlands." He gestured with his goblet. "Ûtgar is gone to build his father's tomb."

Yanámari coughed, and washed down the bit of meat with a sip of wine. "Baron Markha is dead?"

"Murdered these many months, but the baroness did not send word until now, not wanting to burden me. Why should the death of an enemy be a burden?" The king smiled, not in mirth but derision. "Why such concern? Do you miss him?"

"Ûtgar or the baron?"

"Sauciness will only see you punished."

Yanámari pushed her lips into an apologetic smile. "I merely note Ûtgar's absence as I might note the absence of a splinter in my thumb." Then, tentatively, "Why was I not told?"

"When the Wolves arrived with their gifts, why did you not then question his absence?"

Because I mourned my brother.

Imre refilled the king's cup, then Morfran stood and lifted the gold-rimmed goblet. "Welcome, friends! Soldiers! Raise your cups in honor of our guests and the return to brotherhood between our kingdoms."

The company saluted the Dissonay and drank deep of the red wine pressed from grapes grown in the Thynathel Hills.

Leaning back, Yanámari glanced past her father's ornate chair. Austere and grave, the Dissonay captain's profile cut along clean lines like carven stone. He seemed a formidable man. At the salute, he took one small drink of the wine then set aside his goblet and drank no more.

Surely he tasted the challenge in his cup. The Thynathel Hills and other Territories were at the heart of the war. They formed a long, kingless border between the two realms. The Hills were rich in grapes and wool. The Western Wood was a place of magic and mystery. The rest of the Territories comprised all the Calhoun Forest and its wealth of hardwood, fish, and mines. How the Territories remained free for so many generations, Yanámari did not know, but it was said every farmer wielded a sword and every fisherman a bow.

A sudden turn, and the captain captured her stare. His eyes widened as if he asked a question, then the corner of his mouth quirked just enough to be mistaken for a smile. Lifting her chin, she turned to look over the heads of the assembled guests.

A quiet chuckle came from his end of the table.

The king's wolves were brought and chained before the dais. Restless, they snapped tidbits out of the air as Morfran tossed scraps of meat or hard crusts of bread.

"My lord," murmured a loathsome voice. The odor of old incense reached skeletal hands to clutch at Yanámari's throat. Heolstor, the king's hooded counselor, spoke as if some foul creature had stolen his voice but left behind a whisper. He mounted the steps and stood beside the king with only a bare motion toward bowing. "There is one among the Dissonay with ill thoughts toward you, my king."

"I doubt not there is more than one man with such thoughts." Morfran looked at the Dissonay emissary. "Why, High Lord Boorn could be the very one you fear. I can tell you with certainty he has little liking for my wolves."

Lord Boorn's thin smile strained toward civility. "True, my lord. I would not choose such to share my table."

"But it is not your table." A dangerous humor lit Morfran's face.

"And they do you great honor, Lord Boorn, by leaving you unharmed."

"I mean no discourtesy—"

The king cut into a large boar haunch on the platter before him. Fat greased his fingers to the knuckles and coated the ruby and gold ring on his right forefinger as he plucked the meat into pieces. "Look not so fearful, your lordship. Our arrangements for peace have naught to do with beasts." Popping a sliver of roasted meat into his mouth, he smiled as he chewed. "Still, were I you, I would give them wide road."

Tumblers, jugglers, jesters, dancers, singers, musicians and poets diverted the noble company late into the night, but never came too near the dais while the wolves remained.

Yanámari looked for a chance to slip Imre the message, but Heolstor remained. Standing on the dais, staff clutched in an age-withered hand, thin white beard brushing the ground, he appeared to watch the cavorting entertainers, but she knew he was aware of every glance and gesture, every whispered word.

"My lady."

She turned. A Young Wolf stood halfway up the dais steps.

"Yes?"

He approached and bowed. "My servant brought this to me." He held out a bundle of rough cloth.

She hesitated then set it in her lap. Looking past him to where a man in livery stood in nervous agitation, Yanámari nodded for the servant to speak.

"The-the Brother said, 'Silver is worthless, and not even gold will pay.' And then—" The servant cleared his throat. "The Brother said you would know what it meant, my lady."

Her fingers tightened around the bundle. "Thank you. I pray your master reward you for this service."

Acknowledging the not-too-subtle hint, the Young Wolf turned to give the servant a coin, then the two men bowed to her and departed.

Pushing the bundle so that it rested on her knees beneath the table, Yanámari folded back a corner of the cloth. Inside was a piece of linen, threads askew where the embroidery had been sliced. The linen was wrapped around a broken bit of woven twigs, once the handle of a basket. Beneath was a stained, wadded ball of fine blue cloth—a kirtle, streaked with ash, strands of hair clinging to the bloody neckline.

Yanámari clamped her lips against a sob.

A foul breath stirred her hair. "What is it, my lady, fascinates you so?"

She shoved the parcel deeper under the tablecloth, letting the bundle tumble to rest against her feet.

Heolstor stepped back. "Your father begs your attention, my lady."

Forcing back tears, she ignored Imre's questioning glance, turned to the king and put on a smile. "My apology, Father."

"We await your decision." He moved his outstretched arm in a slow arc. "Which of these men will you take to husband?"

"I— How can I—" She struggled to keep her voice unshaken by grief and hatred. "How can I choose on the eve of treaty? There are far more important matters to settle. This is not the time—"

"It is the best time." Morfran grasped her chin in his grease-slick fingers, forcing her to look at him. "Choose."

Shoving her head to the side, digging in his fingers with one last bruising pressure, he released her with a snap of his wrist. The bones of her neck popped.

She strove for impassivity even as tears slipped from the corners of her eyes. With a napkin, Yanámari wiped the grease from her face, lifted her chin, and surveyed the great hall. She scarce saw the faces of the assembled men. On her left, Young Wolves blurred into a line of black tunics with gilt splotches on their chests. To her right, the Dissonay were a bright bar of white and green. Ahead, past the fire on the raised central hearth, were the mingled colors of the provincial barons.

Silence filled the great hall.

She looked along the royal dais and met the eyes of the Dissonay captain. His hand coiled into a fist on the wine-stained tablecloth, his expression alive only in the downward twitch of his brows.

She stood, bowed her head, and bent slightly at the waist. "Answer me one question, Father, before I declare my betrothed."

"Be quick about it!"

Still in submissive stance, she lifted her gaze to meet his. "Do you truly desire peace with our brother kingdom?"

"Indeed. Peace and a prosperous future."

Yanámari straightened. "Then I choose a husband to strengthen those intentions." She pointed at the captain. "I choose him."

Indrawn breaths hissed like serpents, and curses spat from curled lips. Every Skardian man stared at him in anger or disgust. High Lord Boorn glared.

Gaerbith did not look at his men, but saw them from the corner of his eye, putting fists to their mouths or ducking their heads to keep from smiling too broadly. They need not speak Skardian well—or at all—to know what happened.

"My lord the king! Surely you will not let this decision stand!" A fat baron rose, his face red, his voice angry. "He is *that* captain!"

Young Wolves stood and drew their swords.

The Dissonay did not even raise their hands to the hilts jutting over their shoulders. However, those who used their knives to eat now wiped the blades clean on fine table linens or scraped under their fingernails with the blade tips.

Morfran raised his brows.

Gaerbith's sword pushed against his back at an awkward angle, a constant reminder to be alert during the long entertainment, and now the crossguard of the ancestral weapon dug into the back of his neck as he stood. He settled the baldric across his chest and straightened his tunic, taking those brief moments to form a reply.

Desperation crouched in Lady Yanámari's violet eyes. Her father could kill her with little more thought than a man swats a fly. Why did she defy him?

"Lady Yanámari, I am honored by your favor, but I am unfit to be the consort of a queen—"

"Consort? Fool! The man she weds will be king," High Lord Boorn whispered in fierce Dissonay, his face so red that his grey hair looked pure white. "Skardian queens do not rule!"

Gaerbith looked at him.

"Sit down!" ordered Boorn. "You are making a spectacle!"

He could not sit. To do so would insult both Lady Yanámari and King Morfran. Again he looked to where she stood, a rigid column of white. She no longer met his eyes but turned her gaze aside. Her long black hair fell over her shoulder and draped around her arm like the heavy tail of the Dragon broidered on her sleeve.

"I am a soldier of Disson, and a shepherd from the Thynathel Hills. I am not worthy to be the lynchpin of peace, nor do I desire a kingdom. I thank you for the honor, my lady, but pray do not sully the blood of your house."

"You speak well for a dog!" called a Young Wolf, and the others barked, howled, laughed.

The barons sat back with mocking, complacent smiles and drank their wine. One plump baron flicked a hand toward his men. A soldier stepped forward with a crisp bow. The baron nodded once, and the soldier departed the hall with such haste that he set the edges of an arras wavering.

At the mockery from the Skardians, a growling mutter rumbled among the Dissonay, and they half-rose from their benches, but a sharp glance from Gaerbith kept them in check.

Lady Yanámari looked down. "You shame me, captain."

"Pray forgive me, my lady. That is not my intent."

Amusement filled Mad Morfran's eyes. He leaned back in his chair, one forearm resting on the table, and studied Gaerbith.

Gaerbith returned the stare.

The king muttered something then said, "Heolstor."

The old man in the grey robe shuffled forward and removed his hood. Lines grooved Heolstor's face like cracks in the earth when the rains do not come, and his eyes glittered beneath thick, bristling brows. He looked over the king's head, and fixed Gaerbith with a pale gaze.

Gaerbith's heart nigh leaped from his chest. How had he not recognized that carven staff the instant he saw it, and the clawed hands?

He felt a probing pressure in his brain, like fingers digging deep in a knotted muscle. He met the counselor's eyes and pushed back. The pressure waned, but did not release.

Read my thoughts, old man. Read every reeking one, but you shall never find what you seek.

The searching increased, as if a fist clenched around his skull.

You will not rule me as you rule Morfran. I live under Uártha's blessing.

Surprise flared in the counselor's eyes. Gaerbith's mind was released so suddenly he almost stumbled backward. Heolstor's head pulled down toward his grey-robed shoulders like a turtle retreating into its shell. The Master of the Black Hoods clutched his staff and stood still.

"What say you, Heolstor?" inquired the king. "What do you see?"

In the edge of Gaerbith's vision, Turi sat upright and put a hand to the small axe tucked in his belt.

Heolstor was slow to speak. "The captain is formidable," he said in a whispery rasp. "He faces his enemies with full attention."

"So he does. Lord Arien knew that right well." Morfran never took his gaze from Gaerbith's face. "Praise Nar Cahm we did not meet in battle, else I be as dead as my son."

Warning prickled down Gaerbith's spine.

He whirled even as Turi hurled the axe. The weapon tumbled, haft over blade, rousing a small breeze as it passed Gaerbith's shoulder. There was a grunt then a clatter then a crashing thud.

Turi's handaxe buried in the chest of the soldier clad in the fat baron's colors. The dead man's sword tilted drunkenly against the stone wall, and he lay with his feet toward the dais steps, his head hidden by an arras.

"Omwen'din keep you, Turi, you save me again."

"Aye"—Turi grinned, pointing to a broken tooth behind his brown beard—"but I have no wounds like this to mar m'beauty and mark m'great feat."

Warrten snorted. "If that is beauty, me dog's a sweet lass!"

The Dissonay laughed, but they were alone in their amusement.

"Collect this rubbish." Morfran flapped a hand at the corpse. Then he turned his gaze on the nobles. "Baron Hargow, do not forget I am king. I will choose who lives, who dies, and when."

Pale, jowls quivering, the baron slunk down in his seat.

The king added, almost amiably, "I do thank you, however, for attempting to keep the House of Morfran pure. Such loyalty cannot go unrewarded. I will consider the matter."

Turi retrieved his axe before Hargow's men removed the body. Servants emptied buckets of fine-grained sand on the floor to soak up the blood.

Gaerbith still stood, waiting the king's dismissal. Morfran seemed amused by the Lady of Skarda's discomfort. Hands gripping one another, she stood as still as stone.

"A Dissonay soldier, even a captain, is unfit to wed my daughter"— Morfran shook his sleeves back from his wrists—"just as she is unwise to make such a reckless choice. Nevertheless"—he wiped his greasy hands and knife clean on the skirt of the tablecloth before sliding the knife into a decorated sheath at his belt—"her decision shall stand."

"My lord!" A Young Wolf leapt to his feet.

"Sit you down, Gurn Grumësson!" Mofran rose. He glared at the soldier from beneath lowered brows. "All of you."

Men-at-arms and Young Wolves sheathed their swords and obeyed.

"Heolstor shall perform the ceremony at sunrise two days hence." The king looked on Gaerbith with cold displeasure. "On the morrow, a treaty will be born between our two kingdoms, and a wedding feast shall celebrate the peace."

Gaerbith bowed, his teeth clenched.

"Father," Lady Yanámari's quiet voice seemed almost loud in the unnatural silence, "if the matter is settled, I would walk with my betrothed."

"Take Gurn and Rhôn as escort."

Lady Yanámari inclined her head in acceptance.

Imre let out a gusty sigh then immediately bowed in apology. Appearing nowise offended, the king held out his cup for more wine. Gaerbith had recognized Imre but said nothing, just offered a small nod at his smile of recognition. Morfran had no respect for his own family. He would suffer no friendship between his servant and the Dissonay.

Best to study the enemy, not to let him know one's own secrets.

Gaerbith addressed his men. "Warrten and Fremmen, come with me. Turi, choose two men to accompany Lord Boorn then return to quarters. Owen, you and Trag tend the horses."

Servants tried collecting the remnants of the meal, but the Dissonay scooped up leftover bread, meat, and fruit, even confiscated two pitchers of wine before departing.

Owen hesitated once to look back.

Gaerbith nodded. *Go on with you.*

Turning, Owen followed the others.

Lady Yanámari stood, and moved aside her heavy wooden chair. Sinking gracefully, gown pooling around her, she collected a small bundle from beneath the table then rose and descended the dais steps. Her escorts—one surly, one impassive—met her there and bowed. Straightening, Gurn glared at Gaerbith, but Rhôn averted his gaze. He was the only one who had bowed when she entered. He watched her at banquet. Now, he would not look at Gaerbith.

He loves her.

But what could either man do? For reasons known only to herself, the Lady of Skarda had chosen elsewhere.

Gaerbith stepped down to stand beside her, offering his arm. She hesitated—because Rhôn watched, or because the arm belonged to a Dissonay dog? The longer she paused, the more tense he became. Gurn sneered. Rhôn was a blank wall. Behind Gaerbith, Warrten and Fremmen shifted their feet.

Lady Yanámari placed her hand on the back of his, and he realized he had been holding his breath.

Through dim corridors lit by occasional torches, she led the way to a pair of doors carved of stone and graven with a rising Dragon, wings splayed, one wing on each door. Two servants in scarlet threw their weight against a sturdy lever, and the doors swung inward with the same smooth quiet as the city gates. The servants bowed as the small company passed.

The doors led to the thick walls surrounding Elycia. A company of soldiers stood watch, torches at intervals, circling the city like a fiery ring. The light remained on the surface, never penetrating to the dark streets below. A murmur rippled through the guards. Each man dropped to one knee and bowed his head as the Lady of Skarda walked among them.

Yanámari Morfrandötter was no beauty, but her face was one not soon forgotten. In stature, she was like the farm maidens of the Thynathel Hills, but more willowy than those deep-chested lasses. In her white dress, she seemed a pale-barked birch, tall, slender, unbent. He wondered she did not stumble over the tongue of the long girdle circling her hips nor topple forward from the weight of it. He barely felt through the skin of his armor the weight of her hand on his arm.

When their gazes met at banquet, he had caught surprise and haughty annoyance in her eyes. When she chose him, they pleaded. Perhaps her majestic silence now was intended as a reminder of his place. Or a shield against her fear.

"My lady?" asked Rhôn as they passed a broad stair leading down from the wall. "This is the way—"

"Thank you," Yanámari turned to address him, warmth and iron in her voice, "but walls do not interest me. Only windows. I am quite myself now."

By the silent exchange between the Young Wolf and the Lady of

Skarda, some hidden meaning lay beneath her words.

After a moment, she said, "Perhaps the captain wishes to know how well his men are quartered, and the night watch will want fair warning I am coming."

Rhôn flashed a glance at Gaerbith, but inclined his head to Yanámari, and did not speak the objections crowding behind his eyes.

Gurn protested. "Women are not allowed in the Court of Soldiers."

"You think my virtue weak or easily overcome?" Her hand tightened on Gaerbith's arm. "You insult the honor of my betrothed."

"Do you know who he is, my lady? Do you know how many Wolves have fallen before his blade? This is the man who slew Lord Arien! You would ally yourself with your brother's killer?"

She looked him full in the face. "You think, because I am closed in a granite tower, I do not know the outcome of every battle? I am Yanámari Morfrandötter. Neither blind nor feeble, nor wits a'begging. Therefore, Gurn Grumësson, alert the Court of Soldiers the Lady of Skarda is paying a visit."

So it was done. Gaerbith gave a quick tilt of the head to Warrten and Fremmen, signaling them go, and they followed the reluctant Skardians down the broad stone stairs.

Leaning against the parapet, Lady Yanámari hugged the strange bundle to her with both arms. The marks of her father's fingers purpled her chin and jaw.

How could an entire hall filled with men—how could he—not leap to her aid when the king shamed her? Yet, wiping her face, bowing to her tormentor, meeting his scornful eyes and speaking in a clear and steady voice, she had displayed such calm control, such self-possession, that she rescued herself.

"I admire your courage, my lady."

"It is not courage, captain. It is necessity."

Then, "You know Heolstor."

Gaerbith said nothing.

"I have never before seen him intimidated." She studied him a moment. "I do not know your name."

"Gaerbith tha Forba, my lady."

"An old word, *tha*. One might think you a Kel." Then she stood away from the wall. "Come, there is another stair."

"I am no simpleton to go blindly into a new trap."

"A trap will snare us both."

"We have a saying in Disson: Never trust a Skardian."

"We have a saying in Skarda: Never raise your hand to a strange dog."

Gaerbith drew a flat knife from beneath his tunic. "I am not toothless."

She pulled a slender knife from her sleeve. "Nor am I."

"Well, then." He chuckled. "Lead the way."

They sheathed their blades, and he followed her around a tall jutting of rough-hewn stone that obscured a narrow, shadowed stair. The steps abutted the wall on the right, leaving the other side open to the inky pit that was the city of Elycia. Yanámari's gown guided him like the pale shade of Esthenay, who being dead yet guided her husband from the Otherland to life again after his betrayal by a friend. The similarity so struck Gaerbith he almost asked if Yanámari knew the story, but he closed his teeth against it and followed her pallid shape through the chill gloom.

The last steps brought them to a corner of the wall so devoid of light that even her white kirtle reflected neither torch nor moon. He stepped forward. Her hand fumbled for his. Her fingers were cold. Gown swishing across the ground, she led him along an unexpected bit of sward where soft springy turf muffled their footsteps and exuded the brown scent of earth, reminding him of home. A distant light appeared, faint but bright to eyes now accustomed to utter darkness. She released his hand.

They entered a grotto. In place of statuary, hardy young plants sprouted from deep basins mounted on granite pillars of varying heights. Nearby lay wooden boxes filled with earth—raised beds dotted with sprouts.

A bench ran along the walls of the grotto, and she pulled him down to sit beside her. She set the bundle between them. Tears glistened at the corners of her eyes, but she did not speak her sorrow. Their breath hung in the air, but she wore no cloak over a gown that looked like something King Padraig's sisters might wear in summer.

Standing, Gaerbith unbuckled his baldric and belt, tugged his surcoat over his head, and offered it to her. "It has seen hard service, my lady, and it will not keep you much warmer than you are now, but it is mended and clean."

She shook her head, but he held the garment before her until she stood to don the long garment. "Thank you, captain."

Returning his sword to its rightful place and tightening the belt, he said with a smile, "Gurn, I think, bears me no liking."

"Nor me. Not now. Whether or not the treaty council ends the war between your kingdom and mine, my father will never let me be free. He is determined to see me wed into new captivity." Bitterness filled her voice. "If the old gods bless me, I will be a widow soon after."

"You would kill me in my bed?" Gaerbith's smile widened. "I do not surrender to death so easily."

"I will be another man's widow. My father only mocked me by not challenging my choice. He will not let me wed a Dissonay—soldier or noble—unless he sees some advantage to himself."

"What do you require, my lady, that you put us both at peril?"

"Heolstor fears you."

"I am only a man."

"He fears you nonetheless." She gazed up into his face. "Take me with you when you return to Disson." Her words spilled rapidly, as if she feared his denial. "I cannot stay here. I have never been outside these walls. My father would have me die behind them. I have heard there is a great sea north of the mountains, and a broad lowland to the south. There are forests— My brother is dead. There is nothing I hold dear in this place." She laid a hand on his arm. "Please. Take me with you."

"But I fight for Disson, my lady. Your enemy."

"Not mine." Her fingers tightened, gathering the metal links of his mail sleeve. "Is it a matter of money?"

"I am here under banner of truce. How can I steal the king's daughter?"

"You cannot steal one who goes willingly."

"The danger, my lady. A hard journey, even for men seasoned by battle and ill conditions."

"Have you wanted something so great you will sacrifice whatever you must in order to achieve it?"

He had left family and home, set aside his freedom and submitted to a king not his own, to preserve what he loved most. Would it were not in vain.

Yanámari withdrew her hand. "I will leave these walls. Even if I must leap from them."

"Nay, my lady—"

She turned, one side of her face lit by the distant glow, the other side lost in shadow. "That bundle?" She pointed to where it huddled on the bench like a wadded blanket. "My handmaid's garments. She was beheaded for her loyalty to me."

The grim jest among the Dissonay was that only a madman or a simpleton would fight for the Butcher of his own will. All others had to be blind. Morfran had some way of keeping his servants from assassinating him, or the common folk from fleeing the city. Something made men obey him and kept the barons submissive. Something kept the people from rising up against him.

Could a king command true loyalty by fear alone?

"We were going to escape as laborers with a merchant caravan, but the Black Hoods know all, even what we never say. I will not lie to you, captain. If you help me, you risk your life to do it."

"I am a freeman from the Thynathel Hills. For Men of the Territories, freedom is tenuous. We know what it is to live each day as if death were coming each night."

For a long, measuring silence, she looked into his face.

"What do you fear, captain? What steals your dreams and robs your peace?"

The question was an arrow. He almost stepped back from the sharpness of it. "Three brothers and my mother are dead. I dream of home, knowing it will never truly be home again. My brothers are buried in the Hills. Fine strong men, fathers and husbands. One was wounded then captured. At dawn the next day, his broken body was tossed onto the empty battlefield. By his own hand, King Morfran tortured Rabb. He was the eldest, and my father's pride."

"Then you know, captain, why I must leave Elycia." She slid her knife back into her sleeve, and the blade locked into place with a soft snick. "My brother is dead, and now my only friend."

"Lord Arien was a brave man," said Gaerbith. "He fought well. His skill and courage are admired by the Dissonay."

"Gurn told the truth? You slew my brother?"

"I fought him. I was with him when he died."

"You killed him." No emotion, but an intense stillness.

"No, my lady, but I will tell you how he died."

Taking her arm, he led her back to the bench and, knowing he risked much, told of his own grave wounding and the Keepers' gift that enabled him to answer the challenge. When he spoke of the deathblow he dealt Lord Arien, her fingers tightened around one another, but relaxed when he told how he gave the grace of the Keepers to Arien, healing him.

"He spoke, my lady, and perhaps we could have agreed peace in that moment, but a scarlet arrow came from Skardian ranks—"

She laughed, a choked, hard sound. "My father said the man who killed my brother would be at table this night. He spoke true. If it was not my father's hand shot the arrow, then it flew at his bidding."

Rising, she paced the grotto. "Lost to the same evil. Your brothers and mine. Dissonay and Skardian." She looked at him with a slight smile. "No, not Dissonay, but men of the Territories. I envy your freedom, captain."

"A freedom pledged to the king of Disson."

Darkness move against darkness then slide behind an urn on a pedestal. Hôk Nar lurked in the garden.

Gaerbith knelt and, taking the hem of her flowing sleeve, and lifted it to his lips. "Bend down, my lady, and listen well. The Brethren watch us. Smile. Pretend you are pleased with your betrothed."

She obeyed—"It is no pretense"—and touched his face.

The gesture was unexpected. He flinched. Then, seeing the warning in her eyes, he leaned into her touch.

"When we arrive at the quarters," he said, "let my men see you."

Her breath warmed his cheek. "They have seen me already."

"Only as the Lady of Skarda. Now they must see you as a soldier."

"I do not understand—"

"They must find garments in which to hide you."

"In Dissonay colors?"

"You wear them now." Her hand still lingered on his cheek, and he turned his head as if to kiss the palm but looked into the darkness instead. Two more shapes stood blacker than the night. "Do they offend?"

"No. No. But would your men risk so much for me?"

"They would do it for me." The words stabbed. He had already asked too much of his men.

"And why would *you* do this, captain?"

Indeed. She was Mad Morfran's daughter. He should not trust her.

Drinking well into his cups one night, King Damanthus confessed he regretted letting his sister Una marry Morfran, thus linking Skarda to Disson. "We might have remained neighbors, looking over the fence on occasion and exchanging greetings, but now—" Damanthus had sighed, cradling his ale cup lest he spill it. "Now, we are brother kingdoms. There is no feud so bitter as that of blood."

But Damanthus was dead and Padraig was king. He might give his cousin refuge.

"You are my king's kinswoman, and half Dissonay. Such strength as yours should not be stricken from his house."

Her cool hands cradled Gaerbith's face, and she lifted it until their gazes met. The purple of her eyes deepened—perhaps only the trick of shadows—and he could not turn away. With soft lips she kissed his brow then his cheek then his mouth.

His heart jolted, not with fear but with something he did not know.

"It is only a kiss, captain"—she smiled—"not a viper's sting."

"Forgive me, lady. I—"

Best say nothing more. He rose to stand beside her.

She pulled the Dissonay surcoat over her head and handed it to him, picked up the bundle bearing her maid's bloodied kirtle, and said, "We have lingered too long. Let us go, and see the care my father affords your men."

Captain Gaerbith offered to escort her to her chamber, but she bade him remain with his men.

She gathered the skirt of her gown and, the bundle tucked under her arm, walked through the kneeling soldiers with her head high and her steps firm. Past the light from the lanterns, she moved through darkness, her feet finding the low-walled path leading to the door in the royal tower.

From the shadows came the odor of stale incense and a whisper like leaves before the wind. "Well done, my lady. One might almost think you as cold as Mount Cathál, and as strong."

Heolstor barred her way. In one hand was his staff, and in the other a horse-head candlestick, the silver gleaming in the light of distant torches. "One day, I must initiate a formal Sisterhood so you may join the ranks of the Black Hoods. It would be shameful to waste such power."

"Out of my way, Longbeard. I am tired."

With a raspy laugh, he bowed and stepped aside.

She hastened through corridors and up stairs to her chamber. She pushed open the heavy door banded in iron, shoved it closed again and bolted it, then sank to the cold stone floor and rocked back and forth, pressing Elta's bloody kirtle to her breast. No sound came from her aching throat or poured from her open mouth. Tears, hot and stinging, spilled down her face, wetting her gown.

When sound finally came, it was strangled and shrill, a mass of pain pushing through the narrow opening of her throat. Her head pounded, every heartbeat a stab to her brain.

She crawled to the stone fireplace, placed the bloody rags in the center, then dropped a rolled scrap into the fire—the message to Imre, now nothing more than a cruel jest. Then she stirred the coals and added tinder, raising flames, then added wood. The fire grew. Tearing off the fine white gown, she tossed it, too, into the flames, watching the fabric wrinkle and writhe as it was consumed.

The embroidered Dragon on the sleeve seemed alive for a fractured moment before it disappeared.

24 ~ Sleep, At Last

Lady Yanámari left the Court of Soldiers. Rhôn stood, a palm resting loosely on the hilt of his sword, expression still unreadable. Gurn swaggered forward. Gaerbith met his stare and said nothing.

After a long silence, Gurn broke the stare. He signaled Rhôn and walked away.

Rhôn glanced back and nodded. Grateful understanding, or unspoken warning?

"Captain?" Turi crossed his arms. "Best quarter with us tonight."

"Mad Morfran commanded I sleep in the tower."

"Then I guard yer door."

"I need you here."

Turi's mouth opened, but Gaerbith shook his head, refusing any more questions.

Servants arrived with the blankets and pillows Lady Yanámari had ordered brought. None had been provided for the stone benches that served as beds. The Fourth had slept rougher, but she insisted that courtesies be observed.

Basins and pitchers rested in shelves carved above each bed, and a large drawstring bag sat on a raised hearth in the center of the longhouse. Powdered fire, one of the Skardian soldiers said, and showed Owen how to sprinkle it across the hearth and ignite it. It emitted a thin heat.

The Fourth settled for the night, and Gaerbith spoke to Turi quietly, standing on the far end of the longhouse, well away from doors and windows. He relayed Yanámari's request, and Turi nodded. The matter would be handled.

After reciting the warrior's prayer with the men, Gaerbith left the longhouse and passed through the dispersing crowd. Striving to mask his limp—fed by exhaustion until it had grown beyond a small hitch in his stride—he headed toward the tower.

Each man had his own reasons for coming to Elycia, but what they were, Gaerbith did not ask. Even those new-come to the battlefield had lost friends and kindred. How many comrades lay with their feet toward the west? How many more had been burned on battlefield pyres? Like Turi, how many had gone to war because the battle had marched to them, rending their lives but not their courage?

Gaerbith stopped.

The king's wolves lurked in the shadows, tongues lolling, eyes gleaming. The beasts sat on their haunches and returned his stare. In his brief time on the Isle of Morga, he had read of such creatures. They were ordinary wolves taken from their litters just after birth and fed dragon's-milk, a concoction that armored them until their fur was like iron, their teeth and claws like knives. Only a few such wolves could exist at a time. They tended to slaughter one another.

Although kings of old had used natural wolves in battle, Morfran kept his monsters as pets. Why were they here, and not with their master?

"Well, lads," Gaerbith said, "I am tired, and if you do not plan on eating me, go your way. I have no sport for you."

A robed figure materialized from the darkness and uttered a sharp command. The wolves did not obey. The Hood said spoke over his shoulder, and a muscular man arrived carrying three large chains. He whistled. Still the wolves did not respond. He uttered a curse and whistled again.

Gaerbith jerked his head—*go*—and they rose, but languidly, and turned their attention from him.

Neither the Black Hood nor the wolves' keeper acknowledged the captain. As soon as the beasts were secured on their chains, the odd little company vanished into the night.

Gaerbith glanced around. How many more of those apparitions calling themselves Brethren skulked out of sight?

A servant passed with a torch. Gaerbith held out one of the few Skardian coins from his purse and asked the man to illuminate the way to the stables.

Kraekor seemed glad to see his rider, and accepted an apple taken from the banquet, lipping the slices of crisp fruit from Gaerbith's hand one by one, prolonging the treat. There were many seasons for fresh apples, and this was a late winter apple, sharper on the tongue than those grown in the Thynathel Hills. Gaerbith rubbed the horse's neck and chuckled when Kraekor butted his hand, searching for more sweets. "When we reach home, old fellow, we will eat all the apples we want."

Wine apples, honey apples, apples tart as autumn sunshine, apples golden as summer afternoon, green as spring—red as Yanámari's lips.

That was a dangerous road.

Patting Kraekor's scarred withers, Gaerbith bade him goodnight then followed the impatient servant to the tower, where another servant led him up the many stairs to his chamber.

"Wait," Gaerbith said as the man moved away with the torch, and pointed toward Lord Boorn's door. "Where are the guards?"

The man shrugged, sketched a bow, and departed.

Gaerbith knocked, and heard a curse. Boorn had not brought a servant with him, claiming the need for utter secrecy on such a mission, and was likely stumbling around in the dark to find the door.

The bolt scraped back, and the door opened. "Captain." The emissary frowned. He blinked as if the candle in his hand burned too bright. One side of his head was dusty, like a fur fallen in a corner where the servants had not cleaned. "How fare the men?"

"They are well, your lordship. Where are your guards?"

"I sent them away. You must have missed them in the dark."

"I must search your chamber, my lord, for anything harmful."

Boorn stared at him a moment then moved back to let him in. "Be quick about it."

Then, in a tone scarce masked by amity, "It is a strange thing that the king should indulge his daughter's whims. Surely you do not expect to marry her?"

"It is not my place to make such a decision."

Gaerbith searched room and balcony, opening cupboards, tossing back bedclothes, pushing aside curtains, examining the walls behind tapestries, until the emissary bade him stop: "If an assassin were here, he has had ample time to kill me. If one were so foolish as to enter now, he would surely be put to flight by all your noise. Go! I can defend myself from the little ghosties and beasties in the night."

"I cannot perform my duties at a distance, your lordship. It is wiser for me to sleep on a pallet in the chamber or in a chair near the door."

"Go!"

Gaerbith bowed. "Sleep well."

Boorn uttered a filthy oath and barred the door behind him.

One beside each doorway, torches lit the corridor, and the air near the ceiling was thick with strange smoke. Gaerbith opened a shuttered window at the landing, and breathed deep of the crisp night air. Stars glittered in a cloudless sky, the vapor of his breath providing the only misty shrouds. The city below steeped in darkness. No candle flame or torch could he see but the small fires atop the walls. Carved from the Craydaeg Mountains, the city of Elycia was a great granite square, one wall being mountain itself. There was nothing round or gentle here.

Gaerbith longed to see the clover-scented hills of home with their pale stands of birch or dogwood in the north, and slopes draped with vineyards in the south. The red-black grapes of the Thynathel Hills were prized in both Skarda and Disson for their rich wine. Until tonight, many a moon had passed since he had let it roll along his tongue, savoring its sweet bite. There is nothing more tantalizing or frustrating than the scent of fresh warm bread to a hungry man who may not eat it; the brief glimpse of a beloved face; the skim of a short cool breeze on a sweaty brow. In the gilt-rimmed cup, he had tasted home and memory. It were better he had drunk nothing at all than be brought to this melancholy.

High Lord Boorn had married into the wealthy vintner Clan Lunnt, makers of superior wines and hearty meads, and brewers of fine ale. He was a man of vast ambition. His vineyards consumed smaller ones until all the wine in the Hills might someday be his.

Gaerbith closed the shutters and went to his chamber, so small it had likely been something else once, perhaps a cupboard. It had a window, though, and a hearth on which burned one of those weak powdered fires.

He worked his right arm, feeling the tightness around the scar on the back of his shoulder. The weal on his right hip throbbed. Why had the Voice closed the wounds but not taken the pain?

Early in the war, Gaerbith had been knocked from Kraekor and attacked before he could stand upright. It was the first time Turi had saved him, throwing an axe that caught the Skardian high in the chest. Later, Gaerbith gave Turi the man's weapon, a fine blade with an edge harder than granite and sharper than a biting north wind.

"It is not an axe," Turi had said, hefting the sword and sighting along its lines, then shrugging and scratching his beard, "but it might do as a razor."

Gaerbith smiled at the memory. Give Turi a longsword, an axe, and a bow, he was a lachmil all to himself.

After washing his face and arms in a basin of icy water, Gaerbith put aside his surcoat, removed the throwing knives concealed beneath the tunic, and shed the mail. His boots he set side by side at the foot of the bed, and his sword beside him on the coverlet. He lay back on the narrow bed, tucked his hands behind his head, and stared into the dim shadows above. Would there be true treaty tomorrow, or renewal of war? Dare he accept Yanámari as she seemed, or did she play some deep game?

The only women he knew well were his sisters, a few neighboring farm lasses, and his brothers' widows. As for his mother, Uártha had been unusual. Even when he was a young child held in her lap, she spoke to him as to an equal. She treated no one with more courtesy than another, and spoke with an honesty so direct and kind that it was a balm rather than a sting. Uártha had been strong of heart.

So was Yanámari.

What a queen she will be.

His eyelids grew heavy. Turning onto his side, Gaerbith pulled the thick coverlet over his shoulders. Just a little while. Just a little rest before standing watch agai—

25 ~ THE DARK OF HOPE

The cage door scraped open at the prisoner's touch, but he did not step out. Vile darkness clogged his sight, stung his eyes and throat. Hot fumes filled the cavern. Above his head, a glow emanated, so high in the clouds of ash and smoke it seemed a star in the heavens—the Dragon's breath, waiting behind its teeth like a hidden beast, flaring just enough for the prisoner to see the mouth of the nearest tunnel leading away from the cavern.

How long had he been here, embraced by Dragon-spew? How long might he live, now his lungs were heavy with smoke? The Brethren seemed no-wise harmed by it, but their faces were always covered with damp cloths smelling of herbs.

He put one hand beyond the bars, then a foot, then his whole body.

The Dragon did not stir except to breathe. Its great green eyes were narrowed to sleepy slits, not at all interested in the prisoner's movements.

Emboldened, he straightened from the bent posture forced on him by the cage's short confines, and stepped toward the tunnel.

A massive talon appeared, its razor point gleaming through the haze.

He stopped. He scarce dared breathe. His heart thudded. He closed his eyes. When the Dragon's claw closed around him, he did not want to see it happen.

A great sigh—a foul wind—buffeted him, then silence.

He opened his eyes. The talon was gone, and the way to the tunnel lay cleared of smoke.

Syra tugged the blanket around her shoulders, enfolding her son in what scant heat radiated from her thin body.

The weekly ration of powdered fire had been withheld, and no flames warmed their hearth since the king's men took her husband, Rubin. They accused him of burning wood. King Morfran alone had the right to the Craydaeg Forest. It rose across the River Thrayne and was so arduous to reach that few Elycians welcomed their turn to hew wood for the king's fire.

No one was allowed outside the city walls except in guarded groups of laborers to burn refuse, quarry stone, husband livestock in high mountain meadows, tend the terraced gardens across the river from the city, hew trees. Merchant caravans were searched for anyone who dared try escape. Did a brave soul actually flee, he was soon captured, for the Hoods and their Nar'ath were guided by the dark arts and seemed to know one's very thoughts.

Syra touched her son's hair, brown as a pinecone, just like his father's.

Poor Rubin.

No. Fortunate Rubin. He was already free.

26 ~ A Bartered Crown

Lord Boorn brushed cobwebs and dust from his robe. "Captain Gaerbith searched the chamber. He did not find the secret passage, though his hands passed over the door twice."

"An unusual man, the captain." King Morfran gestured at Imre to pour a goblet of wine for the emissary. "I have never seen Heolstor discomfited before this night. Who is this Gaerbith?"

"Nobody. A mere shepherd."

Imre waited until Lord Boorn made himself comfortable in a chair piled with cushions, then he offered him the wine. The emissary took it without a word and held the goblet to his nose. "Red honey grape."

Morfran raised his cup with a slight smile. An unwitting man might have thought it friendly. "The finest treasure in the Hills. Excepting the Royal Boorn grape, of course."

"My sons' sons shall be royal born indeed."

Imre grimaced at the poor jest.

"If I did not fear boredom as some men fear death, I might have ended this war sooner." A yawn threatened to swallow Morfran's words. They were Dissonay, a tongue the king loathed to speak, but Boorn's Skardian was stumbling and rough. The king's Dissonay was flawless. "Does not Damanthus know he is defeated?"

"He is Dissonay, my lord. For him, no lesson is easy."

"How does such a man become the protector of freemen? Does he want the Territories for himself? He says not. I might be tempted to call him a liar but for his straightforwardness in battle." Morfra gestured with his goblet and Imre refilled it, the wine as dark as blood inside the cup. "Were he more subtle, I might have cause to fear him."

"You are Bachaná, my lord," said Lord Boorn. "You need fear no one."

The king slammed the cup on the table. "Never," said Morfran, "call me that again."

Pale, Boorn inclined his head. "As you wish, my lord. Forgive me."

"You are neither kin nor comrade, High Lord Boorn, nor have you stood against my blade." Then, as suddenly as he had grown angry, the king spoke again in composed tones as if he discussed the coolness of spring or the quality of a sword. "We are merely merchants, you and I, haggling the price of a kingdom."

Boorn drained his cup then held it up for Imre to fill. The emissary's hand shook.

"If I may inquire, my lord," he ventured after a short silence, "why let Lady Yanámari's choice stand?"

Leaning his head against the high back of the massive wooden chair, Morfran stared up at the ceiling. "Yanámari." He almost looked pleased. "Would she were a man and took her brother's place. She kicks at confinement, but the struggle will only make her strong. And strong she must be, if she is to be queen of Skarda."

Boorn almost choked on his wine. "She is to rule?"

"On the day Lord Arien fell and all hope for my house seemed lost, Heolstor came to me on the battlefield. My house will rule until a blue sun rises in the west."

"A blue sun? Rising in the west? It will never happen."

"Indeed, it shall not." Morfran's eyes glittered in the firelight. "Through my daughter's strength and through her children, the House of Morfran will rule forever."

"Should Damanthus's son Padraig survive your *peace*, he might be persuaded to wed her."

"You would have me embrace a serpent?" Morfran swirled his goblet. "Padraig is strong enough to husband her, but she is not a quiet consort who will wear a crown merely for ceremony. Yanámari is her mother Una's blood, proud and scarce tamed. Pity she could not have been born pure Skardian."

High Lord Boorn fidgeted, knocking a cushion to the floor. "My lord—" He hesitated. "You are known for craft and treachery, yet you called us the breadth of Skarda to meet you in treaty."

He looked at the king as if expecting chastisement, but Morfran merely waited, expressionless.

"Did I not know our dealings were secret, I would have feared discovery by Captain Gaerbith. He asked questions, my lord, and he expected your men or the Nar'ath to attack us once we reached the mountain passes."

Morfran chuckled. "I expect no less of him."

A dry sound rustled near the door of chamber, and from the other side whined the wolves chained there. The door scraped open. The wolves lay down, chins upon forepaws, as they watched an old man in a long grey robe enter the king's chamber.

Heolstor stood just outside the fire's direct light. He leaned on a staff of carven wood, his thin white beard casting off a faint reflection of flameglow. The room filled with a musty smell.

Morfran set aside his goblet. He stood and opened a shutter. Cold air gusted into the room, swirling flames in the fireplace. The king breathed deep as if he relished the crisp air and, resting an elbow on the broad sill, looked out into the night. "Nar'ath flew to the House of the Brethren after banquet."

Heolstor shuffled forward, holding out a small scroll still tied with the leather string that had recently bound it to the leg of a Nar'ath.

Morfran snatched the scroll from Heolstor's bone-thin fingers and tossed aside the string. Holding the parchment to the light, the king first read it silently then held it out to Imre to later record into the annals.

My Lord the King,

Your servant will soon run to ground the murderer of Baron Markha, my lord's cousin. In my pursuit, I happened upon a handful of Kels in the eastern reaches of the Kelcey Forest. They were duly executed, none of them possessing the skills my lord requires. There are rumors of the Kel-child. They might be true, or nothing more than the wishful memories of old men. Pray Nar Cahm will guide my steps and deliver my lord's enemies into his hands.

Teag

Teag was the king's best hunter of Kels, those dregs of an ancient royal house whose line had fallen a thousand years past yet remained scattered throughout the kingdom like nits to annoy whoever held the throne.

There were countless stories of the Kel-child Morfran sought. Imre had heard them before he had been pressed into the king's service, and even now they were whispered in the city: the Kel-child was dead, he was alive, he had never existed. He lived in Disson and was the real reason for the war. He was a bandit who led the group of rogues known as Kip's Boys. When he returned to take the throne from Morfran, children would hunger no more and all Men would be free.

Whatever the truth about the heir of Kel, there was no doubting he was the only man able to make Morfran uncertain of the crown.

Since the fall of the House of Kel, kingship in Skarda had been a precarious thing. There were rare families who held it for three or four generations, but most lost it within two.

Vegeir, once a wise warrior, had gone mad almost the moment the Dragon Crown touched his head, yet none among the nobles pressed for a new king until Vegeir inexplicably came to himself. Then Morfran, merely a baron's nephew, came forward with such force that he must surely have been aided by Nar Cahm himself. The only way Vegeir could keep Morfran from gaining the throne was by giving it away. So he sought a Kel from the direct line of the old house of kings.

The best Imre could understand from the hodgepodge of stories, Vegeir's men found a boy in whose veins flowed near-pure Kellish blood and in whose hands burned Kellish fire. The king sent for the child, and the boy and his guardian began their journey to Elycia to receive the crown, but Morfran learned of it and ordered them slain. Before he found them, however, man and boy disappeared.

Once the kingdom was wrested from Vegeir, Morfran hastened to find the one true threat to his throne. He plundered villages, burned farms, tortured anyone suspected of knowing the child's whereabouts, but no one in the kingdom had any knowledge of a small boy who carried blue fire or bore a curious mark on the back of his neck.

The mark of the House of Kel was legend: a sword crossed by a small flower. The sword was Azrin, lost these thousand years, and the flower was dragon's-bane, said to be so rare and costly that a few petals were worth more than a bag of gold. It healed wounds no other medicine could touch, and it killed faster than the strongest poison.

If the Kel-child still lived, he was no longer a boy. He might be in exile, or he might be secretly massing an army to take the throne.

High Lord Boorn stood. "The Dissonay are more likely now than ever to aid any who stand against Skarda."

Heolstor fixed a cold gaze upon him. "You heard this in council?"

"Nay, your excellency, but I know my people."

"How fortunate for Skarda that you do not also love them."

Lord Boorn blinked, the insult sliding home like a new-honed knife. "I would serve them as their king."

"A king with a bought crown. A crown you will never own. Skarda will always be your master."

"Only one who holds the lost sword, your excellency, can speak with such confidence. Show me Azrin that I might know my master."

It was the greatest part of the legend, the one Imre feared most, lest he happen upon the sword and die. Only a Kel could touch the metal from which Azrin was forged, and any Kel could make it glow, but only one could command the sword reveal its hiding place.

Heolstor warned, "If Azrin were shown to you, High Lord Boorn, you could not withstand its power."

"You forget," declared the emissary. "Diluted though it might be, Kellish blood taints the royal house of Disson. Therefore, through her mother Una, Lady Yanámari might be called a Kel. Be careful, lest she find the sword and take power over even you, excellency."

Fury in his eyes, the counselor said nothing. King Morfran smiled. Silence ruled the chamber.

Imre shifted from foot to foot, praying the Unknown would direct everyone to retire to their beds before his legs stiffened in place and his knees bent no more.

"I trust Teag's skill. He will bring me the heir of Kel." Morfran gestured to the grim garland draped above the fireplace: patches of dried human flesh displaying the brand of the House of Kel, trophies of the hunt and of the caverns. "He has brought me more of those vermin than any other spy."

Boorn nodded. "A fine rat-catcher."

Morfran reached up like a captivated child. "Yes." He touched the desiccated skins. "Yes, he is."

27 ~ Defying the Woodsman

He dreamed the wind whispered his name.

"Gaerbith?"

A sleep-fogged moment passed.

"Captain?"A woman's voice.

Snatching up his sword, Gaerbith rose from the soft embrace of the coverlet and strode on unshod feet to the door. An unsteady light flickered back and forth beneath it, a guttering candle or a torch crossed by shadow.

"Captain?" Tentative but urgent.

He pushed aside the bolt and opened the door the merest crack.

A servant girl waited, her hair and face shielded by a white kerchief and her shoulders swathed in a woolen shawl. "The Lady of Skarda sends word to meet her near the great hall."

"At such an hour?"

"She said you would know why."

"Wait here." He closed the door.

The servant lied, but he would go nonetheless. A trap foreknown is a trap disarmed, but he found little comfort in that.

Crossing the room still warmed by the woodless fire, he sat on the edge of the bed and donned boots, a leather jerkin, and a plain brown tunic. The mail shirt he left. It was heavy, and he wanted to be able to move quickly and quietly. He worked his left shoulder a little to loosen it, but there wasn't much he could do about the limp. Stiff muscles, too little sleep—he would be fortunate not to topple down the stairs. Sword on his back, knife strapped under his tunic, he joined the servant girl in the dim corridor.

Her candle was the only light. Torches had been extinguished, but the faint taste of strange smoke hung in the air.

A small sound, the slip of cloth against stone, slid out of the darkness. He whirled, shoving the girl aside.

A blade extended toward him. A Skardian battle sword.

"Leave the candle," the unseen man ordered.

The girl stood wide-eyed, hand trembling, wavering the flame.

The sword twitched.

She set the candle on the floor then ran.

"Come away from these chambers," said the man in the shadows. "We will settle this without witness."

"We settle this here, Gurn, and have no more quarrel."

"Very well. We will rouse the entire household and give the king cause for wrath." Gurn stepped forward, blade leveled at Gaerbith's throat.

"Be quick about it."

Young Wolves were renowned for their skill in battle. They preferred fighting ahorseback but were even more skilled afoot, and wielded their strong, thin, single-edged blades with precision, finding the joints of armor, exposed flesh, any small weakness in an enemy's protection, and sliding their swords home like an archer's arrow finds its mark.

Gaerbith caught the end of Gurn's sword in his fingertips and turned it aside. "You do not want to kill me."

"No?"

"Why send a servant? Why not take advantage when my back was turned, before I knew you were here? Why not thrust the blade home the moment you held it to my throat?"

The sword whipped back into place, this time pressing against the side of Gaerbith's neck. "Pray tell, dog, why I do not kill you now, easy prey to Woodsman Death's sharp axe?"

Like a forester harvesting trees from his domain, the fell Woodsman walked the earth and culled from it the lives of men. Across his chest he wore a horn slung on a strap made of woven reeds as frail as life. When a man heard Death's horn, he knew he had but moments before the Woodsman cut him down.

"Either you fear the consequences, or you are curious." Blood trickled down as the blade cut the skin. "You hesitate even now."

The two men stared at one another. Killing heat simmered in the Young Wolf's eyes.

Then the pressure eased on Gaerbith's neck. Gurn stepped back.

Gaerbith took a breath. The Woodsman gathered other souls this night and did not trouble himself to blow the horn for one foolish captain.

Or, perhaps, he merely delayed.

Gurn took a long rushing step forward, bringing his sword up and around in a swinging arc.

Omwen'din, hear my cry. Gaerbith saw the gleaming edge, heard it sing through the air. *May I die a soldier—*

Stepping forward, bending a knee, he ducked under the sword and caught Gurn's hands, using the sword's momentum to twist the hilt from his grasp. Gaerbith rose, holding both the Skardian battle sword and the Dissonay longsword, blades crossed to take the Young Wolf's head from his shoulders. Then Gaerbith waited, watching fear expand in Gurn's face.

After a few moments, Gaerbith slid the blades apart, letting their edges grate against one another in a menacing rasp. Lifting the Skardian sword over his shoulder and hefting it as he might a spear, he sent it hissing past Gurn's head. The Young Wolf flinched, but the blade passed harmlessly into the darkness beyond, clattering and sliding along the stone floor.

"Sleep well, Gurn Grumësson." Gaerbith sheathed his sword. "Come morning, we lay enmity to rest."

Eyes almost closed, sword at his side, he watched the wall open.

A figure in a dark robe stood in the opening, head turned toward him for a long searching pause, then stepped backward and closed the secret door with the barest sound.

Gaerbith rose from the bed and opened his chamber door a little. The abandoned candle still flickered in the corridor.

The hooded figure did not reappear for several moments. When it did, it came from the emissary's room, looked around, then pulled the door shut before disappearing down the shadowed stairwell at the far end of the corridor.

Gaerbith bolted his door once more. In the dark, he ran his hands along the wall between his chamber and Lord Boorn's.

His fingertips caught at a fracture in the stones.

28 ~ STORYTELLER

Yawning, High Lord Boorn held high his candle, illuminating the narrow-staired passage that followed the broad outline of the square tower. The outer wall was pierced by narrow openings through which probed fingers of cold air. Could anyone on the city walls or in the streets below see this small light flickering? If so, what did it matter? Him they could not see.

Mice—or rats—scampered somewhere ahead of him. Dust webbed the air. He pinched his nose to keep from sneezing.

A winemaker and a merchant, he knew earth and money and how to gain both. King Damanthus and his son Padraig were mere soldiers who thought of little beyond the next battle. They had neither vision nor ambition. They did not see the power and wealth waiting to be plucked from the Territories. They defended them from Morfran, but did not covet them. Nay, Damanthus and Padraig wanted only what they already held.

Once Boorn became king—after dispensing with the current Dissonay king and royal family, of course—he would expand the borders of Disson southward into the Calhoun Forest. Perhaps he would take even the Mynoth Mountains, whenever Morfran was not looking. Boorn might also turn far west to lands across the sea, hidden by the swell of waves and the arc of horizon. He would be as cunning as Morfran, making secret alliances and taking what he wanted. Simply because a man began his days as a powerless, landless commoner, must he be denied a place among kings?

As for magic and ancient swords and elusive Kels, they concerned him not. Let Morfran heed every tale and rumor. Let Heolstor have his spells and myths. Boorn would not begrudge a man his beliefs. He might even find a use for such superstitions.

He reached the hidden door, marked on this side by a crude carving of a beast that appeared half Man, half Dragon.

When I am king, I shall be a patron of artisans and craftsmen, and elevate them beyond this childish scraping.

The seal of his house. Hm. Grapes would figure into it, of course, and a crown. Yes. Not only would the seal hang above his throne, it would adorn the royal ring and be marked on all his correspondence. The royal seal must be impressive indeed.

He pushed the heel of his hand against the rough carving. Stones moved sluggishly. Then, with the soft scrape of contracting mechanisms, the door slid open.

He put out an arm to push aside the heavy tapestry.

"Good morning, your lordship," said Captain Gaerbith.

The emissary paled. His mouth opened and closed. The candle wavered in his hand. "How— The chamber door was barred!"

"Come." Gaerbith drew forward a chair. "I will tell you a tale."

High Lord Boorn set the candle in a tall iron stand. He stood a moment, his expression changing, anger replacing surprise, then disdain overcoming all. "I have no time for tales, captain. The sun soon rises."

"Did you agree a fair price after bargaining for a kingdom?"

Boorn's face became sickly grey.

Gaerbith shrugged. "I have been long hours with little sleep, and may have misheard the king's voice, mistaking it for yours."

A growl gurgled in Lord Boorn's throat. He lurched forward, drawing a knife from his belt.

Gaerbith plucked the haft from the emissary's hand. With the toe of his boot, he pushed the chair into Boorn's path.

The emissary fell into the chair as if his legs were strings. He rested his forearms on the carved necks of Dragons, and his hands gripped the snarling heads, obscuring the bulging eyes. His head fell back against the etched scales of Dragon-skin, and he looked up with weary apprehension.

Gaerbith moved nearer the fire, standing with his back to the flames so he could see the emissary's face without revealing much of his own expression. It put Lord Boorn at a disadvantage but aided Gaerbith. He was so exhausted that his body trembled from cold. His shaking voice might be mistaken for fear.

Staring down at his boots, scuffed, stained, sole-worn, Gaerbith gathered his thoughts then lifted his head, looked at High Lord Boorn, and began to speak.

Greed is a fickle master, but a man need never regret his honor.

I am, like your lordship, a man of the earth. You tend vines and press grapes. When I am not a soldier, I tend sheep.

I know where are the best meadows, know when the streams run too swift for the sheep to cross safely. I know when to move the herd so they do not crop the grass too closely. I know where ravines cut the hills, and do not let my sheep venture near the cliffs lest they fall.

Being captain is not unlike being shepherd. A captain must know how to provide food and weapons for his men, where to lead them, how to keep them alive when the battle goes ill. I am not as good a captain as I am a shepherd. I have led my men into this place, and none of us may survive.

I care nothing for thrones or wealth or power. I want my own land. I want to live in peace. If such were possible, I would fly on the wind to the Thynathel Hills and pray Omwen'din wipe His hand across my memory so that war and death might never again follow at my heels.

But I am here, looking into the very face of betrayal.

Nay, your lordship, do not rise. I have your knife, and will return it when my tale is done.

It is the one deadly skill my father taught me—how to throw a knife. I can split an apple in a tree; he could pierce an acorn.

He once loved a highborn woman whose husband killed her when he discovered she had given her heart to another. My father fled that province, found a woman as broken and lonely as he, and married her. They lived in hiding for many years.

I was born in a cave, as were all my sisters and brothers but one. Bandits invaded our home, and we fled, bringing our herd of sheep from the wilderness and grazing it on the lush grass of the Hills. There we built a cottage and a farm. We forgot the mountains.

Then Skarda's king brought war to the Territories, and we freemen begged aid of Disson. I left my father's house, thinking I might serve it better as a soldier than a shepherd. My brothers followed me, even the youngest. We pledged our lives to keep our freedom. Three of my brothers now lie on a soft green slope, their feet westerly so their souls might travel on the setting sun.

How many times have your comrades fallen at your side, High Lord Boorn, or died in your arms? How many times have you run toward the battle, not certain if the war horn called you to victory or to the Woodsman? Where are your scars?

You are the king's High Lord, chosen as his emissary, trusted to speak and act as if you were Damanthus himself. You, then, are as the king to me and cannot be harmed.

Unless you first harm the king.

You betrayed his plans of attack. You took his gold and smiled to his face and played the counselor and close friend, then held out your hand to the enemy and haggled for a kingdom. You sold the lives of my men and countless others for a shadow crown. For a semblance of power.

Be not alarmed, lordship. This is a habit of mine, tossing and catching knives. I mean nothing by it.

Look. The sky lightens in the east. The sun soon rises.

It is not much of a tale, is it? No magic, no beautiful women disguised as hags, no piles of gold appearing as rubbish unless the beholder's heart is pure. Not a rousing tale, but true nonetheless. And mark! You paid close heed throughout. Perhaps I should become a storyteller.

No? Ah, well.

Here, then, is the lesson hidden in the tale: Choose your king.

If you do not speak for Disson this day, you will never walk your vineyards again. Even your bones will go begging a resting place, for I shall not carry your corpse nor ask it of my men.

"You do not threaten me." High Lord Boorn laughed, the sound high and thin. "I know Damanthus is dead and Padraig lies on the brink of death. He may even now tread the paths of the Otherland."

Aye, Boorn would not have been so eager to turn traitor if the old king still held the throne. Everyone knew the fist of Damanthus fell swift on those who stood against him.

"I am named a guardian of Disson. Such a place holds sway over yours, emissary. Do you tempt my resolve?"

"You convince me to consider this mercy you offer." Sarcasm cut the fear in Boorn's voice. "If I refuse Morfran, how do I return to Disson? Free, as the king's emissary? Or chained, as a traitor?"

"As a man who prefers his vineyards to the royal court, and chooses to live his days in quiet retirement, far removed from the constraints of power."

"Constraints of power?" Boorn smiled. "Power is power because it is *not* constrained."

"Oxen yoked plow the field. Water channeled turns the mill. Wind captured sails the ship."

"Your point, captain?"

Gaerbith flicked his wrist.

The emissary drew a sharp breath. The knife stuck fast in the carved wooden back of the chair, the haft quivering a breath from his left eye.

"Power, your lordship. Under constraint."

29 ~ Escape

Syra and her son, clad in rags and unremarkable among the other laborers gathering before the city gates at dawn, stood near a merchant caravan preparing for departure.

Boxes and bags, most of them empty now the goods had been sold, were stacked in carts built narrow to traverse the dangerous road between the Lowlands and Elycia. Beneath the carts were slung sacks of tools or bars of iron, should wheels need repair. Scarlet-clad guards prodded at baggage and opened boxes. Finding neither stowaways nor contraband, they turned to organize the laborers into groups.

Syra stepped backward a little at a time, gripping Evan's hand so tightly that he whimpered in pain. She loosened her grasp.

A pair of horses moved in front of them, between the workers and the caravan. Syra pulled Evan beneath a wagon and out the other side. When she stood, the boy was hidden beneath the folds of her cloak. It was patched and faded, but it might escape notice among other travel-worn cloaks.

Picking up baskets that had been tumbled by the guards' search, she endeavored to appear busy while standing in one place. Evan clung to her, bending when she did, remaining motionless when required.

Good lad. Brave lad.

Sunlight blazed, sudden fire skimming the top of the wall.

"Open the gates!" came the cry, and open they did, swinging wide, revealing wide sky and vast distance.

Freedom.

30 ~ Disguise

Rage scalded the emissary. His hands shook.

Captain Gaerbith was gone, but fear held Boorn captive, blade still buried in the wood beside his head.

His own knife. His own reeking knife.

By the old gods, he is an arrogant puppy!

A soldier should have more respect for his superiors. He should know his place and hold his tongue. None of the other half-witted Dissonay would have thought to search for hidden passages, much less eavesdrop on secret councils.

High Lord Boorn pulled the knife free—it took more effort than he expected—and stood staring at the wall.

A man of coin and words, am I, and not a man of action? I rose from penniless peasant to one of the wealthiest vintners in the Territories. Eh, Captain Nobody, with the stink of sheep still so strong on you I can scarce draw breath?

He tightened his fist, and the jeweled haft bit into his palm.

I will be king.

He pushed aside the wall hanging and searched until he found the one stone that gave way beneath his hand. The hidden door slid open with a whisper. Knife ready, High Lord Boorn stepped through the opening.

Into an empty room.

Gaerbith opened the shutter on the stairwell window. Grey light limned the edge of the eastern sky. *Omwen'din—*

What should he pray? That war end? That Lord Boorn be thwarted?

Light flickered on the edge of his vision. A candle moved in the upper reaches of the abandoned King's Keep. The prisoner, too, watched the eastern sky.

Gaerbith turned from the window. High Lord Boorn would not heed his words. He sighed. Given a second chance, few men took it. Mercy was seen as weakness, and reprieve considered license.

Beside his chamber door huddled a bundle, his few belongings bound together by the bedcover. He slung it over his shoulder and made his way to the Court of Soldiers.

In the Dissonay barracks, all the stone berths were filled, so he lay on the floor. Cold seeped from the stones, but he rolled himself in the thick blanket and waited for his muscles to uncoil. His eyes would not stay closed. He watched dawn-light creep across the floor.

His body relaxed enough to let him sleep. Just before midday, he woke to the loud voice of a crier who stood in the common outside the soldiers' quarters and announced the treaty council would begin in two hours.

Gaerbith drew Turi aside and told him all that had happened in the night. He listened in grim silence, nodding at the murmured instructions. Neither man said anything to the others lest the Skardians overhear.

Food was brought, a great pot of fragrant soup slung on a pole borne on the shoulders of two men. Another servant carried bowls in a wide basket and handed them to the Fourth. Perhaps it was the servants' anxious goodwill, or the way the Skardian soldiers watched without watching, but something warned Gaerbith this was not common fare.

He held the dripping ladle to one servant's lips and bade him take the first taste.

Clamping his lips shut, the man turned his head.

"Come now! Savory meat? Thick broth? You refuse it? One taste, and then my men will eat."

"It is unseemly for a servant to eat in the presence of honored guests."

"We are simple men," said Gaerbith, "and have no need of fine food. We will eat whatever yon soldiers eat."

The servants bowed, gathered the bowls, and departed, taking the soup with them.

A short time later, provisions were delivered to the Skardians. The

Dissonay—without asking permission yet offering thanks all the while —took three baskets of the plain fare. Startled, the Skardians protested, but the Fourth smiled as if they did not comprehend the hurled insults.

Two fellows drew their swords. Turi stood before them, axe gripped in one huge fist, and shook his head. Scowling but quelled, they stepped back and sheathed their weapons.

Gaerbith broke his fast, eating bread, cheese, and dried meat, drinking poor wine that the men heated until it was warm as a blanket and only slightly more palatable.

Owen brought out a heavy satchel emitting the dull clank of metal, and Gaerbith slung the bag over his shoulder. He turned his back to the watching Skardians and quietly addressed his men. "Make ready."

Gaze intent, he smiled wide, as if in jest.

Quick to their captain's lead, the soldiers chuckled.

Good lads.

"Eyes sharp as your father's swords, and ears keen to the Woodsman's call. We leave this day."

They laughed louder still.

"We may have to fight our way out. Though we be freemen, make them pay dearly for our lives."

Great roars of laughter rolled through the courtyard.

"Turi knows my mind in this. If matters go ill with me, he is your captain." For the benefit of watching Skardians, he shrugged. "Pray Omwen'din the gates are open when we come."

"Pray Omwen'din we live," muttered Turi.

With a last look at the Fourth, Gaerbith departed.

He visited the stables, feeding Kraekor and the other Dissonay horses, and refreshing their water buckets. Stableboys watched, some halting mid-task, some standing with arms folded. They stared in sneering silence or exchanged jests. They thought it odd, demeaning, that a soldier did the work of a servant. The opinions and boasts of untried youth.

Gaerbith hung an empty water bucket on its hook beside the well in the stableyard then turned to meet the mocking eyes of the largest stableboy. Others ceased speaking, as if words froze in their mouths.

The lad's bravado faltered, gaze flickering toward something just past Gaerbith's head. Bítan's hilt jutted over his shoulder.

Gaerbith reached up.

The boy tensed, eyes wide, fists curling.

Gaerbith scratched his jaw, grinned, and asked in perfect Skardian, "Have you a razor I might borrow?"

Surprise then anger flared in the boy's eyes. He stepped forward, fists raised, but one of his fellows grabbed the back of his tunic. "Mind, you! He is *that* captain."

The boy stopped short. Gaerbith waited, hands loose at his sides. The youth's his fists relaxed, and a reluctant smile tugged at one corner of his mouth. "Perhaps our master has what you need."

"Now I think on it"—Gaerbith gave his beard one last scratch—"it is colder here than in the Lowlands. I do not borrow that razor after all."

The youth inclined his head. "As you will, captain."

Then, even as he turned to go, he swung back around. "Why did you tend the horses?"

"See the old scarred one? A warhorse, long in years and ill-acquainted with peace. He deserves no less care than my men. Beside, none of you tended them, and we are guests of your king."

Pale, the boy stammered, "Your pardon, captain—"

"There is no need for the king to know."

"Th-thank you, captain."

Gaerbith nodded, and the stableboys returned to raking away soiled straw and spreading new, a mix of dried grasses from mountain meadows.

In the cover of Kraekor's stall, Gaerbith strapped a sheathed knife upside-down under his left arm, buckling the two thin straps over his shoulder and across his chest. Two more knives were tied—one on each leg—beneath his court tunic, and yet another was shoved into his boot. The throwing knives had been given by his father as defense against beasts attacking the flock. Being a shepherd had been his best preparation for this day. Mayhap his destiny lay here, and he would never again walk the Thynathel Hills.

Be it as Omwen'din wills.

Kraekor's ears flicked as he watched his master's preparations. Gaerbith pushed the horse's shoulder and Kraekor shifted, allowing more room in a front corner of the stall. Gaerbith stowed his pack there under the fresh straw then stood and patted Kraekor's neck. "Stand guard, old friend."

Hoisting the satchel given him by Owen, Gaerbith sauntered into the tower, nodding and smiling at the busy servants preparing for the treaty council or the wedding feast. There were no Young Wolves about, and the nobles likely kept to the other side of the tower, well away from servants and common soldiers.

Reaching the corridor where lay High Lord Boorn's chamber, he peered around the corner. Guards stood at the door. The emissary's allegiance was proclaimed as loud as a trumpet call. Not only did he refuse the protection of the Dissonay, he chose the enemy's own men to stand in their place.

Gaerbith drew back to the far side of the stairwell and, shielded by passing servants, climbed to the next floor. That corridor was empty but for a pair of Black Hoods walking shoulder-to-shoulder, their hands hidden in their sleeves, their heads bowed.

He went up another turn of the stair. Time was short. He must find the Lady of Skarda without drawing attention. She might not be in her chamber, but waiting in the great hall for the council to begin.

With too little rest, and bearing the weight of a satchel filled with metal, he quickly tired of all the stairs. He had lived too many years among hills or flatlands, and his body did not yet recall the clear, sharp air of the Grimë Mountains, or the way his sturdy young legs once climbed the rocky heights as easily as running.

Resting at a turning of the stair, Gaerbith leaned against the stones. A patch of light from the window beside him made a bright square on the opposite wall. He stared at it, his thoughts elsewhere.

Someone hummed a bland little tune.

Gaerbith glanced around the corner. A man carried a basket filled with fresh candles and torches, which he used to replace the spent ones in sconces and brackets along the hall. Gaerbith approached in smiling innocence. Letting his Dissonay accent wax thick, he asked in stumbling Skardian where he might find the Lady of Skarda to give her a gift from her Uncle Damanthus.

The servant frowned. "Do the king know of it?"

"Oh, aye"—Gaerbith nodded cheerfully—"but he were so concerned with other matters, he did not tell me the way. A great man cannot be bothered with the likes of me."

The man still looked doubtful. "True. The king do have much on his mind this day." Then, "You have a familiar look." His eyes widened. "You be that captain!"

"Ah, you mean m'brother." Gaerbith shrugged, and slapped his forehead with the heel of his hand. "I be the simple one."

The servant studied him in narrow silence. "I heard tell of such things—one face, two bodies."

Gaerbith grinned. "Aye, that be us. Point me the way, and I leave y'to your matters."

"Up those stairs one turning." The man gestured. "Her door be marked by a boss graved with strange letters, but do not read them."

"Evil words?" Gaerbith affected fear, kissing the knuckle of his right thumb to ward off dark magic.

"Aye, a spell." He moved onward and continued his work.

Gaerbith found the door. New wood marked where the latch had recently been replaced. Kellish words were carved into the iron boss.

Fril Nythna Gruës

It was no spell at all, but an ancient blessing. Cayn the Keeper had spoken it over him the day Gaerbith arrived on the Isle of Morga—

Voices sounded in the stairwell.

He knocked, calling "my lady" in a low voice.

No answer.

He dared speak no louder, but knocked again. "My lady?"

Still no answer.

A tendril of smoke curled out from under the door.

Yanámari watched yet another shoe slide from her foot and tumble toward the river. She leaned forward, reaching a languid hand, but the shoe was already lost to the roiling water.

Wind tangled her hair, knotting it around her neck. Garments— she could not see them—clutched at her limbs, fabric hands to hold her captive. Chill mist rose from Brona's Veil.

She flew.

The River Thrayne churned.

Brona's Veil roared.

She grew warm, strangely untouched by the frigid wind.

She had left the tower at last, and she was unafraid. Why did she never before think to simply fly away? Turning onto her back, she spread her arms and closed her eyes against the sun. Which direction to the Otherland?

No.

She opened her eyes.

Darkness. Fire without light.

Roaring. A voice not the river.

She could not breathe.

She fell.

Choking, Gaerbith dropped the satchel, ran to shove open the shutters, then tore down one of the heavy bed curtains and used it as an unwieldy fan to clear the air, but the smoke only spiraled in sluggish coils. It tasted metallic and bitter. He fell, brought to his knees by muscle-straining hacks that left his throat raw and his ribs aching. Stinging ash blinded him. He shook his head, blinking.

He heaved the thick fabric, but the curtain flopped, stirring the cloying ash without dissipating it.

Something leapt at his mind. Clawing deep, it dug for knowledge, plucking bits of him, inserting despair into the gaps. The invader rifled his memories. Images flashed behind his eyes.

Help, Omwen'din—

A small pouch hung above the flames in the fireplace. He dropped the curtain, crawled to the hearth, and yanked the sack from its hook. Each cough seeking to turn his lungs inside out, he crawled toward the open shutters, pulled himself up, and dropped the pouch through the window.

A breeze caught the bag, scattering a powder the shade of gloaming. Smoke sucked out of the room like brigands chased, and disappeared on the wind. Fire followed the wind, leaping from the hearth, trailing coals and sparks that died even as they flew.

Cold, clean air.

Gaerbith slumped to the floor, his back to the wall, and leaned his head against the cool stones. *Thank You. Thank You.*

The mining of his brain subsided then ceased.

The chamber door stood open, invitation to curious passersby. He forced himself to his feet, shuffled past the bed—and stopped.

Yanámari lay as still as a corpse. Her arms were flung out from her sides. Hair wrapped her throat. There was no rest in her features. Forehead wrinkled, brows drawn together, mouth contorted, she appeared frightened by evil dreams. The bed covers had been tossed aside. Gaerbith touched her arm. Her shift was damp with sweat yet her skin was cold. He felt her throat for a heartbeat. It was shallow.

Female voices approached.

He grabbed the satchel and stepped behind an arras, holding back the edge just enough to see the chamber. There were still three ranks of bed curtains drawn closed. Perhaps the servants would not see—

He stepped to the bed, twitched the covers over Lady Yanámari, and kicked the torn curtain under the bed, returning to the arras just as a knock sounded on the half-open door.

Servants entered, chattering in whispers, asking where Elta was, saying 'twas fortunate they were accustomed to bringing water every day, was it not, else m'lady would never be tended.

"Such a fine thing is Elta, she cannot be troubled to wake m'lady or bring her breakfast?" grumbled one woman, her work-reddened hands deft as she rolled the bathing tub from its corner and turned it upright. "Well past midday, it is."

"Was a feast yesternight," someone reminded her, but the woman just harrumphed.

Another woman swept scattered coals from the hearth, laid fresh wood in the fireplace, sprinkled something then snapped her fingers, and flames sprang to life. She swung out the sturdy arm of an iron hook—attached by a bolted hinge and stored snug against the stones inside the fireplace—and hung a large cauldron from it.

The rest of the women bore buckets of water, two each, hung on ropes suspended from either side of a wooden yoke balanced across the shoulders. They poured their burden into the cauldron and, when it was full, the remaining buckets were set on the floor near the hearth, and the servants started to quietly clean the chamber or settled near the fire for a whispered gossip.

Blood and bone and all the fires of the Void! Gaerbith strove to keep himself still, but he wanted to do nothing more at that moment than toss every one of the women out into the hall.

Gossip continued, however, until one of the servants discovered the torn curtain. One scarlet fold of it snaked from under the foot of the bed. She grabbed up the fabric and thrust it toward the sour-faced woman. All of the women turned to look at the bed. Their leader stomped forward and yanked aside the other curtains. Light fell full on Lady Yanámari's pallid face.

"Should we wake m'lady?" asked a stick-thin young woman. "She looks a mite sickly—"

Gaerbith strode from behind the tapestry and plied the women with what he hoped was a charming smile.

"Who do you be?" demanded the young woman, wide-eyed.

"The betrothed of the Lady of Skarda."

Looking him up and down, the older woman snorted. "Vira, call the guard."

"He speaks the truth," said a timid voice behind her. "M'lady chose him yesternight at banquet."

"Aye." A tall woman nodded. "The king consented. Though you, Master Dissonay, did not seem happy about it at the time."

Still smiling, Gaerbith spread his hands wide. "She convinced me."

All but the sour-faced woman covered their mouths and looked sidelong at one another, descending into bawdy giggles and muffled whispers.

"Now we know why Elta is not here," came a sly comment delivered with a laugh.

His ears burned. "Pray finish your task. I shall attend the lady."

The woman studied him with narrow-eyed suspicion while the others poured the heated water into the tub and laid towels and soap on a chair. Empty buckets were gathered and the cauldron stored before the woman released him from her glare, muttering about lovers hiding behind tapestries. She stomped after her charges—who looked at him over their shoulders with wary, curious, or flirtatious glances—and closed the door.

Gaerbith leaned over the bed and touched Yanámari's pale throat, hovered a hand over her mouth, then pressed his palm over her heart.

He clenched his jaw. Let her soul journey to the Otherland. Her body would leave the city.

"May your feet find the golden path, and Omwen'din welcome you home," he murmured, tucking one arm behind her shoulders and another behind her knees to lift her. "Farewell—Yanámari."

"Yanámari."

That word was a wind. Air, clean and harsh, rushed into her, drawing her upright, scouring her throat, yanking her back to life.

Unseen hands fumbled as they wrapped something warm around her shoulders. She grasped the edges to draw it tight to her body, and felt the rough skin of those hands scrape along her fingers and quickly withdraw. Felt the loss of heat, the shifting of weight, as whoever was near moved elsewhere. Looking up through damp tangled hair, she saw a crumpled and much-mended stained white tunic and a battered scabbard.

"My lady"—the tattered voice spoke Skardian with a slight Dissonay accent—"forgive my boldness, but we have little time."

She blinked at the radiance filling the chamber through the north-facing window. If the light was so strong, glinting off the snowy peaks, then the sun was high and the day far spent.

The man stood with his back to her, his posture rigid.

"Who are you?" The words croaked from her throat.

"Recall your handmaid, my lady, and your request of me?"

Elta. Yanámari pressed her lips tight to keep from crying.

The man—what was his name?—turned just enough for her to see his profile. "Your new garments are beside you."

On the bed, a Dissonay uniform was laid out as if the wearer had melted away during his repose.

She touched the cool metal rings of the mail birnie. "Gaerbith." Her voice rasped like two sticks rubbing together. "You are Gaerbith. A captain."

"Aye, that I am." His words held a frown. "Someone meant to magick you or poison you, my lady."

Heolstor.

"Are you well, my lady?"

Yanámari put a hand to her aching head. "Well enough."

He strode toward the rear wall of the chamber. He limped a little.

"Where do you go, captain? The door is here."

"I go to admire the fine view from your window, my lady." He stood in the light, broad-shouldered and upright "The bath is ready. It may be your last for many days."

Shivering, yet hot with embarrassment, she reached for the chamber pot. This was no time for niceties and court manners. Finished, she covered the pot with a towel and slid it beneath the bed.

She cast a glance at the captain's straight back, then shed her undergarments and scurried to the tub. Steam still rose from the water. She sank into it with a grateful sigh, sliding below the water then sitting up again.

"Captain?"

"My lady?"

"Cut my hair."

"Now?"

"Yes."

He did not reply.

She waited, listening for any sign that he moved.

"I—" His feet shifted, grating on the floor. "I will see you, my lady."

My, but had he not seen much of her already? Her sweat-soaked shift had been little shield. She placed a towel over the mouth of the tub, covering all but her head and shoulders. "I trust you."

There was a small catch in his stride then his shadow fell across her.

She draped the damp waves of her hair outside the tub then held herself motionless, sensing more than feeling as he caught some hair in his hand.

"How short, my lady?"

"To the shoulders. Like yours. I would look as Dissonay as possible."

A knife tugged through her hair.

"Instruct me how to appear less conspicuous."

"Lift your head, but let your hair hide your face. Do not speak. When you walk, swing your arms and let your shoulders carry you forward. Walk with purpose. Never show your hands. They have no calluses or scars."

Rough fingers brushed her back as he scooped another hank of hair. She shivered. Reaching down beside her arm, he touched the water. "Just a few more cuts, my lady, and you may finish bathing before it cools."

Free of the weight of hair that once reached to her knees, her head felt light and her neck as loose as ill-spun thread.

Down on his knees, the captain gathered the shorn hair, sweeping it up with his hands. Ready to rise from the water, she glanced over her shoulder and met his gaze. He held a fistful of her hair.

He looked so ill at ease that she smiled.

"For birds," he explained, striding to the window and releasing the hair to the wind. "Nests."

He faced the window again.

Startled when she had risen from the bed with a great rasping noise, he had been himself again in an instant, ready with a task and a plan. This was battle, and she was merely another warrior. Her hair, however, and bare shoulders—

Maggot wit. She is not for you to see.

A residue of the strange powder clung to a stone framing the window. He almost brushed it away, but pulled back his hand just before his fingers touched the glittering substance.

"I have managed the garments, and this padded shirt," she said behind him. "but how does one put on a birnie?"

"Roll it," he said, not turning around, "until it is gathered near the neck opening, then—"

"Show me."

He did, guiding her arms into the holes where sleeves should be, and pulling the rest over her head. The mail was heavy, and her first movements were awkward.

"You will grow accustomed to it"—he helped her don the white and green surcoat—"until being without it seems unnatural."

The less like a noblewoman she appeared—the less like a woman at all—the more at ease he became. He buckled a short sword at her side, trying to ignore the clean smell of her hair or the warm fragrance of her skin.

"This is not right." She gripped the hilt.

"I could not hide a longsword in the satchel, my lady, nor was there one to be had. Behave as if it is only fitting that you wear a different sword, and no one else will mind the oddity."

Yanámari pushed her hands into a pair of leather gloves Gaerbith had worn many times in battle. They were stained with old blood, sweat, and the grime of long use. She drew herself up, straightening her shoulders, planting her fists against her waist so that her elbows crooked out from her sides. "Do I look a soldier?"

No, not at all. She might resemble a youth without his first beard, but her shiny black hair still hung in damp waves that were almost curls, and her build, slender and tall, was still feminine and her gestures graceful. If he mentioned such things, however, he might steal her confidence, so he smiled and said, "You need a few scars and a healthy beard, but at a glance, aye, you do look a soldier."

He held up the satchel that now held only bread and a bit of dried meat. "Eat what you can. Bring only what you need."

While she tore at the meager food with strong teeth and filled the bag with a few items, he opened the door. Standing in its recess, he looked around the corner into the corridor. Empty.

Subdued voices echoed, and he went to look down the stairwell. It was alive with finely-dressed servants and even finer-clad nobles, all descending to the treaty council.

"There is a hidden passage," Lady Yanámari said at his shoulder. "It leads from the stairwell below to an alcove behind the dais. From there, another passage leads to the door of the great hall."

"Who uses the passage?"

"Elta and I." Her voice thickened, and she cleared her throat. "Perhaps Heolstor. We risk meeting him there, but if we join the march of nobles and walk behind them with proper courtesy, they will not heed mere soldiers, no matter the color of our tunics. The main staircase is the quickest way."

Her features were stern, determined. She would not falter.

"Very well, my lady. Now. Walk bold."

They did walk bold, striding behind the nobles and their servants and guards, just near enough to be noted but not closely observed. Yanámari's heart thudded then raced. What if her father or Heolstor recognized her? The captain was safe—he was expected at the treaty council, so his walking with the others was a matter of course—but she was the Lady of Skarda, clad in the guise of a Dissonay soldier, and she defied the king.

The barons and their men halted their progress and parted to stand along either side of stairwell, looking upward, back the way they had come. Echoing down the stairs, King Morfran's voice responded to the scarce-audible whisper that was Heolstor's.

Yanámari bowed her head, hoping the fall of hair would be sufficient shield against keen eyes. *Please*, she prayed the nebulous unknown, *let him pass me by.*

Claws clicked on stones, followed by the wolf-handler's heavy tread.

The captain nodded to a baron then stepped backward into a corridor, making room for another man. Face still partly obscured by her hair, Yanámari did the same, and the baron drew back from her, as if the brush of her surcoat would taint his. As she passed, he murmured to a companion something about how fine-scented soap did nothing to rinse away the smell of dog, and the other man muffled his laughter behind a closed fist.

Anger flared, heating her face. The look in Gaerbith's eyes told her he had heard, but where anger should have been was only somber quietude, and in his gaze a warning to keep silent.

They stood in the empty corridor. As the voices of Morfran and his counselor drew nearer, everyone's attention riveted on the stairs above, and Gaerbith took another step backward. Then another. Dissonay boots were low-heeled, and they made no sound. The captain stopped at the recessed door of a chamber. It was locked. He jerked his head, and Yanámari joined him, their backs and heels pressed against the door. No one looking down the hallway would know they were there.

Eager whines rose from the wolves, and their handler cursed them for pulling his arms "nigh from their sockets, ye reeking great beasts!"

The wolves would not be calmed. Not the king's sharp words nor even Heolstor's raspy command quieted them.The rustle of stiff garments and the sound of uncertain breathing told Yanámari the noblemen lining the stairs were as frightened as she.

"My lord," puffed the handler, "all these folk about—send them ahead. The wolves have not been fed."

"Not fed? Why?" The king's sharp voice boded ill for the servant.

"Yesternight, my lord. They were not hungry until now."

A wolf growled, and another answered with a snarling snap. Yanámari flinched. Her scabbard scraped against the door.

The wolves grew insistent, their whines eager.

Yanámari closed her eyes, as if shutting out the light would hide her in darkness. Captain Gaerbith squeezed her wrist.

"No one there, my lord," declared the handler.

A long silence, then "Baron Jaspa, walk with me," Morfran said.

Feet shuffled, garments brushed stone, and the jostling sounds soon faded as nobles followed the king down the stairs.

Captain Gaerbith released her. She looked up. He raised his brows.

Passage, she mouthed.

He nodded.

She looked around the corner. Corridor and landing were empty.

Then came the eerie soft thud of paws.

31 ~ Betrayed

Syra walked beside the wagons, here where the road broadened for a bit. Evan walked in step with her, never complaining, although he surely found the air close and difficult to breathe.

One of the mercenaries rode past and looked pointedly at the extra pair of small legs trudging along under her cloak. Syra's heart stumbled but she met his gaze. At any moment, he could reveal her. Or, in return for keeping her secret, he could make demands of her.

His mouth slurred upward at one corner then he moved on.

Do not think me inconstant, dear Rubin. Soon or late, I will see you. Until then, forgive what I do to save our son.

Drawing his longsword, Captain Gaerbith stepped out from the doorway and stood in the center of the corridor, feet planted. With a jerk of his chin, he signaled Yanámari go.

Terrified but determined, she shook her head.

Wolves thudded up the stairs and halted on the landing. Light glinted along their fur, each hair sharp and strong as iron. Teeth bared, the wolves braced their forelegs wide, pulling against their collars. Behind them came the breathless handler, so broad he blocked the light, and in his meaty fists he gripped the heavy chains that the wolves stretched taut.

The handler's voice rumbled. "A bit scrawny, that one, but the fellow with the sword, now, he might make a tasty meal."

He bent down to unhook chains from the wide iron collars.

The man grunted, one shoulder dropping. Yanámari's silver-handled knife impaled his thick-muscled chest, just above the heart. He clapped a hand beneath the wound, surprise in his heavy face.

"Well done." Admiration warmed the captain's voice.

Yanámari licked her dry lips. "My brother taught me."

The handler loosened his grip on a chain, and one of the wolves lurched forward. The man cursed, anger and amazement in his eyes. "My lady?"

Blast! She had been warned not to speak.

Captain Gaerbith stepped in front of her, sword ready.

Grimacing, the handler let out a length on the wolves' chains. Blood ran bright down his tunic. "Ye chose an ill protector, my lady. Cannot even—"

The smell of blood made the wolves even more eager, and they milled. Attack the two people in front of them, or the bleeding man from whose hand they received food and drink, and whom they served second only to the king?

"Go!" the captain ordered Yanámari.

"My knife—"

"Go!"

The captain's sword scraped across wolf hide, the metallic sound ringing above the snarls and snaps.

Still she hesitated. Brona Wanderer would not let him fight alone, nor would Arien be pleased by lack of courage.

She skirted the embattled captain and the preoccupied wolves. Watching her, the handler pulled the knife from his chest and tossed it aside. He wrapped the chains around his forearm.

She grabbed up the knife, took a running leap, hooked her legs around his wide waist and one arm around his thick throat. He peeled her arm away from his neck. She reached over his shoulder with her other arm, and plunged the blade in again and again.

Releasing him, she dropped to the floor and stumbled, the satchel on her back pulling her off balance. He, too, staggered. Swayed. Toppled. The wolves, losing interest in the captain with his annoying sword, fell upon their handler and tore at his flesh.

Yanámari stared down at her crimson hand, gloved in more than just leather. She was detached from her body, scarce able to think or feel. Blood fouled the silver knife.

"Do not look at it." Captain Gaerbith took the knife, wiped it clean on the hem of his surcoat, then slid it into the sheath on her arm. He headed toward the stairs. "Where is the secret passage?"

A few steps down was a stone a fraction darker than the other grey stones around it.

A stale odor curled up the stairwell, and footsteps whispered, accompanied by the tap of a walking stick.

She pushed the latch stone, frustrated at the leisurely way the door sighed open, a narrow section of wall sliding backward into cold darkness. Beside her, Gaerbith stood with his sword drawn, looking down toward the approaching footsteps and intermittent tapping.

Yanámari scraped through the uneven edges of the opening. Her sword belt caught on an edge and pulled her up short. Tugging frantically, she freed herself just as a bloody-jawed wolf bounded into view. It slipped on the smooth stones and nigh lost its footing, claws scraping for a hold.

"Now!" Yanámari cried, and Gaerbith jumped sideways from the stair, crashing into her with bruising force, knocking her down. Her breath pushed out in a gust.

Joined by its companions, the wolf lunged after Gaerbith. He kicked it in the nose. The wolf drew back with a yelp but returned with a snarl.

The other wolves scrambled to enter the narrow space. One of them caught the captain's boot in its teeth. Gaerbith cursed as the gleaming fangs gnawed the thick leather. His longsword was useless here. He drew a knife.

Pulling out from under the captain's bulk, Yanámari fumbled for the carving that would close the door.

Over growls and snaps came the approaching tap-tap-tap.

Yanámari felt along the wall. As soon as her fingernails scraped across the key, she twisted it and the door moved, pushing the wolves toward the open stairwell.

Gaerbith swiped at one of them but the knife blade scraped across the iron hairs, not even parting the animal's fur. The wolf's jaws closed on his mail-clad forearm but the moving door caught its legs, knocking it sideways. Gaerbith stabbed into its open mouth, and the wolf bowed, choking. The captain kicked its body the last small distance out to the stairwell just before the opening sealed shut, enclosing the passage in utter darkness.

There was a rustle of clothing and clinking of mail, and then the scrape of metal on stone. The captain had found his sword.

Wolves scratched at the stones, whining and snarling. The rasping angry tones of Heolstor consigned them weak and stupid creatures.

He knew of the passage—he could open it again and set the wolves on them—but pained yipping, the grinding of metal on metal, and a moist rending sound told a gruesome tale: two wolves feasting on their fallen companion.

"My lady?"

Yanámari found the captain's hand as he reached for her. She placed it on her shoulder and started down the narrow steps.

"I will go first," he said, "lest we meet an armed enemy. Keep your sword drawn."

She pressed against the wall, and he squeezed past her. From the uneven sound of his steps, his limp had worsened. She placed a hand on his back then drew her sword. Her eyes had grown accustomed to the darkness, and she detected his shape as a deeper black. Or perhaps, in such profound lack of light, she sensed rather than truly saw him.

From childhood games of spying and hide-and-seek, her brother would have known better than she which path to take out of the tower, which way led onto way.

As a soldier, Arien had gone seeking danger, taking the most perilous tasks for his own, leading his men into the fiercest fighting. When he returned once to Elycia for a respite, Yanámari urged him to take care. She asked why he plunged into battle like a madman. Did he seek the fearful reputation of their father?

His smile had been bitter. "No, sister. I seek to escape him."

Then he embraced her, something he had not done since childhood. It was so foreign that she held herself still at first then let her arms creep around him and let her forehead tip against his chest.

"Your lot is worse than mine." He rested his cheek on her hair.

"What do you mean?" Yanámari's voice was absorbed by his tunic pressed to her face.

"When you walk, when you turn your head or smile, you look like Mother. He cannot endure it, so he imprisoned you. I made myself like him so I could be free. I am a coward."

"No."

His arms tightened around her shoulders. "When I become king—" but he never finished the thought.

Arien had run toward death, Elta had sought life, but both were gone. Now Yanámari had forced the captain into a dangerous alliance. He had mentioned parents and siblings. Did he have a wife, too, and children waiting in the Hills? Had she stolen from him a precious future? It were better she stumbled through this alone than snare more lives in her miserable net.

Yanámari drew a quick breath to stave off tears.

He halted at once, touched her arm then her face.

"I am well."

Still Gaerbith hesitated.

Blinding light flooded the passage. She shielded her eyes, squinting to see who stood behind the one-eyed lantern. The hand holding it was white as bone and wore a heavy gold ring set with a ruby. A Brother of the Black Hood.

"My lady, you are not in proper attire for the treaty council."

"You prefer I wear a winding sheet and funeral spices?"

"Call off your dog, my lady, and set aside this foolish scheme. Your father forgives the death of one wolf, but he will not do so again."

Gaerbith lunged, but Yanámari caught a fistful of his tunic. "You cannot kill one of the Hôk Nar unless you behead him."

The Hood chuckled, a cold empty sound. "I pray your little blade is sharp, captain." The lantern swayed. "I have little patience to wait while you hack at my neck."

Gaerbith tilted his head as if listening to a voice Yanámari could not hear, then he smiled. "Omwen'din. The Voice, you name him. Or, perhaps, an even more ancient name—"

The Hood shrieked, thrusting out his palm, his fingers hooked like Nar'ath talons.

Gaerbith spoke the name. "Mymna Tor."

The lantern clattered to the stones, the oil still burning.

Then he said something in a tongue neither Skardian nor Dissonay, yet akin to both.

The Hood fell to his knees, clawing at his ears, mouth open and twisted in soundless agony. Blood ran from his face and over his hands, twining down his arms, dripping to the floor.

In an instant of silence so profound Yanámari feared she had gone suddenly deaf, the corpse crumbled into ashes then disappeared.

Her heartbeat throbbed in her ears, then hearing returned. The captain's breathing was harsh, rapid, and he slumped against the wall. She touched his bowed head, then pressed a palm flat to his chest. His heartbeat shuddered along her arm.

"Captain?"

He sagged against her, so heavy that she sank to the steps, his upper body across her lap.

With unsteady hands, Yanámari smoothed his hair and rocked a little, as if cradling a child. "There is a waterfall, Brona's Veil, named for a woman like me who wanted more from life than these walls. And remember the legend of Esthenay, whose shade led her husband from the Otherland when he arrived too soon, cut down by the treachery of seeming friends? As she stood on the threshold of life and death, Esthenay had but to whisper his name and send him back into his body to complete the appointed days of his life. Only his name."

Love was the power in that tale. Between Yanámari and the captain, however, was only respect and the desire for freedom.

The lantern oil burned out, and darkness returned. The captain's breath quieted. His heartbeat slowed.

"No." She rocked side to side. "No, Gaerbith, you cannot leave."

The man had escaped the Dragon's den with help from the creature itself, but now he was prevented by the Brethren.

Several tunnels met under a large irregular dome, a great hall inside the mountain. Torches flickered. Despite the smoke they birthed, he could see well enough. Down each tunnel flared sudden fires or roars, and the whole cavern filled with noxious fumes.

From a peg in a ritual room, he had stolen a black robe. In the garment, he blended with the shadows but was afraid to move from his bit of darkness. He wore no ruby ring nor were his hands as pale and uncallused as those of a true Hood. Besides, he did not know which tunnel led to the open air. Still, he must try.

A group of Brethren converged in the center of the cavern and appeared to be in prayer. A low hum filled the air, not unpleasant but compelling. It rang in the man's ears like a thousand insects. From the other tunnels emerged more and more Hoods until he counted thrice the number of his fingers. Then, like a flock of crows wheeling in sudden flight, the Hoods turned toward what seemed a solid wall of stone. As they approached, it opened to them, and another tunnel appeared.

Tugging the edge of the hood down to cover his face, he tucked his hands into the arms of his robe, fell in line behind the Brethren, and hoped no one turned around.

Turi waited as long as possible, but High Lord Boorn sent a message for the soldiers to attend the treaty council at once. The message was addressed to Captain Gaerbith, but he had not returned from aiding Lady Yanámari. Turi stepped forward to claim the folded scrap, and in so doing signaled the men that plans had gone ill and he was now their captain.

Their scant belongings had been packed since Gaerbith departed at midday, and these they carried with them to the great hall, making no secret of their readiness to be done with this business and leave Elycia. Old Kraekor and the few packhorses would have to wait in the stables until the last moment.

Owen bore the Dissonay standard, and Turi led the way.

The king was late.

Imre set out a goblet and an ewer of wine. Next he placed a silver tray on the table, and arranged freshly sharpened quills, a block of scarlet wax, a lit candle in a short heavy candlestick, and the king's seal—the Dragon of the House of Morfran. Duties accomplished, Imre could do naught but stand beside the king's empty chair and wait.

Skardians of highest rank bore one of two titles: baron or lord. Morfran's young cousin, Ûtgar, had distinguished himself in battle and gained the rank of lord. Gone home to Markha Province to build a tomb for his late father, Baron Markha, and to search for his father's murderer, Ûtgar was among the few Skardians who had ever rightly called themselves by both titles.

There had been more lords before the war with Disson, but they had defied the king and been slain by the Brethren. By that example, Morfran ensured the loyalty of the lesser nobles now gathering in the great hall. The barons smiled at one another and inclined their heads in greeting, but it was mere mummery. They each wanted to be the one Morfran leaned upon for wisdom, and would cut down their closest allies if necessary.

Did none of them see they were useless to the king? They were ornaments to his presence, silent witnesses to his brilliance and cunning.

The Young Wolves arrived as a troop, casting the other nobles in shadow with their swagger and finery. Were it possible, they gleamed.

Next came High Lord Boorn surrounded by stern-faced Dissonay led by a man the size and appearance of a bear. Imre recognized him as the soldier who had slain Baron Hargow's man at banquet yesternight. In their white-and-green tunics, the Dissonay arrayed themselves throughout the hall. They spoke to no one, not even their comrades, but stood near the wall, arms crossed or thumbs hooked in belts. Every soldier wore a longsword strapped to his back.

The bear-like man stationed himself beside the emissary's chair on the dais. A battleaxe hung beside his longsword. A wide thick leather belt wrapped his girth, and the head of the axe rested in a pocket at his back so that the man need only reach over his shoulder and slide the axe free as he might the longsword.

The backs of longsword scabbards were either wood or lapped leather, with the sides wrapping around the blade only enough to keep the sword firmly in place. Above the long enclosed tip of the sheaths was an open V-shape that allowed the Dissonay to quickly pull then twist their blades free without having to clear the entire length of traditional closed scabbards.

Imre almost hoped the treaty council went ill just so he could see the Dissonay in action.

Black-robed scribes rimmed the room. Some lay out clean parchments, sharpened quills, uncapped inkwells. Others set up easels and arranged pots of paint. Still others simply stood, hands hidden within their sleeves, faces covered by their cowls.

Dusty rays of afternoon sun slanted across the dais.

Imre's thoughts turned toward Elta. He had not been able to find her in the garden grotto that morning nor had other servants seen her in Lady Yanámari's chamber. No one had seen her at banquet last night. As the feast had begun, and before the king's daughter arrived, Imre had been sent to the cellars to select more wine for the king's table. When he returned, he endured a few sly remarks from Morfran about flirting with kitchen maids. It seemed the king toyed with him, as if knowing Imre held an unlawful attachment.

A thick-bodied Brother of the Black Hood entered the great hall. He gripped two chains stretched taut by eager wolves. Where was the man who kept the beasts?

Once the chains were fastened to iron rings imbedded in the stone floor, the wolves paced, alert intelligence in their eyes. Red dappled the grey fur around their mouths and across their chests. No need to wonder the absence of the third wolf. Or their missing keeper.

Baron Jaspa, a troubled look on his face, took his place among the other barons and smiled only a little when addressed.

Morfran arrived without escort, a ceremonial sword strapped to his side. He seemed nowise surprised by the lack of one of his wolves, although he did stare at the beasts for a long moment, anger leaping in his eyes then fading as quickly as melting snow.

"Wine!" The king mounted the dais steps and stood with outstretched arms, a capricious god in a pillar of light. "Wine, I say!"

Imre filled Morfran's cup while other servants poured wine into silver goblets set along the lower tables. Morfran waited until Imre tasted his wine for poison—a small smile lit the king's eyes—then seated himself but the nobles stood, raising their cups: "To the king."

He lifted his gold-rimmed goblet. "To treaty. And to the Lady of Skarda, whose marriage shall seal peace between Skarda and Disson."

"To Yanámari," echoed the guests, but with subdued voice.

The Young Wolves did not keep anger from their faces, and some refused to drink. The king chuckled quietly behind his cup.

A treasonous thought charged through Imre's mind. He wished the wine were poisoned after all.

At King Morfran's salute to peace, Turi crossed his arms and planted his feet wide. *Come, Bachaná. Lure us to yer slaughterhouse.*

Standing, High Lord Boorn withdrew from his sleeve a small scroll sealed with the Oak of Disson pressed in green wax. "Damanthus, king of Disson, bade me give you this brief expression of sympathy for the loss of your son, Lord Arien, and he wishes a favorable resolution of this war. Damanthus regrets he is unable to be present—"

Morfran waved a hand. "Your king's absence speaks his wisdom, and his letter is likely far briefer than your speech!"

The nobles laughed, and High Lord Boorn's face flushed.

Morfran took the proffered scroll and broke the seal. "Let us see what good will Damanthus imparts."

Lord Boorn resumed his seat.

Turi surveyed the hall. What delayed Captain Gaerbith?

In the silence, Rhôn Bergsson and Gurn Grumësson entered and took their places among the other Young Wolves.

Not looking up from the letter, King Morfran asked, "What kept you, my young friends?"

Rhôn sat still.

After a warning look at him, Gurn leaned forward, his forearm on the table, and said, "We were speaking with the guard, my lord, and seeing that the Dissonay soldiers lacked nothing." He flicked a glance up at Turi. "They are from our brother kingdom, after all. Once the treaty is signed, we will owe them no more enmity."

"You were spying on my daughter. You will not find her near the Court of Soldiers. I assure you, she slept in her own bed yesternight."

Tossing the open scroll onto the table, Morfran addressed the entire hall. "This is a rare day." He tapped the parchment with a ringed finger. "We who are of noble blood, royal blood, are asked to heed the words of a mere commoner." He stared at High Lord Boorn, a question in his dark eyes. "A captain in the army of Disson. My daughter's betrothed."

Murmurs rustled through the hall. Lord Boorn remained silent, mouth tight, brow creased.

"Were I you, I would have read every dispatch before arriving here so that I might anticipate my enemy's slightest move. Ah, but I forget. The letter is written in Skardian, which you speak roughly but cannot read. And where is the good captain?" demanded Mad Morfran. "What is he to Damanthus? A bastard son? A royal in disguise? A wizard with the power to vanish us all?"

"The captain is likely sleeping off last night's wine, my lord," replied Boorn. "As for what he is to Damanthus, I know not."

"Last night's wine?" Morfran's mouth twitched. "He scarce tasted it. Heolstor, what say you?"

The old man glided forward to stand between the wolves. The beasts whined and lay at his feet. Around him floated a strange odor, pleasant yet repulsive. He fixed his gaze first on the emissary then on Turi. The soldier felt as if his very soul was being probed. He could do nothing to stop it nor could he look away from the pale gaze.

"This one is almost as innocent as he seems," the ancient uttered at last. "Despite his obedient demeanor, he dislikes his duty." The odd eyes turned toward Lord Boorn. "This one knows the trust Damanthus places in Captain Gaerbith. It is not a trust imparted to the emissary."

Morfran toyed with his rings. "Why command a lord do a

commoner's bidding? Why send the servant as the master?"

"Damanthus keeps his own counsel, my lord," replied Heolstor, "and I cannot read his purpose in this. He is too distant for me to sense. A ghost on the edge of my vision. Of one thing I am certain. No one but the king of Disson knew the contents of the scroll."

Hands together, palms facing, Morfran rested fingertips against fingertips and studied the emissary.

Lord Boorn's mouth was rimmed in white.

"We are agreed upon settling the treaty?"

The emissary inclined his head in a slight nod.

"Skarda stands ready. What are Disson's terms?"

Scribes waited, quills poised over inkwells, to record the council. Turi dreaded what might come next. His homeland was at stake.

Boorn stood. "Damanthus, king of Disson, requires the freedom of all Territories under Dissonay protection, including the Thynathel Hills, the southern reaches of the Calhoun Forest, and the Western Wood. He must be assured Skarda will make no further attempts to overtake them."

Turi clenched his jaw to keep his expression blank.

Morfran leaned back in his chair. "Does my wife's brother think me a simpleton? Those are prime lands. Great trees in the Calhoun. Fine grapes in the Hills. Fertile farmland near the Wood. I must let them go merely because he *requires*?" His face hardened. "Does he now rule me? Were it that simple, why spend years in war? Why trample the farmland that would yield me rich crops? Why battle among orchards and vineyards stripped bare of their wealth? I will not retreat from this war for such slight reason."

Boorn replied, "Damanthus hopes the remembrance of former friendship will speak for him. He asks you to recall the oaths of brotherhood uttered when you fought side-by-side against those who sought to destroy his royal house. He bids you remember the day you first saw his sister, the lady Una, and vowed to make her your queen."

"That slattern?" Morfran roared, slapping the table and leaning forward. "She smiled on me while giving herself to a mere provincial! She preferred a commoner to a king! The only good that came of her were my children, but Damanthus took even them from me."

He leaned back again, as if suddenly mindful of all the onlookers. Shaking his sleeves down over his wrists once more, the king grimaced a tight smile. "He will not succeed with Yanámari. Despite her choice of a commoner for her betrothed, she still belongs to Skarda. She will not yield the crown to Disson."

Lord Boorn set a soft woolen bag on the table. Its contents thudded on the wooden surface. "If friendship and kinship will not win peace, I give this in exchange for the terms. It is worth twice the entire contents of Skarda's coffers, and likely more."

He drew from the bag a pearl the size of a fist.

Turi saw his own questions reflected in the faces of the Fourth. They stood alert. A nod, a flicker of his eyes, and the men would attack. He moved his chin, shaking his head but only accomplishing half the arc. *Patience. Let us see the traitor's full plan.*

"Mahyla," breathed Morfran, speaking the legendary name as if in prayer. "The Sea Stone."

The emissary nodded. "The gift from the people by the sea. A close-guarded heirloom of the House of Rhobarrd, it now comes to the House of Morfran in kinship and peace."

Turi's hand worried the hilt of the dagger at his belt. No king would freely part with the Sea Stone.

Light swirled beneath Mahyla's surface, changing hue with each subtle movement of the emissary, putting to shame the light surrounding the king. The stone seemed only a bauble, worth little against forestlands and fields, yet it was said to hold the very power of the gods, and the mortal who unlocked its secrets would live forever.

Something in that tale must be true. As long as Mahyla remained in the keeping of the House of Rhobarrd, every descendent had lived years longer than most other Dissonay, many of whom had survived more than a century, robust and hale to the end of their days.

With the passing of the treasure to Skarda, Morfran would become even more formidable.

From the careful expressions on the faces of the nobles and the Young Wolves, they did not know how to react—in jubilation, suspicion, or fear. Morfran frowned as he stared at the Sea Stone, but High Lord Boorn looked smug, like a man playing at *jhyla* whose toy-soldier *lachmil* has just conquered the board.

Heolstor's whispery voice ended the silence. "My lord, let us council together and consider this great gift."

Morfran stood. Feet shuffled and robes rustled as the nobles and the Young Wolves did the same. Waiting as the king descended the dais, they then formed two lines behind him. The wolves and their keeper preceded Morfran, but Heolstor walked beside him. The Hoods gathered their things in swift silence, and swooped out the door like wind-driven smoke. The king's youthful servant piled a few items on a tray and hastened through an opening behind the dais. Soon, the only ones in the hall were the Fourth and High Lord Boorn.

Still holding Mahyla, the emissary wore a look of mingled panic and puzzlement on his dignified countenance.

Turi drew his axe. The air sang with the sliding ring of drawn swords as the Dissonay strode forward.

High Lord Boorn stuttered backward, pale. Turi plucked the Sea Stone from his hand and laid it gently on the rumpled woolen bag.

Boorn fumbled for his knife. "This is treason!"

"Nay, yer lordship, this is justice. Owen, take Mahyla and guard her well. She is in yer charge until we restore her to Disson." Turi gestured. "Fremmen, bind his hands."

32 ~ OUT OF THE DARK

The warm smell of honeyed porridge embraces him. His brothers are already breaking their fast. They are young again, and living. His sisters—twins—laugh at his haste and make room for him at the table. Father, humor in his eyes, says nothing. Mother smooths Gaerbith's hair then pours a mugful of frothy milk.

A dream. Or the Otherland. Either way, he will savor this grace as long as it lasts.

He has traveled great distance yet is not weary. The journey was the length of thought but the breadth of eternity.

No matter. He is home. He smiles at his brothers' teasing. Food he once thought bland and poor now tastes as rich as any served in a king's hall.

Father rises from the table and kisses Mother. "Haste, lads," he says, grasping his staff and settling a brimmed hat on his head. "Now the sheep are shorn, they may cross the stream to the north meadow. Gaerbith, stay and help Neighbor Rimm when he comes for the wool."

"Aye, Father," he replies in a child's voice.

How young he is, and how young his father. How small the hands of his sisters, and how beautiful his mother.

She has a quietness that absorbs troubles and reduces them to nothings. She teaches him the power in unseen things and guides his study of their mysteries. From her he learns the names of Omwen'din.

"Wake up," she says in a voice not her own. She smiles, but her tone is heavy with tears, and her features blur. "We cannot linger."

He drinks milk but tastes ashes. He drops the cup.

With a jolt, he sat up. Arms released him. He blinked. Darkness.

He shifted away from Yanámari and sat on a lower step. A metallic stink jarred his senses after the sweetness of her neck.

"Gaerbith?"

What a fool he had been. Not only his battle wounds but every injury since childhood had flared to life. Yet, in courage born of anger and arrogance, he had smiled at the Hood and uttered the names of Omwen'din. In a moment of reckless pride, he had spoken words of such power they nigh slew him even as they drove the Black Hood mad. The translation was simple, almost childlike, but the language was ancient, and power lay in the full depth of the original meaning. He was an infant swinging a club, as likely to harm himself as to actually touch the enemy.

Lady Yanámari moved. He heard the dull grind of mail rings rolling against one another. She had removed her gloves, and now brushed his face with soft fingertips. "Captain?"

He leaned in to her touch.

No.

He pulled away from her and stood. The wounds on his hip and shoulder burned.

"You are well?" She sounded uncertain.

"I am well."

He regretted his sharp tone. She had likely feared him dead just now.

"Give me your hand, my lady."

After an uncertain moment of grasping only air, he found her fingers and helped Yanámari to her feet. His boots crunched across lantern glass.

"They will be waiting for us, my lady. We will fight our way out."

She squeezed his hand. "Twice you saved me from the Void. You will escape Elycia. Your prayers protect you."

"Prayers are not incantations, my lady. Omwen'din does not serve me as magic serves the Hôk Nar."

"Why then do you pray?" Her voice was brittle.

"Not only protection, but strength and wisdom and peace. Sometimes I listen and say nothing. I will do all I can to leave this city and take you to a safe place beyond the reach of your father and Heolstor. But if I do not survive, so be it. I serve Omwen'din—He does not serve me. He may do with my life as He wills."

There was a small silence.

"I wish I had your assurance, captain. I wish I could understand it. I regret endangering you with my selfishness."

"You fear the dying. But you are descended from both Skardian and Dissonay kings, and the Dissonay, as you well know, are afraid of nothing." He smiled. "They challenge the fell Woodsman as most men challenge one another at dice. Would you not rather go gloriously to the Otherland than await it in the slow death of daily despair?"

"You are a poet, captain. Is it with such words you rouse your men to battle?"

"Nay, my lady. I lead them."

"Fool!" hissed Morfran, rounding on Heolstor with such force that his fur robe swirled in a wide bell. "Fool!"

The two men faced one another in the center of the king's chamber.

"All that power you claim, yet you turn your back on the Sea Stone. Do you not take it up, I will. Then, perhaps, will the throne of Skarda no longer be subject to the whims of an old man so unable to gain what he most desires that he must make use of stronger men. Yet, once the old man has drawn the vital forces from his tools, he still does not have what he seeks." Morfran gripped the hilt of his sword. "A pity, is it not?"

Heolstor glared at the king. "Do not threaten me. I am the reason you wear the crown—"

"I am the reason you continue to live. My life has allowed you a score of new years to seek the sword of Kel."

"I am the reason you are in power!" Spittle flecked Heolstor's lips and glinted in his thin beard. "I captured the Dragons!" He pointed his staff toward the open windows. "To me the Dragons rendered their scales! Yet I forbore to keep such magnificent gifts, and gave one of the scales to you."

Heolstor's raspy voice grew in strength until it sounded like two giant stones grinding pebbles to sand. "The greatest weapon a mortal could ever hope to wield—power over a Dragon! Long life and great strength! All the knowledge in the world! And yet, in impatience and boundless arrogance, you rushed the binding and destroyed the link. Without that golden Dragon's desire for vengeance compelling it to find the Kel-child, we may never find the sword."

Hunching, Heolstor became a bent old man again, his gnarled fingers wrapping the carven wood of his staff like ribs folded around a heart. His voice diminished. "It is to me you owe the throne. Remember your debt."

Morfran's gaze flicked aside. It was a tiny submission.

But the Sea Stone—how did it threaten Heolstor? Its power was legendary. Was Mahyla, like Azrin, death to touch? Yet High Lord Boorn, no man of magic, had held the great pearl with neither fear nor ill consequence. Perhaps what protected the emissary was what prevented the counselor—Mahyla's warm light at war with Heolstor's dark arts.

Morfran lifted the crown from where it hung on the back of his chair. He had not worn it since his return to Elycia.

"Tell me, Longbeard," he said, running his fingertips across the etched scales of the Dragon Crown, so old their edges were no longer sharp, "what did you read in the mind of the captain yesternight?"

"He possesses a strong gaze and a stronger will."

"Curious, then, that he was not at the council. He turned away your savory poisoned stew and bade his men eat peasant fare."

"The Dissonay are simple folk."

"Yes." Morfran set aside the crown. "As simple as foxes."

"They would say the same of you, my lord."

"I will send for the captain, then for Yanámari." Morfran turned to look out a window. "Prepare you pen, Imre."

"Imre is not here."

Morfran wheeled, his gaze sweeping the chamber. "Where is he?"

Heolstor bowed. "Allow me to summon him, my lord."

Gaerbith almost stumbled. Expecting the next step, he encountered level ground. The echo of his footsteps implied an ample room. He could see nothing, but the space felt broader and the air fresher than in the passage.

Lady Yanámari tugged at his hand, and he released his grasp.

"No, captain." She took his hand again, leading him across the room. "Now it is your turn to follow."

Light—sudden, sharp, and blinding—cut the darkness.

Drawing his sword, he stepped between her and the light.

A slight figure stood in the doorway. "Captain?" Imre, the messenger. "Is Lady Yanámari with you? Is Elta?"

From behind Gaerbith, Yanámari spoke. "Are you alone?"

"Yes, my lady."

"Haste! Inside!"

Imre reached beside the opening. When he stepped inside, he carried a torch. He pushed a carving. The opening sealed. The youth did not appear to be armed—in one hand he bore a tray, in the other the torch—but Gaerbith did not lower his sword.

"What is your purpose here?"

"Morfran dismissed the council while he ponders a matter."

"But why are you here?"

Imre hesitated. "Is Elta with you?"

Yanámari stepped from behind Gaerbith, and Imre gasped.

"A disguise." The lady plucked at her tunic.

"Where is Elta?" he demanded.

She put her hands on his shoulders, and said in a voice thick with unshed tears, "Oh, Imre. Do you not know?"

"Know what, my lady?" Panic raised the pitch of his voice.

She bowed her head. "The Black Hoods—"

The tray and its contents clattered to the ground. Gaerbith caught the torch as Imre fell to his knees. The young man was pale and dry-eyed, shock and despair in his face. Dropping her satchel, Lady Yanámari knelt and embraced him. Like he, she did not weep.

Gaerbith spoke. "Imre, were you followed?"

He shook his head. He removed Yanámari's arms from around him, his movements slow, his expression a stark blank. "The council went ill. I must go attend the king. Heolstor will know why I tarry. He will know where I have been."

Imre wore a messenger's scrip on a long leather strap that crossed his chest. He gathered the tray and the other items from where they lay scattered on the floor and stowed them in the bag, then he stood.

Yanámari stood also. Grief and anger tightened the planes of her face. "The captain killed a Hood." She shouldered her satchel again. "Heolstor claims he knows when the Brethren die, because their essence disappears. If that is true, he will be here any moment."

Lest they know him for a fraud, even beneath the thick covering of the black robe, Rubin stopped following the flock of Brethren and sought another way out of the labyrinth of caves.

Torches guttered in their brackets. Air—great draughts of it—came from somewhere.

This tunnel?

Rubin put his hand into the darkness. Air, like breath, moved around his fingers. Perhaps this was the way back to the great golden Dragon who had helped him find his way through the smoke, but the stench was gone. Instead, the air smelt of flowers and green grass. Entering the tunnel, hand guiding him along the wall, he ventured into a blindness as profound as the Void.

Syra, is there a place still set for me at table? Does Evan sleep curled by the fire, waiting for his father to carry him to bed and tuck the blanket under his chin?

Rubin could never return home. To do so would kill them all. Perhaps, in disguise, he could see his family from time to time. Perhaps he could still go forth with the laborers and send his few coins to Syra. There was a loose stone beside the door of their hovel. It was the perfect place to hide little gifts—

A silken sound smoothed the air. Warm fragrance like a summer breeze breathed in the depth of the mountain.

WELCOME, RUBIN KYRINSSON. A glow pulsed in the heart of the cavern. YOU ARE COME IN GOOD HOUR.

As unsettling as thunder on a cloudless day, as deep as the chasm of the River Thrayne, rich as milk, lyric as birdsong, the beautiful voice resonated in Rubin's ears and sent him to his knees.

BOW NOT TO ME. I AM NEITHER GOD NOR NOBLE.

"How do you know me?"

I AM DRAGON-KIND. I KNOW MANY THINGS. I KNOW YOU WERE OFFERED TO ANOTHER DRAGON. HIS STINK STILL CLINGS TO YOU. I KNOW YOU SEEK A WAY OUT OF THIS MOUNTAIN.

"Do you know the way?"

WITH YOUR HELP, I WILL MAKE A WAY.

"What help could I be to a Dragon?" Until being imprisoned, Rubin had thought as everyone else did—that Dragons no longer existed—but now a Dragon sought aid of him.

THE HÔK NAR SENT THIEVES EAST TO THE DRAGON LANDS AND STOLE SCALES, EGGS, AND YOUNGLINGS. ALL CLANS

LOST YOUNG. The creature sighed. I AM TOO LATE TO SAVE THEM.

"But how can I help?"

BETWEEN OUR CLANS IS ANCIENT ENMITY, EVEN OLDER THAN THE ENMITY BETWEEN MEN AND DRAGONS. IT WAS NOT ALWAYS SO. HATRED HAS OPENED A DOOR FOR EVIL. THE DARK POWER OF THE HÔK NAR OVERCAME ME, AND WHILE I LAY POWERLESS, THEY STOLE ONE OF MY SCALES. YET A SCALE WILLINGLY GIVEN BEARS MORE POWER THAN ONE TAKEN.

Held between two great talons, an iridescent silver disk came toward Rubin.

NOT SINCE THE PRYMMIDDION AGE HAS A SCALE BEEN FREELY GIVEN TO MEN, AND FEW WERE SO HONORED EVEN THEN.

"I am only a woodcutter—"

TAKE THE SCALE, AND COME WITH ME.

33 ~ SACRIFICE

Gaerbith led the way down the corridor. Turi strode into view, face grim, axe dripping blood. He halted when he saw Gaerbith, who drew his brows together in question. Turi shook his head.

High Lord Boorn had chosen himself above his people.

"To the stables," Gaerbith ordered as the Fourth gathered. "We will leave our enemies afoot."

Surrounding Imre and Lady Yanámari to hide them among their ranks, the Fourth ran through the great hall, along passages, and down the shallow steps leading to the Court of Soldiers. As he ran, Owen tore the Dissonay standard from its staff and discarded the wooden rod. It rattled to the ground, and someone trod on it, snapping the staff. Owen stuffed the banner into his tunic.

"Here," said Yanámari, pointing, and the Dissonay turned, approaching the stables from the rear, out of sight of the barracks.

Gaerbith saddled Kraekor, and tied his pack behind the saddle before mounting. The men, Imre, and Yanámari bestrode their own horses or the blooded animals belonging to the nobles. The last man was settling into the saddle when Young Wolves swarmed from their quarters and from the tower, filling the stableyard with the deadly glitter of drawn swords.

Kraekor surged forward, eager to bear his rider to battle. Gaerbith held him back and glanced at Turi. The man nodded. Fremmen drew alongside. The Dissonay gathered shoulder-to-shoulder, facing outward in a bristling circle. To Gaerbith's right, Lady Yanámari drew her sword.

"Fremmen," said Gaerbith in a low voice, "follow her. I will clear a path. Lead the men around and behind."

The Skardians advanced. Among them, Gurn Grumësson grinned

at the captain as if claiming him for his opponent, but Gaerbith did not oblige. He tapped Kraekor's sides with his heels. The old roan bounded forward from the circle, knocking down two Young Wolves even as Bítan hissed through the air and dug a groove into one of the highborn soldiers.

"To me! To me!" cried Yanámari. Her mount leapt through the opening Gaerbith created, and Fremmen called the other men to follow.

Gaerbith hacked at his attackers, felling them more by the weight of his blade than by any grace. He could not swing the full arc lest he catch his men as they passed.

They thundered down a narrow street that Gaerbith and Turi then closed with the bulk of their horses and the sweep of their weapons. A longsword and an axe were not meant to be used a-horseback. While one man laid about with his blade, the other dismounted. In moments, they stood side by side, an effective barrier.

The Wolves ran at them, but most were cut down before the elegant Skardian swords could slip inside the long reach of the Dissonay blades. Bítan parsed a man at the waist, tumbling the torso to the ground. Turi was so tall that his battleaxe took limbs and heads with ease. Piled bodies formed a low barricade. Blood slicked the cobbles. Still the Skardians came.

Time reduced to each move of Gaerbith's sword—slice, block, slash, cut, block, block, cut. Breaking one sword, Gaerbith then knocked another aside, taking the man's hand with it. The Young Wolf's mouth opened, his eyes widened, yet he made no sound as he stared at the space where his hand used to be.

Gaerbith could scarce keep his feet on the gore-covered stones, but Bítan leapt with a will of its own and cut down enemies despite his uncertain footing. He slashed through a scarlet surcoat and felt the grating resistance of mail along his blade. The Skardian fell, dropping his sword.

Pain streaked like fire up an oiled wick. Gaerbith's leg gave way. The bruising shock of the fall jarred along his spine and into his skull. He saw the brilliance of sunlight, the ponderance of blood, the greyness of the narrow street. It was a grave shroud, unfurled and waiting.

He looked down. The remainder of the sword he had broken was buried deep in his thigh. He cursed and tried to stand.

Turi still fought, his long arms adding crucial length to the reach of his axe. Blood streamed down his cheek and arm, however, and cut a bright swath across his white surcoat, testament to the great skill of the enemy.

Gaerbith tried again to stand. Where were his men? Pray Omwen'din they were not surrounded.

He shook his head to clear his sight. His thoughts grew fuzzy.

With a wordless shout, a Young Wolf pointed his sword at Gaerbith.

Gurn Grumësson.

The Skardian strode forward, arms loose at his sides, his advance without haste or uncertainty.

Again, Gaerbith struggled to stand but could not. Blood pushed up around the stump of the blade in his thigh.

His father's voice came to him through distant memory. "Go not to Elycia. Though it bears a fair name, it is a foul city."

"Why, Father?"

"Nobles walk there as if free, their chains unseen. They are bound by wills stronger than their own. For common folk, freedom is a fable they wish they could imagine or had the courage to pursue. In Elycia reigns the servant of Nar Cahm, and he thinks himself a god. Nay, my son, go not to Elycia. Death walks there."

Forgive me, Father.

Gurn smiled, drawing near.

Motes of dust and flecks of blood moved through the air with equal languor. In almost detached anger, Gaerbith cursed the city, High Lord Boorn, Heolstor, King Padraig, himself. He had known the danger when half-delirious Padraig sent him to this forsaken place. To what purpose? To learn something of his enemies? To expose someone Padraig already knew to be a traitor?

The craftiness of the plan struck him like an arrow. Even as Gurn arced his blade to strike off Gaerbith's head, Gaerbith laughed.

Mad Morfran, thinking the battle over and himself the victor, had not thought to look behind him when he withdrew to Elycia and sued for peace, itself a mockery of his enemy. King Padraig—pretending on parchment to be his father Damanthus—had played the trusting Dissonay that Morfran expected. Had sent an emissary to keep Skarda distracted while Disson strengthened its armies.

Well, then. Gaerbith would do his part.

He steadied his hilt in the hollow of his hip and levered the blade upward. The force of Gurn's sweeping attack carried him forward. Realization paled his face, but he could neither stop nor turn back. He plunged to the hilt, his last breath a wet gurgle.

The weight of him knocked Gaerbith onto his side and tore Bítan from his grasp. Pain seared his leg, and he cried out. Turi called to him, but he could not answer through the agony.

Where were his men? Were they caught? Killed? Captured by Heolstor's magic?

He strove in vain to free Bítan from Gurn's body. He grabbed the dead man's lighter sword just in time to stab a Skardian's foot and draw a deep red line across another's sword wrist. His strength waned, but he fought on. He caught the Skardians at their knees while Turi maintained a stalwart stance above him.

"*Omwen'din Pyrva!*" With a many-throated cry, the Dissonay attacked. They surrounded the enemy, who were still trying to take the narrow street.

Yanámari brandished her sword and shouted as loud and wild as a warrior woman of old. Teeth clenched, Gaerbith almost smiled.

Arrows rained from the city wall.

"Turi!" Gaerbith's voice sounded faint in his own ears. "Fall back!"

No longer able to sit upright, he lay on the stones, striving to remain aware, alive.

Yanámari dismounted and knelt beside him. She reached for the hilt of the broken sword.

"No!" He stayed her hand. "Lead the men to the gate. Take a way the Skardians will not expect."

Arrows skittered across the cobbles.

"What of you?"

"Turi will signal the men. They will follow you. Now go!"

She hesitated, her left arm covered in blood. "Have you seen Imre? I lost sight of him in the fight."

More arrows filled the stable yard. Turi grabbed her around the waist and tossed her onto her horse, yet still she turned to look back at Gaerbith.

"Go!"

She did.

The yard and the mouth of the street cleared as Dissonay and Skardians alike fled the arrows. What fool captain would shoot on his own men? Perhaps the order came from Morfran himself, who cared not who was slain so long as his enemies lay dead.

Gaerbith lifted his head and pushed himself up until he was propped against a mound of bodies. He looked for green-and-white surcoats among the fallen but saw none. If any Dissonay had been among them, their bodies had been taken when his men retreated.

Blood wicked along his leg and up into his tunic. Removing his belt, he wrapped it above the wound to stop the bleeding, but his hands were clumsy and his arms weak.

He would rest, aye, lie here on the cool stones—

"You must rise," a familiar voice urged. "Here is Kraekor."

The warhorse bowed his head, snuffling Gaerbith's cheek and testing the scent of the wound then slowly kneeling beside him.

"Come, captain. Up with you!"

Grumbling a curse at the voice's persistence, Gaerbith pulled himself astride Kraekor, and the horse heaved upward to stand unsteadily on the islands of cobblestone surrounded by rivulets of blood.

"Thank you, old friend." Gaerbith patted Kraekor's neck.

The ground was littered with fallen men and horses. Whose voice had he heard? Imre's? But why would the lad be here and not with the Fourth? Did Gaerbith but dream, now that he left so much of his own blood on the stones?

"Come, Kraekor. Let us find our friends."

Across the stableyard, smoke boiled like gathering rain clouds. Black-robed figures appeared, walking toward him with unhurried steps.

Smoke coiled around Kraekor's hooves, hobbling him. The horse snorted and stamped, trying to pull free. Gaerbith slumped forward. He fumbled to draw a knife strapped beneath his surcoat, but no blade would cut magic.

Like a ghost in the darkness, grey-clad Heolstor walked through the billows of smoke, stopped, and planted his staff.

"The moment you resisted me at banquet, captain, I knew you as my enemy. Uártha is dead these many years. How do you even know her name? Was she your teacher? But how could she be? You are much too young to have learned even a tenth of the knowledge Uártha could impart." Then, with an examining squint and a voice grown almost thoughtful, "Your secret is ancient, as old as the mountains, and there is that in you which holds memories captive, sights no Man living has seen. I ask you, captain—how did you acquire your magic?"

Annoyed, feeling the sun warm on his back and wanting only sleep, Gaerbith mumbled, "Not magic. Listening."

"Listening? To what?" Heolstor gestured skyward with his staff. "To the wind? Look at you! Powerless. Nigh dead. Does your hearing bleed out like your wound?"

Gaerbith struggled to stay alert. *Omwen'din, hear my cry—*

"Your prayers are as useless as your magic."

—and give me strength like the oak—

"Ah. You are that boy. Uártha's son. Whatever happened to your mother's little book of words? They cut but did not kill." Heolstor laughed. "Uártha. How foolish."

Anger roiled in Gaerbith's chest.

"The darkness hobbling your horse is a strand of the Void, and the Void is a dread thing"—the counselor smiled—"where men go shrieking with none to hear. Every ill deed, every ill word, every regret, every grief, shreds your soul until that agony outruns anything else your flesh endures."

The smoke touched Gaerbith, and he sucked in his breath at the sudden, sharp pain.

"Tell your secret, captain, and your death will be quick. The Void will not have you."

Gaerbith tightened his grip on the reins.

"So be it. Come, Brethren, he is yours."

Three Hoods appeared through the smoke clogging the air around Heolstor. They approached with hands raised, palms out. His arm hooked through the reins, Gaerbith scarce kept his seat when Kraekor rose to strike at the robed figures. They did not flinch from the attack, nor did Kraekor's hooves do more than batter the air.

"You fear to slay me by your own hand?" Gaerbith taunted. "Coward."

Pale eyes ablaze, the Master of the Black Hoods strode past the Brethren, pulled Bítan from Gurn's body, and drew back the blade. "To the Void with you!"

"No!" A blur darted out from behind a tangle of bodies. Imre leapt between the captain and the counselor.

No, lad. No—

The sword sliced through him from left shoulder to right flank, yet no blood spilled. Even as the blade passed, his body faded and disappeared.

The sword glowed white. Heolstor dropped it, screaming. The staff, too, clattered to the ground. The whips and clouds of smoke evaporated. He grabbed his wrist, screams ripping from him shrill as the rasps of a saw through hardwood. Flame burst in the palm of his hand.

Gaerbith closed his eyes. Let the Woodsman come; he need not sharpen his axe.

A breeze ruffled Gaerbith's sweat-dampened hair. He drew a breath sweetened by the scent of wildflowers. Blinking open his eyes, he gazed on the green hills of home. But where were the vineyards and farms? Gentle waves, laced in foam and so blue they might have been the offspring of the sky, caressed golden shores sloping gently up to meet the Thynathel Hills.

No. Not the Hills. They did not lie near the sea. He looked on the Otherland.

In the distance, a horn blew clean notes in the afternoon air. Lifting his head, Gaerbith smiled, and his gaze sought what he had longed his whole life to see.

"My lord Dragon"—Rubin bowed in the direction of the beautiful voice—"have you a name?"

TAKE THE SCALE, AND YOU SHALL KNOW IT.

Thin and transparent, hard yet yielding, the scale glittered like sunlit snow. Rubin closed his fist around the silver disk, and it warmed his palm.

The name came as if he had known it from birth. "Áredan," he said in wonder, "and your sister is the queen of the Fredek kindred. You said you were not noble."

BEING QUEEN AMÉLI'S BROTHER IS NOTHING IF I DO NOT LIVE IN MY OWN RIGHT. I WAS COVETED BY HEOLSTOR BECAUSE I AM A RARITY—A FREDEK WARRIOR. NOW WE WILL BE FREE BECAUSE YOU ARE ANOTHER RARITY IN THIS PLACE —AN HONEST MAN.

Boldness grew in Rubin. Awareness such as he had never known filled his senses. Where once he saw only night, his sight waxed keen, and he discerned the Dragon's massive shape. He felt the darkness of the Black Hoods, but he also felt Áredan's will pushing against it.

"They know something has changed," Rubin said as the evil sought to retake the Dragon. He saw, with sight not his own, fingers of smoke grabbing at Áredan but slithering off without being able to take hold of him. "They will be coming soon."

COME, RUBIN KYRINSSON. A great silvery claw appeared.

He obeyed, climbing a scaled leg as warm as mortal flesh. Áredan's neck was a gleaming column, his wings a pale sheen. A shallow bowl formed where the bones of the wings met the Dragon's back, and Rubin settled there. Leaning forward, the scale clasped tightly in one hand, he reached his arms as far as they would go around the back of the Dragon's neck, and closed his eyes.

Áredan roared. Rocks tumbled, and fragments rained down on Rubin's back. A fresh wind tugged the black robe he still wore. Upward the Dragon surged, into air so crisp it burned Rubin's lungs. He lifted his head and opened his eyes. Pale blue sky stretched above him, and below gaped the broken cavern and thrust the rugged peaks of the Craydaeg Mountains. Hope welled in his chest. The sun shone over his shoulder, and Rubin laughed.

Then the Dragon wheeled around a crag, and in the west rose the tall grey towers of Elycia.

"Where are you going!" Rubin shouted, fighting a lightning strike of fear. "We will be captured!"

NAY, GOOD RUBIN. WE ARE WILLINGLY BOUND. NOTHING HEOLSTOR AND HIS BLACK HOODS DO WILL HARM YOU. LISTEN. HEAR IT.

Timeless assurance hummed from somewhere deep in Áredan, like a song sung by distant voices, the air clear but the words lost. Here, between the steady beat of Dragon wings, above the Craydaeg Mountains and beneath the smiling sun, anything was possible.

"We go to aid Skarda's enemies."

WE DO INDEED.

"We may already be too late."

WE GO NONETHELESS.

A cut slashed her upper arm. Pain pounded with her heartbeat, but Yanámari did not linger while Turi set men to bind wounds. Instead, she kept watch from behind a wall that hid a pile of rubbish from the street and obscured the Dissonay from the Skardians massed before the gates.

The city wall rising on her left was free of archers, who were gathered above the gates, and below them were troops of foot soldiers, defined by their colors: Baron Vaikhar's men stood beside Baron Chennam's men who stood beside Baron Hargow's, and so on. A few mounted Young Wolves formed a line in front of them, and at the fore was Rhôn Bergsson. He looked across the square, back into the city. The expression on his face was not one of suspicion or anger such as he wore yesternight, but one of grave melancholy, as if he kept watch for something he did not wish to see.

Smudges of shadow, Hôk Nar stood among the foot soldiers. Yanámari did not see Heolstor's grey robe or her father's height. Were he present and mounted on his tall black, Morfran would draw all heed to himself.

In her mind she saw a strong face grown pale despite skin browned by many suns, and a pair of eyes, sharp and blue. Captain Gaerbith expected to die. Fear and grief fisted in her throat. To save his men, he sent them away, and he trusted her to lead them.

Were it not for her selfish request, he would not have pledged his honor, and the Dissonay might even now be leaving the city under banner of peace. But many were dead, their bodies tied across their saddles. Turi refused to leave them lying in Elycia.

They had died because of her. Elta, Gaerbith, maybe even Imre, and all who died today—they were lost because of her.

Yanámari looked over her shoulder at the Dissonay, mounted, somber, silent. What manner of men were they to leave their captain to die? They only followed her because he ordered them to do so. Perhaps the better question was this: What manner of man commanded such obedience?

Dismounting lest the noise of hooves alert the Skardians, she left her horse and walked back to Turi. He watched her without apparent anger or resentment, waiting like his men.

She halted, words and thoughts tangling. "You are a people renowned for fierce boldness in battle," she said in a low voice, wishing she had spent more time learning to speak Dissonay rather than merely reading it, "but this day requires more than force alone."

Had she just insulted them? Their faces betrayed nothing. She did not mean to imply they were not keen-witted.

"You do not follow women to war, and I have never led an army—"

How could she ask for their loyalty? She was here because their captain was dead.

Turi's smile was small, weary. "Aye, my lady, but ye be mistaken in us. When we sleep at last beside fires of wood and not of magic, we will tell ye of the women of old who led our clans to war." As he spoke, he smeared salve on her wound and bound it. "Ye know the city, all its streets and byways. Ye led us to the gates. Command us."

A horn sounded, clear and high, its ringing notes splintering, caroming from wall to wall until the last echo died.

"Our only advantage is surprise," said Yanámari. "There are

archers on the wall and Black Hoods among the soldiers. Only a few Young Wolves are with them, but you know well what they can do. And now my father comes."

Again the horn sounded.

"Turi, keep as close to the wall as you are able. Cut through the foot soldiers. The archers will be forced to overshoot you, for the wall is wide over the gates. The greatest mass of soldiers is in the center, because the center must be protected at all costs if we are to be kept inside the city. The gates are so precisely balanced that the strength of one man can push them open. "

Turi glanced around at the Dissonay. "Any man who reaches the center opens the gate."

They nodded.

"Move on my signal," said Yanámari. "When I kneel before the king—"

"My lady!"

She looked at him.

Turi lowered his voice. "He will kill ye."

"What is it you say in Disson? As Omwen'din wills?"

Though his expression tightened, he said nothing.

"If you surrender, no quarter will be given. I wear Disson's colors and have bloodied a sword against my own people, but I am still the daughter of Morfran, king of Skarda. He may yet have mercy."

She returned to her horse and leaned her forehead against his shoulder. Only yesternight she had told Gaerbith she would sacrifice anything to be free. It seemed an age ago, and innocent.

The Skardians in the square uttered a resounding hail, and the king's deep voice rose above the shout as he ordered everyone to look upon the corpse at his side. Yanámari lifted her head but could not see past the rubbish wall. Mounting the horse, she gazed over the heads of the men ringing the square. The sight stabbed her as sharp as any blade.

"Captain!" breathed Turi beside her.

Gaerbith slumped forward, head bowed, hands slack. The scabbard on his back was empty. Blood covered his legs and warhorse as if they had been dipped in red dye.

"This," Morfran declared, "is the fate of all who defy the king of Skarda!" The gold broidery on his sable surcoat gleamed in the late afternoon light. He made a fine-clad executioner. "Bring a cage. Hang the bones of this Dissonay dog for all to see. When the laborers return at sunset, let it be in solemn order and silent contemplation. Let this carrion feast remind the people they are but Men. Let them know I will not be defied. "

A wind came, sweet with pine and wildflowers brightening the slopes of the Craydaeg Mountains. A breath from the world beyond.

Rhôn Bergsson nudged his mount forward. What he said to the king, Yanámari could not hear, but the young man received a nod from Morfran and departed the square.

Heolstor appeared, one hand bound in a thick bandage and cradled against his chest. The men rolling out the cage ceased their action and stood still.

Yanámari glanced back at the Dissonay. The men touched thumbs —hooked like shepherd crooks—to their chins, mouths then brows. Turi nodded. She drew her sword, still stained with Skardian blood, and gave it to him. She could not approach Morfran with a weapon. His daughter or no, if she wore a sword she would be forced to fight him. Unarmed, there was a small chance she might live.

"If I fall, leave my body on the stones and flee. Do not die for me."

Then she rode out from the sheltering wall. Heolstor's gaze found her in an instant, then the king's. All eyes watched her deliberate approach. Hair short, tangled, damp with sweat and stiff with blood, she did not expect immediate recognition. The Young Wolves had not known her when she led the Dissonay to surround them. Now, despite the torn bloody surcoat and her altered appearance, someone murmured in amazement, "Lady Yanámari!" and men fell to kneel on one knee, heads bowed.

"Yanámari?" Morfran's brows drew together in a confused frown. "What is this?"

"My lord, I come to beg the body of Gaerbith of Disson."

"Explain this madness!"

"He was my betrothed. Grant me leave to bury him"—she inclined her head in a small bow—"then I will return and obey you in all things."

"In all things?"

"Yes, my lord."

The king's eyes narrowed. "Why such attire?"

She dismounted. "Gaerbith was a soldier. Let me do his memory the proper service. Then I will attend you, my lord, and learn what you will teach so that I dishonor my lord and father no longer."

Uncertainty filled Morfran's eyes, but Yanámari did not allow herself to hope. Heolstor stood nearby. He could turn the king's mind in the span of a blink.

"Skardian blood wraps you in its reek," rasped the counselor. He moved forward, the hem of his grey robe stained red. "You lifted your hand against your own people, yet you live. Did they recognize the Lady of Skarda and turn their weapons aside lest they slay you and anger their king? In that moment of mercy, is that when you struck?"

No, she wanted to say, *none knew me*, but his words stole her resolve. Guilt drove her to her knees.

The instant she touched the stones, "Omwen'din Pyrva!" resounded, echoes taking it until the Dissonay cry seemed to come from everywhere. Captain Gaerbith's horse pricked his ears and danced sideways, eagerness in every line.

The horse behaved as if his master lived.

Yanámari rose to her feet, hope surging. Leaping astride her mount, she grabbed Kraekor's reins and turned toward the gates.

Chaos filled the square. Morfran's personal guard gathered around him. Heolstor and his Brethren were so pressed by other soldiers that they were unable to lift their hands and summon the Void. Or, perhaps, they had used it in the earlier battle and drained their power. The Dissonay strove to beat back the Skardians, but were nigh swallowed by the greater number of foot soldiers. Even longswords could not overcome the reach of spears.

Yanámari pushed her mount through the fray, leading Kraekor and praying the captain did not fall. She could see their goal—the center of the gates—but the heaving, stabbing wall of bodies prevented her. She had no weapon, the captain's sword was missing, and she was taken by a sudden crushing panic.

Rhôn Bergsson, his scarlet surcoat bright as blood among the tunics of the barons' men, angled his mount toward her.

A sword clove the air between them. "You are the House of Morfran!" bellowed the king. His massive warhorse knocked aside foot soldiers and spearmen, and Yanámari's mount shifted its hindquarters to the side to keep from being slammed by the bigger horse. Morfran aimed the tip of his sword toward Yanámari's chest. His eyes blazed with anger and madness.

"You are mine! You belong to Skarda! The House of Morfran will rule forever!"

A Dissonay longsword crossed the king's blade.

"If you slay her, my king, your house will die." Rhôn's voice was flat. "If you let her go, she will soon learn that the crude ways of the Dissonay do not suit her, and she will return to you, willing to accept whatever you command."

"You dare instruct me with a Dissonay sword in your hand? You dare prevent the king?"

"I dare remind the king his son is dead. M'lady is the only heir."

Fire flared on the city wall. Screaming balls of flame—burning archers—fell among the foot soldiers. More fire ringed the square. Cursing, Morfran wheeled his mount and shouted for Heolstor.

Rhôn looked at Yanámari, and what she saw in his eyes saddened her.

"Rhôn, I am—"

He slid the blade into the scabbard on Gaerbith's back.

A shadow fell across the lowering sun, and a fresh wind swirled through the square, bringing with it an uncommon fragrance. Another blast of flame rained on the square. Yanámari looked up. A great silver beast with translucent wings wheeled overhead. Battle-hardened men fell back, terror on their faces. Ranks broke as men fled the square. Warriors and Brethren alike sought refuge in the shadowed streets. Morfran shouted his fury, but a blast of flame herded him in the direction of his men.

Aside from Yanámari and Rhôn, only the Dissonay remained in the square. Fire rose high between her and them. Heat scorched the air. Her mount reared in fright, but Kraekor seemed unmoved by the flames.

"Turi!" she called over the roar of the fire. "Go! I will find a way!"

The big man's face wavered behind the heat. He gave her a long look. Then he turned and gestured to his men. Gates opened. The Dissonay galloped beneath the stone arc.

The Dragon hovered like a shield, its wing beats scattering the flames, pushing them hither and thither until every street leading to the gate was blocked by fire. Then the Dragon stretched out its neck and opened its mouth.

Yanámari closed her eyes.

A great swirling wind sucked away from her, and the air grew cool. All was still.

She opened her eyes. Lumps of ash marked where men once stood, and the stones were streaked with soot. Flames still prevented anyone from entering the square, but the fire near her was gone, as if the Dragon wheeling overhead had swallowed it.

Through the drifting remnants of smoke, she saw beyond the gates. The Dissonay waited there.

"You will not be coming back."

She glanced at Rhôn.

"Go," he said. "I will not hinder you."

She held his gaze. "I will not forget."

Then she kicked her mount's flanks and the horse leapt forward, followed by Kraekor, and galloped through the gates.

IV

CAPTAIN, FARMER, ORPHAN, SPY

Thryffin carries a bundle of sticks for the cooking fire, and his mother works in the garden, sunlight on her golden braids. She looks up at him and smiles.

Yellow-clad soldiers fill the yard. The baron's men grab Mother. She kicks, screams, scratches. Dropping the wood, Thryffin runs toward the cart. Two other women lie in it, arms and legs bound. Mother is tossed in beside them.

"No, Thrfffyn! Stay back!" she cries, but he scrambles up the slatted side of the cart.

A soldier lifts a sword, and Thryffin turns to see the hilt descend. Mother screams. The world disappears.

Thryffin wakes. Stars shine. His head aches. He lies in the road, cursing the baron and the Voice. Then he weeps. When tears are spent, he collects the fallen sticks and carries them into the cottage.

His father is not there. Thryffin searches for him from farm to farm until daybreak. He stumbles into Shea, and there he sees a silent crowd gathered at the mill. They part for him.

Beside the grainery door stands Miller George, frowning. His wife touches Thryffin's shoulder and murmurs, "Your father was out of his head. He said you were dead and your mother taken. We tried to calm him." A tear slips down her cheek made pale by a dusting of flour. "He lay quiet, so we left. We thought he slept."

Thryffin walks into the cool, dim room where the grain is stored. The dark figure of a man hangs from a thick beam. Thryffin stares up at it for a few moments then returns to the sunlight.

"He cannot be laid in the kirkyard," someone mutters. "Not for self-murder. Even the old ways do not allow for that."

"The poor lad has no money for a burial," says another.

"He has no home, either. The land is Baron Markha's. Someone should take the lad in."

Looking on him with pity, they all stand aside as Thryffin passes through the crowd. He goes to the kirk, and sits on the topmost stone step. Leaning his head against the rough wooden door, he sleeps.

35 ~ JEALOUSY

Maggie gathered her comb, fresh undergarments, and a bar of yarrow-and-lavender soap, then closed the low cupboard and descended the ladder from the loft.

"Most folk will be at the square, I think, starting the dance a bit early, as they always do." Mother Crumb set the mending basket beside the chair near the fire.

One hand on the latch, Maggie hesitated at the door.

The old woman smiled and waved her away. "Best go, child, before someone else has the notion to bathe."

Maggie left the protecting hedge of the healer's garden and ventured into the mist-ribboned darkness of the forest. She breathed deep of air sweet with roses, clary, and jasmine—more flowers blooming early in the unusual warm spring—and allowed the scented night to clear her mind.

Reaching the river, she dropped her things on the shore and removed the laced leather shoes she had worn to town. Bright music on the eve of the Faere skipped through the dark, and she almost put on the shoes again.

Nay, that would be foolishness.

She loosened her braids then stepped put of her clothes and into the water, shivering as its cold rippled over her feet. Soap in hand, she waded out until her shoulders were covered. She took a deep breath and sank below the chill flow. The water weighted her hair, pulling on her neck as she broke the surface. She rubbed soap into her hair and along her limbs. The action helped warm her. Tossing the bar ashore, she lay back in the water and floated a bit downstream.

"Washing away the blood rite?"

Startled, Maggie floundered, choking on river water.

"Witches do not drown, do they?"

She gasped for air, feeling around for safe footing. Her toes encountered a stony shelf, and she crouched on it, only her head above water. Upriver and across from her, Kathleen Donnegan perched on a rock, arms wrapped around her knees, so still she seemed a part of the rock.

"Kieran Smith is stubborn, and he cannot see what is best for him, but he attends kirk when Father Donovan is here. I have heard the priest pray over him. So I will not fear you, Maggie Finney"—there was mockery in Kathleen's voice—"even if you do burn babies or dance with the Dark One. You will not harm me, because doing so would harm your plans for Kieran."

Shivering, Maggie pushed her hair away from her face. "What do you want?"

"That hand."

Maggie plunged her crippled fingers below the surface.

Kathleen laughed, her head thrown back like a wolf to a waxing moon. Then rancor replaced mirth. "How did you bewitch Kieran that day in his shop? You left a token—your apron around his neck. Some sort of strangling spell to choke away his reason?"

"Any spells cast are yours. Are you not, after all, his betrothed?"

Kathleen tossed her hair over her shoulder. "I must marry him. It is what Father wanted. I am the only Donnegan sister left unwed, and it is Kieran's duty to take me to wife."

"If you must marry him, then you must."

"You mock me?" Swinging her legs over the edge of the rock, Kathleen let them dangle toward the water. "You who can give no proof of birth or rank? You who have never revealed your past? I am the elder daughter of a respected freeman. You. Are. Nothing." She leaned forward. "If not for Mother Crumb, you would have died, alone and unwanted."

True. Maggie had been huddling in the snow when the healer found her, on a night so raw, so stark, that to call it cold was laughable, yet the old woman braved the white darkness because she said she heard the voice of one in distress.

Maggie had never uttered a sound.

Kathleen leapt from the rock and disappeared among the trees. Her voice pierced, even at a distance: "Kieran Smith is mine, Maggie Finney!"

Maggie dressed on the riverbank then hastened back to the cottage.

Mother Crumb did not ask what had happened. She rubbed balm into Maggie's crippled hand then poured a cup of warm tea, settled into the chair by the fire, and took up the mending once more.

While Maggie sipped the tea and stared into the flames, the healer, in a voice weighted with calm comfort, recited the benefits of elfwort leaves.

Next morning, Shea thronged with revelers. The Faere leapt to life. Dancers whirled to pipe and drum. Magicians performed tricks. Tumblers tucked and twirled. Farmers circled livestock pens. Traders and craftsmen displayed wares. Mother Crumb had ventured from her cozy garden and come to sell her healing potions. A bright-striped canopy fashioned from odd bits of old cloth sheltered her sturdy table. To Maggie, standing at the window in an upper chamber of the inn, the Faere was a tapestry, like the rich curtains around a silk merchant's stall.

Across from the inn and down the street, the smithy door stood wide, and smoke rose from the chimney. A steady march of people in and out of the shop bade well for Kieran's purse.

His behavior the other day still stung. He had turned his back as if she were a thing despised.

She turned from the window and tucked fresh sheets on the bed. The chamber was foul with soured cheese and spilled wine. Soiled linens overflowed her basket. Whoever made merry in this room yesternight, she did not begrudge his sore head.

Finished cleaning, Maggie picked up the basket and hurried downstairs. With a farewell to Mistress Clem, she departed through the back door. Head slightly bowed, she searched the Faere crowd for soldiers—men clad in yellow or scarlet. She saw none but a minstrel perched on a stool. Wearing both colors, he plucked a lute and sang mournful love songs, a gaggle of girls at his feet.

Ah, you innocents. Old stories and pretty songs. The only place you shall ever find love.

"Maggie Finney!"

Kathleen Donnegan stood in her path, arms crossed, black hair falling over one shoulder. She wore a simple kirtle, the color mimicking her blue-grey eyes, the subtle fashion drawing attention along her shape. People turned to watch. Maggie's skin chilled. She lifted her chin and tried to continue her course, but Kathleen was too quick, thrusting out an arm to block her passage.

"Thinks she is of better blood than the rest of us. Thinks she can have any man she wants."

Maggie stepped to the other side only to be prevented once more.

"Prances about, and wears her hair in a queen's coil."

"Careful," warned a voice from the crowd. "She is a witch."

Kathleen's eyes glinted in cold triumph. "Baron Markha hates witches."

Maggie knew well his hatred. He had killed a poor peasant woman one autumn, just before harvest, because she had served as midwife in a perilous birth. Against a noble apothecary's prediction, mother and child survived. The miracle was deemed witchery, and the baron left the midwife's body hanging in a tree along the Cameron Road.

"One death for two lives," he pronounced at the execution.

None questioned aloud the terrifying backwardness of such pompous, foolish ingratitude.

Maggie looked at the unfriendly faces surrounding her. Beyond them, a white-bearded man in a green cape pulled coppers from behind children's ears and smiled at their giggles. He made kittens vanish from his conical hat and reappear in the folds of his robe.

"Is he someone you fear?" Maggie nodded toward the old man. "Is he a warlock, plotting to change those children into hideous creatures to serve as his familiars?"

"Tricks, nothing more." Kathleen dismissed the magician with a wave of her slender hand. She pointed to Maggie's crippled one. "But you bear Nardha's blessing."

Maggie waggled contorted fingers at her tormentor. "Oh, aye, lassie! And just what do you want to be turned into today?" She smiled. "You will do nicely as a cat. Then, when you scratch a kindly hand, none will think twice about it."

Kathleen pulled back, eyes wide.

Maggie advanced. She thrust out her hand, and fright grew in that beautiful face.

"You groom yourself and lie about in the sun, disregarding all who might love you because you find none who adore you quite so much as you adore yourself."

Kathleen cringed as if expecting to be transformed at any moment.

Maggie let her hand fall to her side. Shaking her head, she said in quiet disgust, "Go your way, Kathleen Donnegan. We have no quarrel."

Kathleen pushed through the crowd. The onlookers moved away, some muttering dire warnings, others looking back over their shoulders with baleful glances and curled lips.

Maggie stood a moment, gathering her calm, then grasped the basket with both hands once more.

She passed the minstrel. Their gazes brushed against one another, and the gift came in a confusion of questions and close-guarded secrets. There was something familiar about him, but she could not put his face to a specific memory. He bowed his head at once, fingers stumbling over the lute strings, voice faltering as he sang of love.

He knew her.

36 ~ DANCE

Teag swore. His mouth sang romance, but his mind fogged with profanity. He must beware the gift. She had not learned to wield it at will—or with any degree of skill—but he saw the knowledge leap into her face despite his rush to shield her from his thoughts.

Did she recognize him? Would she flee again?

This was the second day of the Faere. The blacksmith still walked free. He had disappeared yesterday afternoon, only returning to his shop near sunset. Teag should have sent word to Captain Nelek, but he made the excuse to himself that he needed more time, more information. He was not afraid. Not he, most successful of Morfran's spies. His grisly trophies decorated the king's own chamber.

Where had the smith gone yesterday? What had he done? Today, he opened his shop with the boldness of an innocent man whose mind was free from troubles. What was his game?

It was as if both he and the laundress knew Teag's purpose and were determined to thwart it, for Maggie Finney had kept herself hidden, too.

Why was she here? Why so close?

From talkative villagers, Teag had drawn out various useless versions of how Maggie came to be in Shea. Why had she not fled to Cameron, that rogues' den? Or across the Plains to the Calhoun Forest? There were more of her kind there. Why live in Shea, mere days from the Markha manor? Even more mysterious, why live among those who feared her? Avoided her? Openly spoke ill of her?

Sweltering in the sun, pouring forth musical treacle and smiling at the moonstruck maidens at his feet gained Teag nothing. Offering flirtatious promises to return on the morrow, he kissed each lass on her cheek and sent her on her way.

Slinging the lute across his back, he set forth for the inn and a tall tankard. And a new plan.

Kieran forced himself to maintain a pleasant demeanor while Faere-goers drifted in and out of the shop, buying hinges or bolts or other small items he kept in half-barrels outside the smithy. A few people ordered tools, and some brought things in need of repair. His mind was not on his work or shallow conversation. He listened with real interest only when more rumors were repeated of the invisible flying monster.

He strove to appear convivial to customers, but his thoughts were filled with plans to leave the village, and whether or not he should say goodbye to anyone. Being seen with them might put his friends at risk. Mother Crumb's revelations and his own questions held private converse, a pervasive chatter in his head.

The night before, Kieran had concealed the bracelet inside a charred log on the hearth in his room, and returned the dagger to its hiding place beneath his bed. Today, every time he shook hands with a customer, he was afraid the blue sparks might return and reveal his identity—or, at the very worst, harm someone. He longed for dusk, for then he could put away his tools, hang up his apron, and close his door against the world.

When twilight came, however, and after supper at the inn, he stood in the shadow of a weaver's shop to watch the Match Dance.

Torches and candles in tall candelabra rimmed one end of the village square, illuminating the dancers. A wooden platform had been erected, and the dancers' leaps and steps pounded on the echoing surface. Laughter magnified. Pipers and drummers played heartily, their faces glowing with perspiration, torsos and arms contorting to the rhythm of their music.

The dance was an ancient custom celebrating spring. Earth's fecundity and a couple's fertility were once conjoined in a prolonged ritual—thus the seven days of the Faere—but the only remaining nod to that ceremony was the gathering of young couples awaiting the itinerant priest's blessing. Married folk looked on, clapping hands or tapping feet, some even dancing in the scant shadows away from the platform, for only the unmarried could join the Match Dance.

Would John Oakley finally win his bride, or would Kathleen

persist in refusing the young farmer?

Were she wise, she would accept John and be done.

Straightening his shoulders, Kieran stepped into the street. He nodded to the few people who greeted him. Nothing seemed amiss. He walked back toward the smithy.

"Eh, Master Smith!"

He turned.

A youth hailed him from among a group of other young men in the innyard. "Do you dance?" It was John Oakley's brother, Nathan.

"Nay, my friend." Kieran smiled. "I am too green and am forbidden to stay out past moonrise. Next year."

Nathan raised his cup. "You heard him, lads! More for us!"

"Best keep your wits about you, or you may find yourselves harnessed before sunrise."

Far from sobering them, Kieran's warning roused a cheer. "To the priest!"

Aye. After all those vows, Father Donovan would be hoarse by morning.

The smithy door opened under his touch. Strange. He thought he had locked it.

Arms encircled his neck from behind. He whirled.

Kathleen smiled up at him, kissed him, buried her fingers in his hair. The men at the inn roared their approval.

Kieran stumbled backward, disengaging her fingers, and pushing her away. Her full lips turned down at the corners. Laying a hand on his arm, she leaned toward him again. "Come! Dance!"

"No."

"But, Kieran," she whispered, her breath warm on his neck as she toyed with the laces of his shirt, "the Match Dance."

He grasped her shoulders and pushed her from him.

Her eyes narrowed. "Is it that laundress-witch? I saw you with her by the river. Are you waiting for her to dance? You will be cooling your heels 'til dawn. She hates men."

"I wait for no one."

Kathleen softened, lips smiling once more. "Come with me."

He shook his head.

Her fingers dug into his arm. "Jenny said to be patient. Give you room to breathe and think. You have taken all that room and turned around."

"We spoke no promises, you and I. Our hearts are free. John Oakley—"

Her eyes blazed like those of a cat caught in torchlight. "John Oakley was a diversion until you came to your senses. Jenny is wed, so who is left? I! The pretty one!" Loud with outrage, her voice caromed off the buildings around them. "Why do you not want me?"

"I will take you!" cried one of the tipsy lads. "Pretty or no!"

Onlookers to the dance turned in the direction of the smithy. Kathleen continued her tirade, arms stiff at her sides.

"You were nothing when Father took you in. He raised you as a son. You did not even have a name!"

She was right. In this one thing, he had failed the man he lived to honor. Yet some part of him resented the obligation. He could not dance with her, an act of promise, then stand before Father Donovan and utter vows he did not cherish. They would be lies.

She awaited his reply. He said nothing.

Tears streamed down her face and glittered in the torchlight. Her palm stung the side of his face. Then, wiping the back of her hand across her cheeks, she stalked to the square, her back rigid.

"Wait, fair lady! We will dance with thee!" Laughing, the wine-emboldened youths linked arms and wound their serpentine way to the dance.

Kieran rubbed his smarting jaw. He stepped into the smithy and walked in darkness toward the forge hearth to coax fire from the banked coals. Perhaps a simple repair could be wrought, or a small item crafted. Something, anything, to calm his troubled thoughts.

He tripped over something, stubbing his toes. Limping and cursing, he applied the bellows, but its belly did not fill and air whistled out of it. He blew the coals to life with his own breath, put a knotty stick of wood to the fire, and held aloft the torch.

Tools littered the floor. The bellows had been slashed, rendered useless. Ashes had been scooped from the hearth and scattered, coating all they touched with a fine grey veil. Narrow footprints disturbed the ashes. On the corner of a worktable, a ragged scrap of cloth hung from a nail. Smooth texture. Thick, excellent weaving. Perhaps there was a bit of silk in the threads, interwoven with fine wool. Rich man's cloth. Kieran held it up to the torchlight.

Scarlet. Teag.

He shoved the cloth into his scrip, and went around the outside of the smithy to his room. The door gaped open. Table and chair were overturned. Shattered crockery crunched beneath his feet. On the hearth, the charred log lay broken and chopped apart. The bracelet was gone.

Kieran knelt beside his bed. The cot lining had been reduced to ribbons, the bedclothes hanging to the ground like the entrails of a gutted cow. He pushed open the inner side of one leg, and a little wooden scabbard swung outward. Removing the dagger, he slid it into his boot.

There was no use closing the door behind him as he left. The latch had been destroyed.

Someone grabbed his arm.

He held the torch like a sword.

Harry's merry smile crinkled the corners of his eyes. "Where are you bound in such high dither?"

"To catch a thief."

Harry's smile dissolved. "Here? In Shea?"

"Someone ransacked my shop."

"What did he take?"

"He seemed more bent on destruction than looting."

"Likely one of the farm lads, drunk and out for a bit of fun. We will soon have it to rights." Harry took the torch and poked his head into the smithy. He whistled. "Or not."

Giving the stub of torch back to Kieran, he reached behind the door, procured the broom, and proceeded to raise more dust than he gathered. He stumbled coughing from the shop and dropped the broom. "I have had a bit to drink."

"And you do not yet sing?"

Harry squared his shoulders. "Only had a bit to drink. I am not yet on the moon." He sat on the bench in front of the shop and pulled a round, dark-colored fruit from his scrip. "A fine early crop." He held it up before slicing pieces from it and offering one to Kieran. "Some say blue apples cannot be grown." He snorted. "Lazy sods! Takes a bit of work, is all."

Kieran bit through the crisp slice, surprised at the tangy sweetness bursting on his tongue. "Good. Very good."

"A bit subject to the blight, but they produce two harvests, early and late. Well worth the work." Harry cut another piece. "Never seen you so agitated. You can scarce stand still."

"I made something."

The words were out aforethought. Mother Crumb's warning rang in Kieran's mind: *Tell no one. Not if you value their lives.*

"Oho! Yon blacksmith has *made* something."

"You, my good friend, should join the performers. You make an excellent clown."

Harry stood, sheathing his knife. "Aye, and if I am such a good friend, you will be telling me what you made?"

"Someday."

"Someday?"

"Aye," Kieran fell in to Harry's jesting tone to keep the darker truth at bay, "and that is all you get 'til then!"

Harry feigned offense. "Paltry show of friendship, you great lump!"

Whereupon Kieran slung him over his shoulder and spun around until Harry threatened to disgorge blue apple down Kieran's back.

Nelek's soldiers camped without fires in a clearing deep in the western Kelcey. Men concealed armor with cloaks or wore none at all, for the gleam of moonlight along metal might draw attention. Such silence was maintained that Teag was halted by the tip of a sentry's lance before he heard the man's footsteps.

The grunt, he assumed, was a request for the password.

"To the coming age," he replied.

The steel point dug at his chest for a long moment before the sentry stepped aside and let him pass. Teag ran his fingers over his tunic, feeling for holes in the fabric. He admired the guard's diligence, but this new suit of clothes had cost a month's wages at the finest tailor in Romney-town. A nail in the smithy had already torn a small piece from his cloak, and soot likely besmirched his expensive garments. Relieved to find no further damage, he walked along rows of soldiers sprawled or curled in their cloaks or hunched on the ground in attitudes of rest.

Nelek stood outside a spacious tent. He gestured for Teag to enter, closed the flap behind them and lit a candle stub, shielding the flame with his hand.

"So," said the captain in a low voice, "you have it?"

Teag removed the leather pouch from his belt and overturned it. The bracelet landed with a solid thunk on the table.

Nelek's eyes glittered in the candlelight. The small flame glinted along the hard grey surface. "This is etherium?"

Teag stared at the circlet, puzzled. It had shone blue when it fell from the blacksmith's scrip yesterday, and a faint color had remained when he found it in the fireplace tonight.

Nelek frowned. "You were taken in by a clever peasant who saw opportunity in your tales to bring one to life."

Teag used the blade of his dagger to lift the bracelet. "See the ash still clinging to the engraving? He hid it inside a charred log."

"All well and good for one of your stories, but what are we supposed to prove with it?" Nelek held the flame close to the metal. "According to legend, Azrin was blue. This is less ordinary than a rock!" He plunked down the candle stub, and wax spilled on a stack of parchments, spattering the pages with leprous spots. "So. The blacksmith is not a Kel. Unfortunate. I relished a chance at his blood."

Teag slid the bracelet back into the leather pouch, drew the strings tight, and knotted them. "I maintain he is a Kel, and any man as clever as he must surely suspect why we are here."

"Why you are here." The captain reclined on a low campaign cot. "Either he was wary ere you arrived, or you make a clumsy spy."

The minstrel's fist tightened around the hilt of his sword. "Pray make yourself plain, Captain Nelek."

The soldier used the toe of one boot to loosen the heel of the other as he removed his gear. "You are too eager for this." He looked up at the spy. "What fires fill your belly?"

Teag refused to answer.

The captain shrugged. He swung his feet up on to the cot and balled his cloak into a pillow. His sword lay beside him, and his dagger still rested in its sheath on his belt. "Did you know your blacksmith went wandering about the forest yesterday?"

"Did he?"

"My men lost him until he returned to the village."

Nelek tapped the fingertips of both hands together, forming a tent over his chest. "I wonder what he was doing out in the forest. And on the day before the Faere." He cast a mocking glance.

Again, Teag refused to answer.

"Well, then, do you know any legends regarding grey-bodied birds with blue wings? It seems the blacksmith disappeared at just the moment they arrived."

Teag drew a sharp breath, chills marching across his skin.

Nelek's brows rose.

Teag shrugged. "There is a child's story or two about trees and forest creatures aiding the return of the Kels, but only fragments of tales. Likely your men were merely distracted by the birds, and Kieran Smith did not disappear. He simply kept walking while their attention was elsewhere."

"My soldiers are inept? Do they lie?"

"The truth involves neither legend nor magic."

"Tell that to the men who watched your blacksmith appear on a forest path where no man had stood a moment prior."

An urgent voice at the door of the tent relayed news. A woman at the edge of the camp demanded to speak with Teag.

"A woman. In our camp. I wonder, how did she find us, Master Spy?" Nelek waved a hand, dismissing him as one does a servant. "Snuff the candle before you go."

Teag knocked the candle to the ground. The flame drowned in its own wax.

Nelek chuckled.

Grinding his teeth, Teag jerked aside the tent flap and followed the messenger through the camp.

The woman stood beside the sentry, who watched her with steady attention. It was not the awareness of a man for a maid. Common soldiers were forbidden natural affections. Mad Morfran demanded full allegiance in all things. No man went willingly into the king's army. He had to be taken. The river of his mind was turned to course down different channels until he no longer remembered who he was before the king became his god. Married men never returned to their families, for they knew no wives or children. Their innate need for companionship was either suppressed or destroyed—Teag knew not which—and the sentry's stare was only vigilance.

"Teag?" Kathleen embraced him.

His heart stuttered. It should not. She was only a woman. Sharp-tongued, seductive, dangerous—no more than he—yet she frightened him. Excited him.

"Come with me," Teag murmured against her hair scented with violets, like silk across his cheek.

Taking her hand, he led her back into the forest until there was just enough moonlight by which to see her outline as she stood in the center of a small glade. He dried his palms on his tunic. "How did you find me?"

"I followed you. Who are these soldiers? Why are they here?"

"King's men."

"Kieran is right. You are a spy."

"How did you find me?"

"At the dance, I saw you go to the smithy. I kept Kieran distracted so you could escape his room. Then I followed you."

"How did you know it was I you followed, and not another?"

"Who else wears a feather-cocked hat?"

He chuckled. "Indeed. But why follow me?"

"Why not?" The timbre of her voice sent shivers down his spine. "If you are indeed a spy, I could tell you more about Maggie Finney."

"I know all I need."

"And Kieran Smith?"

"My questions have been answered."

"Perhaps." Placing a hand on his arm, she said in a breathy murmur, "Did you know he has a mark on his back? Just above his left hip. I doubt even he knows it is there. I saw it once when we were children, when Father Donovan taught us to swim."

Her hand led his thoughts down other paths, but he strove to keep his mind on her words. "Continue."

"You know how, when you swim, your clothes become heavy with water?" She tugged at the brooch clasping his cloak. The fabric fell away from his shoulders and puddled on the ground. "Kieran climbed out of the river, and we all laughed when his breeches slipped."

She pulled off his cap and dropped it on the cloak. "There was a shape like a flower, then a slash that could have been a scar. Father Donovan told Kieran to take more care to keep his clothes about him. I thought little of it all these years, but there may have been more to the priest's reprimand. He knows who Kieran is."

The hairs on Teag's arms stood up. His pulse thrummed in his ears. The priest lied. Recompense would be required of the old man.

"I think my dear foster brother was a servant branded by his master." Her hand slid to his shoulder as she stepped closer, and her breath brushed his ear.

"There is many a freeman wearing an old brand from past years of servitude." Teag's heartbeat played tricks. "What kind of flower? Are you sure the slash was a scar? Not a sword?"

She shrugged. "One appeared to cross the other."

"Why do you tell me this? What do you stand to gain?"

Lacing her fingers behind his neck, she whispered, "I stand to gain your good pleasure."

A heady fragrance informed his senses of the expense she paid for the first night of the Faere.

"But what of your young farmer?" he asked. "Surely he awaits you at the Match Dance. Why come here to impart news that could have waited until the morrow?"

"To see you." She pulled him to her and kissed him. "Dear minstrel, sing to me."

"One song or many?"

"As many as you know."

"Would take a lifetime."

She drew back. "Return with me to the Match Dance."

Clever girl. "The dance implies marriage."

"Indeed." Her breath grazed his ear once more, sending shivers along his spine. "It does."

Thoughts scattered, he tried to be logical. "Are you not promised to Kieran Smith? John Oakley? Someone?"

"If that is so"—she kissed his chin—"why am I here?"

She offered herself from spite and jealousy. In clear day, she might regret her choice.

Her words turned bitter. "There are those who will not do what is expected of them, so I must find others who will."

"You speak of Kieran Smith."

Both hands on his chest, she shoved him away. Whispering only added venom to her words. "The man I want will never give me the attention I deserve, and the man who wants me is a slave to his devotion. I want a man who will adore me yet think for himself. If I stay much longer in my brother-in-law's house, I fear I shall go mad. Soon no man will want me."

"I have no home," Teag said, "nor place for a wife. All I offer is tonight."

Kathleen hesitated, then stepped forward and gave him a kiss he was reluctant to end.

With Harry still flopped over his shoulder and shouting threats if he were not returned to solid ground, Kieran searched for Jenny amid the onlookers at the Match Dance. She stood on the edge of the circle, swaying with the music.

"Your love." Kieran deposited Harry beside her.

The farmer staggered, clutching his head and moaning.

"Too much ale, or too much blood to his head." Kieran grinned. "Although I doubt there is too much of anything but air in that skull."

Jenny laughed. She led Kieran aside and inquired about Kathleen, and he told her.

"Father should never have asked that of you." Then she slipped her arm through his and tugged on it. "You are going to be an uncle."

"When?"

"Winter."

He lifted her in a crushing hug, then immediately put her down, asking if he hurt her.

"Nay, nay." Then, with a hint of wistful sorrow, "You are more my brother than Kathleen has ever been my sister. I wanted you to know first, before we told anyone else."

Her words humbled him.

She nodded toward her husband who watched them with a bleary but amused expression. "What he must have gone through, trying not to let the secret slip until I could tell it." She walked to him, took his hand, and kissed his cheek. "Come, Harry love."

They joined the other married couples dancing near the shadows.

Jenny the pragmatist and Harry the clown. They laughed together. They debated how to spend or hoard their few silver coins. They worked side by side to restore overworked fields and yield a prosperous orchard. Would that all could suffer such a pleasant fate.

Father Donovan stood before a group of young couples. Watching the ceremony, face set in a scowl, stood John Oakley. His gaze met Kieran's in a sharp stare. Kieran's fists closed in instinctive response to the challenge, but he forced himself to relax, drawing a deep breath, nodding to John across the crowd.

The farmer shifted his stance so Kieran was no longer in his line of sight.

Several young women cast the blacksmith inviting smiles, and some reached out to touch his arm. His resolve weakened. He looked for Maggie Finney, knowing she would not be there but also knowing he would not hesitate to dance if she were.

Sally from the inn sidled up to him, her usual serving dress replaced by an embroidered kirtle cut deep at the neckline.

Neckline? Kieran blushed. It was nowhere near her neck.

She shooed away the other girls with a flap of her hand then smiled up at him, leaning against his arm. He felt dizzy.

"I saw Kathleen. She refused to dance with John, then she left. Did you quarrel?"

"I, um, aye, we did."

She pressed closer. "Dance with me?"

His thoughts far from honorable, he almost said yes.

In his silence, her playful expression faded.

Kieran gently extricated his arm from her grasp. "I cannot."

"Just before I came up to you, your eyes were fixed out there." She gestured toward the shadows beyond the dance. "Your heart is not in Shea. Another village, perhaps?"

"No one holds my heart. Yet." But he thought of Maggie Finney, of how she looked in the smithy, and down by the river, and standing still in the grey dawn. "I lack the charm."

"It can be acquired." A teasing light returned to her eyes.

"Then I shall remain bereft, for I cannot seem to learn."

Sally shook her head. "Never. When we maids are old and matronly, you will remain to tempt us into thinking we could have had you once."

He smiled. "Meantime, you are young, and you must let that beautiful gown be seen."

"See? You can be charming. You should try it more often." Standing on tiptoe, Sally planted a kiss on his stubbled jaw, and he wished he had cleaned up a bit before coming to the dance. "There is always next year."

Then she climbed the few steps to the platform and stood against the rail, watching the dancers, swaying to the music.

He turned from the merriment, walking toward the forest behind the village. In the darkness, trees formed a wall of intertwining limbs, a dark tangle like his thoughts.

He walked the edge of the forest, neither truly inside its realm nor inside the village bounds. The trees rustled in a wind he could not feel, whispering things he almost understood.

An ancient tongue murmured on the edge of his ken—*D'urnythn, D'urnythn*—the word from his dream. It was the first word he remembered the day he was found as a child on the Romney Road. He clung to that word until, with time and distance, he forgot. Now it resounded in his brain like the jangling bells on a mummers cart.

Pale silver flickered among the trees as birds flew from branch to branch, following Kieran. He lingered, built a small fire, listened to the forest. Then, saving one brand he kept for a torch, he buried the fire and turned in a new direction.

Folk who wandered into this part of the forest told of hearing voices or seeing pallid faces among the foliage. In autumn, leaves here bore deep reds, deeper than anywhere else in the forest. Sometimes bones were found, as if ancient executioners had no time to bury the dead. Even as a boy, Kieran had never feared ghosts. He played elsewhere because he knew what was buried here. Somewhere on the western side of the Romney Road lay a tree-bordered hillock marked by a mound of stones. One did not play on a grave.

His steps grew muffled on a lush sward. The birds quieted, and hush settled around him. Moonlight slipped through the canopy of trees like a wraith, lighting upon a moss-grown jumble of stones pierced by spears of grass growing up through the cracks between them. Tree roots gnarled the slopes of the hillock. The stillness seemed a prayer.

No mark indicated the position of the body in the grave, but tradition dictated the head always be higher than the feet, the easier for the soul to rise and take its journey to the Otherland.

Wedging the torch between stones, Kieran knelt at the foot of the mound. "Were you my father?"

The breeze withdrew.

"Were you a man of honor? What loyalty kept me beside your corpse? Did you save my life? Did I have nowhere else to go?"

Branches swayed overhead as the breeze freshened.

"What did I see that stole my memory of you?"

A blue-winged bird with a silver-grey body alit on the topmost stone and cocked its head, blinking.

"I am called Kieran Smith, but that is not who I am." He set a new stone atop the grave. "My name died with yours."

Air stirred as if someone stepped past him. Birds swirled up from their branches. Tree limbs swayed, revealing the moon, and then grew still. The glade once more lay shrouded in silence.

He returned to the jumbled smithy. By the light of the torch—another sap-rich stub of fragrant pine—he set the tools to rights, and laid the repaired or new-fashioned articles on a workbench. In a small metal box he placed a fistful of silver crowns and all his coppers, then closed the box. With a narrow chisel, he engraved *Thryffin* on the lid.

Then he filled a bag with a few basic tools and short lengths of iron, and added a fresh tunic, bread and cheese wrapped in a cloth, and a small corked bottle of Mother Crumb's special cordial.

He would miss them all: Thryffin and Mother Crumb, Father Donovan, the Clems, Harry and Jenny. Maggie. Thinking of her made his throat ache. After a hesitant moment, he packed the shirt she had used as an apron. It still smelled of herbs.

He extinguished the sputtering torch. Settling the rucksack on his back, Kieran looked around the room one last time. He had thought it confining. Now it seemed the safest place in the world.

He closed the door.

37 ~ GONE

Nelek strode about issuing orders. Men cleared a large wain, distributing its cargo elsewhere, and secured an empty iron cage in the center. A team of oxen stood in their traces, waiting to be hitched to the wagon. Two soldiers yanked a hooded prisoner to his feet, his tattered breeches and ragged blouse bloodstained by a recent whipping. They pushed him up the wooden steps into a cart. He stumbled, falling in the dirty straw.

Just inside the trees on the edge of the camp, Teag gave Kathleen a kiss and a warning to wait out of sight. She kissed him again then tugged his tunic into place, straightened his belt, and smoothed his sleeve. "Hurry back."

He approached the captain. "It is only morning of the third day."

"And you have had two days to act on what you already know." Nelek rested the heel of his hand on the hilt of his sword. "What of the farmer spreading discord in the pub?"

Hapless Farmer Connor in the Blue Oak, and his imprudent suggestion to attack the baron. Toothless drunkenness.

"I thought it subordinate to our purpose, which is to exterminate Kels, not to seek out disgruntled commoners."

"He spoke of raising arms against Baron Markha and King Morfran. A messenger heard it from the villagers, and informed me. I should have heard it from you. You are, after all, the spy."

"The farmer was drunk. It was frustration, not sedition."

"If the people think they can speak freely against the king, what other freedoms will they assume? Who else will they infect with their poisonous speech?" Nelek's mouth twisted in disgust. "You sympathize with them."

"Sometimes, in pursuit of prey, it is wise to let small game go free."

"A running rabbit or a startled bird will warn a hind the hunter is near."

"A skilled hunter raises no alarm, even among the birds."

"Just before dawn, I saw an odd sight. A strange light shone from the bracelet. Only a little light. Very faint. Most definitely blue."

The spy's mouth went dry. "But last night—"

"Last night you spent in the arms of a willing lass."

Teag had no reply.

"Find Maggie Finney," said Nelek. "I shall obtain the blacksmith."

Teag would far rather arrest Kieran than the laundress. Her untrained power could soon be more than even the great Heolstor of the Black Hoods could overcome. "The girl is easy enough to find by her crippled hand, but you have not seen the smith—"

"No more words."

"You will not know Kieran Smith. It is perhaps better if I—"

Nelek drew his blade and held its tip under Teag's chin. "I am a captain in the king's army. You will not speak to me again as if I serve you. You will not debate my orders. You will obey as if you were one of my soldiers. Do this, and you shall live."

He turned aside the sword. "You say threaten whom he loves, and the smith will come to heel. I will be ready for him. If he tries to resist, his blood is mine. If he escapes"—he sheathed his sword, the sound slithering in the air—"yours will do."

Pausing her work, Maggie looked out the window. Market stalls had multiplied in the square, and entertainers performed, their enthusiasm charming coin from pockets. Livestock pens, formed of rope and hastily-driven staves, were filled with sheep, cattle, horses, donkeys, and pigs. Mother Crumb's striped booth was busy, but no smoke rose from Kieran's shop.

Maggie tucked a clean sheet under the straw mattress, plumped the new-cased pillow, and pulled bedclothes into place, smoothing and tugging until the blankets lay flat across the bed. This was the last room, not as smelly as the others, finally vacated by the late-rising wealthy merchant whose underlings had probably been manning his Faere booth for hours.

The ebony trunk lid let slip an overflow of fine velvet, and a silken robe draped across a chair. She guessed the man sold cloth, but he could just as well have been a thread merchant or a carpet weaver. Wools? Silks? Maggie wondered what dyes he used, and how many strands did he wind for his thread? Did he provide a good strong twine, or did he cheat his customers?

She folded the slippery shimmering robe and placed it atop the velvet tunic, then closed the trunk lid. Many a moon had passed since she had touched such rich material. Mayhap she would visit the Faere —just for a few moments—and torture herself much as a starving man stares at a meat pie in someone else's hands, yearning for what he cannot have.

The noise in the square stilled with a thunderclap of silence. Again she looked out the window. Scarlet-cloaked soldiers surrounded the square, penning the villagers and Faere-goers like fenced cattle. None of the soldiers wore helms, nor did their mail or uniforms bear the marks of recent conflict. They shone like new-struck coins.

King's men.

Maggie left the overflowing basket of dirty linens in the hall and ran downstairs, nearly knocking over Master Clem as he passed the bottom step on his way to the great room. He steadied her.

"Wait." The innkeeper reached into his scrip and drew out a coin, Maggie's pay for the week. Then he drew out another coin and pressed both into her palm. Shaking his head against her protests, he said, "It is my own money. I will do with it what I will. You cleaned while we slept. It is worth something."

"Thank you."

Bidding him good day, she departed out the kitchen door at the back of the inn and hurried down the hedge-bordered path behind the village. The edges of the coins bit into her tight-clenched palm. Past the kirk, she tied the coins into a corner of her apron then pulled up fistfuls of kirtle hem and ran to the mill bridge. Once across the river and in the sheltering forest, she entered one of her secret paths.

Only then did she slow her pace, lungs pleading for air, sweat sliding down her back like the baron's thick, hot hands. She could almost smell the heavy incense that pervaded his chambers and seeped into his skin.

The Plains to the west were too open. If she went north, she placed herself even closer to the king. If she fled to Cameron, she must pass near Donnelly, Baron Markha's ancestral seat, but the thick-forested east was her best hope.

A leather-clad hand clamped over her mouth and a strong arm encircled her waist. Another set of hands gripped her legs, and yet another twisted her arms behind her and bound them.

The back of a knuckle caressed her cheek. "Teag at your service, collector of histories, companion of gossips, erstwhile comrade of Baron Markha." He chuckled. "Of course, I was younger then, and more handsome. Why seek the company of bondmaids when I could comfort the noblemen's neglected wives? But youth and beauty are not at issue now. Is Baron Markha at court? Is he fighting on the Dissonay border beside his fellow Skardians? Has he renounced all his worldly goods, taken the cloth, and become a cleric?"

Hooking an arm under her midriff, he turned her on to her side. She blinked up at his thin handsome face. The minstrel from the Faere. She sensed the false bravado he wore to mask his fear. Her own fear poured in tears of frustration and shame.

"Ah, but Baron Markha is murdered, stabbed by your sewing shears. He—or was it his son?—gave you the witch's claw, and ruined your ability to use those shears for their right purpose. Ironic."

He unpinned her braids, loosing them, running his fingers through her hair. "Waves of fire. These will be lovely against the walls when Morfran hangs your head atop the city gates."

Standing, he said, "She is an example. Make it plain."

A leather-gloved fist struck her face.

Mounted soldiers dressed in scarlet, the color of the king, drew their horses into a circle, surrounding the village square like winter cardinals come before their time.

From his hiding place behind a wine cask, Thryffin saw the long look the captain gave the villagers. The arrogant way the man sat his horse, the proud tilt of his chin, irritated the boy the way a midge's bite itched on the back of his leg. The sight of soldiers filled him with dread. They might say they were here for taxes, but what if they took men as well? They would surely choose Kieran Smith.

Master Smith was strong and broad. He would fight them. Aye, he would!

None of Morfran's soldiers were anything without their swords, because none were as big as the blacksmith. Certainly not their leader, who looked as if he enjoyed frightening folks, his bold eyes measuring them as a hunter measures his prey.

"I am Captain Nelek!" he shouted. "We collect a war tax. Your king would have you remain Skardians rather than fall into the hands of the dreaded Dissonay. If you refuse the tax, we take your sons in payment."

Fear showed stark on the faces of young men, as if their skin stretched tight over their skulls, and they watched the soldiers' hands for the chains or lengths of rope announcing a conscription patrol.

Why did the villagers just bow their heads?

Someone should make the king pay.

Someone should kill the ones who killed boys' mothers.

The only people who seemed unmoved by the ring of soldiers were the mercenaries, armed men serving as guards for the merchants. No caravan of traders traveled without a small band of warriors to protect them from brigands on the road.

An ox-drawn cart lumbered into the square and bore an iron cage. Two men pulled a hooded prisoner from it and pushed him up the steps to the platform used for the dance. The captive's hands were bound behind him, and streaks of blood lined the back of his torn tunic. A soldier yanked the hood off the prisoner. Blood matted his beard, and both eyes were swollen shut, black with bruises.

"This man spoke sedition against Baron Markha. Words against his cousin are words against the king. To ensure this man never falls into such temptation again"—the captain gestured to the soldiers, one of whom pulled down Farmer Connor's lower jaw—"his tongue is forfeit."

People turned away their faces from the horrific sight. Mistress Connor fainted. Bile rose in Thryffin's throat.

"Should you forget this lesson, we leave a reminder."

Another soldier took a flaccid bloody object from a pouch and held it to the railing as another man nailed the tongue in place.

The captain turned his mount, searching the crowd. "Who among you is Kieran the blacksmith?"

Thryffin glanced toward the smithy. No smoke rose from its chimney.

"You vermin, do not think you can hide him."

A breeze caught the surcoats of the soldiers, twisting and billowing the scarlet. Villagers and Faere-goers looked at one another or studied the ground in silence.

Nelek wheeled his horse and waved a hand. A soldier hoisted a long cloth-wrapped bundle over his shoulder and strode forward. He held the bundle before him and, with a quick movement, unfurled the cloth. Kathleen Donnegan tumbled into the dirt.

People gasped. Tears dripped from Thryffin's chin. He rubbed the back of his hand across his nose. John Oakley ran to the body, heedless of the captain, and knelt, feeling for breath, a heartbeat. He took Kathleen in his arms and rocked her back and forth, pushing the hair from her face, repeating her name.

Nelek nudged his horse forward and halted beside the grieving farmer. "A regrettable waste, but certain sacrifices must be made."

The girl's body slipped to the ground. With a roar, John Oakley surged upward, knocking the captain from his horse.

In an instant, foot soldiers surrounded the farmer, drawing their swords, blades at his chest and back. The point of one sword dug into the flesh over John's heart, puckering the cloth around the sword tip. A red stain appeared.

The mounted soldiers tightened their circle, pushing the Faere-goers close together. The captain regained his feet and whipped his dusty cloak away from his sword. The blade hissed into sight.

John's face twisted in a grimace of despair and anger "Why?"

A flick of the sword, and a thin red line slashed the farmer's throat. *No. No. No. No. No.*

Muffled cries rose from the villagers. John Oakley clamped hands to his throat. His knees buckled.

"Neither the king nor his emissary will be mocked." Nelek wiped the blade between his gloved thumb and forefinger, then sheathed his sword.

Blood spilled from John's fingers, staining the pale skin of Kathleen's outstretched arm. He toppled beside her, his face slack, eyes staring.

Anger thundered in Thryffin's brain.

A disturbance arose at the edge of the crowd. Three mounted men and a stumbling prisoner entered the circle. At the head of the small party rode Teag the spy. He dismounted, untied the prisoner's lead from the saddle, and yanked her forward. He ascended the steps to the platform, leading the captive by a rope looped around her neck. Another length of rope lashed her hands behind her. When she tripped at the top of the stairs, Teag jerked her upright by the red-brown hair spilling over her shoulders, and shoved her next to Farmer Connor. The two prisoners jostled one another. Their bodies slumped, as loose and limp as cloth dolls missing their straw.

Thryffin knew the second prisoner by her hair and her grey kirtle. Blood veiled her features and stained her gown to the knees. For the first time since she came to Shea, he pitied Maggie Finney.

Teag spun her around. He grabbed a fistful of her kirtle and ripped it to her waist. Ridges of scarred flesh crisscrossed her back. Thryffin's stomach queased.

Then Teag turned Maggie forward. The torn kirtle slipped off one shoulder, but she could not bring her hands forward to cover herself. Thryffin winced in shame for her. Then she lifted her chin and looked upon the gathered villagers and Faere-goers. A gash marred her forehead and her bottom lip was split wide. Both eyes were blackened and swollen.

Thryffin clenched his fists. Master Smith should be here. He would rescue her. But if he were, he might have been as reckless as poor John Oakley—and as dead.

Captain Nelek said to the villagers, "You gossip about the baron. You wonder where he is, and hope he does not attend the Faere this year. You pray he does not come for your wives or your daughters. Lay those fears to rest, good people. You shall see him no more."

He struck Maggie's face with his gloved fist, and she stumbled sideways. Fresh blood poured from her mouth.

"This is the face of a murderess! Mark it well!" He gestured broadly, like the lead actor of a mummers troupe. "A new baron shall soon ride through the province, and I trow he will be far less understanding than his father. Baron Markha was a gentle master compared to his son. Lord Ûtgar will prove it is possible for the branch of a mighty oak to be made of stone."

Nelek smile, planting his hands on the railing and leaning forward. "You think I speak madness and you are afraid. So should you be. Your troubles are only beginning."

It was then Teag the spy saw Kathleen's body.

His face grew as pasty as unbaked bread. He leapt over the rail, knelt, cradled her in his arms. Her head lolled. The torn sleeve fell away from her arm, exposing above her elbow an angry red ring, as if someone had clamped fire-hot iron around her flesh.

Teag looked up, rage gathering in his face. "Nelek!"

"She served me well." The captain waved a hand toward John Oakley's body. "Your blacksmith fell into the trap."

"Imbecile. This man was just a farmer! The smith is not here!"

"No matter. That strumpet stood in the way of your duty."

Teag lay her body down, then stood and drew his sword.

The captain cast down his plumed helm. Whirling, he descended the platform steps and unbuckled his sword belt, passing it to one of his men and drawing the subordinate's blade. "My steel is far too worthy for traitor's blood."

Thryffin clenched his fists, enthralled by the contemplative, lethal dance as soldier and spy circled one another. Teag lunged, his sword deflected as Nelek sidestepped, their blades sliding against one another with a sinuous ring.

Nelek tapped his chest. Teag took the challenge. It was a clumsy charge, and Nelek nicked the spy's cheek. Teag recovered his stance, and the two men circled again.

The minstrel wore no armor, but the captain was clad in mail. Teag had little skill, but Nelek seemed to expand with confidence. He expected to win.

Pounding his fists on the wine cask, Thryffin muttered, "Careful! Watch him!" as if he could commune with Teag.

Blade countered blade, flashing in the sun. A dazzling spectacle. Thryffin could not turn from it.

Nelek's bold smile slipped as Teag imitated the captain's way of dancing just out of reach of his opponent's sword. Teag returned wound for wound, and blood poured down both men's faces. Chest heaving, Nelek bared his teeth. Teag smiled.

They came together with clanging force, hilts locked, sweat-drenched bodies almost embracing. Muscles strained, lips pulled tight, feet dug into the dust. Neither man gave ground.

An oddity drew Thryffin's attention. While the soldiers watched the swordplay, mercenaries moved to the back of the crowd, standing between the people and the mounted soldiers. Some mercenaries reached up as if scratching the backs of their necks, and some placed closed fists over their chests, adjusting baldrics. No man seemed to acknowledge the others.

Nelek broke from Teag with a sudden heave and hooked a foot around the spy's ankle, landing him on his back. The fallen man's breath expelled with a grunt.

"Farewell, old friend." The captain lifted his sword.

Shouts rose from the king's men. Stabbed then yanked from their mounts by mercenaries, some soldiers fell without a cry. Mercenaries filled their empty saddles. Villagers screamed, scrambling out of the way as king's men charged hired men. Issuing a wordless bellow, Nelek rushed into the fray.

The air filled with dust and defiant cries. Soldiers were run down by their own horses. Men naked of armor slashed at men whose mail made their movements sluggish by comparison. Heads were cloven and limbs hacked. Blood muddied the dust.

Thryffin flinched when a dagger, thrown wild, thudded on top of the wine cask. The blade bit a groove in the wood. Splinters flew up, one lodging at the corner of his eye. Blinking and cursing, he ducked behind a stack of crates and probed his teary eye with none-too-clean fingers. It took some time to rid himself of the sliver of wood. He crept back to the cask, pulled the dagger from it, and slowly raised his head to see the battle.

Farmer Connor and Maggie Finney no longer stood on the platform. Teag was gone.

Blood-streaked, the mercenaries shouted, swords raised high in triumph, as the king's men fled north out of the village along the Romney Road. The iron cage rose and fell with the jouncing wain, but Thryffin could not see through the clouds of dust whether or not it held any prisoners.

Farmer Harry and his wife knelt by Kathleen. Nathan Oakley ran across the square. He hefted his brother over one shoulder, Harry lifted Kathleen, and together they bore the bodies toward the kirk.

Silent, bent in postures of uncertainty, villagers, entertainers, merchants, and tradesmen crept back into the street. They looked around at one another, at the fallen soldiers. Then, as if a grim jester ran among them, they shouted in raucous celebration. The corpses of soldiers were dragged about the square and stacked in a gruesome heap. Each layer of bodies was separated by a row of split wood. Heedless of catching the village on fire, someone doused the pile with a bucket of tar and set it alight. Laughter filled the air, and people danced to tabor, lute and pipe. Foul smoke rose from the pyre.

Numb, Thryffin turned from the spectacle and went to the smithy.

━┿━━━━━

Kathleen Donnegan and John Oakley were buried at sunset.

New religion had supplanted archaic traditions, yet many stayed rooted in the collective memory. Even priests in Father Donovan's abbey still observed the custom of evening burials, begun when folk worshiped the earth and believed the rays of the setting sun guided a soul's journey to the Otherland.

Kathleen's body was draped in linen and lowered into the grave amid a soft rain of petals scattered from baskets. Custom dictated the flowers be red and yellow to mimic the setting sun. John, too, was wrapped in white linen his body strewn with the blue-green leaves of lover's-heart. The plant remained flowerless until late autumn. Then, when all hope seemed gone, it bloomed brilliant red and orange.

Father Donovan fought to keep his hoarse voice from giving way.

At the foot of the graves stood young Thryffin, a small metal box in his hands. His bare feet and tattered trousers were grey, as if he had played in an ash heap. Tears washed his dirty face.

As the Donnegan family guardian, Kieran Smith should have offered the death blessing. In hushed voices, villagers wondered if he, too, had been taken by the king's men, and they waited for someone to step forward in his place. Mayhap he had been called away to a farm and did not yet know of the tragedy. Mayhap he lay injured or ill deep in the forest. The forest folk were said to steal mortals and imprison them in the hearts of trees. 'Twas true, for their moaning whispers could be heard when one passed through the forest alone. Did not trees clutch at travelers and beg freedom for captive souls?

Farmer Harry put a fist to his mouth. Then, dropping his hand and squaring his shoulders, he recited the death blessing.

O One who sees beyond the darkness
and hears the unuttered words of Men,
receive to Your embrace these souls
who tread the golden path,
and turn them not away.

When we who live at last must go
to stand upon the shining strand,
receive to Your embrace our souls
who too-long fettered be,
and turn us not away.

In the silence, Father Donovan made the sign of the Shepherd, then he placed a comforting hand briefly on Harry's shoulder.

"Do you keep the truth from us, Father? Is Kieran dead?"

Father Donovan shook his head.

"He will come back?"

"That is for the Voice to decide."

"The Voice allows this?" Harry gestured to the graves. "What god does that?"

He turned to embrace his wife. Father Donovan could answer his questions, but the young farmer would not hear him—not in truth. Anger deafened Harry's heart with its consuming roar.

Earth arched in low mounds as the gravediggers covered the bodies. Each year on the anniversary of the deaths, stones would be placed on the graves until, after many years, they would be cairns, but at this moment the raw dirt smelled sharp of fear and grief.

Mother Crumb stood between the graves, opened a pouch stitched with red and gold threads, and poured a coarse powder over the loose earth. "Seeds, that life may grow from death."

Thus were Kathleen and John mourned.

Villagers filed out of the churchyard in silent procession, the women's heads covered in white kerchiefs. It was tradition to prepare a grief feast and tell stories about the ones just buried, but awareness had settled over the villagers, as thick as the foul black smoke still rising from the pyre. They would pay dearly for this day.

Lingering mercenaries boasted their prowess over ale at the Blue Oak. Father Donovan could hear their merriment even in the kirkyard.

Only Mother Crumb and Thryffin remained by the graves. The healer seemed suddenly withered, a bit of old root severed from its tree and left to dry above the ground. Her movements were stiff, lacking their accustomed grace. The lines in her face were chasms to channel her tears.

"How fares Farmer Connor?" asked Father Donovan.

"I fear you will be standing over his grave on the morrow."

"What of Maggie?"

Mother Crumb wiped her eyes with the corner of her apron. "I cannot hear her."

He understood. Her gift did not sense Maggie's. For healers connected by their very essence, such a loss was nigh death.

"Kieran? Does the gift hear him?"

"He is gone north, I think. Perhaps west to the Ruins."

"Did he bid thee farewell?"

"He said nothing to anyone." Mother Crumb reached a hand to Thryffin, but he stayed where he was. "He did it to keep you safe, lad. He did it for all of us."

The boy turned and left the kirkyard. The priest gazed after him, wishing he had wisdom for such times.

The healer sighed. "Better to be with Kieran, safe or no. Now the lad cradles a great hurt. It will fester like a rotten wound."

Aye. Father Donovan knew the bitterness of cherished wrongs held tight for too long. He stood beside the new graves, heart heavy. This day had welcomed the evil from which he longed to protect the people, yet he could neither prevent nor alter what had been foretold.

Risá El ethem, Mymna Tor, prayed Mother Crumb.
Risá duru Nar Cahm enkára lenë llumim
Risá nen, o pyrvië grimladh

Power resonated in the sound and rhythm of the Kellish words. Father Donovan repeated the ancient prayer in common Skardian:

Rescue Your people, Mighty Lord
Rescue from the Dark Enemy seeking our lives
Rescue us, and vanquish evil

Soon Mymna Tor and Nar Cahm would shout at one another, and all the world would hear.

V

Outlaws, Murderers, and Thieves

When broken be the throne of Kel
and silent be his voice,
When Dragons rise in stormy flight
and Nardha's hounds rejoice,
When Men in fear and darkness dwell
and children cry to God,
Then look to where the day meets night—
the Warrior walks abroad.

told to Skardian children to frighten them into obedience
in the early days of the Traitors' War

38 ~ Harsh Mercy

Into a vast clearing in the Calhoun Forest on the easternmost edge of the Territories appeared men ragged and silent, stepping from thickets and dense undergrowth, slipping along paths so faint and narrow they could scarce be seen, the discreet highways of beasts.

The men's silence was not born of despair or fear, but of caution. Though arching limbs screened much of the clearing from the sky, Nar'ath had been sighted.

Padraig rested one foot on a moss-covered stump. Woodcutters no longer came here to the eastern reaches of the Calhoun, not since the beginning of the war. He leaned forward, resting his forearm on the upraised knee. The arrow wound had long ceased seeping poison, but weakness plagued him still.

During the first days of the retreat, he had wavered between fever and delerium, between deep regret and cold reason, sometimes questioning his sense in naming Gaerbith and Turi as guardians of Disson but then sending the Fourth Lachmil off to the enemy's city, yet sternly reminding himself the ruse was necessary to keep High Lord Boorn and King Morfran unaware of his plan.

The guardians guarded best by keeping the enemy away.

Padraig had called Gaerbith brother, but would he have sent a brother of his own blood into enemy territory?

Yet a king must make sacrifices. Gaerbith was a warrior, sworn to serve Disson. If he knew what uncertainty tumbled in his king's mind, surely he would look on Padraig in puzzlement—and the captain could say much with silence.

Across the clearing, royal servant Thael used hand gestures and face contortions to direct the placement of Padraig's possessions. The king's tent was still rolled around its poles and pegs, and would remain so. No tents tonight, nor fires. A pity, for Thael had been industrious of late, attentive to his duties.

Yet Mahyla, the Sea Stone, was missing, and then there was the curious frequency of Thael's unexplained absences.

Captain Yerrin approached. The faded remains of a large bruise surrounded a red puckered scar on his forehead near the temple, and his eyebrow and eye drew up on the outer points. What would Padraig's sister—the beautiful, vain Astra—think of her bold young captain now that he bore the visible marks of battle? Would she still see the worth of the man and not his battered face?

A man wearing the fitted green tunic and brown leggings of a woodland runner stumbled from the trees, a hand clamped over a broad dark blotch spreading from his side down his leg. Padraig caught him as he fell.

"Bos!" Padraig lifted the man's head. "Who did this?"

Bos clenched his jaw in a grimace of pain.

Padraig lifted the strap of the message bag over the runner's head, and thrust it at Yerrin.

"Skardians." Bos looked past Padraig, eyes wide. "Here."

A low word from Lord Symon, another from Lord Áben, and the lachmil dropped their tasks and obeyed, as fluidly as water pools and flows. Healers and servants did the same, disappearing into the forest. In moments, the clearing was empty.

With Bos slung over his shoulders, Padraig followed a Keeper and two apprentices up a small slope to where a tree had fallen in the recent past, clods of dirt still clinging to roots that fanned up and out. He lay Bos in the gap beneath the massive trunk, then moved back while the healer hunkered down beside the unconscious runner and the apprentices pulled dry moss from the trunk to pack into the wound.

Thael, Lord Áben, and a servant joined the small group, drawing weapons, taking posts a short distance from the tree. Áben's somber garments and black-and-silver hair melded with the gathering twilight until he became almost invisible. His servant crouched beyond him, behind a wide bush. Thael fidgeted, just enough to rustle whatever twigs lay underfoot, then he, too, stood still.

Padraig drew slow breaths. His eyes grew accustomed to shadows and shapes, his ears attuned to the forest's pulse. Standing behind a pair of young pines allowed him wide vantage of the slope leading down to the clearing.

The Keeper and the apprentices slipped down beside Bos and grew still, nothing more than mounded shapes of undergrowth.

Stars glittered like pale, bright fish caught in a net of branches. Padraig preferred the darkness. For the freemen and the Dissonay, the Calhoun was home, but any light would help the Skardians.

A breeze freshened, teasing the treetops, becoming a wind. A drift of clouds scudded across the stars. The air smelled damp. A storm lurked.

Thael startled then relaxed.

Padraig turned his eyes without turning his head. Black shapes crept from the direction of the clearing. They carried small shields and slender swords.

Padraig eased his grip a little on Rhobarrd, letting the venerable blade's rag-wrapped hilt breathe before the battle. *Come to me, you spawns of Nardha.*

Thael had only a dagger, so his letting the Skardians pass seemed natural and wise, but then the servant's head tilted forward, toward the enemy, then lifted again in a brief, almost invisible, nod.

The enemy replied in kind.

No. Padraig lifted his sword. *By Omwen'din, no.*

He allowed the Skardians to approach until they drew even with Lord Áben, then Padraig filled his lungs and bellowed, "*Omwen'din Pyrva!*"

Sound erupted in the forest, shouts and clanging swords and the rush of running feet. Surrounded, the Skardians did not surrender. Had they been some other opponent than Skarda, Padraig might have admired their valor, but his anger thundered like the storm gathering above, and he heard the murmur of ancient voices, long-dead warriors urging the blade Rhobarrd to cut down its enemies. They fell before him like sheaves of summer wheat bowing before the arc of a sharp scythe, like trees felled by the blows of a mighty axe. He was the Woodsman.

Caws and shrieks came dim from the sky, the sounds blunted by his fury. Pain in his forearm sang anew.

Someone careened into his shoulder and he whirled, blood flying from the edges of his sword. Staggered but standing, Lord Symon lifted a warding hand. "It is I, my lord."

Lightning webbed the sky, and the foul odor of charred Nar'ath drifted down as if carried on the cold rain. In the clearing, a chanting Hôk Nar Brother stood with bone-white arms upraised.

Nar'ath dove, Padraig ran, and the Black Hood stretched forth a claw-like hand. Padraig drew back his sword and struck off the monk's head.

"Run!" he shouted, sprinting for the trees.

Any able man sought the protection of the forest. Nar'ath attacked the rest—living or dead—until the archers let loose their arrows. Only two birds escaped the clearing.

Someone chuckled in the darkness nearby, and Padraig turned.

Captain Yerrin leaned against a tree. He lifted his sword in a wavering salute. "One request, my lord."

"Aye?"

"A bit more warning before we take another brisk evening stroll."

In the rain, he walked the row of sodden prisoners, their arms bound. Among the scarlet surcoats of footsoldiers knelt a man in the green and white garments of Disson. Stopping in front of the prisoner, Padraig pulled off the man's blindfold.

Thael jerked backward, blinking against the torchlight. "Please, my lord! Four generations have we served the House of Rhobarrd—"

Padraig clenched his fist around the blindfold. "Had you cared more for your duties than for your dice, I might look with leniency on your debts. Were your betrayal limited to selling the Sea Stone to High Lord Boorn, I could tell your father you died in service to Disson"—looking into the servant's pallid face, Padraig felt no twinge of sympathy—"but you betrayed us to our enemies, and there can be no forgiveness."

Padraig opened his hand, and Captain Yerrin took the unfurled cloth, tying it again around Thael's head. Cringing, the servant clamped his lips tight, muting a whimper.

"For your father's sake, your death will be as clean and painless as the edge of a sharp sword can provide. It is the only mercy I can give."

39 ~ A False Sun

Light seared her eyes, but squinting gave life to the pain in her battered face. Her mouth was so dry that no spittle remained. In a twisted fashion, Maggie welcomed the lack of moisture. Wetting her lips only stung them.

Short, full sleeves loosely held her torn kirtle in place, but her long hair hid what cloth did not cover. Flies buzzed around the ropes binding her raw wrists, and blood crusted her arms to the elbows. Her hands had been tied in front of her after Captain Nelek ordered her to tend the wounded.

Captain Nelek and his men fled their shame as tormented souls flee the hounds of Nardha. A few furlongs north of Shea, the soldiers had stopped fleeing and returned to an ordered formation. Fasolt stood before them, using his dark power as a Black Hood to calm and control them. They waited on the Romney Road for the supply carts and the captain, who berated them round and long, cursing them for softheaded fools and cowards, unfaithful to Morfran, their god and king. Captain Nelek declared their unworthiness in blistering language then said he would do an unheard of thing and show mercy. Rather than killing them all by his own hand, he would command the services of a healer on their behalf.

Maggie was dragged from the cage and her ropes cut only so her hands could be rebound in front, giving her limited movement to tend wounds and apply medicines. Though still only an apprentice, she was bound by the ancient oath of all healers, and could not turn away any who needed aid.

Fasolt followed her from wounded man to wounded man, and was in turn followed by a servant bearing a healer's box. How did a Black Hood come by such a treasure? It was stocked with many medicines

Maggie knew, a fine supply of clean bandages, and a pair of scissors with which to cut them. No ragged torn edges for the king's men.

Her task complete, she hoped she might be given aid as well, but Fasolt withdrew with the precious box and Maggie was returned to the cage.

She existed in a lethargy of pain, hunger, thirst, and shame.

The cage swayed as the cart lurched over a rock. Maggie steadied herself against the bars. Not the first cage to hold her, it would likely be the last. As soon as King Morfran pronounced judgment, she would be executed.

Mother Crumb, Father Donovan, Kieran Smith, Master and Mistress Clem at the Blue Oak: would they suffer because of her? What punishments would be met upon the villagers of Shea?

Pray You, Mymna Tor, keep them safe.

Could it be called faith, this sudden spate of prayer that bubbled up like a spring, unstoppable in its purity? She who believed in nothing called upon her friends' god.

The faces in the square had been a blur. Did Kieran witness her shame? In the past, the gift had revealed his unguarded thoughts. He did not mind her crippled hand, nor was he indifferent to her. Yet, even if he believed her innocent of murder, could he bear look on a savagely-marked woman whose deepest scars remained unseen?

Such questions did not matter. She went to her death.

The wain groaned to a halt. Greetings were exchanged near the head of the column, then a dialogue ensued between two voices. The words, however, were lost.

Moving stiffly, muscles cramped and bruises tender, she stood. The swelling around her eyes limited her sight. Leather creaked as someone dismounted. Metal-heeled boots dug into the hard-packed earth of the road. She saw a face she had hoped never to see again.

A cold face, and fierce. A golden beard lent years to it, though it belonged to a man not much older than she. Thick brows the color of warm honey surmounted a blue gaze as hard and clear as a frozen night. His face was the falsity of sun in deep winter.

Ûtgar stared at Maggie, one murderer greeting another. "So, this is she. The reason I am sent to build my father's tomb."

"She will be duly punished. There is no escape from the cage."

"Then loose her, Captain Nelek, that I may deal vengeance."

"She goes before the king."

"I am both baron and lord, for my cousin has made me so." His voice was fat with conceit. "I will do what I will."

"Consider, Lord Ûtgar. My men serve Morfran. Morfran alone. Their purpose cannot be thwarted. You would die ere killing her."

The younger man smiled, white teeth gleaming behind his beard. "And yet these fearsome soldiers set to their heels, fleeing a ragged band of mercenaries and common villagers. I indeed have reason to fear."

Ûtgar bent his gaze on Maggie once more. "She was a comely lass. Once. A favorite of my father, although I doubt he was so favored by her." He stepped closer. "Would you do it again? Would you kill my father, knowing your own death followed hard upon?"

Baron Markha's leering jests and grasping hands, hot breath on her cheek, moist lips on her neck—

"You did what none else dared, for they valued life above dignity. I have slain a dozen—a score!—who crawled to me, begging for their lives, promising to do whatever I asked just so long as they lived. Craven pleas. I heeded them not." Ûtgar paused. "But you do not beg. You waited long for your revenge. Such patience is extraordinary."

He hesitated, and his voice quieted. He was afraid. "Who are you?"

Maggie widened the chink his emotions. What brought him here was more than his father's death. Little love had existed between Ûtgar and Baron Markha. Ah. His mother. The baroness governed the province in his stead, her cruelty different but equally brutal and grasping. She would not give up power now, not after having held it for so many months.

Ûtgar's cold blue eyes widened as he sensed Maggie's presence in his mind. "Witch!"

He thrust his sword through the bars. The blade whispered past her ear, slicing a lock of tangled and blood-crusted hair. The strands fell across her arm like wispy spiders.

Nelek clamped a sinewy hand over Ûtgar's and wrested the sword from his grasp. The blade rasped along the bars. Nelek tossed it into the grass beside the road. "You may be Lord Ûtgar and the new Baron Markha, but I am Captain Nelek, and she goes to the king."

The two men faced one another. Ûtgar's chest heaved and his nostrils flared. A great battle waged—his pride against the knowledge he was not the superior swordsman. "You dare humiliate a noble!"

"I have suffered too much shame to be afraid of yours."

Ûtgar smiled. "You ran from common mercenaries. The great Captain Nelek, who has never turned from a fight. So. You scurry off to the king with your prize, hoping to win a pat on the head like a faithful dog."

"The last man to stand against me I pinned to the ground with a borrowed blade"—not quite true, because Nelek had been distracted by the mercenaries before he could deliver the killing blow—"and if there be any more talk of dogs, it will not be from a young pup who does battle from a distance, sending his men to fight but never leading them himself into the heart of the fray.

"Now, m'lord"—his tone grew almost companionable—"perhaps we help one another."

Ûtgar picked up his sword, his face set in fell lines, his pride sore wounded. If Nelek had not possessed the advantage, Ûtgar would have struck. He stood with sword unsheathed, point downturned, the flat of the blade resting against his leg. "What aid can you be to me?"

"Your father is dead at her hand, and the people of Shea gave her refuge. Those same people hired brigands to fight my men. A farmer spoke treason against the baron and the king. We both have cause to burn the village to the ground."

Maggie gripped the bars.

"There is another matter," Nelek continued. "A Kel remains in Shea. A blacksmith. The king is collecting such as he for a secret purpose. Do you know aught of it?"

"You already have a prisoner to deliver."

"Aye, and turning back will cost many days' travel." Nelek sheathed his sword. "But would you not agree that revenge is better than punctuality?"

Ûtgar glanced back at Maggie. "That I would agree."

40 ~ The Ghost and the Dragon

Kieran throve on the minor adventure of climbing small hills or rounding bends in the road or standing at crossroads. He pondered taking other ways, but remained on the road to Romney-town.

A slight edge of fear sharpened the excitement. He never knew if approaching merchant caravans or farm wagons might instead be king's men or Kip's Boys. He hid until the carts rumbled past, and traveled for a time among the trees before returning to the road. Despite that, he felt released, as if invisible shackles had been broken, his feet set free to wander whither they would.

Aside from the blue-winged messenger birds, his traveling companions included the occasional red fox, watchful rabbit, or striped badger. A small herd of deer grazed in a glade yesterday, but a winged shadow overhead sent the timid animals fleeing deep into the Kelcey Forest.

The Renfrew River sang just inside the trees on the eastern bound of the Romney Road, and the music drew Kieran with its drowsy peace. Beneath the shade, the clear water reflected brown stones below and green forest above. Birds settled on branches around him. Intelligence gleamed in their bright, inquisitive eyes.

Kieran shed the pack, waded into the shallows, and bent down, his hands just above the water, waiting for unsuspecting fish. He caught one—more by luck than skill—and cooked it over a small fire. Then, his meal ended, he stretched out in a hollow on the sloping riverbank and fell asleep.

When he awoke, twilight spread its shadowed net through the forest, snaring sound, filling the air with silence. A sense of old magic crept among the trees. The birds were gone, but a small white bloom with a delicate fragrance lay near him as if placed there with purpose.

Where had he seen it before?

Sitting beside the river, twisting the flower stem between thumb and forefinger, he thought of Maggie. She had not Sally's curves or Kathleen's dark beauty, but Maggie's face—her eyes, her rare smile—compelled his gaze and now his thoughts. Had she been at the Faere, he would have asked her to dance.

Night reigned.

He tucked the flower into the ties of his shirt, picked up the rucksack, slung it over one shoulder, and took to the road stretching pale and broad through the forest. One of the few high roads maintained for the swift travel of the king's men, it was raised slightly on a firm-packed bed of stones so that rainwater would drain off on either side, keeping the road from becoming too muddy and soft for wagon wheels or marching troops.

He would have to leave the road soon. Somewhere on the Plains to the west lay the Ruins of Kel. There he would begin his search for the lost sword. Others before him had sought in vain for Azrin, and he had little hope of finding it among the tumbled stones, but where else might it be? Lost to the Black River? Hidden in the royal treasury? Niether Mad Morfran nor any Skardian king before him could touch the sword. Unless he was a Kel.

Did Morfran hunt his own kind lest they prove closer blood than he? If so, 'twas a twisted, vile plan.

Putrescence and decay filled the air.

Kieran looked to the sky. Stars rippled. Stench grew. He leaned against a tree and vomited, then rinsed his mouth with water from the skin.

Wind circled, and a blue glow surrounded him.

Blast!

He unslung the rucksack. He had untied the dagger from his leg and tossed it inside the bag to keep from losing it when he waded into the river to catch his supper. Blue radiance leaked from the seams.

Tainted wind bent the trees. The Dragon flew lower, lower. Dust whipped from the road, stinging Kieran's eyes.

Light increased until the leather of the pack was only a thin veil for the dagger within. He covered the sack with his body, hunching over it like an old man bearing a burden, and backed farther into the trees.

The forest seemed naught but a stand of twigs in the forceful wind tangling his hair and tugging his clothes. Across the road, a wide-spreading tree cracked, its thick trunk felled as if by an unseen axe.

The air grew still.

Tremors vibrated through his feet and up his legs. Each successive thud was the sound of a giant treading the earth.

The Dragon was aground.

Kieran pushed deep into a thicket. A twig snapped. He halted. The thudding stopped.

He willed his heart to slow, but it disobeyed. His breathing sounded in his ears as loud as a storm.

Darkness undulated. Where once it roused the forest at its coming, the Dragon moved toward him silently, fluidly.

Revolting breath, hot and sour, enveloped him. His eyes watered. He heard the distinct whiffling sound of an animal sniffing its prey. A hot exhale ruffled his hair.

Kieran had never counted himself among the faithful, but now he screamed in his mind. A prayer came, as clear as rain falling on stone. He moved his lips in concert with the words, speaking in silence.

Risá El ethem, Mymna Tor
Risá duru Nar Cahm enkára lenë llumim
Risá nen, o pyrvië grimladh

He did not remember the meaning. It lay hidden before he was found, a young child with a mind wiped almost clean by shock, a dagger in his hand and a dead man at his feet. Yet the words were familiar to his mouth, comfort to his mind.

A blue light pierced the northern sky.

The Dragon rose. Air shuddered under the beat of monstrous wings, and trees twisted in the vortex of wind. Dragging in its wake the stink of its passing, the Dragon flew south.

A fresh breeze cleansed the air, and the night seemed brighter. Kieran dropped to the ground and lay gasping, arms outflung, the rucksack beside him unlit and ordinary. Just as it should be.

Mother Crumb had said only Kels could speak to etherium, and only to Kels would it answer.

Aye, but how did he keep it from betraying him?

Maggie stood on unsteady legs and walked the cramped enclosure of the cage. Bruised ribs made that difficult, but she needed to move.

Campfires sprang up near wagons lined on the road. Horses were staked out to graze the lush grass, and soldiers spoke in low voices. Lord Ûtgar's yellow-clad men-at-arms avoided the scarlet-cloaked king's men.

Ûtgar stepped from the shadows. A guard barred his way with a sword. "No one approaches the prisoner. Captain Nelek's orders."

"Out of my way."

The sentry did not stir from his stance. Ûtgar tried to push aside the sword, but still the guard stood fast.

"Wasted caution," Ûtgar jeered. "Were she guard and you captive, she would not hesitate to kill you."

"Be that as it may, you must leave, my lord."

"Your lord? You—" Ûtgar looked up.

A blue light shot from the mouth of the scrip on Nelek's belt. Maggie knew that glow. It resembled the light of the stone she had found at the riverside and now carried in her apron pocket like a secret. The stone warmed, answering the light.

The sulfurous odor of fire and decay filled the camp a moment before wind bent the trees. Wagons swayed. The cage rocked. Soldiers sprang to hold the team of oxen still hitched to the wain. Horses tossed their heads and reared. A pair of fine draft horses hitched to an empty cart broke free. A man leapt into the back and imperiled his life by climbing across the seat and wagon tongue to grasp the flapping reins, pulling them back with such force that the horses' heads bowed and the cart slewed sideways, almost overturning.

The stench rendered some men ill. Others grasped weapons and looked for the source of the foul storm. Stinging wind drew tears to Maggie's eyes. She hooked her elbows through the cage bars to keep from being battered side to side. The force strained her bound hands, and the rope bit deep. Hair whipped about her face, and her torn kirtle pulled taut around her.

Lord Ûtgar ran to Captain Nelek who stood fiercely calm, sword drawn, cloak billowing behind him like a strange wing. Nelek smiled.

"What is this?" Ûtgar shouted, gesturing to the sky.

"It is, I believe, a Dragon."

"What?"

The soldiers nearest Nelek stared at him, surprise and fear on their faces. The wind switched direction then switched again, moving in a circle. The blue light increased.

"Torches!" shouted the captain. "More wood on the fires!"

Flames leapt to life throughout the camp. The shape of a massive wing flashed on the edge of Maggie's vision, and light curved along outstretched claws.

Fire shot from the sky. Men shouted, and horses screamed. Oxen bellowed, jarring the wain, and the cage lurched, throwing Maggie against the bars. She cried out in pain and fell to the floor.

The grass kindled beside Captain Nelek, yet he stood laughing at the sky. "Come to me, you brute!" he shouted. "Show yourself! Show the Kel!"

Trees caught fire. In the light of their blaze, a face as pale as mist watched the captain.

The southern sky flared, dancing with the fickleness of flames. Then a blue spear pierced the underbelly of night. Against his calf, the etherium pulsed.

He felt the essence of another like him, as profound as the stillness just before lightning strikes, proof without evidence.

Leaping to his feet, he heard a voice. It did not call to him, but repeated a plea directed to no one in particular. The distance was too great or the thoughts too faint to capture the meaning.

His fingertips prickled. When he touched them together, sparks leapt. A knowing hummed along his bones and resonated through his skin. His senses stretched taut. Did he imagine the cries? The sounds of confusion? The increased warmth on the night wind?

Kieran shrugged the rucksack onto his back.

The flames disappeared, snuffed like pinched candlewicks. Even the moon darkened. Blinded by the sudden gloom, he blinked. The shaft of blue did not fade, however. It shone all the brighter for the lack of other light.

The dagger glowed again, throbbing like a heartbeat.

Kieran ran.

Nelek delighted in watching Maggie Finney's damaged visage behind the flames. She bent like a degraded garment, too limp to stand upright. *Let her be afraid! She is all too proud, that one. Too*

proud and too cunning.

Blue light still pierced the sky like beacon. His grip tightened on the leather-wrapped sword hilt.

The trees crackled like giant torches, pitch popping and hissing. No longer foul, as if somehow cleansed by the fire, wind flailed the flames with unseen hands as if cracking a multitude of whips.

"Come to me!" he shouted to the Dragon. "If you are here, can the smith be far? Or have you consumed him already, and come to boast your victory?" Throwing back his head, Nelek laughed. He was master of all. Nothing could touch him.

The earth shook. A storm of wind shoved Nelek to the ground, snuffing the flames as a strong breath slays a candle. Even the stars grew dark. Undergirded by acrid smoke, the odor of decay returned in rolling waves.

Surprise rather than fear held him to the ground. He watched in detached concentration as a great claw materialized in the etherium's glow. Then a sinewed leg appeared, covered in glittering golden scales. Next came a wing, outspread, its ribs like beams, the flesh between them as translucent as gauze. Thick as stout timber, a ridged neck arched above Nelek. Last appeared the green eyes of the beast, for the Dragon chose to show no more. Its baleful gaze severed the captain's breath.

DECEIVER.

Captain Nelek heard the melodic voice with a shock of fear.

YOU ARE NOT THE KEL.

"You have not killed the blacksmith?"

BLACKSMITH? I SEEK A KING.

"Were you not sent to destroy the Kellish smith in Shea?"

IF HE IS A KEL, HE WILL BE DESTROYED. BUT I SEEK THE TRUE HEIR. HOW IS IT YOU CARRY ETHERIUM, MADMAN?

"As proof of the smith's lineage."

IT IS YOUR DEATH.

"Nay. My triumph!"

YOU HAVE LET SLIP YOUR MIND.

Nelek leapt to his feet "I will slay you, then, and regain it, for only a lunatic would hold discourse with a Dragon!" He raised his sword.

The creature laughed, a thunder both harsh and soft. A BROTHER OF THE BLACK HOOD. I SENSE THE DARKNESS OF HIS PRESENCE. The green eyes searched the men huddled on the road.

A shadow separated itself from the night. It bowed to the Dragon, who bent near, but what passed between man and beast, the captain could not hear.

He resented being ignored. *This is my Dragon! It shall lead me to the true king, and then we shall see who wears the crown in Skarda!*

Nelek stepped toward the creature, but a flicker of warning in the emerald depths—or perhaps the tug of his own imaginings—pulled him up short, and he stood uncertain.

An uncomfortable thing, uncertainty. He did not have to endure it for long. A ghost stood before him.

"You look well, Captain Nelek." The familiar voice was strong and mocking, scarce to be expected of an apparition. "Would you not say the same of me?"

Nelek tightened his grip on the hilt, wondering if a sword was any defense against a phantom. He had already dispatched the man once with a blade.

Perhaps a pike this time? Flail? Battleaxe?

"You are but the fabric of nightmare," Nelek declared, shaking off fear with laughter. "I see you not."

The ghost smiled.

It touched a livid slash across its cheek, and the corresponding cut on Nelek's face pained him anew. No. No. He only imagined.

"You are dead. I killed you. Your soul escaped with your breath. You abide in the Otherland now, or howl in the Highlands. The Dragon has conjured you to frighten me."

The shade replied, "On the contrary. I still draw breath." It paused, as it had been wont to do in life, gathering the power of silence to add strength to its words. "And will continue to do so after you are long sped to the Otherland."

Panic rose, a surging gorge.

"Ah, you are come," said Fasolt the Black Hood, turning from the Dragon to the ghost.

The shade's smile was empty of goodwill.

The Hood bowed slightly, then addressed Nelek. "Captain, surely you recognize Teag the minstrel."

For Teag it was, his once-fine clothes torn and dirty, a bloody rent in the breast of his tunic, his eyes shadowed as if set deep in a fleshless skull. He was Teag and not Teag: skin pale, wrists and hands bony, clothes hanging from his frame as if from a tailor's dummy, yet he moved with the same eloquence of manner

"How—?"

"How indeed." Teag pointed to the captain's scrip. "You will answer for your use of the bracelet. I will haunt your every step until penance is paid. You murdered Kathleen."

"Foolish girl!" Nelek spat out the words as he might rancid meat. "Sloppy with infatuation, and ready for revenge. "

Anger twisted the minstrel's face. "Did you smile at her as you slid the cuff on her arm? Did you hold it in place while it burned her flesh and stole her mind? Did you take pleasure in her pain?" He grabbed Nelek's throat. "Did you watch the light leave her eyes?" Tears slid down Teag's death-like face. "My love is dead, but I cannot die."

"Love," sneered Nelek, knocking Teag's elbows to break his hold. "As insubstantial as one of your stories. Nothing more."

"Kathleen is dead. Therefore, you shall not die until every last drop of bitter justice has been extracted from your bones."

Nelek felt his first twinge of regret.

The king's men seemed impassive, but Lord Ûtgar's soldiers stared in slack-jawed horror at the massive beast.

The roving green gaze stopped, searching Maggie. She filled her mind with petty things: the brilliance of the blue emanating from the captain's scrip, an idle curiosity about the breadth of the Dragon's wings, the desire for a drink of water.

The green gaze moved onward, and Maggie drew a deep breath.

But the mellifluous voice returned. *I SHALL FIND YOU, KEL.*

Maggie knew the legend, mostly bits of story recalled from childhood, from the people hunted by Mad Morfran. She was not one of them. She was not a Kel.

THE CAPTAIN BELIEVES YOU A BLACKSMITH.

Nelek said something odd to Ûtgar earlier—something about a Kel who was also a smith. Did he speak of Kieran?

Once more, the emerald eyes surveyed the group held thrall by fear and awe. Did the soldiers heard the Dragon's voice, too?

THEY HEAR ONLY THEIR OWN FRANTIC HEARTBEATS. Then came a short, gruff bark of laughter. *AH. A WOMAN. A HEALER.*

The Dragon moved forward, stretching its neck toward her. *YOU ARE NOT THE MOLDER OF IRON, BUT ARE IRON ITSELF.*

Soldiers scrambled out of the way. Horses screamed and reared in fright. A clawed foot descended, silencing the bellowing oxen hitched to the wain. Maggie's stomach heaved at the grating of pulverized bones and the wet sucking sound of the Dragon stepping free of the bloody pulp. Breath snorted out of the beast's nostrils, enveloping her in a noxious cloud.

IRON BARS PREVENT ME NOT.

The Dragon reared back, great neck arching, massive jaws open, heat radiating from them in rippling waves.

Maggie prayed for quick death.

41 ~ Dying

Captain Nelek was mad. Teag saw it in the manic widening of the soldier's eyes and the pugnacity of his out-thrust chin. Nelek carried the etherium bracelet inside a leather pouch, safe from the deadly metal's burning touch but not from its power. The blue light filled the night, glinting along the Dragon's scaled neck, imparting an Otherworldly cast to the faces watching the confrontation between Dragon and prisoner.

The beast hovered over her, poised to wither her with fire or consume her in one crushing gulp. Maggie Finney closed her eyes. Did she cry out in her mind for aid, or did she have other magicks to bring to bear? The gift would be little use now.

There had been a guarded look on Kieran Smith's face that night in the Blue Oak when Teag had questioned him about Maggie. As Kels, did the laundress and the smith communicate by the gift? How much control over it did she possess? Did it gain power when used among those with strong attachment to one another?

Teag glanced once more at Captain Nelek's crazed face. Kathleen would be avenged.

Vengeance was why the Dragon loomed in the camp. Vengeance against the descendents of Kel High King for the death of Attor kin-Dragon, centuries past.

Attor had been slain by an etherium sword.

Etherium only glowed blue in the presence of Kels.

Held captive in a cave, a Dragonking was only interested in Kels.

Maggie Finney was the object of a Dragon's interest.

Ah.

Maggie Finney was a Kel.

"You cannot kill her, Dragon!"

CANNOT? The massive head whipped around to face the minstrel. I DO AS I PLEASE.

"She is essential to the man you seek."

WHOM DO I SEEK?

"The true king of Skarda, descendent of Kel High King, and slayer of Attor, your kin-Dragon." Teag shrugged. "But I could be mistaken."

The Dragon growled low in its chest.

"Will you execute him yourself, or will you bring him before Morfran to do the king's bidding?"

Steam exploded from its nostrils. I SHALL ENLIGHTEN YOU ON THE SUPERIORITY OF DRAGONKIND.

Teag stabbed a thumb toward Maggie. "Spare her as bait for the man you seek. His blood is truer than hers. The guilt of Kel High King flows thicker in his veins. Let him see her, and you will not have to hunt. He will come to you."

AM I FEEBLE? The mellow voice roughened and grew harsh. I AM DERA, MATE OF SCUR ATTOR-KIN, RULER OF DRAGONS!

"Then why dispute with me, O Queen of Wyrms? I am but a man." Teag inclined his head. Then he made use of Nelek's madness and embellished his tale: "A man with the black blessing, for I cannot die. Nothing you do can harm me."

I COULD EAT YOU.

"A most foul meal I would make, brittle, tasteless, all bones and no meat. Besides, you would only vomit me up, and we would be back where we started."

Dera's laughter thundered and delighted. Teag joined her. Maggie Finney stared as if puzzling out the reason he preserved her life.

VERY WELL. BEWARE YOUR CLEVERNESS BE NOT YOUR DOOM. Dera disappeared, claw and leg fading, then wing and neck, until only the unnerving orb of one green eye remained in the air above the camp. I SHALL BIDE ONLY 'TIL THE SMITH COMES FOR THE HEALER.

"You will not be disappointed, O mighty one." He offered his most flamboyant bow, doffing with a flourish a nonexistent cap. His red-feathered hat had gone missing. He missed its jaunty tilt atop his head.

One last rumbling chuckle, and Dera vanished. Not even the trees gave sign of her passing. The air grew clearer, though, and the night less dark.

Someone lit a torch. A few men removed the remains of the oxen hitched to Maggie's wain. Others collected scattered supplies or ministered to their fellows who had breathed too deeply of the Dragon's smoke. Some of those would die. They might recover for a time, but their lungs were seared. Fire and brute strength were only the most obvious weapons of a Dragon. Subtler dangers prevailed: cough, exhaustion, diminished sight. Such was the nature of a Dragon's destruction.

Teag watched the restoration of order. Captain Nelek sheathed his sword and joined the efforts, but Lord Ûtgar stood aloof, giving orders, mouth curled as if an unpleasant odor assailed his nostrils.

Maggie Finney's claw-like hand gripped the bars. "Why?" It was a hoarse whisper, filled with suspicion.

"Why not? I am, after all, a minstrel. I will do anything for amusement. There is vengeance to be had. And, somewhere in his etherium-addled mind, Nelek knows it."

She breached the barrier of his mind. *You need not fear me. I shall not reveal your other secret.*

Jolted, he said nothing.

Her tortured mouth worked into a distorted smile. *Not yet.*

The sharp scent of charred wood lingered in the air, but the beam of blue light had disappeared, and the Dragon reek faded.

Kieran?

Maggie? His feet pounded to a halt. The tool bag jangled against his back. *Where are you?*

Why did you come? she asked.

Why are you here?

Why? Did she speak aloud, she might have sneered. *Were you not in the village square the day the king's men took me? When they nailed Farmer Connor's tongue to the rail? When Nelek tossed Kathleen's body into the dirt and slew poor love-blind John Oakley?*

Bitter words.

He tore the rucksack from his back and dug out a rod of iron the length of his forearm. It would do for a weapon. He had the dagger, too, and a sheathed knife on his belt. *Where are the king's men?*

Almost at your feet.

Who else did they take? Jenny? Sally?

I am alone.

He forced himself to think it, to ask it, despite the gall rising in his throat. *Is the baron with you? Has he— Has he harmed you?*

Kieran felt her leave his thoughts as palpably as if she walked past him on her way out of a room.

Maggie? Maggie!

I killed Baron Markha.

At first he did not comprehend, then he smiled. The baron was dead? Cause for rejoicing!

Again, she seemed to step away from him, closing some part of her mind. *He whom Teag the spy wants more than me is a Kellish smith. Are you the one he seeks?*

Now was his turn to run from truth, but he did not. *Aye.*

He would use me to capture you. Do not come for me. My life is not worth yours.

Kieran stowed the rucksack beside the road, and moved forward into the oppressive darkness.

No! Go home, Kieran! Why are you doing this?

Because I must.

He strode forward.

He felt no obstruction—solid or otherwise—but his next step knocked him to the ground. He landed on the road, a rock gouging his back. His lungs compressed. He breathed nothingness.

All sense of Maggie fled. His mind clouded with disjointed images and muted sounds. He gulped for air but drew none.

He was dying.

The link snapped.

Maggie tried to bring him back, straining her body as if physical effort could control thought, but Kieran was gone. He had bowed to her wishes.

She told herself she was glad. He would be safe from the king's men and—she hoped—the Dragon. She would not be the baited hook.

In that brief connection, however, she had felt cageless. Relieved. Kieran had not seen her humiliation in the square nor her disfigured face. Pray Mymna Tor he never did.

The wind returned, but this time the air felt heavy with rain. In the darkness, a hooded figure stood alone in the center of the now-silent camp. Pallid hands raised to the sky, Fasolt murmured a chant. Chills skittered along Maggie's skin. She did not comprehend the words, but their intent was clear: *Here is magic.*

Warmth spread from her apron pocket all the way up her back and through her arms, down her fingers to the tips. A soft glow pulsed inside the pocket. Here, too, was power.

Fasolt whipped around. "So you are the one."

She did not learn what he meant. An angry cry broke the stillness, and shadowy shapes moved against the dimly lit walls of Captain Nelek's tent.

Two men burst from it, swords glinting. A manic cry identified one as Nelek; the pale hair of his opponent proclaimed Ûtgar. Rain fell as sentinels emerged from the darkness and soldiers rose from sleep, swords drawn. Troops divided into opposing lines like the ragged remnants of armies.

"Hold back your men!" commanded the captain.

Replied Ûtgar, "I cannot keep blood from answering blood!"

Nelek advanced, sweeping a sword down upon the other man. Ûtgar leapt aside, bringing his blade up, gripping the hilt with both hands to maintain his stance against the blow vibrating through the steel. He pushed back the captain's sword, and the blades slid apart. The opponents stared at one another. Then Nelek laughed, slicing toward Ûtgar's side as if to sever torso from legs. Once more, the nobleman thwarted the captain's slashing attack.

"Ha!" Nelek grinned like an impish child. "The puppy bites!"

Teeth bared in fury, Ûtgar screamed, "Cut them down!"

Markha men rushed forward, meeting the king's men with crashing force. The scarlet surcoats pushed back the yellow, but men fell on both sides.

Fasolt stood with upraised arms, chanting. Drenched and shivering, Maggie hugged her arms to her body.

A wrenching cry pierced the noise.

Bloodied, weary soldiers halted their fighting and stumbled back from one another. Bodies scattered the ground. In their midst stood the captain and the nobleman. Nelek's tunic was slashed, and blood lay like black welts across Ûtgar's surcoat. The nobleman went down on one knee, flaxen head bowed. Captain Nelek rested against his sword, leaning on it as one leans on a staff, its point pushed into the earth. He gasped for breath. Soldiers on both sides were intent on the kneeling Ûtgar, bent low to the earth as if pressed beneath the burden of their scrutiny.

Fasolt was silent. Teag, arms crossed, leaned against a taut rope anchoring the tent and looked on with a sneering smile.

Nelek planted a foot against Ûtgar's shoulder, and shoved. The man fell on his back and did not move. "Puppy," said Nelek.

The remaining Markha men attacked. In moments, they lay dead, cut down by king's men.

"Collect their weapons Take anything of use. Leave the bodies for the carrion birds." Nelek pointed his sword at Maggie. "You! Attend me."

42 ~The Keepers

A hard rain battered the western reaches of the Kelcey Forest. Ro'Ar, cloaked head downbent, followed Draken's lead, his boots slapping through the wet undergrowth overreaching the narrow woodland path.

After him came Hetta and Craddoch and the horses. Ro'Ar glanced back. Her hunched shoulders and struggling steps spoke Hetta's weariness; Craddoch's somber face spoke his.

"Draken, stop at the first suitable shelter."

"As you wish, Eldest."

There was a note to Draken's voice—not resistance, perhaps, but distance.

He had wrangled with Madda over which of them would go on the journey. They had brought the dispute to Ro'Ar, and he reminded them that the Voice required only one hunter among the travelers. They agreed to a challenge: the first hunter to bring a deer, a rabbit, and two fowl back to the Ruins would be chosen.

They left in the dark of morning, two ghosts slipping among the trees. They returned at midday—deer slung across their shoulders, fowl and rabbits dangling from their hands—trotting through the main gate, side by side.

An archery match ended in similar fashion, as did a footrace and a climb to the top of the tallest Guardian.

The night before the travelers set out from Havyn duru Asryn, Ro'Ar drew lots. The hunters dropped colored stones into a jar then stepped back and waited, arms folded. Draken was impassive, but Madda fidgeted with the haft of her knife. Ro'Ar knew, before uncurling his fingers, the stone he clutched in his fist was marble, veined blue and grey, and he was tempted to drop it back to the bottom of the jar, but others would hear the clatter or see his heart, and his honor would be lost.

Be it as Mymna Tor wills.

When he opened his hand, revealing the stone, Madda slammed her knife into its sheath and stalked out of the room. Draken's gaze followed her.

"The Narrows lie ahead," Draken now said over his shoulder. "A road passes between them, but the stones and ledges reach far into the forest. We can shelter there."

Ro'Ar knew the Narrows well—as a soldier, he had employed them in attacks centuries past—but he said nothing. Let Draken lead. The hunter had not liked winning by lots. Had he bested Madda in the contests, his present temper might be sweeter. Whatever ailed the man, he must sort it out himself.

A small cry spun Ro'Ar around. Hetta knelt in the path and Craddoch bent over her, a hand on her shoulder. Ro'Ar slogged back to crouch beside her. "Are you injured?"

She shook her head.

Grasping her by the elbows, he helped her stand. Mud clotted her kirtle from knee to hem, her feet sank into the muck, and she clung to his arms to keep from falling. Craddoch lifted her by the waist so that her feet dangled in the air, and Ro'Ar removed globs of mud from her skirt and pulled off her shoes.

"Brythn is the least burdened," he said, and Craddoch set her sideways on the horse. She clutched Brythn's reins in one hand, the strap of a pack in the other, holding herself upright.

Ro'Ar tossed the shoes into the undergrowth. Mud had coated them inside, and one seam was burst. Ah, well. They had never been suited for such a journey.

Brythn was a good, gentle beast, but Ro'Ar walked beside, just in case. When Hetta first came to the Ruins, she arrived on foot, carrying her few possessions in a patched cloth sack slung over one shoulder—all that was left to a baron's daughter who had defied her father to obey the Voice. On the rare occasion she left the Ruins, she rode in a cart or walked. Brythn seemed to sense her unease. Even in mud, he set his hooves sure and kept the pace easy, neither tossing his head at the slap of stray branches nor tugging at the reins to join the other horses ahead on the path.

Ro'Ar patted Brythn's neck. Excellent understanding. Would more

Men were like this beast.

"Why do you smile, Eldest?"

He looked up at Hetta, and rain dripped into his eyes. *Because sight of you gives me hope.*

His far sight sharpened. Warriors, their shoulders slumped yet their feet carrying them forward. Young, old, men, women. Outlaws, villagers, and farmers mingling with seasoned soldiers. "Soon we meet the ones who will bring an ugly history to an end."

The rain eased, moving east as day drew toward evening. Ro'Ar slogged in silence. Holding aside the supple limbs of a flowering thorn bush lest they injure Brythn's legs, he looked up. Hetta's fingers had loosened on the reins. She would be a rider yet.

She had no choice. He had thrown away her shoes.

Some time later, soft, almost as if speaking to herself, she said, "I have read much in Wyn's library. He has a folio of letters from Uártha. There are gaps of many years between them. I may not have the gift of far sight, but I do know we journey to meet her son."

Uártha. It meant *silent*. She had been well-named, for she never revealed her greatest secret. It was the reason Kels were hunted and executed, the reason Heolstor of the Hôk Nar had killed her, the reason her son Gaerbith refused the oath.

"I have heard bits of stories about Uártha," continued Hetta, "but never from you, Eldest. Wyn said you knew her best."

Uártha had drawn people to her yet somehow always stood apart. Her smile could hold compassion, even affection, and she listened with great attention, but one always had the sense she heard a voice other than one's own—that she heard all the words not spoken, all the thoughts unrevealed. What a burden she must have carried. Little wonder she sought to lay it down by fleeing to the mountains and living in obscurity, the wife of a shepherd and the mother of many.

"Uártha had the gift of far sight." Ro'Ar pushed aside a branch. "She was a wanderer and a scholar, but also a healer and a runner, carrying messages among the Kels and the other Keepers. She was, perhaps, the most powerful Keeper to ever hear the Voice. I know of only one other—Sibyl—who approaches her in knowledge, gifts, and wisdom, and, as did she, seeks quietude and namelessness."

"Is that not selfish?" Hetta leaned forward along Brythn's neck to avoid another low branch. "Should not those with the greatest knowledge walk among us? One would think the Voice demand Sibyl return to the Ruins and impart her wisdom—"

"Wisdom is more than knowledge."

"I took the oath two hundred years ago, and I am still learning both."

How many centuries since his own oath? Only a fool ceased to gain understanding, aye, but Hetta's words needled him.

"Do you think me selfish, then, for going where Mymna Tor sends? For keeping watch on the Highlands rather than lingering among the Ruins?"

"No, Eldest, I—"

"For all we know, Uártha did not run from her oath but kept it as the Voice willed, far from us, perhaps even keeping us safe by doing so. And Sibyl is doing as the Voice commands. In her solitude, she keeps watch over the Kel-child, though he does not know her purpose nor even the truth of himself. Before being sent to that village, she taught the healing arts to scattered Kels. She has always been required elsewhere than with us."

A short, tense silence, then "I spoke without thinking," Hetta said. "Forgive me?"

Ro'Ar gripped Brythn's bridle and stopped the horse. "It is I must ask forgiveness."

He glanced toward Craddoch and Draken, who pushed onward without looking back, leading the other horses.

Quiet, quick, before he could talk himself out of it—"Hetta, is there anyone?"

She said nothing.

His face and neck heated. Thank Mymna Tor the light was gone. "Does Draken— Is there anyone who holds your promise?"

"No. No one."

He felt as if he had just run uphill. "Would you—" He caught his breath and tried once more. "This is not the best of times, but—"

"Are you asking for my promise?"

He nodded.

She touched the edge of his rain-damp hood. "Then you have it."

Kieran choked on a sweet draught of air.

"Ah! He wakens," said a sprite-like voice.

Soft hands patted his face. His eyelids snapped open.

"Now, Ella. You frighten him."

Four pleasant faces—one male, three female—looked down at him. The women reminded him of Mother Crumb, ancient yet youthful, with wise smiling eyes.

"Welcome, D'urnythn," said the man, equally old in appearance, his voice warm and deep. He said *D'urnythn* with a soft hesitation between syllables, *Deh-UR-nithin*.

"How—" Kieran's voice sounded like a coarse rasp scraping across metal. "What happened? Is this the Otherland?"

"Time enough for that," said one woman with a smile. She wore ribbons in her hair. "How do you feel?"

He ached. Every old injury from childhood onward throbbed to life, from the scar slashing his palm to the recent bumps on his head, but he breathed. He lived. "Grateful," he croaked.

The elders moved back as he struggled to sit upright. His bed, piled with pillows, stood in the center of a glade. Little tables, shelves, and drawers rimmed the edges of the clearing, and were filled with jars, mortars and pestles, pots, spoons, bunches of dried flowers and herbs. A small cauldron hung over a modest fire in a brazier. An entire apothecary—out of doors.

A sturdy cart stood nearby, flanked by a pair of grazing mules. A pale canvas spread over the glade like a broad tent. Somewhere rain rattled leaves and pounded earth, but it did not fall here.

"Where is this place?"

"The Kelcey Forest," replied the man. "Just through those trees there"—he pointed—"lies the camp of the king's men."

"Maggie!" Kieran swung his legs over the side of the bed, but swayed dizzily when he stood. The old women caught him as if he were a child and laid him back on the cushions.

"Too soon, D'urnythn." The man touched the scarring flesh above Kieran's brow. "How recent is this?"

"It should have healed already."

"The Void has a way of opening old wounds."

"The Void?"

"Both shield and portal. King D'urnythn, you may have to walk through it to defeat it. Dark arts. Very dark."

At the word king, Kieran pushed himself up again. "What else do you know of me? Why do you call me D'urnythn?"

"I am Aldred." Placing a hand over his heart and bowing slightly at the waist, the man said, "And these are Ella, Monca, and Ailis. We are Keepers."

Each woman nodded in acknowledgment of her name. Ella was the one with ribbons threaded through her white braids.

"We call you D'urnythn," said Ailis, who wore the simplest garments of the group, "because D'urnythn is who you are."

"I am Kieran, a blacksmith."

She bobbed her head. "Oh, aye, a blacksmith, but your name is D'urnythn."

Monca, an apron tied around her waist, placed one hand flat on his chest and another on his back, between his shoulder blades. She laid an ear to his chest and commanded him take a deep breath. Startled, he obeyed. After two more breaths, Monca nodded then moved to a table and set to work grinding something in a mortar.

Ailis continued as if there had been no interruption, "You breathed quite a lot of Void before we reached you."

Kieran winced as Aldred probed the still-tender flesh around the gash on his brow. "What is the Void?"

"Nothingness. A taking away. To breathe it is to subtract life."

He heard, but his mind was still on Maggie. Once more, he swung his legs over the edge of the bed. "I will repay your kindness, but my friend has been captured by the king's men, and I must go—if you will tell me how to get past the Void."

"Not tonight." Aldred folded his full sleeves back from his wrists and leaned forward to slather ointment on Kieran's scar. "The Void circles the camp." Aldred passed the pot of ointment to Ella, who passed it to Ailis, who stowed it on a tiny shelf. "For the moment, it is as much our friend as our enemy. Its presence blinds outsiders to the soldiers, and the soldiers to us. They cannot hear us, nor we them."

Kieran coughed, and a shadowy puff of smoke escaped his mouth. He was in no haste to experience again such crushing breathlessness. There must be some way to circumvent it. "How do I recognize the Void so this does not happen again?"

"Listen. Watch the animals." Ella sat beside him. "They sense it. 'Tis a rare creature enters the Void."

"The Brethren almost never erect it where travelers might stumble into it. Too chancy, leaving bodies about. So someone must know you are on this road"—Aldred rummaged through a small leather pouch —"and would prevent you."

"Or keep the king's men safe from Dragon-folk," suggested Ailis.

Aldred muttered to himself, patting his robes, pulling out hidden pockets. "Ah!" Triumphant, he held up a small scroll of thick paper, then immediately began again the process of looking for a lost thing.

Kieran stood. This time, the strength of his impatience kept him from falling. "What am I to do about my friend?"

Ailis's wise eyes held understanding. "Wait."

Helpless anger pounded at his bones like a prisoner demanding release. He could not stay here.

"Wait," Ella echoed Ailis, her grip surprisingly strong as she pulled him back down to sit beside her. "The Void has no power here. The Hood traveling with the king's men establishes the Void around the camp. Here, however, it cannot touch you."

Aldred had found a quill and a small inkwell, and now scratched something onto the paper. He did not look up as he spoke. "The Void sucks the soul from the body, and makes you a slave of Nar Cahm. But the Voice has spoken into you, and the Void cannot overcome the Voice. Unless," he added grimly, "you choose to walk the dark ways."

Ailis smiled. "Do we weigh you with too much arcana?" To her friends, "We throw knowledge at him, and buffet him with the wind of our words. Allow him a few moments to grow accustomed to it."

Patting his arm with a reassuring smile, Ella rose and joined the others at the table.

One hand behind his head, the other resting on his chest, Kieran lay back and closed his eyes.

Despite Father Donovan's homilies or Mother Crumb's stories, he had never quite believed in a power greater than the cruelty he witnessed in Baron Markha, in King Morfran, or in the king's men. Powerful men prospered; humble men struggled. Yet the humble seemed eager and willing to believe in something higher than themselves. They clung to the notion that there were forces at work beyond mortal comprehension.

This very night, a Dragon had fled from words spoken in a language Kieran did not understand, and something that wasn't there had tried to steal his soul.

If there is a Void, there must also be an overflowing. If a Dark Voice, then a Voice of light. If evil, then good.

Why, then, was good so weak? Why did the Voice no longer speak to Men?

If a Dragon, then a Dragon-slayer. If a tyrant, then a rebel. If a captive, then a liberator.

Opening his eyes, he sat upright. "You say my name is D'urnythn. It was my name before Donnegan adopted me, but how do you know it?"

"We are Keepers." Ailis brought him a small cup smelling strongly of honey. "There is little we do not know." She placed the cup in his hands. "Drink."

He held the cup away from his lips. "I will drink only after you tell me what you know of me."

The Keepers looked at one another. After a long moment, Aldred nodded. "Very well," he said. "'Tis a wide tale."

A wide tale. Mother Crumb had said that.

Kieran set the cup in the grass, settled back on the luxurious cushions, and listened.

Vegeir was a bold warrior from a clan of Ethem who had moved north from their traditional land in the Plains to settle on the shores of the Dävra Sea. Skilled in strategy, cunning in war, he took the throne from the crushing fist of Ugbor, who grew more corrupt the longer he wore the crown.

Soon after becoming king, Vegeir changed, talking to himself, spouting bizarre battle plans, heeding only an old counselor with a raspy voice. Vegeir had never before bowed to the words of any man. Despite his madness, his campaigns succeeded against upstart clans or the despised Dissonay. His army obeyed his commands, no matter how absurd.

Then one day he cast aside the Dragon crown. Vegeir declared he had not been himself but would strive against the madness and return to the tradition of the High Kings. This plan, however, bred outright rebellion. High Kings belonged to the ancient but overthrown House of Kel.

Vegeir's counselor, though still at the king's side, turned his attention to a brash young warrior from the southern reaches. Morfran had been raised in the home of his uncle, Baethan, baron of Markha Province.

Morfran craved power. So did his cousin, Cathla. Always, always, the counselor kept to the background, insinuating, whispering. In the end, Cathla proved weak, easily distracted by women, horses, and other entertainments, and became baron when his father died. Morfran was ambitious, gaining favor with his kinsmen and amassing an army to challenge Vegeir.

With the counselor's attention so divided, Vegeir's sanity returned. He knew what the old man schemed, and sought to thwart it. The kingdom would never be free unless the throne was claimed by someone with an inarguable right—the true king, who could stand against the evil counselor and banish the darkness that had shrouded all rulers since the Traitors War.

Vegeir did the unexpected. Rather than hunting down Kels to slaughter them as his predecessors had done, he disguised himself and escaped the counselor's watchful eyes to meet the Kels in secret, searching for one with closest blood to the first High King, striving to convince them of his selfless purpose. Reluctant, fearing betrayal, yet hoping to restore the kingdom to what it once was, the Kels agreed to help.

Morfran issued challenge and war ensued. Time ran short.

At last were found the closest kin to Kel High King: two children, both orphans with no living close relations, one of direct descent, the other from a near branch of the family. To Elycia was sent a guardian with the child from the direct line. The boy carried irrefutable proof: a dagger chased with etherium, a metal none but Kels may touch, and the mark of the House of Kel on his hip.

The guard tried to appear unobtrusive, simply another traveler of no great importance to either Morfran or the counselor—surely not a threat. He would skirt the battle lines in the Plains and take established roads north once he reached the eastern provinces. That was the plan.

It worked until a band of rogues saw the guardian as rich game. He was robbed and killed, but the child disappeared. That was all the world knew of him these twenty years.

Despite Vegeir's death and Morfran's rape of the countryside in his search for the child, the Keepers' hope is not defeated, for the Voice will not be thwarted, and the sword Azrin can only be called forth from hiding by the descendent with truest blood.

The child was proof the ancient royal line still existed, and the blood was not so diluted that the gifts of the Kels were lost. He spoke the old tongue, and could call blue fire from his hands. Whatever broken object he touched, he knew how to repair, and even at a

young age, he crafted beautiful things.
The child's name was D'urnythn.

"All this while, I was in the village, in plain sight." Kieran rose, and walked to where trees encroached on the clearing. "Anyone in Shea could have told Morfran I was there. Why didn't they?"

"They did," Ailis said. "But your story had been told so well and so often that it seemed the truth, and you were not marked as a Kel on the nape of the neck but on the back of the hip, and no one thought to look there."

The mark again.

Kieran turned. "What became of my father and mother?"

Aldred shook his head, great sadness in his eyes.

"What became of the second child? The next nearest Kel?"

"That child also disappeared."

"Surely there is a chance he yet lives?"

"She. And, aye, there is." Ailis offered the cup, and closed his fingers around it. "Now drink. Sleep reveals secrets and resolves questions, and wakens you to new light."

Sometime in the night, Kieran woke just enough to hear rain hitting the canvas, but he was warm and dry and drifted back to sleep.

43 ~ An Answer

Kieran woke on the ground. It was dry around him in a broad circle, but the grass beyond and the trees glistened with the soft sheen of last night's rain. Mid-morning sunlight filled the glade. The Keepers were gone, along with every trace of their presence. He listened for sounds from the camp of king's men, but heard nothing more than birds warbling in trees.

He turned his head. Beside him lay his rucksack, dagger on top, a scrap of thick paper skewered on the blade. Removing the paper, he sat up and unfolded the short message.

Ru tahn aerkha ven á ru fril let dynë drannahh tae.
Cayn. Asryn dyn gra.

He read it aloud, his tongue stumbling over the strange words. Then he read it again, more confident as the cadence and sound of the language became familiar. A third time, and he began to understand. A fourth, fifth, sixth time. The seventh time he read the message, his eyes opened to its meaning: *The sword disdains all but the one who may command it. Call. Azrin will answer.*

Pressing a hand to her aching lower back, Mother Crumb stopped collecting dandelions and stood. A basket of leaves and flowers rested at her feet. A small jug of drinking water waited on the low stone wall of her garden. Two bees hovered near the brim of the jug, and more bumbled around vines and flowers still damp with dew. A lovely morning.

Why, then, did the sun seem shadowed?

She rubbed an aching knee. The old complaint. When had it begun? Oh, aye. The reign of Meresh, who would rather spend his days and nights atop his roof, studying the heavens, than warring with rivals for Skarda's throne. His mother, Iasmeen, had entranced the people with her dark beauty, but she had disappeared on the cusp of peace, and the ache of foreboding began to plague Mother Crumb's bones. The healer had been young then, before common folk began calling her mother and still greeted her as Mistress Sibyl.

Now I am old. Very old. And there is so much yet to be done.

She had been busy the first two days after the king's men fled the Faere. Mercenaries had been injured. She bandaged their hurts, measured out herbs to subdue their pain, and hoped to send all of them on their way with the merchant caravans. Some lingered, however, demanding payment from the villagers in return for protecting Shea from further attacks.

Sally had returned to her father's house, but only as long as the mercenaries remained at the Blue Oak. She might be a comely lass with a shape that stirred men's lust, but Sally was no strumpet. On her way home, she had visited Mother Crumb to buy a balm for her mother. Color high, back straight, she declared, "Stabbed one in the hand with a meat fork, I did." She smiled. "Squealed like a pig. Teach him to sneak his hands up a maid's skirts!"

"What will Master and Mistress Clem do without you?" Mother Crumb tied cloth over the mouth of the medicine pot.

"'Twas they sent me away. I would stay just to spite those filthy animals, but Mistress Clem will not hear of it. She worries." Sally paused. "But my family needs the money I earn."

The healer touched the girl's hand. "You will return."

Tears glimmered in Sally's large eyes.

The mercenaries' belligerence added a twisted measure of oppression. Anger and frustration seized the healer. She wished war and death far from them, but it was well past time the people rose up and refused to wear the yoke. They must act with reason and courage. Did they not understand? Or did they refuse to see?

The brief triumph in the village square would either reap such retribution that they would be broken for generations, or it would increase their desire for freedom. If freedom, such a thirst could not be slaked by anything less than absolute victory.

If Kieran led them, he must believe in it more than they did.

Ah, Kieran.

"How can I complete this task" Mother Crumb looked toward the treetops. "How can any of us?"

She was the last Keeper living among Men here, for all the others have been summoned. They, too, had a task to fulfill. She understand. But why had the Voice chosen her to be alone?

Not since the death of her beloved had she felt so isolated. Even Father Donovan was gone searching for Kieran and one last adventure, and Thryffin followed him, bent on setting Maggie free. Foolish boy and foolish priest!

What if they were caught? The king's men would discover Donovan's true name, and there would be no saving him then.

Father Donovan had held a sword many more years than he had held sacred texts, and proved the saying that old habits were rarely laid to rest.

Old habits. Mother Crumb chuckled at the unintended jest.

"Mymna Tor be with us all, and keep the travelers on their way." Lifting a corner of her apron, she patted perspiration from her face.

"And preserve that foolish priest!" She shook her head. "He is old, and regrets his youth." Tears formed, and she wiped them away with the apron. "My years are grief and solitude. I cannot see how my desolation serves Your purpose, and my faith falters."

A breeze, scented with blooms and forest, wended through her garden and brushed her face. The trees took to whispering, and the river's song grew in sudden chorus.

FAITHFUL CHILD.

"Mymna Tor?"

COME.

"Where must I go?"

HAVYN DURU ASRYN. THEY ARE WAITING.

Mother Crumb covered her face with her hands and wept.

44 ~ Outlaws

Kieran kicked the ashes. Wisps of smoke curled up, and beads of heat flared deep within the charred wood. The king's men had not been gone long.

The site was surrounded by fire-scarred trees, and the prints of some massive beast pushed so deep into the earth that rain had not softened the claw marks originating in the forest, crossing the camp, marring the edge of the road.

Bodies, stripped of armor and weapons, lay pale and bloody beneath the morning sun. Scavenger birds circled overhead. A few intrepid ones tore at the carcasses despite Kieran's presence. He yelled and waved his arms to frighten them away.

No doubt other creatures lurked in the trees, waiting for him to leave so that they might feast.

He walked among the dead, searching for Maggie. He had seen death before, but not so grotesque or brutal. Severed limbs lay scattered. Stench clotted his nostrils and roiled his stomach. The earth was dark with blood. It stained the road, turned the grass brown, and left an unmistakable stink. Why were the bodies unburied? What great hatred had fed the slaughter?

Fresh wagon tracks and the prints of shod horses showed the king's men moved north. Even if Maggie was dead, she would not have been left behind. The king's men would take her body to hang it from the walls of Elycia.

He glanced one last time around the camp, seeing the slight quaver of a bush, the sway of a branch. He sensed watchfulness, other eyes in the forest. Kieran put his arms through the straps of the rucksack, settling it on his back. He made a show of checking the knife at his belt, the strips of cloth binding the dagger to his leg. With a last direct look at the undergrowth, he set a pace north along the Romney Road.

The watchers followed him.

The blue-winged messenger birds reappeared. *Lynneth.* They were *lynneth.*

One, larger than the rest, flew at the head of the flock and bore a white blaze on its grey breast.

"Oradh." Spoken, it was *oradth*, whiteness.

"Ora." *White.*

"Lûvym." *Trees.*

"Lûvië." *Tree.*

They were returning, words spoken in that half-remembered soft voice in his head. His mother?

"So." *Wind.* No, something more. *Gentle wind. Breeze.*

Kieran felt more than heard the laughter from the hidden watchers keeping quiet pace with him. "Come forth so I may know whom I entertain."

"He speaks to himself, and now he addresses the trees." The voice was gruff yet merry. "Come, lads. Meet the lunatic."

Undergrowth trembled to life as green- and brown-clad men stepped from the forest. Some wore swords, some bows and quivers. One man had a crossbow strapped to his back, and another a wicked mace swinging from his belt. Two carried axes. All wore leather armor of some kind, sewn with metal rings to afford limited protection.

A tall slender man—he of the deep mocking voice—stepped forward and hooked his thumbs into his belt. "Ye do not have the look of a rich man, nor do ye be a common traveler."

"Blacksmith."

The bandit studied Kieran. "A freeman, then?"

"Aye."

"From the sound of ye, an Eastman."

"Aye."

"Now that is settled, do ye ken who we be?"

Kieran looked around at the gathered outlaws. Twenty years past, thieves had killed a man and left his body in the road. They left a small boy alive. Those men would be old now—imprisoned, in hiding, or dead. This was a new band of rogues. These might also be the men responsible for the carnage in the clearing, where the king's men and the baron's had camped, but though their clothing was travel-stained, it bore no visible marks of blood or recent battle.

"Playing at being Kip's Boys, are you?"

"Playing?" A smile grew in the outlaw's eyes. "Nay, giant. We be in earnest, eh, lads?"

A rumble of agreement rose from the men. A slight man wearing a hood that covered his face stepped from beside his comrades. He said not a word, but crossed his arms and took a stance beside the leader.

"Nameless here, he never jests." The leader gripped the man's shoulder. "Fiercest one among us. A Kip's Boy to the very tips of his swords."

Aside from the dagger, Kieran had nothing worth taking. His clothes said as much: simple patched brown breeches of light summer wool; a long, loose, once-white tunic belted by a plain wide leather belt; and old leather boots with soles so thin he felt every rock in the road. Last winter, he gave his cloak to Thryffin, so he did not even have that bit of finery, usually the best piece of a freeman's clothing because it must withstand all manner of elements.

"A bit young, are you not? Kip's been dead these twenty years." Irritation crept into his voice. He needed to be on his way, to go find Maggie. "Where are your black horses? The hounds given Kip by Nardha himself? You certainly are not carrying about human heads as torches."

The tall man's grin turned up the edges of his brown beard. "It still be day. Wait 'til nightfall."

The outlaws laughed.

"I be Robby Finney, and I lead this rabble."

At the name *Finney*, Kieran's fist clenched. It was an instinctive thing, as quickly done as undone, but the bandit saw it and raised his brows.

"D'not like me name, eh?"

"Have you a wife or sisters?"

The outlaw tipped back his head and let loose a deep, round laugh. His men joined the merriment. One gasped between chortles, "Wife!" and clung to a fellow's shoulder, the two men leaning on one another in a fit of laughter.

"Nay"—Robby Finney wiped his eyes—"no wife, nor babes, nor ma or da or kin to call me own." Crossing his arms, planting his feet wide, he looked at Kieran. "We find wives enough in Cameron or some other such city set apart for thieves like us. What has that to do with me name?"

"Nothing. Now."

"Yer name?"

"Kieran Smith."

Robby Finney tipped his chin, and one of the rogues—a beardless youth—produced a broken sword, holding the hilt in one hand and the blade flat across the other.

"Be ye a true smith," said Robby, "make it one again."

Taking the hilt, Kieran studied the broken sword. This was fine work, finer even than Baron Markha's sword. A golden-brown gem glittered in the pommel, and tooled leather wrapped the hilt. The crossguard curled up on either end, each set with small jewels of deep yellow hue. He turned the pieces, fitting the edges together like a puzzle. The blade showed signs of recent battle: crusted streaks of dried blood, bent tip. "Whose is it?"

"Dead."

"Killed by whatever broke his sword?"

Robby Finney did not answer. Nameless shifted his stance, moving between the outlaw leader and the blacksmith.

Hefting the blade, Kieran maintained a loose grip on the broadest end, feeling the weight of the weapon. Tingling in his fingertips sang through the metal in a soundless hum he heard in his core. The metal was alloyed and folded, strong and flexible. Such a sword could slice through metal like a knife through pudding. How, then, had the tip blunted? The greater mystery was how such a blade came to be broken. An unimaginable force had been exerted. He could not hope to simply weld the blade. It would have to be made anew by a skilled craftsman.

"I am a blacksmith, not a swordsmith."

"What be the difference? Metal is metal."

"I have never done any work of which I am not proud. The sword will never be the same. The broken ends must be ground down, preparing them for the weld, and then there must be a good overlap of steel to join the two pieces, but that causes a thickening in the blade. It can be smoothed, but the weld will always be seen, even if performed by the most skilled smith. The sword will be shorter, too, and who can tell if the weld will hold?" Kieran returned the broken weapon to the youth who carried it. "I would not trust my life to such a blade."

Robby Finney nodded, a small smile twitching his mouth.

A man with flame-colored hair stepped forward. One long braid hung down the side of his face. A well-trimmed beard thrust out in opposition to his unkempt hair. He stared with stony suspicion. "If he is but a traveling smith, why did he search the soldier camp like a scout or a spy? He knows who did the killing."

Robby sent Kieran a questioning look.

Nameless placed a casual hand on the hilt of one of his three swords, this one at his waist. The other two hung down his back.

Kieran ignored the red-haired man's stare and Nameless' posturing, and kept his attention riveted on Robby Finney's face. Despite his amused expression, there was a constant play of thoughts behind the outlaw's eyes. Kieran would gauge the length of his future by those eyes. "The king's men captured my friend."

The red-haired man grunted. "Rescue him with that fancy little knife?"

"In a forest. After dark. Against men encumbered by armor. I might."

Muscles tensed along Robby's jaw. "They go north to Elycia. What did yer friend do to so rouse Morfran's ire that the king would send his personal soldiers?" He paused, studying Kieran. "King's men be not often defeated, as ye saw right well."

"They are men nonetheless, and can be killed. I know not whither they take my friend or why. Your pardon. I am unable mend the sword. I must be going—" He took a step forward, but the red-haired man blocked his way.

"I do not trust you."

"Any enemy of the king be a likely friend, Helmut," said Robby. "Kieran Smith, ye will never catch them. Not afoot. Come downriver with us. Put ourselves a day ahead of them." The outlaw grinned. "Pick them off as we will."

Kieran was hemmed on all sides by armed outlaws, forced to walk with them, but as they apparently shared the goal of finding the king's men, he did not object.

"Do not be thinkin' to stick that dagger in any of us," added Robby, striding forth. "'Twould do ye no good. We have bigger weapons and better aim."

They stayed on the road for some time. *Lynneth* birds accompanied them until the bandits took to the forest, then the flock rose above the trees and out of sight. Kip's Boys followed the Renfrew River until they came upon several boats on the bank. Pointing to one, Robby pushed an oar into Kieran's hand.

Kieran took a wobbling step into the vessel and dropped to the rear bench. He had never rowed a boat. There were none in Shea. Near the village, the river was shallow and slow, and no one needed boats to fish or cross. Only eastern shepherds used rafts propelled by long poles to float bundles of wool downriver in fine weather, to the Faere or to the weavers in Shea.

"Wide end goes in the water."

Kieran looked up into a sneering, scarred face.

The man repeated, "Wide end. Water."

"I, um—"

The man sucked his tooth, shook his head, then climbed into the boat. He pushed an oar against the riverbank, and the boat moved backward, swaying as the water embraced it. He dipped his oar, first on one side of the boat then the other, positioning the vessel toward midstream. Then he told Kieran to row the left side while he rowed the right.

There was no reason to propel the boat—the outlaws were not trying to move upstream or across the river—but rowing kept the boat from veering too far toward one bank or the other, or from being tipped or turned by the current. Balance, however, took more effort than Kieran first thought, requiring muscles he had not imagined. He found a center and stayed there.

The forest glided past. Boats slipped through shafts of green light and shadow. The river seemed another world. Deer, fox, hare—all manner of animals visited its waters. Curious creatures watched the strange sight of men floating along in what must have appeared to them as fallen logs.

Kieran closed his eyes and listened. The Renfrew grew deeper and swifter the farther north it sped, its song muted, its voice stolen by the depths. Wind caught at leaves. Birds trilled. He heard the occasional familiar warble of the messenger birds.

"Oar," commanded the outlaw.

Startled, Kieran jerked, tipping the boat to one side. The other man cursed but kept the vessel upright. Steadying himself, Kieran thrust the oar back into the water, alert to his task for the rest of the journey.

It ended mid-afternoon with the drawing up of boats on the riverbank, and a scramble up the steep slope. At the top was a tidy camp near which several horses were tied, and a deer roasted on a spit over a fire. A few outlaws sat or lay about the camp, nodding as the travelers arrived.

Someone stirred a cooking pot and asked without looking up, "Any sign of the king's men?"

"Aye, fair Aidan, but not the soldiers themselves." Robby Finney paused to catch his breath, the climb from the river being steep work, and smiled. "But we be close upon them."

The person stood. A young woman, long brown hair in a thick braid down her back, she dressed like a man, short sword at her side. Nearby, a bow and quiver leaned against a tree.

"Who is this?" Aidan stared at Kieran. "A stray giant?"

A hated flush stole up his neck and face. "Kieran Smith, Mistress Aidan. A traveler."

She walked around him, arms crossed, eyes appraising. "Not the usual kind you drag in, Rob."

"Do not be mistaking him for an innocent." Robby leaned forward and said in a loud whisper, "Wandering blacksmith. Very dangerous."

Kieran's rowing partner stepped past him. "Lost in his own thoughts, he was. Forgot to row. Imagine trying to paddle a boat with this monster in it. Left me right frightened."

"Have done, Leidolf."Robby chuckled. "Show him our forge. He can show us his skill."

Leidolf sucked his teeth. "This way, giant."

A rusty anvil stood canted near the crude forge, nothing more than a large, hollowed stone filled with old ashes. Nearby, an elm sapling was blackened but for the very top, which still bore green. Leidolf shrugged. "Sometimes the fire rebels."

Holding back a smile, Kieran shed his rucksack. "For proper work, I need charcoal, but seasoned hardwood will do."

Leidolf cast a sideways glance. "Could bring the king's men down on us, using such precious wood without paying for it."

"And how would you explain the deer over yon fire?"

"With a blade through the heart of the man who asked." Leidolf's hard expression dissolved into an answering glint of humor, although the scar still pulled his mouth into a sneer. "You do not fear us now, do you, giant?"

"I see no cause." Kieran cast about for promising trees. None lay near for the plucking, but here there were no foresters such as those he bribed into chopping down a tree or two for his charcoal pit in Shea. "Rogues you may be, but not murderers."

Leidolf looked puzzled at such a thing, then he scowled as if affronted. "We kill our share."

"Are there no craftsmen among you?"

"Some. We all tried our hands at smithing. No skill." Leidolf waggled thick, callused fingers. "Aidan says we should keep at least one man among us who knows his trade. We found you."

Well, then. "I need an axe."

Leidolf jerked his chin—"Ilari!"—and a youth trotted toward them across the camp. "Cut some wood for the giant." Leidolf looked up at Kieran. "How much you need?"

"As many pieces as you can cut to about this length"—Kieran held up his hands in a rough measure just wider than the hollow in the stone—"good, dry wood. In a forest this old, there will be thick branches that have fallen. Use those."

With a short nod, Ilari trotted back the way he had come, stopping long enough to grab an axe, then disappeared among the trees.

"Do you have any oil? Enough to fill a bucket?"

Leidolf looked around as if expecting to find just such a bucket in the bushes. "Aidan may know."

He departed, and Kieran knelt to clear the undergrowth around the crude forge, setting aside a goodly stack of twigs and branches to start the fire.

Leidolf returned with a basin of thick whitish paste and a bucket of water. "Rendered fat." He hefted the basin. "Closest to oil we have."

Kieran set the basin on the ground—"It will do"—and placed the water beside it.

"Smith?" Ilari stood nearby with an armload of wood. Kieran gestured to a spot, and the youth tumbled the cut sticks and split logs into a rough pile then trotted back for more.

Leidolf crossed his arms, a man prepared to watch, not work.

Kieran cleared away the piled ashes, and arranged wood for a fresh fire, leaving a gap so coals could be fanned. When he looked up, a ring of silent outlaws surrounded him, some standing, some half-kneeling, most with a hand ready to draw a weapon. He had not heard them approach.

He lit the fire with a flint. A short while later, a pile of coals glowed, fanned awkwardly by Leidolf using a woven mat tied to two sticks.

Kieran laid out his tools on the ground then looked around at the outlaws. He put his hands on his hips and waited.

One of the men pulled a stirrup from a leather satchel and thrust it forward. Kieran took it, turned the stirrup over, saw where the weld had cracked. Anyone putting his foot into the ring would land on his back. Kieran looked at the owner and nodded. An easy fix.

Three loose knife handles, two bridles with warped rings, another broken stirrup, a snapped clasp, and a new belt buckle. By the time the outlaws stopped giving him work, Kieran's fingertips were tingling until he sweated as much from containing the blue sparks as he did from the heat of the forge fire. He cooled the buckle one last time, tested the metal against the heel of his callused hand then opened the tongs, dropping the buckle at the feet of its impassive owner.

"Wait a bit before you touch that."

The man turned it over with the toe of his boot, picked up the still-hot metal with his glove, studied the simple fastener, then nodded and walked away. Others followed.

Leidolf wiped a sleeve across his brow. "Well, now, giant. You certainly know your trade."

He looked toward the cook fire. "A sharp one, our Aidie." His voice dropped when he said her name.

Aidan laughed at something Robby Finney said. Her head tipped to one side, and the long brown braid swayed against her back. Leidolf's scar lay stark and white against his sun-red skin. He turned and strode into the forest. Aidan looked up, smile slipping as he disappeared through the trees.

Kieran spread the coals to cool them, then collected his tools into the rucksack. He propped the sack against a tree, knelt on one knee, and removed the threadbare shirt Maggie had used as an apron once. Raising it to his face, he closed his eyes and breathed in the fragrance of herbs.

He reached for her in his thoughts but grasped only emptiness.

Footsteps scuffed the earth, stopping a short distance from him. "Ye said something to Leidolf?"

He lowered the shirt, fingering the worn fabric. "Nay."

"Ye looked at Aidan."

"Aye." Kieran met Robby's gaze.

"Do ye want her?"

"Do you?"

"Every one of the Boys wants her. Does not mean she wants any of them." A glimmer of humor returned to his eyes. "But I wager fair Aidan be safe from ye." Quirking his brows, Robby tilted his head to one side. "Ye repeated a woman's name in the soldier camp. Maggie."

Kieran smoothed the old tunic over his thigh, examining every stain and patch as if in them he might see Maggie's face. "The king's men have her."

"Yer—friend?"

He folded the shirt and returned it to the bag. "A healer." Kieran stood. "Maggie Finney."

"Ah." Robby chuckled. "Finney." He shook his head. "Be at ease, giant. She be none of mine."

He turned toward the fire where his men drank ale, cut meat from the spit, traded jests. "Be not deceived by their laughter, smith. The first Boys killed and robbed for sport, but these men hate." Robby's voice grew grim. "They have good cause. Each has a tale, and a name he keeps to himself. We only know what a man chooses to tell."

Filled with the drone of insects, the murmur of the river, the rustle of leaves in a warm breeze, silence grew loud between the two men standing on the edge of the camp. Tense energy clenched Kieran's muscles. Were it not wasted effort, taking him back over distances already traveled, he would this instant seek out the king's men.

"A smith and a healer be but common folk." Robby Finney hooked a thumb through his belt and shifted his stance to look at Kieran. "Why should the mad king set his sights on such?"

Borrowing from Aldred and Mother Crumb, Kieran replied with a half-smile, "That is a wide tale."

Nameless stood nearby, hood still shadowing his face. He kept a steady watch. Kieran nodded, but the man did not acknowledge the greeting.

"What of him? Why call him Nameless?"

"'Twas a jest at first—to make him talk."

"And did he?"

"Mayhap he cannot."

"You place great trust in such a secretive man."

"He has proven his worth." An enigmatic expression came over Robby's rugged features. "What of ye?" His quiet gravity held a note of challenge, but an almost formal reserve as well. "Ye be more than a blacksmith."

Kieran looked away. Dusty shafts of gold-green light gilded the soft air beneath the trees.

"Kip O'Kelpie was a rogue," said Robby, "but he was more a father than me own. Such be the way of master thieves. They find hapless children and feed them, give them a home, teach them the trade. I was Kip's brightest pupil. Nimble fingers and quick wits. Never rattled by the unexpected. But Kip would never let me learn that other side of the trade—killing for hire.

"He did take me on patrols of the king's roads. We cut many a rich man's purse, and even those of a few commoners who thought themselves Kip's equal.

"One patrol, though—one patrol in early spring I remember well. I was but fifteen. If I had been born a farm lad, I would have been courting a rosy-cheeked lass and building a cottage of me own. But that day I saw a man die.

"When 'twas done, a tiny lad ran from the forest and stood over the corpse. We thought him a wizard. Blue sparks shot from his fingertips. He pressed them to the dead man's chest and chanted in a strange tongue, but nothing happened. Then he shouted at Kip. Shot fire. Kip only stared down at him. The fire disappeared, and the boy drew a dagger. Kip caught his arm, said something I cannot recall, and left him standing in the road.

"Soldiers searched for a lost lad with an unusual name. They said he carried a fantastic dagger and bore the mark of the House of Kel." He looked at Kieran. "I would fain hear the tale of how ye remained lost for so many years."

First Mother Crumb, then the Keepers, and now Robby Finney. The story of Kieran's life was carried by others and was not his own.

"What makes you think I was that boy?"

"I heard the words ye spoke on the road. They had the sound of the words the boy shouted at Kip. I cannot speak for the mark, but I ken that dagger ye carry. Fit for a king."

Robby nodded toward the fire. "Come, giant. Eat, drink. Soon we meet the king's men.

They joined the circle. Outlaws cast measuring glances at Kieran, and a few tossed out their names: Alwin, Bannon, Cort, Rinc, Vili.

Ilari engaged Kieran in conversation about weapons he had known. After a long space of listening to the young man's reminiscences, Kieran sat on an upturned piece of hewn log, trying to ignore his stomach's rumbling, uncertain of what was accepted as polite behavior among rogues. With a sympathetic smile and a droll face while Ilari was not looking, Aidan handed Kieran a mug of cider.

"Ilari." Vili, a sturdy man of deep-chested, muscular build, shook his grizzled head and wiped the back of his hand across his mouth. A scar slashed diagonally down his neck. "Man's hungry."

Ilari flushed, and looked down at his bowl of stew.

Vili sucked the meat juices from his fingers then wiped the fingers dry on his breeches. "If you keep listening, giant, he will keep talking."

He left the circle with a few muttered words about scouting the Romney Road.

Ilari ate his meal in silence without looking up again.

Kieran was reminded of Thryffin, whose grave eyes had seen what too many other children in the Markha Province had seen—the death of hope and kin. Who had taken in Thryffin? Sympathy often extended no further than words, and the villagers had their own troubles and fears. The lad likely still slept on grain sacks and fed Miller George's chickens. Mother Crumb and Father Donovan would not let the boy go hungry.

Robby Finney sliced a chunk of haunch from the deer on the spit, and passed it to Kieran, sliding the meat from one blade to the other. Kieran nodded thanks then bit into the tender flesh.

The outlaws grew silent, staring at him. Kieran stopped chewing, looked back at them, wondered what unspoken rule he had violated. Then he glanced down at the meat. It was choice, one of the best cuts. The outlaw leader might as well kneel at his feet and swear fealty.

As if he saw neither Kieran's discomfort nor the flaring anger in Helmut's face, Robby cut another sizable piece of haunch for himself and ate with relish. After a few uncertain moments, conversation renewed but not as loud as before.

"Rob says you travel with us." Aidan sat beside Kieran, holding her mug in loosely-clasped fingers. She set him at ease, for she reminded him a bit of Sally with her direct speech, but Aidan's ways were more practical than provocative. "We could use a giant."

Kieran had just taken another mouthful of savory venison. He tried to chew quickly and swallow before offering a response.

Aidan's lips quirked into an almost-smile. "Less haste, giant, and a sweeter stomach."

"Aye," he managed at last. "I have eaten whatever fish I could catch—which were not many—so this is a feast."

She laughed, her brown eyes crinkling at the corners. "If this is a feast, I think 'tis best you keep with us, else you will be but bones by the time your journey ends."

"I wish I might, Mistress Aidan." He wiped the back of his hand across the corner of his mouth. "I have a task that must be done beyond the Kelcey."

"What is this task"—Helmut stood, and gestured north with his knife—"that takes you in the direction of the king?"

Robby, too, stood. "Helmut."

"Who is he, Rob? He could be a spy!"

"Aye. Any one of us could be a spy."

"What are you saying, Rob?"

"He be one of us."

"One of us." A snarl curled Helmut's lip as he looked again at Kieran. "Has he seen his family slaughtered by the king's men? Has he met vengeance upon those vermin or wet his hands in their blood?"

"He hunts king's men. You hunt king's men. They killed your love. They hold his love captive."

"A story told to a willing ear."

"Helmut, ye do not want to be saying that."

"What do you know of him that makes you his champion? You gave him your meat!"

"What I do with mine be my concern."

With a last hard look at Kieran, Helmut stalked away from the fire. Robby watched him go then turned back to the circle.

"A good man, Helmut," the outlaw leader said, and returned to his meal.

Aidan ventured a quiet question of Kieran. "The king's men truly hold your love captive?"

He stumbled at the word *love*, but said, "Aye, they do."

Leidolf lunged from the forest, Vili running at his heels. "Soldiers on the road! The king's men will be at the Narrows by nightfall!"

Men leapt to their feet, tossing on the fire the dregs of their meal, and left the circle to mount horses and check weapons. Robby wiped his knife across the thigh of his breeches then sheathed the blade and turned to Kieran. "We have few horses. Y'ride mine."

Kieran tossed back the last of the cider. "Never found horses quite suited to me."

Robby gave a curt nod and departed, Nameless at his heels.

Others doused the fire and removed evidence that the clearing had served as a recent encampment. Aidan and another outlaw cut the roasted meat, and placed the pieces into heavy sacks that they then tied to pack horses.

Kieran emptied the forge stone of ashes and buried them, covering the hole with leaves and branches, the detritus of the forest floor. Then he tipped the heavy stone from its base and slid it so that one side rested on the ground, giving the appearance of long disuse.

He retrieved his rucksack.

Leidolf appeared at his side and held out a sword. The hilt showed age, but the edges of the blade glittered from fresh whetting. "No scabbard."

Kieran took the sword, its weight pulling on his arm. "Longer reach than a dagger."

Leidolf grinned.

Silent and swift, the outlaws moved through the forest, Robby in the lead, Nameless at his side. Kieran was not the only one afoot, but the close-set trees prevented the horses from outpacing the men who walked. Helmut kept to his left and slightly behind him, appointing himself watchman of the newcomer. Leidolf, on the other hand, did as he had in the boat, and put himself in front of Kieran.

"You trust too much," hissed Helmut.

"You trust too little," murmured Leidolf.

Robby uttered a low, sharp word, and the men fell silent.

The sun was lowering when they reached the Narrows, an oddment of land like a forgotten fragment of stony mountain through which passed the Romney Road. Trees grew thick along the road, closing in like a rope around the mouth of a sack. Robby Finney issued commands in gestures, arraying Kip's Boys along either side of the way, in undergrowth or behind trees or on sturdy branches.

Aidan was not pleased to be sent to hide ahead on the road, to guard the horses and the supplies, but when Leidolf nodded, she went. Ilari followed, staggering under the weight of Kieran's rucksack.

Kieran found a spot behind a thick tree and leaned against it, closing his eyes and willing his heart to grow calm.

"Ye will not be killing many soldiers like that," said Leidolf.

"I have never killed anyone."

"Ye will today."

Ro'Ar halted in the middle of the road, and Brythn's nose bumped his shoulder.

Craddoch looked around. "What is it?"

Ro'Ar turned, looking back the way they had come.

"A whole day in the wrong direction?" Draken asked.

"No. No, the foothills of the Craydaeg Mountains lie north, where the Voice said go, but—"

How could he explain the tug in his mind? It was not a whole thought, really, or a vision. Somewhere back along the road, near the Narrows—

"Other Keepers answering the Summoning?" Hetta patted the horse's neck.

"Perhaps." Ro'Ar clicked his tongue at Brythn, who did not need the pull of the reins to compel him forward.

45 ~ At the Narrows

Captain Nelek laughed to himself, and he laughed out loud. He laughed awake, and he laughed asleep. When he did not laugh, he brooded. When he did not brood, he spoke nonsense.

He only spoke sense when necessary.

Meantime, he sang ditties of his own making or muttered outrageous schemes to take the throne from Morfran.

The minstrel-spy-ghost was to blame. Had he performed his duty without being distracted by village slatterns, Teag would be the one with the cursèd bracelet. Teag would be the one who struggled against the etherium's call.

"Etherium can prove your right to the throne," whispered a voice Nelek recognized, dimly, as his own. He had as much right as Morfran. In truth, no right at all. "Blood is a weak argument against strength of arms."

"I did not hear you, Captain Nelek." Teag rode up on a magnificent animal, certainly one of Lord Ûtgar's horses. "Do you address me?"

Nelek snarled.

The other man chuckled.

"Where is the mincing Lord Ûtgar?" Nelek sneered. "Gone prancing off on his own?"

Teag gave him a curious look. "Do you not recall last night's skirmish, captain? You wounded him nigh death."

"You lie! Where is he?"

"You were sore wounded, too, and forced the murderess to tend your wounds because she is a healer. Remember?"

"I would never let such a one near me!"

Teag studied him with empty ghost eyes. "Very well, then. There is no fooling you." The minstrel's tone was brisk. "Lord Ûtgar rides with his men. He found your conversation—lacking."

Nelek uttered a short, snorting laugh. Turnabout, he found the young pup lacking. In every way, in manner as well as spirit. Just as well. Nelek had little use for him. *When I become king, I shall have him executed as a nuisance.*

Humming one of his favorite new melodies in honor of his impending coronation, the captain reached into his scrip to caress the bracelet.

"'Twill kill you," Teag warned.

Nelek waggled gauntleted fingers at the spy.

"Ah." Teag smiled. "Armor. Very good."

He should find new clothes. The colors, the rips, the bloody tear in the chest of the tunic: all kept fresh the memory of the day the minstrel died at Nelek's own hand. Teag held the reins loosely grasped in long fingers. Tattered sleeves fell away from bone-thin hands, accentuating his ghostly appearance. Rather like him to be so dramatic.

"Before you did your best to dispatch him to the Otherland," said Teag, "Lord Ûtgar planned to deliver justice to the peasants back in Shea. Or, more precisely, he would exact vengeance while you redeemed your honor. What broke your alliance?"

The captain remained silent. He only remembered bits of dreams.

"You would not let Lord Ûtgar kill the wench in the cage. He will not be content until he can sate his thirst for revenge."

Nelek smiled. "He will have to wait his turn. The king's right comes before all. And there is the Dragon."

"Ah, yes. The Dragon. How do you think to control her?"

Nelek opened wide his mouth and issued a long, shrill noise. All humor fled Teag's face. His pallid death-look returned.

The shriek of rage disintegrated into discordant laughter as Nelek tipped back his head and let loose his mirth. "What wisdom the spy speaks! But he cannot rule me with his silvered tongue. Oh, no. I am familiar with his tricks." The captain shrank down into himself until his shoulders hunched about his ears. His voice dropped to a whispered growl. "I am Nelek, master of Dragons, possessor of etherium, leader of men, killer of enemies, and"—he giggled —"squasher of spiders."

The bracelet warmed. The circle of faint heat pulsed, a heartbeat. He cast a sidelong glance at Teag, whose staring eyes watched him with hateful spyness.

"You want it, do you not? The fabled blue metal that shines in the night?"

Teag shook his head with a look of disgust. "Keep it."

"A man who does not know how to fight is too dangerous to let loose with a sword," Helmut growled. "Too costly to coddle."

Kieran disliked few people. He hated the baron and the king, true, but they were far away. Few men challenged him, and he had not been in a real fight since childhood when he and Harry traded blows like brothers. This Helmut was bothersome.

"What can you teach me now," asked Kieran, "so I am more ally and less foe?"

Helmut sneered and did not answer.

Leidolf chuckled low in his throat. "Remember the oar, giant? Broad end in the water? Same with the sword, except sharp end in the enemy."

Anticipation and dread hummed along Kieran's bones, sparking from his fingertips. He snapped tiny flames back and forth as a man lost in thought might toss a pebble from hand to hand. At a sharp oath, he closed his fist and looked up.

Leidolf drew back, wide-eyed.

Helmut's face slackened. "Are you a wizard?"

Kieran shook his head

"What is that, then?"

He shrugged. "It returned to me a few days past."

"Returned?" Helmut frowned.

"I had forgotten it was there."

"How is it possible to forget such a thing?"

Another shrug.

Leidolf leaned forward. "Show us again, giant."

He did.

"What can you do with it?"

"I killed a fly once, but that was pure happenstance."

Helmut dropped a beetle into the light web, and uttered a low oath when it fell to the ground a smoking husk. Leaves, twigs, scraps of cloth cut from tunic hems, wisps of hair, a snippet of leather: all followed the beetle into the lightning, and all became charred crisps.

"Does it hurt, having that come from your fingers?"

"Tingles a bit."

All three men bent over Kieran's sparking hands like boys fascinated by insects or toads.

"Lads."

Startled, they looked up. Robby Finney stood over them, amusement dancing behind the warning in his eyes. In a trice, Helmut and Leidolf turned around, their attention on the road.

Robby motioned to Kieran and led the way deeper into the forest behind the outlaws. Stopping beneath a towering fir and planting his feet wide, Robby crossed his arms.

"Heed me, giant," he said in a stern quiet voice, all humor gone. "Should ye be king, ye may remember this day and toss me into a dungeon, but that cannot be helped. I lead these men. We kill soldiers so we can cripple Mad Morfran and take whatever prizes there be— weapons, provisions, horses. I will not have ye playing games when ye must be alert and ready. Whatever trick or magic ye command, lay it to rest. We be at war."

Kieran looked down. "It will not happen again."

"Ah, giant, ye need more pride than that if ye plan to rule a kingdom." He clapped Kieran on the back. "And ye can say me name. Rob."

Leidolf grinned when Kieran returned to their hiding place.

Kieran smiled a little. "Not as bad as it might have been."

"Remember being switched on the backside by yer da? Well, Rob can raise a welt just by looking at ye sharp-like."

No, Kieran had never been switched by Donnegan, though the older man had sparred with him, a friendly exchange. He saw fathers cuff or curse their sons, and wondered why Donnegan was different. When Kieran was especially willful, he had been made to do extra work in the shop or clean the cottage with Mistress Donnegan while Kathleen and Jenny had a free afternoon.

I was raised by fine, good people. What would they think of me now, consorting with outlaws and ambushing soldiers?

There was no time to think on it. The music of approaching battle: clinking bridles, rumbling cart wheels, jangling mail, marching boots, the steady thud of hoofbeats. He tightened his grip on the borrowed sword.

"Stay with me, giant," said Leidolf.

As the sounds of the king's men grew loud, the outlaws grew still. In the twilight, foot soldiers appeared around a bend, just before the road entered the Narrows, and behind them were mounted soldiers, then carts and more foot soldiers. Their surcoats were stained and ragged. A handful of men wore bandages, but no wounded rode the carts. Rather, the wagons were piled with bloodstained weapons and heaps of broken mail, folded tents, and assorted camp items.

At first, Kieran felt almost sorry for the soldiers who marched so wearily into a trap—then he saw the wain. It bore an iron cage with a domed top. In the bottom lay a bloody, bedraggled figure, a woman with her wrists bound and her russet hair spread across the straw.

Kieran tasted rage like metal on his tongue.

A bird trilled, low and sweet.

The outlaws waited. The king's men entered the Narrows.

The bird trilled again.

A ringing cry, wordless and many-voiced, burst upon the king's men. The forest poured forth swords and longknives, torches and arrows. Mounted soldiers wheeled their horses. Footmen crouched behind shields. A driver tumbled backward into the bed of a wain and cowered there, hunched down between the seat and a pile of swords spilling from their covering of tent cloth.

Kieran roared, rushing down the slope past Leidolf, heedless of lances or swords. The dagger blazed at his belt, and blue fire twined his fingers and the blade of the borrowed sword. His one aim was the iron cage, and he thrust aside anyone who prevented him. There was no obstacle, no sound, no sight but his goal.

Something bit his sword arm. He tossed the hilt into the other palm and continued hacking at impediments. He gave no thought to strategy or skill. He relied on brute force, using his sword more like a club than a blade.

Tripping over a body and slipping on the blood, Kieran clutched the edge of the wain. The cart lurched. The heavy horses hitched to it were frightened, scarce contained by the driver. Arm muscles bunched, feet planted against an angled board meant for a footrest, he stood, pulling back on the reins. If the driver gave the horses their heads, they would trample everyone in front of them—king's men and Kip's Boys alike.

A blade flashed toward Kieran. He flinched. It hissed past his throat. He grabbed the mail-clad arm wielding the sword and twisted until the arm wrenched loose. An agonized scream sounded in his ears, but it seemed faint, heard from a distance. He released the arm. The soldier fell, senseless.

Kieran thrust his sword up through the lock on the cage door then thought better of it—why damage the blade? He pulled the sword free, and closed his fist around the lock. Blue lightning danced. With a quick, hard yank, he sundered the hasp, and the lock fell into the straw piled in the bed of the cart.

"Maggie! Maggie?"

He touched her bruise-mottled foot. Heat radiated from it. Kieran climbed into the wain and felt for broken bones.

A soldier swung a mace, but Kieran kicked him in the chest. The man tottered backward, toppling a comrade in arms. An axe bit into the bed of the wain.

Keiran hoisted Maggie over his shoulder, gripped the sword, and leapt from the cart. Two soldiers confronted him, one standing slightly behind the other. In frustrated fury, Kieran let loose the lightning.

It wrapped the sword in arcs of blue flame. Soldiers and outlaws alike stumbled back from the rage of light, forming a clear path. Chests laboring for air, sweat and blood streaking their faces and arms, they stood and stared at Kieran in amazement.

Battle ceased.

A tall robed and hooded form emerged from the shadows. It opened its hand, palm outward, and flung a cloud of darkness deeper than night.

46 ~ Fasolt

Kieran turned to flee, but the small black cloud expanded, enfolding him.

"You can breathe, hear, be heard, see, be seen. But if you try to escape the Void," said the dark monk, "it will consume you."

The blue tangles of light still crackled along Kieran's hand and sword, the dagger still glowed, but now he felt an answering pulse from something inside Maggie's apron pocket pressed against his shoulder. Perhaps it was only her fever burning through him, the heat of combat cool in comparison. The fever was the only sign she lived.

"What do you want with me?"

"Morfran, King of Skarda, has need of you, blacksmith."

"Of what use am I to Mad Morfran except dead?"

"One does not question the king of Skarda."

"Then stand aside and prevent me not."

"There is no king but Morfran."

"Not as long as I live."

"There is no king but Morfran!" The skeletal fingers extended, and the Void shrank tight around Kieran. "Any claims you make are empty and foolish. You are but a blacksmith. There is no king but Morfran."

Kieran recalled Robby's words before the skirmish: *Ye need more pride than that if ye plan to rule a kingdom.*

He straightened his spine. "I am D'urnythn, descendent of Kel High King and heir to Azrin, the sword that slew the Dragon Attor and united the clans a thousand years before the Kingdom of Skarda was born. I am king."

"Fool!" The veil darkened. "There is no king but Morfran!"

"If your king has need of me, you cannot kill me."

"I can imprison you until the Dragonqueen returns. But will your little murderess live 'til then? Healers are sworn to save lives, not take them. No matter. She has served her purpose."

Fresh fury coursed through Kieran. Blue fire sparked anew, arcing to touch the veil. A tear appeared in the black cloud. He raised his flame-wreathed sword and sliced through the tissue of Void. It folded away from the blade, dissolved, disappeared.

In that instant, searing pain leapt through him, and blood poured from the wound on his right arm. He fell to one knee, dropping the sword.

Red light grew within the ring on the monk's white hand. "There is always a price for crossing the Void."

Every joint ached, every muscle screamed. Sweat dripped into Kieran's eyes. His teeth clenched.

Leidolf shoved through the silent combatants and reached for Maggie with blood-spattered hands. Kieran's left arm tightened around her.

"Let her go, giant."

No. No.

"I know, but you must. Let her go, man, and stand."

He loosened his grip.

Leidolf lifted her from his shoulder and stepped back, cradling her close. Kieran gathered his breath and his strength, gripped the sword, and pushed himself to his feet.

The dark monk chuckled. Ring flaring, he held out his hand toward Maggie. Her body convulsed until Leidolf could scarce hold her, spittle foaming white at the corners of her mouth.

Kieran ran, swinging the sword with every dram of anger and grief, striking the monk's head from his shoulders.

It was done in an instant, yet seemed separated from time. Everything happened in measured increments. He lifted the sword—it was weightless and heavy at once—and drew his arm across his body, the sword stretching high over the opposite shoulder. Then it whistled through the air. He felt the yielding resistance of thick cloth, the clawing scrabble of skeletal hands, the tug of flesh, the scrape of metal on bone, and finally the release as his blade swung free.

He stared down at the monk's crumpled body and the still-hooded head. The red light waned, and Maggie lay quiet.

A twining black cloud swirled around the pieces of corpse,

wrapping them, concealing them, sucking all light to itself. Then, in a shock of silent thunder, it disappeared. Nothing remained—neither head nor body nor garments. Nothing but ashes and a gold ring.

It rolled to a rest against the toe of Kieran's boot. He picked it up, feeling the weight of it, watching the light shrink deep inside until the ruby dulled. Freshets of air eddied around him.

In the Narrows, the king's men milled in muttering amazement and confusion, as if wakened from long sleep. They repeated names, perhaps those of wives and children, perhaps their own, and looked around, asked comrades where this place was and if they knew the way to such-and-such a village.

Armor was shed. Swords clattered to the ground. Alone, or in twos or threes, the soldiers walked into the night. The priest who held them thrall was dead. They were no longer the king's men.

Kieran touched Maggie's throat. An erratic beat pulsed beneath the fevered skin. He tried to lift her from Leidolf's arms, but the outlaw shook his head.

A hand clamped Kieran's shoulder. Robby Finney's eyes gleamed in his battle-grimed face. "Come, giant."

"There went your blacksmith," said Teag. "Better Fasolt's head than yours, eh?"

Captain Nelek canted to one side, pale and in obvious pain. Blood seeped through the bandage Maggie Finney had applied yesternight to his wounded side. More blood from a fresh arrow wound soaked his thigh. Growling wordlessly, he sheathed his sword without bothering to wipe it clean. His mind was well and truly gone if he could not recall even simple soldierly matters such as cleaning a blade to keep the metal from rusting.

Unwilling to resist another dig at his enemy, "Did you hear?" Teag said. "He declared himself king! Best run to Morfran and tell him you now serve another."

"There is no king but Morfran," grunted Nelek. He peeled off his leather gauntlets, ruined by blood and burst seams.

"Not if you find the sword first," replied Teag.

"Spawn of Nardha!" screamed Nelek, grabbing a broken pike and waving it in Teag's face. "Get you gone, foul demon!"

"I have promised to haunt you, old friend"—Teag stepped aside, and the pike soared past his head—"and I am a man of my word."

Looking around the clearing, empty but for a scant dozen soldiers who still hadn't come to their senses, Teag whistled a sentimental old tavern tune about young men gone to war. He grinned when Nelek shot him a snarling glance, but he did not stop.

47 ~ Embracing the Fire

Kieran cut Maggie's bonds. The ropes were rank with blood and corruption. If the corruption could not be stopped, her hands must be severed to save her life. That would not be a kindness.

Aidan handed him a waterskin and a soft bit of pale fabric. "She needs a healer."

"She is a healer." He fought for steady hands, pouring water over Maggie's wrists then wiping her face with the damp cloth. "Have you any salt or herbs to purify the blood?"

"I traded with a traveling merchant for something the old fox claimed was a plant used in the Keldon Age. Dragon's-bane. Rare, he said." There was a shrug in Aidan's voice. "Old Beagan is a liar, but I was curious, so I gave him my best hair ribbon for a pouch of it."

Rare indeed, if it could be purchased with a mere ribbon. Kieran poured more water on the cloth and pushed Maggie's tangled hair back from her face. "How is it prepared?"

"Powdered root, I think."

"Put a pinch in a tea pouch. Boil water and make a weak infusion. If it does not make her more ill than she is already, then make it stronger."

"You would risk her life that way without knowing what will happen?"

"She dies already. What more can I do?"

After a long, uncertain look, Aidan put a kettle on the fire and prepared the medicine.

Kieran combed his fingers through Maggie's hair, feeling it catch at his knuckles, tugging free the tangles. He brushed callused fingertips across her forehead, avoiding the swollen bruises around her eyes. Her jaw was black. Her torn kirtle had slipped. Ridged scars curled over her shoulders like crow claws. He slid a hand beneath her back and felt the cross-hatches of raised flesh. Anger again twined his fingers.

Robby Finney laid a hand on his shoulder. "Let me bind that arm before ye be as ill as she." The outlaw opened a flask of strong spirits, shoved a strip of thick leather between Kieran's teeth, and said, "This might sting."

The spirits set fire to his wound. Kieran almost bit through the strap. Rob did not release him when he tried to pull away from the burning, but poured more until the blood washed away.

When the leather was removed from his mouth, Kieran regretted he did not know rich, florid curses to call down upon Rob's head. He had to be satisfied with gritting his teeth while the outlaw wrapped a wide band of clean cloth around his arm and secured it with a knot.

"Ye want to knock me to the dirt now"—Rob grinned—"but that will pass."

He poured the last of his flask over Maggie's wrists, but the putrescence remained.

Kieran continued to bathe her fevered skin, murmuring to her, urging her to waken, to delay her journey to the Otherland. She gave no sign of hearing. Her shallow breaths hardly moved her chest, and only a flutter pulsed in her throat.

Aidan brought a steaming mug of fragrant tea. Kieran lifted Maggie, letting her head fall back so that her mouth opened, and Aidan spooned a few drops between her lips. Maggie swallowed. Hope flickered.

Kieran poured the tea on her wounds, too—perhaps that was how the medicine was supposed to be applied—and prayed he did her good not ill.

Rob greeted the outlaws returning to camp, the dead or wounded on their shoulders. Three corpses were laid out in a neat row. At the next sunset, they would be buried, and their souls prayed into the Otherland. Tonight, the living ranged themselves near the fire, tended weapons or wounds, and flicked glances toward Kieran.

"Giant, why do they look at you so?" murmured Aidan. "They seem afraid. What happened on the road?"

Kieran needed time to understand it himself. "We met an emissary of Nardha, and I killed him."

Aidan sat back on her heels and stared at him.

Maggie sighed. Her body slackened.

Kieran leaned over her, willing her eyes to open. "No. No. No." He held her to him. "Come back, Maggie. Wait for me."

He reached for her thoughts, for that intangible proof that had come to him on the Romney Road when he ran to find her yesternight.

Silence.

He rested his cheek against hers, still hot with fever, and stroked her tangled hair.

Just beyond the outlaw camp, by the light of a small torch planted in soft earth, Aidan knelt beside the pallet of moss and young tree limbs where Maggie Finney lay, and washed the dead woman's body. Aidan had sent Kieran away. His grief reminded her too sharply of the men whose wives her mother attended in childbirth.

Rather than scoffing at strong farmers reduced to tears of joy or sorrow, to tense bouts of pacing or tossing back ale, Aidan understood them. Although she had been privy since childhood to the mysterious, frightening, promise-filled world of the birthing room, she was never at ease there. In the presence of so much life and hope, she saw dreams fall and shatter like delicate sheets of ice, melting and evaporating as if they had never been.

A twig snapped as someone approached. Aidan twitched the torn kirtle over Maggie's torso and glanced up, recognizing the shape if not the shadowed face.

Leidolf squatted on the opposite side of the body, looking down at the outspread hair tangled with leaves. He plucked one. "Why did you send him back to camp?" He twirled the leaf between his thumb and forefinger. "And why did he go?"

"He can do no more than I do now." Aidan poured more water on the rags but she did not use them. She touched the dead woman's battered face. "She is still warm, as if she yet lives."

What was the light inside Maggie Finney that had drawn the giant? She bore on her back deep scars from a savage whipping. The damage looked enough to kill a large man. How had she survived? The crippled hand reminded Aidan of old tales about the black blessing. Twisted limbs were sometimes seen as Nardha's mark, the outward sign of a twisted soul. What had put her afoul of a Black Hood and a troop of king's men? If she truly had been of Nardha's fold, why did her own turn against her?

Nay. Maggie was none of theirs. Not if she belonged to the giant.

Aidan sighed. She felt a great emptiness. "Is there no happiness, Leidolf?"

He leaned forward and looked on her with such naked longing in his scarred face that Aiden turned her gaze. She could not unlock her soul and let him see every secret cowering inside.

With a muttered curse, Leidolf rose and returned to camp.

Kieran stood apart from the other men, one foot in shadow, one in firelight. His clothes stank of battle, the rank odor of blood and sweat. He had taken life, but he felt no remorse. He was hollow.

Leidolf returned from the darkness, wearing a determined expression. He sat on the ground and used a whetstone to hone the edges of his sword. Helmut, Ilari, and the rest of Kip's Boys engaged in similar pursuits, making ready for the next skirmish. As always, Nameless took a post near Robby Finney, watchful even as he worked.

The three slain outlaws had been laid out just beyond the firelight. Their hands clasped their swords, hilts on chests, blades pointing to their feet. They would be buried in shallow graves mounded with stones. Maggie would rest beside them.

Anger clenched Kieran's fists. If he had not left the village, if he had delayed one day—one day—he might have been able to prevent her being taken. Perhaps he could have fought off her captors, hidden her, kept her from that cage.

But what good was remorse? All that was left to him now was vengeance.

A certain quality of stillness, of unheard but knowable presence, made him look up. A great green eye, hovering over the clearing like a malevolent star, peered down at him.

The air grew heavy with Dragon-stink. Someone whimpered in fear. Outlaws scrambled out of the way of enormous claws, and crashed through the undergrowth as they fled. Two men let fly arrows and a third threw a short spear, but the weapons glanced off the Dragon like blunted toys off a rock.

Firelight reflected off the Dragon's golden body; the sun seemed almost to shine again. The massive head swung down toward Kieran, jaws opening and snapping shut, emerald eyes wide as if in delight.

YOU HAVE THE LOOK OF KEL HIGH KING, BUT NOT HIS SWORD. YOU HAVE THE BLOOD AND THE WILL, BUT NOT THE WEAPON TO SLAY ME.

The voice was rich, pleasant.

I AM DERA DRAGONQUEEN. IN THE NAME OF MY KIN-DRAGON WHO FELL BENEATH AZRIN, SWORD OF KEL, YOU WILL PAY THE KIN-PRICE.

A blue glow enveloped Kieran, and the dagger grew warm.

THAT? The Dragonqueen laughed, revealing teeth larger than pikes, longer than spears. AZRIN THE YOUNGER, PERHAPS? YOU SHOULD HAVE WAITED UNTIL IT WAS FULL-GROWN.

"Are you made only of words?" Drawing the dagger, he offered it across his palm. "Or are you afraid?"

YOU WELCOME YOUR DEATH?

"I am at your mercy, Dera. Crush me, tear me, consume me with fire. I cannot stop you. After all, I have but a weak blade decorated with etherium. Pick your teeth with it after spitting out my bones."

Her scaled upper lip curled back in a Man-like sneer. I WOULD NOT COME NEAR SUCH VILE METAL AN IT WERE GROUND TO POWDER AND BORE NO EDGE AT ALL. FILTH IT IS, UNFIT TO TOUCH DRAGON-KIND.

She rose up, arching her neck to glare down at him from an even greater height, and drew in a deep breath.

He ran.

Hot breath swept over him, and a ball of fire set his path ablaze. He flung his arms across his face, turning his back to the flames. Heavy smoke stifled his breathing.

GO THROUGH THE FLAMES, said a voice in his ear.

Kieran blinked against the scorching bite of the smoke. Loathsome holocausts surged on all sides, forming a ring, blocking any possibility for escape. Heat seared his skin.

Had it been less than a sennight since the Faere began? Since he refused Sally's invitation to dance or heard Mother Crumb's fantastic tales? Now he would never know the name of the man buried in the grove beside the Romney Road. Never again would he listen to Harry's jokes or hear Jenny laugh. Why had he not asked Maggie to join him in the Match Dance?

There was no way out, nothing to do but wait for the belt of fire to tighten around him.

Go, the voice repeated.

Why wait? Why not meet Death and be done with it?

Drawing back his shoulders, Keiran walked into the flames.

Fire enfolded him. The blast and tumult subdued into a dim and distant noise. He stood inside a corridor of shifting light, colors playing over him in bands of red and gold as if he walked through the heart of the sun. Kieran reached out, and his hand passed through flames as if through cool water. They rippled around his fingers as water eddies around rocks.

He looked back. A handful of outlaws had been halted in their flight by the fiery wall, and now their faces wavered behind the heat of the blaze. Shock widened their eyes and slackened their jaws.

He turned and stepped out onto the sandy riverbank and into another world. The Dragon was gone, the fire dead, the other men nowhere to be seen. He felt as one in a spell, cast into a world between the living and the dead, all senses gone but sight.

FOLLOW ME.

"Where?"

WHEREVER I LEAD.

"Depends on the matter."

MATTERS ARE NOT ALWAYS AS THEY SEEM. DO YOU TRUST ME?

"You brought me through the fire."

DO YOU TRUST ME?

Kieran hesitated.

THERE ARE MANY MORE FIRES TO COME.

"Who are you?"

I AM THE VERY AIR, PRESENT BUT UNSEEN, AND YET YOU BREATHE. IF YOU TRUST ME, I WILL GUIDE YOU. I AM THE VOICE.

The world blurred and shifted. Fire sprang up behind him. Wind blew. Trees bent. Shouts carried through the forest.

Feet sinking in the damp earth of the riverside, Kieran ran. The dagger glowed in his fist, and the Dragon shot a stream of flame after him. It sizzled in the river, boiling water into steam.

He struck across the river, slogging through the shallows until the water deepened, forcing him to swim. Waterlogged clothing weighted his limbs.

I cannot do this!

The Voice did not reply.

Fire rained.

He dove, but shards of light pierced his watery shield, heating the water. Dead fish floated past, and upside-down turtle shells bumped his arms.

Lungs near bursting, he broke the surface and scrambled on to the bank, crawling under a large thornbush that clawed at him. He covered the dagger with his body, diminishing its glow, and waited.

The Dragon passed overhead in ever-widening circles. YOU CANNOT HIDE FROM ME, KEL. WATER MAY WASH YOU CLEAN FOR A MOMENT, BUT YOU WILL ANSWER FOR YOUR FOREFATHER'S CRIMES.

Dera's voice softened, becoming almost alluring. YOU CANNOT RESIST YOUR DESTINY. IT IS ALREADY FORETOLD. DRAGONS WILL HAVE THEIR VENGEANCE ON MEN.

HAVE YOU BEEN TO THE RUINS, KEL, AND SEEN THE DESTRUCTION OF YOUR ANCESTRAL HOME? THERE IS NO LONGER A THRONE, BUT A RUBBLE OF LOST GLORY AND BROKEN STONE.

A ball of fire shot from the sky. He flinched, but she missed. Flames consumed a small tree then died without further nourishment.

The etherium had obeyed him at last, and did not glow.

She can hear me, she can smell me, but she cannot see me. He sat upright. *The Voice—*

Dera roared. ALL YOU LOVE WILL BE DESTROYED.

She flew east beyond the river. The wind fell. The fire died, as if unable to sustain fury in the absence of its creator, leaving behind charred trees and heavy ribbons of stinging smoke.

Kieran forced himself to stand on legs so weak they shook. He took a few steps, but had no strength to swim back across the river. Where did the camp lay? Would the Dragon return to harm Kip's Boys?

Sinking to the ground, he closed his eyes and composed curses he was too weary to utter.

48 ~ NIGHT

Some time in the cool depth of night, after midnight and before dawn, destruction rained on Shea. The Blue Oak exploded into wild flames as casks and cellar caught fire. Cottages, the smithy, the weaver's shop, even the tanner's shop outside the village, all were destroyed in the enveloping wrath of the Dragon.

Mother Crumb sensed its coming, felt its darkness and rage, and by that frustrated vengeance knew Kieran lived. Gathering her medicine casket, implements, and a few other medicines into a bundle, she hastened across the mill bridge before it came under the Dragon's fury.

Screaming villagers fled to the stone kirk and cried for mercy. Mother Crumb tended their burns and other hurts, praying all the while. "Keep Kieran, and guide his steps. Keep Father Donovan and Thryffin. Cover them with Your hand until Nar Cahm be overcome."

There were no words to grieve for Maggie whose voice she no longer heard.

49 ~ Morning

The boy scratched the stiff grey hair behind the donkey's drooping ear, and wished once more for a fine strong horse, a longsword, and the proper direction of those dogs calling themselves king's men, but he would settle for finding Master Smith.

Nay, *settle* was the wrong word. Truth niggled at him like a worm wriggled through dirt. He would rather find Master Smith than anything else. That, and rescue Maggie Finney. If she really had killed Baron Markha and rid the province of that menace, she deserved high honor and the first place at every table.

"Thryffin," called Father Donovan, emerging from the forest, "be Sibley saddled?"

"Aye." Thryffin tugged at the saddle blanket, flattening a wrinkle lest it rub the beast rudely or raise a sore. "All packed."

"Thee ride first, lad. These old joints need limbering."

The boy pulled the reins over Sibley's head and used them as leads. "I will walk with you, Father."

They traveled in silence beneath boughs meeting like fingers loosely clasped over the road. The dawn-light seemed magical, and for once Thryffin welcomed the fey feeling. Now he understand Master Smith's love for the Kelcey Forest. Were it possible, his anger had eased, enough that he was grateful to Master Smith for giving him a reason to embark on this adventure.

'Twas true, the only other travelers he had encountered were farmers or merchants without even a hint of outlaw about them, so there had been no confrontations or excitement in that regard, but a freeman two nights past told of hiding in the forest to skirt a troop of king's men. They were mingled with Markha men-at-arms, and a great iron cage stood in a cart on the road.

"A woman were in it," the freeman had said, "all bloody-like and bruised. I fear to think what had been done."

So did Thryffin, but he kept silent. Father Donovan shared their bit of supper with the man, then moved to make camp elsewhere that night, far from the road and without a fire.

Midday, a great stink grabbed Thryffin by the throat, and Sibley balked.

"Stay with him, lad," commanded Father Donovan in a grim voice. He slid a sword from the old leather-wrapped sheath strapped to the donkey's saddle, and slipped through the trees like a wraith, his rough brown robe disappearing in the shadows.

Thryffin stroked the old donkey's nose and murmured soft things to the one good ear. It twitched to alertness, turning to follow the slightest sounds.

"A fine beast you are," whispered the boy. "A fine brave beast. Father Donovan will return soon, and his caution and your fear will have all been for nothing. Just you wait."

He said it more to reassure himself than to calm Sibley. The priest's swift confidence and stealth unsettled him. Should a man who served Mymna Tor be so at ease with a sword? Thryffin had never considered Father Donovan had been something else before taking the cloth.

When he had overheard Mother Crumb in the kirk trying to dissuade Father Donovan from this quest, Thryffin crawled from his hiding place beneath a bench and announced that he was going, too.

The healer had looked at him with her mysterious blue gaze that seemed to see all he thought to hide, and she smiled just enough to wrinkle the corners of her eyes. She gathered her medicine box and a bundle of old rags then limped past Thryffin, saying, "Come to my cottage once you are ready. I have medicines for you."

Father Donovan had dispatched a message to his abbot, telling Father Alister his intentions, then set about gathering proper clothes for Thryffin, even shoes.

In the year since his father died, the boy had worn not but the tunic and breeches in which he was clad the day Baron Markha took his mother. Master Smith had long ago stopped trying to put him in different clothes, although the blacksmith did insist Thryffin bathe on occasion and accept the man's own cloak when winter cold turned the world silent and white.

The cloak was with him now, wrapped inside the blankets tied to Sibley's back.

Another scent pushed through the sickly sweet stench. It was acrid and familiar. A fire had burned recently nearby, sharpening the air like a thin knife.

"Hush," soothed Thryffin as Sibley jerked his head and backed away. "Hush, now, Sib. Shhh. I am here."

The old donkey's good ear flicked forward. Father Donovan reappeared, the corners of his mouth stern and white. The scar slashed its pallor down his sun-browned face, lightning in a dark sky.

He sheathed the sword. "Have thee a strong stomach?"

As a traveling priest, Father Donovan carried with him all manner of small sturdy implements to aid his journey. Thryffin had been amazed many times by the tools and collapsible cooking utensils stowed in Sibley's saddlebags. He watched now as Father Donovan unfolded a shovel and locked the hinged places in the handle with iron pins.

"Cover thy nose and mouth with this." The priest handed him a lavender- and mint-soaked cloth. "It will keep away the flies and help a bit against the smell."

Thryffin covered the lowere portion of his face, and knotted the herb-infused cloth behind his head. "What are we going to do?"

"Bury the dead."

Reluctant to move toward what frightened him but refusing to be left behind, Sibley followed Father Donovan with hesitant starts and stops. Thryffin stroked the donkey's neck as they walked around a bend in the road. The stench overpowered the herb-scented masks. The sight roiled Thryffin's stomach.

"Two or three days," murmured Father Donovan. "The scavengers have already been here."

"Is it bad to burn them rather than bury them?" Thryffin struggled to keep his gorge from rising at the sight of so many dead bodies. "Is a pyre against the new ways?"

"Nay, Mymna Tor cares not. Thee be right, lad. A pyre might be quickest, but I do not want to set the forest alight."

"Looks like someone already tried that."

"Aye, it does."

After a few silent moments of staring at the carnage, "Well, lad, it must be done," Father Donovan said at last. "Let us be about it."

"Aldred!" Mother Crumb wept to see Keepers walk the high street, garments ethereal in early morning light. "Ella! Monca! Ailis!" She hobbled to meet them. "How did you know to come?"

Tears shone in Ella's eyes. "Are you hurt?"

"A tumbling wall knocked me down"—Mother Crumb rubbed her hip; it and her leg were tender, covered with large bruises—"but I will be well."

Aldred, tall and grave in a flowing white robe, surveyed the dirty exhausted men gathering the charred detritus of their village. "We knew the Dragon is awake. We did not know we would find such destruction."

Women cooked over open fires, and children huddled together. Many people wore bandages, limped, leaned on walking sticks. Some wore slings binding arms close to their sides. A wide strip of cloth covered one man's eyes and part of his burned face.

"We came to take you with us, Sibyl."

Mother Crumb pulled back from the Keepers. "The miller may not live long enough to see his mill rebuilt. The innkeepers are both badly burned. The weaver and his family were all killed. The tanner, too. There are many more dead." She pointed to the dooryard of the kirk where stacked bodies wrapped in sacking and covered with flies waited interment as the most able men dug one great grave nearby. "The Dragon did this. The only hope I have is that Kieran Smith lives, else the Dragon would not have poured its wrath on us."

Ailis took Mother Crumb's hand. "'Tis little consolation."

"Aye, but if I do not hope, I die."

A boy with large somber eyes stood in the road and stared up at Aldred. The old man smiled down at him.

"Are you Mymna Tor?" the lad asked.

"I am His servant."

"Did Mymna Tor do this?"

The Keeper bent to look the child in the face. "Does a good father harm his children?"

The boy shook his head.

"Sometimes even good fathers cannot stop evil."

"But Father Donovan says Mymna Tor can do anything. Were we bad?"

Aldred placed a hand on the crown of the boy's head. "Nay, you did nothing to bring this upon you. Just as no man can summon the rain, no man can prevent its fall. We do not always understand the ways of Mymna Tor, but we can always trust He cares for us." Aldred glanced again at the destruction. "Some things are, lad. They simply are."

Then, reaching into his rucksack, he brought forth a loaf of bread. "Take this to your mother."

The boy bowed as if to a nobleman and ran to where a woman worked beside men stacking fire-scarred rocks. She spoke to her son then looked where he pointed. Nodding thanks to the Keeper, she called other children to her and divided the loaf among them.

"How many farms were lost?" he asked.

"A dozen, perhaps more," said Mother Crumb. "All but one of the trees in Farmer Harry's orchard were burned."

"You are weary," said Ailis, "and weighed by grief. Come."

Mother Crumb led them to the kirk. In the cool dimness, injured villagers lay on the floor or sat on the narrow benches. The Keepers offered what aid they could before joining Mother Crumb in the priest's cell.

Her friends around her, she began the story with Kieran Smith's growing knowledge of his past, told of the king's men and the mercenaries, and ended with the night the Dragon laid waste the village of Shea.

"Some mercenaries died in the Blue Oak fire. Those who survived fled." She stared down at her hands, gripping one another until the knuckles turned white. "I prayed Mymna Tor take them away. This is His answer?"

Ailis put a hand on her shoulder.

"Just when he is needed most, the priest is gone on a mad quest to find Kieran. These people— My going would seem abandonment. I midwived their births, cured their ills, washed and anointed their dead. I am a healer. I must stay."

"Aye, you are a healer"—Ailis leaned forward and laid a hand on her arm—"but you are also a Keeper. Surely, Sibyl, you have heard the Voice. The Summoning is begun."

Mother Crumb nodded, her throat tight. "I thought He had left me comfortless and alone." Her voice hoarsened, and tears dripped down to darken the fabric of her kirtle. "He takes the only children I might have called my own, a son and a daughter—takes them without any promise of return. I cannot hear Maggie's voice."

Bent by deep, wrenching sobs, she covered her face with her hands and rocked back and forth.

Warm hands touched her back. Gentle voices murmured words in fluid chant. No one tried to stem her tears.

A feather brushed his face. He swatted at it.

It touched him again.

Kieran opened his eyes, blinking against the sunlight. A *lynneth* perched on a slender limb bobbing in the breeze. The bird cocked its head and looked down at him.

He groaned, pushing himself to a sitting position then onto his knees. His head pounded. His arm throbbed. Joint, bone, and sinew rebelled. Leaves clung to him, and he ran a hand through his hair, displacing two twigs and a beetle.

Bracing a hand against a tree, he pulled himself to his feet and looked around. The lynneth lifted from its branch, skimmed past him, and flitted into sunlight then back to shadow, behind a tree, above a bush. It wanted him to follow.

Walking was not sufficient to keep pace with the bird. Kieran forced his aching body to run, his stride uneven and clumsy. He stumbled over rocks and roots, caught his clothes on branches or thorns, but soon his movements became sure, his stride long. The forest opened up before him, and the sloped riverbank no longer tilted. Something—or someone—seemed to bear him up, giving strength and grace where he had none.

He came upon a fallen tree, once a great majesty of the forest. Its roots fanned in a vast display, covered in moss and sheltering several small creatures that scampered at his coming. The log hung out over the river, but did not touch the other side. A mounded cluster of large rocks supported the end of the log, however, and they marched the rest of the way to the riverbank.

Alighting on the fallen tree, the bird waited for him, blinking, cocking its head, hopping a bit as if impatient. Kieran climbed up the roots and stood on the log. The bird flew across the river.

Kieran remembered games from childhood: chasing Jenny across a log far smaller than this, fighting Harry with a stick for a sword, telling each other stories just as twilight deepened into night.

The *lynneth* abandoned its branch, flew once around his head, and then back across the river. *Haste*, it seemed to say.

He walked the broad back of the fallen tree. How he had ever swum the river yesternight? As it flowed north, it grew wide and deep and silent. Its swift current had carried him far downstream. He missed the song it sang through the stony shallows near Shea.

To which village did Father Donovan travel now in his circuit? Who had prayed the death blessing over John and Kathleen? Who would say it over Maggie?

Stepping from log to rocks, seeing his thoughts instead of his way, Kieran lost his footing on the slick surface and plunged into the river.

Without the Dragon's fire to heat it, the water was lung-stabbing cold. He clung to a limb hanging down from the log, but the branch snapped. His shoulder and wounded arm slammed into one of the boulders. Gasping against the pain, he wedged his upper body between the rocks, but the current tugged greedily at his legs. There was nothing for him to hold but the wet, smooth sides of the stones. He spread his arms around one of them, but his hands found little purchase, sliding down into the water. First his feet, then his legs, grew numb.

He forced open his jaw clenched against the cold. "Is this how it ends?"

He struggled to keep his head above water. "If You are the almighty Voice, why have You done this to me? Why do You take everything away and leave me nothing? If You are Mymna Tor, defender of the defenseless, why is Maggie dead?" His voice broke, but he gritted his teeth and refused to shed tears. "What of Thryffin's parents? Mistress Donnegan? John and Kathleen? You defend no one! You are untrustworthy! Evil! I will not follow You!"

A wind grew. Like the Dragon's wake, it pushed him, surrounded him, churned the water, bent the trees. Kieran was pulled loose from the rocks. Flailing and grabbing at air, he spun out into the center of the river. He tried to turn himself, to take control of his body and swim for shore, but the numbing cold held him prisoner.

I SAVED YOU FROM THE FIRE. AM I NOT ABLE TO SAVE YOU FROM THE RIVER?

"You ask for trust when there is no reason to trust!" Kieran shouted skyward, coughing on a mouthful of water. "You toss me into the unknown and tell me to find my own way home!"

I TELL YOU TO FIND YOUR WAY.

Mouth, ears, and eyes assaulted by water, Kieran managed to free his arms enough to keep himself afloat in the once-placid river now chopped by the wind. As the Renfrew swirled through a rocky narrows, he went under but swam upward, gasping.

READY?

"Who will go with me?"

I WILL.

"Then I am alone."

TRUST ME.

"I am afraid."

The great wind gentled.

The surface of the Renfrew River calmed, and Kieran no longer tried to swim. He lay back, floating in the water's embrace. "No matter who I was born, I was raised a blacksmith. Others are more suited to kingship. Is there none else to take up the sword of Kel?"

AZRIN IS YOURS. IT BELONGS TO NO ONE ELSE.

His left hand and foot dragged the river bottom. An eddy pulled him toward pebbled shallows. He crawled onto the grassy bank, his clothing heavy with water, his body clumsy from cold and fatigue.

"Mymna Tor?" he inquired of the air. "Voice?"

Silence.

A wide band of sunlight warmed him. Feet and legs burned as if pricked by flaming needles. He rolled to his side, forced himself upright, and stood swaying on legs like wooden blocks.

The *lynneth* flew west and north.

Kieran stumbled into a run.

50 ~ Under the Sign of the Weeping Hart

He stepped onto the hard earth of the Romney Road. The day was not yet half-spent, but Kieran was weary, hungry, and wishing he could soar like the birds. If he, too, had wings, what would he see from blue heights and cloud mountains?

But he was an earth-shackled mortal, and he pushed against the restraint as a dog pulls at a leash. Every battered muscle leaned forward, willing him to rise. The cords tensed in his neck, and his hands lifted from his sides.

Head tipped back, eyes closed, he called to Maggie, wherever she might be. How high did a soul fly to reach the Otherland? Did she see him on her journey? He said things that never passed his lips. What he could not express in words, he painted in images, and let tears fall for friends he had lost, for past griefs he had held so tightly that his fingers ached.

Watch for me. He opened his eyes. "Wait for me."

Where was he going? And how?

He had lost his coin and Fasolt's ruby ring to the river. He still had a knife and the dagger, but his clothes were rags. What respectable inn would take him, and how would he pay? His rucksack full of tools was still in the outlaw camp, so he could not work to pay for shelter or clothing.

He set an easy but distance-eating pace northward. An hour or two past midday, he rested in a glade filled with small white flowers. For no reason he could name other than an oblique familiarity and the little bit of healing lore gleaned from watching Mother Crumb, Kieran picked blossoms, filling his scrip, their delicate scent lingering on his fingertips. It was the same frangrance as that of the medicine he had given Maggie yesternight.

The sun traced its gilded path, and day faded toward evening. Trees grew scant beside the road and, in the spaces between, framed the Plains beyond, the grasses undulating like a vast golden hoard of mounded coin.

Where would Azrin have remained hidden for a thousand years? Would the sword be suspended in eternity, pristine, preserved from the ravages of weather and time? Or would it be a rusted sliver, useless and disappointing?

What would he do when he found it? The sword would draw people to him to stand against Mad Morfran, but who would come? How would they know to gather, and where and when?

But he had not yet found Azrin. He was like the foolish smith in one of Donnegan's fables: He worried over charcoal, the size of the forge, wondered what the baron would think of his work, but he had no iron.

"Do today what you can. Tomorrow will wait 'til then," was a common saying, and Donnegan lived by it—until his wife had been taken and killed. From then on, he had few wise words or the will to speak them. He sent Kieran to live behind the smithy and shut himself inside his cottage until little Jenny scolded her father for selfishness, for leaving his children so soon to join his wife in the Otherland.

The smith had heeded his daughter and returned, slowly and with uncertain heart, to his place in the smithy.

Kieran grew tall and strong, and soon became the one whom villagers accepted as the blacksmith while Donnegan performed tasks once assigned to the apprentice. It grieved Kieran to watch the man shrink in stature and situation, robbed by the baron's lust and by his own grief.

The old smith was not the only man to experience such loss, nor the only man to fold into himself, compressing life until it extinguished. Thryffin's father had done the same. The boy never spoke of it, but the image of Farmer Grinden's body hanging from a mill beam still lurked in Kieran's mind.

He had offered the boy a place with him, but Thryffin preferred to sleep on the grain sacks in the mill and to help Miller George with small tasks. He was a sturdier lad than he appeared, his thin body and ragged clothes hiding a sharp mind and a strong will.

The villagers were only a fistful of lives when held up against other provincials oppressed by Baron Markha, or when compared to the countless numbers lost in the entire kingdom since the beginning of Mad Morfran's reign. Common folk were trampled and taxed beyond hope. What happened in Shea alone was reason enough to find Azrin.

Farmers, tradesmen, craftsmen untrained in warfare—what chance would they have against the armored and skilled king's men? Would their spirits still rise to action?

Kieran's pace quickened to keep stride with his thoughts. *I will send messengers to gather all those willing. Robby Finney and his outlaws can teach us how to fight.*

His eagerness faded. A man need not leave home to be killed. Many a villager had died on the edge of a blade simply for being in the way. Why would anyone go seeking death?

'Twas foolish to think too high-mindedly of war, yet he could not do nothing. Surely there were more like him in Skarda, men who considered freedom from oppression more gain than a life lived under injustice.

He traveled far past sunset. The moon rode high when he saw the first lights of Romney-town. The air smelled of tilled and tended earth. As he drew closer to the village, however, the sturdy brown pungence of ale overcame the scent of the fields, and sounds of merriment rang in the night.

He entered the broad street lit by multitudes of torches, and jostled his way through a dancing throng of revelers. Some wore masks, others leafy wreaths or crowns of flowers. Loose tassels flew in brilliant streams as women whirled, their hair unbound but threaded with blossoms and ribbons. Men wore garments unstained from the fields, as fresh as new-grown grass.

He found an inn and thought to find refuge inside, but the great room was boisterous with people. The innkeeper and his servants were as merry as the customers, and Kieran had to shout to be heard.

The host shook his head. "No beds free. Try the Weeping Hart"—he jerked his chin in the direction—"along the Cäldon Road. Best place for a traveler during the Faere. Quieter there."

Kieran thanked him, squeezed back out into the crowd, and followed the high street north from Romney.

The Cäldon Road bent in a great bow and turned west. In the bosom of the curve lay the Weeping Hart. The inn was large, two-storied. A torch high on a pole near the road lit the innyard. Over the door hung a carved sign: a horned deer pierced behind the shoulder by an arrow. The hart's neck tucked forward so its head touched its forelegs, and lurid red paint traced the tear-shaped drops of blood falling from the mortal wound.

The door stood open to the mild night air, and Kieran stepped inside to an empty great room. "Good even," he called.

From the kitchen came a woman, tall, thin, sleeves pushed up past her elbows, little curls of hair drifting out from beneath her white cap. Deep lines fanned the corners of her eyes and cupped her mouth. She smiled wearily at him and wiped her hands on her apron. "Good even."

"Have you any beds this night?"

"All of them." She waved a hand. "Faere began yesterday, and the inn empties come sunset when everyone goes to the festival. Come morning, we will have more custom than we can take, and folk sleeping on the tables."

"Are there any tasks I might do in exchange for a meal and a room? I have no coin—"

"A criminal, are you"—she glanced at his wounded arm—"running from the king's men?"

"I fell among thieves, and had a bit of adventure finding my way here. This is the only coin I have." He opened his scrip and removed a fistful of the white flowers.

She stilled. "Where did you find them?"

"South, somewhere along the road."

"Did you search long for them?"

"I happened upon it in a glade when I stopped to rest."

"Beside the road? Few ever find such a treasure, and always where others look but do not see." The woman reached out a hand so slender that each joint, bone, and tendon lay sharp beneath the skin. "How long since I saw this last?" She touched one blossom, releasing its fragrance. Looking up at Kieran, she said, "You know its value, then?"

He shook his head.

"Rarest of healing plants, most powerful medicine. You could stay here for a week on the strength of a single blossom, and complete plant is equal to a gold crown. This many blooms could make you a friend of kings."

"But what is it?"

"Dragon's-bane."

Kieran set it on the table then dropped to a bench. Aidan had traded a mere ribbon for this medicine. Was it real dragon's-bane tea he had given Maggie, or a paltry fraud? Even were it real, would it raise the dead?

A strong hand took his shoulder. "Are you well, traveler?"

Head bowed, he nodded.

"We will use a bit of your precious herb," she said, "and put a fresh bandage on your wound."

The innkeeper returned with a bowl of steaming water and a roll of linen.

Kieran took a deep breath, rubbed his palms on the thighs of his torn breeches, and sat up straight. "Have you any clothes left by past travelers? Perhaps in better repair than mine?"

"Perhaps I can alter my husband's clothes to fit you."

"Thank you, mistress."

She smiled, the lines on her face not so deep this time. "My husband's name was Holt. Folk here call me Widow Holt."

"But what is your name?"

"No man but her husband calls a married woman by her own name."

Aye, his foster mother was Mistress Donnegan, and the innkeeper's wife at the Blue Oak was Mistress Clem. Kieran could not remember ever hearing their true names. Yet his sister was known simply as Jenny, not Mistress Harry. She was not alone. Other young matrons were also known by the names their mothers gave them— Mary of the dale, Cara the weaver's wife, Thryffin's mother Doreena— and none thought sideways about it. Mayhap the northern reaches were more proper in their address than the southern provinces.

He could not bring himself to call the innkeeper widow. It made her seem stoop-shouldered and elderly.

"Your pardon, Mistress Holt. I am a stranger here, and clumsy with customs." Standing, he placed a palm flat over his heart and bowed, almost introducing himself as Kieran Smith of Shea before realizing it was the name Teag and the king's men would know. He must begin a new life and leave Kieran Smith behind.

"D'urnythn of"—he hesitated, all names of small villages fleeing his mind—"of Kel Tor."

"Welcome, D'urnythn."

She rolled up his sleeve and tut-tutted the state of the cut on his upper arm. It should have been stitched. After washing it and placing a few lightly-crushed petals of dragon's-bane over the cut, she bound a fresh cloth around his arm, securing the ends with a firm knot.

Then she brought a supper of chicken stewed with vegetables. Perhaps not as good as Mistress Clem's cooking, it was hot and filling. The apple cider was hard and sweet.

Mistress Holt brought out a basket and sat near the hearth, letting out the seams of her late husband's tunic and breeches. While she worked, she talked. Kieran learned a bit about Romney-town's Faere, similar to Shea's in all ways but the nightly festival. Shea held the Match Dance each night, and Father Donovan solemnized the marriage rites, but the villagers of Romney flung wide their arms and danced for the pure pleasure of it. They had a resident priest who lived at the kirk but never traveled outside the little circle of farms ringing the village. Mistress Holt was surprised to hear priests still went from hamlet to village to town in regular circuits. Such had not been known in Romney since her grandmother was a child.

"He has not told me so, but I think our priest would like to settle in just one village." Kieran pushed away the empty mug and leaned his elbows on the table. "He has plans for the apple orchard near the kirk."

"We keep an orchard here at the inn. My youngest son used to tend it."

"Where is he now?"

The corners of her mouth tugged downward. "My sons and my husband were taken into the king's army two years past."

She spoke with such quiet calm that she might have been relating news of her neighbors or discussing the weather. She did not even look up from her sewing.

"Who helps you run the inn?"

"Children without homes or families. Young women whose husbands were taken into the king's army. Lads not yet grown who fear being taken themselves. We help one another."

After knotting the thread, Mistress Holt bit it in two. She held up the tunic, frowned in thought, snipped at another seam, and rethreaded her needle. "Have you been traveling long? Or have you no wife, D'urnythn of Kel Tor, to make your clothes?"

His ears grew hot. He could not tell her he was a freeman and a blacksmith, or that he was more at odds with his tattered clothes than he might seem. Muscles tightened in his neck and jaw. He could not tell her of Maggie.

She completed her sewing by the time the first revelers arrived, drunk but ready for more. Mistress Holt scooped the dragon's-bane from the table, summoned the servants, staved off complaints by offering hot crusty bread to soak up the ale, then showed Kieran to his room where a large tub of cold water waited. She left him with the clean clothes and a pair of boots she said might fit him.

Heating the bath took a long while—one pot of boiling water at a time poured back into the cold tub—so that when he finally bathed, the water was only lukewarm. Still, his muscles eased and his eyes threatened to close. The soap was harsh but cleansing.

The old garments were tossed in the fire.

He tried the ones left by Mistress Holt. She had given him fresh undergarments, perhaps loose on their original owner but just fitting him. The breeches were snug in the waist and thighs, and he did a few rapid squats to see if the seat would tear. The seams held. After being worn a day or two, the clothes would loosen. As for the tunic, the shoulders were broad enough but the chest was not as deep as he required. Although there was room for his arms to move freely without ripping the fabric, he felt confined. He could not sleep in these strange clothes.

He laid them on a chair then crawled between soft sheets smelling of outdoors and lavender, and stretched out on a down-filled bed His arm throbbed and itched, and the great hall below rang with the merry jests and bawdy songs of the returning revelers. Yet, strangely lulled by the noise, he fell asleep.

He dreamed.

Sweat streamed down his back as he plied the bellows. The smithy door stood wide, and the many windows were unshuttered, allowing a breeze, but heat rolled off the glowing coals. Donnegan nestled a rough-hammered iron bar in their heart.

Two little girls ran screaming into the smithy. Tears coursed down their faces as they cowered behind the anvil. Crouching, Kieran put an arm around each girl. They clung to him, their tears soaking his loose tunic.

Donnegan rushed out to the dusty yard. Men tossed Mistress Donnegan into a baggage wain.

Time skipped, and Kieran stood outside. The wain lurched

forward.

"Save the people, Kieran," Mistress Donnegan said. "Save them all."

Other voices threaded his dreams. He listened but did not understand.

Prayer rose in violent chorus, cried in fragments by frightened voices. Terrified people ran past him, leaving him—a child scarce able to walk—sitting on the ground amid a field of white. He smelled burning and saw flames. No one reached down to lift him into sheltering arms, but he did not fear. Mother and Father would come soon to carry him.

When someone lifted him at last, it was a man with a sad face. He came as the fires died to a glow, after men on horses had galloped behind the fleeing people and disappeared into the night.

The boy felt safe, held against a rough cloak that smelled of the forest, the soothing rumble of the man's voice vibrating through his chest.

Again time skipped.

He stared up at a circle of armed men—

He jolted upright. Bedclothes entangled him. His heart hammered. Sweat slicked his skin.

A firm knock sounded on his chamber door. "Are you well, D'urnythin?"

He stood, rubbing his face with both hands, shamed that he was still so easily taken by dreams.

The light from Mistress Holt's candle flickered below the door, groping tentative fingers across the floor. "Shall I make mint tea? Or hang dried wormwood from your door? It chases away evil dreams."

"No" Embarrassment sharpened his words. "Dawn will be here soon."

She yawned. "Too soon."

The fingers of candlelight withdrew, leaving Kieran in darkness. He stirred the embers in the fireplace, but decided against adding wood and livening the fire. Darkness suited him.

When he woke, the sun was high. He dressed hurriedly. His old boots were sole-worn and broken down. He left them beside the fireplace. Mistress Holt had provided boots with thick soles and sturdy legs. He tucked the dagger into one boot leg and the knife into the other.

Combing long tangled hair with his fingers, he wished for a proper trim and a shave. Though no longer in the itchy beginning stage, his beard was uncomfortable and unfamiliar.

He opened the door. A small upside-down bundle of dried wormwood hung on the handle.

Mistress Holt arrived with a tray of food. Kieran backed into the room as she entered, a grim expression on her face. "Come away from the door," she said in a low voice.

A youth brought a bowl of warm water, a razor, a comb, and soap. Mistress Holt removed one of the bed sheets, draped it around Kieran, and told him to sit on the chair.

Mistress Holt lathered his face then applied the razor to his beard. "A maid will meet you in the apple orchard. Take the horse and continue your journey. Do not go east."

She wiped his face with a warm towel then combed and trimmed his hair. The servant swept the trimmings into the fireplace.

"Who came looking for me, Mistress Holt?"

In the mid-morning light, she looked older than she had in yesternight's half-shadows and firelight. "Someone is seeking a tall, broad-shouldered blacksmith, or anyone hailing from Shea in Markha Province."

"A minstrel?"

She nodded. "He looks for a man wearing old garments and with a bloody bandage on his arm, who was seen at the Faere yesternight."

Mistress Holt removed the bed sheet from around him, and brought him the tray laden with a half-loaf of crusty bread, a wedge of cheese, a bowl of sauced apples drizzled with honey, and a mug of fresh milk still frothy from the pail. "A messenger waits on the road even now, watching for anyone leaving the inn."

Kieran stood. "I will not endanger your household—"

"Eat. My servants are loyal and very quiet."

Holding the tray in one hand, he dipped bread and cheese into the applesauce, drank the milk.

"The maid will give you the sword and baldric passed from my father to my eldest son. May it serve you well."

"A family relic—"

"I do it to avenge my husband and sons."

Finished, he handed her the tray. "Thank you."

"To the orchard. Get you gone."

The serving boy gestured for him to follow—past other rooms along the hallway, down the stairs, past the great room half-filled with hungover revelers, through the kitchen warm with fragrant cooking smells, past the scrap heap behind the inn and around the horse paddock, behind a tall row of garden plants, and into the leafy shelter of the apple trees. The boy turned back to the inn without a backward glance, as if concealing fugitives were an everyday task.

The serving maid was as self-possessed as the boy, and as quiet. She lifted a longsword from the ground and reached around him to pull the baldric over his right shoulder and under his left arm, buckling the wide leather belt halfway between his shoulder and his waist. Then she handed him a sack fitted with a single broad strap.

Slinging it over his other shoulder, he followed her to where a sturdy brown horse stood waiting. He hesitated. He was not a skilled rider. He preferred shoeing horses to riding them.

The horse turned its head, looking at him.

The sound of distant hooves and a veil of dust rose along the road leading from Romney to the Weeping Hart. More than one horseman approached.

Taking a deep breath and planting his foot in the stirrup, Kieran pulled himself into the saddle. The horse shifted but did not try to throw his bulk off its back. A good sign.

He looked down at the girl. "Thank you"—he smiled—"and Mymna Tor be with you."

With neither an answering smile nor any change of expression, she stepped past a half-filled bushel basket on the ground and reached up to pick early apples with their skins of half-green, half-rose.

Galloping hoofbeats drew ever nearer, and dust billowed up in a growing cloud.

With a last glance back at the inn, he turned the horse southwest.

VI

The Blood of Dragons

The tunics of the king's men are as red as the blood staining the flagstones at the abbey's wooden door.

"An enemy of the king hides within your walls. Stand aside."

The abbot does not move. "No enemy is sheltered here."

"The stones cry out."

"A lost lamb was sore wounded in the forest, and we tended his hurts. Brother Dryus will show you the sheepfold."

They exchange long stares. Then, scowling, the captain gestures, and his men turn from the abbey. The abbot makes the sign of the Shepherd and closes the door upon the soldiers. Monks step from the cloister. One holds a bowl filled with water so red it might be blood itself.

"How fares our lamb?" inquires the abbot.

"I doubt he sees sunrise. He has the look of—" At the abbot's raised brow, the physician amends his words. "He appears underfed, Father Alister."

"Then we prepare food along with our prayers. Come, brethren. We still have gardens and orchards to tend, and sheep."

As the others return to their work, the physician murmurs, "It is he."

"Aye," the abbot replied, "and soon he shall be another."

51 ~ ÁREDAN

Yanámari did not know the passes her father used to traverse the rugged mountains, but she guided the Dissonay as best she could recall from maps read in secret. Ink faded, edges crumbling, the parchments had showed remnants of old paths used in ages past, long before Elycia was built, when only tribes of mountain folk lived in the reaches of the Craydaegs, each way rough and strait.

She led the Fourth away from the River Thrayne's narrow chasm and into mountains seamed with cuts and caverns on the slopes leading down to the southern foothills and a forest called Kelcey. Near sunset, they entered another cleft, this one marked by grey stone veined with brown-red streaks, as if a giant hand trailed bloody fingers along the mountainside.

A Dragon followed, gliding down and filling the passage behind the battered troop. Perhaps the horses were merely too weary to care, but they seemed unafraid of the creature. The men, however, cast wary glances over their shoulders. The Dragon's wings fanned, filling the air with a pleasant fragrance, then folded to its sides in silken pleats.

Turi lifted Gaerbith from his horse and laid him on ground Fremmen swept free of stones. Removing her gloves, Yanámari knelt beside the captain. Owen crouched opposite her. The men gathered, silent and grim.

I CAN HEAL HIM.

Yanámari looked up. Warm breath fanned her hair, and she stared into a great eye as purple as twilight, set in silver.

I AM ÁREDAN OF THE FREDEK KINDRED, continued the beautiful voice. WE ARE A CLAN OF SCHOLARS AND HEALERS.

"How do we know you will not take what little life remains in him?" demanded Owen.

I SAVED YOU FROM THE SKARDIANS.

The youth dipped his chin in grudging acknowledgment.

Yanámari untied the rough dressing around her arm and held it toward the Dragon in challenge. Laughter rumbled from his massive chest. Lifting a white-hot talon, he touched the curve of it to the wound. Her skin grew warm, then her arm. Heat spread until her body seemed scarce able to contain it. Vistas opened in her mind, and she felt the pressing weight of a vast knowledge kept at bay. Square towers rose stark and pale. She gazed on Elycia, seeing as the Dragon saw, feeling the heavy tug of servitude as if the chain that had once bound him now circled her ankle. Then she hung on the wind like a bird, and looked down on the broken terrain of mountains and on rivers streaming from snow-melt lakes, flowing down to disappear in forests or feed broad plains. No course promised safety or escape.

What lies before me?

NONE CAN TELL.

No one passes this way.

THEY KNOW NOT WHERE IT LEADS.

Surely the Nar'ath know.

WHAT NEED HAVE BIRDS FOR STONE AND EARTH? THEY FORGE THEIR PATHS THROUGH AIR AND CLOUD.

Guide me. Tell me what I should do.

LISTEN.

Listen? To what? To whom?

Áredan withdrew from her mind, and with him he took the visions. Yanámari blinked. She stood in a dim and fading glow.

She touched her arm. A smooth scar closed the wound, its edges clean, unpuckered, as if the skin were merely a bit paler in that particular spot. She gasped and looked up.

Were it possible, the Dragon lifted a brow.

Yanámari nodded at Fremmen, and he tugged loose the belt around the captain's leg as she pulled free the blade.

Blood gushed from the wound, but a glowing talon thrust into the gap, stopping the flow. Arms flung out from his sides, the captain arched, his back bowing like a bridge. Light glowed beneath his skin, illuminating his body from within, and his ribcage expanded as he took a great breath. Light pulsed as if it were his heartbeat. Slowly, his body eased and the light faded.

GIVE HIM WATER. LET HIM SLEEP. Áredan's massive head turned as he looked among the Dissonay. NOW, WHO WISHES MY HELP?

Weary men shuffled forward, some limping, some leaning one their fellows. Questions lay plain on their haggard faces: How had such a creature come to help them—and why?

Turi and Owen settled the captain away from the others and lit a small fire. Yanámari took a waterskin, dug a cloth from her satchel, and knelt beside Gaerbith. Color crept along his skin, and his chest rose and fell in deep, even breaths. She dampened the cloth and squeezed a few drops of water into his mouth.

Arrows rattled in Fremmen's quiver as he squatted nearby, using his unstrung bow as a staff to steady himself. He said nothing, but surely he saw her clumsy hands, recalled she was accustomed to being the served and not the servant, and concealed his contempt behind a bland face.

He would be right to disdain her. Who was she but the half-blood daughter of a mad king and a disgraced queen? Not a lady, not a warrior. Nothing.

The captain muttered something, a mix of Dissonay and Skardian and a tongue she did not recognize.

"He thinks he still fights in the Lowlands," said Fremmen. "He gives orders to men long dead."

"I am the cause of all this. If I had not asked his help—"

"Without you, we might still be in the city. Dead. And so might he be, if no one trusted the Dragon."

A man in a dusty black robe slid from the Dragon's back and down a giant silver-scaled leg. He seemed a little unsteady on his feet, and he smiled uncertainly at the staring Dissonay.

"A Black Hood," someone spat.

HE IS NOT OF THE BRETHREN. RUBIN KYRINSSON SET ME FREE.

Áredan straightened, and his ears turned as if capturing sound. Then he spread his vast wings and the sky veiled. MEN AND HORSES, GATHER BENEATH MY WINGS. THE NAR'ATH SEEK US.

Just as day turns from rosy sunset to deepest night, the Dragon's iridescent silver became grey and black, brown and shabby green, losing its sheen and taking on the dull hues of the stones and the stunted trees growing in the cleft. Men moved with measured steps, gathering close the animals. Saddles and bridles were handled with care—only faint jangles or creaks. Fires were banked.

Owen gave Yanámari a coarse blanket that had been tied behind the saddle of a dead man. It smelled of old sweat, of blood and dust, but she beat it against a rock until the blanket was as clean as it could be without washing. It could not compare with the fine fabrics covering her bed in Elycia, nor were the leather and mail and tunic she now wore anything like the soft garments that once caressed her skin. She doubted she would ever wear such rich clothing again.

The captain turned his head a little as Lady Yanámari, wrapped in a blanket, settled down beside him. Her hand fell beyond the covering and rested against the captain's shoulder. Owen watched with an unreadable expression.

Someone coughed great hacking rasps. Turi turned. The robed man hunched over a rock, his body taken in violent spasms.

"Drink." Turi offered a waterskin.

Rubin held up a hand as another spasm took him. Turi waited until Rubin sagged, limp and quiet, against the great stone. Again Turi offered the waterskin, and the man took it, hand trembling, and tilted the skin toward his open mouth.

"What ails ye, friend?" Turi asked in a mix of Dissonay and halting Skardian.

"Smoke. Ash. Áredan helped me escape."

"Turi of Braemon's Well, cartwright by trade, soldier by choice."

"Rubin Kyrinsson, woodcutter by trade, but I have never had a choice. Until now."

"A woodcutter, eh? Then ye will know all about axes."

Rubin gave him a curious look. "Indeed."

Turi grinned. "And would ye know which kind the Woodsman carries?"

"The Woodsman?"

So, in murmured and hoarse conversation while the camp settled to rest, the two men talked in jumbled dialects of old tales, of wood axes and battle axes and the best employment of each, drawing pictures in the dirt when words failed, until a short spit of flame from the sheltering Dragon sent them to their blankets and to sleep.

Evan started awake in the rag pile where he lay hidden.

"Shhh," Syra whispered.

Kneeling outside the firelight that descended in a wavering line along the winding mountain road, she broke bread into small pieces. She had stolen it from the back of a cart containing several loaves, small wheels of cheese, and a haunch of meat. The meat Syra left undisturbed, for its richness might make them ill, but a loaf of bread and a quarter-moon of cheese she took, begging silent forgiveness of any soul who might go hungry this night.

Evan stuffed his mouth with the crusty bread.

"Slowly," she cautioned. She let him sip water from a cup she had found among the empty baskets. Poor mite. He had traveled all day without whimper or complaint. Brave lad.

Syra marveled at her audacity. She had never been so far from Elycia, nor had she thought to miss the few friends she had made among the other women when they worked the king's gardens, or spun thread and loomed cloth in his workhouse. Her parents had died in the king's cages. Rubin never knew his true parents, but was claimed as the grandson of an elderly couple to replace a child who had been lost to the cruel cold one winter's night. The thought of something other than grief, loneliness, and forced servitude seemed too daring for a common Elycian to dream about, let alone pursue. Yet here Syra was, hiding with her son, a day's journey from the city.

But how long before someone in the caravan discovered them? She had not seen the guard again who had noticed Evan hidden beneath her cloak. Had he told anyone? Would he come for her in the night?

Evan smiled at her, and she smiled back. Perhaps when the sun rose, if they were still free, she might let herself think of another life.

Finished with the scant meal, they wrapped themselves in piled rags that in the darkness appeared no more than mounded stones or scrubs of undergrowth.

Evan fell asleep. Syra lay long awake and thought of Rubin.

52 ~ King's Commander

The dying sun shed blood on the mountains. Pools of darkness filled chasms and hollows below the city, and in the tower, King Morfran was cloistered with his counselor and his madness.

Frantic laughter had overtaken him as he watched his daughter ride from the gates, then he had looked into the faces of men he knew well and asked them if they could please tell him where was his queen? Had anyone seen Lord Arien, his son? No answer sufficed. He wandered the streets ahorseback, brandishing his sword and hacking at any folk who dared venture too near, cursing them for Kels, until Heolstor found him and took him away.

In the absence of a leader—for the barons seemed too stunned or unwilling to step into the dearth—Rhôn ordered men into ranks without regard to the colors of their tunics. He set captains then gave each troop a task. One escorted returning laborers back over the bridge to the city from the terraced gardens and the high meadows across the river. Another sorted bodies, separating armor, weapons, and corpses into bloody heaps. A third troop collected scorched remains from the square and the wall, and scooped ashes into tight-woven baskets.

The Brethren of the Black Hood stood with their hands in their sleeves, eyes gleaming from the wells of their cowls. Someone loosed the Nar'ath, and the great black birds swarmed the darkening sky. They circled above the city as if collecting the night on their wings, then turned in a wide westward arc. The city grew grimly quiet.

Rhôn ordered the dead stacked outside the walls. Pyres grew until they resembled the rigid square tower of the King's Keep. Then Brethren glided forward, removed small pouches from their wide sleeves, and sprinkled the contents on the ground, forming a ring around each pyre. The Hoods stepped sideways as they circled the funerary mounds, stopping as they reached the places where they began, and there they tucked the pouches back into their sleeves and bowed their heads. A wind rose, fluttering the black robes but not touching the strange powder.

A tingle crawled along Rhôn's arms, but it did not come from the chill gust swirling around him as he stood on the wall. He had witnessed this ceremony at the end of every battle, yet it never ceased to make him uneasy.

Another Hood walked among the pyres, weaving his way to the center of the double ring of pyres. He lifted his hands, palms forward, as if hushing the chatter of the dead. The wind died.

The other Brethren echoed his movements then turned their palms skyward. The powder ignited. Flames twined the bodies and pushed into the center of the pyres, seeking anything to feed the fire. Heat rose even to where Rhôn stood above the city gates.

Other than a small contingent disguised in Young Wolf uniforms and left behind in the Lowlands to harry the Dissonay retreat, no Wolves existed but him. Of the king's men-at-arms, only a few dozen remained. One baron had lost all his men, and not enough horses remained to mount a ten-man troop. The Dissonay and the Dragon had nigh destroyed the Skardian army.

A Dragon. Rhôn had heard tales of such creatures, but all had died centuries ago, after their exile to eastern lands. Whence had this Dragon come, and how did the Dissonay command it?

An honor guard bore a green-draped body through the gate.

"You know what those dogs did to him, commander?" Seated at a battered campaign table carried to the wall by Rhôn, an old bent scribe waited to record his orders. The ancient was rarity in Elycia: though he was a scribe, he was not a Hood. "They killed the emissary. One of their own. The savages."

"Lord Boorn betrayed them," Rhôn replied, "and did not hide it."

"Dissonay should never attempt secrecy." Morfran mounted the steps to the top of the wall. "They have no skill for it."

Rhôn bowed. The rickety old scribe did not rise from his chair.

The king gazed down at the pyres. His eyes were clear again. He was himself. The honor guard offered Boorn's body to the flames.

"The Dissonay took the Sea Stone. All that power in clumsy hands."

"It is theirs, my lord. Why should they not take it?"

Rhôn would face the king's wrath soon, but a strange mood had seized him since the afternoon's confrontation.

When Morfran had arrived in the square, leading a Dissonay warhorse with the captain hunched over its neck, Rhôn had recognized the hilt of the broken blade buried in the captain's thigh. It belonged to Gurn.

Rhôn approached the king and said that, should the Dissonay's longsword be found, it could be placed in the cage with the corpse and serve as a final insult to the enemy dog. Morfran agreed.

The sharp scent of blood permeated the city near the royal tower, the stableyard was strewn with bodies, and a street leading away from it was clogged with corpses. Blood still ran in the crevices between paving stones, and each splashing step stained the legs of Rhôn's horse. Where were the Dissonay? He twisted around in the saddle, expecting an ambush. Nothing moved but the wind-fluttered garments of dead men.

He found the longsword laying aslant the cobbles, its blade bloody, its hilt marred by a black handprint.

For a long moment, Rhôn considered leaving the sword. He owed the Dissonay captain nothing. In the span of a meal, the man had captured the respect of the Lady of Skarda, and half a day later he had slain a kinsman.

Rhôn stared down at Gurn's corpse. It lay draped over a pile of dead. He turned over his cousin's body. Judging by the wound, a weapon had been driven up from below the ribcage in front and out Gurn's upper back. The opponent had been sitting or lying on the ground when Gurn attacked.

Who else but the captain? Even sore wounded and at great disadvantage, he had fought. Such a man should be buried with his sword.

Rhôn turned back, picked up the longsword, and wiped the blade clean.

Then he returned to the gates and saw a much-altered Lady Yanámari clutching the reins of a Dissonay warhorse, without a weapon in the midst of battle chaos. In that moment, he acknowledged to himself three things. First, he had never expected her to choose any of the Young Wolves, for she had shown no particular favor to any of them. Second, he had become one because of the power and place it afforded his father, not for any wish of his own. Third, he envied the Dissonay.

Now, as he stood on the wall at twilight and watched the funeral fires die, Rhôn could not discern why he should envy his enemies. He only knew he regretted not riding with them beyond the gate.

"The men call you commander now?" The cold anger in the king's stare was meant to chill Rhôn, to quell him and cow his spirit.

Rhôn did not tremble. Rather, he inclined his head in a brief bow and replied, "Yes, my lord, but I do not ask it of them."

"You covet my throne." Morfran drew his sword. "You subvert the loyalty of my men and seek to thwart me."

Rhôn moved his hands away from his sides, away from the hilt of his blade. "Your men are your own, my lord."

"Draw your sword."

"My lord—"

"Draw your sword!"

The old scribe gathered his inkpot, quills, scrolls, sheets of parchment, and stuffed them into a large pouch. Leaving the candle, he hastened down the steps as fast as his limping legs would take him. Only then did Rhôn slide his sword from its sheath and make ready to face the king.

The men were equal in size and strength, but the breath of Nar Cahm shielded Morfran from harm. How else could such a reckless warrior emerge without wounds, battle after battle? Yet, invincible foe or mere mortal, Mad King Morfran would not easily conquer.

Traditional Skardian swords were not two-fisted like Dissonay longswords, but were intended to be used in pairs, one in each hand. Over centuries, the blades lost their twins, and men took to fighting with only one sword while clutching a shield in the hand where the other sword should be. When had warriors decided that boiled hides stretched over wooden forms were better preservers than two strong sharp blades?

Rhôn would have preferred the healthy weight of a Dissonay longsword than the deceptive suppleness of this Skardian needle.

He had not long to ponder the matter. Morfran's blade darted toward his throat and Rhôn twisted, dodging the cut. The sword tip thrust past his ear with such force that even the air felt sharp.

A thrust was strong, but it left a fighter vulnerable, his arm extended and his body exposed to the opponent's blade. A man risked the chance of not recovering his stance before his enemy's sword found its mark.

As the king drew back, Rhôn gripped Morfran's wrist and twisted even as he slid his blade underneath, aiming for the king's armpit. The edge scraped across articulated—and unexpected—plates of armor beneath the king's arm.

Morfran rammed the heel of his free hand into Rhôn's elbow, loosening his grip, then hooked a foot behind Rhôn's knee and hit him in the shoulder. Breath left Rhôn in a grunt. His backbone rattled. It took him a stunned moment to realize it was not his bones but his chain-mail clattering as he fell backward.

"Commander of the king's army!" Morfran declared with a mocking smile, standing over him. "Indeed. What skill is required to lead warriors from the flat your back."

He stepped on Rhôn's sword hand and leaned his weight on it. Rhôn grit his teeth, feeling the bones grind and compress, just short of snapping. He tried to rise up on his elbow, but the king's sword nicked his chin.

"Haste kills, commander."

So does hesitation.

Balling his gauntled left hand into a loose fist, Rhôn punched at the king's knee. Morfran stumbled backward. Rhôn rolled to his side then pushed himself to his feet, taking up his sword in his left hand.

Morfran snarled. His attack was swift, his sword a gleaming snake. Rhôn was forced backward along the city wall, unable to meet the attack with anything more than clumsy blocks and dodges. Sweat stung his eyes, and his breath came in gasps. The funeral pyres no longer lit the night, and no guard fires illuminated the wall. He fought in darkness, seeing Morfran only as a black shape in furious motion.

Rhôn's injured wrist slammed against the stone parapet, and pain leaped up his arm.

Morfran's sword flashed.

Again, Rhôn shifted his torso, and the blade sliced past him. He struck at Morfran's forearm, cutting through the glove, and the force of the blow knocked the sword from the king's hand. It fell to the stones with a crisp ring. Cursing, Morfran drew a dagger from his belt and buried the blade deep in the meat of Rhôn's left arm.

Sucking in his breath, the Young Wolf pulled the dagger free with his injured hand and, with an awkward flick, sent it straight at the king's head.

Morfran caught the blade between his thumb and forefinger. He stood in an attitude of interrupted motion, as if the act of stopping the dagger had robbed him of the ability to move.

Rhôn's right hand throbbed and his left arm bled. He backed away, hoping to catch his breath and regain some semblance of strength before Morfran renewed the attack.

The king lowered his arm and laughed. "Rhôn Bergsson, you dare much and you do not beg for mercy." He wiped the blade clean and sheathed his dagger. "I name you commander of the king's army."

Morfran retrieved his fallen sword and slid it into its scabbard. Rhôn still gripped his own sword, wary. He knew well the king's capricious ways.

"Come, Rhôn, let the healers have at you. I must preserve what army remains to Skarda. I cannot have its commander succumbing to fever in an ill-tended wound."

Rhôn put away his blade.

Morfran seemed in no wise injured by the blow Rhôn had dealt. The king's gauntlet gaped at the wrist, but there was no blood.

By Nar Cahm, what would it take to slay the madman?

Wakened by a callused hand clamped over her mouth, Syra was pulled from her pile of warm rags and half-dragged, half-carried behind a boulder. The guard who had seen her son hidden beneath her cloak shoved her down on a jumble of blankets smelling of strong spirits and sour sweat. A tiny whimper of fear escaped her lips.

"No sound," he ordered, clamping her legs with his knees as he tugged at her bodice. "You serve me, I save your son."

Pressing her lips shut, she held her body rigid and wept silently, hearing him mutter curses as he removed his sword belt. He tossed it aside, eased his grip on her legs, and ran one hand up her thigh while his other hand fumbled with the ties of his breeches, as if he did not know whether to caress her first or to satisfy himself. His touch made her skin recoil, and her legs convulsed, drawing up to kick him away, but he caught her knees and forced them down again.

"Wedded women have hotter blood than maids"—there was breathless eagerness in his voice—"and I wager you are a widow, long without a man."

A thrumming filled the air, the beat of myriad wings, threaded through with strident caws. The man cursed, tied his breeches closed, then grabbed his belt again, unsheathed the sword, and ran toward the caravan, shouting, "Awake! Awake! Nar'ath!"

Guards and merchants were roused at once, some of them pulling on boots or knocking arrows into bows as they ran, looking into the sky. The Nar'ath were so many and so large they hid the stars.

Syra leapt to her feet, gathering up the skirt of her kirtle, and fled back to where Evan slept. She scooped him up—rags, cloak, and all—and sought her stumbling way deeper into the dark, away from the caravan. Behind her came shrieks of birds and screams of men as the Nar'ath attacked. There rose the unspeakable sound of rending flesh and the solid thud of arrows burying into bodies.

"Mother?" Evan awoke, struggling in her arms.

"Hush, love." Snowflakes drifted down, leaving cold kisses on her face and arms. "Do not cry out. Whatever happens, do not cry out."

Heolstor stood before the chained Dragon, uncowed by the fixed gaze of the great green eyes or by the pulsing glow that waxed and waned with the beast's breath. He held a golden scale set in an iron ring and dangled it before the Dragon, letting the leather string on which it was hung slip from his hand until the disk swung back and forth in the smoky air.

"Once set upon a mission, the Nar'ath must have blood. They attacked a merchant caravan, for the Dissonay cannot be found. Come morning, you will kill the Fredek, destroy the Dissonay, and bring to me the man who claims to have known Uártha. He knows where the sword Azrin is hidden. We cannot let him tell anyone but us that secret, now, can we?"

The Dragon's eyes narrowed, and his teeth gleamed just a little where the corners of his mouth pulled back.

"Good. We understand one another."

A rumble that might have been a soft growl or a derisive laugh rolled from the Dragon's throat, but no matter how Heolstor probed the creature's mind, he could not learn the nature of that sound.

53 ~ THE WATCHER

The watcher crouched behind a low wall of tumbled stones and twisted little trees that, were he to stand upright, would reach no higher than his waist. He had been careful in his movements, stepping over rocks, never brushing trees, keeping his arms away from his sides so the fabric of his sleeves made only the smallest sound against his tunic. He carried a satchel, and sometimes the contents clinked. From time to time, one or another Dissonay would stop and listen, as if hearing his breath or sensing his gaze.

The watcher had ridden with them when they fled the city, overcoming squeamishness enough to sit astride one of the horses carrying a dead man. In the camp, the horse almost gave him away, nosing his shoulder and whickering.

WELCOME.

Like the tremor of a breeze through birch leaves, the Dragon's thought-speech sent vibrations through the watcher's brain. The creature had long since blended into the darkness but his eyes still glowed in the night.

The watcher hesitated. How did one address a Dragon?

I am sent to aid Captain Gaerbith.

THEN WE ARE HERE FOR LIKE PURPOSE.

And the Lady is part Kel. She might one day wield Azrin. I owe her much, and would not see King Morfran or his counselor find the sword first and thwart her birthright.

THERE IS A KEL WITH CLOSER CLAIM TO THE SWORD.

The captain?

NONE IN THIS ARMY BELONG TO THE HOUSE OF KEL.

Who, then?

NEITHER THE KING NOR HIS SPIES HAVE FOUND THE KEL-

CHILD. BUT THEY WILL. SOON.

We must warn him!

HE KNOWS.

The watcher pondered long into the night. All he had once embraced was either shaken or destroyed. His love was dead, the watcher himself should be dead but walked about unseen, and now he conversed with a Dragon. Life before seemed only a dream.

Sky lightened in false dawn, and the Dissonay woke. The Dragon's shape grew distinct from the rocks around it.

The watcher wrapped his arms around his middle, seeking to quiet his hungry stomach, wondering how to obtain food and drink—and how he could ride another day sharing the saddle with a dead man.

Yanámari woke to stiff limbs, a sore back, and neck muscles so tense they seemed as unyielding as iron cords. She tried to lift her head and sit up, but every movement brought such sharp pain that she lay still again lest she cry out.

In tiny increments, she turned her head. Her hand rested against Captain Gaerbith's shoulder. His hand lay on his chest. Callused, his fingers were long and blunt. The nails could use a scrub and a trim. Scars patterned the back of his hand.

In her father's great hall, she had often heard boasting and seen the Young Wolves reenacting combat, but never had she seen proof of their wounds. Through the slash in his leggings gleamed the white scar on the captain's thigh, and there were other marks on his arms, chest, even a small cut on his neck. Like a mute teller of tales, Captain Gaerbith carried his stories on his skin.

Yanámari rolled away from his side, almost weeping as muscles shrilled in violent protest. She needed to find a convenient scrub tree for her morning necessary, but it was some time before she gained her feet. Not only was wielding a sword an unfamiliar thing, so was riding a horse for any length of time. She had only done either whenever her father wasn't in the city, or when her brother indulged her insistent requests to teach her something. "What if our enemies dare attack our walls?" she would say. "I want to be ready."

Strange to think on it—she had been the enemy.

Her sword belt held an empty scabbard now. She had given the sword to Turi.

After crouching behind a discreet bush beyond sight of the few soldiers already awake, she returned to her blanket and folded it into a thick pad on which to kneel. Her surcoat bunched around her knees. No longer white nor green, the long tunic was torn, reeking, streaked with blood—some of it Skardian, some Dissonay, some her own. She thought of the wolf handler slain by her knife, and of the Young Wolves she had tried to avoid but whose blades could only be met with an attack as aggressive as theirs.

A pale slash shone through the hole gaping in the sleeve on her upper arm. She touched the scar and saw the face of the man who gave it to her, remembering how his eyes flared then died with his breath, her sword in his side. His weapon had slid from his lifeless fingers, and she truly saw her enemy for the first time: a friend of her brother, and one of the few who had offered sincere condolences for Arien's death. Which of the stains on her tunic belonged to him?

Something squeezed her ribs and compressed her lungs, demanding tears. Taking short, sharp breaths, she strove for control. *Not yet. Not yet.*

She washed her face, but only combed the grit and dried blood out of her hair, fearing to use more water lest the skin could not be refilled. With clumsy fingers, she tied back her hair with a leather string. In doing so, she could almost see again Elta's smiling face in the chamber mirror as the little maid dressed her for the banquet.

Was it only two nights past that Elta had died? And Imre—

Yanámari's eyes stung, but she blinked back tears, took up her comb, and set to work grooming the captain. A jumble of tangled hair would not be smoothed. Muttering minor curses, she cut out the knotted mess then combed what remained. As she attempted to pull the dampened comb through his blood-matted beard, his eyelids twitched and he murmured something unintelligible. Yanámari grew still. He did not open his eyes, however, and soon fell silent. She finished the task then rinsed the comb and stowed it in her satchel.

Sitting back on her heels, she looked at the captain. In the grotto, he had spoken of family. Was there a wife anxious for his wellbeing or jealous for his heart? Did children gather at the door every sundown, looking for him to come home safe from battle?

Yanámari remembered the day she stopped waiting for her father.

She had been perhaps six years old, standing on top of a barrel in the stableyard, holding out her sturdy arms to greet him, but Morfran leapt from his horse and strode to the great hall, there to drink and celebrate with his men the acquisition of a new province in the east, said to be rich in silver and etherium, though only silver mines had been found. King Morfran brought back with him a huddle of chained prisoners he cursed at and spat upon throughout the feasting. The wolves were brought to pace before them.

From behind an arras, Yanámari watched, trying not to cry. Her father had no use for tears. He said as much to Arien, who stood rigid beside him on the dais. No emotion showed on her brother's face, but Yanámari saw the gleam of unshed tears in his eyes.

Morfran shoved the hilt of a dagger into Arien's hand and ordered him to kill one of the prisoners. "Any one you choose, boy," said the drunken king, sweeping the Dragon Crown from his head and gesturing with it. "Learn how to kill and who to keep, and this will one day be yours."

Arien swallowed hard but never moved.

Cursing, Morfran drew his sword, stalked to the prisoners, and slew every one. Then he cut pieces of skin from the backs of their necks and held the bloody patches up for all to see. "This will be the fate of all who bear the mark of the House of Kel!"

Later that night, wakened from a dream haunted by the pale faces of the dead, Yanámari heard her brother shouting in his sleep. She left her warm blankets and ran across the cold stone floor to his bed on the other side of the chamber, lay behind him and wrapped her arms around his shoulders. He grew quiet.

They slept sounder than she could remember, and were found that way by the servants in the morning.

The next night, and every night thereafter, he slept in the Court of Soldiers. Morfran thought him soft, weakened by too much comfort and by the adoration of a young sister.

A breeze whisked near her face as if someone stepped past her.

Yanked from her memories, she looked around the camp. Owen was up and cooking breakfast by a fire. She had neither seen nor heard him rise. Her cheeks burned. How long had she sat, thoughts far away, staring down at Gaerbith?

She dripped water into his slightly open mouth. He swallowed. A strong steady beat in his neck jumped like a flock of goats beneath the skin. She touched the leaping vein, and smiled. Not goats. Sheep.

Then she joined Owen by the fire, and nodded in greeting. He scarce looked up at her, watching instead a small pan he held over the fire. With the tip of his knife, he pushed around pieces of crusty bread in bubbling hot fat that turned each slice a pleasant golden brown around the edges.

Yanámari's mouth watered. "My nurse made this for me when I was a child. She called it ancestor's bread."

Removing the pan from the fire, he set it on a stone, speared a piece of the fried bread, and held it out to her. Without thought that it still sizzled, she grasped it with bare fingers then sucked in her breath, tossing the bread from hand to hand until it cooled. When she bit into its soft, crisp flesh, it was sweeter than she expected.

"Delicious!" she mumbled around a mouthful, something she would never have done in the great hall. Despite her father's coarse manners, he wanted her to be elevated in all things, from the way she spoke to the way she walked, a woman whose delicate hands never touched a sword.

How shocked he must have been to see his daughter shorn, bloody, and in armor. She almost felt sorry for him. Almost.

"Why could you not leave the city before you met the captain?" Owen's harsh question startled her. "Why risk his life for you?"

"I asked more than was my right," she said in bitter honesty.

Owen folded a slice of fried bread and bit it in half.

"Do you fear I will force him to honor a false betrothal?"

Owen stared at his hands, rubbing the palms together in a steady motion. Yanámari finished the last of her bread and removed the grease from her fingers by kneading handfuls of sandy earth between them.

"As for leaving Elycia of my own will," she said in quiet defiance, hating to explain, "that was impossible. The Brethren appeared whenever I ventured too near the gates. My father set them as my guards. He would not even let my brother act as my escort beyond the walls. I dared think someone not of my blood or my house might be safe from the Black Hoods. On the night of the banquet, I sent my maid to prepare disguises so we could leave with the merchant caravan. She was discovered and killed."

Yanámari drew a steadying breath and unclenched hands she had unconsciously pressed into fists. "Even if I had chosen to marry one of his darling Young Wolves, my father would never have consented to letting me leave Elycia. There I was born, and there I would die."

She looked beyond Owen to where Gaerbith lay, his head turned to the side. Owen's expression eased, his rigid posture relaxed. Silence grew between them, neither brooding nor angry.

"I was young when my brothers went to war." His words were almost defensive, as if he confessed a secret that might make her laugh at him.

Yanámari waited for him to continue.

"The one next in age to me— Father did not want him to leave the farm, but he was reckoned a man and could leave if he chose. There was not even a war then, just skirmishes. He carried a message to the king about invaders from Skarda.

"Once the war began, Father let the rest of my brothers be soldiers, but there was something special about that one brother. I wanted him to stay." He glanced around the camp, his hands restless. "I could not understand why he would leave me."

Yanámari recognized the pain in his words. "My brother would have taken me with him if he could."

"Lord Arien was a sight in battle!" Admiration lit his blue eyes. "Reminded me of the captain."

She smiled. "They are alike."

"Aye, they are."

He stabbed another piece of bread. "My sisters' husbands work beside Father," Owen continued the tale between bites, "but I was not skilled enough to suit him. So I followed my brothers to war." He looked down again at his hands. "I was a cook and a messenger. I tried once before, but I never really fought in battle until yesterday."

"Neither did I."

"Dissonay go to battle as young as twelve. I am past sixteen."

"I thought you a seasoned soldier. You are most certainly an excellent cook, and I am still hungry."

Smiling, he gave her a second slice of fried bread.

Turi approached, bringing Rubin Kyrinsson, Fremmen, and Warrten with him. They greeted her and sat cross-legged on the ground or squatted beside the fire.

"Surely we will journey long," she said to no one in particular, "and be far from any court for many weeks. I am willing to learn and be treated as any other soldier among you."

"What ye *will* and what will *be* are different matters." Turi looked up from sharpening his axe. "My lady," he added with a small smile.

Yanámari chuckled.

Like Turi's, Warrten's hands were not idle. With a scrap of cloth, he cleaned a wicked-looking weapon with a long handle that flared to join the head, a fluted metal blossom whose petals ended in spikes and from whose center rose succeeding blossoms, each smaller than the one before, until the very end of the mace was a tiny bulb encrusted with even tinier gleaming thorns. How he did not injure himself as he rubbed away crusted blood from each tiny crevice, Yanámari did not know.

"Turi," he said, never taking his gaze from his task, his thick fingers leaping nimbly among the cutting edges, "how is it ye speak as grand as a high lord? Have done! The Lady of Skarda has turned warrior, sure and certain," and now he did look up and give her a slanting wink, "but ye do not have the manners of a lord, nor would I call ye friend if ye did."

Turi gestured with his whetstone. "Mind yer tongue—"

Warrten lifted the mace and waggled it in the air.

The men laughed, yet Yanámari sensed a restraint. Fremmen glanced at the captain, as did all the men from time to time, their eyes turning toward him then back to the circle around the fire as if they were wary of showing too much concern. Sometimes she caught them looking at her, then their gazes would fasten on something else, but she saw their questions, their reserve, their uncertainty.

Turi murmured something to Rubin, who cast a quick look at her before leaving the circle. He returned a few moments later with a short sword, the one the captain had given her, now cleansed of blood, its edges shining. Rubin held it across his palms and offered it to Yanámari. She did not want it, but stood and took it with a small nod. He echoed the gesture, no expression on his face but curiosity.

"We shall make ye a new sword, one more fitting," said Turi, standing. "When we reach home."

HASTE, warned the Dragon.

Through the overspreading membranes of Áredan's wings gleamed the milky light of morning.

THE NAR'ATH DID NOT FIND US, BUT SNOW FELL IN THE NIGHT, AND THE HÔK NAR HAVE MANY WAYS OF HUNTING THEIR PREY. FIND RUBIN A HORSE. I BEAR NO RIDERS THIS DAY.

The camp scrambled into action, men stuffing the last bits of breakfast into their mouths, saddling horses, stamping out the small fires. Someone had tried to fashion a rough litter to carry Captain Gaerbith, but the Dragon said Kraekor refused to go riderless. For the horse's sake, the captain must be bound to the saddle again. A litter would be cumbersome, slowing to a mere trundle their already hampered flight.

Yanámari gathered Kraekor's reins.

HE IS AN OLD AND WISE BEAST. HE KNOWS WHAT MUST BE DONE.

She tucked the loose reins into Gaerbith's lax hands. Wake up, she wanted to shout at him, but he slept on, his body so slack she feared he would fall despite the ropes securing him to Kraekor. Only Bítan, sheathed on his back and wrapped with the same ropes that looped his torso, served to keep him upright.

SOMETIMES, ALL YOU CAN DO IS TRUST.

But—

YOUR BEAST'S NAME IS REN.

Yanámari patted Ren's black neck and offered him a little sweet grain Owen had given her to dole out rarely, a few grains at a time. The horse lipped it from her palm then whiffled against her hand, seeking more. She rubbed his nose.

Ren, for his raven color, she replied, thinking in Skardian.

REN, FOR MAJESTY, Áredan corrected in Dissonay, gently fanning his wings, shaking snow from them.

Nnow magnified the sunlight but muffled their passing, and the Fourth journeyed in silence but for the clink of shod hooves against stones, the creak of leather, the occasional jingle of bridles. The Dragon flew overhead, his shadow undulating along the stone walls of the defile as the Dissonay ventured deeper into the mountain.

The narrow path turned downward and the way became steep. Blockades of boulders forced them to wind through spaces scarce wide enough for a man, let alone a horse with its rider. Yanámari tried to relax her grip on Ren's reins, yet still pressed her knees to the horse's sides. Ahead, Captain Gaerbith swayed as Kraekor carefully picked his way.

Again Yanámari tried to ease her worry, this time by unclenching her teeth. Her jaw hurt. Her stomach and shoulder muscles knotted. Trust was not an easy thing.

A darker, larger shadow rippled across Áredan's. Along the

column, horses threw up their heads and neighs shrilled the air. Some animals tried to back up or move sideways. Kraekor halted. Ren turned askew of the path and pulled at the reins.

Stench grew until it cloaked Yanámari in the permeating odor of decay. She looked up. A Dragon, golden and fiery as the sun, wheeled overhead, its shape twice the length and breadth of Áredan, who beat his wings and rose above the other Dragon.

A roar, a blast of flame, a piercing shriek, the thunder of two masses colliding in the air.

The Dragons tumbled from sight.

The watcher had been walking beside Kraekor, but now he turned back to Lady Yanámari's mount, cupped the frightened horse's nostrils with one palm, and murmured, "Soft, now, soft," while stroking its neck with his other hand.

Yanámari's brows drew together in a puzzled frown. She looked down, straight into the watcher's eyes. His heart jolted.

No. No, she cannot see me.

But she could hear him. And see his footprints in the snow.

The melded, roiling shadows of the battling Dragons reappeared and swept across the line of soldiers like a fell omen. The twisted scents—sometimes foul, sometimes pleasant—brought to mind the image of roses growing from a dunghill. The golden Dragon slashed at Áredan, but the silver Dragon clamped teeth into his enemy's foreleg. The beast roared in pain, one broad wing dragging along the eastern ridge of the defile. Pebbles skittered down the rocky slope.

A single fat drop of golden rain splashed on a patch of bare earth. Dust puffed around it, then a flame burst forth and just as quickly died, leaving a scorched circle, snow boiling into mist at its edges. More drops fell in a sudden spate. One man cried out, gripping his sleeved forearm as the leather beneath the cloth disintegrated. His fellows threw him toward a patch of snow to quench the flames.

"Dragon's blood!" someone shouted.

The cry was taken up all along the line, but there was little shelter to protect the soldiers. The Dissonay rarely wore helms, and few of them fought with shields, for longswords were wielded with two hands. Even if there was something to hold over their heads or cover their bodies, there was no defense against consuming fire.

More blood rained down in scattered drops. Silver produced shoots of green grass or succulent vines, buds of wildflowers or nascent trunks of trees. From the gold, fire withered the sudden new growth or charred the stones, even licked up the dust.

Stones—set free when Dragon wings, tails, or talons scraped the walls of the defile—bounded and skipped down the slope, striking men and horses. One clipped the watcher's ankle and he stumbled, cursing under his breath.

Invisibility was no shield. No power had been given him but the ability to walk the earth unseen. To what end, he did not know.

He looked over his shoulder. Lady Yanámari, grim-faced and resolute, led her horse and looked neither right nor left. Amid peril, she simply walked on.

A shout traveled down the line. "Cave!"

The cut turned sharply, and there it was: the mouth of an enormous cave, wide enough for many horses to walk abreast. Inside the cool, dim space, the Fourth inspected the legs of the horses for crippling injuries. The men themselves bore ugly bruises from falling rocks, but no other burns from the blood.

No one was allowed to rest. Turi ordered the untying of bodies slung over saddles—dead comrades taken from the city—and these were laid on open ground beyond the cave's mouth. The task was done in haste, that the living might avoid the rain of Dragon blood.

Then they stepped into ranks, forming the shape of a half moon, then gripped their swords point-down just below the crossguards, and held them flat against their chests. They spoke as one voice, reciting the soldier's prayer, the force of the ancient words building until the final plea: *May I look upon Your face and be at peace.*

As the last echoes of the prayer died away, Turi lifted his voice and offered the death blessing: "Omwen'din, we give to Thee the honored dead."

The words had scarce left his mouth when flames blazed downward in a fiery gout and consumed the bodies, leaving only white ash.

Startled, the watcher looked up. Smoke wafted from Áredan's mouth.

He twisted to avoid the other Dragon's attack, but long grooves appeared on his flank. The Dragons tangled in the clear cold sky above, their savage snarls and growls reverberating through the stones. Larger, possessing a greater wingspan, the gold Dragon seemed as wounded and weary as Áredan, yet neither surrendered.

The battle moved beyond talon and tooth. The combatants resorted to fire, a weapon to which both seemed impervious. Surrounded by flames, they fought onward, wings tattered, scaled flesh torn. They bled so much that the defile became a scorched forest. As soon as one Dragon's life force produced foliage, the other Dragon's blood seared and destroyed it.

Rubin Kyrinsson stood clutching something in his fist and muttering, but the words were only a hum on the edge of the watcher's hearing.

The Dragons parted, circling one another, roaring, spitting fire. Were it possible, they limped. They met in one last fiery clash—and tumbled out of sight. Dirt and stones and blood flew up in mingled spume.

The Dissonay stood staring at the empty sky.

Into the quiet echoed a curse from somewhere deep in the cave. "Blood and bone! Is this the Void?"

54 ~ ALTERED PLAN

Rhôn walked along the top of the city wall, watching the agitated barons gather before the gates. With almost no horses, few oxen, and scant soldiers to escort the nobles homeward, commoners had been chosen from among the Elycians to carry burdens back to the provinces. One of the Hôk Nar Brethren accompanied each group to ensure the Elycians returned to city.

The barons had endured an arduous journey to the city, and now they were sent home with neither a treaty nor a proper army. Their new task: muster enough soldiers to return to battle by late summer.

They protested—laborers were needed to bring in the harvests—but the king was adamant: supply soldiers, or forfeit lands. If not, the Brethren would devise whatever magicks necessary to turn the minds of the barons to be like the king's soldiers, forgetting their true selves and living only to serve Morfran and do his bidding. Underneath that threat lay the unspoken knowledge that Disson might regroup before Skarda did, and overrun the kingdom.

Rhôn lifted his hand to signal the opening of the gate.

"A Dragon!"

Rhôn turned. Behind him, Morfran slammed a palm against the fire-scarred parapet.

"Those dogs summoned a Dragon!"

Heolstor gestured with his staff. "Our Dragon is a Gremian, much larger than the Fredek, and many times the warrior. He will slay the Fredek and return the Sea Stone to us. Then he will hunt the Kel-child and slay him."

"What of Yanámari?"

"She is the Lady of Skarda, accustomed to every comfort. Even now, she longs to return to Elycia."

Rhôn doubted that. She was strong of will, and proud. If she returned to Elycia, she would not come begging.

Morfran asked, "Did you never find my servant Imre?"

"No, my lord. No one has seen him in the city, nor was he seen by the workers outside the gates."

"His usual haunts?"

"No, my lord."

The glance the king sent Heolstor was so fleeting it might never have been.

Then Morfran pushed upright from the parapet and turned to Rhôn. "Your wounds, commander. You can wield a sword?"

Pain still throbbed deep in the wound, and though his arm would not return to full strength for some days, it was usable. The Black Hoods had muttered their incantations and sprinkled their powders, and held Rhôn's tortured hand over a fire. Bones and sinews stretched, popped, tightened. Pain, though brief, was so exquisite his breath stopped and his sight blurred. He staggered, but the Brethren propped him up and uttered more chants. When they released him at last, the hand was whole.

He scarce had time to flex it, to catch his breath and recover from the pain, before a Brother thrust the hot, barbless shaft of an arrow into the cut on his arm. Rhôn's sight turned black. When he woke, only a scar remained, ridged and fire-red.

Rhôn vowed to find a common healer to cure any of his future wounds.

He inclined his head to the king in silent reply.

Morfran descended the stone steps abut the wall. "We go to the Keep."

Rhôn hesitated.

Heolstor grabbed his arm, digging skeletal fingers deep. "You may regret the secrets you find within the King's Keep."

"You do not accompany us?"

Heolstor shook his head. "I do not enter above twice in a twelve-month. More power dwells there than most men can withstand. Morfran himself will stagger beneath it. But you are strong. Keep your wits about you, and you may become the next king of Skarda."

Nar'ath cawed, wheeling above the city gate, nipping at scraps of rotten flesh still clinging to bones in the iron cages.

Heolstor lifted his staff, calling down one of the birds to perch on the parapet before him. "Outram," he greeted the raven whose height nearly matched his. "What prevented you yesternight?"

The bird blinked, tilted its head, then squawked and flapped its wings in agitation.

The Master of the Black Hoods nodded. "Ah. I had forgotten that little detail. After sunset, you may not see a Dragon except he wishes you to see him. The Fredek must have hidden the Dissonay."

Heolstor suffered Outram's further complaints about what thin meal the merchant caravan provided, and about the many Nar'ath felled by arrows. The mercenaries were skilled bowmen.

"How unfortunate," Heolstor cut across the croaking protests, "but the task still needs doing. Find the Fredek. He may have survived the Gremian, but he will be no match for a swarm of Nar'ath. Finish what the Gremian could not. Who knows but Dragon flesh is a delicacy to your kind. Once you have had your fill, the Dissonay will be without any defense, and you may devour them as you will."

Outram fanned his wings in anticipation.

Heolstor warned, "Do not harm the Lady of Skarda. She may yet be of use to us. Find the Sea Stone and—if by some chance he still lives—bring the captain who leads the Dissonay."

He clutched the raven's neck, and the bird flapped its wings and squawked. "Do not fail, else you will find yourself the main dish of a one-course feast."

Outram rose from the parapet and gathered his flock, rising in a swirling mass, and led them west and south once more.

55 ~ THE CAVE

Gaerbith cursed his weakness. He strove to lift the waterskin to his lips. Lady Yanámari took it from him, tipping the spout, helping him drink.

"Thank you," he said in a voice hoarse with disuse, and laid his head back on the rolled blanket serving as a pillow. "I saw it. I saw the hills and the sea."

He lacked almost the strength to speak without slurring his words, and was not quite sure he made sense.

She capped the skin. "Skalds say kindred and comrades wait on that shore."

He tried to describe all he had seen, but words were as fleeting as deer in a forest.

"No, do not tell me." She smiled faintly. "From the look in your eyes, it is a wonderful place. I shall see it soon enough."

Gaerbith levered his upper body on his elbows the better to see her. "Show me your arm."

It had healed, marked only by a white scar. She pulled the torn sleeve closed. "The Dragon cured us all."

"Dragon?"

Strands of black hair escaped the tie at the back of her neck as she bent over him to support his shoulders. "Lie back, and I shall tell you all that has befallen us."

Her narration in Skardian was crisp, abbreviated. He was reminded of her sitting in the grotto, clutching her murdered servant's clothing, stricken yet not weeping. She pushed everything down like a tight bundle of wool.

"I was afraid, captain, and wanted to keep you here, so I let the Dragon heal you. Do you resent it, when the Otherland was so near?"

"What a fine hero I will be in stories when we reach home." His chuckle turned to a cough. "Saved by the one I was supposed to save."

She leaned forward, a probing look in her violet eyes. "Who are you, captain? Why does Heolstor fear you?"

"You know who I am, m'lady. Gaerbith, son of Forba, shepherd, soldier, captain of the Fourth Lachmil in the army of Disson." He closed his eyes. "Nothing else."

She said nothing, and he had almost drifted back to sleep when she spoke once more. "We lost Imre in the city. You saw him?"

"Aye, and then saw him not. He distracted Heolstor and saved me." He opened his eyes. Light outlined her profile and caught in her hair. "It was a noble end."

Her chin dipped, and she took a shuddering breath. She stood —"You must be hungry"—and moved beyond his sight.

He stared up into the shadowed vastness of the cavern ceiling.

"Lay-about!" Grinning, Turi squatted beside him, and helped him sit upright. "Y'missed all the sport."

"So Lady Yanámari tells me."

"Should have seen her, captain. Would have made ye proud."

Turi's version of the escape from Elycia was more robust than Yanámari's, rich with detail and the enthusiasm that rises after a successful battle, when a man may take his ease and recall it however he wishes. There was, however, a forced quality to the exuberance. Turi withheld something.

"How many died?"

Silent, Turi helped him sit upright against the rugged cavern wall.

"Tell me."

"Podi, Faxon, Galtero, Ellard, Verner..."

Owen approached, then others, until they surrounded Gaerbith, faces somber as the names of the dead were spoken. Then the men made known to him the quiet Skardian woodcutter, Rubin Kyrinsson, and spoke of the Dragon Áredan's sacrifice.

"There is more." Owen drew from his pack a green woolen bag, and from this he brought forth a pale orb shimmering with restless colors. Its glow lit the faces of the watching men.

"Mahyla! How did she come to be here?"

"High Lord Boorn brought her." Owen lifted the pearl in his palm. Bitterness tainted his voice. "He said Damanthus sent her to the Butcher in exchange for peace."

A lie. Gaerbith's fury burned so hot he could not speak.

Owen returned the Sea Stone to his pack and departed with the other men to the far side of the cave where a small fire had been built. Turi remained where he was.

"You know where she belongs?" Gaerbith murmured.

Turi nodded.

"Mahyla is not the possession of one man or even one kingdom."

"If Disson heard ye speak thus," warned Turi, "they would kill ye."

Gaerbith clenched his fists.

"Captain," Turi said quietly, "why did Padraig send us to Elycia? It was not for treaty, nor to protect High Lord Boorn."

Lady Yanámari knelt and put a bowl on the ground, then her deft fingers broke bread into pieces.

"He knew Boorn could not be trusted, but I could not command anyone to come with me on this journey," said Gaerbith. "I hoped you would all refuse and go home."

"Indeed."

"Aye, and you know it. Why did you come?"

"Because I could not let my captain be a fool alone." A glint of humor lit Turi's eyes, and he nodded toward Owen. "And because a bold young cook dared go."

Yanámari held out a spoon filled with bread sopped in broth. Gaerbith swallowed the food and submitted to having his chin wiped clean of spilled soup. Turi smiled, the wretch.

"Why the pretense? Why not execute Boorn and be done with it?"

"Maybe Padraig did not know the depth of Boorn's betrayal, and sent us to keep Skarda occupied while Disson renewed its forces."

Turi sucked his broken tooth. "On such pitiful reason, he would sacrifice men from the best *lachmil* in his army?"

Yanámari held out another spoonful of broth. This time, she spilled none of it. Gaerbith watched her as he swallowed the soup, but her rigid expression did not change.

"Who better to go to the Butcher's house," he said, "than the ones most likely to return from it?"

"We lost men for no good purpose. Padraig will not become an old king by being reckless."

Gaerbith shook his head as Yanámari offered yet another spoonful. Likely made from boiling dried meat, the broth tasted thin, and he was too exhausted to eat more.

"Skarda will regroup," said Turi, "and meet us with dread vengeance."

Gaerbith's thoughts marched elsewhere than his tongue. Weariness garbled his words. "You—always better—warrior." He felt compelled to say things grown suddenly urgent, he did not know why. "Uártha said—Archive." He lifted a lax hand toward Yanámari then let it fall to lie beside him again. "Brave—queen." His eyes closed against his will. "Dragon?"

His head lolled. Gaerbith felt hands lowering his head and shoulders to the ground then he knew nothing more.

Lady Yanámari set aside the bowl and sat with her knees drawn up to her chest, arms locked around them. Opposite her, Turi sat in watchful silence. Beyond him stood three guards at the mouth of the cave, looking outward. Rubin Kyrinsson's lips moved as if he spoke with someone unseen.

The watcher eyed the bowl of bread and soup. His arms pressed around his middle, and he had already tightened his belt, yet rumbles of hunger threatened to erupt. If only Turi and Lady Yanámari would look away for an instant—

Her voice was tense and low. "If you would not let him go to Elycia alone, why did you abandon him when he needed you most?"

"I did as my captain commanded."

"Would you have gone back into the city for his body?"

Turi looked at her with a sad smile. "He expected to die."

He caught the end of his beard between thumb and forefinger, and tugged it as he spoke. "He told me once of a dream he had when only a lad. He saw himself dying in a place far from home. A place of stone. Almost any other child would have screamed himself awake, but Gaerbith said it reassured him. Glimpsing even a fragment of his fate freed him to meet each day knowing he would live to see another."

"Until he came to Elycia."

"Aye."

"I wonder why he came, then."

"A man cannot always be afraid."

"Was he?"

"Any man of sense is afraid when he goes to battle, but he need not be ruled by fear."

"You were merry in my father's hall, even when Baron Hargow's man tried to kill the captain, yet you blessed the dead. Owen fought beside us, yet he is not a soldier. The captain carries secrets deeper than Heolstor's, yet claims he has no power. You are none of you whom you appear." After a moment, she added, "You speak my language better than I speak yours."

"We are not all of us dogs."

The watcher squirmed. In villages nearest the Territories, a man might have to explain whether the dog he referred to was an animal or a Dissonay trader.

"That is another mystery to me," said Yanámari. "At banquet, when called dogs, all of you laughed. Later, the captain even made light of it."

Turi shrugged. "It has no power except what we allow. We can turn the barbs back on our enemies, or we can break the shaft of each arrow and laugh as we do it."

"How frustrating for your enemies." She smoothed the blanket covering the captain and adjusted the rolled blanket that was his pillow. "Why do you follow him?"

"Ah, m'lady, but I might ask ye the same."

Flushing, she looked away. He glanced over his shoulder toward Rubin and the guards at the cave's mouth.

Now! The watcher snatched the bowl of soup and poured its contents down his throat, swallowing the broth and soggy bread as if it were water. Just as Lady Yanámari started to turn back, the watcher set the bowl beside her. He winced as the wood hit the stone floor, but she only glanced at it and shifted aside, likely thinking she had somehow knocked the bowl.

"Rest," said Turi, rising. "He may sleep for many hours yet, and we will remain here until we find the Dragon."

Linked to Áredan by the scale, Rubin had seen the other Dragon tumble then regain strength enough in his tattered wings to move southward in limping flight. Áredan had then plummeted into a ravine somewhere west of the cave, unconscious but alive.

Searching the mountains after dark would be dangerous and foolhardy, yet only a direct command from Turi had kept Rubin in the cave. "If I die"—the woodcutter's defiance seemed to surprise even him—"what is it to you?"

Standing over him, Turi replied, "It means we lose two friends instead of one." Then he placed a hand on Rubin's shoulder. "We know his sacrifice. We will not forget."

So Rubin stood and muttered and looked up into the sky, rubbing the silver scale, trying to waken Áredan. The woodcutter was either a man who hoped beyond reason, or he was mad.

Defying the snow, the silver Dragon's blood had filled the defile with grass and tender vines, enough to feed the animals. The Fourth had brought bread, meat, and cheese with them, but it would not last past the next day. Though Nar'ath had not found them nor the Dragon slain them, they could still be defeated by the Craydaeg Mountains.

What can I do? I do not know these mountains. Do I venture ahead on the path and find where it leads? Do I search for water and grass? Do I take a bow and hunt for food?

The watcher looked around. Owen sat rubbing oil into the leather of a bridle.

Beside Owen lay his pack, and in the pack lay the Sea Stone.

Arms crossed, Yanámari stood beside Rubin while the woodcutter continued his fruitless examination of the sky. He still wore the coarse robe of a Hood, but the sleeves had fallen back to reveal the old, patched garments he wore beneath. The stitching was precise. What had become of Rubin's wife? His rough hands had not executed such delicate work.

His thumb worried a silver disk as if it were a talisman. A beard of many days' growth scarce concealed hollow cheeks or the sharp line of his jaw. His eyes were buried in their shadowed sockets, shrinking pools of water in the bottom of a drying well.

"Rubin Kyrinsson," she said, and the man jerked, startled from his staring trance.

"My—my lady." He bent at the waist in a formal bow.

She put out a hand. "No need for that here."

He stood upright, an uncertain expression on his thin face.

"When was the last time you slept?"

His gaze slid away from hers.

"Tell me true, Rubin." Yanámari adopted a stern look.

"Yesternight, m'lady. When I was in the caves beyond the city, I could not rest, and did not know night from day."

"Tell me of the caves."

"There are many, my lady, and the Brethren are there, skin so pale it almost lights the darkness. There are Dragons, too. Most are hatchlings." He hesitated. "The king offered me to the gold-scaled Dragon. There was talk of Kels and binding and things I did not understand. The Dragon let me go, but Áredan set me free."

"The fire at the gates."

"Aye, my lady."

"How does my father keep the Dragons?"

"Chains for the full-grown, or cells for the younglings."

"But the old scrolls say no bondage is strong enough to imprison a Dragon, nor is it possible to share friendship between Dragons and Men. How did Áredan come to help us?"

"The Brethren stole one of his scales and used magic to bind him. A scale freely given set him free." Rubin held up the silver disk "I see what he sees, but he has walled his pain from me."

"The others will find him." Yanámari laid a reassuring hand on his sleeve. He became very still, and fear leapt in his eyes. She withdrew her hand. "I mean you no harm, Rubin. I do not share my father's madness."

His brows twitched, and his head tilted. "Do you hear that?"

"Hear what?"

"Rushing water."

"But we are far from the river—"

His eyes widened. "Nar'ath!"

Rubin ran to bring in the horses, and Yanámari drew her sword. "Turi, prepare the archers!"

Men slung quivers on their backs and strung their bows.

"We have few arrows," said Owen. "We will be throwing stones before the end."

"A stone to the eye—instant kill."

"What else?" Turi demanded, axe in one hand, sword in the other, gaze fixed on the sky.

"Cut off the talons. The beaks are deadly, but a Nar'ath without its claws is prey to the others."

The hilt of her sword was slick with sweat, and her body shuddered with the force of her heartbeat.

A limping shape shuffled past her. "Let me pass."

Gaerbith's usual strong voice was thin and lacked breath.

Nevertheless, the men parted ranks until he stood in front, longsword ready.

The wingbeats of the Nar'ath grew louder by the moment.

"Turi, stand with me. Owen, array the archers over there. Rubin, have you a weapon?"

"No, captain."

"Find a place among the horses. You are our only link to the Dragon. Lady Yanámari?"

The Fourth had surrounded then passed her until she stood at the rear. She was unaccountably annoyed by the circumstance. "I am here."

Gaerbith must have heard the edge in her voice, for his own held a smile. "Let her through."

She stepped to his side just as a black cloud swooped across the sky.

56 ~ KING'S KEEP

The massive door near the base of the King's Keep was made of dark stone the color of sky just before a winter storm. Though the sun rode high, the Keep cast a great shadow, and the doors were recessed deep, like the mouth of a tunnel. Rhôn's boots scraped as he followed Morfran up the stone steps leading to a shallow landing. Two Hoods stood beside the doors. Hands tucked into their sleeves, cowls pulled low over their faces, they seemed fleshless columns, forbidding in their stillness.

Beneath a thin layer of melting snow, the landing was covered by a spongy carpet of blue-green moss. As Rhôn stepped onto it, the air grew cold and damp, as if he stood too near the spray of a waterfall. Morfran seemed untouched by the sudden chill.

The Black Hoods stirred from their posts, grasped the great iron rings in the center of the doors, and pulled. Frigid air rushed out in a sharp blast, tasting of winter and smelling of rooms old and dusty.

Morfran strode into the darkness. Rhôn hesitated, hand on the hilt of his sword. The metal felt warm, more alive than his own flesh.

The door to a secret stood wide. Inside the towering hulk of stone dwelt a power large enough to frighten even Heolstor, the Master of the Hôk Nar and the highest servant of Nar Cahm. Only a fool or a madman would go willingly to such a place, yet the mystery beckoned, tugging at curiosity and imagination. To such an invitation, there was only one reply.

Taking a breath, Rhôn Bergsson entered the King's Keep.

Morfran held a torch. A grisly thing it was, fashioned of a thighbone dipped like a candle in human tallow, and with a tooled leather grip covered in human skin. Though the strong fragrance of fire-powder overcame the stench, the smoke was oily, coating the back of Rhôn's throat with a stomach-turning taste he tried in vain to ignore.

Light flickered over the carven walls of the great room, richly detailed, some bearing remnants of tint, flaking bits of once-vibrant paint. Rhôn put out a hand to touch the face of a maiden, her still-crimson lips curved in a mysterious smile, eyes glittering with flecks of enticing blue.

The king knocked his hand aside. "Touch nothing."

Raising the torch, Morfran looked up. Rhôn's gaze followed. Even the ceiling was decorated, the work intricate and fine.

"The final creation of the last craftsmen to live under the rule of the Kels. Stonemasons carved Elycia from the very mountain at its back. Artisans worked their skill upon its walls. Cawthyr, the first Skardian king, brought them from the Plains and here they worked until they died." Admiration swelled Morfran's voice. "Here is proof of Cawthyr's strength. The House of Kel was a blight that robbed the people of their purpose, but Cawthyr gave them guidance. He was a leader. He pushed them beyond anything they accomplished in the past, and he achieved the impossible."

Rhôn knew the history of Skarda as well as any other nobleman's son. Those ancient craftsmen had been starved and beaten. Adwr, the last Kellish king, had been a foolish and a poor ruler, but after him Cawthyr imposed the crushing tyranny that had existed nigh unbroken for centuries. Only a few kings, too-brief lights in darkest night, had risen to rule with any measure of kindness.

Behind Rhôn, the door closed, slowly shutting out the light until only the torch provided a small circle of illumination.

"Do you feel it, commander?" The king's voice dropped to a murmur. "Do you feel her power?"

Rhôn felt only the cold, the physical cloak of darkness.

Morfran seemed to diminish, his shoulders hunched, his voice muted. "She knows we are here."

"Who is she, my lord?"

"A pestilential presence. The bane of my life. Aside from Old Longbeard—who glides about on traitor's feet and speaks in a tortured voice like the last utterance of a dying man—she knows me best and hates me most."

He turned his face from the light. After a moment, master once more of his voice, "Come," said the king and led the way to the stairs.

Halfway up the tower, Morfran halted, and Rhôn sank gratefully down on a step to catch his breath. His legs trembled with fatigue. Sweat dripped from his hair, stinging his eyes.

Windows had once pierced the outer walls of the King's Keep, but they had been filled with rubble cemented in place, all but those in the highest reaches of the tower where the prisoner dwelt. Why just there? If the prisoner was as powerful as Heolstor claimed, why did she not fly away? Break her bonds? Defeat Heolstor in a duel of magicks?

Ah, but the old counselor would not allow his power to be challenged. Perhaps it was not so vast after all.

"Why do you laugh, Rhôn Bergsson?" The king's dark eyes glittered in the torchlight, and his teeth gleamed behind his beard in a smile that was not a smile.

"Stories, my lord."

Morfran's brows lowered.

"I was a child afraid of the dark, because my brother told stories at night. I thought just now how little there was to fear. I have survived terrors worse than my darkest dreams."

Morfran studied him. "What did Heolstor whisper in your ear? Did he promise you the kingdom?" The odd smile broadened. "He did the same once to me. If I defeated Vegeir, the Dragon Crown would be mine. But a boy sought to supplant me. He would be easily overcome —so Heolstor promised. What army would rouse to follow a child of only five years? After all, with the blessing of Nar Cahm upon me, none would dare lay claim to my throne.

"The child was a Kel, however, and the barest mention of him set the people buzzing with stories and portents, as if all their long-dead ancestors rose up to whisper history in their ears and bring to remembrance ancient prophecy." Morfran's mouth twisted as he uttered a bitter curse. "Even my unfaithful queen vomited that filth."

The torch guttered, and he looked up into the waiting darkness. "Rise, commander. While the prisoner's goodwill is extended."

Still not sensing whatever power communicated with the king, Rhôn reluctantly stood and again followed him up the stairs, wondering if the power was only a nightmare drawn from Morfran's madness, suggested perhaps by Heolstor but twisted into reality by the king's fractured mind.

Or perhaps it was a lure to Rhôn's curiosity, a way to draw him up to a great height then cast him down, thus ridding Morfran of a rival to the throne and sending Rhôn to mourn with other murdered souls in the Highlands.

He put a hand to his sword. He would not go easily.

Morfran halted before a narrow wooden door. He placed the torch in a bracket, grasped the ring set high in the door, and let it fall against the wood with a resounding clap.

A warm, beautiful voice welcomed them, humor in its tone.

Straightening his shoulders, taking a single deep breath, Morfran seemed to gather his courage before twisting a heavy key in the lock and pushing open the door. Yet, as the door swung slowly inward, the king did not enter.

Behind him, Rhôn strained to catch a glimpse of the owner of such a lovely voice.

"In! In!" it repeated, laughing outright, "else the poor soldier—a commander now, is he?—will lose patience and set you aside, dear Morfran."

Against the light of a window sat the shape of a woman, her face cast in shadow. Her hands were busy as she spun thread on a wheel, her foot rocking steadily on the treadle turning the wheel. Beside her, caught in the oblique light of another window, a spindle twirled, growing fat with silver-grey thread. In her lap was piled the wool from which she spun.

Morfran bowed. "We are come to seek your counsel."

"To what purpose?"

The king straightened. Yet, despite his erect posture and lifted chin, he seemed diminished. "My army was destroyed less than a day past."

The woman nodded once.

"What shall we do now to regain our strength and destroy our enemies?"

"What do you offer in exchange for my counsel?"

"What do you need? More wool? Needles? A better loom?"

"I have all I need."

"What, then, shall I give in exchange for your wisdom?"

"My wisdom remains my own. Counsel, however, can be purchased."

"With. What." Subservience no longer lurked in Morfran's voice.

Long, nimble fingers twisted woolen strands and fed them to the spinning wheel. The tap of the treadle and the whir of the wheel grew faint. Rhôn blinked. Shapes and shadows became one. Pulsing blood roared in his ears.

"Did I not warn of a man whose youth concealed ancient knowledge?" Her voice threaded the tumult. "Did I not foretell he would lay Skarda waste though his own life be forfeit?"

Rhôn shook his head and opened his eyes wide, trying to regain his senses.

Beside him, Morfran seemed locked in a similar struggle. "But— Heolstor slew him." The king's words were choked, chopped. "Before he could do any harm."

"He took your daughter, the last of your house. A presence walks with him. He resists it, but he leans on it. He is strong because of it."

"He is dead." Morfran staggered. "A Dragon, not a man, destroyed my army."

"Who controlled the Fredek? Who commanded the Gremian?" The spinning wheel stopped though no hand touched it. Her foot lifted from the treadle, and the spindle turned one last time before coming to a halt. "Themselves. The Dragons controlled themselves. Only a fool would bring Dragons back from exile without proper rule."

Bent, resisting the force pushing him to his knees, Morfran half-drew his sword but could not clear the scabbard.

She was relentless. "Only a greater fool would boast of it."

Unbound, her hair was long and sable. She stood tall, clad in layers of fabric thin as light yet opaque as the dark of a deep well. Such power radiated from her that its weight crushed Rhôn's chest. He heard a harsh gurgle, and realized with dull surprise he was dying.

"Are you unwell?" Calmness lent her voice terrible amity. "Pray, let me help you, commander."

The weight lifted. Rhôn fell to his knees, gasping.

A cool finger traced his cheek. "Heolstor and his little band of Hôk Nar are dabblers, mere pretenders. They flit about in their black robes, and people fear them. It were wiser they feared me."

Rhôn jerked away from her touch.

She laughed, the easy sound of a carefree girl. "Perhaps you have something I want. Rise."

Rhôn pushed himself to his feet. The king swayed beside him.

"Morfran"—the woman stretched out her hand yet did not touch him—"you should not have come. You do not value my counsel. You appear weak before this young man who, if I am not mistaken, Heolstor is grooming to be the next king."

For a long, still moment, the prisoner and the king faced one another in rigid silence. The woman's face remained in shadow, but her profile reminded Rhôn of someone. Again, he shook his head to clear his vision. Is it possible?

"Set me free." Her quiet voice was heavy with restrained emotion. "Set me free, Morfran." She took a step toward him. "Let me stand beside you."

It seemed—for an instant—that Morfran leaned toward her. His hand lifted from his side, and an expression that might have been sorrow crossed his face.

Then his features hardened, and his hand fell to the hilt of his sword. "You bride of Nardha! You spawn of the Void! I shall never set you free!"

She reached for him, but Morfran drew his sword.

The woman rested graceful fingers on the flat of the blade near the tip. "This sword cannot pierce any deeper than the loathing I saw in your eyes that night. You loved me once, or you would not hate me now." Her voice became soft, tender, honeyed with longing. "Our son is dead. Our daughter is fled. Yet did not a seer tell you the House of Morfran would rule until a blue sun rises in the west?"

The sword turned aside just enough for her to step closer.

"It is not too late," she murmured. "We are not too old."

"That man—"

"Lies." She touched his cheek.

Morfran pushed aside her hand. "I came for counsel, not for the past." There was no anger or disgust in his voice. He lowered his sword. "The barons return to their provinces to gather conscripts and rebuild the army. Rhôn is commander, second only to me. Heolstor has been gathering Dragon eggs and hatchlings, and the young are being trained. It is a hard task. Dragons have hated Men since the exile, and the desire for revenge runs deep even in the young.

"But once they are ours"—excitement rose in his voice, and his empty hand clenched—"we need no army but Dragons. The Dissonay will be defeated, and no other enemy will dare raise his head."

Queen Una—it must be so, for she was like Lady Yanámari in form and manner, and in the shining beauty of her long dark hair—walked to a window and looked out, her back to the men.

"What of Azrin, the sword of Kel?" She gestured, and the airy fabric of her gown fluttered like layers of moths. "If the Kel-child discovers the sword before you do, Dragons will die on its edge or flee back to exile."

She turned her head just enough to show her profile and the tips of her lashes. "In fighting my brother for land belonging to neither kingdom, you have been distracted from you purpose. Heolstor whispered powerful words and showed grand visions, but little he promised has come true. Vegeir was a good man before he wore the Dragon Crown. Desiring to serve his people, he cast aside Heolstor's control. Then you became the old man's favorite."

She rested a hand against the side of the wide opening as if to steady herself, and Rhôn—caught up in her voice, in her every move—waited impatiently for her to speak again. The object of her story, Morfran seemed scarcely to breathe.

"I remember when I first saw you," she said, her words warm. "Damanthus took you hunting, and the party was gone for many days. I had only ever heard your name as a curse, for my father acknowledged only Vegeir as king.

"But Father had died, other men sought the throne of Disson, and my brother asked you to join armies and protect his inheritance. Alliance was affirmed on that hunt.

"Eager to catch a glimpse of you, I hid all day in the forest along the road to Sonndin. I expected grand things, but you appeared dirty and tired, and smelled of your kills. Still, I thought you the finest man I had ever seen. At banquet, I tried not to stare, but—"

"I could not keep my eyes from you," said Morfran, "nor did I wish to. You had power even then to bring me to my knees."

She laughed.

Turning toward him, she was again framed by the light, her face hidden in shadow. "Then why are we here, Morfran? End this imprisonment. Set us both free. We can rule together. Heolstor's power is nothing to mine. He will drink all the life from your marrow, but I will be your strength.

"He believes finding Azrin will prevent anyone else from holding power, or that finding the Great Archive will give him the knowledge to live forever. He will no longer need you."

Una took a step. "Together, you and I will find the sword, steal power from the remnant of Kel. Heolstor will have no more hold on you, and he will blow away like the wind that he is."

Another step. "Let us build again the House of Morfran."

Another step. "Set me free."

A whisper. "Set yourself free."

She knelt before him. He raised his sword.

Rhôn grabbed the hilt of his own weapon, but blade fused to scabbard—he could not pull it free.

Gripping his sword with both hands, Morfran lifted his arms over his head.

Frantic, Rhôn tugged at his recalcitrant blade then abandoned that vain effort and reached for his dagger. It, too, refused to slide free.

Una bowed her head, gathering her hair to one side, exposing the white arch of her slender neck.

The sword fell.

57 ~ THE SEA STONE

Syra stumbled, cutting her foot on a sharp stone. She sat on a rock and lifted her foot, wincing, turning the sole upward, resting the ankle on her knee. Blood mingled with dirt and snow, forming a muddy paste. She had lost a shoe while fleeing the Nar'ath. That foot should have been numb from cold but it throbbed, alive with pain.

Evan still wore both his sturdy boots cut from the leather of a pair of Rubin's old ones, and he scrambled over the tumbled rocks, a sure-footed little goat, his dull-colored clothing lending him the appearance of living earth or wandering stone.

Rubin, what a brave son.

Searching the rags in her satchel, she chose the softest strip of fabric and bound it around her foot, then covered that bandage with another made of strong, tight-woven material that might protect her sole for at least a short distance over the wicked stones.

Evan reached the summit of the ridge and lay flat, his body a part of the mountain.

There was a hidden pass the armies used, but she had never seen it. Rumored to cut through the heart of the Craydaegs, it was a great tunnel opening somewhere in the cliffs near the gates.

Syra squinted at the sky. The merchant caravan had taken the westerly pass north of the River Thrayne, where the way was broader and less dangerous than the old pass following the river. When she and Evan fled the Nar'ath attack, they ran back up the mountain, only slowing to a walk when the way grew too steep. Lest their footsteps echo, they walked softly across the familiar arch of the wooden bridge below the city gates. Though the Nar'ath were occupied elsewhere, she still feared the soldiers, but the walls were empty of guards or watch fires. Heaps of ashes smoked near the city walls.

Funeral pyres?

In fleeing one horror, Syra almost condemned her son to another. Fear had robbed her senses. How could she let her feet lead her back along paths as hard as chains, back to the place she abhorred?

Fear is a great deceiver.

Near dawn yestermorn, she and Evan had found a narrow path and felt their way down to a broad terrace rimmed in standing stones, a cave cut into the mountainside. Only when she woke near midday and emerged from under an overhanging ledge did Syra truly realize to which slope of the mountains they had fled.

Stumbling over rocks, seeking escape where no path led, they forged their own way down the southern slopes. Heat from the stones melted away the snow, and Syra was weary and hungry, her mouth so dry her tongue clove to her teeth.

Evan arrived in a slide of small stones and loose earth. "I saw something glittering, like water glitters, and there were green things growing."

"Water will be welcome." She smiled, pushing his hair back from his damp brow. "Is there a way?"

He nodded.

"Well, then"—Syra rose, placing her weight gingerly on the cut foot—"lead on."

What Evan deemed a path was no more than a narrow cut in the mountainside, but it led southward and downward, away from the imprisoning heights where the city crouched, a stone beast waiting to devour all who entered its gates.

Exertion brought perspiration. Damp skin and damp clothes, with no fire to dry them, could bring illness. Syra had left their ration of powdered fire in their hovel in the city, lest using it on the journey would alert the Brethren. If the water Evan saw was surrounded by trees, then perhaps natural fire was possible.

But would the Nar'ath drink there? Would the Brethren use their far-seeing magic and know fugitives sheltered there?

Even if she made no fire, both of them needed water and rest. Without renewed strength, how could they flee again if the Nar'ath came?

A scent drifted to her, faint at first but pleasing, like blooms filling mountain meadows all too briefly in the spring. As the journey steepened and the way curved toward the westering sun, the fragrance grew. Syra's limping gait quickened and her weariness faded. Evan broke into a run, disappearing around a bend, but his excited whoop echoed back to her. Ignoring her injured foot, Syra ran.

Trees—saplings, really—rustled and shivered, shooting forth new growth until they reached the height of a man, and then they slowed. Soft, thick grass caressed Syra's feet. Petals tickled her shins.

Arms outflung, head tilted back, Evan twirled in a mad circle, laughing. Syra stared at all the wonders. Vines drooping from massive stones bereft of soil. Green grass swooping from ridge to ridge, like a cloak draping broad shoulders. Trees dotting the vale, those farthest away being taller than these growing noisily around her. Varicolored blooms, their perfume dizzying.

Where was the water?

She entered a thicket of willowy saplings. Surely the pond or lake was just beyond them. As she pushed through their supple trunks, such brilliance filled Syra's sight she threw up an arm to shield her eyes, yet the light almost blinded her.

Then the water heaved, breathing out more of the beautiful scent.

DO NOT FEAR, and a great wing lifted to shadow her.

Sluggish silver oozed from long tears in the shining massive body, and where it pooled the grass was greener, the flowers thicker. Blinking, she looked up into a wide purple eye.

RUBIN LIVES.

She stumbled back, slipped on the grass, fell, still staring into that strange eye swirling with colors beneath the purple.

HE IS WELL.

"How do you— Who are you?"

I AM ÁREDAN OF THE FREDEK KINDRED. RUBIN SET ME FREE.

Small hands patted her shoulders and her back, then crept around her neck. She clutched her son's sturdy little body and rocked side to side, her face buried in his soft hair.

Rubin lived. He lived. And he was near.

Her throat ached, but tears would not come.

Something warm touched her foot; the pain disappeared.

THOSE WITH RUBIN HOLD A PRICELESS STONE THAT CAN HEAL MY HURTS, BUT IT MUST BE SOON.

Syra looked up at Áredan. "What must we do?"

THE SEARCHERS WILL NOT FIND ME BEFORE NIGHTFALL

She saw in his eye this grassy vale, then the three ridges east where searchers toiled to climb then descend the riven earth.

Four more ridges beyond the searchers yawned a cavern before which men stood, swords lifted and arrows knocked, their faces tilted toward the sky. A black cloud of Nar'ath swarmed. She saw Rubin, his shadowed eyes and despairing look clutching at her tighter than Evan's small hands.

"No," she breathed.

HELP ME, AND I SHALL HELP THEM.

"We will never reach them in time."

I HAVE A LITTLE STRENGTH LEFT. I WILL LIFT YOU TO THE TOP OF THE FIRST RIDGE.

Perhaps a signal fire? But that might alert Morfran and Heolstor. Besides, how would the searchers know who lit it? They might think it a trap and turn back. Was this, too, a trap? Was this creature a servant of Heolstor and the Hôk Nar?

I WAS THEIR PRISONER, SYRA, NOT THEIR FRIEND.

"He smells," Evan declared.

"Do not be rude—"

"He smells like spring."

She offered a distracted smile, her mind still on the image of Rubin in the cave.

Áredan reached out a claw that shook with the effort. Evan did not shrink away from the curved talon, its back brushing his brow.

BUILD A FIRE.

The smallest saplings were pulled easily from the ground, and there were plenty to be had. Syra and Evan gathered all they could, piling the wood before Áredan, who dried it with a gentle heat, and then helped them haul the wood up the ridge until they heaped a stack as tall as Syra. Áredan lit the beacon then propped his head against a boulder.

"They will see it, even in sunlight?" asked Syra, but the Dragon did not reply.

Evan curled inside his mother's cloak, sitting beside his first true fire—one made of wood and not a mere handful of powder—and Syra stood between the flames and the Dragon, her hand resting on Áredan's scaled brow.

How long since he had torn asunder a Nar'ath with his bare hands? Turi had grasped a curved beak and pulled it apart, rending the creature from gullet to tail. The wet ripping sound, the gut-twisting stench, the black blood still lurked in his dreams. The second Nar'ath had been a quicker, cleaner kill—a stone straight through one glittering eye—but Turi would have torn that one, too, if the bird had not tried fleeing.

Sword and axe sheathed, he bent to fill the pouch on his belt with as many stones as he could grab in two swift handfuls. He stood—and met Gaerbith's amused glance.

Turi shrugged. "I blind 'em. Y'cut off their legs."

The captain laughed. "If the archers do not get them first."

Nar'ath dove. Arrows flew.

Turi rubbed two stones together in his hand, pushing them around one another, moving them from fingers to heel and back again, his callused palm impervious to the hard, sharp edges. One for Edwig, who welcomed home her husband with a sweet smile. One for Isak, who laughed to wear his father's shoes.

Pierced in the first volley, the foremost line of Nar'ath tumbled like pieces of midnight from the sunset sky. The leader flew onward, diving toward the Fourth, unhindered by a long tear in one wing. A shriek, sharp as the screech of blade on blade, lanced Turi's ears.

Nay, ye vile beast. Not this day.

He rose, drew back his arm, and threw a stone. The lead Nar'ath squawked, flipped, then righted itself.

Another flight of arrows brought down more birds, but now the Nar'ath were close enough for swords.

Turi threw the second stone. The leader's head snapped back. The neck flopped. The body plummeted. Chuckling in dry triumph, Turi dug more stones from the pouch.

Blood became a black-red mist veiling the defile. Shrieks and caws deafened him. Long dark feathers twirled down, drifting a slow rain over the men.

Young Trag lurched into the air, screaming, lifted by a Nar'ath whose talons punctured his chest. Owen shot down the bird then hacked off its head. Kneeling in the pooling blood, he shouted Trag's name, but Trag did not move.

A Nar'ath raked its claws across Owen's unprotected back. He arched, mouth wide. If he screamed, the sound was lost to the shrieking.

With a wordless roar, Gaerbith lunged haltingly forward. The bird jerked sideways, caught by one of Turi's well-aimed rocks. Gaerbith cut off the creature's legs. Other Nar'ath surrounded it, tearing at its wings and neck as it squawked and strove to escape them, rising straight up from the fray but unable to flee the birds that followed it beyond the ridge.

Gaerbith stood over Owen, fighting off Nar'ath until bits of them—wings, claws, heads—lay scattered about. "Turi! Do you see Yanámari?"

Turi killed three more as he searched for a glimpse of her.

"There!" someone shouted. "The ridge!"

Gaerbith grabbed for an archer's bow, but the man shook his head. "No more arrows, captain."

Turi threw a stone, but it landed short. He could only watch, angry and helpless.

The Nar'ath clamped its talons around her as if it meant to carry her to a high aerie.

Yanámari kicked and twisted, striking with the short sword. The point dug deep, and the Nar'ath shrilled. She jarred to earth, head striking stone, sparks exploding across her vision, lungs paralyzing. Hearing fled until the shouts of men and the skrilling of birds muted, like blades dulled in battle.

The creature clutched her torso, lifting her only to drop her once more. This time, the impact drove breath back into her, a deep gasp of cold air—not clean and snow-crisp, but cloying, tasting of dust and blood.

She stabbed and slashed, unable to see where she aimed. The sword made contact once or twice, but after a few flailing thrusts, it was wrenched from her hand, the blade clattering and ringing as it slid down the slope.

She blinked. Sight returned, but only as a smear of light and color.

Any moment, a strong beak might descend to pluck her eyes or tear her throat. Yanámari loosened the silver knife from its sheath, and drove the blade into a thin pale stick—the Nar'ath's greyish leg.

Claws loosened.

She yanked out the knife then thrust it upward into the creature's chest. Breath screamed from the hole, followed by a stream of foul, frothy lung blood covering her in a heavy, sticky blanket of stench.

The Sea Stone was heavier than the watcher expected.

Now he followed the searchers looking for the Dragon, the scrip bumping against his leg with bruising regularity. Every now and again, Fremmen or Warrten or one of the others would stop and look back, and he would halt, holding his breath. Climbing the ridges was the worst part, especially when he slipped on rivulets of melting snow, or when falls of loose rocks and dirt slid from under his feet.

And when the Nar'ath swooped from the northeast, he almost cried out. The other men cursed and drew their weapons, but the birds did not come nigh them. They debated whether or not to turn back to help their comrades or to press onward and find the Dragon. Argument grew fierce.

A sweet breeze wandered past. Faces lifted to catch the scent. Searchers forgot their sharp words and turned westward. Smoke rose. A shimmer of heat wavered against the setting sun.

At dusk they reached the bottom of the ridge where the fire burned. Above them, a woman and a child jumped up and down, waving their arms and shouting in Skardian.

The searchers reached the top, and the woman greeted them in a babble of tangled words, gesturing at the Dragon whose body lay coiled in a valley abundant with grass, trees, flowers. The silver sides scarce moved. One great eye showed a sliver of purple beneath glittering lid. A dull, tarnished substance crusted long tears in the scaled hide. One wound still oozed a slow pulse of fresh blood.

Grief bowed the watcher's head. He leaned his forehead against Áredan's shoulder, and wept for the destruction of valor and beauty, for the fruitless hope of escape by any other means than death, and he wept for Elta—in grief and in rage that the all-powerful Voice could have spoken a word and saved his love and the Dragon, but did not.

MY UNSEEN FRIEND. The mind-speech was groggy, faint.

He pushed back from Áredan. *You live.*

AYE. A LITTLE.

You are dying. You must not die.

A weary chuckle. *EVERY CREATURE DIES. EVEN DRAGONS.*

Fumbling the pearl as he might baked bread fresh from the coals, the watcher lifted Mahyla from the scrip. Her light blazed brighter than a thousand candles, brighter than the sun. The searchers, the Skardian woman, and the boy stared in open-mouthed awe.

So much for invisibility.

But the watcher heard the Voice. Starting with a puncture wound on the Dragon's neck, he held the Sea Stone close to the injury. All light and heat narrowed to a focused beam, and smoke rose from deep in the wound. Muscle and skin closed, new scales formed to replace the lost, and blood flamed and disintegrated into an ash so fine it disappeared as it fell away from the wound.

He moved along the Dragon's body, holding up the Stone to each injury, his arms growing tired and shaky before he reached the tail, then down the tail and up along the back.

All the while, the onlookers never spoke. They followed his progress, gathering with him on the other side as the watcher closed the last wound he could see. Perhaps there were more on the side where the Dragon lay, but those would have to wait until Áredan could move.

The little boy reached out a hand and ran his fingers along the new scales. The massive sides heaved a great sigh.

Mahyla's light dulled, but the watcher did not stow her away. Rather, he turned and looked toward the Dissonay. Warrten's narrowed eyes seemed to stare straight into his. Had the brilliant light exposed him?

"What magic is this," asked Warrten, "that the Sea Stone follows us all the way here, and of her own power?"

"I heard footsteps," said one of the men. "And breathing."

Fremmen nodded. "As did I."

Warrten stepped toward the watcher. "Who are you?"

Voice? Omwen'din? Help? The watcher thrust the Sea Stone back into his scrip and stepped backward until his head bumped against the Dragon.

YOU SAVED ME.

"Nay, not us," declared Warrten, still staring at where the watcher stood. "What is this magic?"

ALL WILL BE ANSWERED, IN TIME.

Warrten grunted. After one last long keen look, he turned from the watcher. Reaching as high as his height allowed, he trailed a large, scarred hand along the Dragon's side, tenderly, as one might touch the shoulder of a friend or the downy head of a child.

Hands resting on her son's shoulders, the woman asked, "Rubin?"

Warrten's brows rose. "Rubin Kyrinsson?"

Lips compressed but eyes eager, she nodded.

Warrten grinned. "Syra? Evan?"

Covering her mouth, she nodded again, tears spilling.

The watcher wept once more, not in grief but in a strange joy not his own.

IT IS NIGH DARK. Áredan's voice had regained its familiar command. COME, REST IN THE SHELTER OF MY WING. IT IS WARMER THERE.

The men shared their food with the woman and her son, and heard Syra tell—with the Dragon as translator—the story of how Rubin the woodcutter was falsely accused of burning wood from the king's forest, and of how Syra and her son escaped the city.

She worried for the men fighting the Nar'ath, and Áredan struggled to rise, but Warrten said, "They have fought Nar'ath before."

Fremmen gestured at the still-growing trees. "The Butcher will have another fine forest ere he wake in the morning." He grinned, picking dried meat from between his teeth. "Though I wager his whispery old counselor will take all the glory."

The boy, Evan, set a bit of food on a stone then turned his back. The watcher devoured the hard bread and gulped the cupful of water the child left casually on the ground.

Everyone settled down to sleep beneath the arching wing. As the watcher pillowed his head on the soft grass, the boy patted his shoulder. The watcher jerked away, looking up into wide, curious eyes that stared steadily into his.

58 ~ REUNION

Rope was tied around scrub trees and strung across the cut then hung with blankets. It was as much privacy as the Fourth could provide. Rather than changing her blood-fouled garments, however, Yanámari leaned behind a rock, vomiting what little there was in her stomach.

The injury to her head was dangerous, and Nar'ath blood obscured any other wounds there might be. Someone had to examine her. Gaerbith looked around. As a widower still in love with his wife, perhaps Turi could see a woman naked and not misbehave himself.

Gaerbith held out Yanámari's rucksack, but the big man shook his head—"She is not my betrothed"—and walked away, smiling.

Inside the cave, Owen lay on his side with a thick bandage around his upper torso, padding the deep grooves on his back. No fever manifested yet, though the wound was deep and Owen had lost much blood. The other wounded men, Dremm and Arn, twitched in restless sleep, skin hot but dry. There was no medicine. Gaerbith had already given them all the salve meant to soothe Kraekor's scars.

Stench clogged the air. Dead Nar'ath were stacked in untidy heaps out of sight beyond the cave's mouth. Nearby, a tattered blanket covered young Trag's corpse.

Gaerbith rubbed a hand over the ache in his thigh. Snow had begun falling after sundown. Drifts of it encroached the mouth of the cave. The store of twigs and dried scrub was meager. Cold might claim the Fourth long before hunger did.

He held up the rucksack and stared at it, steeling himself. Then he went to Yanámari. Slumped against the rock, she rinsed her mouth with snow then spit it out. She had scrubbed away the blood from her face, but it still coated her hair and neck, and spoiled her clothes.

"There are no buckets or cauldrons to melt snow for bathing."

She smiled wearily. "Cold may be just the thing."

"Wounds?"

"Everywhere hurts."

Gaerbith hesitated. "We have to shave your head."

Her shoulders drooped.

"And burn everything, even your boots."

"I cannot go barefoot."

"Trag's feet are a mite bigger than yours, but his boots are well made. Mind wearing a dead man's shoes?"

Tears glistened, and she turned her head.

He wished he could offer fine clothes, a good meal, a warm place to sleep. Instead, he must remove yet another piece of her old life, another sliver of dignity. She was a king's daughter, not a soldier, but even a seasoned warrior had limits.

He sharpened his knife, cut away locks until her hair stuck up in odd clumps and spikes, then shaved her head. She did not look at him, but tears dripped from her chin. A large bruised lump marred the back of her head, and she sucked in her breath as his blade scraped over it. Otherwise, she made no sound.

When the last of her hair lay in the snow, she looked vulnerable, like a new-hatched bird covered in soft black down.

Arm threaded through his to steady her, she walked with him to the blankets. He pushed them aside. The small fire was little more than a hint, but it gave more than enough light. He joined her behind the makeshift curtains, twitched them back into place, and cleared snow from a rock so the rucksack would not become wet and soak the clothing inside.

The cold was biting. Yanámari shivered, but unbuckled her belt and pulled off the torn tunic. Gaerbith helped remove the chain mail, and then turned as she peeled away the padded vest beneath, and the rest of her blood-soaked garments. Her teeth chattered, and she laughed a little.

"You have to look, captain."

Before he did, he scraped up handfuls of snow, and the added chill cooled his thoughts.

She presented her back to him. As he cleaned away crusted blood on her upper arm, exposing a ridged slash, she said between chatters and stutters, "All that power, and the healing still leaves a scar."

"There is healing of the moment," he repeated Cayn's words from distant memory, "and there is healing that takes time. I may walk with a limp until the day I die—but I walk."

His words were stronger than he. What of the wounds to her heart and mind, the griefs she did not speak?

He scrubbed snow along her skin, from head to heel, and his hands soon grew numb.

She was covered in bruises and scrapes, and punctures marred her limbs and torso where Nar'ath claws had dug deep. Nothing bled, however, and there were no other injuries. Great tremors shook her, and pale skin glowed fiery red, rubbed raw by the snow.

He stepped back and turned. She would have to remove the rest of the blood herself.

After a few moments, "F-F-F-F-Finished," she said, and even that one word shivered.

He handed her the rucksack then ducked around a blanket, removed the boots from Trag's feet, and brought them back to Yanámari. She wore a long, plain gown of thick wool.

He set the boots by the fire. "Wear an extra pair of socks, if you have them."

Using his arm to steady herself, she donned socks and boots then stomped her feet, perhaps as much to chase away cold as to settle the boots.

He pulled down the blankets and wrapped them both around her shoulders. She stepped inside his arms, and it seemed natural to hold her close until the tremors calmed. She turned her head, resting a cheek against his shoulder.

Turi stepped out of the cave and looked their way.

"Go inside, my lady," Gaerbith murmured. "I will be there soon."

Turi came down the cut to meet her.

Gaerbith untied and coiled the rope, then he scattered the remaining coals, dousing the fire, and brought the rope and the rucksack. He dropped them inside the cave.

The men huddled at the back, near the wounded. Exhaustion drew lines on their faces and set their eyes deep in shadowed sockets. Like he, they were loathe to lie down on the chill stone floor, or perhaps their muscles were too knotted with shivering to allow them rest. No one spoke.

A watch had been set at the cave's mouth, and the horses were arrayed there, an added guard against the cold. Every few minutes or so, someone gave a little water to the wounded and checked their bandages.

Still wrapped in the blankets, Yanámari huddled just beyond the others, near a dying fire. He pulled his cloak around himself and sat beside her. She stirred, shifting her shoulder then settling against him with a small sigh. He smoothed her downy head, and rested his cheek against it.

Her body eased, and her eyes closed.

He sat long awake and studied the fire.

She woke near dawn, when the world still wore a cloak of grey and the sun had not yet begun to dull the chill edge of waning night. Her whole body ached, and a large lump throbbed at the back of her head.

One arm still around her shoulders, Gaerbith sat with right leg stretched out but left knee raised. He kneaded the thigh muscles of the outstretched leg and winced.

Cold overtook her, and she shivered.

"Are you well?" he asked in Skardian.

"A skirmish engages in my head, and my entire body aches, but, compared to poor Trag—" She pushed herself upright, and his arm slid away from her shoulders.

Across the fire, Turi tugged his beard, a smile pulling at his mouth.

Yanámari gripped the blankets tight around her. "You would be right, captain, to wish I had stayed in Elycia."

His brows lowered. "Nay, my lady, I do not wish it."

Even as a pleasant warmth crept along her skin, Gaerbith added, "Were you a man, you would make a fine addition to the Fourth."

She opened her mouth to speak, but had no words. Turi snorted.

"No, my lady, I— I mean no discourtesy—"

Then, clamping his lips shut, Gaerbith slapped her knife, sheath and all, into her hand. The knife had been cleaned, but the sheath still bore smears of dark blood.

Turi folded his arms, teeth gleaming behind his beard. Heat flooded Yanámari, and her face flushed.

Gaerbith stood, and limped toward a fire around which lay three men, each wrapped in several blankets; some among the Fourth had slept cold yesternight. He took from his rucksack two books bound in supple leather, a pot of ink, and a pointed stick, its tip shaped like the nib of a quill. Sitting beside his brother, he opened one book, dipped the stick into the ink, and wrote, unhurried and deliberate.

"He records the names of the men lost when we fled Elycia," Turi said. "We once had an old shield with the names carved on it, but that was destroyed in the last night of battle, before the Butcher—uh, King Morfran—retreated."

"How many names are in that book?"

"I doubt even the captain knows."

"If I had known what destruction—"

"Those who died came to Elycia of their own will, knowing the danger. The three lads there? They lived through the night and will likely grow to be old men, so no tears for them."

Yanámari struggled to her feet, but her head spun and her knees wobbled. Turi gripped her elbow.

"I tell ye true, m'lady. Yer not alone in this ailment." He chuckled. "I never saw the captain so unsteady on his feet—and I do not mean his wound."

Again her face grew hot. There was no use pretending she did not understand his meaning.

"Y'chose well," and his bluff practicality removed any shame.

His face grew somber. "Edwig, my wife, made the worst socks a man ever wore. My sister used to secretly unravel and reknit every one she could find. Saved my feet, I tell ye. Sister sent me a new pair. Last winter, it was. My daughter made 'em. Fine work." He cleared his throat, ran his fist along his chin. "Never wore 'em yet."

They stood a while in silence, morning light expanding, breeze quickening, bringing with it the Nar'ath stench. There was nothing with which to set the dead alight.

Yanámari glanced back. Captain Gaerbith still crouched beside the wounded. He had set aside the journal and now he read from the other book.

"My lady," said Turi, "what is it ye do not ask?"

Looking up, Gaerbith watched the two figures standing near the cave's mouth. When Turi placed a hand on Yanámari's shoulder, something ugly lashed Gaerbith's thoughts. It bewildered him. Why did it matter whom she befriended?

She made him uncomfortable, like a new woolen shirt on his back, creating an itch that no amount of reaching or contorting could quite scratch.

His hand clenched.

The kiss in the grotto—

Only a kiss.

He was Gaerbith tha Forba, captain of the Fourth Lachmil. She was Yanámari, Lady of Skarda and kinswoman to the king of Disson. *There can never be anything between us.*

He put away the log and opened the second book, most of its pages stiff and bubbled from being dropped in the sea many years ago, and a subtle salty smell permeated them. The inks had not run, however, and the illuminated letters marking each new portion were still vibrant, the gilt still glittering. A brittle blade of grass marked his place. In the pale light, he read the first line of *The Historie of Kel.*

In the darkness of the Prymmiddion Age,
when clan fought clan and chaos ruled,
Dragons broke their bond with Men.

With the words came images from dreams and memory: the standing stones on the edge of the heights, the words flying like golden daggers from the book, the bloody warrior who flailed him with urgent pleas to find the Kel-child. He pushed aside those images and read onward, from *Attor Dragonking, a vile creature, worst of his brethren, plagued the people for generations but did not utterly consume them,* until *Kel returned to the mountain to face the Dragon,* just before the legendary battle in which the sword Azrin— Asryn, in the text—slew the Dragonking.

"Captain," came a weak voice.

Closing the book, he looked down, smiling. "Welcome back."

A grimace contorted Owen's face. "No—breath."

Gaerbith tossed back the blankets and tugged at the bandage around Owen's torso. His fingers slid easily under the snug rags. They did not prevent Owen breathing. Troubled, he eased the lad upright, and leaned him back against his chest. The heat of fever burned through the layers of thick cloth.

"Brother." Owen's head lolled against Gaerbith's shoulder, and his eyes closed. "Never told us how Mother. Died. Came home without—

without—"

Without her body.

His father had understood. Gaerbith returned alone, ragged, wounds still raw, but Forba embraced him, gaze filled with mingled compassion and grief. In following days, the two of them walked the Thynathel Hills, their words few. It had been some comfort to the lad of thirteen summers and, perhaps, to Father as well.

"Not highwaymen."

"Nay, Owen, not highwaymen."

Owen slumped, sliding to the side, but Gaerbith caught him with an arm around his middle.

"Cayn. Keepers. All of them. Bright and rising. Children in father's arms."

Throat tight, Gaerbith nodded. "Just so."

On the Isle of Morga in the Dävra Sea lived followers of Omwen'din. They guarded a vast warren of caves filled with treasures of art and scholarship, all manner of crafts and knowledge, hidden in the low, rugged mountains covered in trees and crowned in bare stone. Gaerbith had been meant to become a student there, leaving Uártha's tutelage for Cayn's.

In a small meadow one day, on the lower slope of a mountain, he sprawled, eating an apple, reading, when a man wearing a grey hooded robe and bearing a pale carven staff demanded the whereabouts of the woman who had given him the book. Not waiting an answer, the man attacked. Not an hour later, the book floated in the sea, and Mother was dead.

Owen coughed. Blood flecked the corners of his mouth.

Tugging on a cleanish corner of his tunic, Gaerbith wiped his brother's mouth. "Should have stayed home."

"Would have come anyway."

"Always were stubborn that way."

"Learned it from you."

Teeth clenched, Gaerbith turned his head.

Yanámari looked over her shoulder. Tears stung his eyes. He could not meet her gaze.

"If you stay here," said Owen, "you are in the wrong place."

"You should rest."

Owen whispered a laugh. His thin hand grabbed the loose folds of Gaerbith's tunic. "Go."

Yanámari stood alone. Her expression faltered then her head dipped. After a moment, she turned and left the cave.

Ren whickered at her approach. He stepped forward, extending his glossy neck and bumping her chest with his nose.

"Your Majesty." Yanámari smoothed his forelock. "You greet all females so familiar?"

He chuffed, his breath warm on her cheek.

"I wish you could speak to me as you do the Dragon."

His long lashes brushed her neck.

"I thought Elycia a prison, but were I there again, these men might not be in danger, and you might be in your warm stable."

Ren shook his mane.

"Too much self-pity?" She patted his neck. "I quite agree."

Saddles, blankets, and bags were piled just inside the cave. She found Ren's gear and draped across his back a scarlet blanket edged in gold. Then she took a brush from his saddlebags and ran it along his sides. The action pushed blood into her arms and cold-clumsy fingers, warming them a little.

"Is there a fine-stepping mare back in Elycia or the provinces, mourning your absence? Any foals? Hmm?"

Ren stamped, nodding.

Yanámari chuckled. "I thought as much."

He tossed his head. She gentled her brushing.

"Three days I have known him. Three days. Yet I speak to you because I cannot speak to him."

Hair wild, garments stained and torn, standing at a distance, the captain appeared no taller or broader than any other man. Next to her he seemed powerful, shoulders wide, stance strong. He did not seem a man who needed the help of anyone, let alone the aid of Omwen'din.

He had not taken the Keeper's oath, but he would. Soon. "He argues with Omwen'din," Turi had said when she asked about Gaerbith and his god. "Who but a Keeper would dare such a thing?"

Who but a Keeper would proclaim a power beyond himself? Heolstor and his minions claimed to serve a great and fearsome master, but they were absorbed in forwarding themselves, in establishing place and strength. Keepers served an opposing master. What it must be like, believing a being of unfathomable power was one's friend and defender?

When Gaerbith faced Heolstor again—if he faced him—would that power come to his aid, or was the Voice merely myth, an invention of Men so they need not feel alone in the world?

The captain exchanged a few words with a soldier then stepped into the cut. He walked a short distance downhill, his steps muffled in the snow. "My lady?" Even softly spoken, his words echoed.

On the other side of Ren, she stilled. The horse looked back, as if asking why she stopped brushing him.

Why could she not answer the captain? Where fled their easy conversation? The camaraderie after he saved her from the magic of the Black Hoods, when they fought off the wolves and escaped through the hidden passage?

What had changed?

She ran a hand over her shorn head. Everything had changed.

She tilted her head to watch Gaerbith from under Ren's neck. Kraekor picked his way among stones, neck stretching toward his master, who patted the horse's scarred withers.

"Where is she, old fellow?"

Kraekor shoved the captain's shoulder then nosed along his tunic and lipped at the scrip on his belt, searching.

"No more apples. Perhaps when we reach the foothills, eh?"

It was a good voice, neither as husky as Turi's growl nor as crisp as Arien's precise speech, but as Gaerbith uttered nothings to his beloved warhorse, Yanámari leaned her brow against Ren's neck and closed her eyes, wrapped in that voice.

Then she straightened. She was behaving worse than Elta swooning over Imre— No.

She untangled one more knot in Ren's mane, then stored the brush in the bags and ducked under his chin. "Captain."

Gaerbith looked over the backs of the horses. "My lady."

Words refused to leave her mouth.

His brows twitched downward. "My lady?"

"Tell me— Please, tell me of the Kels."

"A long story, and sad."

"We are here one more day at least, and there is little else to do."

"Aye. Shall we go inside? Near a fire?"

"I would rather be here, in the light."

He chose a wide stone, brushed it free of snow, helped her climb to sit on it, and adjusted the blanket she had pinned across her shoulders with a borrowed broach.

He stepped back, and canted his weight to his left leg. "In the Skardian archives, are there no scrolls telling of the Betrayal and the fall of the House of Kel?"

"The archives reveal only what the Brethren wish revealed, or what previous kings did not burn or order rewritten. I know the House of Kel still exists, though scattered, and that every Skardian king since the Betrayal has sought their destruction."

"What do you know of the sword Azrin?"

"Heolstor seeks it, as does my father, but even if they find Azrin, neither of them can touch it."

"Aye. It is made of etherium. Only a true Kel may wield the sword." He looked at her. "You are part Kel."

"But only part, and that part so thin it might not exist. Too many generations intermingling have diluted it to nothing."

"Diluted or no, there is greatness in your heritage."

Greatness? Ha. Greed and murder, more like.

He hoisted himself up to sit beside her, and his shoulder touched hers. For a time, he neither moved nor spoke.

"My father was a steward in a noble house," he said at last, "and loved from afar his master's wife. She was not wanton, and she sent him away.

"Father wandered from village to village, training horses and doing whatever work he could put his hand to. Mother was a Keeper. She delivered messages and hid Kels. One night she was too late, and watched from a distance as Skardian soldiers burned a Kellish village in the Calhoun Forest."

"But the Calhoun is in the Territories, not in Skarda. Why—"

"An invisible boundary stops no one."

Aye, but invisible boundaries can still imprison.

He shifted, and his shoulder leaned against hers, the rings of his armor a pressing weight. She did not protest. It was comfort.

Gaerbith continued, voice gruff at the edges. "She stood on the Highlands and cried out to the Voice. He trusted her with great knowledge, but warned her it could not be revealed before due time. Then she traveled north to the Dävra Sea, and there she met Forba, my father. After hearing her story, he was so fearful for her safety that he hid her in the Grimë Mountains. And she let him. What brought them to marriage—a beautiful woman with a mission, and a broken man without a future?"

"Perhaps she was weary of protecting everyone else, and welcomed his shoulder to lean on. Even Keepers must grow tired. Perhaps, through their troubles, your parents understood one another."

Sun gleamed over the snowy ridges, long fingers of light scooping handfuls of diamonds. Yanámari closed her eyes against the blinding glitter and lifted her face. Faint warmth touched her brow. Almost she could forget Arien was dead or that she had killed.

Almost.

The captain leapt from the rock. "You asked about the House of Kel, my lady, and I have told you nothing. Wait here."

He brought back a scarf that he draped over her head and wrapped around her throat, and an old book. Then he took his place beside her, and opened to a slightly buckled page.

In the darkness of the Prymmiddion Age,
when clan fought clan and chaos ruled,
Dragons broke their bond with Men.

As he translated the ancient words, the men came closer until they filled the space between the rock and the cave, listening in silence until the end.

On the day the Kels fled was Adwr's family slain, and Azrin
stolen from the dead king's hand. Even now, the one proof of true
sovereignty remains lost.

The last words echoed into silence.

Then, slowly, he closed the book and looked into each man's face. "You have come far, and of your own choosing. You walked into the very den of Bachaná, and laughed in the teeth of wolves. You withstood greater numbers, a fell magic, and the Nar'ath, you lost comrades and kindred, but you fought well."

There were cleared throats and shifted stances, and a few crossed arms.

"Some served Disson longer than I, yet accepted me as captain. Even when I dreamed dark dreams and spoke strange things, still you followed me. For that, I am grateful." He took a deep breath. "Once we reach the foothills, Turi will be—"

A vast shadow rippled across the slopes and wheeled overhead. Men grabbed their weapons and took positions. Drawing his sword, Gaerbith pushed Yanámari from the stone, and she landed in a heap behind him.

"Oh, no you do not, captain," she muttered, unsheathing the silver knife. "You do not keep me from the fight."

"Stay back, my lady."

She flipped back the blanket, freeing her arms. "With all courtesy, Captain Gaerbith, no."

Turi hunched one shoulder, popping his neck, and grinned at her, his axe at the ready.

Glancing at him, Gaerbith frowned.

The shadow returned, sweeping an arc from north and west, bringing with it the scent of fresh grass and spring.

"Áredan!" Rubin shouted, waving his arms.

Indeed, it was. After another swooping circle, the Dragon glided down into the narrow space between the ridges, alighting on the two largest stones and folding his wings neatly to his sides. Whoops and laughter rose behind him, and familiar faces peered around his massive neck and from among the spines above his brow. The Fourth sheathed their weapons and ran to greet their comrades, calling out jests and good-natured threats to the men sliding from the Dragon's back. Gaerbith crossed his arms, watching with a grin, his golden beard and shaggy hair almost hiding his eyes.

A sturdy little boy ran to Rubin, laughing, burying his face against his father's neck. Rubin clutched him close, saying his name over and over.

Áredan reached over his shoulder and lifted down a woman in a faded brown cloak and missing one shoe. She stood staring at Rubin with an expression between tears and joy.

The woodcutter rose slowly to his feet.

"See, Mama?" Evan bounced. "Papa lives!"

Yanámari slammed her knife into the sheath. Turning from the happy meeting, she returned to the horses, and leaned her head once more against Ren's warm neck.

Familiar footsteps crunched behind her, but she did not turn.

After a long silence, Gaerbith left.

59 ~ ASHES

Servants spread cloths on the tables in the great hall, set out candelabra, lit torches, replenished candlestands.

The king's steward approached Rhôn almost on tiptoe, right eye twitching. Gwar whispered, "Commander, have you seen the queen anywhere about?"

Rhôn shook his head, and almost cursed Gwar for making a nervous show. He pitied the man, but he was trying not to call attention to himself, standing half-hidden behind an arras.

"She is angry, to say the least," Gwar continued, "and now the kitchen cannot make the dish she requires. We are short on honey, and she wants sweetcakes."

Rhôn shifted so one shoulder leaned against the wall, putting the steward at his back. Gwar continued his whispered complaint, but Rhôn heard only his voice, not the words.

The queen entered the hall. Black garments floated around her like gossamer razors, each hem gleaming with a slender edge. Unbound raven hair hung down her back. In one hand she held a boll of carded wool, and with the other hand she twisted the wool through her long fingers. Grey thread wound around the spindle spinning near her feet.

The steward gasped and scampered away.

The queen looked around at the servants bowed low in the midst of their tasks, waiting her command. "The king departs at dawn for the Lowlands and war. All menservants are required immediately in the Court of Soldiers. Women, finish here then go to the chambers of Lord Arien and Lady Yanámari, and remove all bed coverings, curtains, garments—everything—and burn them outside the walls. Whatever will not burn, take to the House of the Brethren. The Hôk Nar have ways of disposing what mere mortals cannot."

She paused, but the servants did not move. "Do you not hear me? Go!"

Servants scattered.

Rhôn waited until Queen Una's attention turned elsewhere before moving out from his hiding place and stepping into the corridor.

The Lowlands? War?

Morfran had declared his intention of leading a small troop to pursue Yanámari and bring her back. Unless she and the Dissonay had suddenly grown wings, they were still somewhere in the Craydaeg Mountains, nowhere near the Lowlands.

Rhôn smiled—King and queen in disagreement? Excellent!—then he frowned. Perhaps plans had changed. Perhaps the king's mind was even less his own than it was before he freed the queen.

Heolstor led the way through the empty dungeon lit by smoky torches made of bone and rendered fat, set in sockets on walls streaked with damp and moss and the rusty smears of old blood. Chains and shackles dangled from iron rings in cell ceilings and walls; doors stood wide. From a square pit in the center of the dungeon steamed malodorous fumes.

Rhôn trailed the small party, reluctant to be here at all.

The Master of the Hôk Nar halted beside the pit and looked into it. "Smell them. The younglings are restless. Ready for battle."

"Are they as tractable as your beloved Nar'ath?" Queen Una sounded amused, derisive, seductive. "Your crows failed, Heolstor. They followed their own appetites, and thought armed Men easier prey than a wounded Dragon."

Heolstor growled under his breath.

"Outram their leader is dead, and the Nar'ath do not follow your commands quite so well." Una laughed. "Yet you seek to command Dragons. How ambitious of you."

The old man whirled, his staff raised like a sword, and thrust it in her direction. "I will not suffer mockery from a so-called sorceress who could not free herself from a flimsy tower filled with windows!"

Una hissed. Morfran stared straight ahead, blank-faced, stiff.

Heolstor had not moved a step yet he loomed, a misshapen shadow elongating against a distant wall. He clutched a bronze disc in his bone-thin fingers, and held it over the pit. Light flared in the depths. Smoke coiled, and the stench of brimstone strengthened. Rhôn clapped a hand over his nose and mouth.

From the pit rose a small bronze Dragon. Its wings were like translucent metal yet with the nature of fine cloth, folding then billowing as they lifted the creature into the dungeon. Its eyes gleamed blue, and its talons dug into the wood as it perched on a headsman's block.

The smell of sulfur retreated, and Rhôn uncovered his face, breathing the faint scent of something not quite definable but welcome, like the warmth of baked bread.

"He is of the So'Len, gentlest clan among the Dragonkin." Heolstor looked on the creature as a father might look on his child. "Fredeks are scholarly, So'Lens cultivate the arts, but Gremians love war. He is first of the captured So'Len to kill another Dragon, proof the gentlest mind can be turned."

"You summoned an infant Dragon. Hail the great Heolstor, servant of Nar Cahm."

Fire spurted from the youngling's jaws, and searing heat banishing for an instant the wet chill lurking in the dungeon.

"Show me a full-grown Dragon whose mind is yours, and I will acknowledge your superior skills, Heolstor." Una's amusement flattened to scorn. "Ah, but the king of the Gremian kindred is fled, as is a Fredek warrior. Now no will opposes your own. Save mine."

Rhôn stepped back, recoiling from the hatred blazing in the counselor's eyes.

Heolstor pointed his staff toward a dark corridor at the back of the dungeon. The Dragon's bright blue eyes blinked, then the So'len fanned its wings and glided down from the block. Wings folded close to its sides, it walked into the corridor, tail dragging behind.

"You will regret this day."

Again Una laughed. "Until that day—"

She placed a hand on her husband's arm, and empty-eyed Morfran strode past Rhôn.

At the dungeon's iron door, Rhôn looked over his shoulder. A faint gleam of bronze retreated deep into the dark.

Hours later, Rhôn sealed the last of the letters to the barons then lifted his signet from the warm red wax. The weight of the family mark felt awkward on his finger. Since joining the Young Wolves, he had worn the ring on a chain around his neck.

The mark encompassed a craggy mountain guarded by an ash tree and an arrow. Embroidered on cloth or painted on wood, the mountain would be white, the ash green, and the arrow fledged in blue, but the ring was dull silver, heavy and old, and it left a soft impression in the cooling wax, the mountain's peak rounded and the arrow's tip blunted. Nevertheless, the seal of his house would not be mistaken, and the orders it concealed would be obeyed.

Sliding the last letter into a small leather cylinder, he pushed the toggle through a loop, securing the lid, then he swept his arm across the table, tumbling all the messenger cases into a cloth sack.

A servant leapt to his summons, bowed at the waist, and waited before him with lowered gaze.

"Take these to the rookery, and tell the Brethren to deliver one to each baron." Rhôn handed him the sack. "To the barons, mind, not their provincial seats." The barons were still journeying, having been gone from Elycia only one day. "Royal orders must be answered immediately."

"At once, commander." The servant bowed again then turned, the bag bouncing against his shoulder as he ran.

Rhôn rolled the length of sealing wax into its oiled wrapping then snuffed the stub of candle. He placed both items on a tray, along with a pot of ink, the leftover parchment pieces, and the used quills in need of sharpening.

A servant could have been called to clean up after him, to toss the quill trimmings in the fire, but Rhôn was restless now that the dispatches were done. He watched the bits of feather shaft curl in the flames. He had become like those twisted bits—his senses, his thinking, the very ground beneath him deformed by what he did not understand.

Una was so like her daughter in appearance that, if the queen remained silent, he could almost imagine Yanámari had never left. Yanámari's power had not come from magic or manipulation, but Una seemed to use no other kind. When the queen spoke now, her voice held no music, as it had in the King's Keep, but seemed a sharp north wind that set chimes jangling, dissonant and cold.

When Morfran freed her, his sword had severed more than just Heolstor's will. It had cut the bonds holding back a far greater power.

Rhôn picked up the tray. With any good fortune, the queen would not snare the barons. The words he had written were hers, but his own mingled among them, perhaps lessening her magic: Gather new armies, collect more taxes, appoint additional magistrates and constables to oversee the populace who might become unruly under this heavier hand—but do it quietly. Wait for further word from the king's commander. Only then should the barons send conscripts to the Lowlands or taxes to Elycia.

No need to alert Disson, Rhôn had written, *that the war is far from over.*

He thrust the tray of writing implements at a passing servant and strode from the tower to the wall. Chill night air caught in the back of his throat. Rhôn nodded curtly to the captain of the guard, who bowed in return, and he walked along the top of the wall, the torchlit perimeter between the city and the cliffs, until he reached the corner nearest Brona's Veil. An errant breeze dampened his face with spray from the waterfall.

His fists clenched on the parapet. This was not the life of a soldier. Writing letters and waiting. Constant dull headaches. Separation from himself. King dominated by an ancient menace warring with the queen for power. Friends dead. No army.

No army but untried servants, Heolstor's Brethren, and an unruly, unpredictable clutch of Dragon young.

When the neighboring baron reached home, what would he tell Rhôn's father of all that happened? Berg, once a great mountain of a man, had been too ill to go to battle. He might be proud of a son risen to the rank of king's commander, but what glory was there in a commander without an army?

Pushing away from the parapet, Rhôn descended the rough stair leading from the wall to Yanámari's garden. A Brother of the Black Hood found him there, pacing the dark grotto, and delivered a message: It was done. The Nar'ath were away, the letters sent.

Rhôn stood long in thought.

No going back.

The king read the dispatch then crumpled it in his fist.

"My lord?" asked the scribe at the table. "Is there a response?"

Morfran shoved the small rumpled scroll at him. "You know

Captain Nelek's hand. Did this come from his pen?"

The old man smoothed the thin parchment, made not of calfskin but of tree bark beaten into almost transparent sheets by some magic of the Black Hoods. He glanced at the cramped, almost childlike, writing blotted with ink and filled with scratched out sentences, as if the author had been of several minds about what to write.

To Morfran, King of Skarda

Brother Fasolt is dead, slain by a Kellish smith. The Kel escaped. We will find him.

The serving girl Maggie is dead. My lord's cousin, Baron Markha, has been avenged. Lord Ûtgar, son of Baron Markha, is dead.

Dera Dragonqueen is fearsome, but what good is a Dragon whose fire has no power to kill the king's enemy? I do not trust her.

I bring you etherium, my lord, fashioned by the Kellish smith into a Northman's bracelet. Teag the spy believes the Kel will find Azrin the lost sword.

Shall I kill him?

Written by my own hand
Nelek, captain of the king's men

What had happened to alter Nelek's firm bold script into this wavering scrawl? There was something almost challenging in the tone of the message, something subtle but no longer subservient. The dispatch might not have come from the captain at all but for certain phrases and the enigmatic, bloodthirsty question at the end.

"It is Captain Nelek's, my lord."

The king dismissed the Black Hood, who bowed and left. The scribe waited.

Morfran lifted a hand and touched the garland of skin patches above the fireplace. "Scribe, record the letter into the royal archive. Take the original to Commander Rhôn. Say nothing to anyone, especially Queen Una."

"Yes, my lord."

"And send this reply to Captain Nelek: *If the smith dies—* No. No, do not threaten. Write this: *The blacksmith is to be preserved at all costs. If he is not—* No need to write more."

How was that not a threat?

The scribe did not speak his question but obeyed, writing the brief message to Captain Nelek then copying the original dispatch while the king paced before the fire, drank from the jug of wine, and sometimes muttered. The wolves lay beside his chair, watching him. The more he drank, the more Morfran's boots scuffed along the floor, and the more he reached out to caress the branded scraps of skin.

How had young Imre borne this?

The old scribe had been in Elycia since his sons were taken into the king's army, but for many years before then he had served in the house of a baron who believed a man might be safe from Morfran's meddling if he remained as quiet as possible and sent the taxes and conscripts on time. Such a strategy had worked—but only as long as the baron lived. His son, bolder in manner and tongue, had angered the king and been executed. His family exiled, all property and servants were forfeit to Morfran.

So the scribe had made the long journey to Elycia. Once undergoing the mind molding of the Black Hoods, he was not supposed to have a name. The rite had not held. He learned to erase from his mind anything that might tell Heolstor that all was not as it should be.

He had lived a long life. His sons were gone. Why not let Heolstor know the truth? But something inside him refused to give way.

He set aside the copy, tucked the original and the sealed message for Captain Nelek inside his tunic, stood, bowed to the king who barely acknowledged him, and set out to find Commander Rhôn.

He had scarce stepped out the door when another Black Hood strode around the corner with yet another dispatch, this one inside a small, cylindrical case. The Hood swept past the scribe and into the king's chamber. The scribe followed.

"Message from Captain Nelek, my lord," the Brother said with a bow, offering the case.

Morfran looked up from his contemplation of the floor but did not take the message. "Read it to me."

The Black Hood reached in to draw out the contents then shrieked, dropping the case.

It rolled toward the fire. The wolves leapt up, growling. The Brother clutched his arm. It smoked and disintegrated into ash. For an instant, it seemed the burning had ceased, that only the monk's hand would be consumed, then—with a crumpling sigh—his robe fluttered to the ground, empty but for ashes.

Morfran stumbled sideways as the scroll case burst asunder in the flames behind him. A blue arm cuff rolled from the fire, glowing as if lit from within. Then, as if it were a candle snuffed, the blue disappeared, and the cuff appeared to be dull silver.

The king tipped back his head, black beard pointing to the sky, and laughed. "Teag, you wonderful spy! You have done it! Proof at last."

Coarse fabric rustled over the stones and a musty-sweet smell curled around the scribe. Heolstor walked past him and stood staring down at the empty robe for a long silence, then looked toward the king. "What happened here? What took this Brother? I felt its power."

"If you would defeat the last of the Kels"—Morfran nudged the bracelet with the toe of his boot—"I suggest you make haste."

Anger rolled out of Heolstor with such force the old scribe shrank against the wall.

"Your pardon, Longbeard. I forgot." The king donned his gauntlets. "Even if you do find the lost sword, you cannot make it shine. Pity."

"One day, my lord, you will repent your words, but by then your kingdom will belong to another, and your life will be at an end. She protects you now—it is the only reason you still live—but, ere you die, you will see another wear the Dragon crown."

Morfran squatted beside the hearth and picked up the bracelet between thumb and forefinger, turning it this way and that, letting light gleam along its edges. Then he smiled. Stood. Chuckled. Caressed the metal with his gloved hands.

Threw the bracelet.

Heolstor spun, swinging his staff. The bracelet glanced from the pale wood, careened off the king's chair, caught the end of the staff— slid to a stop against Heolstor's skeletal hand.

A white spark leapt, but no flames ignited.

Heolstor stared at the darkness licking like tongues of fire along his fingers. "No. No."

He tried to brush it away by flapping his hand, but the darkness parted only for a moment.

"No. You did not think this. You thought—" He looked at Morfran in blank puzzlement. "You thought about Lord Arien. Lady Yanámari.

Not about the bracelet."

King Morfran smiled. "You are right about the Dragon crown. I will not wear it again. Nor will anyone else. Your reign is ended."

Darkness rose to Heolstor's chest.

The stones beneath the scribe's feet trembled. He fell back against the open door then forward to his knees. More than the floor began to shake. Small objects teetered, and the king's chair vibrated sideways.

Heolstor lifted, darkness swirling around him like fingers of the Void, drawing into itself. The staff dropped, bounced—first one end, then the other—and clattered to a stop against the legs of the scribe's table. The counselor opened his mouth, but no sound came. His long white beard blackened, curling away to nothing. Smoke coiled his throat and head.

The pillar of darkness spun, contracting into an orb so dense it sucked light inside itself. It gathered speed, power. Shutters tore away from windows, but even the starglow reflecting on the snowfields of Mount Cathál did not penetrate the chamber.

Fire leapt from the hearth, twining the spinning ball in ribbons of flame and ash until all fire was gone, absorbed into the dark.

The scribe scrabbled backward against the pull. He clutched the crossbar on the door, slid it into its cradle, and hung on with both arms. His feet then his legs swept out from under him until his body floated straight out, pointing toward the orb. Sharp pain and a sudden looseness in one shoulder—his arm yanked out of joint.

Morfran flew across the chamber, slamming into the wall between the windows. He pulled himself upright, reached backward, and gripped the outer lip of a window ledge, planting his legs wide and his heels against the wall, but even the king's bulk could not keep his feet on the floor.

Whining, the wolves slid, claws groping for purchase, their gleaming metal-tipped fur standing on end. They careened around the room, smashing against airborne furniture and colliding with one another. The massive bed moved sideways, sliding toward the center.

The orb decreased in size, shrinking until it was no larger than a fist. Chips of old stone and mortar created dusty tangles around it, and other loose items, including the wolves, swirled until soon every flying thing became part of the whirlwind.

All sound ceased—except the roaring of blood in the scribe's ears—and there was no scent but the crisp tang of cold air stripped clean.

Strings of light arced then ribbons of dark, rising from the surface of the orb as if struggling to be free, thick threads yanking themselves out of impenetrable fabric. One strand of light ripped loose, transforming into a translucent shape, a brief ghost. It tore away from the vortex, spun upward with pallid arms outstretched, then vanished. A black form followed—transparent, like a film of smoke—and spiraled outward, mouth opened in a silent howl, then darted out the window.

And so it went—how long, the scribe could not tell—bright souls and dark peeling away from the remains of Heolstor, lives he had taken over centuries in his quest for immortality now abandoning him on their journeys to the Otherland or the Void.

As each soul left, the orb lost a little more of its power. When the scribe's feet skimmed the floor, the sensation was so startling he almost let go of the crossbar.

The last soul filled the chamber with pristine light, a star in an empty sky.

This soul lingered, its brilliance humming in the air like a song held in the back of the throat, and there was such a look of joy, relief, and longing on the shimmering face that the scribe wished he saw what it saw. When the soul rose and vanished, the room seemed blacker than the orb.

The fist of darkness spun faster and faster, once more pulling the scribe's feet off the floor. Just when the pain was too great and his strength almost gone, the ball exploded—a ring of force, blacker than black, a wave of power and sound shocking his chest, his ears, slamming his head against the door.

Smells flooded the air: smoke and fire, metal and brimstone, decay and old incense. But only for an instant. Almost as soon as the darkness sprang outward, it sucked back into itself and was gone. No residue remained.

The scribe let go of the crossbar and sat cradling his dislocated arm. He should be writhing in pain, but exhaustion sublimated all. He looked around the room. Darkness had imprinted itself on the very walls, in the remaining bits of furniture, the old wooden chest, the king's mail armor. He brushed the floor with his fingertips. The stones were not charred and coated with ashes, but swept clean, the sulky color at one with the rock. Even his skin, once pale from lack of sun, seemed burnt. Only Heolstor's staff remained pale, somehow untouched and anchored to the floor.

Groaning, Morfran pushed himself upright, touched the back of his head, and laughed.

He stood, still laughing, picked up the staff from where it had come to rest against the fireplace, and used it to lift down each end of the garland of dried skin, tumbling it to the hearth. He propped the staff against the wall, picked up the strand—twice as long as he was tall—and looped it around his neck into a loose necklace of many strands.

Pain took the scribe, and he groaned.

"Ah," said the king. "Still here?"

He squatted before the scribe, grasped the injured arm, gripped the shoulder, twisted and pushed. A stab of breath-stealing pain, then relief. Morfran dusted his hands and stood. "Well, scribe, off with you. Messages and all that—"

The old scribe struggled to his feet and bowed."Thank you, my lord."

The bracelet lay inside the scorched circle where Heolstor had stood in his last moments. The king crouched beside it, folded his gloved hands, and looked long at the armband.

"So, Captain Nelek. You thought I would put my hand in to remove the dispatch. You thought to kill me." He picked it up and stood. "Well, now. Is my spy in league with you? Or do you act alone?"

With a low sound deep in his throat, he closed his fist around the cuff as if he could crush it, then shoved it into the scrip on his belt.

The crossbeam on the chamber's heavy oaken door flew back from its cradle and crashed to the floor. The door swung open as if flung by a giant. Triumphant laughter entered the room with the swish of soft garments and the crisp fragrance of snow and pine. Queen Una stood before the king.

"You destroyed my enemy. My gratitude knows no bounds." She stepped toward the dazed king, reaching out one slim hand to touch the gruesome necklace. "I will help you capture the Kel you seek, husband. But first"—she took Morfran's hand and led him toward the disarranged bed, its curtains torn and seared—"let me show my gratitude."

Pushing the door closed behind him, the scribe hurried to find Commander Rhôn.

60 ~ PRAYER

A dark shape, broad-winged and vast, rose against the setting sun. Áredan the Dragon bore fragile lives in his talons—Owen and Dremm, returning to the Territories and home.

Though weary from losing much blood, the Dragon had made many flights between the mountains and the foothills, bringing the Fourth, Rubin's family, and all the horses, down from the crags. Then he had gone back for the bodies of Arn and young Trag, and set them in the center of a barren patch of rock on the gentle slope of a small meadow. The Dissonay circled the dead, drew swords, and waited in silence until their captain led them in the death blessing. The Dragon burned the bodies and blew the ashes toward the setting sun.

Owen had wakened and tried to rise. Gaerbith pushed him back down. "Your wounds are healed, but Nar'ath poison and loss of blood have stolen your strength. Áredan will take you home."

"Please." Owen struggled in vain to push himself up. "Please, brother, do not send me away."

"Owen tha Forba. Obey your captain."

Owen turned away his face.

"What is happening—it is not about us. Our will, our wishes, have no place in it." Gaerbith plucked a blade of grass from near his knee and stripped it away, one fiber at a time, then cast it aside. "You serve best by returning home. Be a son. Tend our father's sheep. I must shepherd a different flock."

Then he cupped the back of the boy's head and lifted him until their foreheads touched.

"If I go," said Owen, "you must follow."

But Gaerbith did not answer.

While the brothers talked, and while the others made camp, the watcher returned the Sea Stone to Owen's bag so the great pearl could be returned to King Padraig, and now Áredan's great wings gathered the wind until the Dragon and the wounded were lost to distance and twilight.

Yanámari pulled off her socks and boots, and wiggled her toes in the soft new grass as she looked around the encampment. The men cut green boughs, fashioning them into beds or small shelters, and Fremmen minded the spit over which a deer carcass roasted, sprinkled with herbs.

Every quiver was empty, none of the arrows useful after being fouled with Nar'ath blood, so Fremmen had brought down the animal with a crude spear, and been loudly praised by his fellows.

Little Evan 'helped' the roasting by throwing more herbs at the carcass and asking, "Is it done yet?"

Yanámari smiled as Fremmen's strained but quiet no, the meat would not be cooked for some time became a short, emphatic *no*.

The smell reminded her how little she had eaten since leaving the city, and she pressed an arm across her stomach to keep it from rumbling. She might have been hemmed and threatened in Elycia, but she had never gone hungry or been in want. Freedom demanded its own price, and the debt was far from paid.

Restless, she stood and turned toward the darkening forest surrounding the meadow. She could use a proper bath. If there was a stream in the woods—

She walked on. Shadows advanced among the trees, gathering like the dark ghosts of an ancient army, but she was not afraid. Soldiers were common, trees were not. All her life, Yanámari had only seen them from a distance, either as forests mantling the mountains beneath the snowline or as logs brought across the chasm to feed the fireplaces in the royal chambers. Here trees spoke, reached out to her in welcome, and she wandered among them, trailing her fingers along their rough bark. She traced the edges of broad leaves, held fragrant green needles to her nose, delighted in the feel of dirt instead of stone beneath her feet. Never in her memory had the warmest summer day in the Craydaeg Mountains been as warm as this spring evening in the foothills.

The trees opened onto a clearing. She ran to the center and spun, arms outflung, head back, until she was giddy and fell, laughing, into the grass.

Then, curling on her side, she wept for Arien and Elta and Imre, whose voices she would not hear again, whose comforting faces she would never see.

When tears ended, she slept.

She wakened to utter black. Sitting up in a sudden panic, she almost cried out, but then she caught nearby voices.

Her sight adjusted to the darkness. A couple sat with their backs to a tree, his arm around her shoulders, her head on his chest. They spoke Skardian, but in such low tones that words muted, absorbed into other sounds—a murmuring soft breeze, an inquisitive owl, the distant howl that might mark a farmer's dog or a wolf come down from the mountains. He embraced her with both arms and kissed the top of her head.

Rubin and Syra.

How they had managed not to trip over her in the dark, she did not know, but she would not draw attention. Slowly, gathering the folds of ther woolen gown, she stood.

In the northern sky, it was the time of the Leaping Horse. Head and forelegs pointed west and rear legs stretched back, hooves to the east. The constellation was visible just past the treetops. Yanámari chose her path by its star points and, testing each step, walked back the way she had come.

Her bare foot came down on something sharp, and she clamped a hand over her mouth. Silencing herself only made the pain in her heel scream louder. She eased her foot back to the ground and took no more than two hobbling steps when a shout reverberated.

She stumbled through the undergrowth. Limbs slapped her face and her eyes watered, but still she ran. She ran until she saw flickering light.

Gaerbith stood on a fallen log, its trunk thicker than he was tall, its roots fanning behind him like rays from the sun. He had brought a torch and stuck it in the ground, but the uncertain light concealed rather than illuminated his face.

No enemy beset him. He was alone.

Palm against a tree, she pressed a hand to her side, catching her breath. Was the man mad, shouting at the sky?

He argues with Omwen'din, Turi had said. Who but a Keeper

would dare such a thing?

The captain's words were violent, forceful, punctuated by a finger jabbed toward an invisible adversary, by a fist punching the air. If his deity existed, why did it not strike him down for such audacity? But, perhaps, if truly all-powerful, his god could not be wounded by the resistance of one man. After all, even the greatest storm could not bring down a mountain.

Exhausted, hungry, annoyed, Yanámari used the hem of her sleeve to dab at blood on her cheek, found her direction again by the Leaping Horse, and followed the aroma of roasted venison back toward camp.

She met Turi and others crashing through the undergrowth, torches high.

He looked her up and down for wounds. "How many men?"

"When you said he argued with his god, you did not tell me he argued so loud."

Turi cocked his head to the side, frowned, then turned to the men, grinning. "We run for nothing, lads. Just the captain at his prayers."

Grumbling, the men sheathed their swords and started back.

"Ho, Fremmen," Turi called, "is that venison done yet?"

From the darkness came a teeth-gritted reply, "The next man who asks eats gristle!"

Turi loosed a deep, rolling laugh, and the others joined him.

Yanámari shook her head. "I do not think I will ever understand the Dissonay."

"There is not much to understand, m'lady." He slapped her on the shoulder. "Know when to fight, know when to laugh, and know when to leave alone."

"That one is the most difficult."

"It will come."

61 ~ Turi's Story

Standing watch in the night, Turi had seen Gaerbith return to camp, lie down in a blanket for perhaps an hour, then rise again and return to the forest. Now the captain stood again on the fallen tree, head bowed, in his hand the ruin of a sword—not Owen's hilt, but the broken blade that had been buried in Gaerbith's thigh.

Turi leaned a couple of fresh-cut ash staves against a tree then stepped forward. "Captain?" He held out a chunk of meat and a little bread, wrapped in cloth.

Gaerbith spoke without lifting his head. "You always were the better warrior."

"Aye." Turi laughed. "That is no great secret."

"You will make a fine captain."

Turi tossed the food toward the log then crossed his arms. "Meaning?"

"I am not going with you." Gaerbith looked at him. "Take everyone, and return by the Old Road—"

"Across the Plains? The Nar'ath will still find us, and what about that monstrous gold Dragon? Áredan did not kill him."

"—least expected way. The Keepers use it, and a few farmers or merchants going to market. Disguised as common folk, you should be as hidden as if you kept to the forest."

"Padraig named us guardians of Disson."

"I remain a guardian. More so when I take the oath."

"If y'were not my captain, I would challenge—"

"I am not deserting my men or my post. I will find the Kel-child, then I will face Heolstor, and remove a far greater enemy than Morfran."

"Do not be thinking the Keeper's oath will keep ye safe."

Gaerbith looked down again at the broken sword. Covered in his dried blood, the metal did not gleam, and all that caught the eye was the elegant shape of the guard. "I suffer no illusions, my friend. I know this plan may mean my death. But that, too, is no great secret."

"Cease this talk of dying."

"What do you wish to hear?"

"What becomes of Lady Yanámari?"

"She goes with you. As her cousin, King Padraig will give her aid. Rubin's family will be safest in Disson or the Territories."

"Is that what they want?"

"It is best."

"Like sending Owen away?"

Gaerbith said nothing.

"Told her your plan?"

He shook his head.

Turi reached back and grabbed the staves.

Again, Gaerbith shook his head. "I do not want to fight you."

"A man who shouts at Mymna Tor must be braver than a man who refuses to speak to the woman whose regard for him is plain as"—Turi cast about for words—"as that sun in the sky."

"She is grateful. Nothing more."

Turi held out a staff.

Gaerbith flicked the broken blade. It dug into the earth. He leapt after it, landing with a slight stumble, and took the staff from Turi. He held it across his body. Turi struck his staff across Gaerbith's—not a quick tap for attention, but a call to battle. For a time, the only sound in the glade was the solid, rhythmic thwack of staves.

Gaerbith barked Turi's knuckles. Turi caught Gaerbith in the stomach.

"What if she stays?"

Gaerbith sucked in enough air to reply. "She will go."

"Ye know this certain?"

"Lady of Skarda. Father is king." Gaerbith swung at Turi's knees, landing a sound hit. "She will go to those most useful to her."

Turi staggered but remained upright. He blocked Gaerbith's staff. They pushed against one another, but neither gave ground.

With a mighty shove, Turi broke free and sent Gaerbith tottering backward into the fan of roots rising from the base of the fallen tree. Dirt clods rained down from still-limber tendrils. The captain regained his balance, shook dirt from his hair, and advanced once more.

Talk ceased. The rap and rattle of staves grew louder now, quicker. Gaerbith bared his teeth and stood his ground, his blows so fast and powerful that Turi could only defend himself.

"Ye know nothing of what she wants."

"And you do?" Gaerbith's eyes narrowed.

He scraped his staff down Turi's, raking Turi's hands so that he lost his grip and dropped the length of ash.

Planting his feet, Gaerbith rested the butt of the staff against his instep.

Bending forward, Turi gripped his legs above the knees, catching his breath. His palms stung, and blood seeped from his knuckles. He laughed.

"Yer breakfast lies there, captain. Best eat it before the beetles do."

Gaerbith ate the meat and bread is if his thoughts were far afield. Like a man who wanted something so much that he was afraid to say it, even to himself.

Turi sat with his back to a tree and stretched out his legs.

"My wife was a brave woman. Edwig made her choice and did not shrink from it. M'lady is much like her.

"She was a merchant's daughter. Braemon's Well is a fine place along a good road. I made a decent living. Had a bit of money set by. Still not good enough for Edward Ewartsson's daughter. He planned to wed her to a merchant's son. She had an eye for me, though." He chuckled. "Edward could not keep her from turning 'round to smile at me during prayers or along the street." He tugged his beard. "We never spoke.

"One day, when her father was out of town, she came to my shop to check on the cart I was repairing for him. I knew he would never send her there—he would send a servant or come himself, alone—but I was not about to turn her away. She sat on a barrel. I worked on the cart. We talked 'til sundown. And then"—his chest squeezed, and Turi ducked his head—"then she stood on that barrel, and when I warned her she might fall, she wrapped her arms around my neck, and told me I had best marry her soon, before the dowry was paid to the other merchant. Then she kissed me."

He blinked, and cleared his throat. "She ran off home. I went to the priest. Next morning, just before dawn, Edwig rode a horse to my shop, and with her came a pony drawing a small cart filled with belongings, and one maidservant to drive the cart. The priest married us before breakfast.

"When Edward returned two days later, I paid him a visit. Unhappiest man I ever saw." Turi grinned. "But he paid the dowry. By then, there was no taking his daughter back."

Across the clearing, Gaerbith smiled.

"We had ten years and three children." Turi turned his head, looking to the forest. "Not enough time." Light rambled among the trees. "Not near enough time."

He met Gaerbith's gaze. "Ye may take the Keeper's oath, captain, but that only means y'live past mortal days. Yanámari will die. What does it matter if ye have ten years or two score? They will end. Every day matters."

Gaerbith stood, opened his mouth to speak, stopped. He pressed his foot on the hilt of the broken sword, pushing it into the soft earth until no metal remained above-ground. Then he picked up both staves, dropped them beside Turi, and disappeared among the trees.

62 ~ PROMISE

The Dissonay camp was quiet. Almost quiet. There were occasional mutters, a few grunts, and at least one loud string of curses when a Skardian warhorse objected to its saddle and nipped at Warrten.

The watcher snagged a chunk of leftover venison when no one was looking. Without Áredan for conversation, he felt lost. Not even Evan looked for him. The boy was where he should be—with his father.

The watcher had a father once—he must have—but he could not recall face or voice or laughter, advice or a hand on the shoulder. Perhaps his father had been ill-natured, a drunkard, a ne'er-do-well. Perhaps his father was best forgotten.

"Papa? Papa?" Evan tugged on Rubin's sleeve.

"Careful, son." Rubin turned a shoulder, shielding him from the axe. "This is Turi's. He uses it in battle, but we will use it to cut wood."

Evan sat, elbows on knees, chin in hands. "Wood for fires?"

"A sled." A whetstone hissed along the blade.

"A sled?" Evan's eyes almost disappeared behind his smile. "But this is spring!"

"The horses will pull it."

"I like horses."

Rubin chuckled. With the return of his family, and a little food and rest, gauntness had left his face.

He tucked the whetstone into his scrip, hefted the axe to his shoulder, then nodded to Syra, who sat with Yanámari and sewed together bits of cloth from her satchel. "Tell Mother what we do."

The boy ran to obey, hugged Syra, then caught up with Rubin. "Has Áredan talked to you? Where is he now? When is he coming back?"

"When he is strong again."

495

"I like Dragons."

"Dragons, in their hearts, are no different from Men. There are good, like these Dissonay warriors, and there are bad, like King Morfran. Áredan has enemies among Dragons."

"Who?"

But the watcher did not hear Rubin's reply. The sharp, clear ring of axe on wood cut the quiet.

Surely, if the watcher's father had been like Rubin, the watcher would remember.

Out of the trees strode the captain, an unreadable expression on his face. Turi followed a few paces behind, two staves gripped in one meaty fist. Both men went straight to their blankets and bags, gathering them into rolls before saddling their mounts.

All desultory feeling left the clearing. Men scrambled to prepare their own horses and break camp.

Syra dropped her sewing and approached Gaerbith. "Captain?"

He turned toward her.

"My husband has gone to cut wood for a sled. It might help when Evan grows tired, or if someone is injured or falls ill." She gestured at the armor and weapons of the men who had died. "And we might carry things too cumbersome for riders."

Gaerbith nodded, called to two other men, and they followed him in the direction of the axe blows.

"He does not speak much," said Syra to Lady Yanámari standing near, her hands full of the sewing.

"He can when he wishes."

Syra held open a bag while Yanámari stuffed the fabric into it. "It is to you, my lady, and to the captain, that we owe this reunion. Did the Dragon not help the Dissonay flee Elycia, who knows where he might have flown off to, my Rubin with him?"

Yanámari smiled, warm but sad.

In Elycia, she had been the watcher's friend. She had been the reason he and his love could steal moments together. With Arien's death, however—and Elta's—she had changed. Perhaps even the watcher's own passing into this netherland between life and death had been too much. Yanámari seemed a husk, empty of herself, filled with the essence of a stranger.

She had Ren saddled by the time the men returned from the forest, each dragging long rough-dressed limbs that they lashed into a crude sled and hitched to one of the sturdier horses. No one else was going to ride it, so the watcher settled on that animal as his for the day.

He approached with careful steps, skirting the camp, mindful of his shadow on the ground, and touched the horse's nose. The creature's ears twitched.

"You see me. I am a small fellow, too skinny to add much to your burden. When we pass a village or a farm, I will try to find you apples or sweet grain. Do we agree?"

The horse blinked its long fringe of lashes over large brown eyes, tossed its head in a sort of nod, and whickered.

"Excellent," and the watcher climbed aboard.

Camp broken, morning sun high, the Dissonay ventured south, down from the foothills. By midday, they were deep in a thick forest. By evening, they were still in forest but out of the hills. The moon had risen by the time Captain Gaerbith's low call drew the column to a halt—not, it seemed, to make camp, but to find a way to cross a river.

The watcher swayed, weary beyond thought. Covered in a blanket, Evan had fallen asleep on the sled. Lady Yanámari tipped forward then caught herself. What was the captain thinking, to push onward across a river at night, his people asleep in their saddles?

Turi said something, shook his head, and strode away. Gaerbith stood alone at Kraekor's head, reins in hand, face turned toward the water.

Now, said the Voice.

Suppressing a groan, the watcher forced himself to dismount, then clung to the reins and the stirrup to steady his aching legs. *What do I say?*

Go.

He shuffled forward, heedless of the noise, and when he stopped beside the captain, the words came clear and strong: "Heed me. Mine is the voice you heard call you back from death when Heolstor mocked you and the Void sought to take you."

Gaerbith did not look away from the river. "I remember."

"Omwen'din bids me speak His words."

"I am listening."

"There is one coming to meet you, one you do not expect. Another pursues. You cannot prevent either, nor will you hasten your journey by crossing this river. Wait."

"If I do not?"

"You lose half your men to the water, and none will survive the coming battle."

The captain bowed his head. "Will there be an end of war?"

But the Voice did not give the words, and the watcher remained silent.

"Who are you who speaks for Mymna Tor?"

Almost, the watcher spoke his name but something reined his tongue. "I do what I am bidden. My name is my own."

"I know your voice."

The watcher smiled. "Aye."

Lady Yanámari approached. "Speaking to your god again?"

"Rather, He is speaking to me."

"And what does He say?"

The captain looked at her. "He says wait."

The horses had been tended, the first watch had been set, and everyone else had settled down to sleep. Gaerbith took his place at the edge of the camp, in the shadows, and stood watch until near midnight when the guard changed, and then he slept.

In dreams, the warrior returned, and visions of Yanámari followed. Standing tall in her white gown, defying the king. A kiss in the grotto. Glistening shoulders as Gaerbith cut her hair. Her fierce bravery. There were other images that honor demanded he push aside, but they lingered nonetheless.

When he woke, the forest was coming alive with the sun. He lay for a while, unwilling to rise, and plucked a few leaves of young mint, chewing them as he stared up through the branches.

A sudden stillness drew him upright, and he looked around.

A man, cloaked and hooded, stood in the center of the camp, light spreading from his pale garments.

Gaerbith stepped from the shadows, drawing Bítan as he strode forward.

The man pulled back his hood, letting it fall to mantle his shoulders.

Gaerbith stopped short. "You."

The man inclined his head. His eyes were not bleak, as in dreams, nor were his face and arms streaked with blood. His features were the same, his voice unmistakable. "Hail, Gaerbith tha Forba."

"The warrior."

"You know me?"

"I know your face. Better than I know my own." Gaerbith lowered Bítan but did not sheath the blade. "What is your name, and why are you here?"

"I am Ro'Ar Eldest, First Keeper, sent to oversee your oath."

"And after the oath, another long journey."

Ro'Ar spread his hands in a gesture of resignation. So be it.

"What happens to my men while I go seeking a lost sword?"

"They prepare for war."

"Would they could go home."

"Most will."

Small comfort.

"Others travel with me," said Ro'Ar. "They await us on the road."

Warrten stood beside Gaerbith, mace in hand. "How many?"

"Three. A healer, a hunter, and a warrior." Ro'Ar smiled. "We will not fight you."

Warrten grunted.

"We can, however, shield you from the Nar'ath lest Morfran and Heolstor find you."

"We have a Dragon for that." Warrten slapped the handle of the mace in his palm. "Should be back soon."

"Áredan." Ro'Ar nodded. "He has been delayed."

Alarm coiled down Gaerbith's spine. "Recaptured?"

"Weary, but well."

A woman's voice. "You have seen him?"

Ro'Ar's gentle smile widened. "My lady."

Yanámari inclined her head. Wearing the plain gown, her head shaved, she still stood as regal as she did in her father's hall.

Something squeezed Gaerbith's heart. When she and the Fourth traveled west to Disson, he would never see her again.

"You know me, First Keeper?"

"Mymna Tor spoke of you, my lady. The oil in the fire."

"You come for the captain."

"Aye, my lady."

"To take him away."

"Aye."

"And he is willing?"

Ro'Ar's look held compassion and the keen edge of examination, as if he saw beyond her careful mask. "Ask him."

She spoke without turning her head. "You do this freely, captain, or does your god compel you?"

Gaerbith sheathed his sword. "If it means you live free, I am more than willing."

"You take the Keeper's oath for me, captain?"

"For you and for my family. For my men and their families."

"And what do you do for yourself?"

He stepped toward her. Still she did not look at him

"Heolstor and the Brethren have been the real kings of Skarda. Through puppet kings, they have enslaved its people. Uártha—nay, Mymna Tor—made me guardian of a secret. After I take the oath and find the Kel-child, we will return the lost sword to its rightful place. The true king will be restored." It was harsh truth he must speak, but she had already known imprisonment and injustice. She would respect honest words. "Your father will be set aside."

She nodded. "Even so, he will not yield power. There will be war."

"We know from the Legend of Kel that Azrin itself does not bring war, but peace."

"I am not simple, captain."

He gripped the back of his neck and looked around, casting about for the right words. Everyone had gathered, including Evan, curled on a blanket at his mother's feet.

Turi stood in Turi fashion, feet planted wide, arms crossed. He lifted a brow.

Suppressing a laugh as well as a shaky breath, Gaerbith offered a hand to Yanámari. After a moment, she took it, sliding her cool fingers into his grasp.

She matched his stride down the slope to a tumble of stones and a half-submerged log at the edge of the water. He chose a broad, flat rock that lay at a slight tilt toward the river. Bracing his weight on his good leg, he helped her step up beside him.

She did not withdraw as he expected, but tightened her clasp on his hand. "Take me with you."

He meant to speak, to explain his decision and why it was best she go to Disson, but he could not find breath, much less words.

He stepped forward, embracing her with one arm, and with the other hand cradling the back of her head, the downy hair soft against his rough palm. She wrapped her arms around his waist and bowed her head against his shoulder.

"There will be danger, my lady. We will be in a smaller company, less protected and more hunted."

"You cannot talk me out of it."

"Beyond soldier or Keeper, I am only a shepherd, my lady—"

She lifted her head. "In Elycia, at my father's table, I made my choice and do not regret it."

Many things he longed to say, but words refused to march from his tongue.

Action, then.

With the remnant of the Fourth Lachmil looking on, he bent his head and kissed her.

No quick thing, this. No startled drawing back, as he had in the grotto. This was a promise, and it took long to tell.

Pain tore at him, and he was cold. As cold as if the scorched earth cradling him were a snowbank and he were dying.

He *was* dying. He had lost enough blood to turn the mountainside to ashes.

Scur gathered his legs beneath him, but they shook and wobbled and would not hold his weight.

I AM SCUR ATTOR-KIN, DRAGONKING OF THE GREMIAN KINDRED. I AM NOT SUBJECT TO DISOBEDIENT LEGS OR USELESS WINGS. He strove once more to stand.

This time, his legs held.

When they gave out, he dragged himself across the ground, leaving great scars in the earth. Sometimes, his tattered wings caught enough wind to let him skim the treetops before tumbling him down once more.

THE SILVER DRAGON WILL PAY FOR THIS INDIGNITY.

At the rugged tor called Dragon's Rook, the cave was empty but the scent of his mate lingered. He curled up in its comforting presence, and rested his chin on his foreclaws.

In a nest at the back of the cave glittered a clutch of iridescent eggs. He breathed warmth over them. *I WILL LIVE, AND DEAL VENGEANCE TO MEN.*

The story concludes in
Dragon's Bane
The Lost Sword, Book 2

Author's Note

Dragon's Rook is the result of two decades of creating, revising, learning, re-writing, and generally growing up. The novel began as a dream that became a short story, then soon breached the wall and sprawled across hundreds of pages. It now bears little, if any, resemblance to those first scribbled words.

This book wouldn't exist without my family. My brother, sister-in-law, eldest niece, and father have all had direct impact on *Dragon's Rook*, inspiring fresh ideas, debating plot problems, and choreographing fight scenes. Mom thinks everything I write is wonderful—she might be biased—but she's always ready with spiritual guidance.

Nor would this book exist without the valuable feedback of readers, editors, fellow writers, and friends: Suzan Troutt, Nancy Powell, David Farney, Adrian Simmons, Philip Martin, L.S. King, James King, Johne Cook, Scott Sandridge, Jason Joyner, Damon Ellis, Jennifer DiCamillo, Robert Treskillard, Lyn Perry, Ashley Mendez-Kestler, Tracey Thompson, and Chris Palmer, a young man whose knowledge as a blacksmith saved my fictional smith from an embarrassing blunder.

Thank you, dear reader, for joining the journey.

Last but first, thanks to God for instilling in me a love of story and for introducing me to the greatest Story.

Keanan Brand
Oklahoma
October 2014

ABOUT THE AUTHOR

Keanan Brand is the pseudonym of an award-winning writer and editor who currently resides in Oklahoma. He is at work on several novels of speculative fiction, including space opera, urban fantasy, and the conclusion of The Lost Sword duology.

BLOGS:
https://keananbrand.wordpress.com/
http://penworthypress.com/

FACEBOOK:
https://www.facebook.com/KeananBrandWriter

WEBSITE:
http://keananbrand.wix.com/keananbrand

Pronunciation Guide

VILLAGE OF SHEA

Kieran	KEER-an	**Donovan**	DON-oh-ven
Thryffin	THRIFF-in		

DISSON & THE TERRITORIES

Gaerbith	GAYR-bith	**Yerrin**	YARE-en
Bitan	Bih-TAHN	**Ában**	AH-ben
Turi	TOO-ree	**Bos**	BOSE
Damanthus	dah-MAN-thoos	**Thael**	THALE
Padraig	PAD-rayg *or* Patrick	**Thynathel**	THEE-nah-thell
Mahyla	MY-lah	**Disson**	DISS-ON
Kraekor	KRAY-kor	**Sonndin**	SONN-din
Fremmen	FREM-men	*lachmil*	LOCK-mil
Warrten	WHAR-ten	*jhyla*	JY-lah

SKARDA

Morfran	MOR-fran	**Imre**	IHM-ree *or* EEM-ray
Heolstor	HAY-ohl-stor	**Vegeir**	VAY-gear
Teag	TEEG	**Yanámari**	yah-NAH-mar-ee
Nelek	NEE-leck	**Rhôn Berg-son**	RHONE BERG-son
Fasolt	FASS-olt	**Gurn Grumë-son**	GERN GROO-mah-son
Ûtgar	OOT-gar	**Grimë**	GREE-mah
Arien	AIR-ee-en	**Dävra**	DAHV-rah

Una	OO-nah		**Thrayne**	THRAYN
Elycia	eh-LEE-see-uh		**Craydaeg**	CRAY-deg

KIP'S BOYS

Leidolf	LIE-dolf		**Alwin**	ALL-win
Helmut	HELL-moot		**Bannon**	BAN-on
Aidan	AY-den		**Edel**	eh-DELL
Ilari	ih-LAR-ee		**Vili**	VEE-lee

KELS & KEEPERS

D'urnythn	deh-UR-nih-thin		**Llymduldara**	LHEEM-dool-DAR-ah
Azrin	AZ-rin		**Krûdhírri**	Kroo-DHEER-ee
Ro'Ar	ROH-ar		**Aldred**	ALL-dred
Uártha	oo-AR-tha		**Ailis**	AY-liss *or* Alice
Adwr	ah-DWEER		**Havyn duru Asryn**	Hah-VEEN doo-roo ah-SREEN

DRAGONS & BIRDS

Áredan	AH-reh-dahn		**Fredek**	FREE-deck
Améli	ah-MAY-lee		**Gremian**	GREH-me-an
nar'ath	NAR-ath		**So'Lenn**	so-LENN
lynneth	LINN-eth		**Attor**	AT-tor

DEITY & DARKNESS

Mymna Tor	MEEM-nah TOR		**Nar Cahm**	nar-CAHM
Omwen'din	OM-wen-DIN		**Nardha**	NAR-dtha